Born in 1957, Andrea Japp trained as a toxicologist and is the author of twenty novels. She is the French translator of Patricia Cornwell and has also written for television.

Lorenza Garcia translates from French and Spanish. For Gallic Books she has translated works by François Lelord and Claude Izner.

Katherine Gregor is a writer and translator from Italian, Russian and French. Her translations include works by Pino Cacucci, Pirandello and Pushkin.

The Lady Agnès Mystery:

Volume 2

The Divine Blood
Combat of Shadows

GALLIC

The Lady Agnès Mystery:

Volume 2

The Divine Blood
Translated from the French by Lorenza Garcia

Combat of Shadows
Translated from the French by Katherine Gregor

ANDREA JAPP

Gallic Books
London

This book is published with support from the French Ministry of Culture/Centre National du Livre and from the Institut français (Royaume-Uni) as part of the Burgess programme (www.frenchbooknews.com).

A Gallic Book

First published in France as *La Dame Sans Terre 3: Le Sang de Grâce*
Copyright © Calmann-Lévy, 2006

and *La Dame Sans Terre 4: Le Combat des Ombres* by Calmann-Lévy
Copyright © Calmann-Lévy, 2008

First published in Great Britain as *The Divine Blood*, 2009
English translation copyright © Gallic Books, 2009

This omnibus edition with *Combat of Shadows* first published in 2015
by Gallic Books, 59 Ebury Street, London SW1W 0NZ
© Gallic Books, 2015

English translation of *Combat of Shadows* copyright © Gallic Books, 2015

A CIP record for this book is available from the British Library

ISBN 978-1-910477-17-5

Typeset in Fournier MT by Gallic Books
Printed and bound by CPI Group (UK) Ltd, Croydon, CR0 4YY

2 4 6 8 10 9 7 5 3 1

CONTENTS

SUMMARY OF THE LADY AGNÈS MYSTERY
VOLUME 1

The Season of the Beast
The Breath of the Rose

The Season of the Beast

Winter 1294, Comté du Perche. The recently widowed Agnès de Souarcy takes under her wing Clément, the newborn infant of her lady's maid, Sybille, who has died in childbirth.

Cyprus, 1304. The Knight Hospitaller Francesco de Leone is sent to France. His official mission is to gather information that will help the Hospitaller order anticipate the political machinations of France's monarch, Philip the Fair. However, Leone is guided by a secret quest.

Paris, 1304. Philip the Fair aims to free himself of the Church's authority. Pope Benoît XI is fatally poisoned, and the Pope's personal guard – the twin orders of the Knights Templar and Hospitaller – comes under threat. Philip the Fair, with the help of his most influential counsellor, Guillaume de Nogaret, advances his pawns. He needs to find a docile pope.

Souarcy-en-Perche Estate, 1304. Clément has grown into a young boy with a lively intelligence. He gains entry to a secret library at Clairets Abbey. There he devours all the ancient texts forbidden by or unknown to the Church, and stumbles on a journal belonging to the Knight Hospitaller Eustache de Rioux, which refers to a mysterious Vallombroso treatise, two birth charts and a series of incomprehensible runic symbols … Is there a link between these discoveries and the Knight Hospitaller Francesco de Leone's extraordinary quest?

The body of a man lies in Souarcy Forest. It appears to have been burnt and yet there is no trace of any fire in the vicinity. An emissary of the Pope delivers a message to the Abbess of Clairets, Éleusie de Beaufort. The message contains a reference to the divine blood that washes away all sins. More corpses are discovered, as well as a series of clues pointing to Manoir de Souarcy and Agnès.

On her estate, Agnès, Dame de Souarcy, must also cope with the incestuous desires of her half-brother Eudes de Larnay, who dreams of forcing her to submit to him and is quick to throw her into the clutches of the Inquisition and the bloodthirsty Nicolas Florin. The only person who might save Agnès is Artus, Comte d'Authon, who has fallen in love with her.

The Breath of the Rose

September 1304. Accused of heresy by her half-brother Eudes de Larnay, Agnès de Souarcy finds herself at the mercy of the wicked Nicolas Florin, Grand Inquisitor at Alençon. Florin is ecstatic: this beautiful woman, whom a mysterious shadowy figure has ordered him to kill, drives him to distraction, and he relishes torturing her and watching her suffering. And yet the source of Agnès's greatest pain is her daughter Mathilde, who was ready to betray her, to accuse her of dealings with the devil in exchange for a few trinkets.

October 1304, the Templar commandery at Arville. The Knight Hospitaller Francesco de Leone continues his secret quest. He is searching for a scroll of papyrus – one of mankind's most sacred texts, whose existence he learnt of through his godfather, Eustache de Rioux. The manuscript was hidden by a Knight Templar at one of his order's commanderies.

November 1304, the Vatican Palace. Honorius Benedetti is determined at all costs to retrieve the famous Vallombroso treatise, whose contents must on no account become known. The treatise, which Clément has discovered in the secret library at Clairets Abbey, also contains a reference to Agnès de Souarcy's birth chart.

1304, Clairets Abbey. One by one the nuns are dying by poisoning. The culprit is among them. Éleusie de Beaufort – Abbess of Clairets and Francesco de Leone's aunt – is convinced that the killer's motive is the manuscripts in the secret library …

What is this extraordinary intrigue in which Agnès appears to play the pivotal role? Why is she so crucial to the mysterious quest of the Knight Hospitaller Francesco de Leone that, in a bid to free her, he does not hesitate to slay her jailer, Nicolas Florin? How will Clément, her young protégé, and Comte Artus d'Authon, who has fallen in love with her, protect her from an overwhelming danger? And what is the true meaning of the reference to the Dame de Souarcy's date of birth and astrological sign in the precious manuscripts at Clairets?

MAIN CHARACTERS

Agnès, illegitimate recognised child of Baron de Larnay, widow, Dame de Souarcy.

Clément, posthumous 'son' of Sybille, the lady's maid to whom Agnès gave refuge, unaware that she was a heretic.

Mathilde, Agnès's only daughter, shallow and capricious, frustrated by the harsh life at Souarcy.

Eudes de Larnay, Agnès's half-brother and overlord.

Francesco de Leone, member of the order of the Knights Hospitaller, which has retreated to Cyprus.

Artus, Comte d'Authon, Eudes de Larnay's overlord. Agnès is his under-vassal.

Éleusie de Beaufort, Abbess of Clairets and Francesco de Leone's aunt.

Annelette Beaupré, apothecary nun at Clairets Abbey.

Honorius Benedetti, the Pope's camerlingo (treasurer and secretary).

Aude de Neyrat, Benedetti's beautiful but redoubtable right-hand woman.

Nicolas Florin, Dominican, Grand Inquisitor for the Alençon region.

Esquive d'Estouville, a young girl who crosses Francesco de Leone's path without his suspecting that she is his protector.

Agnan, young clerk at the Inquisition headquarters of Alençon, former secretary of Nicolas Florin. He has joined Agnès's cause.

AUTHOR'S NOTE

Words marked with an asterisk (*) are explained in the Historical References starting on page 601; those marked with a plus sign (⁺) are explained in the Glossary starting on page 611.

Part One:
The Divine Blood

To Janine A. H.,

Tenderness, laughter, reading.
Then such sweet insistent sorrow when you departed.
Rest, our Janine.
Your Ganesh smiles over my work table.

Vatican Palace, Rome, December 1304

The camerlingo Honorius Benedetti's thin lips were white with rage. He had the repulsive feeling that his flesh was gradually being eaten away, that his skin was sticking to his cheekbones. He raised his hand to his nose and smelt it to see whether the odour he had suddenly perceived was really that of his decaying body or simply a distressing illusion. All he could smell was the faint scent of rosewater from his morning ablutions.

They had the upper hand. Once again they had the upper hand. The others. A sudden feeling of dizziness made him close his eyes. How could it be? Benedetti was not afraid of facing the terrible possibility that he had been mistaken all along. That God was protecting his enemies in order to show him how wrong he had been all these years. On the contrary, the camerlingo had only himself to blame for hiring such incompetent henchmen. Any spiritual doubts he might have had were quashed by his absolute conviction that man could not be left to his own devices; that the evil in him would triumph if he were not compelled to be good, because sinning is easier and above all more pleasurable. What a fool he had been to have employed the services of that spectre! As for the Grand Inquisitor, that Nicolas Florin, whom he had learnt had been murdered at Alençon, Aude de Neyrat had been absolutely right. It was madness to have entrusted the execution of such a plan to resentment, envy and bloodthirstiness.

Agnès de Souarcy had escaped from the ruthless clutches of the Inquisition* against all the odds.

Benedetti plunged the tip of the stiletto knife he used as a letter opener into his magnificent hardwood desk. He would pray for the eternal damnation of Nicolas Florin's soul. Although, in reality, the man had no need of his help in order to be condemned to the eternal torments of the damned.

He tugged hard on the braided bell rope that connected his study to an usher's tiny bureau. The man appeared almost instantly in the tall doorway.

'Your Eminence,' he burbled submissively, lowering his head.

'Has my lady visitor arrived yet?'

'This very instant, Your Eminence.'

'Well! Don't just stand there, show her in!' shouted the camerlingo.

The other man stifled a look of dismay. He didn't recall ever having seen the prelate display even a hint of annoyance. Indeed, his unruffled, almost cheerful, exterior was what made people fear him all the more. They knew that the guillotine could fall on any one of their necks without prior warning. Benedetti manipulated this fear and used it to his advantage.

The elegant, golden-haired vision, clad from head to toe in crimson, walked in, preceded by a heady aroma of musk and iris.

Benedetti's tense expression immediately slackened.

'Aude, my dearest lady … You are like a salve that heals all my troubles. Pray, take a seat. May I offer you a glass of fine wine from the foothills of Mount Vesuvius?'

Aude lifted the delicate veil concealing a face so stunningly beautiful that it attracted every gaze.

'Ah … the tears of Christ, its smoothness is renowned.'

'The Lacrima Christi, yes.'

'And offered by you … it is undoubtedly on a par with receiving absolution,' she said teasingly.

He smiled as he filled two tall glasses. He sometimes felt he knew this woman as well as if she were his own creation. A single facet of this piece of perfection with emerald-green eyes, a tiny smiling mouth and a ruthless intelligence remained for ever a mystery to him. Did she really have no desire for atonement or was she hiding a festering wound of remorse beneath her elegant exterior? Benedetti had lived with his own wound for so long he had the impression that it was his most faithful, cruel companion. It would suppurate during the night, tormenting him ceaselessly, tearing his soul apart until dawn.

They took a few sips in silence before Honorius admitted:

'You were right, my dear. Madame de Souarcy is free, cleared of all suspicion.'

'Your henchmen failed.'

'One of them – the Grand Inquisitor – paid with his life.'

'That is something, at least. I do find such people distasteful,' Aude remarked casually.

'They are useful to us.'

'Even henchmen must be chosen wisely. So, the little bastard noblewoman has trumped the most powerful arm of the Church? Well, that's what I'd call a humiliating defeat!'

'If it were only a question of wounded pride, I could live with it. Regrettably, I see in it the nefarious work of my enemies and proof of their mounting strength. It also shows me that Madame de Souarcy is extremely important to them. She must die, and quickly ... That woman must die ... As for her shadow, that little rascal who, according to my spies, is fiercely loyal to her, he must share the same fate.' He closed his eyes and added in a whisper: 'May God bless and receive them.'

'She ... They will die. I will see to it.'

Aude de Neyrat paused and drank the contents of her glass unhurriedly. For once she allowed her worst memories to flood back.

Aude was orphaned at a young age and placed under the tutelage of an uncle. The old scoundrel had been quick to confuse family duty with the *droit de seigneur*. Admittedly not for long, for the toothless scoundrel had died an agonisingly painful drawn-out death – exactly as his ward had envisaged. She had stood over him devotedly, dabbing his perspiring face with a cloth impregnated with poison. At the tender age of twelve Aude had discovered that she had a flair for poison, murder and deceit equalled only by her beauty and brains. She would soon put her precious talents to work in order to inherit two substantial bequests – one of them from an elderly husband. However, she made the mistake of sparing the husband's very young nephew; the boy was so delightful and entertaining that Aude hadn't the heart to send him to an early grave – a serious mistake that would nearly cost her her life. The sweet young collateral heir proved to be every bit as venal as his young aunt by marriage. He alerted the chief bailiff of Auxerre's men to the misfortune that appeared to have befallen all of Madame de Neyrat's relatives, and demanded his inheritance. Aude was arrested. A horde of treacherous rats immediately came out of the woodwork to accuse her of a range of sins from poisoning to fornicating with demons. Honorius Benedetti, a simple bishop at the time, was passing through the town during her trial. Madame de Neyrat's striking beauty had bowled him over. He had made sure he took part in her questioning.

Aude recalled every last detail of their first encounter in the vaulted room at the chateau in Auxerre. Despite the chill of those thick stone walls, Benedetti was perspiring and fanning himself with an elegant fan made of fine strips of mother of pearl, a gift from a lady in Jumièges long ago, he had explained with a knowing smile. The prelate standing before her was slim and small. He had graceful, slender, well-manicured hands; feminine hands. He had urged her to confess her sins. And yet something in his manner had suggested to the young woman that she should do the exact opposite. Aude had confessed nothing and, much to the delight of Honorius – himself a past master at the art of sophistry, had ensnared her judges in a web of lies and deceit. She learnt later that he had done everything in his power to clear her of the serious charges hanging over her, and had even accused the beleaguered nephew of aggravated perjury. The youth, alarmed by the bishop's implicit threats, had retracted his accusation and had begged forgiveness of his dear aunt, whom he confessed to having seriously misjudged. One night, one remarkable and inevitable night, Benedetti had joined her at the town house she had inherited from her deceased husband. Between the sheets, dishevelled by their delightful folly, they had discovered that they were two of a kind, equal in strength. Aude had sensed that she was Honorius's only carnal transgression since taking his vows. In the morning when he had taken his leave of her, she had known – without needing to suggest it tactfully herself – that he would not return. Closing his eyes and smiling, he had kissed her hand and murmured:

'I thank you for this sublime night, Madame, for I do not sense in any way that it was compensation for having taken care of your trial. Thank you equally for having provided me with a few hours of bitter regret and sweet memories.'

A pox on memories.

Aude de Neyrat went on, intrigued:

'My dear friend … Were you really such a sentimentalist that first time we met, when you saved my life?'

'A sentimentalist? Why else would I have saved you when I knew you to be guilty?'

'Because it amused you and perhaps because you desired me a little?'

'All of those things at once. And because you moved me …'

'I moved you?'

'You stood alone against all those men, most of them hypocrites. You were fearless, and yet they would have crushed you. In reality, the choice was a simple one. I could fight on your side, or give them free rein and allow mediocrity to triumph over brilliance. I made my choice.'

'That is undoubtedly the most wonderful compliment I am ever likely to receive and I thank you for it,' she avowed, with unusual earnestness. 'And now I must prepare for my trip if I wish to arrive post haste in the charming county of Perche.'

'You will be stopping off in Chartres on the way, my dear.'

He reached into a drawer and retrieved a fat purse and a few sheets of vellum covered in his small, nervous scrawl.

'Here is enough money to cover your immediate needs, as well as a few recommendations, instructions, names and addresses. I implore you, Aude, do not fail me …'

'I don't recall ever having failed … at anything. We shall meet again very soon, my friend, to celebrate your success.'

A fresh breeze had risen in Saint Peter's Square that lifted her veil like a wing. Aude de Neyrat walked hurriedly. Ever since Benedetti had evoked his emotion during their first meeting, she had been seized by a potent desire – unexpected and inopportune, given the number of arrangements she must make before her imminent departure. What of it! She would do better to satisfy her hunger as quickly as possible without another thought, and Aude knew how.

She made her way towards Ponte Sant'Angelo, which spanned the river Tiber. Dusk already provided her with some cover. She entered a maze of streets which, though scarcely squalid, were certainly no place for a lady of her position to be wandering at any time of the day or night. The early evening breeze dispersed a little the suffocating stench of humanity, of dirt and detritus that seemed to emanate from the rows of hovels. A man approached her. She looked him up and down. He was ugly, dirty and too old. As for his rotten teeth, they disgusted her. She waved him away. On the other hand, the lithe young figure she noticed loitering next to the stairs leading down to the seedy Bianca Donna tavern took her fancy. Aude drew level with him. He was handsome, very handsome indeed. He looked not yet twenty. He stared at her boldly and paid her a crude compliment.

Aude retorted in perfect Italian:

'Please don't speak. You will ruin my pleasure.' She pulled two shiny coins out of her purse and said: 'You will do exactly as I say. No more, no less.'

Suddenly sobered, the young man pocketed the money and nodded.

Aude was exhausted when she rose from the bed in the tiny room at the house of ill repute masquerading as a tavern. The man's smell on her skin still excited her, but she would soon find it intolerable. A mallow and lavender bath would wash it away. He lay, asleep, and she looked at him properly for the first time. What a handsome specimen he was with his swarthy olive skin and thick hair descending from his sternum to end in a point at his pubis. As she had hoped, he had been forceful and brutish. Aude would not deny that her taste for virile men was born of the satisfaction she took in bringing them to heel. It was no doubt necessary to her pleasure. And what of it! Who cared about these witless, charmless oafs who died every day like flies?

A voice startled her:

'That was … You ladies are a sight better than any whores or slatterns. You could teach them a thing or two – those whores, I mean.'

The stench was already becoming unbearable. She slipped into her dress and gestured for him to lace up the back. He stood up and tried to run his tongue along her neck then thrust his sex against her. She turned and glared at him. He grumbled:

'All right …' His sulking face suddenly broke into a grin. 'If I'd known … when I saw you going into the Pope's palace …

What a coincidence, eh? I was there. I saw you. It's not often you see a lady go in there. They say that whores sometimes dress up as ladies and slip in, but that mostly it's spies. Are you a spy, then? You've certainly got what it takes.'

'What a pity,' muttered Aude under her breath, in French this time, and, turning, gave him a provocative smile.

'Ah, I knew you wanted more. It's not every day you meet a stud like me!' He pulled her roughly, pressing his body tightly against hers. She manoeuvred him over to the straw mattress.

The young man's eyes opened wide and his mouth gaped as though he were trying to cry out. A red stream coloured his teeth before running down his chin. Aude pushed the dagger in deeper. He collapsed face down on the floor. She bent down to pull the blade from his back and leapt aside, but not quickly enough. A jet of blood spurted over her dress. She let out a sigh of relief. Fortune had smiled on her – red on crimson wouldn't show. She paused, a look of disgust on her face, as she waited for the man's body to stop twitching. Sweet Lord, how she detested watching death at work, even when she was its agent.

Alençon, Perche, December 1304

It was dusk when Agnan, secretary to the late Nicolas Florin, left the Inquisition headquarters. Two weeks had passed since the demise of the Grand Inquisitor, allegedly stabbed to death during a chance encounter with a drunkard. The sickly young man was ready to swear that these were the happiest weeks of his life. He was equally ready to swear on his life that he had been close to glimpsing an act of divine intervention. In Agnan's eyes it had been so remorseless, so unquestionably just that it could not have been anything but divine in essence. Not that he was superstitious or foolish enough to believe that an avenging angel had intervened to slay the beautiful and ignoble torturer. On the contrary, Agnan had gradually persuaded himself that the Knight of Justice and Grace, Francesco de Leone, had used his sword to defend God's lambs. For only a wolf could protect lambs against other wild animals. What other explanation could there be for the Hospitaller's* timely intervention at the start of the torture of this woman who had so overwhelmed the young clerk?

His euphoria caused him to quicken his pace without him even realising it. He whose ugliness made people turn away. His beady eyes, sharp nose and receding chin rendered him unsightly, gave him a weasely look that inspired mistrust, even disgust. And yet that radiant creature, that woman, had touched him, had gazed into his eyes as though she were able to see past his deceptive exterior, his outward mask. Her soul, unbreakable as a diamond, had caressed his, and he would bear its trace for ever. What joy, what indescribable joy he had felt at being so close to perfection.

A charming thought occurred to him. He was surprised that

he hadn't noticed it before: they shared the same Christian name. Agnès, Agnan. This coincidence, though meaningless and trivial, filled him with pleasure.

Agnan shivered, but did not think to pull up his cowl. A stubborn layer of powdery snow had settled on the cobblestones and crunched beneath his wooden clogs. A damp fog clung to the walls, enveloping the houses and closed shops in an eerie silence. A smile played across the young man's face. He was oblivious to the biting cold seeping through his habit of homespun wool and his threadbare cape. He, Agnan, had played a role in saving Madame de Souarcy. The meagre offering of bacon and eggs he had filched from the kitchens and secretly taken down to her cell had helped to give her the strength she needed to resist the shameful trial that had ensued. It was in part owing to him that the knight Leone, whom he had shown to her cell and warned of the imminent arrival of the monstrous inquisitor, had rescued her. He felt his face grow pink with shame. Was it not wildly arrogant of him to assign himself a role, however small, in Agnès de Souarcy's rescue? And yet he needed desperately to believe that he had laboured obstinately and selflessly, despite the fear instilled in him by the beast Florin.

Wrapped up in these, by turns, sad and joyous thoughts, he was unaware of the shadowy figure tailing him at a distance. He turned into Rue de la Poêle-Percée which led to Place de l'Étape-au-Vin, and wandered distractedly towards Saint-Aignan Church. In order to save himself a detour, he decided to cut through a narrow alleyway between two rows of houses made of wood and cob with shingle roofs, reflecting that, if he were attacked by thieves, nobody would leave their homes on such a dark night to come to his aid. He shrugged. Only a fool or a madman would rob a humble clerk who possessed only the clothes on his back, which were scarcely less ragged than those of a pauper.

In reality, Agnan was clear in his mind. He knew that he continually mulled over his encounter with Agnès de Souarcy, obsessively recollecting every last detail, because he was searching for a clue. Veering between hope and despair, he sought proof that his role in Madame de Souarcy's life, however tenuous, had been preordained, and that it was perhaps not yet over.

He slowed his pace, overwhelmed by a sudden sense of shame. How presumptuous, how conceited of him to cast himself in the role of the heroic architect of some plan that far exceeded him!

It was then that he heard the muffled sound of steps approaching down the evil-smelling alley. He stopped dead in his tracks and listened, trying to see into the encircling gloom. His alarm quickly gave way to panic and his heart started pounding wildly. He was too weak to put up a fight or defend himself. He would flee – make a beeline for the small square surrounding Saint-Aignan Church. Despite the piercing cold, beads of sweat had formed on his brow and trickled down his pale cheeks. He took a deep breath to try to stifle the fear that was choking him. He must run, find the courage to move, but his legs refused to do his bidding. He froze like a rabbit staring into the open jaws of his predator. The tall figure approached him, unhurriedly now, slowly becoming visible in the nocturnal fog. Agnan could see the long cape flapping around a pair of ankles, the glint of a sword banging against a leg clad in a thick leather boot. His head swam and he stifled a dry sob. He fell back against the wall of a dwelling, powerless to cry out for help.

The figure came over to him, bent down and pulled him up by his armpits. The astonished Agnan was only just able to gasp:

'You ... knight.'

'Stand up. What's the matter with you?'

'I thought ... I thought you were a brigand ...'

The other man gave a faint smile and said:

'It was unwise of you to venture down such an alleyway at night.'

'I ... I wasn't thinking properly.'

'I will walk with you. Where were you headed?'

'I was going to Saint-Aignan Church to offer a prayer and attend the service for Advent.'[1]

They walked in silence. Leone hesitated. He was searching for a way of formulating the question that had been plaguing him for weeks – for years. Agnan was wondering. Should he risk putting his mind at rest? Who was he to ask this knight, who both fascinated and terrified him, to satisfy his curiosity? His desire to know was too strong, however, and without daring to look the Hospitaller in the eye, he blurted out:

'Was it you ... Was it you, Monsieur, who ...'

'Who killed, or rather executed, Florin? I confess it was, and in doing so I demand your silence. I could see no other way. He left me no choice and, if I am honest, it is no doubt what I was hoping for.'

'I will for ever be indebted to you for this ... gesture, which I sense weighs heavily on you. That wicked creature's disappearance has cast more darkness out of the world. We are too sorely in need of light to allow us to regret Florin's passing.'

'You mean his murder,' corrected Leone. 'It is charitable of you to employ the general, natural term "passing", but this was true murder, Agnan. I stabbed the man knowing him to be unarmed. It would be dishonourable of me to try to shirk my responsibility.'

'Vermin are not murdered, they are exterminated,' the clerk exclaimed firmly.

'With all due respect, it is not for you to judge. Only God can do that and I have already accepted His verdict.' Leone sighed and went on: 'What was Florin, a freak of nature? Or one of those challenges we encounter in life that serve to remind us how we veer between greatness and intolerable failure? Admittedly, had Madame de Souarcy's life not been in danger, I am not sure that I would have soiled my hands with the inquisitor's blood.'

Agnan looked at him for the first time since their strange meeting in the alleyway and pursed his lips anxiously:

'Oh ... You are right. My mind has been in turmoil these past few days ...' Suddenly, he threw caution to the wind, declaring: 'Do you know Madame de Souarcy's true identity, knight? I had ... I had the overwhelming sensation that something not of this world was taking place ...'

'What nonsense! Unless I'm gravely mistaken, it is very much of this world.'

Silencing his doubts and fears, Leone now demanded in a voice trembling with such emotion as to be scarcely recognisable:

'Did you see her blood?'

Agnan paused and, puzzled, asked:

'I beg your pardon, knight?'

'Did you ... see Madame de Souarcy's blood?'

This man, this saviour, this warrior could not possibly request such a detail in order to satisfy some ghoulish appetite. Accordingly, Agnan responded in a choked voice:

'Oh, Monsieur, indeed I did, and I would have gladly shed every last drop of my own rather than dress her poor, tortured flesh. Florin ... rubbed salt in her wounds to stop them from healing and to increase her pain. The fiend was unaware that I knew what the grey powder was that he kept in his gilded phial. I washed her lash wounds with water. I rubbed salve on her torn flesh until the brother at the infirmary took over from me.'

'But did you see her blood?' Leone insisted, trying hard to conceal his unease.

'It streamed down her back and sides, turning her hair red. It covered my hands, knight, and I kissed them.'

'What ...' The Hospitaller's voice was so choked with emotion that he was scarcely able to finish the question: 'What did it look like?'

'I beg your pardon?'

'I mean … Was it like the blood of other victims? Did you notice anything peculiar about it?'

Agnan tried in vain to understand his escort's persistent questioning. He stammered:

'I'm a little lost … it was bright red, full of life … It wrenched my heart to see it turn the water a brilliant scarlet … I confess that I felt a sudden chill. Is this what you wanted to know?'

'Yes.' Leone nodded, clumsily trying to hide his sudden panic.

As he stood before the entrance to Saint-Aignan after taking his leave of Agnan and then walked back the way they had come, he was weighed down by an indescribable sorrow.

Clairets Abbey,* Perche, December 1304

The fire, which, days before, had so alarmed the nuns until it was swiftly brought under control, had scarcely blackened the walls of the guest house. The Abbess, Éleusie de Beaufort, accompanied by Annelette Beaupré, the apothecary nun, carried out her inspection in silence. The guest mistress, Thibaude de Gartempe, bleated:

'You must believe me, Reverend Mother. The blaze was not the result of any carelessness on my part. I don't understand how it could have started in a straw mattress in the middle of the room, so far from the hearth ...'

Annelette looked intently at the Abbess, who nodded discreetly before reassuring the guest mistress with an explanation whose absurdity nevertheless appeared to convince her:

'My dear Thibaude, fires can be fickle things ... It is conceivable that a spark landed on the straw mattress and set it alight. In any event, the essential thing is that the fire produced more smoke than flames and more panic than real damage.'

Presently, the two women left the guest mistress, who, together with a few lay servants, went to work to remove the traces of what had been no more than a diversionary tactic.

They walked in silence back to the Abbess's study. Annelette sensed that Éleusie de Beaufort was using the time to weigh up the pros and cons before revealing her secret. The apothecary had long suspected that their Abbess was concealing a thorny truth, the nature of which eluded her. She followed the Abbess into the freezing study and stood waiting, her hands clasped in front of her.

Éleusie walked around the heavy oak table and slumped into

her armchair. She closed her eyes for a moment and sighed before murmuring:

'I am guilty of a terrible mistake. Hesitation weakened my resolve. I brought about the situation that has allowed this evildoer …'

She leapt to her feet and brought her fist crashing down on the table as she hissed:

'She has not seen the last of me!'

Annelette said nothing, waiting to see what would follow.

'You were right, Annelette. That trifling fire was no more than a ruse to draw us away from here. You were also right when you advised me to trust you that day – how long ago it seems now – when you confided in me. My failure to do so unreservedly is a source of genuine regret. I lied out of fear, which in no way excuses my blunder or, worse still, my error of judgement.'

Annelette lowered her head without saying a word, fearful, almost, of finally learning the truth.

'Upon my arrival at Clairets, I discovered something which at first I believed was a curious coincidence, and which led me to commit what I do not think it an exaggeration to call the crime of failing to inform Rome. Boniface VIII,* our then Holy Father, was not one of our allies. However, when Benoît XI* was elected I did not hesitate to inform him, and I confess that his response astonished me. I had the distinct impression that my discovery came as no surprise … Oh what a silly old fool going off at a tangent when there is so little time!' Éleusie blurted out hurriedly: 'The abbey houses a vast secret library. Hidden safely inside it – at least until yesterday – are a number of works containing writings of such a disturbing and dangerous nature that they must never be allowed to fall into the hands of evildoers or those motivated by greed.'

'A secret library? Here at the abbey?' Annelette repeated, astounded. 'Where?'

Éleusie glanced over at the tapestry covering one wall of her study and limited herself to one word:

'Behind.'

'Of course, I should have guessed,' the apothecary said ruefully. 'That long wall with no doors or windows that extends from your chambers … When was it built?'

'Judging from the plans drawn up on a piece of parchment I keep locked in my safe, the library was included in the original plans of the building a century ago.'

'So the murderer wanted the parchment, not your seal. At last, her actions make sense.'

Annelette's initial amazement at the Abbess's confession gave way to a burgeoning curiosity, a feverish excitement. She went on hurriedly:

'Does the library by any chance contain any … scientific works?'

'Yes, many of which are extraordinary and challenge even our most long-held beliefs.'

'May I … I hardly dare ask your permission to consult a few of them, that is if … You see, so many of the explanations we are given appear incomplete, not to say illogical.'

Éleusie paused again. What if she were committing an even graver mistake by trusting this woman? After all, besides the apothecary's own word, what other proof of her honesty did she have? What if she were simply a spy in the pay of their enemies? What if she were indeed the murderess – as Yolande de Fleury, the sister in charge of the granary whom life had treated so unkindly, had claimed shortly before being fatally poisoned?

'Our late lamented Pope Benoît's orders were categorical. Nobody but I must enter the library under any pretext.'

The apothecary nun's plain face grew sullen, and Éleusie stifled a feeling of growing resentment.

'Now is not the time for this type of discussion or, worse still, this squabbling,' she replied sharply. 'What I am about to tell you is so crucial, so appalling, as to render any temper tantrum on your part entirely out of place.'

Annelette looked at her and smiled apologetically.

'You are right, Reverend Mother. Please forgive me. My only excuse, if such it is, is that I would give anything to gain even a little more knowledge.'

'Knowledge can be a terrible thing,' Éleusie pointed out.

'No. It is what mankind does with it that is terrible. Science is not to blame if men choose to use advances in the knowledge of anatomy to become better torturers rather than to invent better cures.'

An unexpected tenderness lit up the Abbess's face and she observed:

'You remind me of my dear nephew when you speak like that. I wish he would come back to me. I feel so defenceless ... There I go again with my foolish self-pity!' Suddenly, she appeared resolved and declared:

'I have spent the past few days making a scrupulous inventory. Three of the manuscripts in the secret library were stolen during the diversion. The choice of works comes as no surprise to me and proves without doubt that the arsonist knew exactly what he was looking for. I caught him red-handed, disguised in a monk's habit, his cowl drawn over his face. I tried without success to grab the manuscripts.'

'Is that why you ordered all the exits to be locked and a thorough search of all the sisters, as well as their bundles and carts?'

'Yes. And it won't surprise you to know that "he" was in fact a "she". The blow I received was fierce, but it didn't have a man's violence behind it. The manuscripts have not yet left Clairets and we must find them as quickly as possible.'

'But the abbey is so vast ...' the apothecary began, before

Éleusie interrupted her with a confession that left her reeling.

'Of the three volumes, one was a large notebook belonging to the knight Eustache de Rioux and my nephew Francesco. In it were recorded decades of research and discoveries – both ours and those of our predecessors, the Knights Templar* – concerning our quest. During the fall of Saint-Jean-d'Acre, shortly before the slaughter of thirty thousand souls, Eustache de Rioux and a Knight Templar helped a small group of women and children escape into the tunnels under the citadel. I am unaware of the exact chain of events, but the women demanded to surrender to the enemy, believing their lives would be spared, and the Knight Templar chose to accompany them. Before returning to what would become a bloody massacre, the Knight Templar handed his notebook to Eustache, and beseeched him to carry on the sacred quest that he and a few brothers had kept a jealously guarded secret. The stolen notebook belonging to Francesco records all of these clues, all of our findings.'

'Its loss is a catastrophe,' breathed Annelette, her eyes wide with fright.

'And I haven't yet mentioned the nature of the other two works,' Éleusie commented. 'The second is a guide to necromancy of the most depraved kind, written by a certain Justus. Listen: I have been unable to bring myself to peruse its corrupt pages. However, I know that it did not simply aim to establish contact with the hereafter, already an unforgivable sin in the eyes of the Church, but to enslave souls in purgatory and employ them to evil ends. Francesco purchased it only in order to destroy it, thereby ensuring that it would not fall into the hands of scoundrels. He kept postponing hurling it into the purifying flames that would reduce it to ashes, and now … If it were to fall into our enemies' hands, if they were to make use of the terrible formulae within …'

'Oh dear God …'

'Wait. The worst – or at least the most worrying – is yet to come. The third work is known as 'The Vallombroso Treatise'. It ...' Éleusie went silent, uncertain whether she should go on, already fearing the consequences of what she was about to reveal to Annelette. 'It ... It claims ... Come on, I must take the plunge. It proves categorically that ... that the earth moves round the sun; it spins round the sun, always following the same trajectory, as though held aloft by some unknown force.'

'What! Are you saying that the system described by Ptolemy in which the earth is fixed at the centre of the universe is false?'

'Totally erroneous. Of course you realise that, if anyone overheard us speaking about this, we would be accused of heresy?'

The apothecary, dazed, ignored the caveat. Deep in thought, she appeared to have forgotten everything else – the murdered monks, the fire, the theft, the threat hanging over their quest. Suddenly she cried out, exultant:

'Now I understand everything ... What an idiot, what a fool! And I call myself a scientist! The true scientific mind must never cease questioning. If the earth were fixed in the centre of the heavens, how could the changing seasons, the tides, day and night, the stars be explained! What a privilege, what joy, I thank you from the bottom of my heart, Reverend Mother, for this extraordinary revelation!'

Éleusie's irritation got the better of her and she retorted sharply:

'Leave your rejoicing until later, daughter – that is, if we are still alive.'

The reproof brought Annelette's jubilation to an abrupt end, and she lowered her head. The Abbess went on:

'The workings of the scientific mind are clearly beyond me! The monk at the Vallombroso monastery* who drafted the treatise paid for it with his life. I wonder whether the unfortunate "accident" that caused him to fall and split his head open against

36

a pillar was not the work of our enemies. In any event, the treatise holds the key to the two birth charts you are already familiar with. These charts were discovered by the same Knight Templar who entrusted his notes to Eustache.' Éleusie broke off, then went on in a faltering voice: 'The shadowy figure is now in possession of these notes and of the treatise crucial to their understanding. Our enemies have been hounding us for centuries. Our sole advantage was their slowness to react. We have always been one step ahead of them. Now, I'm afraid …'

Annelette, in a state of extreme tension, tried to make sense of this sudden onslaught of information. She veered between euphoria and despair: euphoria because, despite the labyrinthine path that was taking them there, they were advancing towards the Light; and despair at the thought that she had so long been deprived of these secrets whose enormity she was only now beginning to grasp. She made a supreme effort to impose some order on the chaos of her thoughts:

'We are alone on board a ship lost on a raging sea. Benoît has been fatally poisoned and nobody can say whether the next pope elect will be friend or foe. In short, we must count upon our own guile to recover the manuscripts and exterminate the snake that has killed our sisters.'

'I'd wager my life that the thief and the murderess are one and the same person.'

'So would I, Reverend Mother. Even so, and notwithstanding your doubts about me – which I fully understand, for the feeling was mutual – if I am to form a complete picture of events, I need more facts. If you want me to make some sense out of this muddle, I implore you, be frank with me. We are not friends, I know, and it pains me to say so, believe me.' She stopped the Abbess's nascent protest with a gesture before continuing: 'However, we are … two survivors whose lives are in danger.'

Annelette stifled the unbidden sorrow welling up inside her;

for the first time in her life she regretted the lack of friendship with a fellow human being. No doubt it was too late to aspire to it now. No matter. She went on in a more decisive voice:

'Regarding the two birth charts. Am I to assume that they can be correctly calculated using Vallombroso's theory rather than Ptolemy's?'

'Yes.'

'And that they relate to events or people. I suspect one of them concerns Madame de Souarcy.'

'We believe it does. Madame Agnès was born on 25 December, the date indicated by one of the charts, which specifies that the person we seek was born during an eclipse. However, the eclipse was only partial on the night she was born.'

'Was it essential that the eclipse be total?'

'We don't know.'

'This explains the Inquisition's ruthless treatment of her,' reflected Annelette. 'Agnès de Souarcy is a threat to our enemies and therefore she must die.'

'That is what we believe.'

'Why?'

'My dear Annelette, if we had even the slightest inkling, the Light would already be within our grasp.'

'And yet, according to you, the incestuous desires of her half-brother, Eudes de Larnay, were at the bottom of the monstrous plot that led to Madame Agnès's arrest.'

'Oh, they were. Nonetheless, I am convinced – as is my nephew Francesco – that, unbeknownst to that conceited scoundrel, a far more formidable intelligence was at work behind the scenes. The baron is not a clever man. It wouldn't surprise me if Florin had not also been the victim of somebody more cunning than he. He paid for it with his life. An excellent outcome in his case.'

'Do you believe that Madame de Souarcy's life is still in danger?'

'If our theories are correct, then yes, without a doubt. Indeed, it almost makes the Grand Inquisitor seem preferable …'

Annelette finished her thought for her:

'Because at least we knew where the threat was coming from.'

'Precisely. At present we are in the dark and have no idea who will strike Agnès de Souarcy next – or when.'

'Do you know who might be behind this?'

'I have an idea, at least,' Éleusie replied after a brief pause. 'In Francesco's view, whoever is pulling the strings also ordered Benoît's murder …'

'Damn him …' breathed Annelette.

'I doubt the term even applies to him. He is cunning, extremely intelligent and what is more, my daughter, I am certain that he is not driven by personal glory. His influence in the Vatican must be enormous in order for him to have been informed of the papal emissaries' missions to Clairets, to have made such an impression on Florin and to have enabled his henchman to gain access to our late lamented Pope.'

Annelette stared at her aghast for a moment before it dawned on her. Suddenly she whispered:

'Not him! The camerlingo, Honorius Benedetti?'

'Who else?'

'Then all is lost.'

'What makes you say that?'

Now it was Annelette's turn to hesitate. She had spent sufficient time in Benoît's entourage when he was still only Nicolas Boccasini, Bishop of Ostia, to know something of the complexities of episcopal or even archiepiscopal politics. If the Abbess, blinded by her unquestioning faith, believed that nominations and elections were the expression of a higher, divine will, then she was very much mistaken. In reality, the apothecary almost envied her the angelic naivety that recent events had not completely managed to eradicate. Finally she spoke:

'When Boniface VIII died, it was rumoured that Bishop Benedetti had set his sights on the Holy See. To tell you the truth, it came as a terrible shock when Benoît was elected. Everybody was expecting the camerlingo to be the new Pope.'

'And why wasn't he?'

'I would like to be able to say that a miracle came to our aid, but the real reason had more to do with politics. I wonder whether the majority of the cardinals in the conclave weren't ...' She closed her eyes and shook her head, suddenly uneasy. 'Honorius Benedetti is a fearsome man. He is at once inspiring, inscrutable, intransigent. His so-called allegiance to Boniface VIII also caused concern, I believe. Unduly, for Benedetti is nobody's servant. He is a strategist, a thinker. The relationship between the two men was more like an extraordinary collaboration, for I doubt that Benedetti felt any sort of friendship towards the overbearing Boniface. In my opinion the camerlingo does not seek personal power. He likes to think of himself as being above worldly gain. The fact remains that certain people were tired of Boniface's dubious reputation,[2] his oppressive authority, and they voted for the benevolent, gentle Nicolas Boccasini. Perhaps they thought that he would be easy to control. They were mistaken. Benoît's infinite goodness and purity made him steadfast and unyielding.'

'Dear God ... Are you suggesting that Bishop Benedetti could be our next Pope?'

'I fear so. Astonishing though it might sound, I am hoping that the King of France's need for a docile pope will cause him to interfere in the coming election. If he does, Benedetti will be ruled out. Philip the Fair is no fool and his counsellor Guillaume de Nogaret* still less. Honorius Benedetti is the breed of man who will not be swayed by bribes, flattery or threats. He is a past master of the art of trickery and cannot be duped or seduced. If you are right – and I believe you are – he will stop at nothing to achieve his goal. Yes ... I want the King's Pope to be elected.'

Éleusie's face froze with shock. She stammered:

'So, you would sacrifice the Church, my daughter!'

'No, I am simply hoping for a reversal that will save Christianity and more importantly Christianity's message, which seems to me far more urgent, not to say imperative.'

A heavy silence fell. One thing troubled Annelette. Order. How to order the various elements the Abbess had given her and make sense of them. Finally, her concerns took shape:

'So, the Vallombroso treatise, written by that poor monk who was probably murdered, found its way into Boniface VIII's papal library. As for the two birth charts, they were discovered by the Knight Templar at Acre. We might infer from this that Honorius Benedetti's scholars never managed to decipher them, otherwise Madame de Souarcy would have long since been killed, assuming she plays the crucial role suggested by one of the charts.'

Éleusie studied her daughter, wondering what exactly she was leading up to. She nodded. Annelette went on:

'In that case, given that they no longer possessed the astrological calculations with which to identify her, how did the camerlingo's henchmen find her so quickly and plot her destruction?'

Expounded in this way, the error was so glaring that Éleusie was speechless. Her first thought was how to warn Francesco as swiftly as possible of Annelette's irrefutable conclusion. She whispered:

'Dear God, Annelette, you are right! Could we have been manipulated from the very beginning? Has the camerlingo placed a spy among us? I shudder at the thought.'

Faces, the sound of voices, snippets of memory flashed through the Abbess's mind. Who? Could an evildoer have infiltrated their small group of initiates? If so, Benedetti knew their names, as well as Agnès's. And, if he struck, their quest would be thrown into turmoil. It would never survive. Who? For safety's sake, they had kept their identities secret from one another.

'Does Madame de Souarcy suspect how important she is?'

'How could she, given that we ourselves know so little? We only know that Agnès plays a vital role, but we don't know why.'

'If only the chart pointed to her unequivocally.'

'Indeed,' agreed Éleusie.

'Let us go back to Eustache de Rioux, Reverend Mother.'

'Is this a cross-examination?' retorted Éleusie de Beaufort, who was growing increasingly uneasy.

Annelette was under no misapprehension. The Abbess's sudden sharpness was a sign of her continuing mistrust.

'Without a doubt. Time is running short. You said so yourself. Suspicion is a luxury we can ill afford. I am your only ally. Moreover ... Consider quickly what I am about to say: if I were one of them, now that these precious documents have been stolen, I could kill you this instant.'

With a deftness that took Éleusie completely by surprise, Annelette pounced on her and held to her throat the tip of a short dagger[3] she kept hidden in the pleat at the front of her robe.

'What! ... Good heavens!' cried the Abbess.

Annelette stepped back, replacing the knife in the cloth scabbard sewn into her robe, and said, tetchily:

'Pray, spare me a lecture on the impropriety of a woman of God carrying a weapon. I refuse to be a sacrificial lamb. I must continue my mission – which is to protect you. I owe it to God and to our dear departed Benoît.'

Annelette was mistaken. Éleusie had no intention of preaching virtue to her. The possession of a dagger by one of her daughters, which only days before would have angered her, comforted her now, although she reproached herself for negotiating with her faith.

'The Knight Hospitaller Eustache de Rioux was Francesco de Leone's godfather in the order. Not only was he a formidable soldier but one of the Hospitallers' most respected theologians.

Is it not an extraordinary coincidence that the Knight Templar chose to entrust him with his notes in the tunnel under Acre moments before the final battle that ended in bloody defeat?'

'Indeed, it seems extraordinary to us in our ignorance. However, it further proves that this is all part of a greater plan, a plan so complex that it is beyond our understanding. What else did the Templar's notes reveal?'

'They contained a curious sentence: "Five women and at the centre a sixth." As well as a runic prophecy.'

'What did it predict?'

'The runes gave advice to the warrior of light who took up the quest – in this case Francesco de Leone. They warned him against his enemies who are powerful and ruthless, and against being mistaken. This was no doubt a reference to the first erroneous astrological calculations. Before escorting the women and children out of the tunnel under the Saint-Jean citadel and perishing in the act, the Knight Templar mentioned a text –"a scroll of papyrus in Aramaic purchased from a Bedouin" – which he went on to describe as one of the most sacred texts in the history of humanity.'

'Do we know what it contains?'

'No. The Knight Templar hid the scroll in a safe place, he said.'

'Do we know where?' Annelette continued, a catch in her voice.

Éleusie, in a last act of prudence, refrained from mentioning that the Templar commandery at Arville was at the centre of the mystery. She simply shook her head.

'Is that all? Don't try to conceal anything more from me, Reverend Mother; time is our most implacable enemy.'

'That is all I know – except that the key to deciphering the ancient text surely lies in the astrological discoveries contained in the Vallombroso treatise. But they are complex and time-consuming and Francesco has not yet finished studying them.

For it appears – and again the scientist in you will be intrigued – that in his treatise the monk not only alluded to the earth moving around the sun but also to the existence of other celestial spheres than those hitherto identified. Three,[4] to be precise. Since the first calculation of the birth charts did not take them into account, it was necessarily false.'

'God Almighty … Other planets, unknown to the great scholars! … I feel honoured to be privy to such extraordinary revelations. I thank you from the bottom of my heart, Madame,' declared Annelette, her eyes brimming with tears. She quickly regained her composure and went on: 'Does the second birth chart refer to an event or a person?'

'In all honesty, I have told you everything I know. If it does indeed refer to a second person, what makes him so important as to justify this many deaths in order to guard his secret? Francesco is convinced that the key lies in the ancient scroll in Aramaic. Perhaps he is right.'

Annelette stood up, declaring in a threatening tone:

'If the treatise and the notebook leave these walls, this important person, if indeed he exists, will be doomed. They will destroy him. And if it isn't a person but a miraculous event, then Benedetti will make sure it never happens. In other words, these two works must under no circumstances leave the abbey.'

Suddenly prey to a fit of nervous rage, Éleusie all but shouted:

'Oh really? Do you think me too old or too foolish to have reached the same conclusion? And just how do you suggest we go about it, by scouring every square inch of the abbey grounds?'

'Of course not. We haven't time.'

'Give me a better solution, then.'

'I'm afraid it will hardly surprise you. I agree with you that the thief and the murderess are one and the same person. All that remains is for us to find her.'

'Many long weeks have passed since Adélaïde Condeau's

death, during which we have tried, *you* have tried, unsuccessfully to track her down,' the Abbess corrected, in an accusing tone.

'That is true,' admitted Annelette, her pride wounded. 'However, if you hadn't waited so long to confide in me, I would have known where to look, instead of groping around in the dark.' She added spitefully: 'And, if I'd been better informed, perhaps Hedwige du Thilay and Yolande de Fleury would still be with us!'

A wave of sorrow engulfed Éleusie, and she lowered her head in order to hide her eyes, which were brimming with tears, from the apothecary. She murmured almost inaudibly:

'The thought plagues me every night. Forgive me. I beg you, forgive me. Even though I am entirely undeserving and my actions have been unforgivable.'

Annelette felt a wrenching sadness, and rushed over to the distraught woman, embracing her and whispering in her ear:

'No, Madame, it is I who must beg your forgiveness. I am bitter and resentful because I despair of ever receiving your friendship. No, do not speak. I … I am the one who has acted foolishly, but I am too proud to admit it. I was excited by the prospect of a battle between me and this snake. Blinded by my own arrogance, I aimed to prove that I was the more cunning, the cleverer of the two. I looked for the subtlest ruses, the cleverest way of trapping her when what mattered was swiftness and efficiency. In short, I confess to having selfishly engaged in a battle of wits, forgetting that the most important thing was to find and destroy the culprit.'

With these words she left, devastated by the extent of her own recklessness.

Éleusie remained alone, beside herself with sorrow, speechless and unable to move.

Ayoung novice who had recently arrived looked up as Annelette Beaupré came hurtling out of one of the guesthouse doors into the herb garden. She watched the tall woman stop to catch her breath and raise her hand to her chest. Esquive d'Estouville paused, waiting for her 'mission' to approach. She must protect Annelette and Éleusie de Beaufort and at all costs find the thief who had stolen the manuscripts before they left the abbey. She had been chosen because of her talent for disguise as much as for her expert swordsmanship. Éleusie de Beaufort was the aunt of the beautiful archangel whose life she had protected with her sword in Mondoubleau Forest, whose body she had protected from the cold by holding him close as he lay unconscious. Two months ago. An eternity it seemed to her.

Annelette walked on, stifling the urge to burst into tears, to slump to her knees and pray for forgiveness. Caught up in her sorrow and shame, she did not notice a young novice crouching down in order to turn over the earth, and tripped over her. The young woman stood up, stammering an apology:

'Forgive me, sister. I was so busy digging the frozen earth I did not hear you approach.'

Annelette studied her, shaking her head. She didn't recognise the beautiful face. No doubt she was a new arrival. An offering to God,[5] perhaps. Her eyes lowered in a show of humility, the young woman asked:

'Are you not Sister Annelette, the apothecary nun whose skills are much praised? I have yet to distinguish which names, faces and functions go together.'

'It is the herbs that deserve praise, if anything. My talent consists merely in their preparation. And who might you be?'

An immense pair of pale-amber, almost yellow eyes looked slowly up at her.

'I am new here. My name is Esquive, but when I have the indescribable joy of being received into your order, I will take the name Sister Hélène.'

'You have chosen well. She was a remarkable woman and a true saint.'

With these words, she left the young woman and went to shut herself away in her herbarium, her world. A few yards from there, Esquive d'Estouville dropped her hoe – a tool unsuited to the season – and, unhindered by the short sword lying flat against her thigh, walked nimbly over to the scriptorium. She had attained her first goal and been prudent. She had coiled her unruly mop of wavy hair under the shorter veil worn by the novices in order to conceal it. However, her remarkable eyes were unmistakable and could give her away, for the Spectre whom she had seen off with her sword was hiding within these walls. Each time Esquive met one of the sisters – a rare occurrence since she had shrewdly requested to be assigned to the more onerous outdoor tasks – she lowered her eyes in an appropriate display of humility.

Annelette closed the shutters, bolted the door and began sobbing in the unwelcoming gloom.

How long was it since she had wept like this? How long since she had felt so deeply wounded? A lifetime.

An unbidden image broke through her despair: her father and brother sitting bolt upright behind the table in the main hall, staring at her critically, callously sizing her up. She did not feel hurt by their lack of affection, for it had never been forthcoming in her case, and she assumed that she no doubt deserved the coldness that had surrounded her for as long as she could remember.

That day, her mother had not deigned to leave her chambers where she prayed day and night, scarcely raising her eyes from her psalter, a bleak smile on her lips. The impossibly tall, lanky young woman sat with her hands clasped in her lap, awaiting the verdict of her father and brother, which was swift.

'Are you mad, daughter? You, assist your brother in the art of medicine? You must have taken leave of your senses.'

'But, Monsieur my father, I am well versed in the art of science and medicine.' In a last-ditch attempt to convince them, she had said, almost imploringly: 'You have on many occasions seen for yourself that I can be of considerable help.'

'What impudence! How dare you, Mademoiselle! Why, you ought to be ashamed of yourself! Have you forgotten that you are a mere woman and that women understand nothing of science? Their minds are incapable of understanding such complexities. Admittedly, they are good at remembering and imitating certain procedures and gestures. But when it comes to analysis and diagnostics ...'

The old physic, who considered himself an *aesculapius*,[6] despite having more medical blunders to his name than successes, had turned with a smile of complicity to his son who was an equally lamentable practitioner:

'If you're not careful, Grégoire, this conceited young woman will be giving you lessons on how to bleed a patient!'

Grégoire had laughed smugly, then looked his sister up and down with disgust before declaring in a bored voice:

'What of it ... If she cares to wash dirty linen and prepare ointments, it will save me an apothecary's wages. She can also help my wife with the children and the housework.'

'That is a generous offer, son. What do you say to that, Mademoiselle? Remember that you aren't getting any younger and I can't afford to keep an ageing daughter. As for finding you a husband …'

Annelette couldn't help but notice the look of malicious glee on the two men's almost identical faces. What pleasure they derived from humiliating her at such little cost to themselves. Suddenly, it had dawned upon her. The enormity of the revelation had struck her like a bolt of lightning: they had been afraid of her all these years. Her keen intelligence, her capacity to learn and to use her knowledge terrified them. Thanks to her, they had been forced to face up to their own limitations and they'd never forgiven her for it.

Curiously, this painful truth had freed her. She no longer belonged there because they didn't want her. She had no place among them. She had declared firmly yet calmly:

'I refuse the offer.'

Her father's mouth set in an angry grimace and he threatened:

'Well now … We're no monsters and we can't force you. In which case, Mademoiselle, I see only one other solution …' At this, he had turned to his son and sniggered before adding sarcastically: 'Unless of course a frog miraculously appears and turns into Prince Charming!'

Grégoire had imitated his father, giggling at the unkind joke.

'There is one other solution,' repeated the man whom she now knew to be heartless. 'A nunnery, my child.'

'As you wish, Monsieur. It is my duty to obey you.'

She had been unable to stop the irony from showing in her voice and her father had exploded with rage:

'God's wounds, girl! You cause me to regret bitterly the education you have received …'

She had received nothing but humiliation and shame. She alone was responsible for the knowledge she had assimilated through being observant and attentive.

'It just goes to show what an ungrateful girl you are. And as for your impudence, well, it bears out the growing doubts about the sense in educating young girls.'

She had left the room.

Four months later she became a novice at the Cistercian abbey at Fervaques,[7] founded in 1140 by Sénéchal de Vermandois.

Annelette wept, gasping for breath, wiping her nose on her sleeve, smothering her mournful sobs with her hand for fear a sister or novice might pass the herbarium and hear her.

Stop. Stop this instant, you big gangling fool! Pull yourself together at once. They didn't love you, not even your mother, whose only desire was to leave the world as soon as possible and join the angels in heaven. And what of it! Nearly thirty years have passed. They may all be dead. Will you carry these absurd regrets with you to your grave? Will you continue making a fool of yourself by trying to show them how wrong they were not to love you? They didn't care about you and it is time you stopped battling ghosts. Death is stalking you. Fight. Fight for your quest, for yourself, for Éleusie de Beaufort, for Madame Agnès. Stop fighting a memory, people whose faces have become faded images in your mind's eye.

She sat down on the small stone bench beneath the herbarium window and remained motionless for a long while, her mind drifting. Gradually, her sadness ebbed away and was replaced by a familiar weariness.

How long did she sit there? She could not say. When she finally stood up she thought she heard the bell for vespers.[+]

Figures, gestures, voices that she had seen, observed, heard a thousand times flashed through her mind. Blanche de Blinot, the senior nun and prioress as well as the Abbess's second in command. Blanche, whose deafness and senility had always grated on her nerves. Curiously, the warm compassion she had felt for the old woman had gradually been replaced by a feeling of contempt. Blanche's obsessive fear of being poisoned made her seem even more like a dying woman clinging pathetically to life. Annelette wondered whether the old nun's hysteria when she learned of the deaths of Hedwige du Thilay and above all of Yolande de Fleury didn't reflect her fear of being the next victim rather than her attachment to the treasurer nun[8] or the kindly sister in charge of the granary. Jeanne d'Amblin who sipped her soup so slowly that it felt as if she would be there all night. The dreadful events that had taken place at the abbey in the last few months had brought Annelette closer to the extern sister, whom she had hitherto unfairly resented. It was Jeanne's task to collect donations from charitable souls or those ordered by law to give alms as a penance for minor misdemeanours. As such, she was not subjected to the cloister – unlike, among others, the apothecary – and was allowed to savour the outside world each time she left the abbey. Berthe de Marchiennes. It was true that Berthe had lost some of her pompous arrogance and no longer wore that perpetually pious expression. Annelette had to admit that the cellarer nun[9] had shown some measure of bravery when she confessed to having joined the nunnery because her family had rejected her, and she had no prospects of marriage or any future. And yet she was still suspicious of Berthe and was not entirely convinced by her willingness to help find the murderess. And what of Thibaude de Gartempe, the guest mistress? Thibaude bustled about between her beds and wore herself out sluicing the blackened walls as though in an effort to prove to them all that she was not to blame for the fire. Thibaude, whose madness lay dangerously close to the surface. Annelette could still picture the woman shortly before Hedwige's demise, screaming hysterically and demanding to leave the abbey at once, digging her nails into the apothecary's arm until she was forced to slap her. What if her extreme behaviour was merely a clever ploy, an act? And the stout, sullen Emma de Pathus, who Annelette suspected took out her perpetual ill temper too readily on the novices and on her students, since as schoolmistress she alone had the authority to raise her hand to them. Annelette had noticed many a tearful eye and reddened cheek bearing the mark of Emma's hand. What had she and the infamous Grand Inquisitor been talking about when the Abbess had discovered them in conversation? And the doe-eyed sister in charge of the fishponds and henhouses, Geneviève Fournier? With whom might she have discussed her missing eggs? Geneviève, who could no longer be heard singing canticles at the top of her voice to encourage her hens to lay. Her joy had been silenced for ever, it seemed. And Sylvine Taulier, the sister in charge of the bread ovens, the tiny, stout, tireless woman who churned out loaves as if her life depended on it? And the others? What a woeful inventory. Whom could she trust? Jeanne, perhaps, or more probably Elisaba Ferron who had, at the apothecary's insistence, replaced Adélaïde Condeau as the sister in charge of meals and the kitchens. This middle-aged widow of a wealthy merchant from the Nogent region had recently taken her final vows. Elisaba was big enough to knock out any villain attempting to meddle with her pots and pans. As for her hardened character, it befitted a strong woman who concealed a compassionate nature beneath her stentorian voice and no-nonsense shop owner's manner.

Who? Who, then?

Annelette had started off on the assumption that the murderess was intent on stealing the Abbess's seal. She must think again. All the same, she was not to blame for her mistakes, which were born of the Abbess's mistrust!

Annelette gave a faint smile. Good. She was becoming angry and bellicose again.

She must now reconstruct the various elements, starting with the killer's true motive: the secret library and its precious works.

Annelette walked over to the tall cabinet and took down a bag of *Ricinus communis*[10] whose oil she only occasionally used as a depurative, on account of its toxicity. She spread the grey seeds streaked with reddish-brown on the table she used for weighing and making up her preparations, and sat down on the little stool. She slid one seed to the left: Adélaïde Condeau, their good-natured, if rather witless, cook, who had been fatally poisoned with aconite in a cup of lavender-and-honey tea meant for Blanche de Blinot, the prioress and guardian of the Abbess's seal. She placed a second seed beside the first: Blanche, who scarcely left the steam room and spent so much of her time snoozing that the sisters would occasionally look in on her to make sure she hadn't died in her sleep. Curiously, the aconite used in the tea had not been taken from the cabinet in the herbarium, as Annelette had first feared. The apothecary placed a third seed above the other two: Hedwige du Thilay, the treasurer nun. Next to it she placed a fourth: Jeanne d'Amblin, whose intelligence Annelette deemed worthy of that name. Admittedly, Jeanne had been one of her main suspects up until she herself was poisoned. The fact that she had been on one of her rounds when the yew powder was stolen from the herbarium was further proof of her innocence. Had both friends been targeted or had either Jeanne or Hedwige partaken of the poisoned drink meant for only one of them? In this case Annelette was certain that the murderess had used yew powder stolen from her store in the herbarium. Hedwige's symptoms proved it, as did the convulsions, shaking and vomiting Jeanne had suffered before falling into a semi-permanent slumber. Annelette felt a vague sense of sorrow as she placed a fifth seed beside the others: Yolande de Fleury – sweet-natured, jolly Yolande who had lived only for her dream that little Thibaut enjoyed health and happiness. Who had been lying to her for two long years by bringing her good news of the dead child? Why?

Annelette then made a little mound out of several castor-oil seeds to represent herself, Éleusie, Madame de Souarcy, the Pope's emissary and the contaminated rye discovered by Adélaïde in the herbarium shortly before her death. She contemplated it at length then demolished it with a flick of her finger before forming it again. No. She had left out at least three seeds: Emma de Pathus, the schoolmistress who had been seen talking to the fiend Florin; Thibaude de Gartempe, for who was better placed than the guest mistress to create a diversion by setting fire to the guest house? And finally, the shard of glass which had become embedded in her shoe next to Jeanne's bed. Glass was a precious commodity, and its presence in the dormitory was puzzling to say the least.

She fingered the seed representing Yolande. Strangely, the death of the sister in charge of the granary had affected Annelette more than she could have imagined. She missed the plump young woman's joviality. And yet she had always considered her permanent good spirits a sign of shallowness. Most of all, she regretted her attempt to use Yolande's dead son in order to force her to tell them who had been bringing her news of him. The bright-red streaks on Yolande's deathly pale corpse resembled scratch marks. Annelette's first thought had been strangulation: two hands or a strip of cloth tightening around her neck. Upon closer examination, she had concluded that strangulation had not taken place. Moreover, what woman was strong enough to strangle a healthy person like Yolande without a struggle that would have woken up the entire dormitory? No. Yolande, like the others, had been poisoned. Several other factors supported Annelette's theory, one of which was the reddened patch extending up from the base of her neck to just below her nose. No cord or strip of cloth would have left this sort of mark.

Think. Yolande de Fleury hadn't had the strength to leave her bed or cry for help, suggesting that she was too drowsy to move or perhaps even paralysed. She had almost certainly died of asphyxiation. Either that or heart failure. Was it aconite poisoning as in Adélaïde's case? Think. When Adèle de Vigneux, the keeper of the granary, had discovered Yolande's dead body, it was already stone cold, which meant that she had been dead for hours, even taking into account the freezing-cold air in the dormitory. She had lain there with her mouth open, one leg dangling out of the bed, the other tucked under her buttocks, and despite the cold her arms had been outside the covers. Had a sudden attack of fever made her want to cool down? It was possible. And yet it didn't explain the position of the lower limbs, still less the patch of red rising from the base of her neck right up past her mouth. The stiffness of the limbs was what perplexed Annelette. It couldn't have been due to rigor mortis, which sets in three to four hours after death, beginning in the small muscles of the neck and spreading throughout the entire body within twelve hours. However, judging from the time Yolande attended the last service, she couldn't have died much more than four to five hours before she was discovered. And yet her corpse was cold and stiff. Few known poisons could act so swiftly. Annelette racked her brains to no avail. She had a vague recollection – something relating to an animal, she was sure. Still, one thing was certain: the murderess hadn't taken the poison from her cabinet otherwise she would have recognised the effects.

An animal. Yes. A large animal. Dangerous. What was it! Think. She had read about it once. Why had she with her prodigious memory and ceaselessly active mind mislaid this piece of information?

With an angry gesture she swept aside the castor-oil seeds.

Artus d'Authon had been in a state of extreme nervous tension for the past two weeks. This man who was known to all as even-tempered – though in particular to the household servants, who were better placed than anybody to know their master – would fly off the handle over the slightest misdemeanour, blowing up out of all proportion things that would normally have made him laugh.

The humble folk attached to the chateau kept a low profile, remaining as quiet and unobtrusive as possible. He had scolded a laundry woman for a crease in an undershirt, and one of the cooks thought his end had come when he overspiced the hippocras. As for the farrier, Artus had accused him of mistreating his beloved Ogier and pushed him roughly against the forge wall simply because the horse had shaken its mane when the man approached.

Everybody was concerned. The older servants remembered with dismay the Comte's terrifying grief when his son and sole heir, Gauzelin, had died; they had seen murder written in their master's smouldering brown eyes and in his every gesture. Some even went as far as to speak to Ronan, for whom their master felt a special attachment that was unusual for this undemonstrative man. The old man had known the Comte since he was born, and had virtually brought him up. He alone had dared approach Artus while he was mourning the loss of his son. Now they came to Ronan again to ask if he knew anything, if he could offer some explanation perhaps. Ronan had replied that their master was simply suffering from an attack of spleen and assured them it would pass.

*

Ronan was aware of what was eating away at the Comte, robbing him of the desire to eat, drink, even to sleep: Madame – for this was what he called the woman he knew was no ordinary lady. Ronan had never met her, but he knew of her from young Clément's devotion and his terror when his mistress was imprisoned, from Artus's peaks of joy and sadness, from the chief bailiff Monge de Brineux's flattering remarks, and even from the Comte's physician Joseph de Bologne's enquiries about her health.

Ronan knocked on the door of the little rotunda library which the Comte used as a study. A gruff, irritable voice rang out:

'What is it now? Must I flee to the middle of a desert in order to enjoy some peace around here?'

The faithful servant entered the room, pretending not to have noticed Artus's foul mood:

'The cook begs to know your requirements for supper. You have lost weight, my lord. Your breeches, even your chausses are loose on you.'

'I'm not hungry and I don't want any supper. The man is beginning to annoy me. And so are you, fussing over me like an old mother hen.'

Ronan lowered his head in silence.

Artus could have kicked himself. What sort of a brainless oaf was he, abusing one of the few people who formed a link in his life, a link to his past, one of the few people he truly loved? He sighed with frustration, and mumbled:

'I've always had a special fondness for mother hens. I find the way they fuss over their own and other hens' chicks utterly charming. However … I am not in the mood for company.'

Ronan looked up at the man whom he would always consider his 'little boy' and responded to Artus's veiled excuses with a shy smile.

'My Lord Monge de Brineux doesn't understand your desire

for solitude. Perhaps a talk with your faithful friend might …'

'Brineux wouldn't understand,' thundered the Comte. 'And, besides, how could I explain to him what I myself am at a loss to comprehend. God's wounds! When I think that she refused my hospitality, which was entirely justified after her ordeal in that dungeon! It couldn't possibly have given rise to any gossip.'

Ronan paused, aware that he was treading on dangerous ground, and then, out of love and respect for this steadfast, courageous, yet at times exasperatingly morose man, he ventured:

'Unlike your hospitality, gossip needn't be legitimate in order to spread. I expect Madame's attention was required by various tasks at Manoir de Souarcy. I expect a sudden and open … association with Authon would not seem proper to a lady of her standing and distinction. I expect …'

'Why do you all insist upon calling her "Madame" as if she were the only one,' Artus interrupted, at once puzzled and irritated.

'Isn't she, my lord?'

'In whose eyes?'

'In yours and, as a member of your entourage, in mine.'

'Why do I still feel like a six-year-old boy sometimes when I'm with you?'

Ronan's face lit up as he recalled:

'You were a mischievous, disobedient little rascal. You were already fearless then. Dear Lord, the pranks you got up to! I thought I'd die of fright the day you climbed onto the pigeon loft to see for yourself that the sun rose in the east. You gave us a terrible scare. You flatly refused to come down. And the night you went out into the forest to find the white unicorn in the fairy tale … And that time you nearly drowned yourself trying to stay underwater to see if you would grow gills. God only knows where you got all your ideas, but there was no stopping you. There were times when I thought I'd go out of my mind.'

The Comte's mood softened a little as he recalled his childhood follies – some of which, indeed, had nearly cost him his life. He continued in a calmer voice:

'Everybody. You, Clément, the clerk at Alençon ... that Knight Hospitaller Francesco de Leone, whom I know only by name, even my physician who asks after "Madame's" health and sends ointments for her which he makes up himself from a secret recipe.'

Ronan was no fool. His master's sole concern was the knight. Was he angry with the man for having stepped in and saved Madame de Souarcy? Or was this simply the jealousy of a lover? Realising that his lord felt truly unable to discuss his fears with Monge de Brineux, the loyal servant cautiously broached the explosive subject of his master's emotions:

'Ah ... the knight ...'

'What about the knight? His was not the only name I mentioned, was it?'

'No, of course not.'

The Comte studied him for a moment before conceding defeat:

'Come and sit down, Ronan – since your stubbornness is equal only to the turmoil I have been plunged into for days. And after all, who better to confide in ... besides "Madame", that is,' he added, smiling for the first time in days.

The old man perched stiffly on one of the tiny armchairs, moved by his master's evident display of affection and trust.

'Well, yes ... the knight. I don't know what to make of him, my dear Ronan. I am assailed by the most foolish notions. Clément assured me that Madame de Souarcy had never met the man before he visited her in prison, and I believe him. I am also convinced that his sword killed Nicolas Florin. What could drive a Knight Hospitaller of his rank to assault a Grand Inquisitor? How did he find her in Alençon, and why? His mission was to save her, I'd wager my life on it. Why did Agnan, the dead fiend's clerk, babble incomprehensibly about Madame Agnès, giving the impression that he was in love with her? Why does everybody, man and child, including myself, I confess, worship her to the point of risking their lives to save hers? Why, why this knight from Cyprus? What does he know of her?' he exploded angrily.

'Do you fear that he … how should I say, that this man who has taken a vow of chastity might have formed an improper attachment to her?'

'And why not? Why wouldn't he fall in love? Didn't I fall for her body and soul from one moment to the next?' the Comte retorted in a voice filled with irony.

'Do you remember when you used to ask me questions to which I did not know the answers? And you champed at the bit, insisting: "There's a solution to every problem. You only have to find it."'

'What are you trying to say?'

'Would it not be best to confess your doubts to "Madame"? By all accounts she does not appear to be an evasive woman or one prone to playing foolish games.'

'What, and make a complete idiot of myself? I'm not even sure that she sees any … attraction in me aside from my position and fortune. And you see, in her case that wouldn't be enough for me; what is more, I doubt that for a woman like her it would be either.'

'What better opportunity to find out? And at the same time grasp the nettle.'

'You don't mean with her …?' Artus was indignant.

'Indeed no, my lord. What did I teach you about never handling a lady directly?' Ronan chortled. 'It is far too dangerous. No, indeed. I had in mind the knight de Leone. You might approach him and obtain an explanation. I've heard these monk-soldiers aren't easy to broach, but your name and reputation might encourage him to listen and save you a humiliating rebuff.'

It was so startlingly obvious that Artus gaped at Ronan – as though surprised to see him sitting there. When he finally spoke, he sounded more like his old self:

'Do you realise, my dear Ronan, what a weight you've lifted off my shoulders? Why, good heavens! Of course, I will speak to the knight ... I hope he hasn't already left for some far-off land. Pray, send for Monge de Brineux. He may be able to help me. He has men posted everywhere.'

'What about "Madame"?'

The Comte's self-assurance suddenly faltered:

'Well ... Your advice is sound ... But I need more time to weigh up the advantages and disadvantages. I ... I am perfectly capable of grasping a whole bunch of nettles. But approaching a woman of such distinction is another matter. You see, Ronan,' he went on, adopting a slightly didactic tone, 'women are such complex – not to say unpredictable – creatures, whereas we men ... well, we are more ... straightforward, more approachable somehow.'

The wrinkled face, which years before had watched over him through many a feverish night, broke into a smile.

'At least that is what we men like to believe. Is it not simply because women expect different things of life that we deem them unpredictable ... not to say irrational?'

'Well! Are you saying that I'm talking nonsense?'

'Why, I wouldn't dare, my lord,' the old servant replied, a hint of triumph in his voice. 'With your permission, I will take my leave and send for Lord de Brineux.'

'Go.'

No sooner had the old man so dear to his heart left than Artus acknowledged what he had spent two weeks trying to avoid, preferring instead to fret, bridle, brood and rage. But he had not counted on Ronan. Ronan who had always known how to handle him, how to cajole him patiently into doing what he didn't want to do: to sit down to meals, wash, go to bed, say his prayers, study at his desk and now, as a grown-up, to reflect.

He gave a sigh of impatience. Of course he would need to demand explanations from this mysterious Hospitaller. Was it possible for a soldier of God to form a sentimental attachment to a woman – albeit not just any woman? Artus was honest enough to acknowledge that his unease was in part due to jealousy. 'Madame' had stolen his heart and mind so swiftly, so completely, that he had barely had time to register it. So why not another man's? What other explanation could there be for the knight's readiness to kill without compunction a man of God, a Grand Inquisitor, the Pope's representative – however depraved – in order to save her?

He charged furiously round the modest-sized room, like a caged lion, the tiny, uneven panes of glass rattling in the windows as he strode past.

Clément had assured him that his lady knew nothing of the knight before his unexpected arrival at the Inquisition headquarters.

'God's wounds!' he mumbled through gritted teeth. It made no sense at all. Nothing about Madame de Souarcy made any sense. He froze at the thought. What scheme was being hatched around her?

Meeting the knight would be of no use to him, at least not yet. He had no choice but to do what Ronan had shrewdly suggested – to pay her a visit. His enthusiasm was tinged with dread. What if she sent him away? What if she were evasive? What if he discovered that she didn't share his feelings? Yes, but what if she did?

He needed a pretext. It would make him appear less foolish. He wished to enquire after her health, and after that of young

Clément – whose energy and enthusiasm were indeed missed at the chateau. In fact, Joseph seemed positively to pine for the boy's constant probing.

Should he announce his arrival? He recalled Agnès's annoyance, her stinging rebuke, the day he had arrived unannounced and caught her dressed in peasant's breeches as she harvested her honey, her long, lissom thigh muscles tensing beneath the coarse cloth as she mounted Ogier. Goodness! The woman had not left his thoughts for a single moment since their first meeting.

Should he announce his arrival or not? It would certainly be more respectful, although as her overlord he was under no obligation. However, he thought he would discover what he wanted to know more quickly if his visit were a surprise.

Château de Larnay, Perche, December 1304

Jules stood twisting his cap lined with rabbit fur between his hands. He was trying to keep as much distance as possible between himself and his terrifying master, but had been ordered by the other man in a slurred splutter:

'Come closer! Come closer, you wretch. So, my good foreman, what have you to report?'

The serf was only foreman by default, and his title did not spare him from his master's blows or save him from starvation.

'Come closer, I said!' bellowed Eudes de Larnay, hammering the table with his fist. 'Answer me this instant or I'll have you horse-whipped by your brothers in misery, who will be only too glad to punish you for your recent arrogance towards them. You're nothing but a bunch of useless scoundrels intent on robbing me!'

'No, good master, no,' stammered the terrified man.

'If you and your fellow scoundrels aren't robbing me blind or idling like slugs, then where is my week's quota of iron ore? Not in the paltry sack you brought me earlier, I hope?'

The other man just nodded.

'Yes? Are you making fun of me or what? Why, there's little more than a stone's weight in there! Where is the rest? You've sold it, haven't you …?' He glowered. 'Ah, I see … You're robbing me blind to pay your taxes, your tallage[11] or, worse still, your emancipation. Confess or I'll skin you alive!'

'No, my lord. You're mistaken. That sack's worth is all we could get out of the mine, I swear on my soul. The mine, it's … well, it's …'

Jules's words petered out. He was trembling with fright. His master's temper had already claimed several lives. It was rumoured that he'd wrung that strumpet Mabile's throat for her. Mabile had recently returned to the chateau after spending some time with the master's half-sister, Madame de Souarcy. She was a comely wench, that temptress, but a nasty piece of work.

'The mine? What about it?' Eudes growled.

'It's finished, exhausted, there's nothing left in it. Not an ounce. It's not our fault, master. We've dug until our hands bled. There's no ore left. It's finished. I swear it on my son's life.'

Baron de Larnay leapt to his feet, overturning the bench he'd been sitting on. Jules thought his last hour had come, and stifled a cry as he crossed himself. Eudes roared:

'Out of my sight! Out of my sight this instant before I change my mind!'

The foreman didn't wait to be told twice and raced out of the main hall, thanking heaven for his life, which for the time being was out of danger. After all, he possessed nothing more – not even the liberty to leave.

Eudes flopped against the edge of the table. It was true. If he had flogged the men in recent weeks, it was only in a vain attempt to deceive himself that there was some ore left, enough to keep the King happy for a while.

The mine had for generations been the source of the Larnay family's relative peace of mind vis-à-vis the royal powers, as well as their family fortune – of which only a few tawdry relics now remained. His ancestors had cleverly negotiated with the French kings while continuing to court their enemy: the neighbouring English. The implication was guarded but clear: the ore would go to the more munificent and 'congenial' monarch. Thus his grandfather had summed up their situation with the bonhomie of a wealthy draper: 'A man's wife is never as attractive as when she is pleasing to other men. And men are generous only to women who please.' The bonhomie had run dry and the 'attractive wife' was barren. The mine had already begun to show signs of decline shortly before the death of Baron Robert, Eudes's father.

With a shaking hand, he picked up the pitcher, splashing wine onto the dark wood as he filled his goblet. He staggered, grabbing the table just in time to steady himself.

Mathilde! That stupid, vicious little harlot prancing about the chateau in her aunt's faded finery, giving orders and scolding the servants as though she were their future mistress. They all detested her. He detested her! It had all gone wrong because of her stupidity during the Inquisition trial. Mathilde … Was she expecting him to deflower her in the marital bed? Was that what she was waiting for? Strangely, although it had been his intention, the thought no longer excited him. Mathilde no longer existed if he were unable to use her to hurt Agnès. He belched then laughed raucously. What need had he to court a young maiden with tender kisses when he could mount as many girls as he wanted who would do exactly as he pleased? If Mathilde's stupidity was to blame for the failure of her beloved uncle's plans, then she would have to pay. She would pay for that and for everything else. In his drunken rage it didn't matter to Eudes that a total stranger had stabbed the inquisitor to death. The fault was Mathilde's. She was to blame for everything – even for not being more like Agnès.

Yes, the little fool must pay. Then perhaps he would be able to get some sleep.

He reflected. His face broke into a smile as he had a sudden inspiration. He called a servant, who was also careful to keep her distance.

'Go at once and inform Mademoiselle my niece that I wish to see her.'

The girl curtseyed hastily before obeying.

Mathilde had requested a few moments to make herself look pretty before receiving her handsome, beloved uncle. She had pinched her cheeks and chewed her lips to make them pinker, and debated at length whether or not to let her hair down. No. A lady only unbraids her plaits or uncoils her hair when going to bed with her spouse or lover. She had hurried over to the little stool beside the dressing table and adopted what she hoped was a languid yet elegant pose, with perhaps even a hint of provocativeness.

One look at her uncle's sullen face had told her that she would not be discovering any carnal secrets that night. She had sat up, frustrated. Eudes had seen through her charade, and been overwhelmed by a feeling of violent loathing. The little slut. She didn't even have the defence of poverty, which he recognised in other women while taking full advantage of it.

'Dear Uncle, how glad I am to see you again.'

'I fear you won't be for very long, my dear, sweet child.'

'You frighten me.'

'I'm desperate. Your mother is still blighting our lives.'

'What!'

'She demands your return. It is her privilege, since the outcome of her trial, however unjust, did not strip her of her rights.' Thanks to you, you little wretch, he thought before resuming: 'I fear she will wreak revenge on you for your bravery and your affection for me, which warms my heart. I know her well. Underneath all that innocence lies a ruthless woman. Oh dear God ... When I think of you in that pigsty, Manoir de Souarcy – your pretty hands ruined by drudgery, your lovely figure swathed in rags ... it wrings my heart.'

It wrung Mathilde's equally. Indeed, the mere thought of it turned her stomach. No! She would not go back to Manoir de Souarcy, to her mother, to that filth, those evil-smelling serfs and the unbearable coldness of those ugly stone walls. She wanted merriment, fine food, lights, tapestries, servants, beautiful clothes and jewellery.

'I won't go! I won't go back to that stinking Souarcy.' Panic-stricken and near to tears, she implored: 'Please, Uncle, I beg you to let me stay here with you.'

'It is my dearest wish, sweet child. But how? I cannot fight your mother. Not any more.'

'But ... I will come of age soon,[12] in less than five months' time to be exact.'

'Where can I hide you all that time so that you may come back to me afterwards?' Eudes drew close to his half-niece, lowering his head meekly before driving home his advantage: 'Madame, it took several goblets of wine for me to pluck up the courage to make this confession. Is it not extraordinary for a man who fears only God?' the coward lied.

The young girl became dizzy with expectancy at his sudden submissiveness and use of the word 'Madame'. She simpered:

'You're scaring me, Monsieur.'

'And yet that is the last thing I wish to do at this moment. You ... Surely, in your wisdom, you must have noticed that I have developed an ... attachment to you that cannot be explained by mere blood ties, which, on the contrary ... make it difficult, unthinkable even.'

Mathilde's heart missed a beat. Finally!

'Monsieur ...' she gasped, clasping to her mouth her hand, which bristled with rings belonging to her dead aunt, Madame Apolline.

'I know ... But it is too late now for me to turn back. I understand that our blood ties repel you. I have thought about it long and hard. I stand before you, defeated, helpless, hopeless. Do you wish me dead? I give you my life.'

Ah ... What eloquence! Mathilde had spent nights on end dreaming of such a declaration. Did she harbour a guilty love for her uncle? Indeed not. She scarcely liked him. Mathilde loved nobody but Mathilde de Souarcy, whom she found more and more beguiling. Even so, he was rich – or so she believed – and she found the scene stimulating; she had become an inaccessible goddess before whom men prostrated themselves. What a delightful idea! She stretched out her hands for him to kiss.

'Dead? Never, Monsieur. What must I do to remain always by your side?'

'Do you mean that you …'

'Shh,' she cut him short. 'One should never ask such a confession of a lady.'

'I am an unpardonable oaf, Madame. I apologise a thousand times over. But you have stirred me to the depths, brought me back to life. What must you do? After giving it much consideration I have found only one simple solution. If your mother gets hold of you, she will make your life a misery. You are young and lovely, while she is growing old and has no other prospects than the thankless toil at Souarcy. Her jealousy will know no bounds. She senses that you have won my heart – without doing much, it is true.'

The image he evoked of her having seduced him in opposition to her mother so pleased Mathilde that she accepted it unthinkingly.

'What is this simple solution, dear Uncle?'

'Call me Eudes, please. Do not evoke those ties that wrench my heart.'

'Eudes … I have practised saying your name a thousand times over, Monsieur. Tell me, what solution is this?'

'A nunnery, my beauty. You will be a guest at a nunnery for five short months, until you come of age.'

'I will go to a nunnery?'

'Not as an offering to God, but as a guest. This form of religious retreat is fashionable among the grandest ladies, including the King's daughter, Madame Isabelle herself.'

'Madame Isabelle, really?'

'Indeed, and many others besides.'

'Five months is a long time ... Nunneries are such deadly places.'

'Five months and you will be free for ever. You, I ... But your beauty and elegance will one day take you from me ...'

'Don't be silly, Unc— Eudes, dear Eudes,' she assured him, even as she reflected that Château de Larnay would soon fail to live up to the glorious future she envisaged for herself. What was more, her half-uncle would never receive dispensation from the Church to marry her. 'Very well, sweet Eudes, I agree to go on a brief retreat. But please, I beg you, find a nunnery less dreary than Clairets!'

'I already have one in mind,' he lied as he racked his brains to think of a place as far removed as possible from Larnay and Souarcy-en-Perche. 'You will need to draft a brief letter explaining your wish to leave the world[13] for a spell in order to be closer to God ... It will help me to defend us against Agnès's wrath.'

Eudes's immediate choice was Argentolles, a Cistercian abbey founded by Blanche de Navarre and her son Thibaut VI de Champagne. It satisfied his requirements perfectly: it was far away, buried in the heart of the Champagne region and the rule drafted by Saint Benoît was particularly severe, requiring extreme poverty, strict observation of the cloister and a special emphasis on manual labour.

Your pretty nails will be torn to shreds from scrabbling in the earth, my little coquette; your back will ache from stooping to collect firewood and you'll have to break the ice in your washbowl every morning.

'You may dictate, Eudes.'

As he carefully chose the phrasing that would best give the impression that his niece's decision was final, he envisaged her sitting naked on a hard stool in a freezing room. He saw a nun's razor approaching her beautiful chestnut locks and slicing them off before shaving her head. He saw them fall to the ground in long wavy clumps. He saw the tears running down Mathilde's cheeks and dropping onto her tiny breasts. He could almost feel the roughness of the long linen shirt as it slipped over her head. The whore!

By the time her mother found her the insufferable little flibbertigibbet would have come of age and then nothing and nobody could intervene to save her from the convent. Especially since he intended to be a generous donor, and releasing her might involve having to return the money. He was counting on being able to convince the Abbess that lust was leading the young girl astray and that he as her uncle and guardian was concerned for the purity of her soul, and trusted that God and discipline would keep her on the path of righteousness. How could the good woman who was about to do him such a great favour possibly find out that he wasn't the foolish girl's guardian?

The whore!

Aude de Neyrat stretched, gazing with satisfaction at her milk-white skin, which was slightly flushed after her rose-and-lavender-scented bath.

Wearing only a pair of embroidered silk shoes, she was studying her reflection in the small mirror in her private chamber. Perfect. She always looked perfect – from her toes right up to her lovely domed brow, which was accentuated by a subtle shaving back of the hairline in accordance with the fashion of the day. This was not vanity or conceit. Together with her intelligence and guile, her body and ravishing face were her two most powerful weapons, and as such deserved to be taken good care of.

While she awaited the arrival of her visitor, she decided to cross the communal baths in her simple attire. It was a test she liked to perform occasionally.

She stepped nonchalantly out of her chamber holding a goblet of mallow tea, and pretended to examine the recent arrivals as though she were an elegant lady searching for a relative who was meeting her at the baths. A dozen or so pairs of female eyes fixed upon her, looking her up and down, more or less discreetly, weighing up her beauty. Reassured, Aude returned to her private chamber. There is no harsher critic of a woman's beauty than another woman, for a man's judgement is quickly clouded by desire. Ten women!

These furtive evaluations were one reason why Aude frequented bathhouses. A woman of her position could afford to bath at home. The second reason was more strategic. Women gossip openly among themselves, even with complete strangers they have only just met at the baths. They exchange secrets of the boudoir, recipes, marital or financial problems and occasionally let slip an anecdote that might be useful to those who know how to bring down the powerful. Aude frequented bathhouses as a means of garnering information. Moreover, what better place to receive a female visitor whom she did not wish passers-by or servants to see entering the town house Honorius Benedetti had rented for her in Chartres. What better place for secret meetings than these rooms ringing with banter and laughter?

Mixed baths existed in those days when nudity was not considered shocking. Some were the setting for amorous trysts and, regardless of whether money changed hands, were little more than brothels. Aude avoided such places, some of which were high-class establishments where tables were beautifully laid out with food and wine in front of screened-off baths so that couples meeting for a few hours might replenish themselves between love-making sessions. With the exception of an occasional, yet burning, physical need, the pleasures of the flesh, whose every trick and ruse she was familiar with, had long since ceased to interest Madame de Neyrat. Her body had become a means like any other of achieving her ends.

Aude stretched out on the little day bed in her chamber and closed her eyes.

Honorius, dear Honorius. She had found the camerlingo older, shrunken, on her last visit to Rome. It was strange how some men's appetite for power is never sated. They seize, devour, absorb fresh morsels of power, which leave them ravenous.

She opened her eyes and sat up straight. A woman was staring at her. She wore a robe that was not warm enough for the time of year and a bonnet, no doubt covering her shaven head. Aude stood up, slowly picking up the bath sheet that had slipped to the floor. The other woman studied the blonde mass of hair framing the charming, perfectly oval-shaped face, the flawlessly domed brow, the big emerald-green upward-slanting eyes and the heart-shaped mouth. She felt an immediate hatred of this too beautiful, too self-assured, too casual woman who was an unwittingly cruel reminder of everything she lacked, which had tormented her for so long.

Aude de Neyrat asked in a frosty but polite voice:

'I see no bundle, nor any package, Madame. Does this mean that you have not yet recovered them? Our mutual "friend" will be most upset when he hears.'

'No. I have them.'

'All three?'

'Yes.'

'What joyous news. Where are they?'

'At Clairets Abbey. It took me a long time to find the whereabouts of the secret library.'

'Do you not receive generous compensation for your pains?'

Aude retorted with deceptively casual irony before going on: 'So, the much coveted manuscripts are still at Clairets ... This hardly constitutes progress.'

'You see, our Reverend Mother has ordered a thorough search of every cart and every person leaving the abbey, regardless of their destination or their duties. I couldn't risk ...'

'This is an infuriating setback, which will displease our Italian friend. As for your Abbess, Madame de Beaufort, she is becoming more and more of a thorn in our side. We must have these papers urgently. Is there any chance of her lifting the restrictions soon?'

'On the contrary, I'm expecting her to order a careful search of the whole abbey any minute now.'

Aude de Neyrat's mouth set in a fold of displeasure.

'What an appalling thought. Do you think she might find them?'

'I don't think so ...'

'But ...? Isn't that what you were about to say?'

'There have been a lot of strange goings-on recently.'

Aude raised her pretty eyebrows quizzically. Her guest went on:

'The suspicious death of the Grand Inquisitor who was meant to help me ... to help you – I don't believe for one moment in those rumours of a violent encounter. The unconditional pardon granted to Madame de Souarcy in the name of God. That accursed apothecary, whose self-importance is proving more dangerous than I had thought. The rape and strangulation of the servant girl Mabile, who belonged to Eudes de Larnay's household. Mabile was of great use to me. She led her master right where I wanted him, to the late Nicolas Florin's door. She also procured several pieces of glass for me from a window in Madame de Souarcy's antechamber. Crushed and added to a meatball or a slice of bread, they become a lethal weapon. If necessary this could be used to further incriminate Madame de Souarcy, thus killing two birds with one stone. There again, I'm not convinced by the theory of a murderous vagabond. Mabile was not easily fooled. At the very least she would have fought tooth and nail to defend herself. Another thing bothers me. When the bailiff's men found her body at the forest's edge, they noticed she was wearing several layers of clothing, as if she were preparing for a long journey. Something's being hatched, Madame, and I'm worried.'

Aude studied her in silence for a few moments. Honorius had shown an astonishing lack of judgement in recruiting this woman. As she had commented during their last meeting at the Vatican, fear and envy were the traits of a coward and it was folly to trust in them. She insisted, again in a polite voice:

'You must get the manuscripts out and bring them to me as soon as possible so that I can take them to our friend.'

The other woman felt a sudden rush of anger and snapped back:

'Do you think it's as easy as clicking your fingers? I'm the first to be affected by this sudden imposition of the cloister at the abbey. I should have followed my instinct and moved the money I've earned through my thankless toil to a safer place.'

'Thankless perhaps, but lucrative nonetheless.'

'Do you consider killing an easy task?'

Genuinely taken aback, Aude replied:

'The first corpse is the only one that counts. Thereafter it is mere repetition.'

The other woman breathed in disgust:

'You're …'

'A monster? Perhaps.' Madame de Neyrat, suddenly wistful, added: 'Even so, few are born monsters. Most I have met turn into them.'

She quickly pulled herself together and pealed with laughter:

'Oh but guilt does not become me. Moreover it causes the face to wrinkle prematurely. I confess that in my case the whole process is quick and relatively painless. Going back to the subject of Madame de Beaufort, she is growing … tiresome.'

She noticed the other woman grow tense, and remarked softly:

'You have turned quite pale.'

'She's an abbess.'

'What of it! Doesn't this tiresomeness to which I refer blight the days and nights of an archbishop soon to be Pope?'

'But … That hag of an apothecary watches over her like a hawk.'

'We all have our cross to bear. However, I have something that will lighten yours.' She pointed to a velvet purse sitting on a flimsy table in her chamber.

As the other woman snatched it greedily, Aude ventured:

'A piece of friendly advice from a stranger: be sure to earn it.'

The woman perceived the implied threat behind the casual delivery, and assured her:

'I'll do my best.'

'Do it, and do it quickly and efficiently. After that we'll need to talk – on an equally friendly basis, I hope – about another obstinate acquaintance: Madame Agnès. What is she like, this woman whose elegance I have heard praised so highly?'

'She is beautiful and clever if that's what you want to know.'

'Indeed. The description is a terse one. Could you elaborate a little, please? I'm dying to know more. Describe her to me.'

'She is quite tall, taller than me, slim but strong. Like you she has fair hair, but with a coppery sheen. Her blue-grey eyes are striking and her skin is as pale as befits a lady of her standing, even though Madame de Souarcy is content to work outside in all weathers like a serf,' she added curtly.

'A very pretty picture so far. Why then do I have the impression that portraying her displeases you?' quipped Madame de Neyrat. 'Pray, do go on.'

The other woman's face tensed and she replied through gritted teeth:

'I'm sick to death of that Souarcy woman! The whole world it seems is ready to jump to her defence. Everybody sings her praises and lists her endless virtues. But what is she, this Souarcy woman? She's comely to be sure, and pious and elegant and erudite and undeniably intelligent.'

'Goodness! And yet you complain that she is undeserving of praise?' Aude de Neyrat declared mockingly. 'My dear woman, jealousy and envy are unreliable weapons. Do not trust them.'

'What do you mean?'

'Jealousy drives weak people to look for the source of their failure or unhappiness in others when it lies within themselves.'

The scarcely veiled insult stung the woman, and her cheeks flushed. She detested this pretty monster and would gladly have made her swallow her words. But she detested *and* feared her. Aude de Neyrat went on:

'Rest assured. Madame de Souarcy will soon cease to be a thorn in your side … I have a few excellent ideas on the subject.

But ... all in good time. Haste makes for poor workmanship. Let us meet a week from now in the same place at the same time ... this time with the manuscripts. We will celebrate Madame de Beaufort's finally joining her beloved husband with a slice of delicious jellied apple with walnuts. After all, are we not doing her an immense favour?'

La Haute-Gravière, Perche, December 1304

A cold, damp wind had risen and was gusting into the throats of the two intrepid travellers, who were reckless enough to have ventured out as night began encroaching upon the remains of the day.

Agnès gripped Clément tightly with one arm while with the other she controlled Églantine, the powerful grey-black Perche[14] mare. The horse stood higher than a man, at over fifteen hands, evidence of the breed having been crossed with stallions from Boulogne several centuries earlier. These powerful dray horses, bred for their strength and stamina, could carry a French knight to the Holy Land, keep up a slow trot and hurdle obstacles. But they tired easily at a gallop and consequently the journey from Manoir de Souarcy had been a slow one.

Agnès patted the animal's powerful neck, praising her:

'Good girl, Églantine. We're here.'

The mare came to a halt and waited patiently as Clément slid down her foreleg to the ground and Agnès jumped from her side-saddle, equipped only with one left stirrup. As she landed, her feet sank into the reddish mire. She winced and the young boy enquired in a concerned voice:

'The wounds that fiend inflicted on you aren't yet healed, are they, Madame?'

'Besides the scars left by the lash, I bear scarcely any trace of them, thanks to Agnan's kind attentions, and to the monks who took turns nursing me, but especially to the well-nigh magical ointment sent to me by my Lord d'Authon's physician, your beloved Joseph. However, I do occasionally get twinges in damp weather. But don't worry, the worst is behind me.'

The young woman lifted the front of her skirts and walked

forward a few paces. She gave a nervous sigh as she cast her eye over her bleak inheritance. A bed of angry nettles had colonised the ten acres of arid land. No other plant was tenacious enough to grow there. The approaching darkness only added to the desolation of the place, which was battered by incessant winds and rain.

The sound of Clément's breathing distracted her from these depressing thoughts. The young boy was gasping, as if he'd been running. He murmured:

'Now that we're here, I feel afraid. Afraid that I'm mistaken, that my intuition is only a fantasy.'

Clément's discomfort roused Agnès, who stood up straight and declared in an almost scathing tone:

'Well, we're here now, and it's too late to start worrying. Let's see if your excellent Joseph de Bologne's stone can tell us whether this barren soil contains any iron ore.'

'Monsieur Joseph showed me how to carry out a simple experiment using this remarkable instrument. He asked me to treat it with care for it is rare and priceless, and to keep it a secret as a precaution.'

'I see. And you refer to this big lump of rough-hewn stone as an "instrument"!'

'Yes. As I already explained to you, it comes from Magnesia, in Asia Minor. The history of this stone, known as magnetite, is a troubled one. Five thousand years ago, a shepherd by the name of Magnès[15] left his flock grazing below while he climbed onto a boulder to watch over it. The metal tip of his crook appeared to stick to the rock, and when he let go it remained upright. He was terrified and thought it had been bewitched. Even Lucretius and Pliny the Elder attributed magical powers to the stone.[16] A dozen years ago, my mentor Joseph came across a letter drafted by a man called Peter Peregrinus[17] detailing everything that was known about magnetite yet still unknown in our kingdoms.[18]

According to Monsieur Joseph there is nothing magical about the stone's properties; it is a fascinating scientific phenomenon we have yet to comprehend.'

Agnès listened attentively to the explanation then summed up:

'So, if the crook stayed upright on the boulder, it follows that the stone … somehow fastened itself to the metal?'

He smiled, pleased at rediscovering her agile mind.

'Yes, Madame, it attracts metal.'

'I'm beginning to share your admiration for this Joseph whom I've never met. Hurry, it will soon be dark and I want to see this prodigious stone at work. Églantine knows the way home, and my short sword will dissuade any young brigand, but I would prefer to be home before nightfall. What must I do to help you?'

Clément replied enigmatically:

'Nothing, Madame, just watch over me as you have always done.'

She had the almost painful feeling that these words – unrelated to the experiment the young boy was about to carry out – summed up more clearly than any lengthy exposition what their life would be like from then on. They were alone, a woman and a young girl disguised as a boy for her own protection, for both their protection, and yet they were united by a love that was pure and therein lay their strength. Agnès had been given further proof of this when a hideous vision of death had approached her in her sinister dungeon at the Inquisition headquarters in Alençon. How much did Clémence/Clément, still so young, really grasp of this love, of the bond between them? And she, the Dame de Souarcy, what more did she know of it besides her own certainties?

'And as I always will. Even at the risk of my own life,' she whispered softly.

Clément looked up at her with his blue-green eyes and smiled as he nodded. Then, ending this stirring moment that was so intense that words had become superfluous, he declared with forced cheer:

'I will perform the experiment flat on my stomach.'

He rummaged in his satchel and pulled out two long strips of hessian, which he wrapped around his hands and forearms before walking over to the mass of blackish nettles.

'These horrid weeds sting even when they're frozen.'

'They provide an invaluable source of compost.'

'Whose formula was brought back by the Knights Templar. But that doesn't stop them prickling like the devil.'

The mention of the military order brought back the memory of the mysterious Knight Hospitaller. Agnès called out to Clément as he walked away towards the carpet of nettles:

'What do you know about the knight Francesco de Leone?'

'Very little, in truth. I first heard his name when the good Agnan mentioned him the day the Comte and I arrived in Alençon. Then I learnt from you that he is the nephew and adopted son of the Abbess of Clairets, Éleusie de Beaufort. But I'd wager my life he killed that fiend Nicolas Florin. I give no credit to the story of a drunken stranger having stabbed the Grand Inquisitor, your tormentor, to death.' He added in a sharp, almost angry voice: 'Let me tell you, Madame, that he pre-empted us. My Lord Artus d'Authon would have given him no quarter. And neither would I.'

Agnès suppressed a smile:

'I have no doubts as to your courage. You are my brave defenders.'

Clément knelt on the ground and continued:

'Going back to the subject of Francesco de Leone, I've never met the man, but I'm grateful to him for saving your life, even though he prevented us from doing so. I wonder ...'

Clément paused suddenly as he pushed aside a mass of nettles with his swaddled arm. One question among many had been plaguing him since Agnès's return, since her puzzled description of the Knight Hospitaller's visit.

As Clément had sat listening that night at the foot of her bed, the coincidence had seemed so striking that it had made him think. Was this Francesco de Leone the second author of Eustache de Rioux's journal? Having never confessed to his lady about the discovery of the secret library at Clairets, Clément refrained from any comment that would instantly have aroused Agnès's suspicions. He agonised over this petty omission, the white lie of a child afraid of being scolded, since he now considered it a dangerous deception. In addition, he had the vague impression that Agnès was a piece in a vast game of chess – the scale of which he was unable to determine. Both he and Agnès had soon realised that Eudes de Larnay, his lady's half-brother and overlord, was himself being manipulated by a far more powerful and formidable player – a far more ruthless one too. Artus d'Authon had, by a process of elimination, traced their enemy to the Vatican – a Vatican without a pope. In reality, Clément felt uneasy about the chain of events: Agnès had fallen into the hands of the Inquisition and the Knight Hospitaller appeared from nowhere. The wicked inquisitor met a timely death at the hands of an implausible debauchee. The judgement of God was invoked and Agnès was saved. The Knight Hospitaller dissolved into thin air, like a ghost. Clément then learnt that Leone was none other than the adored nephew and adopted son of the Abbess, guardian of the secret library at Clairets where he had discovered a journal belonging to two Knights Hospitaller. The journal, devoted to a 'sublime' quest, contained extraordinary astronomical discoveries as well as two birth charts, one of which fell under the sign of Capricorn. Agnès was born on 25 December. Could one of the charts concern her? And what of the other chart? The pieces were being set up, and he still hadn't understood which game was being played. A game of chess, yes.

'What were you going to say?'

Dusk obscured the look of unease on the boy's face. The young woman was about to repeat her question when Clément cried out:

'Madame, Madame ... Look! It's a miracle!'

Agnès ran over to him. He was kneeling on the ground and holding up a piece of stone flecked with reddish soil. She all but snatched it from him, turning it over in her hands, examining it from all sides, dumbfounded, stifling her relief, the violent joy welling up inside her. She prodded the tiny specks of clay that appeared to cling to the rough surface of the magnetite. The infinitesimal pull, their resistance to her attempts to dislodge them, and the way they clung on again the moment she took her finger away brought tears to Agnès's eyes.

Clément stammered with emotion:

' ... Ah ... The stone from Magnesia attracts the soil! This is the proof, the scientific proof that the soil is rich in iron! It's a mine, Madame. Your barren La Haute-Gravière is an iron-ore mine and you will have the right to exploit it until you die.'

Agnès understood the cutting reference to Mathilde, whose cruelty and betrayal had haunted her for weeks. Her daughter would never enjoy the riches of La Haute-Gravière – if riches they were, and Agnès was convinced of it – not while her mother was still alive, unless she remarried. And neither would Eudes de Larnay. God had given her the passive means with which to avenge herself on her half-brother. She addressed a silent prayer to Clémence, to the voices, the benevolent shades that had helped her during her imprisonment.

She fought the urge to fall to her knees on the soil she had so long despised, loathed, and beg its forgiveness, pay homage to its endurance. No doubt had she been alone she would have given in to this strange act of contrition. Instead, she bent down, dug her fingers into the earth she had so hated, and, grasping two muddy handfuls of clay, lifted them to her lips. She kissed the soil, inhaling the bitter metallic odour as if it were her life blood.

When she opened her eyes, Clément was staring up at her, a small, poignant figure in the middle of the unremitting bleakness.

'Are you all right, Madame?'

'Yes … dear Clément, I am feeling better, and it is a sensation I had long forgotten. I'm just a little overcome … And I'm ravenous!' she added.

'You're getting your health back, then. Let us leave, Madame. Night is falling.'

Agnès led Églantine over to a tree stump, which she used to help her mount the huge mare more easily and less painfully. She called to Clément. The youth mounted in turn and let out a sigh as he slumped against her.

They headed for home, the animal keeping up a steady speed, spurred on by the prospect of the stable. Agnès thought aloud:

'Let us suppose – for I still feel it is too good to be true – that La Haute-Gravière really does contain iron ore. And, speculating further, let us assume that the mine is rich …' She trembled with nervous excitement and whispered: 'What would we do with it? I mean how do we extract the ore? How do we turn it into knives, swords and coulters?'[19]

'Monsieur Joseph once again comes to our aid. Believe me that man knows everything – he even knows about the laws governing mining! We'll need large amounts of fuel, which your forests will supply. We'll also need miners, but we can find those among your serfs and labourers,[20] providing you respect the law that prohibits mining and conversion during harvest time because it would be detrimental to the wellbeing of the soil and the subsistence of your serfs.'[21]

'Do such laws exist?'

'They do, Madame, and with good reason.'

'And how in heaven's name do you know all this?'

'Master Joseph told me.'

'Is your Joseph a lawyer too?'

'He is everything, Madame. He insists that to be versed in the laws of the land that gives you refuge is to avoid unwelcome problems.'

'Then he is a wise man.'

Clément went on to list the drawbacks:

'We will also need a river with enough water to drive the mill that will work the bellows and allow us to cool the beaten metal. However, we have no mill or powerful watercourse ... But there are plenty nearby, and with our drays and oxen we can carry the ore to one of them in exchange for a fee and a percentage of our profits, which we will need to negotiate down to the last penny.'

'You have an answer to everything, my clever Clément,' Agnès said, smiling and stroking his hair.

Another thought occurred to her, which dampened her enthusiasm and she added:

'I tremble with rage at being forced to hand over half of all the extracted ore to that scoundrel Eudes, a quarter of which he must pass on to his overlord, the Comte d'Authon.'

As she spoke she was struck by the sudden realisation that Eudes knew about the mine, or suspected its existence. He had not plotted her arrest by the Inquisition only out of resentment and frustrated desire. He had not turned Mathilde against her out of simple revenge. He wanted the iron ore. If Agnès had been found guilty of heresy or even complicity to commit heresy, she would have been stripped of her dower, which Mathilde would then have stood to inherit. Eudes needed only to shower the girl with dresses and jewellery – at no cost to himself since they had all belonged to his dead wife, dear Apolline. Unless he considered it more expeditious to shut the young woman away in a nunnery once he had become her legal guardian.

Agnès felt choked with resentment. She was surprised by her own reaction. Had Eudes's debauchery and perversity – however shameful – excused his actions in her eyes? Perhaps. Perhaps she had excused Eudes in part because she saw in them a sign of mental derangement. In contrast, money, the lure of profit, all the plotting in order to lay his hands on his widowed half-sister's dower revealed that only his rotten, scheming soul was to blame.

After a few moments' silence, Clément remarked in a voice too casual to be innocent:

'I see no way around that – at least while you remain Lord d'Authon's under-vassal.'

Agnès was not fooled:

'You seem very keen to see me wed. Do you wish to be rid of me? In any event ... It is not the custom for a lady to propose marriage.'

She heard him giggle, and then:

'Yes, but it is customary for her to make it known that she favours such a union, especially when the gentleman in question eagerly awaits a sign ... or should I say despairs of ever receiving such a sign.'

'You little rascal!' laughed Agnès, thankful for this moment of gaiety that pushed back the shadows hanging over them.

'Can she make it known?' continued Clément.

'Yes.'

'Without displeasure?'

'Yes.'

'In that case with pleasure?'

Agnès could no longer contain her hilarity and pretended to chide him:

'Stop it this instant! What are you making me say? I'm not

amused,' she spluttered. 'I'm choking with embarrassment. That's enough, you mischievous child, let us speak no more of it!'

Clément's joy at having brought a smile to his lady's face was short-lived. He must tell her the truth about his discoveries in the secret library at Clairets. He could no longer delay his confession.

Clairets Abbey, Perche, December 1304

The shadow slipped down the corridor running alongside the scriptorium, preceded by her steamy breath. She turned the corner when she reached the refectory and listened out. Not a sound. The coast was clear. The guest house was empty owing to the lingering acrid smell left by the blaze. The shadow's accomplice had been clever to think up that diversion. She had started the fire. The shadow had only needed to wait for the resulting confusion on the far side of the abbey to sneak in and steal the manuscripts. As for that fool of a guest mistress, Thibaude de Gartempe, she was annoying everybody with her insistence that she had done her best, that she couldn't understand how it had happened and that she was in no way to blame for the fire that had almost destroyed her little domain.

The figure arrived at the steam room, not far from the bath-house. Blanche de Blinot, who had made the place her own during the past few weeks, had retired to the dormitories where, as soon as her head touched the pillow, she would continue the semi-permanent slumber from which she rarely emerged these days. The old woman was fond of the room where, according to her, she was able to read the scriptures without getting cold and risking a chest infection. The scriptures! Only a fool would believe such a story! Blanche spent virtually the whole day asleep.

The shadow groped her way in the dark over to the cabinet where the ink was placed overnight to keep it from freezing. Sitting on the bottom shelf was a collection of cracked ink-horns that hadn't been thrown away because nothing in that place of voluntary poverty was ever thrown away. The shadow felt a further rush of resentment. The abbey was wealthy, extremely wealthy. Why, then, must they be deprived of everything on the pretext of doing penance and remembering the poor? Did shivering under skimpy blankets make the poor feel any warmer? Did digging the earth or cleaning the muck off pigs improve their lives?

Soon. Soon she would be free to live in the world. To live, at last. Monsieur de Nogaret had promised introductions to the best Parisian society, where the shadow's talents for underhand deeds would be valued by the King's counsellor, who had already employed her to spy on troublesome members of the nobility. What did it matter that the shadow received payment from Nogaret as well as from one of his staunchest opponents, the camerlingo Benedetti?

Paris, how exhilarating! The idea of serving the powerful had finally seduced the shadow. She wanted freedom and wealth. Admittedly, the idea of killing Éleusie de Beaufort was repugnant, but it had to be done in order to retrieve – and above all to remove from the abbey – her pot of money, which included the modest sum that the wretched Mabile had entrusted to her. She had hidden her hard-earned gold in the false bottom of a reliquary – allegedly containing the tibia of Saint Germain d'Auxerre, who had fought against the Picts and the Saxons in England – donated to the abbey by Madame de Beaufort. After all, the Abbess was as stubborn as she was blind. What strange madness causes some people to fight those who are more powerful than they? For the 'Italian friend', as Madame de Neyrat had referred to him in order to avoid saying his name, was one of those dangerous creatures who should never be opposed. The shadow shuddered. Sometimes she had the disturbing impression that the camerlingo was watching her every move, entering her head and rummaging through her thoughts. Childish notions inspired by her fear of the camerlingo.

At last, an end to fear. Was that not true freedom? Madame de Neyrat was free because she was fearless, had no regrets, no conscience. Madame de Neyrat scared and fascinated her. She detested Madame de Neyrat.

She seized the large dark-grey ink-horn, which a hairline crack had rendered obsolete. Red ink had dried along its rough edges, like a trickle of blood. The shadow removed the hemp stopper that kept the greenish-brown powder captive inside. As far as the shadow knew, it came from an exotic Asian fruit roughly the size of an apple. The little-known substance was highly prized by poisoners, despite its exorbitant cost – no doubt justified by its extreme efficacy which, thanks to Yolande de Fleury's unexpected participation, the shadow had been able to witness at first hand. That poor fool Yolande. The good sister in charge of the granary had come bleating to her in the registry[22] after her violent encounter with the Abbess. The pretty little goose had cried on the shoulder of the person she thought was her friend, had sworn she hadn't given away the name of her kindly informant, had explained that she had seen through Éleusie de Beaufort and Annelette Beaupré's wicked ploy, insisting loudly that as his mother she would have known if her little Thibaut were dead. That same night she had joined him!

The shadow considered the meagre amount of powder that was left, and wondered whether there might not be enough for both the Abbess and the meddlesome apothecary, Beaupré. Was it not too much of a risk? Was it worth incurring the wrath of that pretty monster Neyrat in the event that Madame de Beaufort survived the poisoning? Certainly not.

The shadow emptied the contents of the ink-horn onto a small square of cloth, which she tied carefully before hurrying back to the dormitories.

Compline[+] was long over by the time Agnès and Clément arrived back at the manor. A pleasant languor slowed the Dame de Souarcy's movements. One of the farm hands rushed over to take Églantine to the stable and a well-deserved meal of hay.

Agnès detained Clément, who was heading for the kitchens to get some food:

'Stay, dear Clément, and share my supper. I don't feel like eating alone.'

'Madame ...'

'Does my company displease you?'

'Oh,' he breathed, frowning at the mere suggestion. 'It's just that ... It is such a privilege ... What will the others think?'

'What others? Poor Adeline? We're virtually alone. Every day I fear Brother Bernard, my chaplain, will announce his departure.'

'Why should he? You've been cleared of all suspicion.'

'Yes, but even false accusations leave a mark. The poor young man was terrified that people would give credit to the tales of heresy and carnal dealings with me. I wouldn't blame him for wanting to leave Souarcy.'

'And yet he seems like a man of faith and honour.'

'May God hear your words, for he would be sorely missed in the village, and I doubt that others would be hammering at the door to replace him.'

Adeline appeared. The sudden departure of Mabile, Eudes de Larnay's spy and one of his numerous lovers, appeared to have jolted the stocky young girl out of her usual ineptitude. She had embraced her new post as mistress of the kitchens with enthusiasm – if only to prove that, armed with pots and pans, she was equally capable of producing marvels. Her curtseys, however, remained as clumsy as before. She curtseyed then, tottering slightly, and declared:

'Seeing as it's Advent and a fasting day to boot, and cold as death outside, I've prepared gourd[23] soup with almond milk. Upon my word, it's as smooth as mayonnaise. After that I've made horse bean and onion purée to go with the trout Gilbert caught to liven up your fasting day, Madame. For dessert ... well, there's a slice of dried layered fruit tart left over. Dried fruit, that'll perk you up after a ride. I haven't got much to finish ... A goblet of mulled wine, perhaps.'

'It all sounds very tempting, Adeline. Thanks to your talents our Advent meal promises to be as delicious as that of any feast day. Lay a place for Clément next to me.'

The young woman was so thrilled at the compliment that she appeared unsurprised by the young servant being singled out for such an honour. After all, everybody knew of Madame's fondness for the boy.

They ate their soup in silence, a silence Agnès at first attributed to their exhaustion and the emotion of their discovery. And yet something about Clément's demeanour and his lack of appetite intrigued her. She waited until Adeline had served Gilbert the Simpleton's fine trout en croute and then, unable to contain herself any longer, she questioned him. The steaming pastry gave off a delicious smell of clove and ginger.

'I sense that you are pensive, serious. You're picking at your food. What's the matter?'

The young boy looked down at his trencher[24] in silence.

'Come now, Clément, is it as bad as all that?' Agnès insisted.

'Yes, Madame,' he whispered, almost in tears.

'Tell me, quick – you are frightening me.'

'I ... I lied to you and I am terribly ashamed of myself.'

'You lied to me? That's impossible.'

'It's true, Madame. I was afraid you'd be angry and ... the longer I kept it from you, the more difficult it became to tell you the truth.'

Agnès's incredulity gave way to a feeling of unease. She ordered:

'Tell me this instant. I demand that you stop shilly-shallying and confess.'

'I ... I sneaked into Clairets Abbey at night.'

'Have you taken leave of your senses?' Agnès whispered, stunned.

'I discovered a secret library.'

'Clément ... Have you lost your head?'

'Oh no, Madame, I have not. How do you think I knew about Guy Faucoi's *Consultationes ad inquisitores haereticae pravitatis* and about that slim volume describing the terrible torture methods used by the Inquisition?'

'A knowledge that helped me to survive,' Agnès added. 'Carry on.'

'Nobody but the Abbess appears to know the library exists. I went back there night after night. If only you knew how many marvels, discoveries, advancements for mankind are hidden within those windowless walls!'

Overcome with panic, the Dame de Souarcy exclaimed: 'How could you have been so foolish! The Abbess would have thrashed you if she'd found you there!'

'I know.'

'I should be furious with you for being so disobedient, so devious ...'

'But are you, Madame?' asked Clément woefully.

'I should be! However, I am unforgivably weak where you are concerned.'

The young boy stared into her eyes, and a look of immense

relief appeared on his face as he saw a smile play across her lips.

'Indeed, I find it impossible to stay angry with you for very long. Moreover … Had you not warned me about those inquisitorial ruses, I would have fallen into every single trap Florin laid for me.' A twinkle of amusement lit up her grey-blue eyes, which were trained on him, and she said in hushed tones: 'And, besides, I have an insatiable interest in books. Tell me. Tell me about everything you found there.'

He revealed every single one of his discoveries, and was enthralled by the changing expressions on her face: concern, surprise, awe, joy, anger and dazzlement. He told her about the earth moving round the sun; he described the marvels of Greek, Jewish and Arabic medicine; assured her that unicorns, fairies and ogres did not exist; and finally he spoke of the knight Eustache de Rioux's journal, of the predictions and birth charts it contained and of the Vallombroso treatise, which still eluded him. She listened, leaning slightly towards him, open-mouthed, and he reflected that she was without doubt the most over-whelming, the most magnificent mortal created by God in his infinite goodness to light up the lives of others. When he had finished, she remained silent for a few moments then said:

'It's astonishing! I'm speechless. All of a sudden I feel cold. Ask Adeline to add a few logs to the fire.'

'I will do it. The poor girl must be exhausted, not that she complains about having twice as much work to do since that rat Mabile's departure.'

'You're right. Tell her she may go to bed and that we enjoyed her meal very much. And tell her that her cooking is as good if not better than Mabile's.'

'She'll swell with pride.'

'Pride, provided it is fleeting, can be a salve, especially to a wretched girl to whom life has not been kind. And besides, if her pride remains focused on her soups and roasts, I see no harm.'

He obeyed. During the ensuing moments of solitude, Agnès sat, the earthenware goblet of mulled wine in front of her, her mind empty. No, not empty. Far away. All of this confirmed what she had long suspected but had been unwilling to admit. What exactly was she afraid of? She couldn't say. The truth, perhaps?

Her thoughts drifted. Mathilde, always Mathilde. The rage that had roused her, despite her exhaustion, when the young girl had tried to send Clément to the stake, had not turned to hatred, despite her prayers. More than anything else, Agnès would have liked to be able to close her heart and mind to the girl. Of course she did not blindly believe that Eudes's villainy was entirely to blame for turning her daughter's mind. Even so, the scoundrel had done his best to foster the bad seeds planted in Mathilde's soul. And, indeed, Agnès herself felt responsible, at least in part, for their very existence. She blamed herself for not succeeding in stamping them out completely. She couldn't pretend that she was unaware of their existence, their origin, their very nature. These seeds were a punishment for the sins of the mother.

Clément came back and sat down beside her, and they watched the fire stir again from its embers. The feeble warmth it dispersed through the cavernous, icy room, illuminated by resin torches fixed along the walls, did nothing to drive out the chill Agnès felt in her bones.

'Speak to me, Madame. Scold me if you must, but say something,' implored Clément, suddenly unnerved by the long silence.

'Dear Clément ... I'm afraid.' She buried her face in her hands and declared: 'A beautiful, brave lady whose Christian name you bear once told me that fear is no defence against pain. She was right, and yet ... I miss her terribly. I've missed her for so long. I tell you I'm afraid of not living up to Madame Clémence de Larnay's expectations of me. She was so fearless, so determined ... and loving and loyal too.'

'But you do live up to them, Madame. You live up to something that is immeasurable.'

'They are sweet words. Forgive me for not believing I deserve them. For you see, Clément, I was so afraid in that evil dungeon. Afraid of death – or, worse still, of suffering. Afraid of giving in, of acting like a coward and denouncing others, of surrendering. Madame Clémence would have held her head high, stood her ground and ridiculed anybody who threatened her.'

'But you didn't give in any more than she would have. I agree that fear is no defence against pain, Madame, but fearlessness does not defeat pain either.'

'What is your solution, then?'

Clément grinned, and Agnès wondered for a split second what he would deduce if at that very moment he caught sight of himself in a looking glass.

'My solution to fearing pain or being foolishly oblivious to danger? To tell myself that it is possible to survive pain, however bad. To convince myself that it is better to have my flesh torn asunder than to lose my soul. Flesh heals, lost souls are rarely saved.'

'Clément … I need to ask a favour of you …'

'Anything, Madame, unreservedly,' he interrupted.

'Finish what I scarcely dare envisage, Clément. I am confused and I know that my confusion is not accidental. Join all the loose strands, I implore you. Link your discovery at Clairets to the knight's visit to my cell, the devotion that made him kneel before me in that evil-smelling mire. He spoke like a man entranced. Don't forget Agnan, Nicolas Florin's young clerk, his passion and how he, too, was willing to die in order to save my life. None of it makes any sense. No visible sense, unless these two men know or perceive things that remain a mystery to me.'

'A mystery? And yet what you say makes it clear that you are nearing the answer, although we still do not possess the key to this mystery. I've told you all I know. I, too, am haunted by an intuition, which I have no real means of verifying.'

'What are you talking about? What intuition and how did it come to you?'

'I don't know. I believe that we are – that you are – in the centre of a storm, the scope of which we are only just beginning to grasp.'

The boy's remark stunned Agnès. So, Clément shared her exact feelings.

'What storm?'

'I wonder whether the first birth chart might not refer to you.'

'It's absurd! What? An illegitimate noblewoman, a widow with no fortune who barely manages to keep her household afloat by bartering the honey and wax she wrests from her half-brother and overlord in exchange for grain, and by rearing pigs and growing buckwheat and millet? Such a woman as I would appear in a notebook belonging to two Knights Hospitaller, one of whom fought at Saint-Jean-d'Acre? Fiddlesticks!'

'A widow with no fortune whom a Grand Inquisitor was intent upon destroying and who was saved by a Knight of Justice and Grace who fell from the sky. Come, Madame ... I am as confused as you. But you must confess that some coincidences are too great to be simple coincidences.'

Agnès was silent for a moment before confessing:

'I know. I know and I am terribly afraid.'

'So am I, Madame. But there are two of us.'

'I'm behaving like a silly fool tonight,' she began in a faltering voice. 'Do you believe me, Clément, when I tell you that one day you will find out the truth about these charts?'

'In order to do so I must lay my hands on the Vallombroso treatise.'

'And return to Clairets in order to consult the notebook, too, I suppose?'

A smile flashed across the young boy's face and he corrected her:

'No. During my last visit to Clairets what seems like an eternity ago, before your trial, I carefully copied out the two birth charts and the prophecy, as well as some of the other notes, onto a piece of paper, which I have hidden in a safe place.'

Agnès did not know where the immense feeling of relief came from that caused her to let out a sigh. She spoke but did not understand the meaning of her own words:

'All is not lost, then.'

'The fact remains that I do not have the Vallombroso treatise and without it I have no hope of making any progress. I will, with your permission this time, take advantage of the approaching Nativity celebrations to slip back into the library and look for it – if it is even there.'

'Tomorrow I will request a meeting with Madame de Beaufort. We might learn something from it.'

Éleusie de Beaufort had hesitated at length. The thought of having to meet Madame de Souarcy made her uneasy. And yet she could not refuse to see her without giving an explanation. She rose to her feet with a sigh and made her way to the reception room where Agnès was waiting. The young woman got up from the small bench beside the fireless hearth and stretched out her arms, a joyous smile on her face. Éleusie immediately regretted having agreed to meet her. How would she avoid answering the questions Agnès was sure to ask? Would she be capable of concealing the truth? A sudden feeling of dizziness forced the Abbess to sit down. This young woman had no idea how incredibly important she was and she mustn't find out.

'Thank you for seeing me at such short notice, Reverend Mother. I know how full your days are.'

'Don't mention it. You come and see us so rarely. Are you recovering from the ordeal of your iniquitous trial? And how is that little rascal Clément?'

'He has been wonderful and is a great comfort to me since ...' She did not finish her sentence, certain that the Abbess would understand the allusion to Mathilde. 'As for the trial, I am trying my best to put the whole experience behind me, although I fear I may never ... I have to tell you about the astonishing visit I received in my dungeon ...'

Éleusie listened attentively, pretending she knew nothing of it.

'Your nephew, the Knight Hospitaller, came to see me.'

'Really?' the Abbess replied, clumsily feigning ignorance, and making it clear to Agnès that she already knew.

She went on:

'Ah ... I thought perhaps that you had sent him to comfort

me. I must confess that I don't understand how he learnt of my imprisonment. Indeed, I was unaware that he even knew of my existence.'

The Abbess's pale cheeks became suffused with blood and she declared:

'I may have mentioned your name and your troubles at Souarcy.'

'I see ... I thought your nephew was in Cyprus.'

'Oh, he is. I mean, he is based at the Limassol citadel.'

Agnès was growing more and more perplexed by the direction their conversation was taking. Éleusie's visible unease and the fact that she was clearly lying alarmed her and confirmed her intuition. Something was being hatched which concerned her, though she had no idea what it was. She paused; it would be impolite to persist as the Abbess appeared unwilling to provide an explanation. So be it! Éleusie knew something and Agnès was determined to force it out of her.

'You spoke to me of him one day, of the bond between you, and of your motherly love for him.'

'He is my sister Claire's son. After her death at Saint-Jean-d'Acre, my now deceased husband and I, having no children of our own, brought Francesco up as our son. He completed our union. The three of us loved one another dearly ...' She smiled at the memory of her charmed life before entering the stout walls of Clairets Abbey.

Agnès clung to these initial confidences.

'I ... That is why I took the liberty of coming here today ... Sweet Lord, how can I say this ... I thought ... I imagined that fever and exhaustion accounted for the strangeness I felt when I recalled my brief encounter with your nephew. And yet ...'

'Did you say strangeness?'

Something was wrong. Éleusie seemed unsurprised to learn that her adopted son had been at Alençon. And she had not asked about the knight's reasons for visiting Agnès, and yet her face had grown sullen. She was hiding something. Agnès was now certain that the terrible events that had nearly cost her her life were connected. Eudes, her half-brother, had played an insignificant role in a plot that far outreached him. Her voice became sharper as she demanded:

'Madame, I beg you to attribute my persistence to the abject fear I experienced. I need to understand and ... your unease leads me to believe that you might have some explanation.'

She was taken aback by the Abbess's abrupt response. Éleusie de Beaufort stood up. Her pretty face wore an expression of intense pain, and yet there was a look of tenderness in her eyes. She replied curtly:

'Please go, Madame. I must ... There's been a fire and ... er ... some manuscripts have been ... destroyed.'

'No. You ... dishonour your position, your calling, by brushing aside my request in this way. Do you realise what I have been through?'

Éleusie de Beaufort fought back her tears. She composed herself and breathed:

'Oh ... I know, I felt it in my body, to a degree you cannot imagine.'

The Abbess's visions, her incessant nightmares. The lashes raining down on her back, flaying her skin. The indescribable pain of the salt that monster rubbed in her wounds – in Agnès's wounds, which racked Éleusie's body.

'I beg you, don't abandon me like this,' the young woman implored. 'You spoke of manuscripts that have been destroyed? What manuscripts? The Vallombroso treatise?' Agnès declared suddenly, on impulse.

An icy hand stroked her cheek then fell away. Éleusie de Beaufort murmured:

'It is not my place ... not yet, not I. May God protect you always.'

She left the reception room like a woman fleeing, accompanied by the sound of her footsteps and the rustle of the heavy folds of her robe. Agnès sat motionless, stunned.

A novice hurried over to Agnès and offered to help her climb into the saddle. The Dame de Souarcy refused the generous offer with a polite smile and said to the young girl with strange pale-amber eyes:

'You are most kind, but I must manage on my own. I have a ... stiff back, it's nothing serious. Besides, I won't always have you to help me.'

The novice disappeared through an arched doorway in the enclosure wall.

After dragging herself up onto Églantine's back, Agnès was overcome by a wave of fatigue. The huge Perche mare stood patiently as she settled into the saddle.

Ladies' saddles[25] at the time were only a slight improvement on the sambue that was still used in Madame Clémence's day. The sambue was a chair-like affair perched on the horse's hind-quarters, which did not allow the rider any control over the steed, making it necessary for a servant to lead the animal on foot. In fact, the palfreys[26] ridden by ladies in days gone by were trained to walk at a steady pace so that their riders would not lose their balance and fall off. The reason for this was that sitting astride a horse, which was far better suited to trotting or galloping, was considered detrimental to procreation.

Églantine fell into a steady pace. Unbidden thoughts of Mathilde flashed through Agnès's mind. She had received no news of her daughter since the trial. She had tried to imagine how she would react, what she would feel when she stood before her most zealous accuser. Would she demand an explanation from this child whom she had carried in her womb? Would she retreat into silent disapproval? Would she mourn the terrible loss, the destruction of what she continued to believe were some of her fondest memories? Mathilde as a baby, when she began to walk and later on as a little girl. She must stop lying to herself! Loss and destruction certainly – the words were not too severe. As for her fond memories, they had been undermined, not to say destroyed, by Mathilde's hostility towards her during the trial. Her daughter had dissolved before her eyes to be replaced by a ruthless accuser, a merciless informer. She might as well admit the truth: her fondest memories were of Clément, and she had no idea what her reaction would be when she found herself face to face with Mathilde. And yet a terrible realisation had gradually dawned upon Agnès: Mathilde did not only detest Clément and the harsh life at Souarcy, she also detested her mother more than anything. Agnès pursed her lips, holding back the overwhelming sorrow engendered by this thought. Still, it was out of the question that she leave her daughter any longer in Eudes's predatory hands. If necessary, she would ask the chief bailiff, Monge de Brineux, to go to Château de Larnay to fetch her, to drag her back to Souarcy if need be. She intended to write to Eudes without delay and inform him of her decision.

Agnès banished these dispiriting thoughts from her mind, and focused on her strange meeting with the Abbess, which had only served to deepen her confusion. Besides feeling disillusioned and uneasy, she had come away from the meeting certain of one thing: she and Clément were not losing their minds. They had been swept away by a wave whose proportions far surpassed them, had fallen by accident into a gigantic whirlpool that was buffeting them ferociously.

She was wrong.

Manoir de Souarcy-en-Perche, December 1304

An eerie stillness awaited her when she entered the quadrangle. No dogs, no busy farm hands. She felt as if she were stepping into a fairy tale where a spell has been cast turning the inhabitants of a house to stone.

She glanced around and called out: 'Hello. Is anybody there?'

Gilbert the Simpleton shot out of one of the barns and came running over to her with surprising agility for someone so massive.

'He's here, my lady. Oh, dear Lord Jesus … What a to-do! He arrived this afternoon without warning! He appeared out of nowhere!'

'Who did, Gilbert?'

'Why, he did of course,' he replied, flushed with excitement, flailing his arms like an angry goose.

'Calm down, Gilbert dear, and tell me who.'

Églantine did not bridle when he rushed to help Agnès dismount, seizing her by the waist and lifting her up as if she were as light as a feather before gently setting her down on the ground. It occurred to her that this giant, who had the mind of a child, was strong enough to wring a bull's neck with his bare hands.

'Thank you, dear Gilbert. Try to calm down and think. Who arrived?'

'Our lord, my good fairy. "Our lord", that's what Clément said.'

She felt cold with rage as she spoke the man's name through gritted teeth:

'Eudes?'

'No, not the evil dwarf. I'll crush that pest under my boot if he shows his ugly face here again. Our noble lord, from over there on the other side of Authon Forest.'

Agnès trembled.

Ah, dear God ... Lord Artus. But how, why, when? Why had he not warned them? She looked despairingly down at her dress, which had been dragging in the dirty snow, and at her nails, which were stained green from the cheap dye in her riding gloves. She must look dishevelled and dirty – in short, a fright, and Gilbert's admiring gaze would not convince her otherwise. She regained her composure and ordered calmly:

'Take Églantine back to the stable, please.'

Gilbert walked off slowly, whispering in the mare's ear. It was odd how all the animals, even the bees, liked Gilbert. Some invisible bond seemed to connect him to them.

Quick. What must she do? Go to her chambers and clean herself up? No. The Comte must have heard her calling out to the servants. She ought to have been annoyed and resented his unannounced intrusion. She suppressed a smile. He had done it intentionally. Nonetheless, she felt sure he would give her one of those clumsy excuses, which even the most intelligent men were prone to. Was it not endearing how they imagined they could trounce women at their own game? Agnès chortled. Come now, gentlemen, we are so familiar with these ruses that we can spot them a mile off! She would feign surprise and embarrassment, although her embarrassment was real enough ...

She straightened her coat and her veil, lifted up the short train of her dress and walked with a purposeful air towards the main door leading into the hall. She entered, calling out:

'Adeli—'

He jumped up, flustered, from the crockery chest upon which he was seated.

'You, Monsieur!'

'Hm ... Indeed, Madame. I'm afraid that I'm repeating the

same oafish behaviour by coming here unannounced.'

'Monsieur, you insult me. Is my lord not welcome in my home under any guise, and regardless of the … commotion his arrival might cause?'

He smiled and lowered his eyes. Beneath the compliment lay a scarcely concealed rebuke. He had expected nothing less and would have been disappointed otherwise.

'I am failing in all my duties, my lord. Have you been offered any refreshment, some fortified wine perhaps – most suitable on a cold evening such as this?'

'Yes. Your young kitchen girl filled me with delicious cheese bread, the name of which escapes me, and some mulled wine with cinnamon and ginger.'

'A *gougère*.[27] She makes them very well. If you don't mind me enquiring, Monsieur, to whom, or to what happy circumstance, do we owe this visit?' Agnès went on in a pleasant voice.

'To the town of Rémalard. I'm on my way there. Alas, I am growing too old for these long rides,' he said, without taking his eyes off her. 'Ogier is still fresh, but I confess that my back is aching.'

She gave a little smile, which she then pretended to conceal quickly with her hand.

'Are you laughing at me, Madame?'

'Indeed no, Monsieur.'

'Then why did you smile?'

'I … You will think me very forward, but I am not in the slightest convinced by the story of your poor old aching back.'

He failed to notice the hidden compliment. And so it should be.

'The perceptiveness of the fair sex never ceases to fascinate, or should I say unnerve, me. I admit that it was a clumsy excuse. I merely wished to enquire after your health. Moreover, Monsieur Joseph, my physician has charged me with an important mission.

I am to deliver a letter to Clément, but I have seen neither hide nor hair of him since my arrival.'

'Clément? Come here at once, please!' she called out.

The door leading to the servants' privy opened at once, and the blushing boy appeared as if by magic.

'Forgive me, my lord,' he apologised as he bowed before the man. 'If you had asked for me, I assure you I would have come at once.'

'But you prefer to spy on me from behind that door.'

In a polite but piqued voice, Clément declared:

'I'm not in the habit of spying on my lady's acquaintances. I was merely keeping watch.'

'You little rascal! Be off with you before your insolence earns you a clip around the ear!' the Comte threatened, half in jest.

Clément was about to flee when Artus held him back:

'Wait, I have a message for you. The next time, you two wily accomplices can find some other messenger.'

Clément seized the small square of sealed paper and shot Agnès a knowing look before slipping out through the same door.

A silence fell. Agnès considered that it was not up to her to break it, and so she waited. She felt a slight pang of guilt. Artus d'Authon was having great difficulty extricating himself from the awkward situation in which his arrival and, above all, his attraction to her had placed him. She had no intention of going to his aid. She had fallen for this intelligent, honourable, attractive – extremely attractive – awkward man. No doubt it was unforgivable coquetry on her part to leave him floundering in the agonies of courtship, but she was enjoying his lover's embarrassment too much to put him out of his misery just yet. After all, she had been a widow for more than ten years. And as for the elegant, playful banter of lovers, she had always been deprived of it, her deceased husband having been a respectful and courteous man, but not one given to repartee, much less to poetry. She realised that she was feeling rather mischievous when she had thought herself sober and sensible. The playful mood this man put her in was delightfully unexpected. And so she waited.

'Hm ...'

He scratched his neck, cursing himself. God's breath! He was tongue-tied! And yet he'd spent the whole journey there practising how he would broach the matter. What had happened to all the clever, eloquent, if scarcely compromising, phrases he had recited for Ogier's ears alone?

'Did you say something, Monsieur?'

'Er ... The weather's taken a turn for the worse.'

'Indeed, and I fear that it will not improve for many months – it being winter.'

A pox on his clumsiness! God's wounds ... He would end up making an utter fool of himself if this continued. Show some pluck! The worst he could receive was a severe rebuke, but then at least he would know where he stood. And once his wounded pride had healed, he'd ... Well, he didn't know what he'd do. The problem ... The problem was that pride played no part in this.

He should have sought advice from Monge de Brineux, his chief bailiff. Had he not recently wed the lovely, jovial, clever Julienne? He must have needed to seduce and cajole her, for the young woman's father was a wealthy man and she had no need to accept the first proposal of marriage. Were there not tried and tested methods of seduction which gentlemen exchanged among themselves? The elders showed the young how to fight and hunt and even initiated them into the secrets of carnal love. What a fine ambush this was! The hunted had become the huntress and the hunter's only wish was to become her quarry. In short, convention had been turned on its head and he was lost.

For her part, Agnès had entered a world of coded behaviour which an hour earlier she was unaware existed, but which she appeared to find her way about in with miraculous ease. How awkward he looked. Despite how cold it was in the big hall he was perspiring. She threw him a line:

'Will you stay overnight at Souarcy? I must give the order to prepare your apartments.'

'I would hate to impose upon your time and your hospitality, Madame. Especially since Rémalard is near enough to Souarcy to enable me to arrive there before nightfall.'

'You may take my hospitality for granted, and you would honour me by accepting, Monsieur.'

'In that case, I accept,' he replied, relieved.

He was perfectly aware that his relief was due to the fact that he had awarded himself a stay of execution. Now that he knew he was dining at the manor and staying overnight he need not hurry matters. He was astonished by his own cowardliness. He had fought, sometimes one against three, without fear for life or limb, and yet here he was ready to turn tail and run.

He would enjoy this stay of execution. At last he could breathe more easily, relax, engage in pleasant banter about this and that.

Agnès was not taken in. He had retreated so as to have a better run up. Was that not what the most powerful chargers did in order to conserve their strength?

And so they chatted over their mulled wine. She went into raptures over the love songs of Chevalier Hugues,[28] Châtelain d'Arras, who upon leaving his beloved to embark upon a crusade bade her farewell with exquisite grace. In contrast, she railed against Chastie-Musard,[29] an outrageously misogynistic poem that was still recited in certain circles after more than half a century.

'What a hotchpotch of rhyming nonsense, a collection of platitudes! And so filled with loathing towards womankind! I feel ashamed for the author, who was clever or cowardly enough to remain anonymous. What coarseness!'

He smiled, charmed beyond words, only half registering her vexation. How he had missed her, how he had tired of being without her. Life lost its meaning, its beauty, its interest. How could he have come to depend so much on this woman whose existence he had been unaware of up until a few months ago? Did it matter? No.

'I trust I'm not boring you, Monsieur? Forgive me, I get carried away sometimes. It is so rare for me to meet people with whom I can hold a meaningful conversation. No doubt I am trying your patience.'

He was taken off guard, embarrassed.

'Not at all, Madame. On the contrary you delight me. And yet …'

'And yet?' she insisted.

'This loathing of the fair sex is so widespread that it must conceal something else.'

'What?'

'Fear, of course.'

'Fear? Who are we to instil fear?'

'You are different. Indispensable. And men always wish to control what is indispensable to them so that they might never suffer need. Moreover … but these are not appropriate words for a lady's ears.'

'You forget that I've been married and given birth.'

At that precise moment, Artus's vague fear of taking another step, of exposing himself, dissolved. He studied her at length with his big dark eyes, so inscrutable, so serious that they unsettled her, threw her off balance.

'Forgive me if I dare to make a boorish observation.'

She was burning with impatience and with curiosity too, though she would never admit it:

'I can at least listen to you dispassionately.'

'Only briefly.'

'I beg your pardon?'

'You said that you'd been married, and I replied: "only briefly".'

Suddenly plunged into the dizzying world of innuendo, she felt a lump in her throat. Unable to come up with a worthy riposte, she quipped, feebly:

'Can one be more or less married?'

'Do you doubt it, Madame?'

She had not counted on their polite banter taking such a dangerous turn. She stood up gracefully and announced:

'Forgive me, but I must go and see how Adeline is getting on in the kitchens if we wish to dine soon.'

'Ah ... meals, bed or baths, a woman's usual parry.'

'I don't under—'

'You understand only too well,' he cut her short. 'I'll wager Adeline can manage her pots and pans perfectly well without any help from you. Please sit down.'

Agnès reluctantly did as he asked. Her initial amusement had given way to a feeling of panic. In reality she was ignorant of the world of courtly love and seduction. Contrary to what she had wished to believe, being a woman was no guarantee of finding her bearings in these matters. After all, what was she but a noblewoman and a peasant farmer? He knew that world. He must have been at court, and had doubtless known many courtesans whose vocation it was to captivate, to please and above all to endure.

'Am I embarrassing you, Madame? It would grieve me.' She shook her head, forcing a smile. He went on:

'You must acknowledge ... Be so good as to acknowledge that this conversation which is intent upon avoiding the heart of the matter has gone too far and deserves at least a conclusion.'

'We were discussing poetry ...'

'Come, Madame! We were discussing true love – although,

granted, the word was never mentioned ...'

She tried hard to stifle the emotion that was making her gasp for breath, fearing, longing to hear what he would say next.

' ... I cannot summon the words, those words. I have used them rarely and then only a very long time ago. I feel like a simpleton before you. I am ... nearly old enough to be your father ...'

She raised her hand and shook her head once again. He pre-empted her:

'Do not underestimate the importance of such differences. On the other hand, I have an excellent reputation, a noble title and a large fortune. I am Comte d'Authon and Lord of Masle, Béthonvilliers, Luigny, Thiron, Bonnetable and Larnay ...'

'Are you drawing up a contract, Monsieur?' she interrupted him.

'If I'm not mistaken, your own marriage was a contract.'

She stood up abruptly and said in a stinging voice:

'Is this the boorish remark you warned me about? For your information, I had no other choice.'

'Please forgive my rudeness. And do you have a choice now?'

'Indeed I do.' She studied him, her lips pursed, and added: 'Very well! Since we are engaged in drafting clauses, I wouldn't wish to be outdone. What is it you are trying to tell me by listing the advantages of your social position? Did you think that I was unaware of them? Could I have forgotten that you are my overlord, and that Authon, albeit small, is one of the richest counties in France? What more can you add? Your friendship with the King? Your servants? Your tableware, your stables? Your hunting grounds? Your furniture and property?'

Taken aback, he stammered: 'What am I to say ...'

'Tell me the truth, now. The truth that is in your heart!'

'The truth ...? What an abyss!'

She stamped her foot and cried out:

'For pity's sake, Monsieur! It is too late to back down now, you said so yourself. Is this not the real reason you came to Souarcy?'

'The truth … The … passion I feel for you has long since exceeded the protection an overlord owes his vassal.' He raised his eyes to heaven and declared: 'God's wounds … I am not gifted with eloquence, Madame. A pox on words! Women are so fond of words!'[30]

'Three words, Monsieur. That is all. Three simple words and I will give in – I, whom the Inquisition could not force to surrender. Three simple words.'

'And what if … what if you yourself are incapable of uttering them! What if … they stick in your throat because you do not mean them? Words, words and more words! Tell one of your farm hands to saddle my horse at once! I am expected at Rémalard. Do not see me out. I wish to choke on the cold air, alone.'

The sound of Ogier's thundering hooves echoed in the courtyard before disappearing, muffled by the snow. Agnès stood still, unsure if she was about to break down and cry, or burst into hysterical laughter. She bent over, gasping, waiting for the tears to come.

The three words had hung in the air throughout his visit. Had she been able, she would have said them for him, but it was not the custom for a woman to do so.

Her attack of nerves subsided as quickly as it had come. What an unbelievable adventure – to be in love. It had taken her a while to define this dryness in her throat, this knot in her stomach whenever he was near, this erratic breathing, this delicious apprehension. How blind she'd been. And yet, never having experienced such overpowering emotion before, how could she be blamed for not having recognised it?

What an extraordinary and marvellous thing.

He would say those words. He must.

Cyprus, December 1304

A rnaud de Viancourt, Grand-Commander of the order of the Hospitallers and prior of the citadel at Limassol, let out a sigh. He who found the Cypriot heat so insufferable savoured the cool December air now filtering through the arrow-slit windows in his study. The Hospitallers had been allowed to remain on the island after the defeat at Saint-Jean-d'Acre in 1291, despite the misgivings of Henri II de Lusignan, the King of Cyprus, about this military order establishing a base in his realm.

The prior put down the short missive he had just received from his supposed cousin Guillaume. The true identity of this impassioned scholar of angelology was Francesco de Leone, Knight of Justice and Grace, whom Viancourt had sent to spy on King Philip the Fair's* counsellor, Monsieur Guillaume de Nogaret.

The King of France, with Nogaret's keen collaboration, was looking for a prelate whose election to the Holy See he would finance in exchange for an assurance of neutrality in France's political affairs. However, both Viancourt and Guillaume de Villaret, the order's Grand-Master since 1296, had long feared that the newly elected pope's allegiance to the King would not stop there. Philip was absolutely determined to suppress the military orders, primarily the order of the Knights Templar – effectively the Pope's private guard. Viancourt could not help but admire the King's strategy, no doubt elaborated by his most faithful counsellor, Nogaret. Rather than demand the simple disbanding of all the orders of the Knights of Christ, and risk incurring the wrath of the Vatican and that of the young nobles and burghers who were avid supporters of these pure, heroic orders, he intended to unite them under the single banner of one of his sons. This would most likely be Philip the Younger, the only one whose intelligence was deemed worthy of that name. Philip the Fair would thus keep the monk-soldiers in check, forcing them to conform at very little political cost.

> *My dear cousin,*
>
> *I hardly dare inform you that my research into angelology is at a standstill. It saddens me to imagine your disappointment. The second order of Dominations, Virtues and Powers[31] continues to evade me. There is one piece of news, however, which I foolishly hope will please you. I am beginning to gain a clear understanding of the third order of Principalities, Archangels and Angels and now feel certain that the* tempus discretum *for which I have been searching in the documentation available to me relates above all to the Principalities. I need a little more time in order to arrive at a definite conclusion. I apologise profusely for this further delay, which I am sure will prove awkward for you.*
>
> *I reiterate my unstinting desire to persist in this difficult research, and I trust that my next letter will contain news of my significant progress.*
>
> *Your humble and indebted Guillaume.*

Francesco de Leone was informing him that there were four possible prelates contending for the papal throne – an advance on his last letter, since it seemed that two cardinals had already been rejected by Philip the Fair. The famous Archangels and Angels … an amusing metaphor! However, there were no further references to Augustine's 'City of God' as a bibliographical source, which meant that he had decided to leave Monsieur de Nogaret in order to pursue his mission elsewhere.

The slender man carefully reread one last time the missive that lay on his desk.

I apologise profusely for this further delay, which I am sure will prove awkward for you.

An amused smile lit up the Grand-Commander's gaunt face. It was true that Leone would be staying on in France, but was that not why Viancourt had sent him there, without the knight suspecting it in the slightest?

The prior stood up and walked over to the safe in the wall opposite his desk and took out a scroll he had received a few weeks earlier. It was signed: 'G' – Clair Gresson, personal secretary to Guillaume de Plaisians.[32] Plaisians had been Nogaret's pupil at Montpellier before becoming seneschal at Beaucaire. He had joined the King's immediate entourage to work alongside his former teacher a year ago, and had already demonstrated his remarkable talents as a lawyer. In addition to his vast intellect and solid education, he possessed a remarkable gift for oratory. As was rumoured in the corridors and antechambers of the Louvre, he had become Monsieur de Nogaret's *éminence grise* and appeared to share Nogaret's animosity towards the late Pope Boniface VIII. Gresson was one of the most zealous and skilled informers the prior had ever known, and placing him close to Plaisians had been a clever move, which greatly reassured Arnaud de Viancourt. Clair Gresson had written:

My dear Godfather,
I hope that your health has improved. Our mutual cousin is nervous about having to inform you presently of his slow progress in the research on angelology he has undertaken at your request. During his time here with us he has discovered a few details that shed light on his studies.

*The theoretical niceties are lost on me, but I understand
that these findings have indeed aided his progress.*

*Our cousin, who I assure you has worked tirelessly, has
gone to visit a relative whom he has not had the pleasure of
seeing in a very long time. An unexpected death has kept
him there for longer than he intended. But do not grieve,
dear Godfather, for the death was not in the family, which
enjoys perfect health.*

*Believe me when I tell you that our cousin performs
his tasks with a diligence and intelligence that are most
praiseworthy. I am convinced that he will present you with
an end result that will entirely justify your decision to
entrust him with the drafting of this treatise on the discrete
time determining the operation of the angels – on this*
tempus discretum, *this exception between divine eternity
and the continuous cosmic time of material substances,[33]
that is of such interest to us.*

Your devoted and respectful godson, G.

Arnaud de Viancourt smiled again, despite the seriousness,
not to say peril, of their situation. In his letter, Clair Gresson
confirmed that Leone had left Nogaret's entourage. However,
the other information concealed within these lines was at
variance with what the knight had told him, not that this surprised
Viancourt. While in the King's counsellor's employ, Francesco de
Leone had no doubt stumbled upon information that was more
specific than he had acknowledged. He was playing for time and
the prior knew why. Gresson was informing him that Leone had
gone to visit his aunt Éleusie de Beaufort, the Abbess of Clairets,
as Viancourt had predicted; Viancourt was aware that the two
manuscripts Leone had purchased from Gachelin Humeau were
hidden in the abbey's secret library. As for the death he need
not grieve, it no doubt referred to that evil monster Nicolas

Florin, whom Benedetti's henchman had entrusted with Agnès de Souarcy's execution. So, the lady was out of harm's way and enjoying 'perfect health', but for how long? Their enemies would never cede. Agnès was the key figure in a thousand-year struggle, a bloody and ruthless struggle.

Arnaud de Viancourt held both letters to a candle flame and watched the brownish wave devour the vellum. Although unintelligible to the majority of men, he preferred them not to fall into anyone else's hands, especially not those of their present Grand-Master, Guillaume de Villaret.

Leone must continue to be kept in ignorance of the prior's exact role. Neither he nor anyone else must ever know that Arnaud de Viancourt had for a long time been secretly guiding their quest, since before the disaster at Acre even, when the Knight Templar had entrusted his notebook to Eustache de Rioux. Francesco must continue to believe in Viancourt's total allegiance to the Grand-Master of their order. More importantly, he must remain convinced that Viancourt was intent upon foiling Philip the Fair's plots, when in fact those that terrified the little, grey-haired man were being hatched by Honorius Benedetti.

The prior spared a friendly, almost affectionate thought for the knight whom he was secretly guiding, who was still so young, so full of promise – Francesco, his finest warrior. Francesco who must not yet fully understand the irrevocable implications of the battle he was engaged in fighting.

The prior's emotion was short-lived. There was still so much to do, so much progress and so many discoveries to make. So much to fear.

He had been vacillating for weeks now. Should he travel to France in order to continue helping Francesco behind the scenes? This would mean leaving the Limassol citadel leaderless and running the risk that Henri II de Lusignan would use the opportunity to install his men. And might not a sudden voyage also arouse Guillaume de Villaret's suspicions?

What did it matter, if they were right? Everything would soon be turned on its head. The world as they knew it would be transformed overnight. People would no longer hesitate between heaven and hell – terrorised by one, dreading the other.

And what if this upheaval did not occur? What if it was destined to light up not their lives but the lives of those who came after?

Viancourt sighed. He was a mere link in a chain. What did his role matter? It did not. His name would be added to the secret list of those who'd gone before him. He had no interest in personal glory and in this he resembled their most implacable enemy, the camerlingo Benedetti. In reality, tragically, he loved this man whose destruction he was nevertheless intent upon. He recognised in him one of his own. They belonged to the same race. A race that nothing – neither reward nor fear – can discourage. A race that is capable of putting aside its own interests in order to accomplish its mission.

I will crush you, Honorius. I will crush you, but I will mourn your loss. I know you as well as I know myself, Honorius. We are twin souls, even though yours is damned by virtue of your mistakes. I feel as if I have only ever been truly close to you. Do you feel as I do?

Honorius? How can we both be convinced of serving Him with all our might and all our love when our actions are opposed?

Alençon, Auberge de la Jument-Rouge, Perche, December 1304

*A*n almost suffocating silence. The cold, grey light of a late winter's afternoon. The acrid smell of altar candles. Footsteps echoing on the brown flagstones.

Francesco de Leone glided through the interminable ambulatory of the church. His black coat, ornamented with a cross, its eight branches fused together in pairs, flapped around his leather boots.

He was following a silently moving figure, her presence betrayed only by the soft rustle of fabric, a yellow robe of heavy silk. A woman, a woman hiding. A woman almost the same height as he. The candle flames cast an intermittent glow on her undulating hair. A silky wave descending below her knees and merging with her dress. Hair with a copper sheen, like honey. A sudden breathlessness made Leone gasp with pain, even as the icy chill froze his lips.

With his left hand he tried to wipe away the sweat running down his brow, stinging his eyes, and scratched his face with his gauntlet. Why was he wearing it? Was he about to go into combat?

Gradually he had become accustomed to the semi-darkness. By the dim light filtering in through the dome and the flickering candlelight, he strained to see into the enveloping gloom obscuring the columns and engulfing the walls. What church was he in? Did it matter? It was a smallish church, and yet he had been circling inside it for what seemed like hours.

He was chasing the woman, without urgency. Why? She did not try to run away, but maintained an equal distance between them. She kept a few steps ahead of him, as though anticipating his movements, staying on the outside of the ambulatory while he moved along on the inside.

He paused. A step, one step, and then she stopped. The sound of steady breathing. The woman's breathing. As he moved off again so did his shadow.

Francesco de Leone's hand reached slowly for the pommel of his sword even as a feeling of tenderness made him gasp. He looked down incredulously at his right hand clutching the metal sphere. He had aged terribly. Great veins bulged beneath the wrinkled skin.

Suddenly he was aware of a third presence hiding in the darkness. A bloody, murderous presence. A ruthless presence. The woman had stopped. Had she sensed the ferocious shadow? A voice murmured: 'Help me, knight, for the love of God.' A pale feminine hand brushed the sleeve of his long tunic, causing him to tremble with almost intolerable delight. The other hand disappeared into the folds of her dress and emerged clutching the handle of a glinting short sword. He hadn't noticed that she was armed. He whispered, 'I will give my life for you, Madame,' then turned slowly towards her. The saffron yellow of her silk dress was stretched tightly over her belly. She was with child.

Francesco awoke with a start, his mouth open, gasping for breath. The dream, the recurring dream. It was becoming clearer, he was drawing closer. He knew now that the dream was the future. He lay doubled up, sobbing uncontrollably, on the straw mattress in his lodgings at the tavern at Alençon where he'd been since Florin's execution. Dry sobs, sobs of gratitude, sobs of immeasurable relief. He had been so afraid that he was chasing the woman in order to kill her. He was simply following her in order to protect her – her and the child she was carrying. The difference in their ages in the dream proved that, contrary to what he had long believed, the young woman was not Agnès de Souarcy. And yet she resembled her like a sister.

Was this quest that had for so long driven him, borne him, exhausted him nearing its end? What was the exact meaning of the dream?

He got up and stood, naked, in the middle of the murky room. He moved slowly over to the tiny window and lifted the piece of oiled hide, stiff with frost. He came out in goose pimples as a blast of icy air filled the room. He slumped to his knees, savouring every moment of his prayer of obedience and unending gratitude.

The woman. He would give his life for the woman with child. Without demur, without fear, without reward. His life belonged to that woman who had raised her sword in an unknown church to protect her unborn child. It was the child.

Jeanne d'Amblin had returned from her rounds a few days before, exhausted, trembling with fever and racked by terrible fits of coughing. She had tried in vain to resist Éleusie de Beaufort's injunction to rest a little in order to aid her swift recovery. Owing to her state she had been apportioned two thick blankets, and Annelette had brewed a succession of curative decoctions and chest balms. The apothecary was well aware that the extern sister's symptoms were as common to severe illness as they were to more minor afflictions, and that she must do her utmost to stop the infection spreading to the other nuns.

Jeanne handed her the empty bowl that had contained a chest remedy of cabbage water, beech wood and borage.[34] She screwed up her face, protesting:

'Why do all your remedies taste so foul?'

'Even though I added spices and honey to improve the taste,' Annelette remarked. 'I will leave you to rest for a while. After that … you must agree to a few inhalations.'

'Oh no, not one of your fumigations with nettle and lovage, please!'

'They work best.'

'But it's for horses!'[35]

'And for humans too. Decidedly, you are not a good patient, dear Jeanne.'

The other woman replied with an apologetic smile: 'Forgive me, kind Annelette. I'm bored of being in bed. There's nothing wrong with my legs; it's my head that feels as if it's in a vice and my lungs are roaring like a furnace!'

'I sympathise. However, you must understand that an untreated cough can turn into something more serious, and besides you're contagious. Isn't it curious how diseases spread ... Is it only the breath that is infectious? I'm not so sure. We are all aware, for example, that one can become infected by wearing a sick person's underclothes. A fascinating problem.'

Jeanne, who otherwise had little interest in science, said in a concerned voice:

'Are you saying that I might infect you?'

'Not this big old lanky carcass! But if you do, I will lie in the bed next to you and we can keep each other company,' the apothecary retorted.

She plumped up her patient's pillow and enquired:

'Are you certain you have everything you need, Jeanne? Your jug of water contains essence of mallow ... I don't think there's anything else ...'

'I've lost my handkerchief. It must have slipped down somewhere.'

Annelette looked under and around the bed but could not see it. She pulled a replacement out of the reticule attached to her belt, which, besides a handkerchief, contained a phial of antiseptic, a long needle for removing splinters and some tiny pieces of cloth soaked in pine oil.

'Here, this one is clean. I'll bring you another later.'

She left Jeanne who, despite her protests to the contrary, was visibly frail and began nodding off. She was careful to lower the thin curtain that screened off her cell from the rest of the dormitory.

Annelette Beaupré walked down the long corridor leading to Éleusie de Beaufort's study. A familiar figure overtook her. The slim novice turned and gave her a radiant but shy smile. Ah yes, what was her Christian name again? She had said she wanted to take the name of Constantine's mother, Hélène. Annelette had forgotten. It was not important.

She knocked loudly on the door and was greeted by a violent fit of coughing.

A pox on these chest infections, she thought. They spread like lightning. The Abbess's age and frail constitution made her an obvious target ... Well, now she had a second patient under her charge. She could only hope that there would be no more casualties and that her Reverend Mother would be more cooperative than Jeanne.

The apothecary recalled one spring when she had ministered to over thirty nuns and almost as many lay servants suffering from vomiting, diarrhoea and stomach cramps. She had managed to avoid infection herself, but had feared she might die of exhaustion.

She found the Abbess slumped behind her desk, her head in her hands. Annelette knew she was right the moment Éleusie de Beaufort looked up. Her eyes were streaming, her nose was red and she was sniffing pathetically. The Abbess said in a hoarse voice:

'This is all we need, my dear Annelette. An epidemic.'

'So far only Jeanne and you have been infected. Let us hope that it does not spread.'

The Abbess blew her nose loudly and said:

'I need some fresh bits of cloth. These ones are ... terribly soiled. I scarcely have the strength to stand, daughter, and ...'

'Of course. I will go to the linen room at once. On my way back I'll stop at the herbarium and make you an infusion ... Jeanne says they taste foul, but I promise to add an extra dose of honey, ginger and cinnamon to take away the bitterness.'

Half an hour later, Éleusie de Beaufort set down the bowl which Annelette had made her finish down to the last drop, and exclaimed:

'Sweet Lord, what unpleasant medicine indeed! Is it not the

height of injustice to be ill and have to swallow such foul potions as a punishment! Light the oil lamps for me, daughter. Night is already falling and I can barely see. I feel so weak. I hope a good night's sleep will restore me. Have you advanced in your investigations, in your analysis?'

'Not as I would wish. Please do not think me indiscreet, but I understand that a messenger came to you this afternoon and ...'

The Abbess gave a faint smile:

'Some good news, at last. My nephew is on his way here. What a relief!' Suddenly, her pretty, finely lined face darkened.

'I sent a message back explaining the recent events here at the abbey.'

'How is it that I didn't see your nephew during his last visit? Heavens, it would have been a catastrophe if that wretched Florin had found out he was here!'

The Abbess's face flushed with pride and she declared:

'Francesco is cunning. He can slip in and out like a cat. Not a wall or door exists that can keep him out.'

A sudden fit of coughing caused the Abbess to choke. Annelette rushed over to slap her on the back. Finally the spasms abated.

They spoke again of the murders and the threat hanging over their quest. Then Éleusie described Francesco in such terms that it seemed to Annelette that she had mistaken him for an archangel, and she marvelled at the power of a mother's love. The apothecary was about to leave for the dormitory when something in the Abbess's manner alerted her. Her teeth appeared clenched and her jaw muscles jutted out beneath her pale skin.

'Reverend Mother, are you quite well?'

Powerless to unclench her jaw, Éleusie shook her head. An interminable list of symptoms ran through the apothecary's head. A trismus, this was what was known as a trismus. It was found in certain types of tetanus infections or after an inflammation of the tonsils.

'Reverend Mother!' Annelette cried.

Éleusie appeared to jump out of her chair. She fell to the ground like a dead weight. Annelette ran over to her and tried to pick her up, but the tiny woman's muscles were rigid. She was gasping for breath, suffocating. The sweat was streaming down her face, soaking the neck of her robe.

Then it dawned on Annelette. She leapt to her feet like a madwoman and grabbed the empty bowl. She tasted the dregs and thought her legs would give way under her. The excessive bitterness told her that something had been added to her mixture of herbs. She bent double, letting out a sob of grief. She herself had administered the poison that would end the Abbess's life. That monstrous poisoner had turned her into an unwitting accomplice. For the first time in her life, Annelette was overwhelmed by the desire to kill. She hated her, she wanted to see the murderess dead at her feet.

She knelt down beside Éleusie, who was fighting for every breath, struggling to control her arms, which were sticking straight up in the air. Annelette wanted to take her hand, but just then a terrible convulsion seized the Abbess's frail body, causing her back to arch before she collapsed again.

'Are you in pain, Madame?' the apothecary whimpered. 'I don't recognise any of these symptoms. What did the fiend use? Madame, I beg you, please don't die, don't leave me! Oh Madame … I lied to you … I'm not nearly as strong as I pretend to be. I only stood firm in order to reassure you, to prove how indispensable I was to you. Don't leave me, I beg you! Stay with me! I'm afraid, Reverend Mother. What will I do without you?'

A teardrop fell on the Abbess's pristine white robe, then another, forming tiny damp circles. Only then did Annelette realise that she was crying. She felt as if her life were ebbing away at the same time as that of the dying woman. The apothecary curled up beside Éleusie on the floor and intoned: 'Bless you, my sister, bless you, my sister … God loves you. He loves you …'

She had no idea how long she remained there. Her thoughts had strayed far away.

The dying woman's cry made her leap to her feet. Éleusie, teeth still clenched, was staring at her intently, trying desperately to tell her something. Annelette drew close to the Abbess. Another cry resounded from her throat. The Abbess pursed her lips with difficulty and murmured between gritted teeth:

'Sa— The … sa—'

'Your safe.'

'Fran … ces—'

'Your nephew, Francesco.'

'Let—'

'A letter, or letters for your nephew in your safe.' Éleusie managed to blink one eye.

'Se— Se … cret.'

'It will remain a secret, I swear on my life.'

'Key … Libr— secr—'

'The key to the secret library is also there. Who must I give it to? Francesco?'

The Abbess blinked again.

The dying woman's rasping breath puffed her cheeks out sharply at intervals. In a panic, Annelette was unable to think clearly. Should she leave the room, run for help? No. Éleusie could not be left to die alone in that sinister room.

A hoarse sound, then another. Her arms still sticking up in the air, her legs jutting out from under her dress revealing her ankles, Éleusie waited calmly for death. She did not mind being conscious, experiencing every last detail of death. Dying was not as terrifying as people made it out to be. On the contrary it treated her, its new victim, almost with compassion. For Éleusie clearly felt the presence of her beloved sisters by her side. Claire's laughter pealed in her memory, Clémence's lips brushed her soul and Philippine's fingers stroked her cheek.

Henri, my sweet husband … At long last I will join you. I encountered many obstacles along the path I took to reach you. And my journey was often a lonely one. I always felt so cold without you. Now, at least I feel warm again.

One last effort, only one.

She managed to open her lips:

'Live … my … friend. Live.'

A final, terrible exhalation. Her chest was motionless. It felt as though a huge red wave had unfurled in her head, blurring the edges of things.

A last gasp. Her body rose in an arch from the icy flagstones, resting only on her heels and the back of her head then slumped to the floor, lifeless.

'Madame, Madame?' sobbed Annelette. 'No. No, it cannot be! No, it isn't fair, it isn't fair! It's my fault, it's all my fault. I was in such a hurry to prepare her decoction it never occurred to me that the rascal might have mixed her powders in with my herbs. My stupidity and negligence are to blame!'

And all of a sudden she was seized by a terrible rage. She crawled on her hands and knees over to the door and screamed at the top of her voice:

'Die, you monster! Die! Rot in the darkest depths of hell for all eternity, even if I have to send you there myself!'

There was a sound of running feet, and the door burst open. The two women stumbling upon the grisly scene cried out as one. Thibaude de Gartempe and Berthe de Marchiennes, the cellarer nun. Thibaude knelt beside Annelette who was still hysterical. The apothecary, who was raging uncontrollably, struggled to free herself from her sister's grasp:

'Die! I'll kill you if I have to …!'

'Annelette, I beg you! Calm yourself. It is over. Calm yourself. *Annelette*, stop! We must attend to our Reverend Mother's body.'

The apothecary's hysterical screams ceased abruptly, and she stared wildly at the guest mistress. Then the dark cloud obscuring her pale-blue eyes cleared and she murmured:

'My God ...'

With Thibaude's help she rose to her feet. Berthe was standing motionless, inches from the Abbess's corpse, her face as white as a sheet. She stammered:

'This place is cursed. I am sure of it now.'

'You foolish old woman!' growled Annelette. 'The only thing in this place that's cursed is the poisoner. I need your key to the safe; it was our Reverend Mother's final wish. Give it to me quickly and leave here at once, both of you. I shall call for you later when it is time to destroy the seal.'

'But ...'

'That's an order!'

Berthe feebly attempted to counter her:

'Given the advanced age of dear Blanche, our senior nun and guardian of the seal, and until such time as a new abbess is nominated, I am the ...'

'You are nothing!' the apothecary shrieked violently. 'Nothing but a suspect. Now give me the key.'

The cellarer nun's sour expression became a scowl. She grabbed the leather thong from around her neck and hurled it into the other woman's face before leaving the room, accompanied by Thibaude.

Annelette Beaupré lifted her robe and untied the small piece of cord around her waist, attached to which was a second key.

As she knelt beside the Abbess's body, it occurred to her that the hardest part was yet to come. And yet she was overwhelmed by a feeling of infinite tenderness. She lifted the dead woman's head carefully and slipped her hand down the neck of her robe. Death had relaxed the obscene rigidity of her limbs and jaw, restoring to Éleusie the dignity of a handsome woman in middle years. Annelette retrieved the third key and sat for a moment with the head of the friend she had discovered too late resting on her lap.

Éleusie's last words to her had been: 'Live, my friend. Live.' They were the apothecary's recompense for a life of bitter, self-imposed isolation, which she had only recently realised how much she detested. She stroked the dead woman's brow, still damp with sweat, and kissed it before getting up to open the safe with the aid of the three keys. In it she found a heavy key – no doubt a copy of the key to the Abbess's chambers – and another smaller key. The Abbess's seal lay on top of a bulky letter. On it she had written in the long hand Annelette knew as if it were her own:

> *To be given to my dear nephew Francesco de Leone on my death. Should anyone go against the will of the deceased and read this letter, they will answer with their soul. God is my Saviour and my Judge.*

Annelette leafed through the other documents: acts of purchase or sale of land or buildings, transfers of forests or mills. With the intention of hiding it, she took the parchment containing the plans the Abbess had mentioned. The only safe place she could think of was the library. She pulled the tapestry aside and discovered the low door.

Armed with one of the oil lamps she had lit what seemed like an eternity ago, she entered the vast, high-ceilinged room. She felt an icy draught on her head and looked up towards the horizontal arrow-slit windows at the top of the walls. Despite her wrenching grief, she gasped with emotion at the sight of the hundreds of volumes before her, scarcely daring to approach them.

Breathless, her mouth gaping in astonishment, she struggled against the superstitious fear that was paralysing her. Suddenly she hurled herself feverishly at the shelves. She devoured the titles, sighing with admiration, moaning with envy at the thought of all that science, of all that assembled knowledge. My God ... To be allowed to remain in there for months reading everything, learning everything ... She was gripped by a sudden panic: what if the newly appointed Abbess[36] decided or was ordered to destroy these marvels? Annelette shuddered at the thought. She would keep the key until the knight Leone's return. His grief would be terrible, far greater than her own. Annelette knew how much Madame de Beaufort had loved her adoptive son and she did not doubt that her feelings were reciprocated.

She must act quickly in case Berthe and Thibaude came barging in again. Those two fools were quite capable of imagining that she was taking advantage of being alone to forge documents using the seal. Petty souls frequently project their own guilty desires onto others.

As she was placing the letter and plans on a shelf, her foot struck an object. She stooped in the semi-gloom, which was barely illuminated by her lamp, and discovered the wicker basket full of sachets and phials of toxic substances from the herbarium which she had entrusted to the Abbess. So, this was where she had hidden them.

What was the fast-acting poison that produced such convulsions and stiffness of the limbs? She was convinced that the same substance had been used to kill Yolande de Fleury. The sister in charge of the granary must have scratched her own throat in an attempt to breathe before the paralysis spread to her limbs.

An animal. The poison was connected in some way to a large

wild animal. No memory stirred. Perhaps the answer lay in one of these books.

No! They weren't just scratch marks. The discoloration was too extensive, reaching right up to below her nose. Éleusie had cried out every time Annelette touched her. Had the merest contact caused her pain? Annelette imagined the murderess that night in the dormitory. The fiend! She had gripped Yolande's neck with one hand and gagged her with the other. She had stood there watching her sister die. She would receive no mercy in this world or the next. Annelette swore on her life, on her soul, that the killer's punishment would be swift and terrible.

Another piece of the puzzle fell into place: the murderess hoped that by killing Éleusie the ban on leaving the abbey and the systematic search of people, bundles and carts would be lifted. The manuscripts. They must under no circumstances be allowed to fall into the hands of their enemies. Annelette would do her best to foil the poisoner by any means possible – even if she had to compensate for her lack of any real authority by blatant aggression, as she had done with Berthe and Thibaude. Despite her age and feeble-mindedness, Blanche de Blinot had every right to claim the position of Vice-abbess. However, the apothecary was sure that the assassin would have no difficulty in manipulating the senile old woman. As for Berthe de Marchiennes, even divested of her former pride, she, too, was fool enough to be swayed by eloquence and clever flattery.

Annelette Beaupré tried hard to fight off a creeping sense of despair. She would find a way to keep the restrictions on leaving the abbey in place.

As she made her way over to the low door, which she had left ajar, another thought struck her. The handkerchief! Conscious of the fact that certain illnesses – notably pulmonary infections – are passed on by contact with a patient's garments or personal effects, the murderess had no doubt stolen Jeanne's handkerchief while she was asleep, and placed it within Éleusie's reach. The Abbess's frail constitution, in addition to her exhaustion and the anxiety she had suffered over the past few months, had done the rest. The snake only needed to follow the progress of the infection and poison the remedies she knew Annelette would use to treat the Abbess.

She would kill her – with her own bare hands if necessary. Annelette knew she was capable of it. Worse still, she longed to see the life snuffed out in that devil's eyes, as she had seen it die in those of Éleusie de Beaufort.

The apothecary walked out quickly, locked the low door and pulled back the tapestry. She left Éleusie's study, locking the door behind her. She would attend the removal of the body. She would prevent anybody from remaining in their deceased Reverend Mother's chambers until a new Abbess had been appointed and installed, for then Annelette would have to hand back the keys.

Oh dear God ... I beg you: make Francesco's return swift.

Vatican Palace, Rome, December 1304

The camerlingo Honorius Benedetti studied the earnest expression on the shiny face of the French prelate sitting opposite him. Archbishop Foulques de Marzin was waiting for his advice. It was not long in coming:

'My dear brother ... my friend, what can I say? Naturally the King of France and the other European monarchs will use all their political might to influence the outcome of the forthcoming papal election, but ultimately the decision rests with the conclave. You will receive the vote of all the French prelates who do not wish to see an Italian elected to the Holy See – at any rate those humble enough to recognise that they themselves would not make good popes or those who refuse to cast their votes in return for ... compensation.'

'And how many of them do you suppose there are, Your Eminence? I mean who cannot be bought – that monstrous word – or are not driven by ambition?'

Marzin amused Benedetti – in an unpleasant sort of way, he had to confess. This bishop, who would stop at nothing to snatch the Holy See from his rivals, frowned and puckered his lips in distaste when he spoke of their greed for power and glory. A disturbing thought occurred to the camerlingo, which he attempted to brush aside. In the end, did he not have more in common with those 'others', his hidden enemies who were fighting for the coming of what they called the Infinite Light? They, too, believed that their lives were of no importance. That only the future mattered. Of course, they had chosen the wrong side, for men were men and no miracle, no sacrifice by the son of God who died on the cross would make them change in any enduring way. They sobbed, prayed, implored until the memory of the martyr's purity began to fade, and then they continued their scheming, wicked ways.

Benedetti looked again at the man whose face reminded him of jellied fruit dipped in rancid syrup. He could not resist taunting him, although his good political sense told him simply to dupe the man.

'Do you want the truth?'

'I would expect nothing less from you, with respect.'

'Very few.'

The syrupy expression faded, and Foulques de Marzin's face, tumid and purple in colour from an overindulgence in rich food, became visibly distraught. How amusing he was indeed, this flabby lump who preached abstinence in a booming voice. Monseigneur de Marzin's pressing need for money was common knowledge – money that allowed him to keep his voracious family, as well as a few exceedingly pretty and exceedingly young mistresses. Did he really imagine that he would be able to install them like a harem at the Vatican Palace? And why not? It wouldn't be the first time. Marzin had come to him for support, for his vote, in exchange for which he was willing to make a great many concessions.

Suddenly this scene, which previously would have delighted the camerlingo to the point of making him draw it out as long as possible, ceased to amuse him.

He wanted this whining maggot out of his sight this instant. His presence suffocated the camerlingo.

'My dear friend, you know how much I respect you. You are one of the lights of our church. Rest assured that you have my vote.'

The flabby face quivered with emotion, contentment most of all.

'If it pleases God to make me His next representative on earth, believe me, Your Eminence, I will not forget your good deeds and your innumerable virtues. I will need men of faith by my side whom I can trust. I thank you most graciously.'

'No, it is I who must thank you, dear Marzin, for being that candidate for whom I can cast my vote without fear of making the wrong choice.'

Honorius stood up to signal that the meeting was over. Believing he had achieved what he came there for – the vote which the camerlingo had already promised to a dozen or more French and Italian prelates – Foulques de Marzin hurriedly kissed the hand that was being held out to him.

Rid of the loathsome schemer at last, Benedetti was able to engage in one of his silent monologues. These were infinitely precious to him. In whom had he confided for so long if not the son of God?

What did you imagine? That the blood that flowed from Your hands and feet would save the world? It was a beautiful dream. But nobody is able to save the world. All we are able to do is to postpone its destruction. There are so few righteous people in Your kingdom, Sublime Lamb of God. Your flock is reduced to a tribe of individuals who are being killed, who are suffering because others prefer to revel in sin, which they maximise and which makes them rich and happy. Sin can be so enjoyable, so easy, while virtue is harsh and arid. Whom can it tempt? What is that You say? That my hidden enemies are also part of Your little tribe? You are right. And yet You know that I am too, and that I would die a thousand deaths for my love of You. However, I do not entertain the foolish hope of changing men. The day men stop fearing the consequences of their actions, nothing will stop them. Their madness, their barbarism will become law. The weak will have their throats cut or be turned into slaves. Only the cruel and bloodthirsty will remain. The future will become a terrible nightmare if we let them have their way. I aim to keep their fear alive. I aim to strengthen the leash that restrains them. I will be hated. What of it? My life is pure torment since Benoît's murder. Do You know what I sometimes think? That this world is in fact hell. That there is no other.

Honorius Benedetti despised them all, or nearly all. They disgusted him. Why had he loved Benoît so, despite the deceased Pope being his most stubborn adversary? Why did he feel like such an outsider, so different from his innumerable allies – willing or not? Was it his punishment only to feel akin to, like a fellow soul of those whom he must crush, eliminate?

The arrival of an usher interrupted his train of thoughts.

'Show him in at once.'

The diminutive young man bowed before him. And yet nothing in his demeanour suggested servility.

'Pray, take a seat, Clair.'

Clair Gresson, Guillaume de Plaisians's private secretary sat down. His long journey from Paris had left him with dark shadows under his eyes. His coat was covered in the whitish dust of the roads.

'I came as soon as I could, Your Eminence. Please excuse my dishevelled appearance.'

'You are excused, Clair. Do you bring important news?'

'Indeed. Far too important to entrust to any messenger. I must leave again without delay. My absence might arouse suspicion and alarm my master, Monsieur de Plaisians.'

'Have you some names at last?'

'Oh, I have better than that! A single name.'

'Quick!' cried Honorius, unable to contain his excitement.

'Monseigneur de Troyes.'

'Renaud de Cherlieu?'

'Yes. After much hesitation between Monsieur de Got,*

Archbishop of Bordeaux, and Monsieur de Cherlieu, Cardinal of Troyes, Guillaume de Nogaret and my master have decided in favour of the latter. From a purely mercenary point of view, I am not sure that they have chosen wisely, for de Got would have brought the Gascon vote with him. However, Monsieur de Got seemed ill disposed to the idea of a posthumous trial of Boniface VIII, who was his friend, although he proved more amenable over the matter of the order of the Knights Templar.'

Clair Gresson confirmed what the camerlingo's spies had told him about a list containing two names. Even so, considering the support he would receive from the Gascon prelates, Honorius would have backed Monsieur de Got's candidature as the winning one. However, his political intelligence notwithstanding, if the archbishop had refused the King's demands in exchange for his covert support, he had de facto lost the Holy See.

The camerlingo felt a sense of relief that was almost unsettling because it was so unusual. At last he knew whom he must fight. He had no lack of means at his disposal. Spreading rumours at the right moment of Nicolaism, dealings with the devil, heresy or tolerance of religious deviance would defeat Cardinal de Troyes's candidature. Honorius would be elected. Not that the papal crown held any attraction for him, but he was prepared to resign himself to it if necessary in order to further his mission. In addition, Renaud de Cherlieu's influence was not far-reaching enough to pose any real problem. Even so, Honorius would have to dig deep into his war chest, dole out promises, threats even, liberally, while pretending to be as meek as a lamb, if he had any hope of being elected. He would see to it that he was.

He felt a warm affection for the young Clair Gresson, who had been won over by his arguments without any need for remuneration. He was pure. Pure in the way Benedetti was pure, since purity has many faces.

'My friend, I thank you from the bottom of my heart. How

strange, I utter that word "friend" twenty times a day without ever meaning it. I needed to say it to you in order to rediscover its wonderful significance. Go and rest. Thank you. Thank you for having brought me this reprieve from anxiety.'

'I must leave again at once, Your Eminence.'

'Very well.' Embarrassed suddenly by the oft-repeated gesture, Benedetti took a purse from the drawer of his magnificent desk, pausing before handing it to the other man. 'I ... Take this. It is neither payment nor reward, it is simply ...'

Gresson's face flushed, and he stood up, declaring abruptly:

'You insult me, Monsieur. I may be poor, but I am not for sale. If I wore out my hired horses in order to arrive here as quickly as I could, it is because I believe in your vision. Men are incapable of governing their lives. Without our guidance they would live in turmoil. Does the wish for peace – or at least a practical approximation to it – require payment? That being so, I will accept the cost of my journey, which I can ill afford. But nothing more. The satisfaction of working for the future is the only reward I need.'

Benedetti knew it, and had expected, counted on Gresson's refusal. Perhaps the camerlingo had needed this rebuff in order to convince himself that he was not entirely alone.

'Truly ... your visit will be the only pleasant experience in my entire day, or should I say in a series of very long days,' he commented, accompanying the young man to the door leading out of his study.

Alone once more, Honorius gave in to a brief surge of emotion. That exhausted young man had no idea to what extent his visit had calmed the camerlingo. Of course, the information he had brought was of the utmost importance. But aside from this clever piece of espionage, Gresson's integrity, his scrupulous honesty, vindicated Benedetti's struggle. Power and intelligence were so isolating that it became easy sometimes to lose sight of the measure of what was at stake. And the camerlingo was occasionally plagued by doubts, by the fear of being mistaken, of having sold his soul for the wrong cause.

Gentle Jesus, I too wish to save them. To save them from themselves, to save them for You. Like You I wish to save them from their lust for murder, villainy and cruelty. But I am a mere man, not the Son of God, and I fight with the weapons of man. They are corrupt, I know. But I have no others.

Clair Gresson crossed Saint Peter's Square with a heavy step. A flutter of pigeons accompanied his passage, their wings brushing boldly against him as they took noisily to the air. He scarcely noticed them.

Honorius Benedetti would range his impressive forces against Monseigneur de Troyes, who would never recover. The path of Bertrand de Got, Archbishop of Bordeaux and the King of France's true choice, would be open. Generously aided by Philip the Fair, his election to the papacy was almost guaranteed, thanks in large part to the Gascon vote. And Bertrand de Got would never abandon the military orders, certainly not the Hospitallers. Behind his rather nondescript appearance he was a skilled diplomat who knew how to keep his head down and weather the storm. He was an expert at inaction, continually promising, never delivering until he was absolutely certain. The elaborate game of hide and seek that he would soon be playing with the King would not change this.

Arnaud de Viancourt, the Grand-Commander of their order, would be relieved. Viancourt was by no means glad to turn his back on the order of the Knights Templar. They were enemies yet brothers. Brothers in spirit. Brothers in battle. Blood brothers. However, he would go to any lengths to save the order of the Hospitallers.

Clairets Abbey, Perche, December 1304

Francesco de Leone scaled the steep abbey wall adjacent to Notre-Dame Church. His coat tails flapped around him like two great black wings.

Gripping the rough surface of the stones, the agile figure advanced a few feet. When he was a yard from the top, the joyous prospect of seeing his aunt brought a smile to his face, despite his exertions.

The sky, heavy with the promise of snow, was his unwitting helper, obscuring the moon; if anybody spotted him he would be hard pressed to justify his nocturnal presence in a Bernadine abbey.

He reached the top and lay flat on the broad stones for a moment, catching his breath before jumping down the other side. He hugged the wall of the abbey church, preferring to cut around the back and through the kitchen garden, where he was unlikely to bump into anyone at that time of night. All he needed to do then was slip between the side wall of the library and the scriptorium and he would reach his aunt's chambers.

He hoisted himself up onto the ledge of one of the high, narrow windows in his aunt's study and whistled to her as softly as possible. No reply. Could she be sleeping so soundly? He whistled again, louder. The window opened. A tall, heavily built woman stood facing him. Francesco's surprise was shortlived. The woman urged:

'Quick, knight! If one of my sisters sees you, all is lost.'

He jumped into the study, bewildered:

'Who are you, my sister in Christ? Where is your Reverend Mother?'

The woman's face became tense as she replied: 'Annelette Beaupré, the apothecary nun.'

Francesco heaved a sigh of relief. Éleusie had mentioned their unexpected ally in one of her last letters. She had praised the woman's intelligence and tenacity.

He grasped her hands affectionately and murmured:

'There is no greater pleasure than the sight of a friendly face. Is she sleeping?' he added, pointing at the closed door to Éleusie's bedchamber, which was almost as Spartan as a prison cell.

The woman stared at him, her jaw clenched, her pale-blue eyes frozen in a grave expression. She pronounced each syllable:

'She is dead. Dead, do you hear! Poisoned, before my very eyes.'

'Pardon?' he asked, incredulous, desperately trying to understand how the word 'dead' could be applied to his beloved aunt.

'She collapsed in front of me and there was nothing I could do.'

'No!' he cried, shaking his head violently.

'That fiend has struck again. It would appear she mixed poison into one of my remedies for lung infections. It was I who gave your aunt the potion that killed her... The traitor will pay. I have sworn it before God.'

It took a while for Francesco to grasp the full implication of her words, for their meaning to sink in. Dead, poisoned.

He pictured the lovely, graceful lady, hampered by her dress, laughing at her clumsy attempts to teach him how to play *soule*,[37] a village sport that involved kicking, throwing or batting a leather ball into a circle in order to score points. He recalled her veils scented with mallow and lavender, and how he would sometimes bury his face in them before going to sleep. He could almost feel her cool slender hands stroking his brow as a child, as a youth and then as a grown man. Overwhelmed by grief, he staggered over to the long dark oak table and slumped on top of it, his head in his hands.

Annelette stood motionless, devastated by their common grief, incapable of offering a word or gesture of comfort. Grief required time and space in order for it not to be all-engulfing.

She watched him leap back to his feet. He brought his powerful fists down on the table again and again and again, causing it to judder each time. She heard him groan, and repeat in one long breath:

'Accursed wretch, you'll pay for this. Accursed wretch ...'

After what seemed to Annelette like an eternity, his arms fell to his sides. When he turned to face her, he was unrecognisable. The blood dripped from his hands onto his surcoat, red upon red.

'She went to God peacefully,' the woman murmured.

'I am sure she did, sister. But I mean to send that poisoner straight back where she came from, to hell.'

'That is impossible, knight. What is more, you must leave here before daybreak. If I occasionally slip into my late Reverend Mother's chambers, I have no right to be here and you even less so. I have kept her keys. So far nobody has dared ask me for them, discouraged by my legendary bad temper, which it is now in my interests to exaggerate. However, I will have to hand them over to the new Abbess. Have no fear. I will take care of the murderess. We haven't much time. There are many things I need to explain to you. I must give you a letter, as well as the secret plans of the abbey, which you must hide in a safe place, outside these walls.'

For the next hour, under the feeble light of two sconce torches,[38] Annelette told Francesco of the recent calamitous events at Clairets Abbey. Some of them he had already learnt from his aunt, others left him shocked and devastated.

'… And the final wickedness of these monsters is to have denied us our right to grieve. We have no time, you see, we have no time to mourn the dear victims …'

The apothecary's anxious voice trailed off, and she sighed.

He corrected her:

'Unfortunately, I doubt that this will be their final wickedness.'

Francesco was stifling the panic that had threatened to overwhelm him since she announced the theft of the manuscripts and his notebook. For a split second he had been tempted to admit defeat, to lay down his arms and surrender, to stop everything and go back to Cyprus. To retreat for ever inside those forbidding citadel walls on that faraway island. To surround himself with memories of Éleusie and Henri de Beaufort, of his mother Claire, of his sweet sister Alexandrine … Like a beckoning whisper in his mind ravaged with grief.

'No! Never give up. Fight to the death, and beyond.'

Éleusie? Claire? His aunt Clémence, whom he had scarcely known? Or the eldest, Philippine, the warrior so adored by her sisters? He could not say. He had never met Philippine. Éleusie, and Claire before her, had rarely spoken of her, as though the mere mention of her name evoked a magnificent past that only belonged to them. Why did it suddenly feel so urgent for him to remember every snatch of conversation, anything he had been able to glean about her, however insignificant?

Éleusie had remarked one day:

'She knew that she was the strongest, the most single-minded, and she sacrificed herself for us.'

His aunt had soon changed her mind and clammed up, refusing to yield before Francesco's insistence.

Whom had she been discussing with Claire in private that day when he had stood in the doorway to his mother's chambers:

'She is so like Philippine that my heart stopped when I first saw her.'

He was still a child then. The two women had gone silent when they saw him. He had been too polite to ply them with questions.

'Knight? Knight?'

A hand squeezing his arm brought him back to the study where he had so eagerly wanted to be and which he now detested.

'I know that my grief, however terrible, cannot compare to yours, knight. You have lost a mother. I have lost a sister and my only friend. One of our brightest guiding lights has been extinguished, and such lights are so rare that, when one goes out, it causes insufferable pain. But time is running out, knight, I implore you … it will soon be matins.[+] Accompany me to the library so that I can give you the letter and the plans.'

He followed her, feeling as though each step required a superhuman effort. Annelette fetched the precious documents she had left on a shelf and handed them to him. He put the parchment into one of his surcoat pockets and turned the letter over in his hands. He pictured Éleusie behind her huge desk, her eyes lowered, forming the words that he was almost afraid to read. When? Had she sensed that her end was coming? Misinterpreting his hesitation, Annelette suggested in an unusually gentle voice:

'Do you wish me to leave so that you may read it alone?'

He shook his head and declared:

'Please stay, sister. Your presence is a solace to me. It is only that … that …'

'She is so close that she surrounds us even though we cannot see her?'

He stared at her, amazed and moved by how easily she was able to read his thoughts. She added:

'This is what happens with beautiful, powerful souls like hers.

They stay with us and guide us through the darkness.'

He lowered his eyes and broke the seal on the letter, dated a few days before she was murdered. She had known, then.

My darling boy,

When you read these lines, I will no longer be there to kiss your brow. However, you may be sure that I shall continue to watch over you always. God will grant me this favour, I know.

It falls to me now to fill in some of the gaps in your knowledge of our lives – at least those parts of which I alone am aware. If it has taken me this long to make up my mind, it is because we feared that some of this information might lead you astray. Who do I mean by we? Four sisters: Clémence, Philippine, Claire and myself.

I need more time. I sense that any moment now she will engulf me. Who? The murderess, the shadow.

The lives I am about to describe to you are lives full of calculation, strategies and subterfuge. They are also lives full of love, trust, collaboration and self-sacrifice. Have no illusions about me. I am the most mediocre, the most timorous member of this blood-and-soul sisterhood. Curiously, I survived the other three, who were far better equipped to continue. I have wondered over this selection and must admit that I have never understood it.

Before beginning these painful confessions, I want to tell you again how much I have loved you, how much I still love you and will love you for all eternity. Your addition to the happy couple that Henri and I formed was a blessing, despite the terrible damage left by the deaths of Claire and your little sister, Alexandrine. You were our ray of sunshine, our hope. You were my last reason for living. You know that Claire has always remained close to my heart. And yet God knows how much I loved being called Mother, how hard it was for me sometimes to remember that I was only your second mother.

Four sisters, four women, then, including the lovingly obstinate Philippine. Perhaps you were surprised that we never spoke of her, that I was so evasive when you asked about the aunt you had never known. Do you remember how I used to divert your attention with a book, a tree, another story? It was so difficult for me, for us, to lie to you that we preferred evasion ...

The last two letters were faint, as though Éleusie had paused before continuing. The first letter of the next word was a splodge, suggesting that she had thrust her quill too hastily into the ink-horn.

... A jumble of confused images comes flooding back to me. Philippine, the magnificent chimera. She was breathtakingly beautiful. You might have difficulty believing that we all, even your mother, whom heaven had blessed with such an abun- dance of mental and physical attributes, considered Philippine a miracle. Her intelligence was equalled only by her beauty, her goodness and her compassion. The angels vied with one another to bestow gifts upon her at birth. Ah ... Philippine's laughter. What I wouldn't give for the joy of hearing it once more. She had such an easy smile. And yet behind the cheerful nature that lit up the lives of all who knew her lay an exceptionally strong, brave and single-minded woman. Philippine feared nothing and no one but God. I have made one fundamental omission in this otherwise faithful portrait. Like your mother, Claire, though to a lesser degree, Philippine was endowed with the gift of second

sight and, although she never spoke of it, unlike me she did not suppress it. I was terrified by my visions, and like a coward I tried to stifle them. Clémence was spared them, although her extreme sensibility occasionally allowed her to envisage events and people as keenly as we did. Claire explored them. Philippine followed them. To the very end.

Thus it was neither wantonness nor an unfortunate accident, still less a shameful sin, when that man – of whom I know nothing – crossed her path and she knew that he must father her child.

As you can imagine we kept her pregnancy a secret. She spent half of it in Italy with your mother and the other half with us in Normandy.

My eyes are moist with tears, my darling boy, for the end is nigh: the end of this letter, which I can picture you reading, Philippine's end and my own. The midwife declared that it was one of the most terrible births she had ever witnessed. Philippine began haemorrhaging and was confined to her bed. No amount of prayer, remedies or tears helped. I still see her big grey-blue eyes staring out of her beautiful face, her lips dry from fever. One morning I had fallen asleep while I watched over her, and she squeezed my hand to waken me. She declared joyously: 'Stop your grieving, my dear. I am happy. This was how it had to be. I was ready. Remember me in your heart, gentle sister. Take care of my baby. She is more important than any of us.' She smiled and puckered her lips in a last kiss before her head fell back. I remained with her until just after terce.[+]

The child's hungry cries wrenched me from the yawning yet welcoming abyss into which I was spiralling. Certainly the need to watch over Agnès, the chosen lamb, was what enabled me to overcome my searing grief.

Agnès. Yes, you read correctly. Agnès de Souarcy is

your first cousin on your mother's side, the daughter of
Philippine and an unknown man …

Stunned by these revelations, Francesco glanced up at Annelette. The apothecary nun looked back at him. He too had the impression that he was falling into a bottomless crevasse as he tried desperately to process his thoughts.

… It was Claire who decided straight away that Clémence should look after her. With hindsight, I wonder whether your mother had not already foreseen her own death and your coming to us. Baron de Larnay was a dullard and a scoundrel. He had sired so many bastards that one more was unlikely to come as any surprise. We took advantage of the fact that he had, indeed, left Clémence's maid with child. The poor girl was languishing at one of the farms on the estate, waiting – as was the custom, in order to spare the fornicating nobles any discomfiture – for her delivery, which arrived in the form of a miscarriage. Clémence managed to persuade her to pass Agnès off as her child. I do not know whether the maid accepted with good grace. My dear sister Clémence was a firm-handed woman, and was able when necessary to handle dangerous situations. It surprised everybody how soon Baron de Larnay developed a fondness for the little bastard girl. It was our role to protect and educate her. Again it was Clémence who broke down the baron's resistance so that years later, when Agnès reached adolescence, he recognised her as his daughter. She cleverly threatened her husband with the state of his soul, already overburdened with sin. The twisted desire Eudes de Larnay felt, and still feels, towards Agnès is less blameworthy because she is only his cousin. However, it was out of the question that he bed her, as he had so many

others, at the risk of producing another specimen of their delinquent race.

The rest you know, my darling boy, and I can imagine your surprise. I trust, I hope, that you are not angry with me for having kept you for so long in ignorance. Do not think it a feeble excuse when I say that Claire, Philippine and Clémence were adamant that the secret should not be divulged unless there was a danger that it would die out. This is now the case. I am going to die soon and join my beloved ghosts who have accompanied me during these long years. I already miss you dreadfully, my sweet angel, and yet I rejoice in seeing them again. Amen.

Live, my brave boy. Live and fight on, I beseech you.

Your loving mother for all eternity.

Francesco de Leone was stunned. How could they have kept the truth from him for so long? Why? Curiously, discovering his blood tie with Madame de Souarcy made him feel no closer to her. Not now. And then it struck him. This was exactly what the four sisters had wanted, or at least the three instigators of the deception. It was not his cousin Agnès whom he must defend and protect from and for the sake of everybody, but the key designated by a prophetic birth chart. His body relaxed as he exhaled lengthily. The tightness he had been feeling in his chest for the past few minutes abated. They had been right. The circle was closing. Agnès belonged to their family, a family that had safeguarded the quest for generations. Born of a woman who had chosen motherhood outside the sacred bonds of marriage, no doubt because she had followed the sign that led her to the man who must father her child. A girl.

He looked up at the apothecary who was staring anxiously at him.

'All is well, sister,' he reassured her.

He walked over to the little sconce torch she was holding and placed a corner of the letter over the flame. They watched in silence as the chiffon paper slowly blackened. Francesco kept hold of it until he felt the flickering flame scorch his fingers.

'You must leave here soon, knight,' Annelette Beaupré urged.

'I realise that. I won't even have the consolation of spending a few moments at the resting place of my second mother.'

The apothecary nodded before adding:

'She is buried in the nave of the abbey church of Notre-Dame, beside her predecessors.'

'Do you know ... I enjoyed the immense good fortune of having two wonderful mothers whom I loved equally.' Aware that time was running short and that the dormitories would soon be stirring in readiness for the first service of the day, he added: 'The manuscripts ... They must be found. They must not leave Clairets.'

She sighed uneasily as she said:

'I can ensure that they don't for the moment, brother. I have firmly insisted that Madame de Beaufort's final orders should be carried out to the letter, but ... if the newly appointed Abbess is ...'

'One of them,' he finished her sentence. 'And I am sure she will be. My aunt was murdered so that she could be replaced by one of their accomplices. I fear that her arrival at Clairets is imminent. Therefore we have very little time. If you find the manuscripts, destroy the treatise on necromancy. I regret not having already done so.'

'And what about the others? I won't be able to leave the abbey in order to give them to you – that is, if I do manage to find them. The notebook our dear Reverend Mother mentioned to me and ...'

He interrupted her with a gesture. Suddenly his heart leapt. The memory of a smudge of ink at the bottom of a page ...

A torn-out page that had caused him such anguish because it contained their most important conclusions drafted in invisible ink! The thief had unwittingly saved them. He crossed himself and stammered:

'We are not as lost as I had feared. Sister, has anyone else gained access to the library besides my aunt?'

'Impossible. No one else but she knew of its existence – besides the Pope's messenger whom she hid there for a few hours. He was found dead in the abbey environs.'

'Did they find a piece of paper on him?'

'No. There was no trace of the Abbess's letter.'

He was not referring to that piece of paper. He persisted:

'Somebody must have entered here without my aunt knowing.'

He took the sconce torch from Annelette and walked hurriedly over to the stairs leading down to the dark depths of the storeroom used as a workshop. He rapidly descended the steps, grasping the banister so as not to lose his footing in the dark. He moved cautiously across the trampled earth floor, sliding one foot in front of the other until he almost stumbled against the small stepladder used to reach the highest shelves in the library. It had been pushed up against the far wall, just below the narrow barred window that allowed air into the cellar. Francesco stood on the second rung and held up the sconce light. He examined the solid iron bars. The gap was wide enough for a child to slip through. He hastened back up to the library and whispered:

'You teach children here. Do you think one of them might have discovered the whereabouts of the secret library?'

Annelette, who had not moved an inch but had waited patiently, replied to the knight's almost accusatory question:

'Yes, we do receive some schoolchildren here. But they are absolutely forbidden to roam the abbey grounds, and certainly not without a teacher present!'

Francesco, who said nothing, was secretly surprised by

Annelette's naivety. It showed how little she knew children if she imagined that they always obeyed their elders.

'Are you acquainted with any of them?'

'Pardon?'

'The children. Do you know any of them? How many are there?'

'I know some of them by sight, I suppose. The schoolmistress, Emma de Pathus, is in charge of them together with the other teachers. As to how many of them there are, I would say not more than twenty. They are mostly children of the wealthy farmers, burghers and minor nobles who do not have the means to pay for private tuition. They can already read and write when they come here, and we complete their education by teaching them the Gospels and something of astronomy. Not to mention Latin and its leading authors: Cicero, Suetonius and Seneca. Some of the children are very bright, others struggle. My God!' she exclaimed suddenly, clapping her hand over her mouth.

'What?'

'Clément! It can't be ... It is too incredible ...'

'Pray, explain yourself.'

'We accepted Clément, Madame de Souarcy's protégé. He is very bright and avid for knowledge ... Do you suppose that ...? How could he have discovered the library? And why him and not another?' She was speaking to herself rather than to Francesco.

Nevertheless, Leone felt instinctively that the young boy was the one he was looking for.

The circle was beginning to close.

Another coincidence had been added to the string of coincidences that had guided all their lives for so long.

He must find the boy as quickly as possible, and he prayed that the torn-out page had not been destroyed or lost.

The apothecary was growing increasingly anxious, and he realised that she was afraid her sisters would soon stir. He followed her into his deceased second mother's study and waited for her to lock the hidden door. On impulse, he embraced her and whispered in her ear:

'Be careful. You are her only obstacle now. I am infinitely grateful to you, my sister, for having accompanied my aunt during her final moments. I am grateful to you for grieving her death. I will find a way to renew contact with you. Recover the manuscripts before it is too late and, more importantly, stay alive!'

He left through the window he had entered by earlier.

Esquive squeezed behind one of the supporting pillars outside the scriptorium and watched the lofty figure vanish swiftly into the darkness. The bitter chill of the winter evening no longer made her shiver. She placed her fingers, which were numb with cold, over her mouth, stifling her whisper:

'Have no fear, my beautiful archangel. I am watching. I am waiting. The pretty monster will soon arrive. And she is far more terrifying than the one who is already wreaking havoc within these walls.'

Annelette smiled as she tried to remember. Now that she came to think of it, it was the first time. For the very first time another being had held her in his arms without her feeling awkward or irritated. But then Éleusie had confided in her that Francesco did not resemble other mortals, that he was more like an angel.

She walked out into the corridor, cautiously hugging the walls until she reached the dormitory where she lay down on her bed for a few moments before matins. She would not go back to sleep, but would continue her search as she had done the day before and the day before that.

Her eyelids grew heavy and she chided herself as she struggled to stay awake: there was no point in falling asleep for a few minutes; it would only make her feel more tired when she woke up. However, a wave of exhaustion weakened her resolve. Her thoughts dissolved into a chaos of images. Suddenly, a blur formed in her mind's eye, immense, black and threatening. It raised its long powerful claws. She sat up. A bear! A black bear! The poison that had killed Éleusie was used to kill bears in Asia. *Nux vomica*. The powerful drug was extracted from the seeds of an orange-coloured fruit the size of an apple that grew on a magnificent sixty-foot tree. The tree was called *Strychnos nux-vomica*.[39] She remembered now. The poison had no antidote and was unknown in Europe. Half a grain[40] was enough to kill a grown man.

How had that exotic and costly poison found its way to Clairets?

Aconite.

Ergot of rye.

Yew powder. A large dose of it was lethal. A smaller dose caused prolific vomiting accompanied by shaking.

Congestion of the lungs. The handkerchief. She heard her own words: '*Isn't it curious how diseases spread … Is it only the breath that is infectious? I'm not so sure. We are all aware, for example, that one can become infected by wearing a sick person's underclothes …*'

The shard of glass by the dormitory bed that had lodged in her shoe. Éleusie telling her that one of the murdered emissaries had a series of tiny wounds in his throat and had died from internal bleeding.

A sister who was friendly enough to make people want to confide in her.

A sister who was allowed out for long enough periods to be able to procure poison, pass on information and pretend to bring news of a little boy who had died two years before.

A sister who was intelligent enough to elaborate a bold plan in order to steal the manuscripts.

A sister who was close enough to Hedwige du Thilay to learn the nature of the trap Annelette was preparing with the eggs stolen from Geneviève Fournier. This was how the murderess had outwitted her, but she had needed to kill the little treasurer nun who might have revealed her name. And while she was murdering her friend, the fiend had not hesitated to ingest some of the yew powder herself in order to avoid suspicion.

A sister devious enough to find an accomplice prepared to steal poison from the herbarium while she was out on one of her rounds.

The scattered pieces of the puzzle were at last coming together. A plain but pleasant face, lit up by a warm smile.

Jeanne d'Amblin. Jeanne d'Amblin and her accomplice, who had slipped into the herbarium in order to procure the yew powder and put Annelette off the scent by diverting suspicion from the extern sister.

A murderous rage seized the apothecary, who rose from her bed and looked around for Jeanne's curtained cell.

The wicked sinner! She had used the affection and respect she inspired in others and her influence over them to kill them. Annelette was overcome by a terrible grief. Éleusie had been so fond of Jeanne that Annelette had sometimes felt jealous. Jeanne had been her friend and confidante. What had driven her to commit such atrocities? Zeal? Was Jeanne one of their sworn enemies? Annelette instinctively thought not. Was it money? Revenge? Had the poisoner been any one of the other sisters, would Annelette have despised her as much as she hated Jeanne now? Undoubtedly not. Jeanne had nearly managed to pull the wool over her eyes as well. Annelette had trusted her, perhaps even been a little fond of her. And all the while the extern sister had been plotting to kill her too.

The apothecary clenched her fists so hard that her nails dug into the palms of her hands. She felt capable of beating the scoundrel, of dragging her kicking and screaming to the cellar where she would await the arrival of the chief bailiff and his executioners.

She forced herself to breathe slowly through her mouth until her heart stopped racing. She struggled to calm the fury that made her want to hurl herself at Jeanne and thrash the living daylights out of her.

No. Such rashness would be unforgivably stupid. Annelette did not doubt that she could overcome the extern sister by force, but others would soon arrive to take her place.

She would wait. Be cunning like her opponent. Watch her every move until she led her to the manuscripts. There was so little time. Francesco was right. 'They' would quickly appoint an abbess from among their followers. She would lift the restrictions on leaving the abbey so that Jeanne would be able to take the much-coveted manuscripts to the camerlingo. All would be irrevocably lost.

Annelette felt suffused by an icy calm. 'They' must contend with her first. She stifled her panic at the thought that she was now entirely alone and vulnerable.

She would find Jeanne's accomplice. A name came to mind. Sylvine Taulier. Who was better placed than the sister in charge of the bread ovens? She could easily have made bread contaminated with ergot. Or Adèle de Vigneux, the granary keeper? She decided to interrogate Sylvine discreetly, an easy enough task since the woman was not endowed with much in the way of brains. She smiled sadly. The Abbess would have chided her for being uncharitable. The time for kindliness and forgiveness was over, and Éleusie was no more.

Her energy, depleted since the demise of the woman she admired, came flooding back like a benediction. Annelette would fight to the death.

After that, justice would be done.

The innkeeper, his face red from all the wine dregs left by his customers which he made it a point of honour to finish, hurried over to the fine-looking gentleman who was stooping to avoid hitting his head on the crossbeams. He recognised the fellow.

'My lord, my lord, you honour my humble establishment with your presence ... once again,' he declared, bowing.

Artus d'Authon reflected that nobody would now be in any doubt as to his social position. Indeed, this had been the inn-keeper's intention, flattered as he was to receive such an august customer – and a rich and generous one to boot. On his last visit, this noble lord had left his change on the table. Adèle, the slattern who worked in the kitchens, had picked it up, but Maître Rouge[41] had soon made her hand it back. The shameless wretches! On top of free food and lodging they expected a wage! Even her rags were Maîtresse Rouge's hand-me-downs. Yes, his wife, Muguette, in addition to being a buxom wench and spirited in the bedroom, was a charitable soul. Indeed, he would sometimes chide her for it tenderly:

'Maîtresse Rouge, your generosity does you credit, but remember the old adage: give them an inch and they'll take a mile.'

'What of it!' his beloved would reply, wiping her mouth with the back of her hand. 'My bum and breasts will soon be poking out of this tatty old garment. That flat-chested beanpole could make three dresses out of it.'

It was true that the comely Maîtresse Rouge had what it took to whet the appetite of even the most sated innkeeper, and Maître

Rouge drooled at the mere thought of her. He made a supreme effort to concentrate on his prestigious guest.

'What may I offer you, my lord?'

'Your very best wine, and I mean your very best.'

'Naturally, naturally. I know you to be a connoisseur,' declared the innkeeper of La Jument-Rouge, just so that anybody listening would be in no doubt as to his long association with this gentleman.

Artus knew what the man's game was, and thrust home his advantage.

'And bring an extra goblet so that we may share your nectar!'

The other customers looked up in surprise. The innkeeper felt dizzy with delight. What a joy, what an honour! Ah, Maîtresse Rouge would scarcely believe her ears when he told her how a noble lord, or at least a wealthy knight, had invited him for a drink. And who was to say he wasn't a baron or even a count? Ah! Good Lord!

Moments later, when the visibly moved Maître Rouge sat down, he was still pink with pride. Even so, he was not foolish enough to imagine that a count, a baron or even a wealthy knight would request him to sit at his table merely for the pleasure of his conversation. Whatever the reason, the innkeeper had more than one trick up his sleeve. He knew how to speak ill of people without ever compromising himself, how to spread gossip without fear of reprisal and how to tell the truth – but only when it was in his interests. Moreover, if they spoke in hushed tones, it would convince the other customers that they were well acquainted. What a promotion for his establishment! And without him having to spend a centime, to boot.

'Maître Rouge,' Artus began, 'I understand that a friend of mine, a Knight Hospitaller by the name of Francesco de Leone, has been lodging here with you for some time.'

The noble customer's polite tone delighted the innkeeper as it was a mark of the man's regard for him.

'I hear you, but lower your voice, my lord,' he advised, determined not to pass up any opportunity to increase his respect in the neighbourhood. 'Er ... I endeavour to exercise the utmost discretion regarding my more distinguished guests,' he added.

'And it is to your credit. Where is my friend, then? I must deliver an important letter to him from the King's counsellor,' Artus improvised.

'The King's counsellor?' repeated the innkeeper, his eyes out on stalks.

Ah! What a godsend ... when Maîtresse Rouge learnt that he had provided lodging for a knight who corresponded with *the* King's counsellor ...

'In person. Naturally, you understand that I am not at liberty to tell you more.'

'Oh, naturally! The affairs of the realm are ... Well, they're the affairs of the realm.'

'Wise words, to be sure. What, then, has become of my friend, the knight?'

'He left my establishment two days ago.'

'God's wounds! Do you know where ...?'

'I'm afraid not. Your friend the knight was ... He was a Hospitaller. Careful, prudent and silent. If I were the biggest liar in the world, I couldn't claim that he wasn't politeness incarnate. However, my establishment, while enjoying an impeccable reputation, is scarcely accustomed to such good behaviour. Some of the monks who come through here are spirited, not to say lively!'

This brief portrait of Leone, which appeared to grieve the innkeeper, on the contrary went some way towards relieving Artus's anxiety. So, Leone observed his vows, which included absolute chastity. Yes, but what of love? Was it possible to resist love when it raised its head? Artus was living proof of the contrary; he had not even seen it coming.

'I see ... so you have no idea where he might have gone.'

'None whatsoever. He took his meagre baggage, paid his dues and left, vanished. Although ...'

The innkeeper paused.

'Although?'

'Although, one evening, he did invite a clerk to dine with him. A young man with a face like a rat, repulsively hideous if you ask me. I believe the lad is a secretary at the Inquisition headquarters. He might know something. They seemed to be on friendly terms.'

Agnan! The Agnan who had babbled so nonsensically when Agnès was freed.

Artus emptied his goblet and took his leave of the innkeeper as he would a wealthy burgher, causing the man to purr with delight.

Upon which Maître Rouge – who had never so much as offered a stale crust of bread to a beggar, preferring to fatten his hens instead – was overcome by an angelic benevolence and, hands on his hips, flatly refused to allow the Comte to pay for his jug of fine wine.

Manoir de Souarcy-en-Perche, December 1304

Francesco de Leone had been waiting for nightfall in order to take a look around the grounds. During the day the dogs were loose in the courtyard and would quickly have picked up his scent. A brief inspection of the outlying buildings led him to conclude that the little thief Clément did not make his bed there.

He slowly circled the outside of the manor house again at a few yards' distance, gazing up. Two rather dilapidated square towers flanked a modest-sized building consisting of two floors and an attic space. It was common in that region for the houses to be built from north to south so that the east- and west-facing windows enjoyed the sunrise and the sunset.

A little earlier, he had thought he saw the dim glow of a lamp through the oiled hide stretched across a skylight on the roof of the north tower. As he drew closer he was able to make out the lighter patches where the widest cracks had been filled in with mortar. He felt an immense tenderness towards Agnès de Souarcy. She strove determinedly to keep from rack and ruin the manor which, with each new season, threatened to cave in on her and her household. After all, there was nothing surprising in this. The woman whom he had desperately been seeking for so long must be a survivor whom nothing and nobody would ever force to surrender.

Hoc quicumque stolam sanguine proluit, absergit maculas; et roseum decus, quo fiat similis protinus Angelis.[42]

The divine blood that cleanses the sins of he who bathes in it.

Not far from the tiny skylight, Leone noticed a rope coiled round the menacing head of a gargoyle[43] in the form of a fish with bat's wings. These carved stone grotesques jutting from the eaves channelled rainwater away from the walls to avoid damaging the masonry. They were purposely hideous, made to look like creatures from hell, and were intended to taunt or ward off death and death's demons, which were everywhere.

The rope suggested secret forays – by Clément or by another servant? The knight's intention was to find the boy as quickly as possible and retrieve the missing page. What had made him tear it out? It was true that paper was costly and would fetch a good price. However, if that were the motive, why not tear out both of the apparently blank pages? Yet he had taken only the second-to-last page, the most important one. Leone sighed. He would have to spend another night under the stars, a freezing-cold though mercifully dry night.

The birth of the Saviour would be celebrated on the morrow. He had been looking forward to spending the following night praying beside his aunt. He would have recalled those Christmases when as a child he waited impatiently for Éleusie to declare finally that the divine child had been born, fearing that one day the announcement would be cancelled owing to some dreadful event. The little boy felt an overpowering sense of relief when, each year at midnight, she rejoiced with him at the new arrival. Francesco had been unable to eat, even though the fasting for Advent, begun on Saint Andrew's day, had just ended and the kitchens thrummed with the sound of plucking, scaling, chopping and peeling. If the knight had subsequently found out that He was not born on 25 December, that day would still remain miraculous, a day of hope, perennially frustrated, which had the power to change men, to change the world. And yet the very next day the world was in the same state as it had been upon the eve. And, as for men, they would not change unless they were forced to.

If at that moment someone had pointed out to Leone that he was in agreement with his most implacable enemy, he would have drawn his sword.

He moved a few dozen yards from the house and curled up behind the trunk of a massive oak tree, wrapping his fur-lined cape around him and pulling his lambskin cowl down over his head. His limbs were stiff with cold, and his stomach ached with hunger, but he knew how to ward off discomfort and pain. He conjured up all the ills of the world, bared himself to them and above all defied them to weaken his resolve. He imagined for the hundred thousandth time the white and red steps at Saint-Jean-d'Acre. A beautiful woman's decapitated head, a child's bloodied hair. He imagined for the first time the charming lines at the corners of Éleusie's smiling mouth and bitterly regretted not having studied them more closely. Finally he sank into merciful oblivion.

The angry screech of a barn owl woke him from his slumber. He stretched slowly, brushed off the dusting of snow that had fallen on him during the night and warmed his hands with his breath. There was not much he wouldn't have given for a bowl of hot soup or hippocras and a few slices of bread. The pale moon cast a timid light. The rope was still in place, carefully coiled round the gargoyle's head. And what if nobody used it on that day of prayer? Francesco was not sure whether he could spend another day followed by a freezing night outside without any food.

A movement caught his attention. He glanced up at the roof of the square tower. A tiny figure was hoisting itself up through the skylight with the help of the hideous stone head. Was it the famous Clément? The figure uncoiled the rope and let it fall. Leone noticed that it was knotted in places, making it easier to shin up. The knight had to curb his impatience. He was far older and no doubt far heavier than the diminutive figure now nimbly descending the length of the wall, but his strength had not failed him yet. As for the grotesque drainpipe securing the rope, it looked solid enough. His plan, if it could be described as such, was disturbingly simple. He would break into the manor via the attic and search the various rooms under cover of darkness. It was impossible for him to enter through the courtyard on account of the dogs, unless he announced himself.

Clément landed on the ground and straightened his short tunic and his cape. As he had explained to Agnès, he intended to slip into the secret library one last time in the hope of finding the Vallombroso treatise. The nuns would be gathered in the church for the lengthy Christmas services and, if he were careful, he might manage to sneak in before dawn without being seen. He had been worrying since his lady had told him about her strange meeting with the Abbess. Éleusie de Beaufort had referred to the beginnings of a fire and damaged manuscripts. What manuscripts? In which library? In the secret library or the one open to all?

Agnès put on her grey woollen dress in order to attend dawn Mass, which followed midnight Mass.[44] The whole village would be there. She tried without success to banish the dark thoughts that had been haunting her for days, and adjusted the fall of her veil. She would dispatch a letter to her brother the very next day, ordering him to bring Mathilde back to Souarcy at once. She would send a second letter to Monge de Brineux informing him of the steps she had taken, and asking him to be ready to demand the young girl's return if necessary. The Dame de Souarcy was well aware that she would soon lose her authority over her daughter, who would come of age in a few months' time. The young woman would then be free to place herself under the tutelage of her uncle until her marriage. Was five months long enough for a soul to change? Agnès doubted it, and was honest enough to acknowledge that what was most important for her was to know that she had done all she could to save her daughter from her uncle's corrupting influence.

The dangerous direction her thoughts were taking alarmed her. She silently admonished herself. Mathilde, from being one of her greatest strengths, one of her strongest driving forces, was now weakening her resolve, undermining her, sapping her energy. Agnès had striven and toiled, scarcely allowing herself more rest than a peasant. Many a time she had collapsed on her bed at night, choking back tears of disappointment and despair and wondering how she would feed her household in the days to come. And each time she had drawn strength and courage from the thought of Mathilde and Clément. In reality, they alone had obliged her to stay alive. And yet, one day, her daughter had wanted her dead.

Stop. Stop whimpering and lamenting your fate!

I cannot.

You could if you set your mind to it instead of brooding like an old woman. Remember that evil-smelling cell. How did you stop your life ebbing away?

By clinging to my happiest memories. But precisely, Mathilde …

Stop. Other wonderful things have lit up your life. Madame Clémence de Larnay, Clément, and now him.

Him? What do I know of him?

Since when have you needed to know in order to be sure? The charm worked immediately. She could still see Artus, white as a sheet, angry almost and yet so tender and anxious. Their last conversation echoed in her mind:

'*Three words, Monsieur. That is all. Three simple words …*'

'*And what if … what if you yourself are incapable of uttering them?*'

Agnès stamped her foot. The perfectly charming fool! How tiresome men are when they're afraid of their emotions. Even the most intelligent ones become mired in their awkwardness to the point where everything seems impossible.

He would say those three words. She vowed to herself solemnly that Christmas day.

Clément, my angel. Come back to me soon. I regret having allowed you to make one last trip to Clairets. What would become of me without you, dear Clémence?

She began to open the studded door to her chambers then hesitated. She ought to wear a coat – even just to go to the chapel. It had been so cold for the last few days. She pushed the heavy door and it slammed against the frame. She looked around for her cloak lined with otter skin.

A noise. A muffled sound coming from above. Footsteps. Clément had left before dawn, and in any event he was so light on his feet that she never heard him from her room. His flimsy ladder would not take an adult's weight – certainly not plump Adeline or hefty Gilbert. Had somebody broken in from outside? To what purpose? Had the intruder been waiting for her to leave her room before making a move? In that case he had been misled by the door slamming.

A vague fear formed in her head. She was alone at the manor. Who would hear her cries? Adeline had been busy for hours behind the stout kitchen doors, preparing the mulled wine and milk rolls, which would be shared out after Brother Bernard had blessed them. She was well out of earshot of her mistress's voice.

Agnès tiptoed over to the circular annexe extending above the eastern wall of her chamber, which served as a wardrobe and a privy, to fetch her short sword – a gift from Clémence de Larnay. She was no match for an experienced swordsman, but, as her loving guardian had often pointed out, 'A woman determined to defend herself can scare off many a common thief.' Legs slightly apart, eyes trained on the door, she stood in the middle of her chamber waiting and listening to the footsteps above, which stopped, moved off and stopped again. She heard a sliding sound – Clément's straw mattress being moved – followed by a stool being dragged across the floor. Somebody was methodically searching the attic. Surely not a burglar, for one glance around would have told him that the occupant owned nothing of any value. Moreover, what villain would be fool enough to risk being caught inside the manor, knowing that the punishment was death? The noise began again, moving over to the trapdoor above Clément's ladder.

Agnès's breath quickened, and she clutched the pommel of her short sword. There was a snap followed by a dull thud. One of the rungs had given way and the intruder had fallen to the floor. Despite the chill in her room, she could feel the beads of sweat forming on her brow and she dried her right hand on her dress to be sure of keeping a firm grip on her weapon.

The heavy door opened slowly. She tensed, ready to pounce, aware that surprise would be her strongest weapon.

The tall figure slipped into the room, pausing to check the corridor once more before closing the door and turning round. Agnès was flabbergasted, as was the intruder, judging from his sudden pallor.

'Knight?'

'Madame …'

'But … What are you doing here at Souarcy, sneaking into my chamber like a thief?'

He stared at her, unable to speak, veering between a sense of shame and awe. She was … just as she should be. Magnificent, her sword raised, poised to strike yet without a trace of hostility.

The hesitancy in Agnès's voice gave way to sternness: 'Well, knight? I demand an immediate explanation.'

'Madame, I regret that I can offer none that is acceptable.

Nonetheless, my remorse is equalled only by my embarrassment.'

'Do you really believe that your remorse and embarrassment will satisfy me? You have placed me in an extremely difficult situation. You saved my life and my honour. But I cannot tolerate you intruding into my house, into my chambers, like a thief. What are you looking for?'

'To tell you the truth, nothing, Madame.'

'The truth? Really! Are you not telling me lies, Monsieur?' she said angrily. 'If so, you must learn to tell them better.'

'I cannot. I will not.'

A mysterious smile lit up the beautiful face of the man standing before her. He lowered his eyes, shook his head and murmured:

'Why don't you return your sword to its scabbard? I don't suppose that you will lunge at me now. And I would rather die a thousand deaths than shed a single drop of your blood.'

She looked at her weapon as though she were seeing it for the first time, and complied.

'Let us leave here, Monsieur. Walk with me to the chapel. I will overlook the inappropriateness of your presence in my chambers. Dawn Mass is about to begin. However, I want your word that we will resume this conversation where we left off, knight. I insist that you give me your word.'

'It is yours until the end of time, Madame,' he replied with the same smile.

She sensed the enormity of his words without grasping their meaning. Was this man so elusive that she would never understand him? And yet he was made of light. Of that she was certain.

Clairets Abbey, Perche, December 1304

Clément crept along cautiously, his hand cupped around the feeble light emitted by his sconce torch. He hugged the walls, positive that his dark clothes were invisible against the stones, which were enveloped by the gloom. An icy silence pervaded the abbey, broken occasionally by the choir's mingled voices floating out from nearby Notre-Dame Church. Questions to which he had no answers were racing through his head. Had the rapidly extinguished fire reached the secret library? What if the notebook had been destroyed? He ought to have gone ahead and borrowed it. Admittedly, he had copied out in his delicate script the parts he thought were essential. But how could he be sure, given that he had understood so little of the jottings on its pages? What if he were found out? The secret game of hide and seek, which had once amused him precisely because he saw little danger of being caught, made him feel uneasy that night. He lay flat on the ground, squeezing his body through the thick bars guarding the opening to the cellar. He felt for the stepladder with his foot. It appeared to have been moved. Perhaps somebody had needed it in the storeroom. At last he managed to gain a foothold on the top step.

Once his feet were firmly planted on the trampled earth, Clément sniffed the dank air. He could detect no smell of burning. He climbed the spiral staircase towards the library and froze as he reached the top. The door leading to the Abbess's chambers was wide open. His throat became dry with panic and he moved back, terrified that Éleusie de Beaufort might walk in and find him there. He could hear no sound coming from the adjoining room, which he supposed was her study. Slightly reassured, Clément moved ahead cautiously. Keeping close to the wall, he cast a furtive glance into the room. The apothecary nun. What was her name again? Annelette, Sister Annelette, the tall, surly woman he had passed occasionally in the corridors. She was sitting behind a heavy oak desk, her brow resting on one hand, absorbed in a large book that was open in front of her. Since when had she known about the secret library? Could the Abbess have given her permission to consult its works?

Clément held his breath, unable to decide whether to remain there or leave. He stood next to the doorpost for what seemed like an eternity. The chill rising from the flagstones gradually froze his ankles and legs.

He almost cried out in fright when the woman stood up brusquely and began walking towards the door. My God, he was finished! He flattened his body so hard against the wall that the stones dug into his shoulder blades. He closed his eyes, as though not seeing would somehow render him invisible. He heard the door shut and a key turn in the lock and the darkness suddenly thickened around him. He stifled a sigh of relief.

Clément waited for a few minutes before setting to work. He could see immediately that the fire had not affected the library. However, after searching thoroughly for several hours he found no trace of the notebook belonging to the knight Eustache de Rioux and his co-author. A slight misalignment in the bookshelves in front of him caught his attention. He examined one of them from top to bottom. It looked as if it had been pushed back recently. Acting on an intuition, the boy threw all his weight against the solid piece of furniture and managed to move it several inches. One more push uncovered a hole in the ground, a hiding place. His heart beat wildly as he knelt down on the floor. Beneath the glow of his little oil lamp he stuck his hand into the bottom of the hole and pulled out a square of oily cloth which he held up to his nose. Beeswax. A sheath designed to protect precious manuscripts against damp and insects. But what had it been protecting? The famous Vallombroso treatise? He rummaged again in the hope of finding some other clue. A needle-sharp prick to his neck made him gasp.

A woman's deep voice said:

'Stand up slowly, you little rascal. One false move and I'll slit your throat like a rabbit.'

Clément could tell from the calm, resolute tone of her voice that she would not hesitate to carry out her threat if necessary. He rose to his feet and stood facing what he took to be a novice, judging from her robe. The dagger in her expert hand was sizable enough to make one braver than he think twice. He slowly moved his lamp closer to the woman. She was very pretty and young, no more than sixteen or seventeen. But it was her eyes that most intrigued Clément. Two pale-amber pools that cast an eerie glow on her fair cheeks.

'Who are you, young servant?' she enquired in a firm voice.

'Shh … She might …'

'Who, Annelette? She left immediately after locking the library door. Did you not hear?'

He shook his head.

'You'd make a terrible spy. Who are you?' she repeated.

'Clément. I belong to Madame de Souarcy's household.'

The amber eyes narrowed, but the tone of her voice remained unwavering as she asked:

'Madame Agnès de Souarcy? Who nearly died under torture?'

'Yes.'

She went silent before resuming in a calm but threatening tone:

'Do not lie to me. I can see through lies, however subtle.'

'In that case you must know that I'm telling the truth,' he protested.

'Good! Continue and explain your presence here.'

Clément, regaining some of his poise, parried:

'And what about you? How do you explain a novice gaining

entry to the Abbess's jealously guarded library? For, you see, I have a sneaking suspicion that she has no idea that you're here and that, if she did, you'd be in a great deal of trouble!'

A look of sorrow clouded the girl's lovely face:

'You do not know?'

He stared at her intently. She went on:

'Madame de Beaufort died a few days ago. She, too, was poisoned.'

'What? She, too, was poisoned?' he echoed her words, shocked. 'But ... but my mistress went to see her recently and ... well, you say there have been other cases of poisoning ... and yet the Abbess mentioned nothing.'

'Four nuns have now perished, including our Reverend Mother.'

The announcement was met with silence. In the flickering, odorous flame of the oil lamp, Esquive d'Estouville could see a tear slowly trickle down the boy's pale cheek. He blurted out in one breath:

'What is it all about! My lady hauled before the Inquisition, accused, dragged through the mire by her own daughter, murdered emissaries, the Pope assassinated, poisoned nuns, this library, the ...'

He stopped himself just in time, but the young girl finished his sentence for him:

'The Knight Hospitaller's notebook? It was stolen during a fire that was deliberately started as a diversion. Two other works were also taken,' added Esquive, who was no longer in any doubt as to the young boy's sincerity. 'Éleusie ordered the strict cloister to be watched, barring urgent exceptions, and anybody leaving the abbey to be thoroughly searched along with their bundles and carts.'

'Hopefully, then, the stolen volumes are still inside the abbey walls.'

'Hopefully.'

'With all due respect, Madame, who are you, and how did you get in here?'

'My name will mean nothing to you. Let us say … that I am a steadfast friend. I opened the door in the simplest way possible – using a copy of the key which was given to me.'

'By whom?' Clément asked boldly.

'I do not know.'

He had no doubt that she was telling the truth.

'Why are you here and why did you wait in silence? For you saw me arrive, didn't you?'

A faint smile spread across the pretty heart-shaped lips.

'I needed to make a quick inventory before the new Abbess arrives, to make sure that there are no more … dangerous manuscripts here. Annelette arrived so I hid. An hour later you appeared and I was curious to know what you were looking for.'

'The Vallombroso treatise,' he declared bluntly.

'Hm … I thought as much. It was one of the three stolen volumes.'

'Madame, I beg you, what is the meaning of all this?'

'The time has not yet come, Clément, and, besides, I do not have all the facts.'

'My lady was in grave danger …'

'No,' she corrected, 'she is in grave danger. Still.'

'From whom?' Clément was seized with panic. 'Tell me so that I may protect her better.'

Her faint smile turned into a broad grin and she whispered: 'Let me say that I think you are quite capable of protecting your lady.' Growing serious again, she went on: 'You ask from whom? From the others. They have numerous and changing faces. Listen to me carefully, young man. There are few whom you can trust. The Knight Hospitaller Francesco de Leone is one of them. I am another.'

'And my Lord d'Authon?'

'He is not really one of our … friends. But his reputation is too good and solid to conceal any disgrace.'

She looked up at the horizontal arrow-slit windows and said:

'It is almost time for midday Mass. The sisters will be deep in prayer. You must leave soon.'

He nodded. She resumed:

'Clément … I am still not sure who the poisoner is, but I am closing in on her. Trust no one.'

At these words an icy shiver ran up the boy's spine.

'A final warning: the new Abbess, whose arrival at Clairets I fear is imminent, will not be one of our allies – far from it. From now on keep away from the abbey.'

Daylight was beginning to fade by the time Clément returned, exhausted, to the manor. He hurried to the main hall to tell his mistress of his encounter. She was standing near the huge hearth where a fire was roaring. A man seated at the table was slowly and meticulously eating a slice of bread and dripping. He wore leggings tucked into his walking boots, and an old-fashioned mid-length sleeveless coat, over which he must have worn the boiled wool greatcoat lined with moth-eaten rabbit fur that was lying on the crockery chest together with his felt hat. Clément could tell the moment the stranger looked up at him that he was not, as his clothing might suggest, a craftsman or tinker. Indeed, had he been, Agnès would, out of charity, have offered him food and drink, but in the kitchen. Stranger still was the puzzling yet persistent feeling that he knew this man, even though he was sure of never having seen him before.

'The Knight Leone has honoured us with an unexpected and … somewhat unconventional visit,' his lady informed him calmly.

So, this was he. He wanted to run over to this beautiful man and fall to his knees out of boundless gratitude for unhesitatingly taking the fiend Florin's life in order to save Agnès. But the man's deep-blue penetrating gaze dissuaded him – a profound gaze, like a tempting abyss, serene.

'Have you eaten your fill?' enquired Agnès.

'I am sated, Madame, and I thank you for this precious offering.'

'Clément is my confidant. He is privy to all my affairs. Customary courtesy having been observed and Christian charity respected, I ask you once more, knight, to explain your forced entry into my house,' she said in a soft voice.

'Forced entry'? What was she referring to? Clément sensed that it was not yet his turn to speak.

Leone, who knew what it was to go hungry, glanced down at the table and swept up the few scattered crumbs.

'I confess that I'm looking for something that was stolen from me, although the theft was no doubt unintentional.'

'Can theft ever be unintentional?'

'Certainly, when the thief is unaware of the precise nature of what he has stolen.'

'And I am harbouring such a thief in my house?'

'A relatively innocent thief, yes.'

'What is this stolen object?'

Clément felt a growing sense of unreality. A crucial revelation was imminent, he was sure. And yet the conversation, although tense, was being conducted in a bafflingly calm manner.

'I cannot answer that question.'

'I beg you, knight,' Agnès insisted, without the slightest irritation. 'I have a strange feeling that ... none of this is a coincidence. Lord, I am at a loss to find the words to describe what I feel. I sense ... strongly that a web has been woven linking us three, and many other people and events besides – most notably my daughter, my half-brother and the Inquisition – and that all of this reaches so far back into the past that I am unable to follow the trail.'

Leone responded with a deep sigh, whether of relief or dismay she could not tell.

An innocuous or nearly innocuous scene flashed into Clément's mind.

A standing desk. An unused quill pen resting beside an ink-horn. No paper on which to copy out some of the jottings in the notebook –

paper was a luxury and kept under lock and key. The last two pages of the unwieldy notebook. Blank pages. Wetting a corner of his tunic with saliva and wiping away the traces of ink on the quill and on his fingers.

In a soft, faltering voice the young boy declared:

'It is a piece of paper, Madame. The page which I told you I had torn from the knight Eustache de Rioux's notebook. So, Monsieur, you are the co-author?'

'I am.'

'You have no choice now but to break your silence,' Agnès retorted.

'On the contrary, Madame, I am sworn to the utmost secrecy. Do not see in this any scheming or calculation on my part.'

'Isn't this the secret that nearly cost me my life?' parried the Dame de Souarcy.

'I confess that my heart bleeds for the suffering you endured. But if the secret were revealed … who can guarantee that it would ever be fulfilled? So many would be hunted down and killed.' He paused and smiled, tossing back his head, and Agnès had the distinct feeling that he had entered some other wonderful world. He murmured: 'And yet your life, Madame … your life is infinitely more precious than mine.'

'Exactly, and time is running out, Monsieur,' Clément intervened. 'You are aware that the journal has been stolen along with the treatise. Others will discover the secret before we do, and I'll wager they will not be our friends.'

'Stolen?' breathed Agnès, raising her hand to her chest.

Clément went on, his chin trembling with emotion:

'The Abbess was fatally poisoned a few days ago. She is the fourth Bernadine to be murdered.'

Agnès felt her legs give way under her.

'Oh dear Lord,' she wailed, lurching towards the table in order to steady herself. She slumped onto the bench, holding out a shaking hand to take the goblet of water offered by Leone.

'Knight ...'

'I know how it grieves you, Madame, and I know the true affection you felt for my second mother, an affection which I assure you was reciprocated. While your sorrow does not alleviate my own, believe me it is a comfort. I need that piece of paper, young Clément.'

The boy was about to go up to the eaves to retrieve the document from its hiding place under a wooden plank next to one of the high beams, when his mistress's voice rang out:

'No. Stay here, Clément!'

'Madame, with all due respect I must insist. This piece of paper contains vital information,' the knight argued.

'It was blank before I copied out some of the notes onto it,' the boy replied.

'What notes?' Leone urged.

'The ones I was afraid I wouldn't be able to remember by heart.'

'Which ones?' the Hospitaller almost cried out.

'The two birth charts. Some rows of numbers, a strange drawing of a rose, which I imagined must have some secret meaning ... and a fragmented sentence with only a few letters.'

'The rose ... did you copy each petal in detail, in exactly the same order and size?'

'Scrupulously, knight,' affirmed Clément, realising that he had been right about the rose in full bloom.

The change that came over Francesco was visible. His face relaxed. He lowered his eyelids and clasped his hands together. Agnès reflected that she had just glimpsed an archangel. He whispered in a voice so deep that she was barely able to make out his words:

'Sweet Lord, Infinite Love, we are perhaps saved.'

He appeared to return to the world of mortals and reiterated his demand:

'Return the piece of paper to me please, Clément.'

'No,' Agnès countered, calmly but firmly. 'I demand to know what it contains and to receive a proper explanation. I have paid with blood, humiliation and suffering. It is my due.'

'Will nothing I say convince you to change your mind, Madame? Even if I tell you that I know only an infinitesimal part of the secret and that it is terribly dangerous?'

'Nothing. Besides, fear is no defence against pain or danger.'

He recalled his aunt Clémence having one day uttered those words.

'Very well. Run and fetch the piece of paper, Clément, and never forget that your petty act of thievery and your insatiable curiosity might have saved us. Ah, and forgive me ... I'm afraid that your ladder could not hold my weight. Madame, could your kitchen maid bring me a candle?'

Adeline, who was in awe of this stunningly graceful, rather badly dressed man, hurried away, muttering unintelligibly. They waited in silence. Curiously, despite their recent disagreement, Agnès felt at peace in the knight's company. This man radiated an innate strength. She reflected that as a woman she ought to find his long, firm hands, his aquiline nose, his domed brow, his magnificent deep-blue eyes and his mid-blond shoulder-length hair attractive. Admittedly, he was a man of God and a monk-soldier so that any such attraction would have remained purely hypothetical. And yet she felt none whatsoever, although she would gladly have laid her head on his shoulder and rested for a while. She blushed at the inappropriateness of such thoughts and turned her head, pretending to be on the lookout for Clément. Had thoughts of Artus d'Authon filled her imagination to the point where there was no longer room for any other man? Perhaps, but she doubted that this explained the indefinable fondness she felt for Leone.

What nonsense to be thinking at a time like this, she scolded herself. Clément's arrival put a stop to her questioning.

After glancing at Agnès, who gave a slight nod, Clément handed the knight the carefully folded piece of paper. It seemed to take Leone an age to reach out and take it. Finally he held it delicately between his fingers and whispered:

'*Non nobis Domine, non nobis, sed nomini Tuo da gloriam.*' [45]

At once moved and relieved, he studied Clément's fine handwriting. It was a miracle that had made the young boy copy out the two birth charts and the drawing of the rose, which he felt certain contained vital hidden information. He thanked heaven for the intelligence, curiosity and courage of this youth who had inadvertently crossed his path.

Francesco de Leone held the long piece of paper carefully up to the candle. He ran the paper backwards and forwards across the flame until a series of red letters appeared.

'What is this magic?' exclaimed Agnès.

'There's no magic in it, Madame,' explained the knight. 'It is invisible ink made from simple plum juice. Other recipes exist apparently, using citrus fruits from the *Citrus limon*[46] tree, which originates in Asia and grows in Spain. When it is heated, the juice turns red, as it does in a pot.'

Agnès walked over and stood close to Leone's shoulder. An unexpected feeling of wellbeing came over her as she brushed his sleeve. She thought that she could close her eyes and that instant fall into a peaceful dreamless sleep. A brother. He was a brother to her. Did he feel the same? He looked at her, his eyes, the colour of deep blue sea, sparkling with joy, and his lips formed a silent word that she was unable to make out.

Standing on tiptoe, Clément attempted to decipher the letters and numbers that were gradually appearing. A complex diagram, ellipses marked with tiny dots. Planets. He gasped, choking with emotion:

'The Vallombroso theory!'

'The essence of it,' corrected Leone, 'thanks to Eustache's foresight. He was keen for us to be able to do without the monk's voluminous work if necessary. And so we made a summary of what we needed to know in order to penetrate the mystery of the two charts.'

The Hospitaller continued for a few moments to pass alternate sides of the paper over the flame. He urged:

'We mustn't delay in copying out these notes. In truth, I have no idea how long it will be before this ink made of juice fades once it has been exposed to heat.'

'Clément, there is some paper and a phial of ink in my wardrobe. Go and fetch it. The ink shouldn't have dried out as I used it only recently.'

The young boy and the knight sat side by side at the long table carefully copying out the revealed script.

Adeline came in briefly to light the sconce torches in the cavernous room and placed an oil lamp on the table in front of the two copyists before hurrying back to her domain on the other side of the door, reflecting that with a good memory like hers there was no need to write things down.

Puzzled, Clément asked:

'I do not see the fragmented sentence I copied out. This one,' he insisted, pointing to the tiny letters written in his script.

'b...me...re...au...per...t'

Leone turned and stared deep into his eyes before replying:

'It is an unfortunate oversight. However, we may be able to piece together the meaning.'

Clément understood that Leone was deliberately lying and

wanted Clément to know. Leone belonged to a breed of men who were capable of lying provided their duty, faith and honour demanded it. The young boy instinctively refrained from questioning him any further, for he was certain that the knight's only intention was to spare his lady.

Agnès was sitting at the far end of the table, her mind wandering. And yet for once she felt happy drifting. Images of Mathilde, Eudes, Florin and of Hugues's death following days of agony and purulent, swiftly decomposing flesh no longer seemed obtrusive. They flashed through her mind but without staying long enough to cause her pain. The memory of that bathhouse near the cathedral, in Rue du Cheval-Blanc, where she had allowed herself to be led without objection, haunted her still. The memory of the soothsayer's hovel that day during the terrible winter of 1294. The smell of grime and sweat emanating from the mad old witch's rags had made Agnès's gorge rise when she drew near and snatched the basket of meagre offerings Agnès had brought: a loaf of bread, a bottle of cider, a hunk of bacon and a scrawny boiling fowl. Did she regret it? How can one regret the inevitable when it is inflicted upon one?

A husky voice made her jump:

'Milady, the hour has almost come for Christmas Mass. Vespers is long over.'

'Ah … Thank you, Adeline. We will go to the chapel and have supper afterwards. Brother Bernard is invited to join our festive meal. You will lay the table for four. And prepare a bed for our guest in the outbuildings. He will stay with us until morning.'

Leone could hardly take offence; it was unthinkable for a lady – a widow living on her own – to invite a man who was neither a relative nor her overlord to stay in her house.

'Very good, milady. I'll see to it at once. And don't forget the "offering to our lady" last thing tonight.'

'I had forgotten,' Agnès sighed.

'What is this "offering to our lady"?' Leone asked.

She chuckled.

'The offering to our lady is a custom in these parts that will no doubt appear foolish to you. On Christmas night peasants, serfs, farm hands, craftsmen and tradespeople offer gifts according to their means to the lady of the estate as a mark of appreciation for her good offices, her protection and her justice. I am inundated with baby carp, snail pâté, blood sausage, jellied fruit, socks made of boiled wool, gingerbread men and pork-fat rissoles. Occasionally there'll be an embroidered sheet or counterpane made by one of the better-off wives who have time for needlework. We're not wealthy here at Souarcy, but we survive and manage to feed our children and take care of our elderly. The inhabitants of our village are humble, industrious folk. They put their heart and soul into their labours, and do not baulk at hard work.'

'Foolish? On the contrary I think it's an admirable custom. I only wish it were more widespread.' He fell silent before continuing in a solemn but joyful voice: 'If only you knew, Madame, how glad I am at the prospect of praying beside you on this Christmas night. I would never have dared ask heaven for such a gift.'

Agnès had the feeling these words contained far more than simple courtesy.

Clairets Abbey, Perche, December 1304

Shortly before dawn, Annelette Beaupré had heard the clatter of carriage wheels on the cobblestones of the large courtyard separating the enclosure wall from the stables. The clang of metal meant that the wooden wheels were ringed with iron, an unmistakable sign of the visitor's importance. A female visitor, she would soon discover.

Annelette was stunned when she caught sight of the woman who had ordered them to assemble in the scriptorium. She was quite simply dazzling, despite the veil and the austere robe, which could not disguise her perfect figure. Aged twenty-three or twenty-five at the most, she examined them one by one, a rapturous smile on her face. The novices were also present, huddled together in a far corner of the enormous freezing-cold room. When the emerald-green gaze of the woman who was to be their Abbess fell upon her, Annelette immediately understood that the battle would be fierce. The apothecary slowly lowered her eyes. Her gesture was not one of submission or weakness. On the contrary, she hoped to delay revealing her complete mistrust of the other woman. There was a moment's silence, broken only by the rustle of robes, the muffled scraping of feet and a few coughs provoked by the cold air. And then a loud, rather deep, but elegant voice rang out:

'My daughters, what a joy it is for me finally to behold your faces after such a long journey. I have imagined this moment a thousand times over with great impatience and not without some apprehension. Yes, apprehension is the right word,' she insisted, raising an exquisitely slender hand. 'I know how much the departure of your Reverend Mother, who has joined the greater glory of Our Lord God, has wrenched your hearts. I know of her great competence, faith and compassion. I, too, need you to welcome me with open arms. My task will not be an easy one. There are those among you who will no doubt compare me to our dear departed sister, Madame de Beaufort. You should not, though I shall not hold it against you. It is my firm intention to do everything in my power to follow in her footsteps. Shall I confess that I hope one day that you will say of me: "She did not let us down"? I intend, therefore, to model myself on the late Madame de Beaufort, a pious and courageous woman, to whom I believe I bear a certain resemblance. Like her, I am a widow. Like her, I have never given birth. Like her, I believe that during the terrible grief brought on by the loss of my husband another life opened up to me. Your Reverend Mother has perished at the hands of an evil poisoner, our other dear sisters likewise. You can be sure that my primary task is to find the culprit and hand her over to the secular arm of the law so that justice may be done here on earth, pending the justice of God, who will not fail to condemn her a second time.'

The Abbess paused for a moment before resuming:

'What more can I tell you about myself that may be of some importance? My worldly name was Aude de Neyrat. I am so overjoyed to be among you that I am at a loss to think of anything else. It is my most fervent wish that the future Pope confirms my nomination ... It would break my heart if I had to leave you now. You may go, daughters. I have much to do, including meeting some of you and validating my seal in the presence of the senior nun and prioress, as well as the cellarer nun. May God in his goodness watch over us all.'

Annelette took advantage of the sea of white robes to slip towards the door unnoticed, stooping almost, aware that her height made her conspicuous. Of course she would be one of those whom the Abbess wished to 'meet', if only to recover the key to Éleusie's chambers. She must outwit her but she had to be prudent. Benedetti had sent this woman because he knew that she was capable of anything, of the most evil acts, and Annelette was sure that this ravishing creature's guile was matched only by her intelligence and utter lack of scruples.

She jumped as a small, firm hand pressed a note into her palm. A quick look around revealed nothing – a bevy of nuns wearing the white veil of the Bernadines and the grey veil of novices surrounded her. Annelette hastened to the herbarium where she read the message. A few words were scribbled:

'Join me immediately in the kitchen garden. Our lives depend upon it. Destroy this note.'

The apothecary held the strip of paper over the sconce torch and did not let go of it until the last letter had been consumed by the flame. She hurried out. The kitchen garden was on the other side of the fence that enclosed the medicinal plant beds surrounding the herbarium. To begin with Annelette could see nobody. At last, the slim figure of a novice stood up from behind one of the wells in the middle of the spacious vegetable garden. She knew this young woman. Was she not the novice who had told her she wished to adopt the name Hélène after she took her final vows? What was her name again? A pretty name that brought to mind swordsmanship and combat. Esquive.

As she approached the novice, she demanded in a suspicious, hostile voice:

'Why did you ask to meet me?'

The anxious pale-amber eyes studied her. And then a voice that seemed deep for such a small young girl explained:

'We have very little time. She arrived sooner than I expected. Her first act will be to lift the restrictions on leaving the abbey, since this was the reason Madame de Beaufort was murdered.'

'Who …?' stammered the apothecary.

'Who am I? Esquive. Like you I am another link in the chain. You must have faith in me. What can I say that will convince you that I am your ally – your only ally in this place? Francesco de Leone came to see his aunt, unaware that she was dead. You took him into the secret library whose entrance is concealed by a tapestry in the Abbess's study.'

The young girl leant over and pulled a key out from under her robe.

'Here is the copy that was given to me when I was informed of my mission, which was to go to Clairets Abbey in order to help you and to prevent the poisoner from using her talents on both you and the Abbess. Unfortunately, I failed and Éleusie de Beaufort is dead.'

'So, you have been spying on us since …'

'I arrived only a few days before her death. Moreover, it is not my task to spy on you but to protect you.'

'Who gave you this key?'

'Oh, a messenger. I have no idea who had it made and I do not ask. I obey. I obey the magnificence. I know only what I need to know. Nothing more … The rest is unimportant.'

Curiously, these last words were what convinced Annelette. Indeed, what else mattered? All that mattered was their quest.

'I believe you.'

'Have you any strong suspicions as to the identity of the wicked poisoner?' asked Esquive.

'Jeanne. Jeanne d'Amblin, the extern sister. I have no proof as yet, but the sequence of events points to her, assuming that she made use of an accomplice at least once – the day the yew powder was stolen from the herbarium while she was out on one of her rounds.'

'Who might her accomplice be?'

'I thought of Sylvine Taulier, the sister in charge of the bread ovens. However, I must confess that there is only one reason for my choice. Who else could have baked the bread containing ergot of rye that fatally poisoned several of the Pope's emissaries?'

'Ergot of rye?'

Annelette found her bearings in the world she knew best, and undertook to describe the alarming toxicity of the tiny blackish clusters of mould that commonly grew on cereals, especially rye, and which when ingested left the skin looking charred, caused gangrene in the fingers and hallucinations followed by death.

Esquive interrupted her with a wave of the hand:

'We have very little time, sister. So, do you think that Sylvine Taulier is the accomplice?'

Annelette pursed her lips before confessing:

'I admit that I dislike the woman and this makes me mistrust my own suspicions about her.'

'You are right to be prudent. What about Jeanne?'

'Oh, I allowed myself to become almost a friend to her. She is extremely gifted at making herself liked. She is so caring, so thoughtful that heaven itself would open its gates to her without a confession.'

'These are formidable qualities in a killer.'

'Undeniably, and Jeanne is shrewd into the bargain. It was a masterstroke to have her henchwoman steal the poison from my cabinet while she was away on her rounds. I fought back my urge to pounce on her, considering it cleverer to let her move around freely so that she would lead me to where she has hidden the stolen manuscripts.'

'That was sensible,' Esquive agreed.

'Oh, dear God,' the apothecary groaned, 'I was led astray. I wasted time and our Reverend Mother has been murdered.'

'Do not torment yourself. You are not to blame. You were not careless, only too trustful. What kind of world do we live in that punishes trust?'

'The world will change, won't it?' Annelette asked in an almost childlike voice.

'It is what we strive for without reprieve.'

'But do you believe in it?'

'With all my heart and soul. It has to change; it will change. In the meantime, we must at all costs think of a way of recovering the stolen manuscripts before Jeanne d'Amblin, or the redoubtable Aude de Neyrat, manages to take them out of the abbey.'

'I fear that we are being watched. I will return to the herbarium. Meet me there this evening, after vespers.'

Esquive had turned on her heel when Annelette called her back:

'My sister in Christ ... thank you.'

'For what ... for failing to protect Éleusie de Beaufort?'

'For being here. She ... Éleusie appeared so fragile and yet she was unyielding.' She lowered her head. 'I confess ... I confess that I have been terribly afraid since our Reverend Mother's death, I who believed I was immune to fear.'

'Only fools are fearless. Courage consists in conquering our fears. We will meet again shortly, sister.'

Aude de Neyrat, whose most fervent wish was that she should be subjected to the severity of monastic life for as brief a period as possible, shivered beneath her sumptuous coat lined with squirrel fur. Having no intention of taking her impersonation of a Bernadine abbess to extremes, she had ordered her trunks to be brought to her chambers. Shortly before her departure from the comfortable town house where she had been staying in Chartres, she had ordered her maid to pack several splendid dresses, an abundance of toiletries and two warm coats, as well as a bottle of prune liqueur – so invigorating in the cold weather. After they had arrived, Aude had quelled Berthe de Marchiennes's silent curiosity upon glimpsing the various trunks:

'My research books. I devote the few spare moments I have to writing a life of Macarius the Elder.'[47]

Berthe, whom erudition usually left cold, had been impressed.

*

Aude studied her pretty hands while she waited. She had summoned Jeanne d'Amblin, ordering her to come and see her at once. The extern sister's poor performance was beginning to exasperate her.

Jeanne entered, beginning brusquely:

'Why have you come here, Madame? I thought we were supposed to meet at the baths in Chartres.'

'The fact is that our mutual friend is growing impatient,' replied Aude de Neyrat. 'And so he decided to send me here in order to ensure that the manuscripts reach him at the earliest possible moment.'

Jeanne d'Amblin tried hard not to show her anger:

'It is most unwise. You will give us away!'

'To whom? To the other nuns? Don't worry. I shall see that it doesn't happen.' Aude frowned, her pretty mouth setting in a fold of displeasure. 'Moreover, I am not sure I like your tone. Change it.'

The extern sister perceived the threat. Out of obligation but above all caution, she declared, in a gentler voice:

'Annelette must under no circumstances suspect that we are acquainted.'

'Are we? Acquainted? You are in my employ ... for as long as you are useful to me. As for Annelette, you seem overly afraid of her. And yet she was most obliging when I demanded the keys to the Abbess's chambers. She handed them over immediately without protest. I have the impression that the apothecary's bark is a lot worse than her bite. Where are the manuscripts hidden? Hand them over to me in exchange for a princely sum and we will part on the best of terms.'

Jeanne studied her. This beautiful monster was capable of killing her the moment she became expendable. The others, Yolande, Adélaïde, Hedwige, even Éleusie, had been easy prey in comparison. Madame de Neyrat would doubtless fight to the death. Jeanne's death. As for her promises and assurances, the cunning creature lied so effortlessly that the truth must surely burn her tongue. The extern sister replied scornfully:

'Bring them to you? Here? Not a chance. They will leave here with me and we will meet and make the exchange at some other place. You will give me a fat purse and leave with the volumes.'

Aude smiled approvingly:

'I would have responded likewise. Do you know why wild animals rarely kill and eat each other? Because they know that it is in their nature to be wild animals and they instinctively mistrust one another. Very well. I will lift the restrictions on leaving the abbey as of tomorrow. First of all I must present my letters of recommendation to those old fools at the abbey chapterhouse and then validate my seal. We will meet at the same bathhouse in two days' time. My stay here will be extremely short and frankly I won't miss the place. It is bleak … And in my opinion this damp chill is most unhealthy. Must the love of God necessarily involve going to an early grave?'

'I wouldn't know. I have only my own interests at heart.'

'Wise words that ring true, daughter. Now go.'

Half an hour after vespers, Esquive entered the herbarium so soundlessly that she startled Annelette, who was hunched over one of her inventories. The apothecary could not help smiling as she studied, thoroughly this time, the very young girl. She was slim and small, her head scarcely level with the tall woman's shoulder. Her exquisite, almost triangular face gave her the appearance of an adorable kitten, an impression that was enhanced by her large pale-amber, almond-shaped eyes. Her small heart-shaped mouth was ruby red, in contrast to her pale skin. A mass of brown curls now protruded from beneath her short novice's veil. A delicate, perfectly proportioned miniature, and yet Annelette was certain that her tiny hands could put up a ferocious defence and that beneath her smooth, domed brow lay the resilience and pugnacity of a defender of their quest. She shuddered. The world she had left outside the abbey enclosure years before had caught up with her in the form of this girl, and it was a world about which she knew nothing. A world in which she felt powerless, useless and confused; a world where young girls were indomitable soldiers, abbesses were beautiful ruthless whores, killing was easy, lying a pastime and pillaging a whim. It occurred to Annelette that she would never go back to that world. In reality, it had taken these dreadful poisonings to make her realise how much she no longer belonged there or wished to be there.

Esquive went directly to the point: 'I have had time to reflect during the service. There are only two of us, but two are better than one. We must retaliate on two fronts. Firstly we must not allow Jeanne d'Amblin out of our sight for a moment, and secondly we must find out whether Sylvine Taulier is her accomplice. We must prevent the extern sister from entrusting the manuscripts to the other sister.'

'Would she not be more likely to give them directly to the new Abbess? Wasn't this the reason for her prompt nomination?'

'Did you not describe Jeanne as cunning? Placing such trust in Madame de Neyrat would be suicidal. Once Jeanne is no longer in possession of the manuscripts, she will be of no further use to Benedetti and his henchmen. No, the Abbess will allow Jeanne to leave with them at the earliest opportunity. The exchange will take place later. In other words, if Jeanne wishes to retrieve the manuscripts, she must do so tonight, and no doubt she will wait until well after compline when the other nuns are in bed. Therefore it is crucial that we discover whether you are right and Jeanne's accomplice is indeed Sylvine, the sister in charge of the bread ovens. Remember, there are only two of us, and it would be an almost impossible task to trail the extern sister as well as an unknown accomplice.'

'Does it matter?' objected Annelette Beaupré. 'Jeanne is the important one. I doubt she has revealed her secret hiding place to the other woman. While she is retrieving the documents we will pounce on her and take them back.'

Despite the freezing temperature inside the tiny building, the apothecary rolled up her sleeves as though to prove that she was prepared for a physical confrontation. Her declaration brought a faint smile to Esquive d'Estouville's lips, and she dampened the apothecary's zeal:

'I cannot help feeling suspicious. If I were Jeanne, I would only pretend to leave the abbey with my spoils. It is Madame de Neyrat's close association with the camerlingo that makes her dangerous. And if I were Madame de Neyrat, I would hire a few docile brutes to wait for the extern sister to leave and take back the manuscripts without having to pay for them.'

The logic of this approach served only to increase the apothecary's unease: she was out of her depth in these worldly matters.

'In all honesty, I prefer my potions, toxins and herbs. They hold no nasty surprises provided one knows them well.'

'Oh ... It is much the same with human beings,' Esquive contested gently. 'The most common mistake where they are concerned is to think we know them when we don't.'

'In effect, snakes are snakes and doves are doves,' the apothecary remarked pithily.

'Not always. It is equally wise to mistrust doves.'

'How sad,' Annelette sighed.

'Indeed, but what joy when a snake ceases to spit its venom.'

'Is such a transformation possible?'

'Yes, although I grant you it is rare. And I doubt that our two enemies, Neyrat and Amblin, will ever undergo such a change. However, we must postpone our grieving over doves that turn to evil. Time is of the essence and the moment for scheming has passed. We must attack head on; it is our only chance.'

'Attack head on? You mean Sylvine?'

'Exactly.'

'The thing is ... my aversion to her is reciprocal, and I doubt she'll even listen to me.'

'Threat and blackmail often produce the quickest results,' Esquive suggested calmly.

Annelette protested: 'But they are sins!'

'Poisoning an abbess is an even bigger sin,' the young woman replied irritably. 'The purity of your soul is praiseworthy, sister, but it is no longer appropriate. We have until dawn to succeed. If we fail ... I prefer not to think what will happen if we fail.'

Annelette's shoulders slumped.

'You are right. And, besides, did I not envisage strangling the monster with my bare hands?'

'Where do you suppose Sylvine Taulier is now?'

'At her bread ovens, I imagine.'

'So, a little way behind the abbey church.'

'Unless she's in the wood shed. She watches over her trunks and logs like a hawk. She would count every morsel of kindling if she could! She ... Well, she grows more foolish by the day. Imagine ... she dogged our Reverend Mother for months with her demands that the communal firewood be separated from *her* wood for the ovens because, she claimed, the meagre heating in the abbey was eating into her reserves! Are we to build another shed just so that she can keep her logs apart? The silly woman!'

'Ah yes ... I can see that you aren't on the best of terms.'

'Let us just say that we keep our distance in order to avoid ruffling one another's feathers!'

'Perhaps now is the chance to remedy that.'

'Pardon?'

Esquive's extraordinary eyes flashed mischievously:

'Ruffling feathers can be a good thing.'

Annelette chuckled, then, remembering herself, apologised:

'This is no time for laughter. But I will do it. Your idea appeals to me. Let us do battle with the bread maker!'

'Give me a few minutes to reach your meeting place – or battlefield.'

Offended, the apothecary replied:

'I am tall and quite strong enough not to require any protection.'

'And what if you allow somebody else to be the judge of that for once?'

The young woman's observation left Annelette speechless. She was amazed not to feel any need to protest, to insist that she was perfectly capable of confronting any danger. How could such a slip of a girl inspire such confidence in her?

And so Annelette gave Esquive a few minutes to get away from their secret meeting place in the herbarium.

She used the time to try to contain her terrible grief over Éleusie's death, which the intervening days had done nothing to alleviate. She struggled, too, with her fear of the outside world, which she had believed held no more mysteries for her. Where or to whom could she turn if the King or the new Pope, weary of the murderous goings-on at the abbey, ordered it to be closed down and the nuns sent to other convents? In reality, Annelette knew that she was too old to adapt to new surroundings, new faces. She was no longer sure whether she had the necessary strength to struggle, criticise, rail and parry in order to conceal her weaknesses.

Stop moaning, you great gangling creature! Get up, pull

yourself together and get a move on! How sluggish you are growing in your old age. And you look down your nose at Blanche de Blinot and Berthe de Marchiennes? Well, daughter, you're scarcely more vigorous than they! Come on, where's your pride? Show me what you're made of.

The humiliating sermon worked and Annelette got up from her stool.

Château de Larnay, Perche, December 1304

Is that low-born woman threatening me? Eudes de Larnay, whose drinking spree had lasted several days and nights, belched angrily. A warm mixture of wine and bile filled his mouth and he grimaced.

The wretched woman! Who did this bastard offspring of his father think she was? He reread the brief letter that had just been delivered to him, blinking in his drunken stupor in an attempt to stay awake.

> *Dearly beloved brother,*
>
> *You are aware of my feelings for you, as I am fully aware of those you entertain towards me, which you have demonstrated on countless occasions; I need only allude to your selfless generosity and unstinting concern regarding my future and that of your niece, Mathilde, my daughter. I am eternally grateful for your courage in unhesitatingly offering Mathilde shelter when, owing to a flagrant injustice, I was dragged before the Inquisition. God's intervention cleared me of all suspicion, allowing me to carry on my life where I had been obliged to leave off.*
>
> *Believe me, dear brother, I am well aware that life at your chateau is far sweeter than the simple farm life here at Souarcy, which is all I am able to offer my daughter. However, as I am sure you will agree, the rightful place of a girl not yet come of age is with her mother. I would therefore appreciate it, dear brother, if you would bring her to my house. Without further ado.*
>
> *Your loving sister and obedient vassal,*
> *Agnès*

Despite his drunkenness, Eudes was not fooled. Agnès had taken care to detach the last three words so that he would understand that this was not a request but an unmistakable command, which no polite phrasing could disguise.

He sprang up from the bench in a rage, sending his earthenware goblet flying. A plume of wine sprayed out over the flagstones, followed by a muffled thud like distant thunder. He pounced on the unfortunate vessel, grinding the yellow fragments of Perche sandstone furiously underfoot until all that remained of it was dust. Suddenly the grotesque absurdity of his gesture struck him with full force.

This female had the power to reduce him to the state of an eight-year-old boy having a temper tantrum. This female had the power to make him look ridiculous in his own eyes.

So she wanted her daughter. Well, her whore of a daughter was shut away in a convent, and Agnès wouldn't be seeing her again in a hurry. She should be grateful to him for having rid her of such a creature. Mathilde hated her, envied her; she dreamt only of destroying the mother whom she could never resemble.

What was the Dame de Souarcy really after? Eudes's blood?

He doubted it and yet even Agnès's hatred would have been some consolation – being important enough in her eyes for her to want to destroy him. Scant compensation, yet preferable to the indifference he had been struggling with for years.

He had filled the emptiness as best he could with wealth, petty power, young girls and wine. But his wealth and power were waning and only his serfs feared him now. Wine made him feel increasingly ill and, as for women, they sickened him.

He yelled:

'Hey! Come here at once! Must I thrash you all in order to be obeyed?'

A manservant poked his head round the door and, keeping his distance, enquired:

'You called, master?'

'Bring me a pail of cold water, an escritoire and a quill, at once!'

The man vanished, reappearing moments later with a young scullery maid, who trailed a few steps behind him in the hope of avoiding a blow.

The manservant hurriedly set the pail down on the ground.

'On the table, you fool! Do you expect me to sprawl on the floor like a dog?'

The man obeyed, and withdrew quickly. The panic-stricken girl nearly dropped the escritoire and a splash of ink landed on the main table. Eudes followed her every move. After setting down the sloping box, she raised her head.

A sharp slap knocked her off her feet and she fell back onto the bench.

'You clumsy oaf! Clean up that ink with your tongue.'

'Please, good master … for pity's sake, no,' whimpered the petrified girl.

'Pity? Wretches like you don't deserve pity. Clean it up! Unless you prefer to be horse-whipped. Hurry up and decide. I'm running out of patience and you're liable to get both in return for your blundering.'

With tears in her eyes, the young girl obeyed. Eudes stared with fascination at her tongue as it lapped at the dark oak table. She stood up straight, eyes lowered, and swallowed awkwardly, her lips and nose stained black.

Eudes felt a wave of nausea rise up his throat, and he bawled:

'Out of my sight, you hideous wretch! And thank heaven for my leniency. Others would have given you a thrashing.'

The girl hurried away as fast as her legs would carry her.

Eudes struggled not to lose consciousness and managed to drag himself over to the pail. He plunged his head into the water, holding his breath until he felt his legs give way, hoping he would have the courage not to lift his head out and gulp in the air. Once again his nerve failed him.

The cold air in the room gripped his scalp, which contracted as he sat down in front of the escritoire. He wondered whether his wet hair might freeze into an icy helmet that would help him come up with a reply, a riposte.

He creased up with laughter as he recited his opening gambit:

My ferocious little lamb,

I am unable to return your daughter to you having arranged matters to suit us both. Have no fear; your little virgin bitch's hymen remains intact. I had no taste for it – although as God is my judge she was more than willing to give it away, our blood ties meaning little more to her than lark's spittle. The moral of the story being that a woman can be at once a virgin and a shameless whore.

Instead – once his amusement had subsided – he wrote in a heavy, faltering hand:

My dearest Agnès,

Your letter catches me unawares and startles me. Mathilde left Larnay a few weeks ago. She has been touched by God's grace – no doubt as a penance for her indescribable behaviour during your trial. I must take this opportunity to assure you that I, too, was taken in by her allegations. At all events, she wished to join a nunnery, the name and location of which I do not know, but she assured me that she had informed you of her decision and that you had approved.

I do not know what to think of this matter. Should we in all conscience stand in the way of such a devout and powerful vocation? Should we deprive her of her only possibility of redemption?

It goes without saying that you may take my support for granted.

I remain, as ever, your devoted Eudes.

He reread his missive, chuckling aloud from time to time. Go on, my beauty. What will you do now?

Go on. Search every convent in the realm.

Clairets Abbey, Perche, December 1304

Just as Annelette had predicted, Sylvine Taulier was busy counting her logs and muttering to herself. Absorbed in her obsessive, almost daily inventory, she failed to notice the apothecary, who cleared her throat to announce her presence. The sister in charge of the bread ovens swivelled around, scowling. Annelette thought to herself how distinctly unappealing the woman was in every sense of the word. Sylvine Taulier was short and stout, resembling a big square lump with no neck and a pair of beefy arms and legs. Even her face was square and reminded Annelette of that of a repulsive toad with its coarse glistening skin. Two restless, bulbous little eyes completed the unattractive picture. In reality, the physical attribute that most made Annelette bristle was undoubtedly the woman's voice – a booming yet shrill, high-pitched voice that pierced the eardrums and set the teeth on edge. She was exposed to it anew:

'Well, Sister Annelette? Did you wish to see me?'

Why the devil else would I drag myself over to the wood shed? the apothecary cursed to herself, even as she went out of her way to appear courteous:

'Why, yes, and I'm so glad that I found you here. Are you happy with your stocks?' she asked, pointing to the carefully stacked logs.

'That remains to be seen … I could have sworn there were more! Some people are just plain spoilt, always complaining of cold hands and feet,' grumbled Sylvine, 'and so another log goes on the fire, and another stump, all day long until dawn. All I can say is don't come running to me when there's no wood left for baking bread!'

'How right you are,' Annelette sympathised, refraining from

observing that they were surrounded by forests belonging to the abbey, and that whole tracts of low wall were stacked with logs waiting to be used.

'In my opinion, our dear Reverend Mother was far too kind and understanding. May her soul rest in peace as I am sure it does. I mean, this is no town house for ladies of the court; it's a Bernadine abbey.'

Annelette, whose uncharacteristic diplomacy was already beginning to chafe, prevaricated:

'You are right. And you have so much work to do, dear Sylvine.'

'Indeed I do, and I'm very glad that somebody's finally noticed!' the sister in charge of the bread ovens replied, nodding vigorously.

Annelette agreed wholeheartedly:

'I mean, making sure that the logs that are brought in are properly dried and stacked, scolding the woodcutters who would throw them in any old how to be done with it, preparing dough, kneading it, baking it for just the right length of time, overseeing all the different flour stocks ... truly, what a task!'

Sylvine Taulier puffed up with pride, reflecting that perhaps, after all, she had been wrong about the apothecary whom she had hitherto considered ill-tempered and arrogant. Exalted by all this flattery, she added:

'Not to mention all the different types of bread: black bread, bread for holy days, everyday bread, bread for masses; it takes some organising.'

'And spelt bread, corn bread, wheat bread ...'

'And barley and oat and millet, which must all be mixed in the right quantities!'

'And rye bread ... we forgot rye bread, which they say is more difficult to bake.'

'Oh, no more than the others,' corrected Sylvine. 'And,

besides, there's not much call for it. I mostly mix wheat with rye. Rye bread is for journeys. It's filling and less costly than wheat, and more nourishing.'

And more to the point it has a sour taste that masks the ergot perfectly, Annelette thought to herself.

'Really? I thought that we ate a good deal of rye bread. Yes … Did you not bake a batch shortly before our dear Reverend Mother's death?'

'No.'

'I could have sworn you did.'

Sylvine, whom the apothecary's insistence was beginning to irritate, said coldly:

'Well, you're mistaken.'

Counting on the other woman's lack of guile, Annelette Beaupré affected a slight air of superiority.

'I have an excellent memory, my dear. Nobody has ever caught me out in this regard. Consequently, if I recall rye bread being served with the soup, then it was.'

Piqued by this odious great creature encroaching on her territory and telling her what was what, the sister in charge of the bread ovens retorted sharply:

'And of course you're never wrong, are you?'

'In all modesty, I cannot recall a single instance when I was,' affirmed the apothecary with a look of evident self-satisfaction.

This was enough to make Sylvine Taulier fly off the handle.

'Very well, then, this evening your pride is headed for a fall. Follow me.'

Sylvine strode ahead at a march as the two women covered the six yards separating the wood shed from the bread ovens. The shed housing the ovens stood alone, far removed from the main buildings – although in centuries past they would have been adjoined in order to utilise the heat. However, numerous fires had finally discouraged this economical building practice.

Inside an adjacent hut, the oven inventory lay open on a lectern. The suffocating heat indicated that the next day's bread was still baking; it was all very well for Sylvine to rail against people who were sensitive to the cold when she herself spent most of her day in the warm.

The sister in charge of the bread ovens had to stand on tiptoe in order to be able to read the ledger. She turned a few pages and declared in a triumphant voice:

'I record everything, do you hear me, everything! Even the bread the rats get to, which is used to thicken the soup for the poor – provided the dirty creatures haven't pissed on it. Here's the page for the day our dear Reverend Mother … God in heaven, what a terrible thing when I think of it.'

Annelette was surprised to see the woman rub her eyes with her closed fists, a gesture which, however vulgar, showed true emotion. The sister in charge of the bread ovens, who was not used to yielding to her emotions and felt awkward, cleared her throat before continuing:

'I am turning the pages back to before that terrible day and what do I see? Nothing. Not a single ounce of rye bread! Wheat and rye, yes, spelt wheat, naturally, and plenty of oat bread, but no rye bread.'

'I continue to be sceptical, my dear Sylvine, for I have a clear recollection of eating some delicious and very flavoursome black bread.'

Unsure whether to feel pleased by this fresh praise or irked by the doubt cast on her sincerity, the sister in charge of the bread ovens nevertheless softened up:

'Yes, it is very good. The secret is to add a little milk. It makes kneading easier and helps the bread rise.'

'Well, I am sure I had the pleasure of eating some not long ago. May I take a look at your ledger just in order to …?'

'Certainly not!' thundered the dumpy woman. 'How would

you like it if I stuck my nose into your herbarium inventory? And, besides, I've had enough of your insinuations. What exactly are you suggesting? That I have lost my wits and can't tell the difference between wheat and rye?' Her small eyes screwed up as an odious thought crossed her dull mind: 'Oh, I see ... you think I might be making a profit by reselling wheat flour to the bakers in the village and replacing it with rye and oat? Is that it? Come on, I dare you to admit it!'

Hands on hips, head down, teeth clenched and with a wild look in her eyes, Sylvine Taulier gave every impression of being about to charge at her accuser.

Annelette sensed that Esquive had probably been right, and that, on the contrary, the strategy she had chosen was a dismal failure. The time for smiles and cajolery was over. She must now use blackmail and threat.

'Listen, Sylvine. I don't like you any more than you like me. However, I am forced to admit that you bake by far the best bread of any nun I have ever met. Now, let's stop beating about the bush.'

The other woman's beady eyes wandered towards the exit. Annelette threw herself at the door, which she slammed shut before leaning her full weight against it to stop anyone leaving or entering. She pointed a threatening finger at the sister in charge of the bread ovens and declared frostily:

'You will not leave here until I receive an explanation. The choice is simple. Decide quickly. You ...'

'I can tell you one thing. You've lost your mind. Keeping me a hostage and in my own workplace! I will refer the matter to our Reverend Mother, and since she doesn't appear overly fond of you ...'

'Really? You know that, do you? How, may I ask? Secrets confided by your accomplice?' Annelette Beaupré insinuated.

Sylvine Taulier clutched the weighty ledger to her ample

bosom – the only part of her anatomy that was round – and hissed furiously:

'I shan't tell you a thing. We can spend the whole night here if you want.'

'I do!'

'And if you think I'm going to let you poke your nose in my register, you've got another think coming. You have no authority over me. Go on, scowl and glare at me all you like! Keep it for the novices and some of the other nuns – you don't scare me.'

'Which just proves that you're even stupider than I thought.'

'What! What!' the other woman gasped.

'They'll accuse you of being an accessory to poisoning, you fool! The poisoning of several of our sisters and of our Abbess ... Do you realise what fate awaits you? You'll be stripped to the waist, chained like a bear and dragged through the streets of the surrounding villages, where they'll stone you then hang you from the gallows!'

Sylvine Taulier's face drained until it turned as pale as the mound of ash underneath the oven doors. It was not the catalogue of punishments but the accusation itself that appeared to make her reel.

'Accessory to poisoning ...? Not only are you wicked, you're insane! Why do you suppose I sweat over these ovens and haul those heavy logs? It was my dream to be in charge of the kitchens and meals, like our dear Adélaïde Condeau, may the Lord rest her soul.' She sighed regretfully. 'But I couldn't ask for the post. I'm as incapable of bashing an eel's head against a wall as I am of wringing a little rabbit or chicken's neck, let alone murdering or helping to murder one of my sisters or our Reverend Mother ...! You're the fool! Look at these muscles,' she added, raising her brawny arms, incensed with rage.

Something about the woman's protestations, her bearing and the tears in her eyes told Annelette Beaupré that she had picked the wrong target. And yet she thrust home her advantage:

'And you expect me to believe you just because you say so? When was the last time you baked rye bread?'

'Why are you so interested in the rye? Rye never killed anyone.'

'This batch did.'

'That's impossible!'

'Not if it was contaminated with ergot.'

'Ergot?'

'It's a fungus that forms small black clusters on the ears of the cereal. A powerful poison. When did you last bake rye bread, pure rye bread?' Annelette repeated, pronouncing each word clearly. 'Hurry up. I'm growing impatient. If I don't receive a satisfactory reply, I'll inform the chief bailiff straight away.'

Suddenly aware of the seriousness of her situation, Sylvine feverishly turned the pages of the register she was still clasping in case the other woman tried to snatch it from her. She looked up and stammered:

'A month ago, at the beginning of Advent. And then again last October. Let me see … if I go further back … again in May. And before that in February I made a whole batch because we hadn't enough oat and wheat flour.'

May. The Pope's emissary who had brought Éleusie a message and was then discovered having apparently been burnt to death; he had arrived at their door in May.

'That's enough shilly-shallying. I want short, precise, truthful answers, otherwise I will hand you over to the authorities. The sister in charge of the kitchens and meals orders the bread supplies, does she not?'

'Of course. Who knows better than she how much is needed at our table or by the poor?'

'Do you record her name in your register?'

'What do you take me for, a fool? Well, you're wrong. I may

not be educated like you. And I confess to having trouble reading long texts and being put off by difficult words. But I know how to write. I learnt here!' she declared, proudly.

'That is very commendable,' acknowledged Annelette, who was being truthful for the second time since the beginning of their dispute.

'Ah, you see! May. Here we are. I put an A beside each of Adélaïde's orders. There was no point really, since besides her ... Then again, when our Reverend Mother wished to supplement our everyday fare she would sometimes ask for milk and egg rolls, or if one of the sisters were ill, she might tell me to add duck or pork scratchings to the dough. I marked her orders with RM for "Reverend Mother",' she added.

'Yes, of course, you wouldn't put it for "Éleusie". And so is there an A or an RM next to the rye bread in May?'

'Well, that's what's strange. Neither. I've put "A via J-A". Ah, now it's coming back! Jeanne, our beloved extern sister, came to give me Adélaïde's order and she brought a bag of flour with her. I remember it well because I don't think Jeanne had ever set foot in here. One gets very grubby in here and it's insufferably hot during the good weather.'

'I see. I am grateful to you, sister, and as God is my judge I beg your forgiveness. My quick temper makes me overbearing. You are no fool, quite the opposite. You do your job admirably well and I insist that you are the best bread maker whose creations it has been my privilege to taste.'

'Oh ... "creations" is a big word ...' the other woman stammered. 'After all, it is only bread.'

'Ah ... bread ... bread is everything. We fill our hungry bellies with bread. Bread is life, it is sacred.'

'And what of my humiliation, stoning and hanging ...'

'I was mistaken about you and I beg your forgiveness. However ... my only valid excuse is that we are all in danger. Sylvine ...

Tell nobody of our meeting and of your discovery. Nobody! All our lives depend upon it – including your own.'

'Jeanne d'Amblin? Could she ... I don't believe it. Impossible! Could she have substituted that stuff for proper rye flour ... that ergot?'

'Shh! I tell you.'

'I'll "shh" this instant, Annelette. None of this will leave this room, I swear on my soul.'

The apothecary vanished swiftly through the door she had been barricading with her tall body. A figure soon joined her. Esquive.

'Did you hear?'

'Practically everything. Sylvine is not the accomplice we're looking for. But you were right about Jeanne.'

'Where is that other fiend hiding?'

'We must find out.'

Compline was long over. Still night lay over the abbey, broken only by the shrill cry of the tawny owl. The silvery bulk of these birds of prey occasionally flashed into sight as they glided noiselessly through the night air. They nested in the clock tower of the abbey church of Notre-Dame. Unlike other species of owl, they were tolerated, for they were thought to bring good fortune and ward off evil.

Annelette lay fully clothed, her eyes wide open, fighting off her exhaustion and the desire to fall asleep by keeping her mind occupied. What were they dreaming of, these nuns screened off in their tiny cells? Of their former lives? Of the chores that awaited them on the morrow? Of the poisonings and the fear they felt? The truth was, Annelette now regretted having been so uninterested in her sisters. Like poor Sylvine, whom she had scolded so harshly earlier. What did she know of this woman's past life? Nothing. It had taken several deaths for her to realise that the pontificating Berthe de Marchiennes had no illusions about herself and that Yolande de Fleury had borne a son. One persistent question plagued the apothecary. Why had Jeanne, the murderess, brought good news of the dead boy to his mother? What had she hoped to gain from it, since she was clearly not motivated out of pity? And who might her accomplice be now that they had established Sylvine Taulier's innocence? Emma de Pathus, the schoolmistress, who had been on such friendly terms with that fiend Nicolas Florin? Another thought occurred to the apothecary: what if Jeanne had been doubly cautious and perverse and had already poisoned her accomplice so as to ensure her eternal silence? Which of the three dead women then, Éleusie de Beaufort being excluded from her list? Adélaïde Condeau, the sister in charge of the kitchens and meals? No. Adélaïde was a jolly chatterbox and choosing her would show lack of judgement and Annelette readily believed in Jeanne d'Amblin's intelligence. Hedwige du Thilay, the treasurer nun? Certainly not. Hedwige was far too nervous, unpredictable and given to fits of melancholy.[48] Yolande de Fleury? Yolande had been a pure soul. She would never have taken part in such wickedness unless she had been forced to, and perhaps not even then. Yes, but what if her reward had been news of little Thibaut? Heartening news of a mother's adored child in exchange for complicity? It would explain why Jeanne had concealed the child's death. And yet the apothecary was unconvinced of Yolande's participation.

A sliding sound. She closed her eyes, adopting the even breathing of a sleeper. The faint rustle of fabric. The muffled almost imperceptible patter of bare feet on the dormitory flagstones. A nervous sweat made Annelette Beaupré's hands grow clammy. What if Esquive did not back her up, what if she'd been mistaken about the young girl? And how would she manage alone? She was a scholar and a scientist, not a fighter, still less an expert in hand-to-hand combat.

Enough! You're a head higher than Jeanne and at least thirty pounds heavier. Don't be so chicken-hearted! You silly scared goose! You can crush her easily if it comes to it.

Annelette listened out. All was quiet again, a heavy silence interrupted only by the sound of the other nuns' breathing. She got up cautiously and glanced around the enormous room. Jeanne's cell was empty. The coast was clear. She must hurry in order not to lose sight of the extern sister. Clutching her clogs, Annelette Beaupré moved as silently as a ghost. Despite her thick stockings, the bitter cold rising up from the flagstones froze her legs. She opened the door quietly, poking her head out and scouring the length of the corridor, the end of which was plunged into almost total darkness. She glimpsed Jeanne's outline as she turned right towards the relics' room. Could that be her secret hiding place? Annelette hastened after her on tiptoe. Suddenly an arm clasped her round the waist, nearly causing her to cry out.

'Shh,' whispered Esquive. 'Not another word. Come on.'

It was only then that Annelette caught sight of the short sword in the girl's right hand. The relief provided by this weapon, and by the stiletto concealed beneath her own robe, troubled her. It took so little to plunge straight back into savagery.

They in turn passed the corner pillar and reached the staircase leading up to the relics' room. They climbed the bottom steps, crouching out of sight of Jeanne. Not far from them, the flickering flame of a sconce torch danced aloft as though suspended in the air. So, the fiend had thought of everything. A grating sound. The reliquary, thought Annelette. She was opening the reliquary Madame de Beaufort had donated to the abbey, which it was believed contained one of Saint Germain the Bishop of Auxerre's shinbones. A fresh anxiety gripped her. What if she were mistaken again? Even supposing the handsome glass casket, set in an ornately chased silver frame, had a false bottom, as was commonly the case, it could not possibly be big enough to contain three hefty volumes. Another grating sound. Esquive tugged at her sleeve and they backed away hurriedly, hiding behind one of the vast supporting pillars.

They held their breath until Jeanne had gone past, and waited until she was some distance away. Annelette whispered so low that Esquive had to press her ear to her lips:

'She's not carrying anything as bulky as books. And besides …'

'Shh … I don't think she's finished yet. Let's keep following her.'

Jeanne was hurrying down the very long corridor leading to the cellar. She veered left, towards the baths and the steam room. The two women raced after her, only to pull up and fall back a few paces when they discovered that the door to the steam room was open. The extern sister appeared to be rummaging through the contents of a cupboard. They heard the sharp click of a door closing, shortly after which she emerged – this time clutching a large package wrapped in a piece of whitish-grey cloth. The books.

Annelette's body tensed as she prepared to hurl herself at Jeanne d'Amblin in order to snatch the precious booty, but a small iron hand gripped the back of her robe, restraining her just in time. She turned and glared furiously at Esquive who shook her head, placing a finger to her lips. Incensed, the apothecary nevertheless complied. Once Jeanne was out of earshot, the young girl explained in an almost inaudible voice:

'It is too soon to intervene. If she's half as clever as I think she is, she'll find another hiding place – one that's more easily accessible during the day. She must first exact a price for her safety from Madame de Neyrat. And I can't help agreeing with her on that point,' she added with a flicker of amusement in her eye which Annelette judged inappropriate. 'If Jeanne lets her guard down for a second, that woman will make short work of her. We must keep trailing her.'

The extern sister had almost passed the refectory by the time they crossed the gallery giving onto the steam room. The surrounding darkness was so thick that, had it not been for her white robe and the flicker of the sconce torch, they would no doubt have had great difficulty trailing the murderess. Where was she going? Jeanne d'Amblin appeared to be making her way towards the Abbess's chambers. Esquive frowned. Was Jeanne more foolish than she had supposed? Was she naively going to hand over the manuscripts to Aude de Neyrat tonight?

The extern sister paused in front of the door leading to the Abbess's study and bedchamber. She pulled from under her robe a copy of the key she had obtained thanks to her invaluable accomplice. Opening the heavy door a crack, she walked forward a few steps. Her bare feet were numb from the cold. The merry murderess, Madame de Neyrat, was sleeping the sleep of the just in the adjoining room. A faint smile appeared on Jeanne d'Amblin's lips. So far everything was going precisely according to plan. She had recovered from the reliquary her tidy sum of money, augmented by Mabile's more modest one, then fetched the volumes she had recently hidden in the steam room at the bottom of a basket full of old linen that was sent away twice yearly to be mended. She felt smug in her cleverness: nobody would have thought to look in such an ordinary, everyday hiding place. Except perhaps Madame de Neyrat, to whom she attributed a keen intelligence mixed with cunning. It was best, therefore, to move her precious plunder, her safeguard. The bogus Abbess's only weakness was her conceit and Jeanne intended to use it against her. It would never occur to the arrogant Aude that she herself was harbouring the manuscripts she was so desperate to hand over to the camerlingo. As for that odious Annelette, the Abbess's study was the last place she would think of poking around in. Too obvious, not subtle enough for her.

Jeanne d'Amblin moved like a cat, on the alert. Her breath formed wisps of steam. She went straight over to her objective: the stout sideboard where Éleusie had kept her registers. She slipped the three volumes inside, certain that Madame de Neyrat would avoid the dreary task of registering every detail of monastic life, for which the extern sister could hardly blame her.

Jeanne left without making a sound, delighted by her deception. She hurried back to the dormitory and went directly to bed without bothering to make sure that everybody else was present.

Esquive walked up to the heavy door and tried to open it.

'Heavens. It's locked! I was only given a key to the library.'

Now it was Annelette's turn to lift her heavy skirts and rummage around until she produced a key, the spare key she had found in the deceased Abbess's safe. She handed it to the young girl, a glint of triumph in her eye.

'You are brilliant, my dear. You will explain later how you came by it.'

'Being brilliant does not preclude being obedient. I was asked to hand over *one* key, which I did. However, I had two in my possession.'

Esquive inserted the spare key in the lock, but Annelette stopped her:

'One moment. Madame de Neyrat is asleep only a few feet away. We cannot possibly carry out a search. And yet Jeanne left empty-handed. I must confess that she is even more cunning than I'd thought: to hide the works without hiding them. Very clever indeed. The only piece of furniture where manuscripts that size would fit is the sideboard containing the registers.'

'I insist, you are brilliant! Wait here, sister. You can be our lookout. One intruder is less likely to be seen than two.'

The apothecary nodded, acknowledging:

'Moreover, I am not known for my lightness of touch.'

Annelette felt as though she had waited an eternity for the young girl to reappear. When she finally emerged, the apothecary opened her eyes wide and her face froze. She gasped, uneasily:

'Did you not find them?'

'Yes,' the other woman assured her, beaming. 'But I have hidden them temporarily – until tomorrow or the day after – behind a hundred or so books in the library from which they were stolen and to which we have a key. We must fight craft with craft! Later I will have no difficulty retrieving them and returning them to the knight Leone.' Her amber eyes filled with glee as she declared: 'I would give anything to see the expression on the extern sister's face when she next looks in the sideboard.'

'What a stroke of genius,' sighed the apothecary. 'And what about Jeanne? We can't allow her crimes to go unpunished.'

'Have no fear. They say that wild animals never kill and eat each other, which shows a deep misunderstanding of the habits of savage beasts. Annelette, we have gained a glorious victory and I thank you from the bottom of my heart. Without these precious works, our enemies will be powerless ... Well, perhaps not powerless, but they will be unable to discover the second birth chart.'

Unnerved by the girl's solemnity, the apothecary whispered:

'No. Don't tell me that you're about to leave!'

'Yes, my good friend, and it pains me. I regret leaving you alone. Time is running out, as you know. However ... I will stay just long enough to witness the spectacle of our dear Abbess's rage. It should not be long in coming.'

Clément blinked in disbelief.

He had joined Leone in his corner of the barn once the servants in the house had gone to bed. He hadn't even waited to sit down before beginning:

'"b...me...re...au...per...t." What is the meaning of this sentence scribbled in the notebook?'

The Hospitaller did not reply immediately. Finally, after what appeared to be an inner struggle, he said:

'"The bloodline passes down through the women. The blood that is different* will be reborn through one of them. Her daughters will perpetuate it."'

'Agnès?'

'Probably.'

'Why "probably"? The first birth chart is hers, is it not?'

'In all likelihood, if the partial eclipse doesn't exclude her.'

'What do you mean, knight?'

'According to the prophecy contained in the Aramaic papyrus, whose hiding place we have yet to find, this momentous birth ought to have been greeted by an eclipse. The day Madame de Souarcy came into this world the eclipse was not total. I am not sure how important this detail is.'

'What is this lineage?'

'I have already told you far too much, Clément. Our enemies have repeatedly shown that they will go to any lengths to suppress this secret. Madame de Souarcy's accusation and my aunt's murder are only the most recent manifestations of this.'

'Exactly. So, if anything were to happen to you ... would the secret die out?'

After a silence, which Clément sensed was heavy with doubt and fear, the knight finally consented to reveal more.

'I don't know exactly which lineage it refers to. Eustache and I considered every possibility from the most wondrous to the most outlandish.'

'The Sacred Lineage?' suggested the young boy, his heart pounding.

'I've always had my doubts and never more so than now,' said Leone, recalling his aunt's posthumous revelations. 'Madame de Souarcy had no links with the Holy Land, any more than her … mother. Although, some claim that Mary Magdalene came to Gaul. On the other hand, following Christ's death and resurrection the Virgin Mary allegedly fled to Turkey and ended her days there. And yet … You must never repeat what I am about to tell you, Clément – your lady's life no doubt depends on it.'

The young boy, sensing the gravity of his words, nodded. The knight resumed:

'Eustache translated the passages in Aramaic copied out by the Knight Templar at Acre in his notebook. We then wrote them in invisible ink on the last blank page of the notebook – which, alas, you did not tear out. We are unsure whether the passage comes from the famous papyrus, but in any event it speaks of a divine blood that washes away all sin. As in the fragmented sentence I just reconstructed for you, it refers to a blood that is different, extraordinary.'

'Extraordinary in what way?' Clément murmured.

'I do not know. I have the impression that all I can do is repeatedly confess my ignorance. Eustache and I concluded that the answer to this mystery must lie in the papyrus.'

'And what became of it?'

'The Knight Templar maintained that he had hidden it in a

safe place. At one of their commanderies.'

'Do you know which one?'

Something about this boy fascinated Leone. His instinct told him that he would be the only one to whom Leone would reveal the whole truth. He told him plainly what he had held back from Annelette:

'I am persuaded that it is at the Templar commandery at Arville.'

'Not so very far from Souarcy.'

'Indeed, and that accounts in part for my interest in the place.'

'Do you have any clue as to where the papyrus is hidden?'

'No. But I think that the rose is meant to help us find it.'

'That's why it was so important to have copied it faithfully.'

'Exactly. However, I discovered nothing during my brief visit to the commandery, not even when I went inside the Temple of Our Lady.'

Leone and Clément had then spent until dawn studying from every conceivable angle the calculations of the Vallombroso monk whose discoveries had cost him his life.

Just as he was about to fall asleep on the straw, the young boy was roused from his exhaustion by a sudden realisation. He had just understood how to make sense of the astronomer's calculations. He shut his eyes tight for fear the knight would glimpse his excitement. He needed an hour – two at the most – alone with these pages. It would scarcely take him longer to prove his theory, or at least so he hoped.

Feigning drowsiness, he mumbled:

'Knight … My lady must already be waiting for us. Go ahead of me to the trough in the courtyard. The icy water for our morning ablutions will wake us up. I'll use the time to reflect a little more.'

'Provided you don't fall asleep,' Leone said, smiling.

Francesco de Leone carefully folded the page containing the

reddish-brown script, overlapped in places by Clément's spidery scrawl, and left the copy they had made the evening before on the bale of straw they had used as a lectern.

Rather than trying to interpret as accurately as possible the differences between Vallombroso's theory and that of Ptolemy, which still held sway – as Leone and his godfather Eustache de Rioux and the Knights Templar before them had done without success – Clément would use the first decoded birth chart to decipher the second. A short cut which the brilliant Archimedes* would have applauded.

From a purely mathematical and astronomical point of view, the first approach was undoubtedly the more satisfying. However, the vast numbers of extremely complicated calculations it required had thwarted his predecessors. The second, more pragmatic approach would only give him the correct calculation of the second birth chart. However, in the end, was that not the most important thing?

For the hundredth time since the previous evening, he studied the two birth charts whose sun sign was in Capricorn – from 22 December to 20 January. The letters signifying the planets were repeated there: E for Earth, Su for Sun, M for Moon, Me for Mercury, Ma for Mars, V for Venus, J for Jupiter, Sa for Saturn, GE1, GE2, As,[49] with the accompanying symbols representing the different astrological signs and the Roman numerals designating the houses of the zodiac. Two slight differences broke the troubling similarity between the charts: Jupiter in Pisces and Saturn in Capricorn in one and Jupiter in Sagittarius and Saturn in Pisces in the other.

Clément traced a map of the heavens on the trampled earth floor of the barn and added the information from the first birth chart, the calculated date – 25 December 1278, Agnès's birthday – and the corresponding positions of the planets. The simplest task was to banish from his mind Ptolemy's erroneous deductions. Indeed, he needed to consider the data provided by the first birth chart as a sort of zero hour of the universe – the starting point from which all the stars began their interminable journey. He smiled to himself: this amounted to saying that the world began with Agnès's birth. A charming idea. With the aid of the Vallombroso monk's calculations concerning the revolutions around the sun of the three mysterious planets referred to as GE1, GE2 and As, and the only two differences between the two birth charts – Jupiter in Pisces and Saturn in Capricorn in one and Jupiter in Sagittarius and Saturn in Pisces in the other – Clément was able to determine the length of time between them. Using his forefinger as a quill, he tallied up the months, days and years, and arrived at a most curious figure. The second birth was so far in the future that Clément assumed he must have made a mistake. The knight would soon be back. He grew uneasy. Quick, what should he do? Go. He must take the copy with him and go somewhere where he could continue his calculations undisturbed.

He approached the high barn door and glanced furtively out into the courtyard. Leone was leaning over the trough and making loud gasping noises. Clément took the opportunity to slip away.

Where should he go? He mustn't return to Clairets. As for his attic or even the outbuildings, Leone would have no difficulty finding him there. La Haute-Gravière. It wouldn't take long if he cut through the woods, and the place was so desolate that nobody had been there in years.

He slipped between the outbuildings, silent as a shadow.

'Well, you here? Where'd you be off to then, Clément?'

It was Gilbert the Simpleton with his booming voice that carried a mile.

'Shh ... I'm running an errand for our lady.'

'Our good fairy.'

'Yes.'

'Where'd you be going?'

'La Haute-Gravière. But it's a secret.'

'Ooohhh...' breathed the simpleton, placing a finger to his lips.

'Yes. Not a word so as to please our lady.'

'I'll be a carp,' he promised, closing and opening his lips.

Having finished his ablutions, Francesco de Leone walked slowly back to the barn. Clément had had ample time to go off with the copy of the page the knight had 'accidentally' left behind. He had noticed the sudden change in the boy's demeanour. Would he in a few hours manage to make sense of the calculations over which he and Eustache had racked their brains for so long? It was not impossible. The path of their quest had been strewn with so many bizarre twists of fate in the form of unexpected help and strange encounters (like the one with the little Cypriot beggar girl with amber eyes) that Leone had long since concluded that at times he must let himself be carried along by events whose origin he did not understand.

Clément had indeed run off. The Hospitaller was not in the slightest bit concerned. Nothing that the young boy did could possibly harm them, for he would rather die than fail his lady.

The pale winter sun was shining feebly on the frosty tufts of grass dotted about the courtyard as the knight walked over to the main hall. Agnès was already seated before a bowl of split pea and mint soup supplemented with a few pieces of fried bacon.

'Sit down beside me, knight. Did you lose Clément on the way here?'

'It is he who has gone off without me. He left in such a hurry that I didn't see where he went.'

'He often disappears for short periods. He'll be back this evening, ravenous.'

Adeline brought another steaming bowl in from the kitchens, as well as a large slice of bread and dripping. When she had gone back to her den, Leone said:

'He is very dear to you.'

Agnès looked up at him with her blue-green eyes. A wave of tenderness and sorrow engulfed the knight. She had his mother Claire's eyes – Philippine's, too, perhaps, but having never met his aunt he couldn't be sure. His sorrow gave way to astonishment as a different pair of eyes replaced those of Claire in his memory. He swallowed a mouthful of soup in order to mask his sudden unease. No, he was mistaken; he was imagining things. It wasn't possible. The similarity was a coincidence.

'Indeed, he is very dear to my heart. I brought him up. As you know, his mother died giving birth to him. Clément has never failed me, or hurt me. He has always been by my side, as he is now when I am so alone.'

Leone understood the allusion to Mathilde and chose not to respond.

'Dare I ask a favour of you, Madame?'

'Please, go ahead.'

'I would like your permission to return here this evening in order to engage Clément's help in carrying out a plan I have elaborated.'

'Granted, Monsieur. However, I beg you to remember that he is only a child and no warrior like you.'

'Rest assured, I will remember.'

However, she was unable to rest assured, and decided to remind Clément the moment he returned of the boundaries which she demanded he respect for both their sakes.

Alençon, Perche, December 1304

If Artus had imagined that his most difficult task would be to approach Leone and, worse still, to persuade the knight to confide in him, he was soon to be proven wrong.

That evening, as the bleak winter night thickened, he waited in front of the forbidding door of the Inquisition headquarters. For the past hour, he had been pacing up and down and stamping his feet in a vain attempt to keep warm.

He had hesitated at length, wondering whether it might not be best to corner the clerk Agnan in his tiny office. But the certainty that the man would be nervous of eavesdroppers and would clam up had dissuaded him.

At last the studded double doors to the headquarters opened and the puny, desperately hideous young man emerged.

The Comte d'Authon let him walk on a few paces before drawing level with him in three strides. The young secretary turned around, a look of alarm on his face, fearful, perhaps, of an attacker. A smile replaced his startled expression, lighting up his weaselly face in a way that was almost touching. He bowed by way of a greeting, and stammered:

'Monsieur le Comte ... Forgive me. I didn't recognise you straight away.'

'Don't mention it. How have you been keeping since the demise of the hateful Florin?'

'Wonderfully well, my lord. It is as though one of hell's deadliest shades had miraculously disappeared.' He paused, then asked the question that was on the tip of his tongue: 'And Madame de Souarcy, has she recovered from her ordeal?'

Understanding what it was that the young man dared not ask, Artus announced:

'Indeed, she is a very brave woman and God takes special care of her. She remembers you often with enormous gratitude.'

'Does she really?' Agnan stammered, his face turning a deep scarlet. 'Tell her from me that her appreciation is wasted on one as miserable as I. Tell her, please, that I am for ever in her debt. Madame gave me the greatest gift I could hope for. She will always be in my prayers. Please be sure and tell her this, I beg you, my lord, with the utmost respect.'

Artus had the uneasy feeling that this man was speaking to him as though they were both privy to some tremendous, secret mystery. And yet he was still lost in conjecture. He decided to be clear in his mind about it and suggested:

'I would be honoured if you would agree to share my supper. Then I must return directly to Authon.'

'Oh, the honour is mine, my lord.'

'Do you know of a tavern where the food is less deplorable than at La Jument-Rouge, and where we may converse in peace?'

'I do. Auberge de la Serfouette,[50] Rue des Petites-Poteries. I've heard that it is excellent.' Suddenly embarrassed, he added: 'However … being superior, the food is not cheap.'

The remark brought a smile, swiftly suppressed, to the lips of the second richest man in Perche after the King's brother, Monsieur Charles de Valois.*

'I like the sound of it. La Serfouette would seem to be the ideal place to celebrate the death of that rogue Florin.'

L'Auberge de la Serfouette was run with artistry by an outstanding chef, a former lay brother with the Knights Templar. He had left the military order before taking his vows, after the failure of the last crusade. In his words, the loss of Christendom in the East and the Saracens' humiliating victory had discouraged him for ever from following the troops with his cartload of pots and pans. Beginning with the very first course, consisting of sweet wine accompanied by jellied fruits, Artus had nothing but praise for Maître Serfouette, who had returned from his travels around the world with an exotic and flavoursome collection of recipes. The delicate aroma of the second course, a simple consommé made of meat stock flavoured with saffron, verjuice and parsley, confirmed his opinion.

They spoke of this and that – of the recent harvests, of Guy d'Anderlecht,[51] a peasant who had become a sacristan and travelled to Jerusalem after his small business failed. Later, he had returned to his home town, a few miles south of Brussels, where he had died. Curiously, in recent years his memory had attracted a religious following.

Agnan began to relax a little. His pale hollow cheeks were burning from the modest glass of wine he had drunk. He ate slowly, afraid his hunger would show. Artus felt a wave of fatherly affection. Did the monk really think that the Comte didn't recognise the glazed look of satisfied hunger? He, too, had been ravaged by lack of food during his travels around the world. He decided, therefore, to wait until the end of the third course – a haunch of venison marinated in red and white wine, vinegar and quince jelly.

'Sweet Lord, what magnificence,' murmured Agnan, who had consumed a week's worth of food.

Maître Serfouette walked over to their candlelit table to receive their compliments, which were readily forthcoming. An experienced landlord, he soon left – though not before offering them an apple liqueur to aid their digestion before the next course.

Agnan's face was by now bright red, his glowing cheeks no longer a sign of his awkwardness. Artus d'Authon took the plunge:

'Agnan, I believe you are well acquainted with a friend of mine, the knight Francesco de Leone.'

The other man sat bolt upright and replied in a voice emboldened by alcohol:

'He is a man of light, a pure, courageous soul. A messenger sent by God in His infinite bounty. He saved Madame de Souarcy and defeated the creature of darkness.'

'Undeniably. He pre-empted me by a few hours,' the Comte added clumsily, still obsessed by the thought of not having wrenched Agnès from the clutches of the Inquisition.

He was taken aback by the response of the sickly clerk, who retorted in a stinging voice:

'By a few hours, you say? Do you know what a few hours in the hands of Nicolas Florin signified? I know. I heard their screams. I had to put my hands over my ears for it to stop.'

Had the reproach not been entirely justified, Artus d'Authon would no doubt have been offended by his guest's tone of voice. Just then, a fresh-faced servant girl arrived with their dessert and smiled before vanishing again. He was spared the need to respond. They ate their buckwheat crêpes with honey and powdered jujube[52] in silence. Then Artus asked:

'I have an urgent letter for the knight. Do you know where I might find him?'

Agnan looked up and pursed his lips before replying sharply:

'Do not be deceived, my lord. Admittedly, the apple liqueur has gone to my head and should, I hope, excuse my rashness. However, this frail, deformed, rather ugly creature sitting before you is a courageous soul. And he was rewarded a thousandfold for it by Madame de Souarcy.'

Utterly baffled, the Comte d'Authon asked:

'What are you trying to say?'

'With all due respect to your rank, your reputation and your childhood friendship with the King, I do not for one moment believe your story. You don't know the knight Leone and there is no letter.'

The young man's unexpected boldness, not to say impudence, flabbergasted Artus, who breathed:

'Heavens! What candour! Are you aware, young man, that I have run men through for more trifling impertinences than this?'

'Oh, I am sure you have. I'm not afraid,' the sickly man went on. 'I have been in the presence of a miracle. She smiled at me, she touched my hand. I will never do or say anything that might endanger or even displease her.'

This same shared devotion for the woman who had stolen Artus's heart and soul. He felt another pang of jealousy:

'How might my wishing to contact the knight displease Madame de Souarcy?'

'Because the knight saved her, and she must feel a debt of gratitude towards him. What an incredible coincidence. A divine coincidence, I tell you.' Agnan appeared to reflect before continuing: 'Monsieur, I sense that you are a decent man. I have witnessed the trust Madame places in you and it convinces me that I'm not mistaken. You have done me the great honour of sharing this exquisite meal with me, and ... and I am tempted to exploit your generosity.'

'How so?'

'By asking you to honour me once more.'

'How?'

'By telling me the truth, my lord. Nothing can oblige you, I am sure, except perhaps the respect you might have for me.'

Artus looked at him. Agnan did indeed possess a shy but steadfast purity that inspired respect. He spoke:

'Out of respect for you, then. My question is at once simple and extremely embarrassing. Do you think that Madame de Souarcy was acquainted with the knight Leone prior to his miraculous intervention?'

'What makes you ask?'

God's wounds, this was without doubt the most difficult

confession Artus would ever have to make. He took the plunge: 'The anxiety of a lover who feels his age. I speak, I assure you, of a love which the Church would heartily applaud.'

The little pink face broke into a smile. Agnan clasped his hands together in delight:

'What wonderful news! What a magnificent comtesse she will make!'

Suddenly growing serious again, he announced:

'No. I am certain that she did not. Madame de Souarcy had never seen the knight before. As for the knight, I can only base my judgement on instinct, not on fact. I had the impression that she symbolised something of great value to him. A mission, perhaps ... I don't know. Something crucial enough to make him resolve to slay a Grand Inquisitor. When I met the knight again recently, he asked me a very peculiar question.'

'What?'

'He ... I confess that I still don't understand ... He asked me ... what colour Madame de Souarcy's blood was.'

'I beg your pardon?'

'You heard correctly.'

'What did you reply?'

'Well ... what could I reply ...? Red, a red so beautiful, so heart-rending that it made me weep. Blood. The blood of poor victims.'

'What was Francesco de Leone's response?'

'He seemed ... not disappointed, that isn't the right word. Disturbed, fearful.'

'Fearful because her blood was red?'

'I told you, I still cannot fathom the meaning of our exchange.'

Artus found the heady sauvo-crestian[53] they were served next almost sickly – although its richness was equalled only by its smoothness.

Half an hour later, Artus accompanied the young clerk to his lodgings at the Inquisition headquarters to safeguard him against any undesirable chance encounters.

After they had cordially taken leave of one another, the Comte d'Authon was scarcely any closer to his goal. Admittedly, the lover in him was reassured by Agnan's revelations. But the man was lost in a maze of speculation.

E arly that morning the novices had had to break the ice in the tanks in order to heat up some of the frozen water for washing. Their faces had turned pink from the exertion and they tucked their numbed fingers under their arms to warm them.

The daughter of a burgher from Nogent turned to one of her sisters and said in hushed tones:

'We should urinate on them.'

At which the other replied, exasperated: 'Don't be silly, that's for chilblains!'

Esquive had kept her distance from the group and was watching the tall doors that opened onto the corridor leading to the scriptorium and the Abbess's chambers. She had decided not to deprive herself in the name of Christian charity of what she considered the legitimate pleasure of seeing these two wretches confront one another. In reality, she was champing at the bit, although she supposed Madame de Neyrat would win. Hands down.

Jeanne d'Amblin had waited until dawn. Taking advantage of the lifting of the restrictions on leaving the abbey, she strode through the main doorway in the enclosure wall, clasping a package wrapped in yellowish-brown cloth. Once outside, she walked cautiously, taking small steps and glancing around her. She had scarcely covered ten yards when she spotted them slumped against one of the oak trees at the edge of Clairets Forest. Two drunk-looking, threatening ruffians. Two cheap cut-throats hired by Neyrat. Jeanne had been expecting them, yet she was choked with rage. What did those idiots take her for? She had lied, cheated and killed enough times to make her suspicious of the slightest shadow. A few dozen yards still separated them, and so the devils continued pretending to engage in lively banter, mocking one another and slapping their thighs good-humouredly like a pair of harmless fellow travellers. They were waiting for her to draw near, at which point they would pounce on her, drag her into the thicket, grab her package and, no doubt, cut her throat. The extern sister looked around quickly. Not a soul. Nobody to come to her aid – for the porteress nun would never leave her peephole unless ordered to by the Abbess. Jeanne d'Amblin slowed down and, taking a deep breath, turned on her heel and ran back full pelt towards the enclosure wall. The two cut-throats quickly realised that their quarry, and their reward, was getting away. They ran to try to catch up with her. Jeanne could hear their thudding footsteps behind her and cried out:

'Porteress, the door … open the door quickly. I'm being attacked. One of God's wives is being attacked!'

She heard the grate of the long iron bar that secured the high door. She turned round without slowing down. The brigands were now only a few yards behind her. With all her might, she flung the cloth-wrapped package as far away from her as she could. One of the scoundrels shouted to the other:

'Stop, we've got it! We're paid to get the package.'

The two men swerved and pounced on the precious booty.

Jeanne cried out as she hurled herself through the opening:

'Quick, close the door!'

The young lay girl whose job it was to open and close the door gave her a dazed look and gasped:

'Sister … sister … I've never seen anything so dreadful in all my days. What is the world coming to when wretches like these attack one of God's wives?'

Jeanne, out of breath, simply nodded.

'We must inform our Reverend Mother at once,' the other woman insisted, her anger mounting. 'And the chief bailiff too!'

'I will attend to it,' Jeanne lied, trying hard to control her anger, which was causing her to shake every bit as much as the physical exertion.

The silence in the abbey church of Notre-Dame made Jeanne d'Amblin shiver. She had a sudden feeling that the place was suspended between life and death – unsure of which would come. A deathly cold calm permeated the nave and the transept, seeming to flow in waves from the chancel. How had she ever found peace among these huge, forbidding stones, these lofty great pillars? Everything in that place seemed designed to crush all who entered there, to convince them of the futility of their striving, of their desires. She wanted to flee that gloom, pierced only by the pale light seeping mournfully in through the gemelled windows.[54] To flee the apsidiole[55] chapel where she had once found refuge. Refuge? There was none for her now at the abbey. She felt as though every wall, every door threatened to encircle her, to overwhelm her until she was completely engulfed.

She needed a few minutes to calm down, to banish her feeling of extreme unease, which she refused to believe was any sort of premonition.

A calm, icy hatred had replaced the rage and fear she had felt earlier and she resolved to confront Madame de Neyrat. She stood up and walked out into the cold winter morning, every step requiring a monumental effort.

Jeanne d'Amblin opened the door to the Abbess's study without knocking and walked in. The room was empty. The extern sister had prepared no preamble, no riposte, nothing. Had Madame de Neyrat already been informed that the package had been taken from her, that she had been forced to throw it to her assailants in order to reach the safety of the enclosure?

Jeanne d'Amblin stood before the oak door that would for ever remind her of Éleusie de Beaufort. She waited for the bogus Abbess, who was singing to herself in the adjoining chamber, to finish dressing. The memory of her dead Reverend Mother, of the years they had shared in false friendship – on her part anyway – had faded more quickly than the extern sister would ever have imagined. Had she changed so completely? In fact, two years before, Jeanne had had the impression that her life had changed radically. Resignation can sometimes prove treacherous. For Jeanne had resigned herself to the sad life of the nunnery, lacking in grandeur yet secure. She truly believed that she had said goodbye for ever to a life that was freer, more perilous, more dazzling. That was until the foolish Yolande had confided in her, had developed a girlish infatuation for her that was unconditional and, above all, blind. It was true that Jeanne tended to inspire confidence and affection in people. There had been a time, almost forgotten now, when this gift had helped her survive in the outside world, by making a little niche for herself when no one else wanted her – not her parents, still less her brothers. In their defence, the Amblin fortune had been no more than a distant memory to which her father had clung in order not to yield completely to despair. Her ability to ingratiate herself with people had become one of her most reliable weapons. The young sister in charge of the granary had confided in her the story of her passion for the man whom she would refer to as 'her love' until the day she died. She had sobbed as she spoke of little Thibaut's birth and of her sacrifice as a mother, as a woman, insisting that she had never once regretted it, convinced as she was that by taking the veil she had saved her child from a mortal illness. She had told the extern sister that her greatest wish was to have news of her son.

Jeanne d'Amblin, a little bemused, scoured her memory for

traces of the old Jeanne d'Amblin but found none. What had become of her?

Had she visited Fleury, near Malassis, on one of her rounds out of compassion for poor Yolande, or was she already hatching a plot? The extern sister could not remember. What did it matter in the end? The part of her that had died would never come back. Three years ago, Jeanne had tentatively approached Isidore de Fleury, the father of one of her fellow prisoners – as she liked to refer to them. The ruthless old tyrant whom the young sister in charge of the granary had described was already in decline. He was vaguely aware that death was approaching. On the pretext of brightening up his life Jeanne had gradually ensconced herself, made herself indispensable, become gradually more affectionate. The old despot had everything that she wanted: he was rich, remarkably credulous when humoured, and above all he had one foot in the grave. Jeanne had also exercised her talent for making herself liked on Thibaut. The stout, ominous walls of the vast manor house appeared to have crushed the life out of the sweet young boy. He had become a silent ghost, vanishing into the shadows, disappearing from sight in order to avoid vexing his grandfather. When it was time for her to leave, he would cling to her white robe and earnestly enquire whether it was true that all nuns became angels. She had eluded his question a hundred times before deciding to answer him:

'Indeed I hope not, dear Thibaut. For, you see, there is nothing more tedious than the life of angels.'

'When will you be coming back, Madame?'

'As soon as I can, dear child.'

She had been fond of the little boy, who only needed an occasional smile, a sunny garden and a modicum of attention in order to come alive again – all things that his strict grandfather was unable to give him.

The months that followed showed that human intransigence

applies above all where others are concerned. Isidore de Fleury had begun to talk about his own death, his belated regrets, punishment and reward. For the first time since they had met he mentioned his daughter's name:

'Perhaps I was too hard on Yolande, with whom you are acquainted. What have I left now that I am an old man riddled with arthritis? A grandson who is certainly a good boy, but whose constant presence annoys me. Yes, I was too inflexible. Now I have reached an age when a younger woman's presence would brighten up my life. And what would become of Thibaut if anything were to happen to me? His mother would come back and run the estate. And yet I fear that too. Yolande is a slip of a girl and not well suited to serious and laborious tasks. You see, dear Jeanne, it is unthinkable that that rascal whom she fell for, that scoundrel who bedded her like a vulgar servant girl, should lay his hands on one penny of my property!'

Not knowing where the words came from, Jeanne had heard herself blurt out sorrowfully, tears in her eyes:

'So, it is as I feared. You know nothing.'

'What don't I know?'

'Yolande died a year ago this winter, from pneumonia. She did not wish you to be informed. How I hate myself for being the bearer of this terrible news.'

He had stared at her as if she were speaking a foreign tongue.

Jeanne had hurriedly thrust home her advantage:

'You are so wrong, my good friend. You paint an unflattering and unjust portrait of yourself. What Yolande did was a terrible sin. As a righteous father, concerned for the future of his only child, you chased off the wretch who robbed her of her purity. If you want to know what I really think – and God knows it is difficult for me to criticise a dead sister – now that I know you better I am shocked by her harsh judgement of you.'

'Harsh?'

'The words she used to describe you could scarcely have been more cruel, more hateful even ... to the point where I became convinced that you were an unfeeling monster.'

'As extreme as that?' he had asked, turning pale.

'Dear God, forgive me for being the harbinger of this dreadful truth.'

Isidore remained silent, then reached out his hand and sighed:

'No. You have done the right thing. Old age makes us soft. And there was I trying to find excuses for her, tormenting myself with the idea that I had been cruel. Do you realise, my dear, that all I have left is that mischievous little Thibaut. For make no mistake, I am fond of the boy ... But childhood is a distant memory to me now, and I am no longer habituated to it.'

'In truth I find him so delightful that I regret having taken the veil, which prohibits me from bearing children.'

After a very short time, and even less effort, Jeanne had become 'darling', 'my sweet', 'my ray of sunshine'. She in turn had managed 'my foolish old Isidore', 'my secret lover', 'my fearsome lion'. Curiously, Monsieur de Fleury did not find these silly pet names ridiculous in the slightest. As for their physical contact, it was so infrequent, swift and undemanding that the extern sister scarcely felt that she was sinning. On the other hand, it seemed to please him. Indeed, she had cleverly manipulated the situation so that the old man could not fail to accept her reasoning. She was still young enough to be attractive to him, and to care for a small boy as well as an old man. Moreover, the years the extern sister had spent in the convent appeared to mollify Isidore de Fleury – as though they offered him some guarantee of a piece of paradise, which he did not necessarily believe he deserved. After all, Jeanne had long been in God's good graces. Thus she became his promise of entry into Eden. She was familiar with the rituals and obligations and would be a boon in helping him on his upward struggle. And so a wedding date was fixed. The notary was to draw up a contract whereby Jeanne would retain the usufruct of Monsieur de Fleury's property after his death, in return for caring for Thibaut and bequeathing his grandfather's estate to him.

Resignation had disintegrated. Resignation was no more than a hideous mask, a second skin that had been smothering her for all those years. At long last Jeanne was going to live the life she deserved.

And then that old fool had gone and died only a few weeks before the wedding. Suddenly the bottom had fallen out of the brilliant plan she had brooded over for nights on end in the seclusion of her cell – envisaging her disappearance from the abbey to be reborn as the second Madame de Fleury, leaving nothing behind but her detested white robes. That despicable old fool! How could he have played such a wicked trick on her! May he rot in hell!

Once again Jeanne had found herself with no money, no future and no life. But now she was unwilling to accept her fate. She had never again set foot in Fleury, and had only later found out that Thibaut had succumbed to a fever. Yolande had not been informed because she was believed to be dead, and Jeanne had made sure that her fellow prisoner never found out. And why not be honest: the thought of the young sister in charge of the granary inheriting her wicked father's property, which should have come to her through marriage, rankled with Jeanne. Moreover, she did not want Yolande to learn of her true relationship with Isidore from the servants at Fleury. And so she had continued to lie to the woman who considered her a friend, bringing her comforting news of the dead little Thibaut from her rounds. No doubt she also derived a perverse pleasure from the shocking deception and the power it gave her over the other woman.

*

The sound of a heavy trunk closing brought Jeanne back to the present, to the here and now. She struggled to regain her composure. She was in desperate need of it. The confrontation was about to begin. The door opened and Aude de Neyrat emerged, majestic, preceded by a hint of musk, quite inappropriate for an abbess.

'My dear ... what a pleasure to see you again so soon.' Madame de Neyrat's luminous smile suddenly faded. 'Ah, ah ... I see, still no trace of the manuscripts.'

'Does that really surprise you? I can scarcely credit it.'

'Whatever do you mean?' simpered Aude, feigning awkwardness.

Jeanne's heart began to pound. This would be a close match, and she must on no account allow Madame de Neyrat to sense her unease. She forced herself to adopt an even tone, mirroring the amused expression that appeared never to leave her opponent's face – although it could not have reflected less what Jeanne was feeling.

'Please, save these games for others. Perhaps you were unaware that a couple of brigands were lying in wait ready to snatch them from me?'

'That is a grave accusation, daughter.'

'And one that is entirely justified, Reverend Mother.'

'However, you must agree that it was a cunning plan. It saved me having to pay you, for you are becoming increasingly greedy, my dear.'

'Greed rarely diminishes. On the contrary, it has an infuriating habit of growing ... at the slightest provocation.'

Aude de Neyrat perceived the innuendo although she did not grasp its full meaning. She asked in a soft voice:

'What are you saying?'

Jeanne drew in her breath, fearful of stumbling over her words and instantly betraying the extent of her anxiety to her enemy.

'That my joy at having narrowly escaped summary execution has only increased my appetite. And that no expense should be spared when hiring cut-throats. What I wouldn't have given to see their faces when they tore off the covering only to discover a pile of boards!'

The Abbess's perfect face froze, her mouth set in an angry line. The emerald-green eyes lost their sparkle. For the first time since their meeting at the baths in Rue du Bienfait, Jeanne felt the exhilaration of imminent victory. She felt renewed courage. She could get the better of the beautiful monster.

'Have I upset you? Oh I dearly hope not, Reverend Mother. However, rest assured – the manuscripts are not lost but remain in my safekeeping,' Jeanne declared with deliberate irony. 'Let us concern ourselves not with your contentment but with that of "our mutual friend" the Italian. How much do you suppose it is worth?'

Aude de Neyrat passed her tongue over her lips and hissed:

'You were told the figure. Two hundred pounds, a very generous sum.'

Jeanne was thoroughly enjoying herself. The other woman had finally lost her air of superiority.

'Not enough. Not nearly enough, considering that this will be my final mission.'

'How much?'

'You sound so bitter. I would have liked a little more civility from you.'

Madame de Neyrat lowered her head. When she raised it again, the change was subtle yet unnerving. Her features were set in an expression of implacable hardness. Despite her delight at taunting her opponent and pay mistress, Jeanne suddenly felt that the game had gone on long enough and she must put a stop to it.

'Let me see. How about doubling that?'

'Good heavens!'

'I think the manuscripts are worth that much to you. However, I can always look for another buyer.'

'Do not threaten me, Jeanne. I dislike being threatened.'

The extern sister, surprised by this use of her Christian name, went on:

'You will provide me with one of your sumptuous dresses and a coat. I will change in your chamber, then fetch the manuscripts together with a few of my personal effects,' she added, thinking of her hoard of money. 'We will then travel together by wagon as far as Bellême, where we will make the exchange. I will then disappear.'

Aude de Neyrat, a wily predator accustomed to every type of ruse, had noticed Jeanne's eyes wandering involuntarily over to the sideboard. She mentally congratulated the extern sister; such a hiding place would never have occurred to her.

'Only ... I do not have four hundred pounds here.'

'Come, Madame!'

'Very well.'

'Do you accept?'

'Have I any choice?'

'I think not.'

'In which case, I accept with good grace. You may choose any dress you like from my trunk, good woman. One of my loveliest, made of heavy Genovese silk, is laid out on the bed. A crimson robe that should favour your complexion.'

She led Jeanne d'Amblin into her chamber and pointed with a nervous gesture at the garment. The gown with its squirrel-skin trim was so sumptuous that it took Jeanne's breath away. She reached out to touch it, but a sudden instinct stopped her. She swung round to face the Abbess and said sharply:

'I've been told of the devastating effects of certain poisons that work through contact, disfiguring their victims and leading to an agonisingly slow death.'

A smile flashed across Madame de Neyrat's face and she remarked:

'If I were thinking of dispatching you prematurely to a so-called better world, would I not wait until I was in possession of the manuscripts? Still, you are right, one cannot be too careful nowadays.'

She picked up the precious silk garment and buried her face in it before handing it to Jeanne.

'I hope that my little demonstration has put your mind at rest.'

'Yes. May I have a few moments alone in order to dress?'

'Of course, what was I thinking? Forgive me. Call me when you have it on. There's a coat lined with lynx fur in that trunk over there which you should find suitable,' the Abbess suggested. 'Oh, I forgot to tell you that the dress is laced at the back and fastened with two gold pins, in the Italian style. As for the flared sleeves, they're the height of fashion. And look ...' Madame de Neyrat went on, showing her the shoulders. 'They, too, are cleverly fastened with two silver pins, allowing us to change our appearance as we please without destroying the garment.[56] Ah, and this,' Aude said rapturously as she pulled out a tall round bonnet from one of the trunks. 'The best-dressed Italian women swear only by this turret hat, which sets off the veil admirably and will cover your shaven head. Admittedly, it is still a little daring for our beautiful yet austere realm. However, I believe it will soon become fashionable.'[57]

'I ... I haven't had my head shaved for a long time,' Jeanne confessed awkwardly. 'My hair has finally grown back.'

'A woman with foresight,' Aude chuckled as she left the chamber.

Jeanne felt the weight of the sumptuous fabric. A childlike joy made her want to dance. In a few hours from now she would be rich, and for the first time in her life she was going to wear clothes fit for a princess. At last, the world was her oyster. People would nod respectfully as they passed her in the street, children would bow and curtsey before her. When she appeared, conversations would cease. She was no beauty like Madame de Neyrat, but she was attractive and slim and such finery would render even the most ungainly creature elegant. She slipped out of the hated robe. She felt a shiver of delight as her fingers caressed the fine embroidery in gold thread running up the sleeves. Dear God ... a lynx fur coat ...

Jeanne twisted around in a vain attempt to fasten the back of the dress and the sleeves. Desperate, she called out to Madame de Neyrat. Her frustration was short-lived; was it not a delight to have this arrogant female serve her, however briefly?

Madame de Neyrat complied in the most natural way. She pulled the sleeves up to her shoulders and fastened them. Then she walked behind Jeanne to lace up the back of the dress. A shiver of fear now ran up the extern sister's spine. Fiddlesticks. The camerlingo's Abbess wouldn't stab her in the back − not before she had the manuscripts. And yet a sharp pain made her cry out and leap forward.

She swung round to face the other woman, ready to pounce on her and seize her dagger or stiletto.

Madame de Neyrat's face had turned white as a sheet, and the only weapon she was holding was one of the long pointed collar pins, stained with blood. She stammered:

'God in heaven ... I apologise for such clumsiness. These pins are dangerous! Here, let me take a look.'

Now that her fear had subsided Jeanne felt a sharp pain reaching down to her shoulder blades. A trickle of warm blood ran down her back. Had she done it deliberately? Why?

'It's a nasty gash, my dear. Will you ever forgive me? We must treat the wound at once. I have just the thing,' declared Madame de Neyrat, rummaging through a small cedarwood chest under one of the windows. 'This ointment was brought to me from Asia. It both disinfects wounds and helps them to heal more quickly. It might sting a little when applied, but any discomfort is momentary.'

She opened the small spherical seal on the glass phial, making as if to dress the wound that was causing Jeanne to grimace. The extern sister backed away.

'Don't come near me.'

'I only want to help you, to soothe the pain.'

Jeanne d'Amblin stared suspiciously at the phial.

'Oh, surely you don't think that I intend to poison you? Look, this should put your mind at rest. Come over here.'

The extern sister did as she said. Aude de Neyrat tipped the phial into her open palm. A trickle of glutinous liquid, like egg white, formed a small pool in her hand.

'As you can see, I'm still alive. Let's continue the experiment.'

She leant over, appearing to pause for a split second, a strange look of glee on her face. Then she closed her eyes and lapped at the balm before bursting out laughing:

'Good Lord, what a revolting taste! I only hope it doesn't give me a stomach ache. Well? Do you prefer infection leading to possible gangrene – for the gash is a deep one – or will you allow me to treat your wound? What a clumsy servant I would make … I'd be dismissed on my first day!'

Reassured, despite an instinctive mistrust of the other woman's concern, Jeanne yielded. The cold salve on her skin made her come out in goose pimples, but it didn't sting as she had been expecting. Madame de Neyrat finished lacing up the crimson dress, humming softly to herself. She placed the turret hat on Jeanne's head and took the magnificent lynx fur coat out of the second trunk.

She stepped back, tilting her head to one side to assess her efforts, and announced:

'You look simply dazzling! Now turn round, please, so that I can see the back.'

Jeanne turned. She stumbled and had to prop herself up against the wall. Her head was spinning and the furniture in the room was pitching. An intolerable wave of nausea made her double up and she vomited a salty, bitter liquid. She reached out to Madame de Neyrat, screaming:

'Devil!'

The other woman leapt aside deftly and hurried into the adjoining study, laughing:

'That makes two of us, then, doesn't it?'

Jeanne managed to stagger after her, using the walls to steady herself. The front of her beautiful red dress was by now drenched with vomit. How? What trickery had enabled Madame de Neyrat to touch, even swallow the poison without any ill effect while she felt as though her heart were about to burst out of her chest? An antidote. The fiend had taken the antidote beforehand. And Jeanne felt death closing around her, touching her, stroking her brow. Racked by painful spasms, she slumped to her knees, imploring:

'Keep the money. Give me the antidote and I'll give you the manuscripts.'

Madame de Neyrat pointed to the heavy sideboard containing the registers and teased:

'Do you mean the ones hidden in that cabinet? I had a look while you were dressing and found a large package wrapped in linen. It's very kind of you, but a little late, I think. Besides, I'm sorry to have to tell you that there is no antidote to this tree poison.'

'But you … you …'

'Thanks to you I was able to experience a delicious thrill. I was informed that this otherwise lethal poison is quite harmless to the touch or when swallowed. However, I was not entirely certain, and I confess that I was so excited that my heart beat faster for a few delightful moments. There is nothing more exhilarating than defying death. A most intoxicating feeling. Now, what else did I learn that might be of interest to you? Oh yes, I remember, this relentless poison is extracted from a magnificent, sturdy tree called the ako,[58] which grows in Africa and Asia. Its leaves are round and its bark is used to make clothes. Only the sap is poisonous. The indigenous Indians coat their arrow tips with it. One arrow is enough to kill a buffalo in a few long and painful minutes, approximately twenty, or so I'm told. The curious and invaluable property of this poison is that it is harmless to the touch or when swallowed. However, it becomes fatal when it enters the bloodstream – through a wound, for example. You poor woman, the convulsions will soon grow worse, you'll have difficulty breathing, your heart will beat wildly … and then stop.'

Madame de Neyrat groaned apologetically:

'I do dislike watching people die, you see. The only death I really enjoyed was that of my uncle … My excuse is that I was very young! At the risk of appearing cowardly, I think I will leave you for a while and pretend to go about my duties as Abbess. I shall come back when you … when you are no more.'

'I beg you,' gulped Jeanne. 'Anne— Annelette … send … for her,' she managed to splutter between two gasps.

'Oh, she can do nothing to help you,' Madame de Neyrat appeared to lament.

'My soul … the next world …'

'You are an optimist, my dear. Do you really believe that your soul can be cleansed? And if your aim is to denounce me, I doubt anything you could say would come as a surprise to our peevish apothecary. However, I am magnanimous in victory and will soon be shedding this white robe. Let us show clemency! I'll send for her. Try to hold out until she arrives. But first of all I must take the precious manuscripts with me.'

She took the three volumes wrapped in a piece of creased linen from their hiding place and pressed them to her, sighing as she stroked them.

She left the room without a backward glance at the dying woman. Honorius would be pleased. He would retrieve the much coveted works and at the same time be rid of the shady executioner who had become a nuisance to him. As for her, she was happy to have repaid part of her debt to the camerlingo. The rest would come shortly, when the minor noblewoman Souarcy and her little servant boy had been dispatched to a world where Aude, a compassionate killer, hoped they would be happier. Three henchmen, handsomely remunerated, were awaiting the ideal moment to put an end to their worldly travails. The chief bailiff Monge de Brineux's men would conclude that they had been attacked by brigands. Madame de Neyrat's orders had been clear and adroitly peppered with threats in the event of failure.

Annelette hurried to the study. Jeanne's face was bathed in sweat and contorted with pain. She was pressing both fists into her sternum to try to calm the convulsions racking her body, and wailing like a baby in between fits of vomiting that filled her mouth with a bloody saliva that ran down her cheeks and neck.

The apothecary bent over the dying woman, who spoke with difficulty:

'Aude … it was she …'

'What do you mean it was she? She who poisoned Adélaïde, Hedwige, Yolande, our Reverend Mother and the papal emissaries?'

'No,' Jeanne croaked, shaking her head.

'No, indeed, since it was you. Do you mean that she has poisoned you?'

'Yes ...'

'Then she is not all bad, and can even be useful. I hate you, you snake. How could you? I don't know what poison she used and frankly ... I don't care.'

'Bless ...'

'Bless you? That is not for me to do.'

Annelette stood up and walked out. Jeanne's last cry did not cause her to jump. She closed the heavy door behind her.

The extern sister's corpse was swiftly removed from Madame de Neyrat's chambers and laid out in the stables.

Aude de Neyrat went back into her chamber shortly afterwards in order to prepare for what she hoped would be her imminent departure. She carefully put down on the bed the bulky package she had held on to tightly while Jeanne d'Amblin's unsightly corpse was being removed from her study. She sat down beside it and untied the binding holding the cloth in place. She examined the titles: *Collectiones* by Guillaume de Saint-Amour,[59] an obsolete canon; *L'Architrenius*, a lengthy allegorical lament penned by the Latin poet Jean de Hanville in about 1184, which had earned him more popularity than acclaim; and finally an illustrated work expounding the various techniques of trictrac and chess by Nicole de Saint-Nicolas, probably dating from the twelfth century. Madame de Neyrat leapt to her feet and exploded with rage:

'Wretch! Burn in hell! How dare you play such a trick on me!'

Her incisive mind did not spare her; she had made an unpardonable mistake by failing to examine the contents of the package before killing the extern sister. And yet one thing became immediately apparent. Jeanne had known nothing of the substitution otherwise she would have offered the manuscripts and not money in exchange for the nonexistent antidote. Who then? Of course, Annelette Beaupré! Aude de Neyrat charged over to the herbarium, certain she would find the apothecary there.

She burst in and pulled up a yard short of the tip of a stiletto. 'Don't move or come any closer, Madame, or I will not hesitate to send you straight back to where you came from.'

'Do you mean hell? Don't be so melodramatic! We are both intelligent women – or at least I sincerely hope that we are.'

'I'm not familiar with every type of poison, it is true, including the one you used to get rid of Jeanne d'Amblin. However, I know all the different ways they can be administered.'

'Do you suppose that I would poison you and make the same mistake twice in such a short space of time? Do you take me for a fool? I want the manuscripts. Name your price. Don't try to fool me, I know you have them.'

'I don't.'

'You're lying,' Madame de Neyrat said, growing impatient.

'No.'

'No?' she repeated, unsure now.

Annelette explained in an almost amiable voice:

'The manuscripts left the abbey some hours ago, thanks to your lifting of the restriction, for which I am eternally grateful, Madame. They are as we speak making their way in great haste towards their rightful owner. Afterwards, my messenger has instructions to deliver a brief missive to Messire Monge de Brineux, the Comte d'Authon's chief bailiff. In it I have recounted the circumstances surrounding your unexpected arrival at Clairets. If I am not mistaken, Messire de Brineux should arrive here with his men-at-arms tonight or early tomorrow morning. It is up to you to decide whether you wish to be here to welcome him.'

Madame de Neyrat pressed her full lips together before giving a broad, languorous smile:

'I was right: we are both intelligent women. And intelligence also means knowing when one is defeated and facing up to the consequences. I think I will have to forgo the pleasure of meeting Monsieur de Brineux. I shall see you again, my dear.'

'I doubt it.'

'Who knows?'

Annelette Beaupré and Berthe de Marchiennes argued at length before reaching an agreement. Blanche de Blinot had not been consulted because Annelette feared the old lady would become tearful and start rambling. Jeanne d'Amblin's remains were thus buried in unconsecrated ground outside the abbey enclosure, which was the fate of witches and poisoners. Some of the nuns, shocked by Annelette's revelations, insisted on accompanying their extern sister to her final resting place. Few looked up to watch the large covered wagon bearing Madame de Neyrat and her trunks away.

Louvière Forest, Perche, December 1304

A strange urgency had driven Agnès. A sudden anxiety had sent her running to her chamber. She had dressed warmly and without thinking had reached for her short sword, fastening the scabbard to her belt. She had called one of the farm hands and told him to saddle Églantine as fast as possible. The young man had looked at her with surprise and murmured:

'It'll soon be nightfall, Madame. It's not a good idea.'

'Saddle her up this instant!' she had snapped, each wasted moment increasing her anxiety.

She had been riding for a good half-hour. Her fury was beginning to give way to alarm. The fool, the little idiot! Thank heaven Gilbert the Simpleton had told her where he'd gone. What on earth had possessed Clément to go to La Haute-Gravière alone and without his crossbow? What was he planning to do there? Collect more soil samples? It made no sense to take a short cut through the Louvière woods in order to save himself a mile on foot when he could have taken a horse. If only the knight Leone had come back, she could have asked him to escort her. No matter. All the same, she felt nervous. The waning light cast strange and menacing shadows in the undergrowth and the trees towered up like the tines of a harrow.

A thick blanket of snow had fallen, covering all the landmarks that might help those journeying on foot to find their way back. It would soon be pitch dark. It was that time of year when night was quick to swallow up the remains of the day.

Agnès shivered with cold, despite her long cloak lined with otter-skin that was beginning to wear thin – a gift from her deceased husband – and her woollen dress. She reflected that the complete stillness seemed almost unreal. No rustle of leaves, no patter of animal feet running as she approached, only the rhythmic crunch of the powdery snow under Églantine's measured but steady gait. The young woman looked around for any sign of Clément's having passed that way. All of a sudden, the mare pulled her head up abruptly and breathed out loudly through her mouth. Agnès stiffened, pushing aside with an automatic gesture the flap of her cloak covering the short sword that hung from the belt tied around her robe. She calmed her horse with a whisper and squeezed with her leg to make it walk on. For a moment she regretted having ridden side-saddle, for she would be at a disadvantage against a rider sitting astride his horse. Even so, if she had to flee, Agnès was a good enough horsewoman not to be thrown. But Églantine could not hold her own at a gallop against a gelding crossed with an Arab – a much lighter breed – and still less against a destrier. She was letting her imagination run away with her. She chided herself. She must remain calm. She was simply looking for Clément. When she found him, she would give him a proper telling-off, and remind him that he was not to stray so far from the manor at dusk without letting her know. What on earth had come over him? He was usually so thoughtful.

She heard the echo of voices before she saw two, no, three men some seventy yards ahead of her. Her irritation instantly dissolved and she was seized with panic. Judging from their filthy rags, they were brigands – the sort of cut-throats you'd expect to encounter in the forest. And yet she was assailed by doubt when she heard one of them cry out to his fellow henchmen:

'Show no mercy, gentlemen. Our orders are to take no prisoners.'

The tone, the wording, belied her initial impression. These were no ordinary brigands. She pulled up the reins in order to turn back before they saw her. It was then that she noticed, behind the semicircle formed by the three men, the terrified face, the small figure backing slowly into the undergrowth, hunched as though preparing to make a dash for it. Clément.

Agnès's throat went dry. She remained motionless for a few seconds, unable to think.

Suddenly, Clément, who had only just seen her a few dozen yards behind his assailants, screamed out in a piercing voice:

'Run! Run, Madame, it's a trap!'

The mare, alarmed by the cries and by the fear she could sense in her rider, whinnied and pawed the ground nervously.

Agnès whispered in a voice trembling with fear:

'Steady, girl, steady, girl,' and then with as much bravado as she could muster, she shouted at the brigands: 'Let the child go this instant. That's an order!'

They turned as one. Agnès saw the astonishment on their faces and decided to thrust home her feeble advantage. She went on in a strident voice:

'The boy is my servant. He belongs to my household. If you should persist, you will be executed. I will demand it of the chief bailiff. That goes for all three of you. You will be hanged from the gallows then quartered and left for the vultures to pick over.'

The brigands looked at one another. Agnès made Églantine walk on a few paces. Clément shook his head and sobbed:

'Don't come any nearer, I beg you! They're going to kill you too. They're …'

'Shut your mouth, lad!' bawled the one who looked like the ringleader before remarking to the others:

'We're in luck. It's the lady of Souarcy. She's walked straight into our hands. I'll take care of her. You finish off the boy and make sure you're quick about it!'

Agnès felt the world stand still for what seemed like an eternity. What happened next was total chaos. She watched the man stride towards her. She saw him brandishing a hunting knife. She saw the other two move in on Clément. She saw the young boy narrowly avoid tripping over a tree stump. Without knowing exactly what she was doing or being aware of the sequence of her actions, she kicked off her shoe, wound the double strap of the stirrup leather tightly around her left thigh and slipped her bare foot through the stirrup. Then she secured her right leg by sliding it under the strap of the breastplate around the animal's neck, and gripped the raised pommel with the back of her knee. She would use the reins to command the animal. Églantine grew calm, sensing from the renewed confidence and rapid precision of her rider's gestures that she was once again in command. The man came to a halt, grinning, delighted by what he took to be a cowardly retreat when in fact Agnès was preparing her steed to charge. When she was about forty yards from him, the young woman struck the mare sharply on its hindquarters at which it broke into a gallop. She urged it on with a cry. The ground shuddered beneath the ton of hurtling muscle, and the percheron's powerful hooves ripped up clods of frozen earth. Raising herself slightly in the saddle, Agnès drew her short sword with her left hand while controlling the horse with her right and urging it on vociferously. The mare bore down on the brigand, gathering pace under its own momentum:

'Charge, my beauty, charge!' cried Agnès.

The killer's eyes grew wide with fright. For a split second he appeared rooted to the spot. He turned and shouted something to his accomplices which Agnès, deafened by the stampede of the maned colossus, was unable to hear. He tried to flee but the horse was already upon him. All Agnès saw was an open mouth. All she felt was the feeble resistance of human flesh and bone being trampled under the iron-shod hooves as they thundered towards the clearing.

Agnès could hear the horse's uneven, almost laboured breath and she coaxed her steed:

'Go on, Églantine, go on. Don't stop now! Please go on, just a little further!'

She spurred the animal on with her leg and her voice.

Clément was crawling backwards along the ground in a desperate attempt to escape from his killers. Agnès saw. She saw their knives, glinting mercilessly, threatening the child. However, the two scoundrels, unnerved by the scene they had just witnessed at close hand and by their companion's trampled corpse, hesitated a fraction of a second too long. A fraction of a second in which Agnès's mind went blank. She swerved to the left, her body level with the saddle flap, held on only by the stirrup strap now cutting into her left thigh and by her right knee. She urged the mare on towards the brigand who was nearest to Clément. For a moment she thought she would hit him head on. All she felt was the sword jarring her fingers. The man slumped to his knees, his hands clasping his neck, which was oozing blood. Agnès managed to regain her balance in time to pull up her horse, which was in danger of going out of control from sheer exhaustion and the frenzy of the charge. She veered over towards the clearing. The third wretch had fled, leaving Clément sobbing on the ground, his head in his hands. She made Églantine walk on a little, whispering softly and patting the mare's sturdy neck, which was ringed with white lines, then walked back towards the young boy. When she dismounted, sliding down the dark, quivering flank, she thought her legs would give way. She looked away from the man she had just killed and tried to stop shaking. She felt paralysed by an overwhelming fatigue. She forced herself to walk over to Clément. He looked up at her, his face wet with tears, and wailed:

'You killed him. You killed him to save my life! You saved my life …'

She heard herself reply in a calm voice she barely recognised as her own:

'And I would do it again if necessary.'

The enormity of her words shocked her less than their absolute sincerity. She went on:

'They were no ordinary robbers, were they?'

'No. I thought so at first, but their mission – for it clearly was a mission – was to execute us both.'

'Then hurry,' she interrupted. 'We must return to Souarcy immediately. I fear the third accomplice may have gone to fetch reinforcements. Quick, Clément! Get up at once. There is no time to lose. As for your tears, they will have to wait. Get up this instant!'

Agnès walked over to the mare and leant her brow against its neck. She could feel the blood pulsing through the animal's powerful veins tickle her skin. Her mind went blank until the boy came up behind her. She heard a faltering voice whisper:

'Your sword, Madame. I pulled it from his throat and wiped it clean as best I could on … well, on his surcoat.'

She mumbled, exhausted:

'I will say a special prayer tonight. It is the custom the first time a sword is stained with blood. Please help me to mount. My legs feel weak.'

He pushed her up as best he could. Agnès managed to sit in the saddle and then haul him up beside her. He murmured:

'I love you so very much, Madame. Was it not a miracle that brought us together?'

'I love you, too, my sweet child. And no, it was not a miracle. Love is the only eternal miracle. The pity of it is … the pity of it is that we so often forget. Let us be away.'

They did not speak during the first mile of their journey back to Souarcy. Agnès feverishly tried to recall the scene that had just taken place in which two men had lost their lives, in which she had killed twice – but she was unable to. A jumble of images, sounds and sensations flashed through her mind. A mouth wide open, a violent blow to her knuckles, the intolerable pressure of the strap cutting into her thigh, the hollow sound of a body being crushed, her exhaustion as she dismounted. Nothing more. So very little. She was gripped by a strange anxiety. Had she turned into such a monster that these two men's deaths left no lasting impression on her, no pain or remorse? Why not admit that a fit of sobbing or an attack of nerves would have reassured her. And yet her eyes were dry. And as for nerves, she felt completely calm.

She heard herself demand sharply:

'What were you doing going to La Haute-Gravière alone and so late? Your casual attitude is irresponsible, Clément. It isn't like you to be so careless.'

He tried feebly to protest: 'It was a trap, Madame.'

'And what difference does that make? You only fell into it because you left the manor. Those rogues would surely not have been reckless or foolish enough to have gone searching for you there.'

'You are right. And to think that I led you into it too! Oh dear God … if anything had happened to you on account of me …'

She felt his body quiver and regretted her harshness. 'That is not the reason I am upset. Whatever possessed you to do such a thing?'

Clément's shame and retrospective fear gave way to exhilaration. He ventured timidly:

'Oh, Madame, if you only knew … I needed some time alone … The knight would have found me if I had hidden in the outbuildings or even in the eaves. It was the only place I could think of. The calculations are more difficult than I had anticipated … even with the help of the precious information taken from the Vallombroso treatise.'

'What on earth are you talking about?'

'About the second birth chart – the one I copied onto the page I took out of the notebook.'

Agnès grew tense, her curiosity vying with her unease:

'Have you unveiled its secrets?' she whispered despite being surrounded only by thick forest.

'Yes. I went back over my calculations a hundred times, in disbelief. For, unless I've made a terrible mistake, the second person was born on the night of 28 December 1294.'

'God Almighty,' breathed Agnès. 'Why does that not surprise me?'

'Was there a lunar eclipse, Madame?'

'A lunar eclipse? No, at least I don't think so. It was on the night of my birth that the moon all but disappeared. On the other hand, the sun was completely swallowed up for a few seconds just before you were born. An eerie darkness fell. I remember the wild look in the dogs' eyes, their muzzles raised to the sky. One of them growled and put his hackles up and they shrank back, yelping, and lay close together on the ground. Then daylight returned. Many people saw it as a clear omen that the end of the world was nigh. I confess that I thought so too.'

She paused. She had seen it as a sign that the world was ending and that her death was imminent. And, indeed, Sybille had died that night. As for Agnès, had it not been for her nurse Gisèle's obstinacy, she too would have died.

'Eclipses are natural phenomena, admirably explained in Vallombroso's treatise. If the planets travel in the firmament, it is inevitable that their paths occasionally cross, obscuring their luminosity. It has nothing whatsoever to do with curses or omens.'

'I believed it did. I was very young. The winter was so harsh that everybody thought it was a punishment from God. My husband Hugues had just died and ... in short, we had been living for weeks in fear of a final cataclysm.'

Clément was silent for a few seconds before continuing: 'Why are you not surprised, Madame? Do you really think the second birth chart refers to me?'

'I'd stake my life on it.'

'But I'm not the only person born on the night of 28 December 1294.'

'That is true. However, the first chart appears to refer to me.'

'What is the connection? I confess that it fills me with joy, yet I am at a loss to understand why I was born here at Souarcy, by your side, when I could have been born anywhere else or not born at all, given that my mother died during my delivery.'

'I sense that our two lives are linked through a series of coincidences, each one stranger than the next,' Agnès observed, before changing the subject. 'Clément ... Monsieur de Leone wishes to talk to you about a mission he wants you to carry out. That is all I know. If it puts you in any danger, I demand that you refuse, do you understand? Regardless of your extraordinary intelligence and courage, which make me so proud of you, remember that you are only disguised as a boy. Men are stronger than us.'

'We are faster and more agile.'

'More agile, yes, though I'm not so sure we are faster. However, men are more suited to fighting. Perhaps it is by dint of the education girls receive, which I have tried to spare you. Perhaps it is in our very nature as women. In any event ...'

'And yet you fought like a man in the forest, sword at the ready.'

'No. I fought like a woman, indisputably. My first instinct was to flee, while I still thought it possible. There is no dishonour attached to a woman fleeing from conflict. That is how it is. I attacked only after I had seen you. Fear for a loved one, rage against whoever means him harm makes the female of the species more formidable than the male.' Suddenly she declared: 'Don't think you can evade the issue by changing the subject as is your wont. Did you hear what I said about your forthcoming meeting with the knight?'

'I heard you, Madame. It will be as you wish.'

Agnès appeared to hesitate. When she finally spoke, he turned to look at her, aghast:

'Clément, the moment we arrive I want you to go to the chapel and burn the page where your name is mentioned in the register of births and deaths.'

'Madame … ! You …'

'It is an order and not open to discussion, Clément.'

'Very well, Madame.'

They remained silent until they reached Manoir de Souarcy.

Gilbert the Simpleton ran with a lumbering gait towards them, his face contorted with worry.

'My good fairy … It's almost dark! I didn't know where to start looking for you. You're so pale, my lady. What is it?'

As was his custom, he lifted Agnès out of her saddle and his eye fell upon the short sword stained with dried blood.

'Oooh … a scuffle!' Gilbert's jaw clenched so tightly the muscles showed. Suddenly angry, he demanded:

'Where are they? I'll make them eat their teeth!'

He wrapped his broad left hand round his right fist, cracking his joints.

'Two of them are dead, Gilbert. The third got away.'

'Three? Against one fairy?'

Panic-stricken, he twirled her round roughly, making sure that she was not wounded.

'I am unharmed. Églantine was very brave. Take good care of her please, dear Gilbert.'

She tousled the fearsome yet good-natured giant's unruly mop of hair. He instantly calmed down, forgetting his rage and thirst for blood of a moment ago, and purred with contentment.

Clément had not uttered a word. After Gilbert led the mare away, he murmured in a faltering voice:

'Are you all right, Madame?'

'I'm not sure. I scarcely recognise myself. Should I not be eaten up with remorse and regret? I have the strangest sensation that what happened in the forest … how can I describe it … has nothing to do with me. That it is … apart from me.'

'Perhaps it is because of the violent nature of the encounter. You are not a murderer, Madame.'

She smiled feebly:

'Really? And how do you account for the two corpses I left behind?'

'That was legitimate self-defence. You did everything in your power to save us from the hands of what I am certain were hired killers. Nothing more.'

'You are probably right,' she agreed. 'However, I doubt that I will convince myself of it so easily. Come, the knight will be waiting. Go at once to the chapel and do as I asked. Then and only then can you join the knight. I am going up to my chamber to change. These clothes … I cannot bring myself to wear them tonight. I will join you presently. Don't forget your promise, Clément.

Seated on one of the stout crockery chests, the mastiffs lying at his feet, the knight Leone waited calmly, watching the furious flames devour the infamous work on necromancy written by a certain Justus. Next to him lay the creased linen covering. He had discovered the package a little earlier on top of the bale of straw where he had left the bundle containing his scant belongings. The much coveted manuscripts. He had adroitly questioned the two farm hands who were clearing the courtyard of snow that had become compacted and slippery with the comings and goings of animals and carts. The two young men had been glad of a moment's conversation, enabling them to rest their backs and relax in pleasant company, and they willingly answered the Hospitaller's questions. According to them, no stranger had visited the manor that day. Leone wondered for a moment whether the shadow that had slipped unseen into the barn in order to return the volumes to him had not also slain Archambaud d'Arville before he could kill the drugged knight. He raised his head as Clément, who had entered the room, all but roared upon seeing the large notebook with the ugly purple cover:

'The manuscripts!'

'Yes. I found them when I returned to the barn a moment ago. The messenger – or whoever it was – slipped in and out unnoticed. I recognise the work of one of our allies. We have learnt to become invisible. In any event, thanks to you – to that piece of paper – we were able to proceed without the Vallombroso treatise, but it will prove extremely useful for our continuing calculations. As for that ... Justus ...' He turned towards the hearth. 'He has been reduced to ashes, and God only knows how relieved I am. You must hide the other two volumes, Clément. No one must find them. I cannot take them with me; it would be too dangerous.'

The young boy's eyes flashed mischievously and he confessed:

'Oh ... I can already think of an excellent hiding place.'

'That doesn't surprise me coming from you. Where?'

'In the stallion Mariolle's stable. He has a skittish nature and takes a perverse pleasure in biting anybody who goes near his mouth. The farm hands all avoid him, except for Gilbert the Simpleton who, as his name suggests, is unlikely to go looking for complications!'

'Good. And your lady?'

Growing solemn, the young boy related briefly, in a voice that faltered as the memories flooded back, the ambush he had fallen into on his return from La Haute-Gravière. He stressed his lady's bravery, which had saved both their lives. Francesco leapt up and cried out in a panic-stricken voice:

'What? What is this you say? Why did you wait to tell me of this misadventure? She charged on horseback against three armed brigands! The fool! They could have ... they could have ... Dear God, they could have killed her.'

All of a sudden, his alarm vanished and he smiled mysteriously. He closed his eyes and murmured:

'It couldn't have been otherwise. She couldn't be otherwise.' Then Leone asked Clément, curiously: 'Does Madame de Souarcy often worry like that when you disappear, which I understand you do regularly?'

The thought hadn't occurred to Clément, but he understood instantly what the knight was driving at. Since, as he saw it, he owed absolute truthfulness only to his lady, he replied evasively:

'Recent upsetting events have made my lady more readily apprehensive.'

Leone sensed the boy was dissembling and did not persist. So, Agnès had inherited her aunt Claire and her mother Philippine's unusual gift. No doubt she was unaware of it, and felt confused by her muddled intuitions, unsure of how to use them or how to control them. They had so terrified Éleusie that she had suppressed them, seeing in them a mark of something she was not convinced was godly.

What had Agnès sensed? What had compelled her to order Églantine to be saddled at dusk, to ride off armed with her short sword? Did she know herself? Leone stifled his fascination for this mysterious facet of the women in his family, which he, at least, felt sure was a sign of the divine will.

'Do you intend to return the page that you ... borrowed from me earlier?'

Clément blushed to the roots of his hair and stammered: 'Of course, knight.'

'Have you made any progress in calculating the second chart?'

'No, I thought I could, but I overestimated my ability.' The young boy lied so effortlessly that he surprised himself.

'That is a great shame,' Leone murmured, disappointed.

He had almost convinced himself that this strange boy who had crossed his path would succeed where he and Eustache had failed. So, the die was truly cast. The next step was to go to the Templar commandery at Arville. He went on:

'Did Madame de Souarcy tell you that I need you to help me carry out a plan?'

'Briefly. Is it a mission?'

'In a sense. The Temple of Our Lady at the Templar commandery in Arville is a small fortress in itself. It stands outside the ramparts so that the villagers may attend services without entering the commandery, thus respecting the cloister of the Templar monks. It would take a battering ram to break down the great door. However, there is another, smaller side entrance, opening onto a medium-sized vestibule, which the brothers use in order never to have to leave the enclosure. The door has a narrow window with a bar across it, leaving a gap as wide as the one you slipped through to gain entry to the secret library at Clairets. One other important detail: there is a slightly elevated watchtower overlooking the church. However, Arville is a peaceable little town. I doubt that the commander considers it necessary to place a guard there in the unlikely event of an attack on the Temple of Our Lady. Still, I cannot swear to this.'

'So, you want me to break in ...' Clément summed up.

Leone nodded.

'And how will I unlock the door for you?'

'As is common in abbeys and commanderies where they try to limit the number of keys, the side entrance, unlike the great door, has no lock. It is secured by a bar slotted into metal supports.' Leone paused then said: 'Clément, your lady asked me ... or rather she ordered me not to lead you into any danger. I cannot promise you that ...'

Clément cut him short:

'I know. It is not important, Monsieur. My lady is prepared to brave death in order to save me. With all due respect, despite being a peasant boy, I am lucky enough to have been brought up to want to resemble her in every way. It would be absurd and ungrateful of me to wish it otherwise.'

The knight looked at him with his mysterious, shifting, impenetrable gaze.

'I like you very much, young man. In a strange way you remind me of myself when I was your age. As for courage and honour, they are no strangers to the peasant class, young or old. We will leave at dawn. Arville is far from here and your draught horses are slow. It will take us all day to get there. Fetch a warm coat and prepare enough food for us both. Then go to bed. I will inform your lady. We have a long journey ahead of us.'

Clément hastened to the kitchens.

Leone regretted involving the boy in events over which he had no control. However, time was running short and only he could get into the temple. The knight would rather fight than expose the young boy to danger, but he had no choice.

Agnès's entry into the great hall cut short his reflections. Voicing his retrospective concern, he enquired whether she had recovered from her dreadful encounter in the forest. She stood before him, without saying a word, waiting. He understood, and dutifully related the conversation he had just had with Clément.

'Monsieur, if anything bad were to happen to Clément, you

may be sure that – gratitude or no – I would never forgive you for it.'

Leone hesitated, then took the immeasurable plunge:

'He is your son, is he not?'

She swayed. The blood drained from her face.

He fell to his knees before her, lowered his head and whispered:

'Forgive me, Madame, I beg you. Forget. Forget my insolence. Dear God, forgive me. What is important is that you are safe and that your actions in the forest prove – as if it were necessary – that you are ... who I thought you were, for she would never flee in the face of danger.'

'It is too late, knight,' she replied in a very gentle, very weary voice. 'You have said it now, therefore it exists. What would be the use in denying it? Pray, stand up, Monsieur.'

Leone rose to his feet, remaining before her. Agnès studied the man once again, astonished by his perfect beauty. There was such compassion and poise in his bearing and in the solemn way he looked at her that it wrenched her heart. It occurred to her that her life had been the exact opposite of this man's. She had made no choices, taken no direction, followed no path. She had strolled down unaccustomed pathways free of insurmountable obstacles. In reality, she was content simply to have spared herself and her daughters the worst: she had avoided Eudes by marrying Hugues, then by giving birth to two bastards, and finally by disguising Clémence as a farm hand.

She cleared her throat to get rid of the catch in her voice:

'Clément is indeed my child and is not related by blood to my deceased husband. How did you guess? Was it our eyes, which are so alike? Isn't it uncanny? I only noticed it recently.' She walked over to the long table and flopped onto one of the benches. She sat up straight, her hands resting on her thighs, her eyes gazing off into space and said: 'Please do not think that it was ... a wayward act of lust on my part. I cannot even offer that as an excuse. I planned it carefully. I could have changed my mind a thousand times before reaching the door of that bathhouse at Chartres. And yet I was clear in my mind when I crossed the threshold. Nobody forced me, and the man who held me around the waist used no violence against me, on the contrary.'

She paused. The knight's kindly, almost hoarse voice reached her ears as through a thick fog:

'I am quite willing to believe that it was not an act of waywardness. But why ...'

'Swear to me, knight. Swear on your soul and on the blood of Christ that you will never betray my secret, never under any circumstances.'

'I swear, Madame, on my soul and on the martyrdom of our Saviour.'

'Hugues de Souarcy, my husband, had sired no children by his previous wife. He was sterile. He was very old. I ...' She made an effort to suppress her tears and steady her voice before continuing: 'I was a coward. I was perfectly aware that if he died without an heir, I would become the ward of my half-brother, Eudes de Larnay. I wished to avoid it at all costs. I needed a child.'

'Mathilde?'

'She is not a Souarcy either. Like me, she is a bastard born of an adulterous union.' She closed her eyes and murmured: 'Haven't I now become a cheap whore in your eyes!'

'You, Madame ...' he breathed, indignant. 'You are the purest, most magnificent of all women. May God strike me down if I tell a lie. As for whores, I know of none who sells willingly the little they can call their own. With Clément being a boy, why did you not announce him as Monsieur de Souarcy's heir?'

Agnès hesitated only a fraction of a second before lying once more, without knowing why. Leone, unlike Eudes, would not have taken advantage of knowing Clément's true sex. And yet a curious instinct compelled her not to reveal the truth:

'Clément was born prematurely, only eight months after my husband died. Our future hung on a few weeks. I ... For a long time I was plagued by the thought that Hugues's death from being gored by a stag shortly after my second betrayal was a cruel punishment. The ensuing years, right up until my trial, have done nothing to make me change my mind.'

'God can sometimes appear incomprehensible to us mere mortals, but He is just towards the just and towards His most beloved children.'

'I see. And of course I am just and a beloved child of God,' she said laughingly.

'Indeed you are, Madame, to a degree you could never imagine.'

Plunged into the maelstrom of her painful memories, she did not hear him.

When her husband's lifeless body was laid out on the table in the great hall, Agnès had known for some weeks that she was with child. By a courteous, cheerful man without a trace of vulgarity, who had taken her to the bathhouse on Rue Épervier, during her last visit to Chartres. One look between them had been enough to decide her. Oddly, she had known that a child would be conceived as a result of this brief encounter. It had been her aim. She had prayed for a son. The man's name? She had forgotten. Or perhaps she had never known it, she wasn't sure. What was more, she would have been incapable of describing what he looked like to save her life. He was tall, taller than she, his hair was brown and his eyes blue, like her husband's. She knew this even though she didn't remember him. She had chosen him because of his likeness to Hugues, as she had Mathilde's anonymous, almost faceless, father.

She had been so afraid before going to see the soothsayer her old nurse, Gisèle, had recommended. The bad fairy's hovel stank of grime and rancid mutton fat. The ugly witch had come up and snatched the basket of meagre offerings the sixteen-year-old Agnès had brought. A loaf of bread, some fresh cider, a piece of bacon and a boiling fowl.

She had been so afraid until the woman had placed her hand on her belly and looked into her eyes. The witch's face had lit up with malicious glee as she spat out the words:

'It's another girl you've got in there. Not a handsome boy with a tail between his legs!'

Hugues de Souarcy would have no posthumous heir.

Nothing could save Agnès now.

The young girl had stood motionless in disbelief. There was nothing more to say or do.

And then without warning the fortune-teller's humour had undergone a violent change, her spiteful glee had turned to panic. The old hag had screeched and pulled her filthy apron over her bonnet in order to shield her eyes. She had thrown Agnès out, ordering her never to return.

Agnès had left. She had fought off the urge to lie down there in the mud befouled with pig's excrement and go to sleep for ever.

A few weeks later, in the middle of that harsh winter of 1294, on the evening of 28 December, Agnès had contemplated the dying embers of the fire. A deadly cold had assailed man and beast for weeks on end. So many corpses. Souarcy-en-Perche had buried a third of its peasants in a common grave hastily dug outside the village. An epidemic of cholera had struck.

The people shivered. They clung to one another as though the last vestiges of warmth given off by the other walking wraiths would keep them alive.

The survivors prayed day and night in the icy chapel next to the manor, hoping in vain for a miracle, relating their suffering to the recent death of their master, Hugues, Lord of Souarcy.

A silvery layer of ash covered the dying embers in the hearth in her bedroom. The last wood, the last night. She had despised her feelings of self-pity. She deserved no mercy; she had behaved like a fallen woman without even the excuse of hunger or cold.

She had wrapped herself in her beautiful cloak lined with otter-skin and had taken off her slippers made of boiled wool, reflecting that Mathilde, aged one and a half, would wear them in a few years, God willing.

Agnès had descended the spiral staircase leading down to the great hall. Nothing seemed to exist except for the sound of her bare feet on the dark, icy flagstones.

Sybille was waiting for her in the chapel; Sybille, to whom she had given refuge a few months earlier because her advanced state of pregnancy, following her violation by a pair of villainous thugs, made her almost a sister. Sybille, who was wasting away, blue with cold and hunger and fear. A thin chemise covered her body down to her ankles, stretched over her heavily pregnant belly. Sybille, whose fervent desire for purity, which she believed she was about to discover, had made her spirits soar. With an ecstatic smile on her lips, she had promised her lady:

'Death will be sweet, Madame. We will enter the light together. Are you afraid?'

'Be quiet, Sybille.'

They had walked towards the altar. Agnès had slipped out of her cloak and untied the leather thong that held her dress up under her breasts, concealing her full belly. For a moment she had felt numb. Then the unforgiving cold had made her eyes prick with tears. She had stared at the painted wooden crucifix before falling to her knees, her hands joined in prayer. Death had taken Sybille so swiftly. And yet the young girl had intoned up until her last gasp: '*Adoramus te, Christe.*[60] *Adoramus te, Christe. Adoramus te, Christe.*'

Finally, Agnès's body had slumped forward. The icy stone

floor had received her without mercy. She had stretched her arms out in the form of a cross and waited for the end to come, praying for Mathilde's future, repeating over and over to herself that she was sinning against her body, against the child she could feel inside her and that she deserved no forgiveness. She had prayed that only she would be damned. Gradually she had begun to lose consciousness. And then a harsh voice had rung out, ordering her to get up off the floor, to live. Her old nurse, Gisèle.

Gisèle had fought her, forced her to return to the world that so terrified her.

Sybille was dead, the baby girl she was carrying likewise.

But Clémence had been born less than an hour later.

If Clémence had been a boy, Agnès would no doubt have braved the treacherous rumours and presented him as Hugues de Souarcy's posthumous heir – after all what difference would one more lie make? But another girl would not change her fate as a widow with no son. And, indeed, a bastard child jeopardised her dower, which could be taken from her if evidence of her misconduct were furnished – something Eudes would instantly have made it his business to do.

A terrible sorrow that was only too familiar to Agnès made her heart sink. If Clémence ever found out that she was her daughter, would she forgive such a shameful deception? Would she forgive being denied her mother, her rightful place, her social position, however mediocre? The years of lying, of guilt had come to this: the fear of losing for ever the person she loved more than her own life.

'Madame? Madame, are you unwell? You look deathly pale, you …'

Leone's urgent voice pulled her from the morass of bitter memories and back into the great hall. She was trembling. With a huge effort, she managed to say in a relatively calm voice:

'Forgive me, knight. My thoughts were drifting back in time. Those were dark days. However, I would scarcely have the effrontery to demand the light,' she quipped with a bleak smile.

'You are right on that last point: it would be futile to make such a demand.'

She did not understand what he meant, but did not hazard a question. It suddenly seemed essential that she find her footing in the present and renounce these memories that were poisoning her thoughts. She continued in a steadier voice:

'You owe me some sort of an explanation, knight.'

'Do not be mistaken. I am not trying to deceive you or to be secretive. I am afraid … I am terrified of placing you in danger. Such an idea is intolerable to me.'

'Come, Monsieur! I was thrown into the clutches of the Inquisition. Prior to that, a handkerchief of mine embroidered with the letter A was left at the scene of a series of horrific slayings of monks – emissaries of our late lamented Holy Father – in order to incriminate me. No doubt the work of that wicked servant girl.'

'The letter A? Oh … the emissaries did indeed trace that letter, but it did not stand for Agnès – or any other Christian name. It stands for *apokalupsis*.'

'The apocalypse?'

'Not in the catastrophic sense that we understand. The revelation, the coming, the light. A new beginning. A new world.'

'What new beginning? What world?'

'Are you asking me to describe it to you? I cannot. Hope.'

Agnès, becoming irritated, repeated:

'You are in my debt, Monsieur – one secret for another. Mine, as you can imagine, was extremely painful.'

She had the distinct feeling that a barrier had descended between them. He bowed slightly, his hand on his heart:

'At your service, Madame.'

'What was the meaning of the fragmentary sentence Clément read aloud from the page he copied out?' She stopped his protestations with a gesture. 'Please, knight, do not imagine that I believed your story of an "unfortunate oversight". What did the sentence mean?'

That Agnès should attach such importance to this pivotal link in the chain was further proof in Leone's eyes that she had inherited the gift of clairvoyance possessed by the women in his family. He did not hesitate any longer:

'"The bloodline passes down through the women. The blood that is different will be reborn through one of them. Her daughters will perpetuate it."'

A shiver ran up Agnès's spine. Suddenly everything made sense. Her deception a moment ago, when she had allowed Leone to believe that Clément was her son, was justified, as was her urgent demand that he go to the chapel and destroy the page in the register of births and deaths. In an almost inaudible voice, she asked:

'What line is it, do you think? What blood?'

'I would not name it under pain of torture, Madame. Not even to you, despite the infinite love that binds my soul to yours. I beg you, do not persist. I will not be forced to lie to you.'

He left with these words, or rather he fled without taking his leave. The thought that he could vanish from her life so suddenly, so totally, left her paralysed. What bond had grown between them that made him seem so important, so crucial to her?

The bell for lauds[+] had not yet sounded as they saddled their horses.

Agnès took Clément aside and spoke quickly and quietly to him. The boy was surprised by her insistence that the knight

Leone must under no circumstances suspect that she was a girl. Anxiously, she added:

'If anybody had told me that I would one day fear the Hospitaller's shrewdness more than that of my half-brother, I would have dismissed it as utter nonsense. And yet I do. Take care, Clément. He is far more cunning than Eudes.'

'Why should that worry you, Madame? He is our staunchest ally. Together with the Comte d'Authon,' he corrected, 'yet there is much that our lord does not know about us.'

Agnès paused, biting her lip. She could not yet confess to him what she had told Leone the previous evening. She told herself that it was not the right moment. And yet her sincerity had caught up with her: the only thing stopping her was her fear of Clément's reaction.

'"The bloodline passes down through the women ..." and the second birth chart concerns you.'

'But you are the first.'

'Time is running out, Clément,' she said impatiently. 'Please, trust my instinct. He must not learn of your true sex.'

'I promise you, Madame.'

Mondoubleau Forest and the Templar commandery at Arville,
Perche, December 1304

A sort of tacit agreement had led Clément and Leone to make their journey in virtual silence. Their exchanges were limited to an occasional comment about the harsh frosts that winter, which had even split the bark on the trees, or about the simple meal they would prepare later with the food Adeline had packed for them: bread, bacon, some cheese and a little apple brandy to warm them.

A commonplace yet urgent desire had been bothering Clément for the past few minutes. How would he manage? Two hours earlier, the knight had proposed a brief halt. He had walked up to a tree with his back turned, and Clément had envied him his ability to relieve himself so easily. However, he had shaken his head when Leone suggested he do the same, insisting he had no need yet.

Finally they stopped again, after an interminable ride at the slow pace of the draught horses from the manor. Clément dismounted Églantine slowly, afraid that a sudden jolt might make him lose control. In a deliberately cheerful voice, he announced:

'I'm going to gather some fallen branches[61] for us to thaw our frozen limbs.'

'Good idea,' Leone replied, dismounting in turn from his enormous dapple-grey stallion, the skittish Mariolle, who, after slyly trying to take a bite out of his arm that morning, had sized up his prospective rider and been quickly won over.

The young girl's eyes pricked with tears of relief when at last she reached a safe enough distance to be able to pull down her breeches.

When she, he, returned to their makeshift camp with a load of branches and twigs, Leone had spread out the contents of his leather shoulder bag and was heating a metal tumbler of snow between his hands. They ate their frugal meal in silence, warming their hands before the meagre flames.

'You aren't too cold are you, knight?' Clément asked. 'You must be used to warmer climes.'

Leone studied him as he carefully finished chewing his mouthful.

'I am accustomed to many things – to the heat and the cold, to need and plenty, to rain and sun, friendship and enmity – to life and death too. You see, rain never feels so sweet as when the desert sun has been scorching your skin for weeks on end. And the same goes for everything else.'

'Love and friendship are never more precious than when we have been subjected to hate. Of this I am sure. But life? We enjoy life without knowing death.'

'You're mistaken. We carry death within us from the day we are born and we are aware of it. Life is borrowed time, and death a callous and ruthless usurer who always exacts payment.

This is what makes life so precious – our own and that of others. It never ceases to amaze me how easily it can be snuffed out or destroyed.' Francesco sat up straight and said in a more playful voice: 'Bah! Let us speak no more of such depressing things!'

Leone picked up a charred twig and used it to trace a map of their target in the sodden earth next to the fire where the snow had melted. He began by making a large oval shape representing the ramparts, remarking:

'Observe and learn, as I did during my first visit. We are here, before the main gate. To the left are the stables – apparently spacious enough to accommodate fifty warhorses at any one time. The animals are shipped to the Holy Land[62] – or at least they were fifteen years ago. Nowadays, the Knights Templar sell them as draught horses at cattle fairs – a pity considering how valuable these spirited animals are. At the far end of the stables is a kitchen garden that supplies the community with the majority of its vegetables and medicinal herbs. To the right of the entrance, between Temple of Our Lady, our objective, and some outbuildings, you'll see a smallish dwelling. This is the *preceptor*'s[63] house. We must be careful when we go past as they say three sergeants take shifts during the night to guard the arrow-slit windows. However,' Leone added with a grin, 'in sleepy towns it is not unusual for them to nod off at their post. A little further to the right is the watchtower overlooking the temple. It is instantly recognisable by its imposing double-tiered belfry spanned by a lancet arch. The church is made of grey stone and, as I have already explained, stands outside the ramparts to allow villagers to attend services without entering the commandery. It is the small side door that interests us – the one the monks can access without needing to leave the enclosure. In the middle of the enclosure stands the tithe barn.[64] Overlooking the barn is a second watchtower,[65] which is broad and round. This one worries me more. I'll wager that the knights keeping watch inside it are far more attentive than those dozing in the commander's dwelling.'

Clément studied the lines the knight had traced for him in the mud and, pointing to the area behind the tithe barn, asked:

'What is this tiny cross to the right of the second watchtower?'

'Those are the bread ovens.'

'In that case we will avoid both towers by skirting around them to the right, and then edge our way along the left side of Temple of Our Lady until we reach the door in the centre.'

The rapidity of the boy's strategic thinking stunned Leone, who had formulated exactly the same plan.

He looked up. The leafless trees seemed to be imploring the pale winter sun to shine. The Hospitaller stood up and stretched his arms and legs. Clément followed suit. Leone stamped his feet to dislodge the crust of snow under his boots.

'Come along, my boy, back in the saddle. We are nearing the end of our journey. We shall be within sight of the commandery by nightfall, after compline.'

They tied their horses to a tree twenty yards or so from the pebble path leading to the high wall that encircled the various buildings in the Arville commandery. The drawbridge at the main gate had been raised for the night. The blackish waters of the river Coëtron, which filled the moat, glistened softly under the light of the pale moon that was struggling without much success to break through the late-evening clouds. Leone chose to see this as a portent: even the moon was on their side. Clément suggested:

'Nobody will be on the lookout for a little rascal like me. I could go once round the commandery to make sure the coast is clear.'

'There's scarcely any need. Life in a commandery is very ordered, similar to the monastic life. They have supper at sunset after vespers, and retire to their dormitories or to their posts after compline – the last service of the day. Let's wait a few more minutes before going in. Clément ... I gave my word to your lady and with your help I will keep it.'

'Why with my help?'

'Should our exploit turn ... sour ... that is, if we are seen, I insist you make a dash for it without looking back.'

'And leave you to face danger alone!'

Leone stifled the beginnings of a grin engendered by the young boy's objection. He had no idea how much he resembled his mother. He made an effort to be diplomatic:

'I do not doubt your courage. But one or two will make little difference against a hundred or more Knights Templar. My sole aim would be to hold them off long enough for you to hasten back to Souarcy, thus keeping my promise. In any event I would be arrested. I would lay down my arms as soon as you were far enough away. I have no wish to be slain by my brothers.'

Unconvinced, Clément enquired:

'Then you swear that they would not harm you?'

'Of course,' the knight affirmed, praying that the Knights Templar would likewise lay down their arms.

'In that case, Monsieur, I agree. Let us anyway do our utmost not to be caught.'

They followed the moat to the left, slipping alongside the interminable enclosure wall, made of red sandstone from the quarries at Cormenon and Sargé. At last they reached a spot where they had a clear view of the roof of the tithe barn, which they were now behind. It was tiled with shingles made from chestnut – a tree that abounded in the region – that could survive in all weathers for hundreds of years. The broad watchtower stood slightly to the left, behind the barn. Further to the left were the bread ovens, which were lower than the other constructions and therefore invisible from behind the ramparts. They walked on, counting their paces, until Leone raised his hand to indicate that they should stop. According to their calculations, they should now be to the left of the ovens, and out of sight of the watchtower whose arrow-slit windows overlooked the barn.

Leone lifted Clément as if he were light as a feather, and the boy straddled the wall, flattening his body in order to merge into the darkness. He in turn did his best to help the knight up, though he was tall and heavy, despite his graceful body. Indeed, the young boy marvelled at the man's agility, and was no longer surprised at how easily he had shinned up the rope suspended from the gargoyle at Souarcy. They slid down the other side of the wall and squatted, listening out for any sounds. All was quiet. They moved along in a crouched position until finally they reached Temple of Our Lady. Clément identified the famous door, obtruding slightly from the imposing wall, that allowed the monks to go and pray without leaving the enclosure. Just as the knight had said, above it, at head height, was a narrow opening protected by a thick iron bar. It seemed to him that there was less space between the bar and the wall than between the bars on the cellar window at Clairets.

'Do you suppose you'll be able to get through?' Leone murmured uneasily.

'At the cost of a few bruises and bumps, I expect. I only hope I won't get stuck,' the boy whispered back.

Leone gave him a leg up. While he wriggled, Clément reassured himself that if his head had gone through his body would follow. But the sharp flint tore into his shoulders and he had to clench his teeth in order not to cry out in pain. He exhaled, flattening his ribcage as much as he could, then squeezed one hip through, followed by the other. Finally he was inside, the Hospitaller holding him up by the knees to stop him from falling on his head. Despite the cold, Clément was panting. He raised his voice slightly in order to instruct the knight:

'Let go of one leg, but keep hold of the other or I'll crack my skull open.'

He was able to pull himself up and grasp the bar with one hand. Leone then let go of his other leg and he dropped to the floor. He approached the door, massaging his throbbing shoulders. The bar lifted easily and Leone had soon joined him inside.

They walked out into the nave, guided by the pale light of the moon filtering in through the high arched windows. In the distance, over by the chancel, a speck of light – like a minute flickering star – appeared to be hovering a few feet above the ground. Clément pointed to it. Leone whispered:

'Votive candles to the Holy Virgin.'

Clément was overcome by a strange sensation. He could tell from the knight's sudden pallor that he felt the same. It was as though they had entered another universe, outside time. The trepidation that had not left him during the entire journey suddenly dissolved. Even the intense cold in the entrance seemed reluctant to follow them there. His head was spinning feverishly and he blinked, hoping to accustom his eyes more quickly to the darkness. Leone pulled two sconce lights out of his leather shoulder bag. He walked over to the chancel. His tall figure was swallowed up by the gloom. Clément imagined that he was all alone in the universe, in that space inside the massive church. And yet he was not afraid. Two tiny stars detached themselves from the larger one and floated towards him. As he passed Clément one of the sconces, Leone explained in hushed tones, more out of a need for secrecy inspired by the imposing stones than for fear of being heard from the outside:

'You will observe that, apart from the altar, a few candelabra and the wooden figure of the Virgin Mary, there is nothing here that could be used as a hiding place, except perhaps a hollowed-out piece of masonry or a loose flagstone, which would take us too long to find.'

'How can you be sure that what you are looking for is hidden in this temple and not in some other building?'

'My instinct – along with what I know of the Templar mentality which, rivalry aside, very much resembles our own. For a Knight Templar, the commandery is the holiest place in the world. Both our orders show a special devotion to the Virgin Mary. Mary gives birth and protects. Mary knows but doesn't tell. Who better to guard such an important secret?'

'It is a good argument. Then we must search every stone in every wall and pillar, not to mention the floor. We'll never be finished by tomorrow morning.'

'You will leave before dawn. I will find somewhere to hide.'

'In here?' Clément protested. 'How can you possibly hope to hide in here? As you yourself said, the temple is almost bare.'

'There is always the crypt. That's where the commanders are buried and – if the crypt is spacious enough – the members of the chapter too. Let's go and look. There should be two stairways, one leading down from the nave and the other from the chancel.'

The low door leading to the second stairway was situated behind the elegant carved and painted wooden Virgin. It suddenly occurred to Clément that she resembled Agnès with her domed brow, her prominent cheekbones and small heart-shaped mouth.

They emerged into a long vaulted cave. Contrary to what they had expected, the air was dry, though freezing cold.

Six recumbent effigies lay in a row. Clément walked over to the sculpted figures, graceful in their simplicity, their hands joined in prayer. On the base of the first effigy of a small man of slim build he could read the words: '*Frater Robertus de Avelin est preceptor tunc temporis Areville, 1208.*' [66] He moved on to the second figure, which was muscular and youthful – the customary way of portraying people at the time.[67] 'Henri de Couesmes, 1176' was the only inscription. He studied the face of the third effigy, a man with a princely beard, then the fourth – undoubtedly the tallest of the six. The emaciated face, aquiline nose and square jaw suggested a man of authority, and the almost disproportionately strong hands, a soldier. The letters carved in the stone base read: 'Guillermus de Aridavilla, 1218,'[68] the ancient Latin name for Arville. Guillaume d'Arville. There followed an epitaph, which he translated: 'He arrived at sext[+] during Advent and left at nones[+] in the New Year.' That name. Guillaume d'Arville. Clément knew it from somewhere. He felt instinctively compelled to search his memory, but the precise recollection eluded him. He studied the pleated granite robe and the heavy sword lying on the body and reaching down to the feet. On the calf a minute five-stringed viol[69] with two sound holes, as well as a bow, had been sculpted. A music lover no doubt. A curious detail drew Clément's attention. If the stonework he had seen up until then had been remarkable for its austerity, the instrument's sound box was heavily ornate, decorated with finely chiselled lacework. As he leant over to take a closer look, he distinctly felt his heart miss several beats. He suddenly remembered where he had seen Guillaume d'Arville's name: on the building charter of Clairets Abbey, granted in July 1204 by Geoffroy III, Comte du Perche, and his wife Mathilde of Brunswick, sister of the emperor Otto IV. He had read in one of the registers of chronicles in the library – very hastily, it is true, since he was looking for information about the Vallombroso treatise at the time – that Monsieur Guillaume d'Arville had died during the summer of 1229 on his way back from the Holy Land, not far from Constantinople. He could not have been buried at the commandery! This effigy … My God! It was impossible, he must be mistaken! His throat dry, he called out:

'Quick, knight!'

Leone rushed over and knelt down to see what the boy was pointing at.

'God in heaven … The rose. It's the exact same rose. See how the petal on the right is much bigger than the others; Eustache and I assumed that this must be some sort of symbol, a number of paces or cardinal points. Perhaps it is simply there to distinguish the rose.'

Clément told him briefly all he knew about Guillaume d'Arville who, it appeared, was linked to the commandery and to Clairets Abbey. Leone listened intently. After he had finished, the knight continued to stare at him. The young boy, disconcerted, enquired:

'Have I said something …?'

'No … It is simply that you are one of the many extraordinary coincidences that have guided my life – no doubt one of the most intriguing.'

'I don't understand what you mean, Monsieur.'

'It doesn't matter. I scarcely understand myself. Later. We have very little time. Let us consider Guillaume d'Arville's effigy. According to you, his corpse cannot lie in this tomb because he died in Constantinople.'

'There's something else. Unless I'm mistaken, I'm sure I read that the knight d'Arville died in the summer. Why then does the inscription say that he returned at nones in the New Year?'

'It could be a mistake.'

'I hardly think so. It is more likely to be a message and … it may be madness on my part, but I wouldn't be surprised if the precious papyrus you've been searching for isn't underneath this effigy.'

'For the love of Christ!'

Leone leapt to his feet and declared: 'Help me!'

'But …'

'Hurry. We'll remove the metal pins at the corners then ease the lid off.'

'But it must weigh a ton,' protested Clément.

'If not more. But we needn't lift it, we can just slide it to one side.'

The knight squatted and began thrusting the blade of his dagger into the mortar seal between the lid and the base. His panting breath echoed through the crypt. He inched his way around the tomb on his rear. Finally he stood up, his face dripping with sweat, and whispered:

'Now comes the hardest part. I'll need your help. When I give the word, push with all your might.'

He sat on the floor with his back to the lid, his knees bent and his feet flat against the cellar wall to gain leverage. Clément heard Leone breathe in slowly, then he cried out:

'Now!'

They pushed again and again. The unwieldy lid moved only a fraction of an inch at a time. Clément was no longer aware of the stabbing pains in his shoulders. As for his arms, they felt as if they had turned to stone. Breathless and shaky, he almost collapsed as he heard the knight say:

'We've made a wide enough gap for a small hand to fit through. The pleasure is all yours, I'm afraid.'

Clément recoiled, muttering:

'Suddenly I don't feel so brave.'

'What are you afraid of?' The Hospitaller smiled, pushing three fingers through the narrow opening. 'If there were any rats in there, they'd have been dead for nearly a hundred years!'

'There might be a trap.'

'Why lay a trap in the tomb when the sculpted rose is designed to point initiates to it?'

'You're right. Come on, show a little pluck,' Clément cheered himself on.

He cautiously slipped his hand through the gap until his fingers touched the bottom of the cavity. He pushed his whole arm inside and, fanning out his fingers, declared:

'Just as we thought, it's empty, or at least there's no skeleton. Curses! We'll have to push some more, knight. I can only reach a third of the way across.'

They kept going for another good quarter of an hour, sweating and grunting. Clément felt as if his lungs were about to burst and the blood pulsed through his veins, making his head throb. The gap was wide enough now for him to squeeze both his arms and shoulders through. Tears ran down his cheeks as the painful scratches from the flint stone in the entrance scraped against the granite lid. He meticulously inspected every corner of the tomb, feeling blindly with his fingers. He stifled a cry of disgust as his hand touched something soft and yielding, like skin. He made an immense effort to stay calm and drew the 'object' towards him.

Leone all but snatched it from him, unfolded it and, examining what appeared to be a piece of parchment, exclaimed:

'I don't understand! These are the plans of Clairets Abbey – identical to the ones my aunt Éleusie de Beaufort requested be entrusted to me after her death.' Suddenly anxious, he demanded: 'Are you sure there's nothing else inside?'

'I've gone round every inch of the tomb, including the sides and the bottom of the lid, twice. If the papyrus in Aramaic is hidden in this temple, it's not in here. May I?' he asked, reaching for the piece of old vellum.[70]

'You will notice that the secret library is included in these plans, which proves that it was envisaged from the outset,' Francesco de Leone remarked, his voice brimming with disappointment.

'Yes. And look … there at the bottom – a signature … Bring the sconce torch nearer, please. Oh … Gui…l…rmus d…Arid …vill…' he deciphered. 'Guillermus d'Aridavilla! He signed the plans!'

Leone leant over the parchment and said: 'That's strange, the one I have isn't signed.'

Clément continued his examination under the dim light of the sconce torch. Suddenly he saw it, partially concealed by the letter *O* of the word *bibliotheca*:[71] the rose.

In a voice trembling with emotion, he whispered:

'The papyrus is at Clairets Abbey, in the secret library.'

Leone had no doubt that the boy was right. He was overwhelmed by a feeling of deep sorrow. Éleusie, sweet Éleusie. Was she aware in her resting place that all these years she had been guarding a secret so vital, so precious, that it had cost many lives? Rest in peace, beloved Mother. I have taken up the torch now.

When Leone stared over at the partially open lid, Clément said firmly:

'I'm exhausted, knight! My shoulders are aching. It'll have to stay where it is. We haven't desecrated the tomb for it contained no remains.'

'You're right. Come on. We'll steal away under cover of darkness.'

The bell had just rung for nones when they arrived back at the manor, exhausted, half asleep in their saddles. Mariolle had grown skittish with fatigue and was snorting and shaking his mane irritably. Francesco de Leone was not sorry to hand him over to Gilbert the Simpleton. He hauled himself over to the barn and collapsed onto his bed of straw. Clément had disappeared as if by magic and Leone was sure that he was already recounting every detail of their adventure to his lady. He hoped the boy would think to treat his wounds. They had another long night ahead of them. When he awoke from a deep sleep, shortly after compline, his head was spinning. He felt pleasantly hungry.

After his perfunctory ablutions in the icy water of the trough, he proceeded to the main hall. His place had been laid. Agnès and Clément had just finished a dish of minced leek and pork in saffron. For the next course, Adeline had prepared a stew with sparrows that fed on linseed and were sometimes known as linnets. The tiny birds were glazed in lard and then boiled for a few minutes in meat broth spiced with ginger, cinnamon, a goblet of verjuice and red wine. It was delicious but fiddly to eat if one wished to avoid gorging oneself in the manner of a man like Eudes de Larnay. For dessert she had prepared dark nougat with almonds and slivers of dried apple.

'Pray, be seated, Monsieur, and eat,' Agnès bade him. 'Meanwhile, I would like to say a few words,' she went on in a sharp voice. 'You brought Clément back alive and I am grateful to you for it. But his shoulders are covered in bruises and look as if he's been beaten. And I understand you are planning another escapade tonight?'

'I humbly beg your pardon, Madame, and yours too, Clément.

I would have gone alone to the commandery, but I needed his small frame and his agility. Has he told you everything?'

'Yes.'

'Tonight's escapade, as you call it, should be almost painless, for I have the key to the library. Moreover, judging from the manuscripts that were returned to us, the new Abbess must have left as hastily as she arrived. In addition, I have a strong ally there. However, I cannot promise that we won't need to scale a wall or two.'

Somewhat softened, she retorted:

'At least give me your word that you will protect his life as you protected mine.'

'I give you my solemn word, Madame. With your permission we will leave in a few hours. Do not wait up for us.'

'Oh, because you imagine that under these circumstances I will be able to sleep!'

Clairets Abbey, Perche, December 1304

L eone showed Clément the hand- and footholds he must use in order to scale the high enclosure wall without too much difficulty. The young boy's muscles were beginning to flag. He reflected that the profession of spy or thief was not for him. Agnès was right: he simply did not have the physical strength, and it was not by dint of reasoning and logic that one broke into an abbey like Clairets.

They walked soundlessly along the path Leone had only recently taken, before learning the devastating news of his sweet aunt Éleusie's death. And yet he knew that her magnificent soul, brimming with love and courage, had been with him ever since. He tore aside the piece of oiled hide covering the window of the dearly departed woman's study. The room was pitch black. Leone whispered:

'Clément?'

'Yes, knight. I'm here on your right.'

'Clément, I must ask you to carry out a very sensitive mission.'

'You said you had the key!'

'No, not that. I want you to sneak into the nuns' dormitory and wake up the apothecary very gently and very quietly. We need some light and her assistance would be a great benefit.'

'*What?*'

'You heard me. You do know her, don't you?'

'Yes, I mean, I don't think I'll have difficulty recognising her. She's rather ugly. What are you asking me …? Well, I'll be going, then.'

'Clément … If you should happen to glimpse … a naked shoulder or, heaven forbid, a lady's leg – for when all's said and done they are ladies … I trust you will act like a gentleman and turn away.'

This was no time for gaiety, but the young girl had to stifle the urge to giggle.

'Oh, you can rest assured that I will behave like a perfect little gentleman.'

When he had slipped away, Leone made his way into the library, hampered by the lack of light.

He felt somebody behind him. He swung round, his hand clutching the pommel of his sword.

A shadow came towards him, a slim shadow. He drew his sword.

'Do not be afraid. I wish you no harm, I promise.'

A young woman's voice. She moved closer until at last he could see her face. He knew her from somewhere but he couldn't think where.

'Do you remember me, knight? Cyprus, Freya's cross, the runes. It seems like an eternity ago.'

'God in heaven … the grubby little beggar girl. Was it you, Madame? Ah, yes, of course … I remember your extraordinary eyes, which I searched high and low for after you … vanished. My sister, my friend …'

He rushed over and embraced her. Her body tensed. He misunderstood her response and pulled away abruptly, embarrassed:

'Forgive me, I am so happy to see you again.'

'So am I.'

A terrible but brief battle raged in Esquive d'Estouville's mind. Was she the winner or the loser? She would never really decide as to the true outcome of her remorseless struggle with herself. The beautiful archangel would never know that she had killed for him, had stabbed a Templar commander in the back. He would never suspect that she had lain beside him all night long in a dark forest. He would live out his whole life without ever understanding the infinite love she felt for him that made her tremble, made her dream of him day and night. Esquive smiled. In fact, she had undoubtedly chosen the easiest path. Had she confessed, he would have been so kind, so gentle, that she would most likely have died of despair. He would remain for ever her adored, magnificent archangel. She would cherish until her death the unique love she felt, a love so perfect that no other man could ever rival it. He would never know. What need was there for him to know? What did it matter in the end? She was alive, vibrant, thanks to him.

'Did you find the manuscripts?' she enquired in a calm voice.

He grasped her hands and kissed them tenderly. He said joyously:

'Ah … my mysterious messenger. Are you my good fairy, Madame?'

'I hope so with all my heart and soul. Never forget that. Ever.'

'I promise you I will not.'

'I must leave for Paris now, Monsieur. Annelette Beaupré will do everything in her power to help you. Until we meet again – here perhaps, and, if not, then certainly in the next world.'

She walked a few paces then changed her mind and whispered, as though to herself:

'I wish you great and good fortune, knight. I will watch over you.'

He accompanied her to the study door, which he opened cautiously, peering out to make sure the way was clear.

As the Hospitaller watched her disappear down the end of the corridor, he was seized by an almost sweet pain. He would never see her again.

He fell against the closed door, uncertain. The muffled sound of cautious feet running roused him from his momentary torpor. Annelette Beaupré, twitching with excitement, bounded into the study holding a sconce torch in front of her, followed by a breathless Clément.

'Knight …' she bellowed.

'Shh, sister, speak in a whisper, please!'

'Forgive me. Here is the light. I was under the impression from what the little tearaway told me that … oh! Dear God … our goal is in sight. Oh, dear God … dear God,' she repeated, her hand on her heart. 'What joy, what an indescribable honour to be chosen like this. What a tragedy that our dear Reverend Mother is no longer with us.'

'She is.'

'You are right,' she agreed, pointing a finger at him. 'I'm an utter fool! In my defence, I've been a bundle of nerves since I was wrenched from sleep. I will pull myself together. What must be done? I am at your service, Monsieur. Just one thing before we begin,' she added, embarrassed. 'How intolerably trivial! Um … would you mind turning your backs, dear friends? My stockings are down around my ankles. I was in such a hurry to put them on when this young man … and I dared not pull them up to my … above my knees, and I've been treading on them ever since, which slows me down dreadfully and hampers my movements. It won't take more than a moment.'

They obliged.

'The poisonous snake is dead – poisoned in turn. Divine justice exists after all! Jeanne d'Amblin, the extern sister, everybody's friend and dear Éleusie's confidante! Murdered by the bogus Abbess – the beautiful Neyrat with her emerald- green eyes beat a hasty retreat, without the manuscripts, back to whence she came, to hell, I hope. What I wouldn't give to witness Benedetti's anger! There. You may turn round now. I'm respectable and fully functioning. What must we do?'

'Allow me briefly to fill you in, sister. Then we will need to put all three of our heads together. And I know how invaluable yours is.'

Annelette's cheeks flushed. She was so delighted at the compliment that she hadn't the heart to restrain herself as humility dictated.

With a few interruptions from Clément, Leone brought Annelette up to date with their recent discoveries. She went into ecstasies:

'Ah … what marvels you have achieved. There are times when I regret not having been born a man. I would give anything to have been in that crypt with you. I am strong. I could have helped you move the effigy.'

'We managed, sister. Even so, your assistance would have been much appreciated,' Leone assured her. 'Now look at this.'

He spread out before her the old piece of parchment. 'This is the rose that has been guiding me for years. We have long misunderstood its true meaning. Finally, the die is cast. The truth is within our reach. What do you make of this rose?'

Annelette studied the vellum for a few seconds before remarking:

'Is the flower pointing to a secret hiding place? In that case we must calculate its position in the letter *O* in *bibliotheca* on a scale that will permit us to find its corresponding location in the floor or the wall.'

Annelette took out of the reticule on her belt a needle for removing splinters and used it as a ruler. Half sprawled across the long table at which Éleusie de Beaufort had spent so many hours, she measured the distances between the rose in the letter *O* and the lines on the plan representing the walls of the secret library, the staircase down to the workshop and the high arrow-slit windows. She used a quill to jot down the results of her calculations on a scrap of paper. At last she raised her head and announced:

'Well. Now all we have to do is calculate the scale. The inside wall of the library running alongside the cloister is two and a third needles long. Knight, please would you measure the length of that wall in paces and give me the result?'

When he came back two minutes later, he was grinning.

'I had to do it twice because I lost count. Just short of thirty-one and a half feet.'

'Which means one needle is equal to a little over thirteen and a half feet.'

The apothecary then became engrossed in dividing her needle into tenths and fifteenths, muttering to herself as she worked.

Leone smiled knowingly at Clément, who discreetly nodded back at him. In employing Annelette Beaupré's prodigious intellectual powers they had given her a priceless gift. A sudden cry made them jump. The nun clapped her hand over her mouth and whispered apologetically:

'Forgive me … We must be silent, I know. I'm exalted. I have it. The position, I mean. It is in the wall opposite the one you measured.'

Annelette untied the thin piece of cord gathering her robe at the waist and laid it on the floor, instructing the knight:

'Give me your foot so that I can mark the piece of cord against it. This way we will get as close as we can to the actual hiding place.'

They watched her for ten minutes as she placed the piece of cord up against the walls and flagstones. Suddenly, she gestured with her arm, silently pointing to a stone on the wall just below the ring used as a torch holder.

'It's there. Or at least it should be according to my calculations.'

They each in turn felt the wall for any notch or tiny crevice that might activate a mechanism. In vain. With the blade of his dagger, Leone began scratching at the pointing. A good quarter of an hour later, he gave up. Stones that were designed to be moved or removed were not pointed.

Annelette looked dreadfully disappointed and hurried back to the study to review her calculations. The knight looked at Clément and asked:

'What do you think?'

'I think we're looking in the wrong place.'

'How can you be so sure?'

'Because of the epitaph. The solution lies there.'

The apothecary looked up, reflected for a few moments then asked:

'Clément, would you fetch the book of chronicles in which Guillaume d'Arville's death was recorded?'

The young boy did as he was asked. Annelette examined the corresponding page, clearing her throat as she read.

'Hmmm … You see, when they relate to events that have already occurred, the chronicles are sometimes imprecise. On the other hand they are never entirely erroneous since they must be able to be used as evidence. Thus, the chroniclers prefer to leave out details rather then risk including an error. Their "scrupulousness" in these matters is greatly helped by the fact that the falsification of chronicles – which does occur – is punished most severely. They therefore take their task very seriously. If this register says Monsieur d'Arville died in the summer then we can be sure it is true. We cannot know whether it was in July, August or September, but at all events it was nowhere near the New Year and, moreover, he was born in June and not at the beginning of Advent. I have come to the same conclusion as Clément. The epitaph contains some other meaning: "He arrived at sext during Advent and left at nones in the New Year."'

Clément nodded, expanding:

'It is this exactness regarding times that surprises me. It is only in the royal family that precise times of birth are given – and even then not always. Some of us don't know what day or what month we were born.'

Leone added:

'I think that if a code exists, it is contained in the epitaph and we must focus our search there. What do you think we should be looking for?'

'A riddle.'

'A riddle?'

Clément began by summing up his reasoning: assuming that the sentence was a secret code, it must refer to an event that occurred every year at the same time, since the person who devised it could not know exactly at what point in the future the code would be deciphered. The question he then put to his two companions appeared extremely simple on the surface: what is it that returns each year at sext during Advent and leaves again at nones in the New Year? It could not be Advent itself, which ended on Christmas Day. A heavy silence fell on the library. Annelette proceeded by eliminating the events that could not take place during that period:

'No religious festivals, with the exception of the birth of our Saviour. Nothing relating to the land, by which I mean the harvests, for it is the middle of winter ... and, by the same token, nothing that thrives in the warm weather either ...'

Leone attempted to stem this exhaustive inventory:

'Sister, might not a list of events that *could* occur be more helpful?'

'You are right,' the big woman agreed. 'But it will prove more difficult. Indeed, it is only in making such a list that I realise how few things do happen in winter time!'

'I think you have partially answered the question, sister,'

Clément cut in. 'Such a degree of constancy and permanence, for the epitaph was devised at least a century ago, suggests natural phenomena. Storms are too random and tides too remote from here. And I have never heard of either lasting more than a month. The same applies to eclipses. However, the sun and the moon return every morning and every night.'

'True,' Leone argued, 'but they do so all year round and we need a relatively transient event.'

Clément, who was deep in thought, blinked in agreement, before continuing:

'It can't refer to the phases of the moon as they do not coincide.' Suddenly he gave a little leap and exclaimed: 'I've got it! Vallombroso's theory. The Earth's trajectory round the sun. Winter is the season when we are furthest from that planet – hence the cold weather. Light and shadows change! The arrow-slit windows! It is true that their height and horizontality were aimed at making them almost invisible from the outside, but I'll wager they have a double function: they allow the light to filter in at a certain angle, creating circles of light and casting unusual shadows!'

'Sweet Lord, the boy's intelligent!' marvelled Annelette.

'And the word isn't enough to describe my astonishment at your abilities,' Leone added. 'We must wait all night until nones tomorrow, then, for we are approaching the New Year.'

'It will soon be matins,' declared Annelette. 'Go into the library. I will sneak into the kitchens and fetch some provisions before Elisaba Ferron, the kindly but punctilious sister in charge of meals, gets up. Then I will lock you in and join you later.'

Agnès stood facing the hearth that was feebly heating the inhospitable main hall. She did not condescend to turn round, still less to curtsey to her overlord.

'Madame … I … Ogier brought me here at a gallop. I …'

She raised her hand and demanded in a sharp voice:

'Three words, Monsieur. Have you forgotten how things stood when we said farewell, or when you bade me farewell? Three words or you will leave this manor and our lives – my life – for ever. You are a man of honour, and I know that you will not take your revenge on me or my servants because of your own verbal shortcomings. I will continue to pay tribute to you and to pay my taxes without demur, according to my duty. But our association will end there. I'm waiting, Monsieur!'

God in heaven. She took his breath away. She terrified him as nobody ever had, not even when he was five years old. At that tender age he had, as dear Ronan frequently reminded him, done many foolhardy and dangerous things. Later on, ladies, or those who were not quite ladies – that is to say, prostitutes – had honoured him, for it was always an honour, by appreciating his charms.

One of the sweetest memories of his weakness for the fair sex would always be that young whore from Constantinople, who had offered him a night in a bedroom at a dingy brothel in the grand bazaar. She had sold him nothing because he had paid her nothing. She had led him by the hand, laughing: 'I like you. You are witty, my friend. Witty and kind. What more could a girl like me ask for?' Thinking better of it, she had added: 'I know what

I can ask of you. Thank me in the morning as though I were a lady.'

The next morning, he had drawn the sheet up over her and kissed her hand, murmuring:

'Madame, you are an intoxicating flower, whose fragrance I will not forget in a hurry. I thank you.'

She followed him with her pretty hazel eyes as he reached into his pocket for some coins. When he drew his hand out, it was empty. He had covered her brow and feet with sweet kisses that were more precious to this woman than money. Instinctively, this fallen woman who had been bought, sold and bartered had found a sensual eloquence, a dignity that fitted her like a dainty glove. Despite her anxious expression she had declared:

'Monsieur ... If by some stroke of fortune our paths should cross again ... do me the honour of recognising me. I won't ... Well, whoever you are with, I won't mention the nature of our previous encounter. Introduce me as a ... distant acquaintance or a friend's lover or even as a woman of easy virtue – I will not take offence, only ... do not ignore me.'

Understanding instantly this woman's fear of becoming invisible, her struggle to continue being, he had feigned gentle indignation, in order to offer her something that was not silver or gold:

'Madame ... you wound me! Who do you think I am? If, by a stroke of fortune, as you put it, our paths should cross again, I beg ... no, I demand the honour of a dance or at least a brief conversation – which I assure you will not compromise you if you are accompanied. Come, Madame, give me your word this instant. And be sincere, for I will hold you to it ... Let us shake hands on it!'

She had pealed with joyous laughter as she pulled the sheet up under her chin, and it had occurred to him momentarily that she looked like the young girl she must have been when she was sold in the white slave market in Constantinople, one of the most prized in the Middle East. Delighted, pouting graciously, her acceptance remained one of his sweetest memories:

'A dance or a brief conversation? You go too far, Monsieur! Very well … you demand a lady's word … I give it. With pleasure. And I will shake hands on it!'

She had drawn level with him as he stepped through the doorway of the pitiful hovel, which was decorated with pieces of bright-red cloth and tasteless baubles. Outside, the thrumming crowd in the grand bazaar bartered and traded and went about its business. Voices heckled and bargained, exchanging harmless insults. The angry cries and overwhelming stench of the camels – which it was claimed made the Lydian army flee[72] – reached them, as did the clipped phrases of the parakeets, which the stallholders encouraged them to repeat in order to obtain a higher price. The aroma of cinnamon and nutmeg combined with the stench of dung and human excrement, and the scent of musk and iris. The metallic smell of the blood dripping from the throats of the sheep, black with flies, hanging on hooks on the stalls, also helped to produce an olfactory experience unlike any other: that of the belly of Constantinople. The whore, whose name he did not know, had stammered:

'Don't forget … Don't forget! I gave you my word. Pray, remind me should we ever meet again. Just for me … A brief conversation, an almond sorbet, a sweetmeat of honey and rosewater, a glass of tea, anything, anything it pleases you to offer me that day.'

He had kissed her hands once more, murmuring into her soft skin:

'Madame, never forget that it is you who have honoured me. You are the perfect ray of sunshine that brightens the weary traveller's journey. God protect you. And should we ever meet again … I will not hesitate to remind you of your promise, at the risk of seeming like an intolerable boor. You will have difficulty getting away from me, I assure you.'

He was lying. He knew he would never see her again. And yet, in time, it would turn out to be one of the few lies of which he felt proud.

Adeline entered the main hall carrying a pitcher of mulled wine and some sweet bread made with cream, eggs and honey,[73] which she set down hurriedly before disappearing with an inaudible murmur.

'You see … Madame … I feel like a frightened boy and …'

'I'm waiting, I tell you.'

'Three words are what you want,' he resumed.

'What I insist upon. Forget for the moment, Monsieur, that I am your vassal and think of me as a woman. Custom dictates that it is my privilege to give orders even to you,' she declared, her back still turned.

'Very well. I respect and accept your present status. Three words! God's wounds!' he cursed, before continuing. 'Forgive me. I forget myself occasionally and utter oaths that are offensive to the fair sex … It comes with soldiering and being a farmer. Three words … You speak as if it were a business arrangement that must be sealed by spitting and shaking hands! If only it were so simple …'

She remained impassive, silent, as motionless as a statue. 'Well, at least help me,' he cajoled.

In vain.

For the past few moments, Artus d'Authon had had to stifle an irrepressible urge to burst into peals of laughter – he who had not laughed in years. Admittedly, the situation was insufferably frustrating, impossibly unnerving and yet, Lord, he was happy! The woman was intelligent, beautiful and sweet as an angel, but she was resolute and stubborn as a mule. As a pack of mules. He loved her madly and she was taunting him even though he hadn't shown his hand and could still turn back. He was surprised and overjoyed to feel life surging through him again. More precisely, to feel life surging through him for the very first time – for he could not recall ever having felt so alive until he met Agnès.

Very well. This was not about smiting the enemy or running him through with his sword, but convincing a dear woman whom he desperately desired, of the depth and utter sincerity of his feelings. Even so, as an expert swordsman he would have found it easier to fight a single-handed duel with three men. Alas, it was women who tended to choose the weapons of love. Undeniably they were skilled at handling them and understood their subtleties, since love – of whatever sort – was the most important thing in their lives. And Artus hoped with all his heart that it would be for ever thus.

Terrified, fascinated, enchanted, he declared:

'I love you, Madame. I love you terribly, unreservedly, undyingly. Are these the three words you wanted to hear? For I could elaborate on them indefinitely: I await you. I crave you. I want you. I desire you. For all time. With all my heart. Pray, requite my love. Pray, marry me now! Oh … good God, I've progressed to four words!'

Finally she turned round and gave him the loveliest smile he had ever seen. She joked:

'Are you teasing me?'

Curiously, he had no desire for frivolity at that moment. In a serious, almost sombre voice he asked her:

'Madame … I have bared my soul. I wait for you to do the same or … to dismiss me promptly and courteously.'

'Dismiss you? Have you taken leave of your senses?' Suddenly annoyed, she thundered:

'Oh dear God … What they say is true, then! Men in love are

blind, deaf ... and dumb into the bargain! Do you see nothing? Have you understood nothing? How remarkable! A lady madly loves a gentleman who loves her madly back. Heavens ... Is this the first time such a thing has happened?'

'Now I'm afraid that you're mocking me. No matter. I am still waiting for you to utter those three magic words, Madame.'

'The three words? Oh, but I do not fear them. I have felt them deep inside me for a very long time, Monsieur. Would you like me to declaim, sing, whisper or perhaps write them to you? I love you utterly, undyingly, my gentle lord.'

He rushed over to her, arms outstretched, and she stepped back, murmuring:

'I am ... overcome, even a little afraid. Forgive me ... I am scarcely accustomed to ... Indeed ... I'm embarrassed to feel like a maid while being a mother. What you said was true, although it angered me at the time. I was married only briefly and am relatively ignorant of married life. Naturally I'm aware of my ... conjugal duties, but ...'

He kissed her hands, his dark gaze fixed on her big grey-blue eyes, which stared back at him.

'Madame, my beloved, I am conceited enough to believe that I will not impose any duties on you – conjugal or otherwise. I am presumptuous enough to imagine that our coming together will be as lovers, companions, husband and wife, never contractual. I've been waiting for this moment all my life.'

He let go of her hands and clasped her shoulders. She trembled.

'Do you understand? I am not young any more. I know what I've had and what I no longer want. Better still, I know what I want. You.' He closed his eyes and she missed seeing them staring into hers. 'Oh, Madame, I am delirious with joy ... I am not a cheerful fellow by nature. Indeed, my chief bailiff, whom you've met, thinks me far too dour. Everybody does. Doubtless I am not light-hearted or humorous enough. Do you know that it was you who made me laugh for the very first time since I was a boy when you narrated your misadventures with the bees? I should have suspected then that you had won my heart for ever. Madame, you have brought me back to life. I can feel life surging through my veins. It stings, it burns, it intoxicates me. When? When may I introduce you to my proud swans, my gentle albino deer and my stubborn peacocks and explain to them that you are their new mistress?'

Everything was happening too fast. Agnès was beginning to feel fearful. It was all so new, so different. And yet she loved this man. It was a strange sensation, which she was discovering for the very first time, having only ever felt strong emotion towards her two daughters and Madame Clémence. However, Artus was of course a man, and she had loved no other before him.

'But Souarcy, my servants … I cannot simply abandon them.'

'We will appoint a steward. As for your servants, notably that cunning Clément, you will choose those you want to come with you and they will be welcome in our county.'

She closed her eyes and whispered to him up close:

'I love you … I love you … I love you … Oh … how I love saying the words "I love you", words which up until now I only said to … children.'

She felt his lips on hers. The long, deep kiss they exchanged felt like her very first. No doubt it was. She faltered as he drew away, fighting the urge to pull him back towards her, towards her belly. He could tell from her glazed look, and he shook his head slowly, smiling:

'I must leave directly, Madame. Otherwise I will be in danger of committing a sin, a succession of sins, which I would be unable to regret.'

'Must you really go?'

'Don't tempt me. I'm very susceptible to temptation where

you are concerned and I have no desire to resist. I am already making a superlative effort to act like a gentleman. And there was I thinking that women could be trusted to be more reasonable in such matters!'

'Indeed they are. However, you are the reason for this weakness, this madness that has come over me all of a sudden, and which astonishes me, I openly confess.'

He acknowledged the compliment with a slight nod and took his leave, hastily and with great regret.

The idea of the life pulsing through his veins, the strength he felt in each of his movements. The idea that he was alive at last and that the long years of sorrow had vanished like a looming cloud evaporating. The idea that – quite apart from his wealth and status – a beautiful, incredible, extraordinary woman had chosen him as the most important, the only man in her life. He could have demanded and got just about any woman. This woman, whom he wanted more than anything, was hanging by a thread, a taut but stubborn thread, which she had woven and which had led her to him. Nothing would be simple; she was not simple. He laughed as he climbed into the saddle. Ogier shook his mane by way of a greeting. Ronan would reduce him to silence by insisting in a polite but firm voice that 'just because ladies think differently from us it does not follow that they are complicated. In fact experience shows that they are often right.' Life was a miracle. Why had he doubted it for so long? Why had it taken him so long to see it?

'Ogier ... your master is drunk. Drunk with joy. Surely it is better than being sober and sad, don't you think? The sorrow that has dogged me for so long is no more. This is good news, my brave steed. Come. Let us be off before I change my mind and break down my lady's door. I am tempted, sorely tempted. Bear me away. Ogier, sweet Ogier, men's lives are such complex affairs.'

A few dozen yards further on, the Comte resumed his monologue:

'Ogier ... I imagine her hands, her neck, her skin ... Well ... you understand. I imagine her laughter, what she will say when I take her for a walk through our gardens. I imagine her wonderment when she discovers all that will be hers when we are married ... The worst of it all, dear Ogier, is that I am not even sure that she has the slightest interest in worldly goods. On the other hand, I know that the pond, the trees, the flowers, the peacocks and the deer will take her breath away.'

Stirred beyond his wildest imaginings, he philosophised:

'No, you see, Ogier, despite what Ronan says, women's essence is very different from ours. Now, I'm in no way implying that theirs is any less precious, although it is unquestionably more stimulating, at least for a man. However, it must be said that it is very different ... not to say incomprehensible.'

He slumped onto his destrier's mane in fits of laughter as he realised that he was conversing with the stallion as if he were a revered scholar, whose greatest quality, no doubt, was that he couldn't answer back.

The bell for nones had just rung. Annelette had given the pretext of an urgent inventory in order to be excused. Although a relative calm had returned since the death of the poisoner, fear was still in the air. Annelette's inventories in the herbarium reassured the nuns – for through them she could be sure that no further wickedness was being prepared. And so Berthe de Marchiennes, who had been Acting Abbess since Madame de Neyrat's departure, had encouraged the apothecary to continue working in her little den.

Annelette Beaupré was in a hurry. She had decided to go into the herbarium in order to divert any suspicion, and then leave again discreetly once all the other sisters had gathered in the abbey church for prayer. She hastened through the refectory and was about to go out into the vegetable garden when she heard a creaking sound coming from the kitchens. On the alert, she approached the huge door leading to the world to which poor Adélaïde Condeau had been so attached. At first, all she could see was a pair of stockings and the pleats of a robe twitching. A nun, perched on a stool, her back to Annelette, was trying to reach an earthenware pot where Elisaba kept the honey.

'What do you think you're doing, sister?' thundered Annelette.

A cry, the stool toppled over. Annelette rushed to catch the pot of honey, while the other woman fell flat on her back with a thud. Emma de Pathus, the schoolmistress, lay on the floor in an ungainly position, her robe pulled up over her face. Annelette helped her get up and narrowed her eyes as she looked at her.

'What were you doing?'

'I … I … I …'

'Yes, of course, and …?'

Suddenly regaining her air of superiority, Emma de Pathus looked the apothecary up and down, scowling:

'Well! And who exactly do you think you are? Have you perhaps forgotten that you're the daughter of a mere commoner?'

'An utterly inappropriate remark in such a place as this, Madame!' hissed Annelette. 'But I would not expect less, coming from you. I may be the daughter of a commoner, but I'm not in the habit of sneaking in here and guzzling my sisters' honey in secret, and to crown it all while they are at prayer! And I don't take out my grievances on innocent children by slapping them …'

Emma de Pathus opened her mouth in protest but Annelette, beside herself, shrieked:

'Shut up, you greedy pig! Your cheeks are as flabby as your buttocks, which I've just glimpsed, for my sins! Yes, I may be a commoner, but I don't have dealings with demons disguised as inquisitors! Wipe that look of surprise off your face this instant,' Annelette continued haranguing her. 'Oh, I know all about it! Our dearly departed Reverend Mother saw you conversing vigorously with Nicolas Florin, whom God in his wisdom saw fit to punish … You can be sure that I will inform our new Abbess of your misconduct.'

Furious, and determined to deliver the final blow that would atone for the affront she had just received, Annelette Beaupré lashed out one last time, leaving the other woman reeling:

'Don't misunderstand … I'm sure that no guilty affection passed between you. Had the opposite been true then the Grand Inquisitor would not only have turned out to be a monster, but a man of very bad taste and low standards!'

The big fat face quivered like a jelly and turned pale. 'Guilty affection?' she stammered. 'Have you taken leave of your senses? I only spoke to him on one occasion to ask after my brother, who had been an inquisitor at Toulouse and had just been posted to

Carcassonne. Indeed, they had met there before my Lord Florin left for Alençon.'

Despite her desire to believe that she was a liar on top of everything else, Annelette was certain that Emma was telling the truth. However, she hadn't finished with her yet.

'And the honey? Perhaps you were thoughtfully making sure that it hadn't gone stale.'

Emma de Pathus's reaction left her dumbfounded. The schoolmistress broke down in sobs of tears, stamping her feet like a woman possessed, and wailing:

'I'm hungry! I'm hungry! ... I'm hungry all the time. My stomach aches and my legs feel weak. I can't take any more of this fasting – not to mention all the penances, which are even more excruciating in winter. All I can think of from morning until night is food! It makes me irritable and I take it out on the children and I loathe myself for it all the time. I only wanted to love God, not to suffer hunger each day that He creates! It is a torment. Do you hear me? My life is a torment! Instead of praying as I would like, instead of engaging in meditation which I love, I close my eyes and all I see is sausages, crusty bread, jellied fruit, succulent roasts ... I'm damned, damned ...' she sobbed, burying her face in her hands.

Upset at having been the cause of Emma de Pathus's extraordinary yet very real distress, the apothecary was moved to pity. Thrusting into her hands the pot of honey she was still clasping, she said:

'Here, eat it. I won't tell Elisaba that I found you here.'

Annelette slipped into the secret library where she found the knight Leone and Clément staring up at the arrow-slit windows. She walked over to them and whispered impatiently:

'Well?'

'You've arrived at just the right moment, sister,' Leone greeted her. 'Nothing yet – it's cloudy outside. Watch the walls and the floor, Madame.'

Annelette stood in the middle of the cavernous library and did as he had requested, turning round on the spot. She was soon joined by her two companions.

Clément wiped his palms, clammy with anticipation, on his breeches, concluding that these were without doubt the longest moments of his life, and then swiftly changed his mind. No, the longest had been those that had separated him from his lady during her imprisonment.

Clément and Annelette cried out as one. Annelette pointed, wide-eyed, at a set of bookshelves, the sliding one beneath which the knight Leone had hidden the Vallombroso treatise. Leone and Clément rushed towards a splodge of light the size of a hand, the jagged outline of which unmistakably resembled the petals of a rose in full bloom.

'The bars on the windows to keep birds and rodents from getting in and damaging the books,' the apothecary declared. 'We can't see them from here, but I'm sure that it is their shape casting this pattern.'

'Quick, let's push the bookcase to one side before it disappears.'

On the wall behind, at head height, the rose shone at the centre of a large stone. Leone began scratching with his fingernail at the pointing, sand mixed with a tiny amount of slaked lime to keep it from hardening. It crumbled easily and he slotted his fingers into the space he had created and pulled. What they had assumed would be a hefty stone came away so effortlessly that the knight lost his balance and nearly fell over backwards. It was a piece of dressed stone barely an inch thick. Behind it was a hiding place.

They uttered no cries of triumph or joy, nor did they embrace one another victoriously. They simply stood in awed silence.

Leone slumped to his knees and the other two soon followed. They prayed in silence together. Despite the elation he felt,

Leone was fighting off an overwhelming sense of despair. He had finally arrived. For as long as he could remember every day, every waking hour of his life had been dominated by the quest. What meaning would his life have now?

He despised himself for his cowardice and egoism, and rose to his feet. So many had suffered and died for this moment. For the first time in his life, the Knight of Justice and Grace of the Order of Saint John of Jerusalem* felt ashamed.

'Knight … we can't just stay like this,' Clément whispered.

'I know.'

Leone approached the small hollow. With what seemed like a supreme effort of will, he stretched out his arm. His fingers touched a small, rough scroll. The papyrus. His heart leapt into his throat.

'My legs feel like jelly all of a sudden,' Annelette lamented.

'You mustn't faint, Madame,' implored Clément. 'Why not go and sit down in the study and we'll join you there shortly.'

She did as he suggested.

They emerged through the low door behind the tapestry, crestfallen. She sat up, enquiring anxiously:

'Is it not the papyrus?'

'Yes, I believe it is,' replied the knight. 'But, as far as I can tell, it isn't written in Aramaic, but in an unknown language. Apart from one sentence, a single sentence, the last, which I know by heart. "And you shall see the Son of Man sitting on the right hand of the power of God and coming with the clouds of heaven." It is the Gospel according to Saint Mark,[74] which echoes the book of Daniel: "And the God of heaven will set up a fifth kingdom that will never be destroyed."'

'My God …' breathed Annelette. 'The Second Coming? Christ will be reborn to save us all once more. As the Good Book states, there will not be a third. Could it be that …?'

'The papyrus is covered in bizarre, not to say disturbing,

drawings. Strange luxuriant plants and women bathing in large vats of green liquid.'[75]

'Naked women?' asked Annelette.

'Yes. Two of them have bleeding hands, yet they are smiling. The blood flowing from their wounds is green.'

'Is it some sort of silly joke?'

'I don't think so.'

'I mean to say, nobody has green blood!' exclaimed the apothecary.

A soft voice declared:

'True, but what if its greenness signifies that it is different? "The bloodline passes down through the women. The blood that is different will be reborn through one of them. Her daughters will perpetuate it."'

'Different in what way?'

'I don't know,' Clément smiled, his eyes pricking with tears. For a while now, he had been stifling his urge to run away.

Far away, he did not know where. Somewhere nobody would ever find him ... her.

Suddenly Clémence understood everything: Leone's timely intervention during the trial; the death of Pope Benoît XI, who was determined to prepare for the Second Coming; the tenacity of Honorius Benedetti, who knew that such an event would undermine the foundations of the Church, which he and his followers had helped to strengthen; even the fear that had driven Agnès to make the young girl promise not to reveal her sex to the knight under any circumstances.

She, Clémence, was the sixth woman, the one in the middle, surrounded by five others, one of whom was Agnès. Her mother. Her mother, who had fathomed the mystery before them; her mother who had always taken care to hide her, even though she was unsure of the true reason. Her mother who wanted more than anything to protect her from a wonderful yet terrible fate, for the infernal hordes would be unleashed upon the one who threatened to restore the Light. The evil, sinister souls who thrived on the dung heap of the world would destroy anyone who got in the way of their intrigues, their base acts, the evil they grew rich upon.

Who would carry the future child? She or one of her daughters' daughters?

Clémence suppressed the urge to snatch the papyrus from Leone's hands and tear it to shreds.

She must hide this divine blood whose greenness was only symbolic. She did not want it. All she wanted was to hurry back to the magnificent woman who had given birth to her, to fall at her feet, to cover her hands with kisses and weep against her belly. Nothing more.

Leone assumed the boy's painful agitation was a result of their discovery. His own feelings veered between exultation, ecstasy even, and relief. He had found it at last, and yet his quest continued. Agnès, as his dream had revealed, was not the woman, but one of the initial mothers, like Philippine before her. She would give birth to the woman, for he was certain now that the dream that had for so long haunted him was a premonition. The future child was the one he must protect more than his own life.

He felt a warm, infinitely sad tenderness towards Éleusie de Beaufort, his mother, Clémence de Larnay, Philippine and Benoît, all of whom had guided him to this precise moment in time.

Clairets Abbey, Perche, January 1305

Three days later, Annelette, a little guiltily, decided to pay a visit to their poor senior nun, Blanche de Blinot, after nones. Following the dreadful death of the poisoner, Jeanne, she appeared to have become completely senile. In fact, the apothecary was unsure whether the old woman had quite fathomed the extent of the extern sister's wickedness. Blanche slept through the services, nodded off over her bowl at supper and the rest of the time she rambled – asking after their Reverend Mother, Éleusie de Beaufort, whom she had not seen all day. The novices took it in turns to bring her Elisaba's potent infusions. It was all Thibaude de Gartempe and Berthe de Marchiennes could do to cajole Blanche into leaving her steam room when evening came.

Guilty, yes. Annelette considered that she had been uncharitable and unsympathetic. And there were all those dead nuns, recently buried at Clairets, who weighed on her conscience too, for she regretted not having made enough effort to get to know them better.

Annelette Beaupré popped her head round the door of the steam room. Blanche opened her eyes and quickly closed them again – a sleep reflex, no doubt, judging from the steady rumbling of her chest. Annelette called out softly so as not to startle her:

'Blanche, dear. I've brought us a couple of goblets of mallow tea from the kitchen. They should warm us up nicely. I nudged Elisaba's elbow while she was sweetening yours, for I know how fond you are of honey. Can you hear me, Blanche?' she said, raising her voice.

The old woman jumped and seemed to emerge from a coma.

She blinked, then appeared to recognise the apothecary:

'Ah … Annelette, dear Annelette. How good of you to come and see me. Pray, sit down. Wait, I will move up to make a place for you. Pass me those goblets. I'll set them down so you don't scald yourself.'

The old woman carefully placed them next to those she had already drunk during a day mostly spent sleeping. The apothecary was afraid that with her sluggish movements and trembling hands she would drop one of the earthenware cups and that it would break on the floor. However, offering to help Blanche would have seemed discourteous. After all, nobody likes to be reminded that they are growing old.

Now that she was there, Annelette did not know what to talk about with this woman, whom she had never really liked. She said:

'Reading the Gospels is a great comfort, is it not?'

'Oh yes, indeed,' Blanche agreed. 'Every reading reveals new marvels.'

'Yes.'

Having exhausted the only subject for conversation she could think of, Annelette sighed, smiling:

'Shall we drink our tea before it goes cold?'

'With pleasure.'

Annelette made as if to get up, but Blanche held her back with a firm gesture.

'Stay where you are, my dear. It is good for me to move. My old legs are getting very stiff. Allow me.'

With a trembling hand, Blanche passed her the goblet. Annelette raised it to her lips and stifled a frown of dismay. The drink was terribly sweet and cold. The old nun must have mistakenly given her the wrong cup. It would be rude to point it out. No matter. She would drink it down to the dregs, well almost.

For the rest of her life Annelette would wonder about the role the senses played in comprehension.

For a brief moment she watched the tiny wisp of steam rising from the tea Blanche was noisily sipping. It was only when she once again raised her almost ice-cold tea to her lips that her senses alerted her. She looked up. The ruthless eyes staring at her were not those of a kindly old woman, but of Jeanne's accomplice.

Annelette leapt to her feet. The other woman pounced on her suddenly and unexpectedly, throwing her to the floor with her full weight. With extraordinary agility for someone her age, Blanche dug her knee brutally into Annelette's neck and chest and gagged her with her big fleshy hand. The apothecary understood. It hadn't been Jeanne d'Amblin who had held her hand over Yolande de Fleury's mouth when she lay dying in agony on her bed, but Blanche de Blinot. It was Blanche, too, who had brought the poisoned drink to Adélaïde so that she could make out that she had been the intended victim. What better way to divert suspicion away from her? But why Adélaïde? Had the young sister in charge of meals connected the rye bread Jeanne had ordered to the death of the Pope's emissary? Undoubtedly. Blanche was as much of a criminal as the other woman.

Despite gradually being choked, Annelette's rage gave her a sudden surge of strength and she dug her nails into the face distorted by hatred, scratching, slashing, tearing at it as fiercely as she could. The murderous grip loosened. The apothecary landed a violent kick somewhere on her enemy's anatomy and managed to leap to her feet and race over to the door. Blanche, hindered by her painful limbs, had difficulty standing up. She screamed out like a woman possessed:

'I hate you … all of you! Die, you wretch, die! Poor foolish women that you are! You're too stupid to understand how dangerous your ideas of purity are! The world is as it should be.'

Annelette, trembling all over, managed to remove the key

and lock the steam room from the outside. Blanche banged with her hands and feet on the heavy door, shouting and screaming torrents of abuse.

Annelette caught her breath and regained enough poise to shout back:

'You'll never stop us, you devils! You may kill us but others will take our place. As for you, you murderess, the lord chief bailiff will soon be coming for you. You will not escape his judgement and your sentence will be terrible.'

She was wrong. When Monge de Brineux arrived the next morning, escorted by his men-at-arms, they discovered Blanche dead – her bluish tongue protruding from her mouth, her dead eyes staring towards the cupboard where the ink-horns were stored.

In some of the discarded ones, they found dregs of powder of varying hues and odours. Annelette was able to identify the more unusual ones. Poisons that had been purchased outside the abbey or stolen from her cabinet in the herbarium. Blanche had not been sleeping in the steam room. She had been the self-appointed guardian of Jeanne's stock of poisons, and of the manuscripts.

Epilogue

One evening four days after Leone and Clément, with the aid of Annelette Beaupré, had made their astonishing discovery in the secret library at Clairets Abbey, Agnès grew anxious when Clémence, who she felt had changed, had become distant since returning from her adventure, failed to appear. She cautiously climbed the rickety ladder up to the eaves. The moment she pulled herself through the trapdoor, she knew that she was about to suffer a terrible blow. Clémence's clothes had gone. Agnès discovered a brief letter that had been left on top of the straw mattress.

Madame, my dearly beloved mother,

Since I have decided that this letter will be brief I must weigh each word, although I could fill a whole volume with expressions of my undying love for you. Four days ago, when I found the papyrus, I understood the power of your love for me, and this knowledge is the only thing I wish to take with me.

Is it possible to fight destiny? I do not know but, thanks to the courage I have inherited from you, I intend to try.

Ah ... Madame, if only you knew. My dream lasted but a few brief moments, there, when I realised that I was your daughter and how much you loved me. I could see only one thing: the two of us walking at sunset through the magnificent gardens at Château d'Authon. You placed your arm round my shoulder and I clasped mine round your waist. We laughed aloud as you muddled up the names of the flowers we were looking at. Madame ... what bliss! So brief, but can bliss wait? A few brief moments, before

I made up my mind to run away from the knight Leone and his kind, from their absolute faith and their pure love, before I made up my mind to fight my enemies alone, the dream dissolved. I must leave.

Be sure, Madame, that wherever I may be, you will be by my side. God watch over you.

I pray to heaven that you suffer no distress, Madame. The thought of you grieving for me is unbearable.

Live like the magnificent being you are.

Your ever-loving daughter, Clémence.

Agnès's tears choked her. She dropped the letter and slumped to her knees, howling like an animal.

Later, much later, she lay face down on the floor, exhausted. Never! She would find her, even if it meant travelling the length of the kingdom barefoot, searching in every house, in every hovel. She would find her!

Agnès leapt to her feet.

She would never accept being parted from Clémence.

* * *

Artus d'Authon gave Eudes de Larnay no chance to escape. He swooped on his prey like an eagle, pinning him against the wall of the main hall and declaring in a calm but threatening voice:

'You are nobody, Larnay, a stinking scoundrel, rotten to the core. I have the power to crush a criminal like you and I will not hesitate to do so if necessary. It would even give me some pleasure, so do not tempt me.'

Yielding hastily before the unambiguous threats of Lord d'Authon, his suzerain and soon to be brother-in-law, the minor baron Eudes de Larnay named the province where, according to him, his dear niece had wished to find peace with her Lord.

However, he continued claiming that he knew nothing more – if only to avoid finding himself on the wrong end of Artus d'Authon's sword.

When, after a long and arduous search, Agnès finally discovered the exact whereabouts of her eldest daughter, she learned that Mathilde de Souarcy had vanished from the abbey one night, two months earlier, taking with her a few old clothes, not to mention a number of liturgical objects and a dozen or so books that could easily be exchanged for money. Agnès d'Authon understood from the Mother Superior's sighs that no thorough search had been made for her daughter, whose stay at the abbey had left the other novices and nuns with no happy memories. She was devastated by the news, although not as much as she had feared ... or expected. However, instinct told her that, now that her mother had remarried, Mathilde would reappear in the not too distant future, if only to claim her inheritance.

* * *

The knight Leone was delighted to receive permission from the prior of the citadel in Cyprus to prolong his stay in France. Arnaud de Viancourt encouraged him to make contact with Monsieur de Got, the Archbishop of Bordeaux, in order to plead the Hospitallers' cause discreetly. The knight obeyed, glad of any opportunity to watch over Madame Agnès's belly.

* * *

On 5 June 1305, Monseigneur de Got was elected Pope, under the name Clément V. The Holy Father had the political intelligence to keep by his side the camerlingo Honorius Benedetti – about whom, thanks to Arnaud de Viancourt's revelations, there was not much he did not know — for the excellent reason that an enemy out in the open is less dangerous than one plotting behind the scenes.

* * *

Agnès de Souarcy, rather than request a castle, land or ravishing jewellery from her beloved husband Artus d'Authon, asked that he promise to find her little 'rascal' Clément for her. Much to the Comte's astonishment, she finally confessed that the boy was in fact a girl, and therefore deserved protection. The rest of the story being too dangerous to relate, she decided to lie by omission.

A year later, Agnès d'Authon, cosseted by the devotion and ceaseless attentions of her husband, who, in his own words, had become like an 'old mother hen', gave birth to a robust baby boy with his father's brown hair. Scarcely had the little lad opened his eyes than he was thrashing his legs and loudly demanding his mother's milk. The midwife, who was besotted with the bawling infant, held him aloft — as was the custom when a new heir was born — so that all could see 'that he was fully equipped and with a fine member, upon the midwife's word'. Agnès wanted her first-born son to be named Philippe. Everybody saw in this choice a charming homage to the King. She did not contradict them, although it had never even crossed her mind. The name had come to her one morning when she woke up, a few days before she gave birth.

After his delivery, the midwife had declared to anyone who wished to hear, especially those who offered her a generous goblet of wine in the village tavern, that in all her long career she had never seen such a child. 'He just slipped out, I tell you! That nine-pound baby just slipped out of her. I scarcely had time to fetch the basin and there he was – bright red and bawling his head off! You wouldn't think it from looking at her she's so slim, but there's a woman built to have a rabble of brats.'

* * *

Disappointed at the birth of little Philippe d'Authon, Francesco de Leone returned to Cyprus. Arnaud de Viancourt's warm reception heartened him. And yet he was haunted day and night by the same thought: she must have a daughter! The line could only be continued through the female sex.

* * *

Thanks to Joseph de Bologne's invaluable advice, the exploitation of the mine at La Haute-Gravière proved less taxing than Agnès had feared. Although now a rich woman after her marriage, she discovered that the habit of poverty is not easily forgotten, and she put aside the profits from the sale of the iron ore for Clémence. Because her beloved daughter would return, she must. God would not allow Agnès to suffer so cruelly again, not now that they could at last find happiness.

Joseph de Bologne – who it turned out did know everything about everything, as Clémence had claimed – explained to her that she could simply extract the iron ore and sell it – as was the custom – to a local lord or monastery equipped with a forge. However, the Norman Charter worked in her favour for once. In that province powerful leagues of ironworkers had been established,[76] concentrated in the neighbouring county of Ouche. In order to cut out the lords and monks, they exploited the ore in exchange for a fee and a percentage of the profits. Agnès had brought in these Normandy ironworkers and did not regret her decision.

* * *

Under Clair Gresson's orders, Arnaud de Viancourt's spies scoured the kingdom for a young boy called Clément with blue-green eyes. They did not find him.

Part Two:
Combat of Shadows

Auberge de la Carpe-Vieille, Authon-du-Perche, Perche, July 1306

Raimonde gave a contented sigh as she stretched her rheumatic limbs. The offer of a drink, pleasant company – what more did a woman need to lift her spirits? Her foot nudged the heavy basket full of victuals she had haggled over at the market. Those crooks! Everybody knew the harvest had been poor these two years, but good-for-nothing traders kept raising the prices and had you by the throat like brigands. Raimonde would not stand for it, screaming accusations of theft like a fishwife. That was how she came to meet Muguette, who had been standing beside her at one of the stalls. Upon hearing Raimonde's outburst, the young woman had turned and nodded in agreement.

'You're so right, my friend. These thieves get fat on the misery of other folk. When you think that only last Christmas one pound of lard cost a quarter of a denier,⁺ and now it's twice as much. And they're trying to tell us that the pigs have been hard hit by the bad weather! Are they mocking us?'

Feeling vindicated by the unexpected support, Raimonde had launched into another tirade of caustic remarks. Feigning shame, the greedy seller had hung his head and waited for the storm to pass. Though food was scarce, he was not short of customers. He wished the foul woman would cease complaining and move on, but either way his pockets would be well lined by the end of the day. It mattered little to him if paupers could not afford his wares. They could drop dead – there were so many of them that you would barely miss them.

Raimonde and Muguette had taken an immediate liking to each other and decided to seal their friendship with a well-earned pitcher at the nearby Carpe-Vieille tavern. Muguette looked like a well-off farmer's wife, judging by her lace-trimmed bonnet and the amethyst cross she wore on a thin black ribbon around her neck, not to mention her wedding ring, which had a turquoise the size of a little fingernail. In a surge of generosity rarely seen these days, she had said, 'It's my treat!'

Raimonde did not need any coaxing. She was too old and too tired to manage going back and forth to the market for victuals on her own, but Ronan, servant and confidant of the Comte d'Authon, would not listen to her. The kitchen cart and draught horse were reserved for heavy purchases, such as a whole beef, a stag shot in the woods by the master, barrels of wine, or bushels[+] of wheat or oats. Everything else had to be carried in your arms or in a wheelbarrow.

Muguette called the innkeeper. 'Maître Carpe, bring us some good wine. We've earned it.' Then, outraged, she said, 'Profiteering swine! They'll bleed us to death. My husband's a wise man and says there are hard times ahead, and I think he's right. Of course, we've got nothing to grumble about, but it wouldn't be very Christian of us to rejoice while so many others are suffering – not very Christian. At least that's what I think.'

'And that is most charitable of you,' Raimonde replied, emptying her goblet in one draught, followed by a click of the tongue.

Muguette immediately topped her up, encouraging her with a nod.

'So you're in the service of our goodly Comte Artus?' she asked with deference. 'What a man! Isn't afraid to get his hands dirty. We've seen him mowing barley like a simple labourer. And what a fine specimen of manhood.'

'Ah, to be sure,' the old woman agreed. 'And he's just and charitable.'

'We have little cause for complaint, in truth. We might wish for better weather for the harvests, of course, but such is life …'

They chatted at leisure of this and that, swapped secret recipes for various sauces, concoctions to soothe a burning throat, and the best method of sweating snails[77] in order to rid them of their bitter taste. In other words, they thoroughly enjoyed each other's company. Raimonde was sorry when the time came for her to leave, lest she earn another reprimand from Ronan. The man saw and knew everything; it was as if he had eyes in the back of his head.

The women parted at the door of the tavern, promising to meet again on the next market day. Raimonde guffawed. 'I have little means but next time it's on me.'

'It'll be a great pleasure to see you again, my friend.' Muguette said goodbye before vanishing round the corner of the narrow street.

Raimonde walked along, pushing her wheelbarrow, huffing and puffing. Good Lord, it was such a long way! The stony path made it hard for her to go faster, and she stopped regularly to catch her breath. She decided to demand that Ronan send a man to accompany her when she had to go to the market in future. She heard the sound of light running footsteps behind her and turned around. Muguette was rushing towards her, so she waited, smiling. The young woman stopped abruptly a few feet away, her hand on her bosom, out of breath. 'Oh, my Lord, I'm such a goose! My husband won't finish his business until late evening, so I can help you push your load.' She interrupted the faint gesture of protest the old woman was about to make, and insisted, 'No, no, it's the least a woman of my age can do for a woman of yours – hopefully some day someone will do the same for me. Now let me take over for a while.'

They chatted for ten minutes or so, then Muguette stopped. Raimonde took the wheelbarrow from her, and thanked

Providence for sending her such a helpful young woman.

Muguette started to limp and said, laughing, 'Wouldn't you know it! There's a stone in my shoe. Go ahead, Raimonde. I'll catch you up and relieve you.'

The old woman felt better. Thanks to sweet Muguette, the ache in her back had eased. She heard rapid footsteps, and turned her head slightly. Muguette must have got rid of the stone.

At first, for a split second, Raimonde's mind was empty of thought. But then a terrible pain exploded in her breast, pushing her forward. She wondered what wild beast was tearing at her flesh. She hiccuped and attempted to straighten up, open-mouthed, struggling for air. A stream of blood poured from her chest, staining her shert.[78] She wanted to scream and call for help, but her strength had already drained away. Raimonde collapsed, upsetting her wheelbarrow as she fell, oblivious to the fact that her charming companion had just sliced through her heart with a stiletto.

Muguette wiped the blade on the dress of the old woman lying face-down on the ground. Her lips curled in disgust, she rolled down the sleeves of her dress, which she had taken the precaution of turning up in case they were splashed with blood. She hated the denier-sized strawberry mark in the crook of her right elbow. She murmured, 'I'm sorry, Raimonde. God take your soul, my friend. I had no choice. You're an angel now, so I'm certain you forgive me.'

Muguette was about to hasten away from her victim when a thought stopped her in her tracks. All that food! No one finding the body would leave it for the bailiff's men. It was a sin to let food go to waste. Raimonde would not be needing it now. And, after all, Muguette now had to return her dress, her bonnet and her pretty jewels to her patron, and take back her poor rags.

She glanced over the scattered contents of the wheelbarrow.

There was a monkfish wrapped in grass to protect it from the heat. Good God, she had never eaten such a thing. A dish for a prince. And to think that it would go off by the following day. Also, a substantial portion of black pudding – a beauty – she would enjoy that. She gathered up the food without another glance at the woman bleeding her last.

Standing by the tall window of his study, his hands clasped behind his back, the camerlingo[79] Honorius Benedetti stared absently at the bishops' houses[80] that formed the heart of the papal palace built during the short reign of Nicholas III.[81] He hated himself for his uncontrollable impatience but so much depended on the replies he had been expecting for months.

Archbishop Benedetti appeared to be small and slight, an impression which was reinforced by the large desk, inlaid with ivory, mother-of-pearl, and turquoise lozenges, at which he sat. The only son of an important Verona merchant, he was hardly the right material for a man of the cloth, especially given his taste for the ladies and life's pleasures. Even so, thanks to his intelligence, which many described as sharp, he had risen through the Church hierarchy at astonishing speed. His many, albeit cautious, critics whispered that his dazzling talent for calculation and cunning had not done his ascent any harm either. A shrewd politician, he played on the terror he inspired in many. Fear is a wonderful deterrent for those who know how to use it.

As usual, Honorius Benedetti was dripping with sweat. He retrieved the mother-of-pearl fan from one of his desk drawers. Few were aware of the delicious secret surrounding that beautiful object. It had been given to him, early one morning, by a female conquest from Jumièges who he was never to see again. Nevertheless, her fan had been with him throughout his days as a priest. A delightful souvenir from over twenty years earlier. Strangely, it now seemed to him that his mind accommodated two different sorts of memory. A very distant but enduring one contained little moments of no importance but for the happiness they brought with them. His fishing excursions with his elder brother or their great imaginary adventures as they conspired together deep in the grounds of their large family home. His mother's volleys of throaty laughter that reminded him of the song of a rare bird. The soft skin of a few ladies or less-than-ladies. These memories had been set aside the very moment Benedetti had been assailed by divine grace. He had been stunned by a kind of immense, painful love, which he had not expected or asked for and which, had the choice been his, he would have gladly rejected. God had imposed upon him, and everything else had become blurred. So Benedetti had conceived a single aim – that of serving Him with all his might and intelligence. Ever since, during nights of deep despondency when he tried to seek out just one delightful memory banished by these twenty years of all-consuming faith, he could not find it. Instead, he was besieged by his other set of memories of plots, deceit and lies. And murders. So many murders, so many people whose demise he had ordered. Yet only one of these odious scars would gnaw at him till his last breath. The others, he would learn to live with. In fact, he already had. Only one face, one name persisted. Benoît XI,* his purulent wound. The angelic Benoît, whom he had loved like a brother and for whom he would have worked relentlessly, but whose poisoning he had ordered. Benoît had passed away in the arms of his murderer, murmuring fraternal words in his delirious death throes. Benedetti's eyes welled up with tears as he closed them to force himself to see, for the thousandth time, the large stain of bloody vomit on the dead Pope's robes.

Benoît, the much-loved lamb of God. You know, brother, I believe, deep in my soul, that the worst sin I could commit – I, who committed them all in full conscience – would be to seek absolution for your death. I want you to remain my worst nightmare, my damnation, the madness that sometimes creeps up on me and which I struggle against day after day. I want your death throes to torment me until the end of my own.

An usher, stooping obsequiously, put his head round the tall door and said in a plaintive voice, 'I knocked twice, Your Eminence.'

'Is he here?'

'He's waiting in the antechamber, Monseigneur.'

'Show him in immediately.'

Honorius Benedetti suddenly felt an unpleasant hollowness in his chest. What if it were bad news? What if the mission had been a failure? What if— Enough! He fanned himself nervously, making the fragile mother-of-pearl strips creak.

The prelate stretched his hand across his desk and greeted the young Dominican.

'Brother Bartolomeo, I must confess I was impatient ... and somewhat apprehensive about seeing you again.'

'Your Eminence ...'

'Take a seat and keep your news to yourself just a little while longer. You see, there are exceptional moments in life that we wrongly disregard because of our foolish eagerness to bring matters to a conclusion. And yet these moments are the turning points of our existence. Once the doors are shut behind us, they are closed for ever, with no hope of going back. We should therefore acknowledge the profound importance of these moments.'

Bartolomeo nodded in agreement, uncertain as to the exact meaning of the camerlingo's words. These past months had been so tumultuous that sometimes he felt dizzy.

An unknown little inquisitor in Carcassonne, he had obstinately requested an audience with the camerlingo in order to denounce a wicked brother who enjoyed the atrocious tortures he inflicted on innocent people. The pernicious Nicolas Florin savoured every facet of his talent for destruction. He delighted in disconcerting, seducing, intoxicating, conquering and devastating souls who were too trusting, because it strengthened his confidence in his own toxic power. Bartolomeo had been one of those souls. Nicolas had worked his charm patiently, until he had left him with no will to resist an attachment that had nothing brotherly about it. Of course, the sin of the flesh and sodomy had been avoided. However, Bartolomeo was perceptive enough to realise that he would have succumbed had his torturer not grown weary. Nicolas had suddenly found his own seduction game irksome. Every night, Bartolomeo had silently thanked the camerlingo, whose intervention had saved him from the worst and most exquisite temptation by appointing Florin Grand Inquisitor for the Alençon region. He had prayed for this just man who had put so many defenceless people out of harm's way. And then Nicolas had been stabbed to death by a passing drunk; at least that was what Bartolomeo had been told. Even so, Florin's evil shadow had not completely evaporated but had clung to the young Dominican's slightest action for weeks, following him like an insane reproach.

Then he had received a short missive at the Inquisition* headquarters in Carcassonne. Such a surprising missive that at first he thought he had mistaken its meaning. The camerlingo Honorius Benedetti was summoning him to his side, in Rome, where he was henceforth to serve. Far from this going to Bartolomeo's head, on the contrary, he was gripped with fear that he was not up to the task the prelate expected of him. To serve the greatness he had sensed in the archbishop during their brief conversation seemed to be beyond his abilities.

He had appeared before the prelate, insisting that he was probably lacking in competence. However, Bartolomeo's gentle stubbornness had persuaded Benedetti that the young Dominican was what he was looking for, and so he had dispelled the young man's doubts.

'Brother, I've known so many men who weren't what they pretended or thought they were. I have sometimes been unpleasantly surprised and, at other times, happily so. Therefore, let me be the judge of your skills.'

Masking his world-weariness beneath friendly tones, Benedetti had then explained to the young Dominican the meaning and inflexibility of his holy mission: Church order had to prevail, no matter what the cost, in order to rein in the worst human tendencies. Subsequently, the research the camerlingo had entrusted to Bartolomeo had taken up all the latter's attention, and he had not questioned the soundness of the archbishop's convictions. After all, God had chosen to place Monseigneur Benedetti in the Vatican and there could therefore be no doubt that that was where He needed his help. In fact, little by little, the young man had caught a glimpse of Honorius Benedetti's wider canvas, and had felt that his own role, no matter how lowly, could contribute to turning man away from bestiality and drawing him towards the light. And so Bartolomeo's apprehension had been replaced with joy. He was finally serving mankind – all the brothers and sisters to whom he had given his life for the love of Christ. Thus, Nicolas Florin's shadow had crumbled and disappeared entirely.

The prelate's oddly serious tone punctured Bartolomeo's happiness.

'The moment's gone, Bartolomeo, and I have savoured it. And now your news. Is it good?'

'I don't know, Your Eminence. The issues are too complex for me to understand the situation fully, as you will see. Having said that, I believe it's favourable.'

'Give me all the details.'

'As you ordered, I spoke to the Abbot of Vallombroso,* Father Eligius, a kindly, sound man. He's loyal to you and was happy to tell me the whole story. The old mathematician monk, Brother Liudger, who conceived this blasphemous astronomical theory seems to have been an inveterate rebel,' Bartolomeo said disapprovingly. 'Despite warnings from the other brothers, he wouldn't rest until he'd proved that he was right, and that Ptolemy's[82] greatest work was no more than a collection of glaring errors. What presumption!'

Looking stern, Honorius Benedetti approved of the outburst by shaking his head. Sweet little monk. Of course, the Earth moved around the sun, and not the other way round, but no point in disabusing him. The young Dominican had to keep on believing, like others, that he was God's successful project – His crowning glory. Even the planets and the sun had to pay homage to man's Earth by moving around it. There was no end to human arrogance.

'Then the recalcitrant Brother Liudger slipped, probably because his pattens had got soaked ...'

He slipped because I had someone push him – a killer I'd hired and who smashed his skull against a pillar, Honorius mentally corrected. We've recovered the manuscript where he recorded his remarkable advances in astronomy. The Earth is not still in the middle of the firmament but moves around the sun, like the other planets. In addition, Liudger's calculations have proved the existence of three other stars. This veritable revolution in knowledge implies that all the birth charts, and possibly even our astrological medicine, have been established using incorrect data. We were advancing in the calculations that would have allowed us to clarify the second birth chart of the prophecy: 'The bloodline passes down through the women. The blood that is different* will be reborn through one of them. Her daughters will perpetuate it.'

Agnès de Souarcy was one of the women, the first birth chart – the one they had managed to decipher. Everything pointed to the fact that it was she who, some day, would give birth to the new Mother. The number of generations did not matter. There was no doubt whatsoever that the second birth chart concerned one of her daughters, the one who would perpetuate that unique bloodline. And then that damned thief, Gachelin Humeau, had to go and steal the Vallombroso treatise, one of humanity's most valuable manuscripts, as well as other works, from Boniface VIII's* personal library, in order to sell them to the highest bidder.

'... the notebook where he wrote down all his nonsense has vanished into thin air ...'

'Yes, yes, I know all that,' Benedetti said, irked. 'Didn't you gather any new information during your stay in Vallombroso?'

'Yes, Your Eminence, I'm getting there. Even though all this happened over five years ago, Abbot Eligius is still upset by it, and he is still tirelessly pursuing his investigation.'

'He's a brave soul,' said Honorius, thinking he would soon have to find a bishopric as a reward for the said Eligius to ensure the latter's silence and continued gratitude. He, of course, would put up a show of protest and swear that his sole concern was defending the Church. Ongoing play-acting that did not deceive anyone. A prize, but only if the good abbot gave him what he had been seeking for years: a way of accessing the discoveries of the mathematician monk.

'... Brother Liudger's fingers were deformed by an ailment of old age. He could barely tie his sandals, let alone hold a quill. In other words, he could not have written down all the nonsense littering the pages of his manuscript.'

'Then did someone else transcribe it for him?' Honorius asked with tension in his voice.

'Definitely, and yet Father Eligius said that our villainous monk didn't trust anyone, especially after the reprimands and formal demands that he stop his nonsense at once. He could only have trusted someone loyal and well versed in mathematics, and who wouldn't have made any errors in the copying.'

'And do we know who this confidant was?'

'Indirectly, Your Eminence. A young Benedictine went missing from the monastery a few days after Brother Liudger's accident. He had just been ordained, and his master of novices was none other than our ranting astronomer. If I might be allowed to express my opinion, I wouldn't be at all surprised if he'd stolen the manuscript in the hope of making money from it.'

How wrong you are, my charming Bartolomeo, Honorius thought. It is we who recovered the theory after its author was murdered. As for the young monk, he must have got scared, which proves he's not only erudite but also sensible.

'And the name of the young Benedictine?'

'Sulpice de Brabeuf. He's vanished from the face of the earth, spirited away.'

'Then we'll find him. We must, and as soon as possible.'

'Your Eminence, do you think he would have perfect recall of all the many equations he wrote down under dictation, even if he's a skilled mathematician?'

'Of course not. However, paper is very expensive, and monasteries are thrifty. Copyists often practise on blank strips recovered from the bottoms of letters or other writings, in order to minimise mistakes and avoid damaging a nice clean page. Moreover, as you know, scribbling a letter or even just a sentence, delicate as it might be, can take up several hours of copying. In addition, let's assume that our two accomplices must have worked in secrecy and not had much time. In other words, I wouldn't be surprised if there's a rough draft of the work somewhere. If I were in Sulpice de Brabeuf's shoes, I would have made sure to take it with me when I ran away.'

'How shall I proceed in order to find him?'

'You'll receive help. We must act quickly. As quickly as possible. Search the neighbouring monasteries on my behalf. See if a young priest or monk arrived there shortly after this Sulpice disappeared. Having said that, I doubt he's hiding in a monastery. Perhaps he's gone into the world under an assumed name. I don't know, Bartolomeo.' The camerlingo's tone was increasingly one of irritation. 'This Brabeuf must have a family and connections outside the order, since he was very young when this happened. It's possible he sought their help.'

'I'll search day and night, Monseigneur.'

'Don't hesitate to remind any recalcitrants of the consequences of incurring our displeasure. At the same time, gently promise those who help us our prayers and forgiveness for their past errors. Often those who fear for their comfort in the next life become strangely meek.'

Forest of Trahant, Perche, July 1306

Aude de Neyrat held a square of fine linen soaked in rose essence to her nose. The stench in the hut turned her stomach. Black smoke rose from a central hearth that had been dug out of the clay soil towards a hole in the roof, which was made of boughs and thatch. The black hen suspended over the fire by its legs, and whose throat had been cut, had stopped struggling. A few drops of blood were still falling on the firebrands with a sizzle. The witch was fussing by the fire, mumbling without stopping to catch her breath, occasionally throwing into it a pinch of powder that flared up with a green glow.

Aude was growing impatient, trying to control her pressing desire to exit the hovel and breathe some fresh air. Her face tense with concentration, the witch collected a large handful of disgusting viscera from a cauldron and threw them on the brands. The fresh emanation of reeking fumes that spread between the walls of blackened planks made Aude retch. Madame de Neyrat, Camerlingo Benedetti's bosom friend, gratefully in his debt and, therefore, his accomplice, was surprised at Honorius's insistent recommendation of this witch. Did he really believe in the powers of darkness, he who up to then had only used poisoners, including Aude de Neyrat herself?

A gentle sigh escaped from one of the dark corners of the hovel. Aude turned her head and squinted to try to make out the shape of the little girl sitting cross-legged on the ground. Earlier, the stunning-looking child had welcomed her with a charming curtsey, before quickly disappearing into the shadows where she could not be seen. Madame de Neyrat was puzzled by the stark contrast between the witch's emaciated body, her long black fingernails, thick and curved like a dog's claws, her straight hair, so tangled it looked like an ugly mane of suint and grime, and that little blonde angel with limpid eyes. In truth, the little girl could have passed for Aude's own natural daughter, and not for the witch's offspring. Could she be one of those children left to die by poor parents, or a pretty little angel snatched from her cradle in order to be trained to inspire the pity of customers on market days or matrons standing around gossiping in the church porch? Aude de Neyrat had then focused all her attention on the dark woman, who could have been thirty years old as easily as one hundred, and forgotten all about the little girl.

There was another, barely audible sigh. Aude gestured into the darkness. Something stirred and the child approached her shyly. She glanced anxiously at the back of the woman, who was droning at the dying fire, and ventured a slight grimace of disgust. Aude found the way she scrunched up her nose delightful. She smiled and nodded at the little girl to join her. She held out her fine, perfumed handkerchief and the child buried her adorable little face in it, closing her eyes with pleasure. The admiration Aude saw in her eyes as she returned the fine square of fabric made her almost forget the insalubrious atmosphere for a few seconds. She tapped the ground next to the rickety stool on which she was sitting, and the little girl rushed to sit by her.

'Are we making any progress?' Madame de Neyrat suddenly asked, annoyed.

'Yes, we've almost finished,' the witch answered in a cheerful voice.

'Are you quite certain your ... your art is powerful? Since I'm paying so handsomely for it ...'

The woman turned abruptly and froze at the sight of the little girl curled up at the feet of the splendid creature who had entered her foul-smelling lair an hour earlier. A haze of blonde hair framed her perfectly oval angel face. Two enormous emerald lakes, which tapered like almonds towards the temples, stared at her without a hint of fear and, in fact, with a kind of haughty contempt. The witch's mood changed. Did this beautiful young lady think the whole world should bow before her? If so, she was clearly ignorant of the powers of the woman who had been recommended to her, and whom everyone feared.

The woman hissed, 'Go back into your corner, Angélique, unless you want a good thrashing.'

Before she scampered off, the child cast a terrified glance at Madame de Neyrat, whose aversion to the witch was growing by the second. The child back in her place, the hag's manner mellowed and she made an effort to be amiable towards her wealthy guest. The purse the lady had given her was nice and full. Much more than she ever got from local peasants trying to get rid of a wart or make one appear on the face of a rival, those who wanted to conceive a son, or even to do away with a troublemaker without risk of getting caught.

The hag explained, 'I'm not one of those mediocre witches who sell their useless philtres to gullible folk, or those sorceresses who say they can cause miscarriage and barrenness in women and beasts.'

'I'm glad to hear it,' Madame de Neyrat simpered. 'Oh, I nearly forgot … Did you manage to obtain what I wanted?'

'Most certainly.'

The woman plunged her claws into her dirty, oversized dress, and pulled out a small parcel wrapped in thick cloth. Aude condescended to stand and take it, then sat back down gracefully and unwrapped what turned out to be a slender ring with streaks of iridescent grey-white. She turned it over in her hands, her beautiful mouth pursed in an expression of doubt.

The hag tried to justify herself. 'I've followed your orders to the letter! It was hard to find.' Staring at Madame de Neyrat with her jet-black eyes, she murmured, 'In spite of your splendid finery, your bearing and that angelic face behind which I see an abyss, I know I can tell you the truth. Others cannot understand or even bear it ... whereas we both know, don't we? That you must always pay for something you want above all else. Cowards find some prices unacceptable, but you and I know – am I not right?'

Madame de Neyrat merely nodded in agreement. The witch continued in the same calm, almost detached tone. 'I wanted to outshine them all. In order to reach my goal, I had to form a ... a union with powerful allies. Powerful but ruthless and without pity ...' She pointed her sharp talons at the clay floor. 'They have no interest in money, glory or even gratitude. The only thing they find irresistible is souls. So I offered mine in the bargain. I knew exactly what I was doing and have no regrets. I've seen, learnt and heard so many strange and wonderful things. I've penetrated many of the mysteries that surround us. The souls of others are an open book to me.' The witch closed her eyes and an expression of sadness without a trace of anger appeared on her face, making it less repulsive for a fleeting moment. 'Well, Madame, let me tell you that the souls of those who come here, or that I happen to meet by chance, have a powerful stench. So it's no wonder that my ... my powerful allies chose mine. It was pure. I'll wager yours was, too. But that was before. Before.'

Memories. So many memories rushed like a malignant tide into Aude de Neyrat's mind. Her early life had been mercilessly turbulent. It was a miracle that she bore no scars from it. Fate preys on people. It sniffs out the weakest creatures and sets out to undo them little by little. Orphaned when she was very young, Aude had been entrusted to the guardianship of a repulsive old uncle who had stubbornly confused family charity with *droit de seigneur.* However, the villain did not enjoy the bewitching charms of his young niece for very long. Excruciating stomach cramps had soon confined him to bed to die a painful death, while his ward devotedly watched over him. At the age of twelve, she was discovering that her talent for poison and cunning were equalled only by her beauty and intelligence. An aunt, some cousins who stood to inherit and who looked her up and down with the haughtiness of those who have never had to fight for their survival, and a cantankerous, bedridden husband, all soon followed the libidinous uncle to a world Aude wished might be a better one for them.

Madame de Neyrat's head was spinning. She had betrayed, cheated, plotted and killed. God. Would God, in His infinite wisdom, realise that she had been driven to these crimes only by circumstances? Probably not. She forced herself to be calm and stared at the ill-tanned wolf skins hanging from the low ceiling. The strange thought suddenly crossed her mind that they were probably the spoils of recent poaching which could have cost the woman her life. Was she therefore so feared that even her lord had no hold over her? Aude de Neyrat's scepticism of the woman's powers was beginning to diminish.

The witch studied her seriously for a while, perhaps hoping for a response that would prove that, despite their differences, they were two of a kind. Aude de Neyrat sat stiffly and quietly on her stool.

The witch asked, 'Must the child die with the mother?'

'Heavens, no, poor little angel!' Madame de Neyrat replied with irony. 'We're not monsters. In any case, a male heir will not be a problem. What ... what will happen afterwards?'

'It will all go smoothly, and then I'll forget all about you, as usual.'

Madame de Neyrat was insistent. 'Humour me with a few details.'

'A slow, drawn-out illness. The symptoms will start shortly after the little bag I'm about to prepare is placed near the bewitched woman, in her chamber, under her bed, for instance. What usually happens is that she'll lose her appetite and languish until she dies.' The witch hesitated for a moment, then added, 'It shouldn't surprise anyone around to see her health failing. They'll just think it's the curse of the d'Authon ladies. The first Comtesse, and now the new wife, Madame Agnès de Souarcy. A tragic train of events.'

Madame de Neyrat's curiosity was aroused. 'Did you by any chance have anything to do with the demise of the first Comtesse d'Authon and her son?'

The witch looked at her askance. 'Those are secrets I never share.'

'Wise woman. Will she – I mean Madame Agnès – suffer?'

'Except for seeing her life ebb away from her, no. Why, would you like her to?'

Aude de Neyrat was indignant. 'What do you take me for? I just want to get rid of an obstacle, that's all. I have no taste for suffering – not even other people's. To tell you the truth, I don't care for her either way. It takes someone to hurt me very deeply before I enjoy torturing them.'

Only once had she done that, and with great joy, when she had prolonged the death throes of the uncle who crushed her with his weight whenever he felt like it, pulled her by the hair to force her to open her mouth, and slapped her with the back of his hand if ever she protested or wept. She could have hastened his death but, instead, she chose to draw it out. As she washed the old man's hands with cool water, dabbed his forehead with a handkerchief and his lips with a damp cloth soaked with poison, she witnessed the progress of his death with delight.

'What's in the little bag?'

'Some effective ingredients – what they are exactly is my secret. The closer it stays to the lady, the quicker fate will act.'

'Have you thought of a way of getting it close to her?'

'Don't fret. That is all in hand. That's another thing you're paying me for.'

'When will she meet her Maker?' Madame de Neyrat then asked with the flippancy of a lady out on a visit.

'Three to five months, depending on her constitution. It's the price to pay if you don't want anyone to suspect a poisoning.'

'A second pregnancy would be most inconvenient. The Château d'Authon midwife tells anyone who offers her a drink in the nearby tavern that Madame de Souarcy is built to bear children. If she were already with child …'

The witch spoke with some hesitation.

'If it were merely a question of making her womb barren, that would be easy. Do you want her never to bear children? Death is too serious a matter to dish it out lightly.'

'Perceptive as well as moderate,' Aude de Neyrat joked. 'We're in a rush and there's no more time for half-measures. She must die, and quickly.'

'I'll do as you say. You're paying.'

'Have we nearly finished?'

'Here, for the time being, yes,' said the witch, retrieving a little bag of black cloth from under her grimy dress. A smile hovered on her lips as she opened it slightly, pulled six feathers out of the slaughtered hen, and stuffed them inside.

'The spell is cast,' she said. 'Once this little bag is in place, the rest will follow without any need for us to get involved.'

'What a happy prospect!' Aude de Neyrat exclaimed brightly. 'I hate this corner of the earth, with its constant morning mist that never clears before midday. The sun seems to struggle to break through. I can't wait to return to my fiefdom in the south of the kingdom. To hell with the rain that chills you to the bone and makes you feel prematurely old!'

Aude de Neyrat stood up gracefully, rearranged her crimson velvet dress with its fastened sleeves and, in a conversational tone, asked, 'How much for Angélique?'

'She's not for sale,' the hag replied, suddenly turning venomous.

'Why not? Everything's for sale at the right price. You know that as well as I do. One hundred pounds[83] for the little girl. It's a generous offer for an orphan no different from twenty or a hundred or a thousand others around. Especially since she's going to leave you as soon as she's able to. It would be foolish to refuse.'

'She's not for sale,' the woman insisted.

'But you stole her, didn't you?'

'So what? If I stole her, then she's mine.'

'One hundred and fifty pounds. Think about it. You could buy half the town of Ceton, with that. Wouldn't that be sweet revenge?'

'Leave. I've given you what you came for. Now leave.'

'Two hundred pounds. It's my final offer.'

'And my answer is still no.'

'You're making a mistake,' Aude simpered. 'I always end up getting what I want.'

'Take care, I know some frightful secrets.'

Aude closed her eyes. A charming smile lit up her face. She whispered, 'Not against me. So many have wished me dead or afflicted by awful pain. I'll wager some even paid people of your kind handsomely to make it happen. And look at me: I'm alive and in rude health. I'm starting to believe I shall never die or suffer old age. You don't frighten me ...'

Aude's pale eyelids opened lazily and she fixed her eyes, as green as a deep lake, on the dark woman. She continued in a serious, resolute voice.

'... and I will have Angélique. It's a whim and a promise. I like to humour my whims, and I always keep my promises.'

Her countenance darkened as she remembered that two years earlier, for the first time in her life, she had failed to keep her promise. She had promised the camerlingo Honorius Benedetti the life of Madame Agnès de Souarcy, now Comtesse d'Authon, and three manuscripts kept hidden in Clairets Abbey*, and failed miserably. In her defence, it was because of the pathetic woman entrusted with carrying out the killing, an abbey nun who had been recruited by the prelate. The one satisfaction she had derived from her failure was to have finally killed that Jeanne d'Amblin, the extern[84] sister. Those whom the witch had indicated earlier with the tips of her claws must have feasted on that vile soul who had done her so much harm and brought her so little credit.

As for herself, what could she pride herself on? What credit did she still have? Her honour. It was all that remained intact. A strange honour that accepted lies and murder. An honour the rules of which she alone had drawn up. Not a weight heavy enough on the scales to counterbalance her debits. Angélique. Angélique was not just a spoilt woman's fancy. For the past hour, Aude had convinced herself that the charming child with the predestined name was the weight she needed to reduce her debt. She would have Angélique. She would raise her as her own daughter and give her all that the world had conceded to her only after a fierce struggle. After all, if she returned one of God's angels to Him, He would doubtless be more inclined to exercise mercy.

How could she snatch the little girl from the witch when she might still need the hag to rid her of that illegitimate noblewoman? She had to wait and plan. Patience is one of women's most infallible weapons. They excel at it. Moreover, being a cautious woman, Madame de Neyrat had limited belief in the power of sorcerers, no matter how feared they were. Intrigue and poison seemed more reliable and somewhat more real. After all, sometimes lesser things were more powerful.

She took her seat in the covered cart that was waiting about sixty feet[+] away from the hut. Her plan was taking shape. The day before, she had received from the camerlingo Honorius Benedetti the information she had been awaiting for weeks. It was the name of another abbey of nuns, located in Champagne. For once, Honorius's henchmen had done a good job. Of course, the journey would be long and dull, but Aude de Neyrat was already savouring her impending success.

G iorgio Zuccari, chief captain of the Lombards[85] in France,
was sweating with embarrassment in his long rich brocade
coat. His chaperon[86] alone appeared to weigh twenty pounds.
Despite his large bulk, which made it difficult for him to walk,
he had turned his nose up at the boatmen who carried people
and bundles of merchandise between the Tour de Nesle and
the Louvre. Instead, he had chosen to elbow his way through
the infernal bustle in the streets, be shoved by idle passers-by,
merchants and whores, and harassed by clusters of flies rising
from heaps of rubbish along the central gutters. He panted his
way through the maze of narrow streets, shuffling across the
Île de la Cité until he reached the Grand-Pont which led to Rue
Saint-Denis. He had then walked round and round, sometimes
retracing his steps, allowing himself more time to think before
reaching the great tower of the Louvre.

The building works of the Palais de l'Île de la Cité, which had
been decreed by Saint Louis, had not yet begun. All the powers
of the State therefore remained sheltered within the forbidding
citadel that rose beyond the border of the capital city, not far
from Porte Saint-Honoré. It was a little cramped inside what was,
after all, the austere dungeon which Philip Augustus[87] had built
in order to centralise the Chancery, the Accounts department and
the Treasury.

The previous week, Giorgio Zuccari had requested an audience
with the King's close counsellor without, however, elaborating
on the reason for his visit. Nogaret had immediately complied
with his request. Not only was Zuccari the biggest banker in the

Kingdom of France, and you do not fall out with your banker until you are able to repay him, but the captain of the Lombards had a good reputation. A reputation for flawless integrity which suited the rigid Guillaume de Nogaret. The Lombard did not hesitate to extend the terms of repayment to twenty-four months, something few other lenders granted.

An usher pushed the door open and Monsieur de Nogaret walked into his antechamber. Zuccari rose from the armchair into which he had collapsed from exhaustion a few minutes earlier.

'My old friend,' Guillaume de Nogaret greeted him as he approached with outstretched hands in a rare gesture of cordiality.

'Thank you for receiving me so promptly, my lord.'

'I am always pleased to see you.'

A faint smile lit up the counsellor's gaunt face.

Once again, it struck Zuccari, as it had a thousand times before, that Nogaret might only be thirty or so, yet he looked ancient. Short and puny, his strange, statue-like eyelids, without lashes, emphasised the unpleasant stony nature of his features. He wore the long robe of the jurists and the only concession to sartorial luxury granted by his office consisted in a felt bonnet which covered his head and exposed his ears.

'The pleasure – and, may I add, the honour – is all mine,' said Zuccari, bowing his head.

'Let's sit, my dear friend. They should bring us some refreshing grape juice and a few plum cakes soon.'

Nogaret was not known for being especially civil with his numerous visitors, so this was an unusual mark of respect. Respect, but also political shrewdness since, in addition to being the moneylender to the powerful of this world, Zuccari had had the ear of all the popes since the arrogant Boniface VIII, and the current pontiff, Clément V,[88] was no exception to the rule. Men –

even popes – come and go, but the secrets of Rome live on, never to die.

'You have been very unforthcoming as to the object of your visit, my dear Zuccari …'

The Lombard tightened his lips, annoyed, and once again sidestepped the issue.

'It's just that it weighs most heavily on me, my lord.'

Nogaret studied his interlocutor for a few seconds, noting the way he nervously rubbed his small, fat hands together and the perspiration on his upper lip.

'Good heavens!' he said, surprised. 'It's the first time I've seen you ill at ease.' He paused briefly, then added, 'I've seen you feign embarrassment in order to throw people off the track often enough to know when you're truly lost for words.'

Giorgio Zuccari responded to the backhanded compliment with a slight movement of the head, then made up his mind to speak.

'Perhaps it would be best if I tell you everything, my lord. I've just returned from Rome …'

He was interrupted by the unobtrusive entrance of a servant carrying a tray with tall crystal glasses and a small wooden board heaped with plum cakes. Without so much as a glance in his direction, Nogaret waved the man away.

'I beg you, carry on, my friend.'

'Well … First of all, I wish to thank you, as ever, for your … your discreet intervention which allowed me to keep my office as captain. That ugly wart Giotto Capella[89] had been trying to push me out for years, while flattering me and calling me his "kindly uncle".'

Guillaume de Nogaret dismissed this reminder with an elegance that suggested his help to the Lombard had been a mere trifle. However, Zuccari was not taken in. Nothing Nogaret decided or plotted was ever disinterested, except his service to the King and realm of France.

'Let's forget these old memories,' the counsellor replied. 'I disliked Capella, whereas helping you suited me. That angry gout-ridden man stank of carrion. We need that sort to perform all the dirty work but their presence leaves me nauseous. Especially since he had also heartily recommended a nephew to me who ended up leaving me most unpleasantly in the lurch. A certain Francesco Capella, who seemed so affable and helpful. Still, it's all water under the bridge. Let's forget about it and, instead, use these lessons for the present and future.' Nogaret took a large sip of dark-purple grape juice and continued. 'So to what do I owe your visit?'

He was answered by an embarrassed sigh.

'Good heavens! Is it that bad? Obviously, you're not here to collect a debt of the realm – you don't usually find that a difficult task. Come now, my friend, we have a good rapport and I'm certain you wouldn't have requested an audience simply to tell me about your recent trip to Rome … Unless you met someone there whom you and I consider important. And that cannot be our beloved Pope, since he isn't there.'

Zuccari was at the same time worried and reassured by the fact that Nogaret saw through him so easily. Everyone knew the King's counsellor's vast intelligence and icy subtlety, and that made the Lombard's task a little easier. Nevertheless, he stumbled.

'Monsieur d'Authon … Our beloved and highly revered Clément V—'

'Where's the link,' Nogaret interrupted, 'between Comte Artus and our – may God watch over him – Holy Father?'

Suddenly adopting a resolute tone although he wished he could disappear down a mouse hole, the banker gave a little cough.

'The link? It's the murder of the Grand Inquisitor in Alençon. A certain Nicolas Florin about whom, admittedly, there were awful rumours but who, no matter what, was one of the strong arms of the Church.'

Nogaret knew all about it. An inquisitor in Carcassonne, who had distinguished himself by his cruelty, had had a young widow, an illegitimate noblewoman, arrested under suspicion of complicity in heresy, further aggravated by devil worship.[90] The said Florin had been murdered by a drunkard he had picked up in some disreputable tavern, shortly after the interrogation had begun. The judgement of God had been invoked, proving the suspect innocent. Nogaret, a man of demanding and total faith, had been overwhelmed by emotion. God Himself had dispensed justice. He had therefore never entertained any doubt that the woman had been as pure as a newborn lamb. Subsequently, this Agnès, Dame de Souarcy, had married Comte Artus d'Authon, a childhood friend of the King. Naturally, the bond between the two men had weakened over the years. Nevertheless, Artus was the man who had taught Philip the Fair* how to handle arms, as well as how to lead a lady through the night in such a way that she would sigh with contentment amid crumpled sheets the following morning. That kind of bond between two men lasts beyond the years.

'Zuccari, don't tell me Lord d'Authon had anything to do with the murder of this dreadful butcher whose outrageous reputation reached our ears?'

'Yes, indeed, I regret to say. There are two testimonies that point in his direction, as well as a piece of irrefutable evidence the nature of which has not been revealed to me. Equally, the judgement of God could have been legitimately invoked if a stranger, a tramp for instance, had been the murderer ...'

'But becomes less convincing if it was Lord d'Authon, the

lady's current husband, who killed the tormentor,' the counsellor concluded.

The banker stared at him for a long time before speaking.

'And so you see my problem,' he said despairingly.

'Are these testimonies reliable?'

'As reliable as they can be. The most damning one comes from a little street urchin who runs small errands for a few coins. Lord d'Authon paid him to follow the Grand Inquisitor Florin then give him his personal address. This report is corroborated by Maître Rouge, the innkeeper at the Jument-Rouge in Alençon, who saw and heard the Comte d'Authon talk to the boy.'

'From what I've heard, the Grand Inquisitor's valuables were stolen.'

'It's what the murderer had us believe, but that's not the case. Our Holy Father's investigators didn't waste any time. They drew up an inventory of the nauseating contents of the cesspit at the home requisitioned by Nicolas Florin. He had seized[91] it from a wealthy burgher accused of consorting with the devil.'

Nogaret pictured men of the cloth digging in malodorous mud with their hands. He stifled a retch.

The banker continued. 'So these investigators swam in excrement for two whole days, and found the rings that had been stolen from Nicolas Florin. What kind of drunken robber would throw his booty into the cesspit straight after committing his crime? But it may be the signature of a gentleman who protects the woman he loves but would never stoop to robbery.'

Nogaret was losing his footing and, as a man of control, not to mention conspiracy, this was something he could not bear. He returned to the question that had been gnawing at him since the start of this strange conversation – strange and uncalled for, since it had been brought about by a Lombard banker better versed in politics and money than in divine interventions or such matters. He took the time to eat a plum cake and pretended not to understand.

'My dear friend, you're confusing me ... What's your interest in this story of a minor noblewoman whose importance lies only in having married Artus d'Authon?'

The banker drained his glass abruptly and stammered, 'Ah, my lord, if only you knew how difficult this mission is for me.'

Nogaret studied him, unable to decipher his meaning. 'Your mission, my dear Giorgio?' he whispered.

'Certainly – and entrusted by the highest power.'

'The Pope?'

'In person, through the intermediary of his camerlingo, the much-feared Honorius Benedetti, who summoned me to Rome. I must confess I'm puzzled. Why would the outcome of an Inquisition trial of a bastard noblewoman, then Madame de Souarcy, worry the pontiff so much? Especially since I understand the trial itself contained many irregularities.'

Monsieur de Nogaret finally grew impatient and said, without any more pretence, 'What does our benevolent Clément V want, and why?'

'He's demanding an investigation and will not give up on it. If the Dame de Souarcy has wrongly benefited from a judgement of God that turned out to be in her favour, then he wants to know. He's not saying he will demand another Inquisition trial – that would not be a wise political move. You know the people are fond of this kind of indirect trial by ordeal,[92] especially since Monsieur Florin was so detested by the population of Alençon. Nevertheless, the Holy See wants answers and Lord d'Authon is the only one able to provide them. I must insist on this point, my lord counsellor. From what I understand, it's not a question of going back over the outcome of Madame de Souarcy's trial but simply of clarifying the situation. After all, if the lady has benefited from a miracle, then this is an exceptional enough event to attract a keen interest on the part of the Pope and his entourage.'

Nogaret smiled faintly. 'Monsieur d'Authon is a friend of the King, or at least someone the King cares about. The Comte has been shrewd enough not to interfere in the affairs of the realm and not to seek the favour of the King. My master retains a vague but friendly memory of him. In other words, handing him over to the law would be … how shall I put it … inappropriate and not well received.'

Giorgio Zuccari looked down at his plump hands and murmured, 'A favour would be rewarded.'

'Truly? What do you mean?'

'Well … I wouldn't wish to speak for the camerlingo, but it seemed to me that His Eminence appreciated the King's dilemma. An important detail here: the conversation took place in Latin and you know how it is with priests, my lord … they're experts at rhetoric and double meanings that come more easily to those who have mastered the language to perfection. With them, it's better to read between the lines and never underestimate the power of what is insinuated or not mentioned directly. I'm being excessively cautious because I don't wish to distort or extrapolate anything from the camerlingo's words, and thus lead you astray. In brief, it was clearly stated that, should Lord d'Authon explain himself in relation to the two testimonies, His Holiness would mark his gratitude by reopening the discussion about uniting the two great military orders.'

That was one of Philip the Fair's greatest ambitions. Despite the heroic resistance of the Knights Templar* and the Hospitallers,* not to mention that of the orders of Saint Lazarus and Saint Thomas, Saint-Jean-d'Acre had fallen into the hands of the Mamelukes of Sultan Al-Ashraf Khalil in 1291. Most Templars had returned to the West. As for the Hospitallers, they speedily retreated to Cyprus where Henri II de Lusignan, king of the island, had finally reluctantly agreed to temporarily grant them the city of Limassol, on the south coast of the island.

The years which followed the rout at Saint-Jean-d'Acre had seen the Templars' fortune decline, but had spared the Hospitallers since they had always devoted themselves to charity and compassion. The common people resented the Templars for their arrogance, their privileges, even their laziness and lack of generosity. There were rumours that the money collected by the order yielded a profit which was for its sole benefit, and that it amounted to a fortune. Jokes began and multiplied. You 'went to the Temple' instead of the brothel. You were a 'thief or a liar like a Templar'. The military orders, the warrior Templars in particular, hampered the King in his desire to put an end to papal interference in French politics. Guillaume de Nogaret, assisted by his former pupil Guillaume de Plaisians, had considered this issue from every angle. To demand the disappearance, once and for all, of the military orders was a bad move. Young noblemen and the wealthy were attached to the model of devotion, obedience and heroic deeds advocated by the Knights of Christ. On the other hand, the former plan to unite all these orders, which had been initiated fourteen years earlier by Nicholas IV,[93] offered a solution which could kill two birds with one stone. The union just had to favour the Hospitallers, who would then take charge of it, and one of Philip the Fair's two youngest sons had to be appointed at the head of this new order. This way, the French sovereign would avoid clashing with the Pope or public opinion and, at the same time, would muzzle the entire papal pack. There was just one fly in the ointment: Jacques de Molay, the Temple's new Grand-Master. An excellent soldier, a man of faith and a conservative, he would not be deposed without a fight. De Molay's political naivety did nothing to lessen his arrogance. He would kick over the traces, unaware that the dice had been thrown without him.

'Jacques de Molay will strongly object,' Nogaret said.

The Lombard stared over the counsellor's shoulder and replied, 'I didn't get the impression that the camerlingo was frightened at the prospect of opposition from Monsieur de Molay.'

Guillaume de Nogaret savoured a plum cake, taking a few seconds to think. He could not miss the opportunity to take an important step towards uniting the military orders, a cause dear to King Philip's heart. However, he did not like the thought of disposing so casually of a well-respected French gentleman of whom the sovereign was fond.

'My dear Zuccari, you understand of course that I cannot take this decision on my own. This concerns a friend of the King himself. So, just to be sure that I understand you correctly, allow me to recapitulate … The Holy See insists that Monsieur d'Authon be requested to explain himself before a secular tribunal with regard to the two testimonies concerning the murder of a Grand Inquisitor.'

'An Inquisition tribunal,' the banker corrected, swallowing.

'I beg your pardon, but isn't this a question of murder rather than heresy?'

Giorgio Zuccari compressed his lips and hissed, 'No, my lord, it concerns a judgement of God. Did anyone wilfully commit the unforgivable blasphemy of acting in the place of God? You must admit that only the Church can judge the extent of such a crime.'

The Lombard departed, suddenly feeling younger and calmer for having carried out his painful mission. Nogaret finished his grape juice. What were Clément V and his camerlingo plotting? Why did they need to contest a judgement of God which seemed to be convenient for everyone? Why defend so vehemently the memory of an inquisitor whose integrity was so questionable? Had the papacy not suffered enough from the scandal triggered by the barbaric acts of Robert le Bougre?* In what way did the murder of this other rotten apple affect them? Nogaret sensed a trap, although he could not quite make out its form.

The Cistercian abbey, founded[94] in Molin[95] by Blanche of Navarre and her son, Thibaut IV of Champagne, had initially taken in nuns from Liège. The convent had grown so powerful that neighbouring villages would try to negotiate their integration into the independent fiefdom of Molin in order to benefit from its protection. Morangis,[96] for example, had offered its forest in return for this union.

Terce[+] had just rung when Madame de Neyrat was admitted to the workroom. The young lay porteress,[97] unaccustomed to the world and its etiquette, announced, after a clumsy curtsey, 'I'll go and fetch the good mother, Madame. Or maybe her prioress. I can't go and tell your niece directly.'

Aude stopped herself from replying abruptly that she did not care which nun dealt with her request, as long as she was attended to with haste, but she managed to stifle her sharpness, which could have compromised the outcome of her visit.

The journey had been exhausting. She had arrived at nightfall the previous evening and, Rheims being too far, the only place she could find to stay was a grimy inn. Her back was itchy, which meant that, as well as the filth, she had picked up fleas from the disgusting straw mattress on which she had slept badly.

Strange how life sometimes leads down such twisted paths that you get lost. Honorius, dear Honorius. Why had he not plotted better and obtained the Holy See for himself? He certainly did not lack the power or the means, be it gold or intelligence. Camerlingo Benedetti's mind was the only one that Aude felt equalled hers. Therefore, if he had declined to stand in full daylight, it meant that darkness suited his purposes better. Her heart-shaped mouth broadened into a smile. Dear Honorius. Her memories of him were the only truly diverting ones she owned.

*

Denounced by a nephew she had spared because she liked his handsome face, Aude had been arrested by the men of the chief bailiff of Auxerre. They had taken a keen interest in the relentless ill luck that kept striking her relatives. Honorius Benedetti, who was then just an ordinary bishop, happened to be in the city during the trial. The stunning beauty that stood before him had brought back happy memories of his wild youth. The elegant blonde cloud, dressed in emerald green, had answered his questions with a web of lies and false contrite facial expressions which his expert eye had appreciated. He had decided that so much talent and intelligence could not end up severed by the blow of an executioner's axe, let alone burnt at the stake like a witch. And so Aude had been cleared of all suspicion and the young nephew had begged her forgiveness. A week later, Honorius had gone to see her in the town house inherited from the husband she had dispatched to his grave. Honorius's hopes were not disappointed and this indulgence of the flesh – his only one since entering the Church – had not left any bitter aftertaste of error. She had given herself to him with the joyful ardour of a lover, and not like a woman trying to repay her debt. At daybreak, after that wild and delightful night, she had declared in a desolate tone, 'Life is too short to allow it to be ruined by spoilsports. If people had behaved better ... I wouldn't have had to poison them. Swear to me that you're a sensible man, Honorius. I would so hate for you to disappear ...'

Her exquisite threat had sealed their pact. Because, in truth, it was a pact. Of course, Honorius had saved Aude's life when it was hanging by a thread. However, the bond between them was much deeper than mere gratitude. They belonged to the same breed. A rare, dangerous breed, but one capable of risking everything in order to reach a goal. A breed that could not be restrained by fear, or interest, or even by love.

*

She was summoned back from her memories by the rustle of heavy fabric. A puny little woman, wrinkled like a winter apple, was watching her with a serious expression. Aude stood up, bowed respectfully and introduced herself. The other woman responded in a voice lacking any warmth.

'I am Bérengère d'Etreval, Abbess of this convent. They tell me you wish to see Mademoiselle your niece.'

'Indeed, Reverend Mother. I'm on my way to Rheims and, since I was so close to Molin, I couldn't resist the urge to see my niece.'

'It's quite natural for an aunt.'

Something flat and diffident in her tone put Aude de Neyrat on her guard. 'Is she in good health?' she asked.

'In excellent health.'

'Would you allow me to see her? Only for a moment. I am fully aware of the austerity of the rule of Saint Benoît, a magnificent austerity.'

'Yes, unfortunately this is something we've been unable to impress on Mathilde. Perhaps you can instil some common sense and ardour into her unwilling young head.'

'I shall do my very best, Reverend Mother.'

'You will certainly need to. I shan't deny that, had it not been for the obvious despair and insistence of her dear uncle who, as her guardian, feared for his niece's soul and virtue, we would have happily forgone a recruit like her. She hasn't stopped remonstrating, complaining and lying shamelessly since she arrived here. We await as impatiently as a blessing the day he decides to marry her off.'

Madame de Neyrat managed to keep her face impassive. Just as she had suspected, the minor baron[98] Eudes de Larnay had got rid of the troublesome Mathilde by locking her up in a convent. Mathilde de Souarcy, Agnès's only daughter, had compiled a false testimony accusing her mother of complicity in heresy, and she had been summoned by the Inquisition tribunal in charge of judging her mother, or rather sending her to her death. Unfortunately, in spite of all the efforts of Nicolas Florin, who was conducting that mockery of a trial in a masterly fashion, Mathilde's foolishness had caused the plan devised by Honorius Benedetti to fail. Eaten up by jealousy towards her mother, and a desire to send her to the stake, the young fool had got herself entangled in her own statement to the point where her testimony had been challenged. Then Florin had been murdered.

Aude de Neyrat suppressed a smile, picturing the wrath that must have overwhelmed the feeble-minded Eudes de Larnay, Agnès's half-brother, when he had discovered that the Dame de Souarcy had escaped the clutches of the Inquisition. Consequently, he had chosen an abbey far away from Perche, so that Agnès would not be able to find her daughter. What was the real reason for it? Was it a final act of revenge against his half-sister after the failure of the Inquisition trial? Larnay was a rat. From what Madame de Neyrat had heard, he would have been more than willing to rub his belly against that of his blood relation. He had pursued her with incestuous diligence until he could not deceive himself any longer. She would never give in to him and found him repulsive. On reflection, Aude felt almost sympathetic towards the Dame de Souarcy, to the extent that, in her shoes, she would have promptly killed the baron.

Aude assumed a desolate expression and sighed.

'I understand your sorrow and resentment, Reverend Mother. So much effort in vain when the burden of caring for everybody within these walls is already so heavy. How can I put it? Mathilde … Well, let's just say that I also understand my good cousin Larnay's decision to place his hopes in you. Having said that, Mathilde has always been a lively girl for whom the calm of meditation and prayers have never been ... well ... sufficient. Eudes should have suspected that she was too fond of the world for a life of purity and self-denial to appeal to her completely. If I can contribute, however modestly, to quietening her down and urging her to be patient until she marries, then I will do all I can during my short visit.'

'Thank you, my daughter. We'll take you to the parlour where you can both sit and talk comfortably.'

Madame de Neyrat felt an exquisite twinge of apprehension in her throat when a nun brought Mathilde de Souarcy into the parlour. Would she be foolish enough to say, 'Who are you, Madame?' or cunning enough to pretend she was happy to see her dear aunt? As she had hoped, shrewdness won out over surprise in the young girl. Dressed in the ugly grey habit reserved for oblates,[99] her head concealed by a thick off-white veil, her arms outstretched, a beaming smile on her face, she walked to Aude, who was sitting down.

'Dearest Aunt ... What a pleasure to see you. I'm quite overwhelmed.'

'Darling Mathilde ... I'm so happy. I've been thinking of you ever since you retired to a place so propitious to elevating the soul. I beg you, do sit by me. I have so much to tell you. Your Mother Superior, Madame d'Etreval, has kindly granted us a few hours.'

Aude noticed the girl keenly observing her finery, making an estimate of her wealth by her jewels. It was a good sign. When the young nun who had brought her in had shut the door behind her, Mathilde's smile vanished. She leant towards her make-believe aunt, and, tight-lipped, whispered discreetly, 'Who are you, Madame?'

'Will you believe me if I tell you that I'm your best friend?

We have very little time, which I managed to snatch from the Abbess who is, to say the least, disappointed with your lack of dedication, because I promised to knock some modesty and obedience into your pretty head.' She interrupted Mathilde's attempt at a response with an elegant hand gesture. 'In truth, it matters little to me. Even so, you'll have to show yourself to be more pleasant if we are to succeed. Don't worry, it'll only be for a few days.'

'I don't understand what you're talking about, Madame,' Mathilde replied in a tone that was increasingly impatient and wary.

'Well, my friend, you understand that I cannot get you out of this grim place, at least not in the conventional way. I would have to provide a notary's letter, asserting that we are related.'

Mathilde opened her eyes wide, and was all ears.

'Still,' the alluring creature continued, 'to help you, I have recruited three strapping men who will assist you in leaving this enclosure. After all, it's not a jail, although one could easily think it is,' Aude said jokingly.

'Why this concern for me? You don't know me. Who has sent you? That arrant knave of an uncle who has left me to rot here for almost a year? Or my shrewd mother who used me in order to turn the game to her advantage? The pretty hypocrite!'

'Neither.'

'Come now. Who cares if I die between these horrible walls, if I scratch the soil to pull up a few vegetables, scour pots with ash and sand, or if I have to darn such rough and threadbare undergarments that it would be outrageous even to give them to the poor?' She held her hands out to the splendid woman and hissed in a venomous voice, 'Look, Madame. Look at my hands. They are so ruined that I'd cry with rage if I had any tears left to spare.'

'My poor darling,' Aude concurred. 'Most awful indeed! They're the hands of a peasant or an old woman. You are so pretty and distinguished. It's so unfair!'

'So it is!' Mathilde agreed, with tears in her eyes. 'So, Madame, who are you that you should concern yourself with a wretched recluse who has been brought to this place of suffering by other people's jealousy?'

'It's too soon to explain the true reason for my visit and, besides, we don't have time. You're too clever for me to try and pretend that my help is totally disinterested. We'll talk about that later. However, rest assured that I am touched by your ordeal. It's unfair as well as cruel. As for the payment I expect … it's nothing disproportionate or offensive, I give you my word. The Baron de Larnay has made foul use of you in his war against your mother. What did he really want? Was it her or the iron mine in La Haute-Gravière that was part of her dower?[100] I know not. Both, perhaps. The fact remains that you have been swindled, ill-treated and abused. As for your mother, as you said yourself, she has made a clever move. With all her playing at being a poor victim, she's managed to marry a man who not only has a rich estate, but is also good-looking. Moreover, the mine should have gone to you straight after her marriage.'

'Swindled is the right word,' Mathilde hissed through clenched teeth. 'They've robbed me of what was mine by right and by blood. I shall have my revenge.'

'And you would be right to do so,' Madame de Neyrat said with emphatic approval.

It had taken just this brief exchange for Aude to assess this girl on the brink of womanhood. She was foolish, already embittered, arrogant, calculating and selfish. Still, her voracious appetite for life and money made her an asset to Madame de Neyrat's plan.

'Mathilde, we are among those rare people who have known

true suffering but never give in to adversity. We always rise again, heads held high, and never accept defeat. Am I right?'

'Absolutely,' Mathilde replied.

She was seduced by this flattering description of her supposed tenacity. In addition, the fact that she resembled this splendid woman who was so richly adorned and surrounded by heady wafts of iris and musk made her feel smug. Returning to the crux of the matter, she asked:

'So are you proposing to get me out of this antechamber to an alms house …?'

In response, she received an elegant nod of the head.

'And you have kindly told me that you expect something from me in return…'

Another nod of the head.

'I still don't know exactly who you are …'

'Aude de Neyrat – your ally.'

'That's not much to go on, but it will have to do for the time being. I care only about one thing – to escape from this place as soon as possible. I've already tried to, several times. However, not only are these doors better guarded than the Louvre prison, but where would I go? My family has basely abandoned and cheated me, I don't have a sou, or even a decent garment.'

'All that will be taken care of, my dear. You will be welcome in my town house in Chartres. Now, time flies in your company but I must still tell you my plan before one of the sisters comes to interrupt us. I gather from the not so subtle hints of your Abbess that your proud resistance has made the nuns suspicious. We need them to drop their guard so that my men can intervene. So what do you say we give them a performance of sorts? You are going to emerge from our conversation … enlightened and moved by the desire to obey. You will ask Madame d'Etreval's humble pardon, and blame your past excesses on your youth.

You will perform with enthusiasm and good nature the endless chores you're assigned like a beast of burden.'

Mathilde grew more and more sullen at the dreadful list. Aude tried to comfort her.

'It's not for long, my dear. A short week. Just time enough to fool them so that we can free you. The naivety of nuns is equalled only by their desire to believe that they've managed to correct a soul. You will pray with devotion and dedication. You will be charming and helpful to the others ...'

Madame de Neyrat suddenly had a doubt. The girl lacked intelligence, as she had amply proved during her mother's trial, when she had inadvertently contributed to exonerating the very woman she was trying to push towards the torture chamber. What if she exaggerated her behaviour and aroused suspicion instead of allaying it? Aude de Neyrat continued, in a sweet tone.

'I know you're very clever and will proceed with a light touch, so as not to alarm the nuns with too extreme a conversion.'

Mathilde blinked in agreement.

'We hardly know each other, my dear. However, Mathilde, you should know that, like you, I've had to fight against adverse fortune, unfairness and humiliation. I am a few years older than you, and have had years of battle ... But look at me now. I am wealthy, beautiful, loved and feared. I'm afraid of nothing and am my own master. And it's what I'm offering you in return for your help. To train you with the weapons I have forged for myself. They are fearsome and you possess the strength to learn to handle them.'

Astounded and dazzled by this seductive future, Mathilde felt infinitely grateful to this inspiring creature who was saving her from the worst, from the convent, from this life she had thought she would never escape. Her small brain sought no further. She made up her mind to obey this woman in every way, to imitate her, and become as beautiful and powerful as she was. She would have the world at her feet and, in the end, Eudes de Larnay would bite the dust. As for her mother, she'd make her pay for all that had happened. She would take back all that was hers by right and by blood, and more.

There was a slight noise. Aude turned her head towards the door and immediately adopted a soft, serious tone.

'My dear, I am so relieved to see you in this state of mind. It's no wonder, given your sweet nature ...'

Madame de Neyrat feigned surprise to discover the Abbess, Madame d'Etreval. She stood up, immediately followed by Mathilde.

'It's sext[+] soon, Madame. I must ask you to leave these walls.'

Aude put her hand to her mouth in a gesture of apology. The arrival of the Abbess, instead of the nun who should have come to collect Mathilde, suggested she hoped that the young girl would improve.

'I beg your pardon, Reverend Mother. The conversation with my niece has been so long and constructive that I lost track of time.' Aude turned to the young girl with the demeanour of a caring aunt. 'Let your pure heart dictate your actions, my dear.'

Mathilde dropped her head and approached the little woman, murmuring, 'My dear Reverend Mother, I don't know how to beg your forgiveness. I have been foolishly rebellious. Your constant efforts to help me and make me feel welcome should have opened my eyes. All I can use in my defence is my youth, but also the sense of being abandoned by my own family which was breaking my heart.'

Aude was delighted to see the woman's face light up with satisfaction as she gave a sigh of relief – this woman who ruled over a universe of prayer more powerful than a large feudal estate. The battle was not won yet but it had begun promisingly.

There was a persistent drizzle when, shortly after nones,[+] Agnès, Comtesse d'Authon, Dame de Souarcy, dismounted. The armed guard that her beloved husband, Artus, demanded she take with her wherever she went, did the same, remaining a few feet away from her.

Agnès stroked the neck of the beautiful bay gelding,[101] missing her brave Perche mare Églantine, whose coat was a dark grey – almost black – and which she had ridden until her marriage. Églantine's neck stood taller than a man. However, these strong animals were built for endurance so, although they could sustain a trot, they soon tired if they galloped.

She looked at the ten acres of red earth conceded to her by her dower, which used to be depressing. At that time, it was nothing but a mass of stinging nettles. She had hated this constantly windswept, rainy place, and cursed it for not contributing to the survival of Souarcy. That was until the evening when Clémence had used Joseph de Bologne's magnet. Monsieur de Bologne was the Comte d'Authon's Jewish* physician, a very learned man who knew everything about science but was also well versed in astronomy, philosophy and even the twists and turns of the law. That was when Agnès had found out that Eudes de Larnay, the villain who had been trying to bed her despite their blood ties, perhaps also coveted La Haute-Gravière, aware of its rich iron deposits. Having her convicted of complicity in heresy or for committing a sin of the flesh with a man of the cloth, as he had tried to do, would have resulted in her forfeiting all her rights and her dower. He would then have obtained her daughter, Mathilde, as well as La Haute-Gravière. The hatred she felt for him was now laced with boundless contempt.

As usual when she came here, Agnès sighed with surprise at the transformation this arid place had undergone. The nettles had been mown, and the spindly trees that had managed to withstand their rampant growth cut down. Furrows so wide and deep that men disappeared down them had been dug in the earth.[102] Mounds of soil were waiting to be loaded onto carts that took turns, all day long, to ferry the ore to the mills worked by the bellows of smithies. There, a *mesureur*[103] would estimate the load of ore delivered, the cost of the charcoal and the smithy time necessary to transform it. He would then inform Agnès of how much metal she could hope to obtain.

She was very glad she had followed Monsieur Joseph's advice. For once, the law of Normandy, usually not on the side of women, had favoured her. Powerful leagues of iron workers had formed in the province and gathered in the nearby Ouche region. In order to gain their independence from lords and monks, they mined the ore by contract and for a percentage. Unlike most other people, Agnès had called in these iron workers instead of selling the extracted ore to a lord or a monastery with a smithy.

The foreman emerged from one of the trenches and noticed her. He crawled on his knees to pull himself up the hill, and then ran towards her, his hat in his hand. The heavily built man, constricted in a sleeveless leather tunic, bowed low and said proudly, 'Madame, I keep telling you, this mine is the wealthiest in the region. It's a pleasure to shovel when you get rewarded.'

'Thank the Lord, my good Éloi. I used to hate this arid soil so much. It's very charitable on its part not to hold that against me but, instead, to now show me such generosity.'

'Soil is neither cruel not spiteful.' The man waited to get his breath back, apparently reluctant to speak. 'I don't know … We're indentured, after all … Still, you're always very fair to us, so I'll tell you. Some people have been nosing about here for some time, on the pretext of gathering mushrooms.'

A shadow of anxiety darkened Agnès's serene mood.

'Nosing about?'

'First of all, my apprentice Robert and I thought they were petty thieves. Except that those generally come at night. After all, there's always someone ready to buy a large sack of ore. But these people pretend they're just passing. They approach and start chatting. They look like they're from a manor. If you want my opinion, they're too well polished to be honest people.'

Could they have been sent by Eudes? Why would her half-brother be watching the mine? What could he possibly hope for? Or did he take pleasure in tormenting himself further by looking at what he had not been able to get? She felt an unpleasant shudder and tensed up. What was Eudes plotting? Was he insane enough to conspire against his overlord, the Comte d'Authon?

Artus d'Authon had left Eudes de Larnay no way out, and the latter had understood that he was not up to confronting his almost half-brother-in-law. A lazy but sensible man, he had given his half-sister his blessing and publicly rejoiced at her prestigious union. Agnès had not heard from him since. There had been increasingly persistent rumours that the last iron mine in Larnay, exhausted like all the others, had closed down.

'Keep your eyes open, my good Éloi. They could be my half-brother's men ... I know him well and, whatever he has in mind, it's sure to be vile.'

'Fear not, my noble lady. I've seen so many different kinds of prowlers and troublemakers that I can smell them before I even see their dirty muzzles. If they so much as try anything shady, there's fifteen of us strong men here who've not been scared of anything for a while. Let them get a taste of our shovels, our pickaxes and our scythes.'

He helped Agnès back on her horse and said goodbye with a friendly wave before leaving.

Agnès kept thinking about what the foreman had just told her. Should she inform her husband and add to his worries? Come now, she was overreacting. After all, what could Eudes do? A slight smile relaxed her face. He must have choked with rage upon discovering that she had gone from poor, submissive vassal to his overlord by marriage. That was fine revenge, indeed.

Followed by her armed guard, she rode along the edge of the Forest of Louvière. Two years earlier, she had killed two men there – two assassins – in order to rescue her daughter Clémence from their clutches. It seemed an eternity ago. Strange. She did not even remember the faces of those brutes.

Clémence, my darling, my sweetheart, I miss you so much. Where are you hiding? None of our attempts to find you has given me the slightest hope of seeing you again. I picture you beautiful, safe, and obstinately chase away all dark thoughts. It's easy to imagine the worst when the absence of a loved one eats away at you day and night. I want only the best for you, you who were and still are the best of me. I'm scared that they might find you before I do. How could you defend yourself then? Honorius Benedetti's henchmen want to destroy you after they've obtained the manuscripts you're protecting. As for the Knight Hospitaller, this Francesco de Leone, who saved my life and is offering to sacrifice his in order for the prophecy to be fulfilled, he still doesn't know you are that being of light, the very woman he's been searching for with all his devotion and great courage. I can't trust him either. I distrust his love and his purity – perhaps even more than I distrust the accursed servants in the camerlingo's pay.

'We shall spend the night at Manoir de Souarcy,' she said to the armed guard. 'I'll order them to prepare you a straw mattress in the outbuildings and serve you a generous supper.'

She pictured the large farm with its square towers whose stonework had been repaired on her husband's orders. It was strange how she increasingly longed to return to its thick and forbidding walls, its huge, icy rooms which she had once found sinister. Memories of a past life often appear sweeter than reality. At the time Agnès had worried so much for herself, her daughters and her household. She had been so afraid that bad weather, an epidemic or any stroke of bad luck would endanger all their lives. She had slaved away like a peasant, snatching anything she could from the soil, and even then was barely able to feed them. But now she felt a sense of peace as soon as she entered the large courtyard. All her memories of Clémence were ingrained in the place. She revisited them one by one as she inspected the outbuildings, the dovecote, and as she quizzed those of her servants who had remained at the manor. Her memories would rush towards her like cherished ghosts, as she came down to the village of Souarcy and wandered at random down alleys whose houses were built cheek by jowl. It was a maze of narrow streets snaking so haphazardly that a cart loaded with hay would often chip the corner of a roof as it drove along. Like other manors, Souarcy had no right to bear arms. Once upon a time, when the English had not yet been declared friends, and were therefore constantly looked upon with distrust, the only defence against an attack had been discretion and mass inertia. This passive but tenacious response explained the raised township and its position deep in the neighbouring forest. With a certain degree of gall, the high walls of the enclosure, behind which peasants, serfs and small craftsmen had taken refuge, had withstood covetousness and many assaults.

Predictably, Mathilde intruded into the young woman's mind, and she chased away the memory of her daughter's winning smile, temperamental sulking, envy-fuelled anger, her fear of the dark. Though the thought of Clémence filled her with worry, Agnès summoned her image constantly. It had given her the strength and forbearance she had needed over the past two years, when her elder daughter's actions had left her bewildered and plagued with regret. At the height of her rage and terror, when she had had to admit that Mathilde was pushing her and Clémence into the implacable claws of the Inquisition by lying without shame or remorse, Agnès had tried to hate her. Perhaps she had even succeeded for a short while. But she was always plagued by the certainty that it was also her fault if the girl had turned out that way. It's painful for a mother to admit that she has always preferred one of her children to the other, but that had been the case with Agnès and she was far too honest to pretend otherwise to herself. She remembered her laughter and conversations with Clémence – when as a child, she had to be called Clément, when she still did not know that she was not the bastard child of a heretical servant but Agnès's second daughter. She thought of their walks, of their joyous complicity and even the fear of the future they sensed in each other. She might as well admit it. She had loved Mathilde as a child, had raised her, hoped for what was best for her and done all she could to make her life less difficult. On the other hand, it had been a sheer delight to discover Clémence day by day. When she had teased her a little, she had carefully watched her every expression and slightest frown, searching in her youngest for traces of herself, her natural mother.

She nudged the horse with her knee. She was in a hurry to get to Souarcy. Her head was starting to spin a little. She was probably tired after the journey.

The Louvre, on the outskirts of Paris, the apartments of
Guillaume de Nogaret, August 1306

Philip the Fair was listening, his face inscrutable, his metal-blue hawk eyes fixed on Monsieur de Nogaret. He had straightened up, sitting tensely in his chair with its high carved back.

'Coming from you, I suspect this is not a tall story,' the King said icily.

'Certainly not, Sire,' the counsellor replied.

He had shrunk further and further into himself as he told the sovereign about the meeting he had had with Giorgio Zuccari, captain of the Lombards.

Sensing her master's dangerous mood, Delmée, Philip's favourite greyhound, had raised her black-streaked head and was staring at Guillaume de Nogaret with a rather unfriendly expression. She did not like the man's smell and was alarmed by the annoyance she sensed in her master, whose side she never left, day or night. A hollow growl occasionally rumbled in her throat.

'Quiet, Delmée, my beauty,' Philip said. 'Nogaret, have you by any chance forgotten that Artus d'Authon is a friend of mine?'

'If I had forgotten it, Sire, my burden would be much lighter.'

'So this is Clément V, through the intermediary of his camerlingo who ... how can we put this? Requires? Requests? Advises? Demands that Authon appear before an Inquisition tribunal in order to explain himself with regard to two testimonies, one of which comes from a little street rascal, the other from a common innkeeper? Is that right?'

'Yes.'

'It would be hilarious if it weren't so absurd! Isn't Monsieur d'Authon's unblemished reputation – which even his enemies acknowledge – enough to clear him of these ridiculous suspicions? The murder of a Grand Inquisitor – and unarmed! Has our Holy Father taken leave of his senses? It's true that we've drifted apart over the years but of one thing I am still certain: Authon would never have stooped this low. He's a fine swordsman and would have slapped Nicolas Florin, insulted him before witnesses so as to provoke a judicial duel.'[104]

'With a man of the cloth? Moreover, Sire, if I might be permitted this contradiction, assuming that the man who murdered the Dominican wanted to exonerate Madame de Souarcy and invoke a Judgement of God, the Grand Inquisitor's death would have had to look accidental or somehow miraculous. And let's not forget, who had reasons for urgently saving the lady from torture?'

Philip became enraged. 'This is all nonsense!' His thin lips were pressed into a hard line. 'What do you think, Nogaret?'

'What do I think, Sire?' the counsellor repeated, daring, for the first time during this interview, to meet the sovereign's gaze.

'That's right. What are these tales they're spinning us? If we agree to the request of the Holy See, they'll show us their gratitude? Or at least lend a more favourable ear to our demand for unification of the soldierly orders? Why not a posthumous trial of Boniface VIII, may he for ever burn in hell!'

'There was no talk of a posthumous trial, as I said. Only the unification was mentioned. It's what Zuccari reported to me, my lord, and even that with many oratory precautions.'

'Wise man! This all gives me the impression that the Pope and his camerlingo make vain promises. I smell villainy, or at least an attempt to deceive with twisted language. After all, we're used to that, Nogaret. If we agree to their request, all the Holy See will have to do is a volte-face and then pretend that we have misunderstood their wishes, and that there was never any question of repayment.'

'We can always demand ... clearer assurances.'

Nogaret was relieved. Above all, Philip was afraid of being cheated. In other words, he had already accepted the idea of forcing Monsieur d'Authon to appear before a Church tribunal. A man of honour and of his word in his private affairs, Philip conducted those of the realm like a true sovereign: all promises and friendships ceased to exist and he would use any means whatsoever to reach his goals.

Philip mechanically stroked the dog's head. Delmée would not take her eyes off Nogaret. Her long, fearsome jaws could snap the ribs of a hare with a single bite. The counsellor believed that animals were merely creatures God put at man's disposal to use as he pleased, but without cruelty. He wondered for the umpteenth time how come her master – whom he venerated without any tenderness – found pleasure and comfort in the company of his dogs, and more especially Delmée, who seldom left his side.

'I cannot understand this,' the King continued. 'Why, in heaven's name, does the Church object to a small miracle which, in everyone's eyes, attests to the truth of a trial by ordeal? On the contrary, it should be happy about it and fear that it might be overshadowed by suspicion. What does Clément V want with Artus d'Authon, who has never meddled in politics except as far as managing his land is concerned, and of whose very existence he was probably unaware even just three months ago?'

'I've asked myself the same questions over and over again, Sire.'

Philip leant down to his dog and told her, in an almost amused tone, 'You see, my brave girl, your master smells a trap. What troubles him is that he doesn't know where it's concealed and what kind of game it awaits.'

The white dog with the black-streaked head wagged her tail

without, however, looking away from the man who was standing there, waiting for his king's decision.

After a few seconds' silence, Philip spoke in a tone so detached that Nogaret knew what he was about to say weighed heavily on his heart.

'Clearer assurances, did you say? We definitely need them before we proceed any further. Our old acquaintance Zuccari will have to act as go-between, whether he likes it or not.'

'And if we get them, Sire?'

'Then Monsieur d'Authon will have to explain himself before a Church tribunal. Now leave me, my dear Nogaret. I need to think.'

Manoir de Souarcy-en-Perche, August 1306

Agnès looked around. The large courtyard was deserted
except for two Beaucerons which charged at them, baring
their teeth, only to come to an abrupt halt as soon as they
recognised their mistress. She called for her servants and there
was a sudden roar in the outbuildings. The heavy door of one
of the stables was pushed open as though it was just an oilskin.
Gilbert the Simpleton suddenly appeared, his mane of hair all
tousled, and hurled himself towards his mistress.

'Our good fairy's back, finally!' he yelled. 'Sweet baby Jesus,
it's a miracle!'

The giant, whose mind was that of a child, was stammering
with sheer happiness.

The bay horse showed no nervousness when the muscular
figure rushed at it, and did not snort when Gilbert grabbed its
reins. Agnès had always marvelled at the silent bond that seemed
to exist between Gilbert and animals. Even the vindictive gander
that had a habit of charging with a hiss at its human victims
without any provocation on their part would follow him good-
naturedly. As for Mariolle, the Perche stallion that terrorised all
the farm hands with its talent for pushing them to the bottom of
its stall, then administering a kick, or else crushing them against
the wall with its rump, it would wait patiently, somewhat puzzled,
while Gilbert changed the hay in the stable.

'My sweet Gilbert, help me dismount, I'm tired,' Agnès said in
a gentle voice, stroking the tangled mop of hair. 'We've been on
a long errand, so I'll be spending the night at the manor.'

He lifted her from the lady's saddle as though she were a
feather and placed her on the ground with surprising gentleness.

'Take care of our mounts and ask for a straw mattress and a hot supper for my guard, will you?'

'Right away, m'fairy. It'll be as you order.' Then he turned to the guard who watched over the Comtesse during her outings. 'Come, you. What're you sitting there with your arse nailed to the saddle for?'

Accustomed to more civil manners from the Comte d'Authon's people, the man obeyed, rather taken aback. Agnès suppressed a smile.

Adeline burst out of the kitchens, wiping her hands on an apron stiff with grease and grime. It occurred to Agnès that she would need to diplomatically restore some order here. The chubby adolescent bent over in a clumsy curtsey that almost threw her off balance.

'Oh ... Sweet Jesus ... And I've got nothing ready! Oh, dear, Gilbert didn't catch any trout from the Huisne 'cause we weren't expecting you, you see? And it's a fast day[105] on top of everything else,' she said in despair, 'or we could've killed a fowl.'

'Don't fret, Adeline, some soup and a piece of bread will do us nicely. I'll retire to my chamber early, I'm feeling tired.'

'Oh, confound it ... we can do better than that,' insisted Adeline.

Agnès had appointed her as stewardess for kitchens and foods, a rather grand title for a large manor farm like Souarcy, but something to please the poor girl whom life had treated harshly.

Adeline indicated the armed guard with her chin and, lowering her voice, said, as though to justify herself, 'Then he'll go and tell at our master's chateau that I didn't know how to manage when our lady arrived. I'm not being shamed like that! Sooner a colic! I'll go and tell the maidservant to start a fire in the hall and your apartment, Madame. It's very damp.'

With a stubborn expression, she gave another curtsey and charged off to her kitchens.

Lifting the front of her dress, Agnès walked slowly, almost

hesitantly, towards the shallow steps leading up to the main hall. She shuddered. Despite the tallow[106] torches the maidservant had just lit, the large room was plunged into semi-darkness. So many Souarcys had lived within these austere walls that smelt of damp and neglect. She relived scenes from her own life that had taken place here. Her husband, Hugues, disembowelled by a wounded stag, had been laid out on this heavy table after his long-drawn-out death throes had finally granted him ultimate relief. In this hall, she had watched her two daughters, one of whom was unaware of their true blood tie, growing up. An indescribable monster and charmer, a Grand Inquisitor, had come seeking her by this fireplace in order to drag her away to suffering and death. And then a large, serious and fascinating man had become ensnared in her love and her words, and Agnès had discovered the brightness of life and the overwhelming desire to give herself to someone unreservedly.

For almost two years now she had had a life that still surprised her so much every day that she sometimes feared she would wake up from a magical dream. Two years of a passion so complete, so perfect, of a love so total that the sight of her husband in the distance would still take her breath away, just as when, late in the evening, he would crinkle up his eyes and cock his head, seeking her desire with his eyes. In truth, Agnès had been content with her life as the wife of Hugues de Souarcy. Polite and respectful, that honourable man of war had always treated her with consideration and tenderness. However, until she had married Artus d'Authon, she had never known the folly of bodies that seek each other out and give themselves, the nagging, almost painful longing for the other person when he is away for a few hours, followed by the relief at seeing him again and of lacing her fingers with his. She stifled a laugh and shrugged. Good heavens, what a silly goose she was! Her mood suddenly darkened. There was just one crucial thing she needed to make her happiness complete: to find Clémence, to take her in her arms and smother her with caresses, to cover her hair with kisses. She would find her; she would not rest until her child was by her side, safe and sound. Surprisingly, Agnès, who was so wise and thoughtful, had discovered a hidden part of herself that she had been unaware of before. She had glimpsed that dark abyss during the Inquisition trial, when her eldest daughter Mathilde had tried to send Clémence to the stake. Agnès had been overcome with rage, even at a time when exhaustion and hardship should have made her give in. It was a rage with no limits, not even those dictated by pity. She realised she was capable of doing anything to protect Clémence. Reasonable Agnès, who was charmed by the delicate poetry of Marie de France,* delighted by the cooing of a female pigeon and enchanted by a summer downpour, had discovered an unsuspected beast within her. She was so worried by this other part of herself that, subsequently, she had restrained and tamed it in the hope that it would vanish. She thought she had succeeded; that is, until her beloved child had disappeared.

One evening, three days after the extraordinary discovery in the secret library of the abbey by Francesco di Leone, Clémence and Annelette Beaupré, then apothecary sister and now Abbess of Clairets, Agnès had grown worried about the child's absence. She had found her to be somewhat distant and, since her return from that adventure, even quieter than usual. Agnès had carefully climbed up the rungs of the thin ladder that led to the attic, Clémence's den. As soon as she was standing on solid ground again, she had felt that a terrible trial awaited her. Her daughter's farm-boy clothes had disappeared and Agnès had picked up the short letter left for her on the straw mattress. She was so touched by it that her eyes had filled with tears. Every word, every sentence she had read a hundred times was etched in her memory.

Madame, my dearly beloved mother,

Since I have decided that this letter will be brief, I must weigh each word, although I could fill a whole volume with expressions of my undying love for you. Four days ago, when I found the papyrus, I understood the power of your love for me, and this knowledge is the only thing I wish to take with me.

Is it possible to fight destiny? I do not know but, thanks to the courage I have inherited from you, I intend to try.

Ah ... Madame, if only you knew. My dream lasted but a few brief moments, there, when I realised that I was your daughter and how much you loved me. I could see only one thing: the two of us walking at sunset through the magnificent gardens at Château d'Authon. You placed your arm round my shoulder and I clasped mine round your waist. We laughed aloud as you muddled up the names of the flowers we were looking at. Madame ... what bliss! So brief, but can bliss wait? A few brief moments, before I made up my mind to run away from the knight Leone and his kind, from their absolute faith and their pure love, before I made up my mind to fight my enemies alone, the dream dissolved. I must leave.

Be sure, Madame, that wherever I may be, you will be by my side. God watch over you.

I pray to heaven that you suffer no distress, Madame. The thought of you grieving for me is unbearable.

Live like the magnificent being you are.

Your ever-loving daughter, Clémence.

Agnès had been choked by sobs. The sheet of paper had slipped out of her fingers and she had fallen on her knees. She had howled like an animal for what had felt like an eternity. She had never known that she had this animal cry within her, so huge and almost never-ending. Where did it come from? From a boundless, implacable love which had only been threatened by dangers she knew she could fight thus far: Eudes, Clémence's true sex, Mathilde, and the precariousness of their lives. And yet now, extraordinarily powerful creatures with inexorable willpower, the camerlingo Honorius Benedetti's henchmen, were drawing close to her daughter.

Later, much later, she had lain on the floor, exhausted. She had curled up there, kept alive by just one belief: she would find her, even if she had to criss-cross the realm, searching every cottage and every nook. She would find her. Nobody would separate her from Clémence.

She approached the stingy fire that barely flickered in the huge hearth, not expecting much warmth from it. She turned her back to it in the vain hope of chasing away the stiffness she had been feeling for several days now. It seemed that even during a heatwave, the rooms of the manor did not warm up. Agnès had always felt chilled in them but today she was shivering with an inner cold that was creeping under her skin. Would she ever confess to Artus d'Authon the reason for her impatience and her insistence on finding little Clémence whom she had supposedly taken in after her mother, a servant, had died in childbirth? When her husband expressed surprise at her obsession with the sudden disappearance of the adolescent, who he still thought was a boy, she had told a half-lie. After all, she had already told so many others in order to survive. This time, however, lying to the man she loved had weighed heavily on her. She had confessed that Clément was really a girl, and that she had dressed her as a boy to protect her from the predatory desire of Eudes de Larnay and also to spare her from the convent, which often reserved the most menial tasks for low-born orphans and lay servants. Moreover, Agnès had said in justification, she feared someone would discover that the girl's mother had been a Waldensian* heretic. Her fate would have been terrible then. Artus seemed content with that explanation and his desire to please his beloved had done the rest. He had sent his chief bailiff, Monge de Brineux, on Clémence's trail. The search had been unsuccessful up to now, except for a few false hopes which had hurt Agnès even more.

She admonished herself. Enough of this childishness and these bouts of despair – they would not take away her courage. With God's help and Artus's peaceful but steady strength, she was going to find her youngest daughter. Nobody would stand in her way.

Agnès slowly walked up the stone steps to her antechamber, surprised by her lack of energy. She smiled when she entered the cramped room, scantily furnished with a pedestal table and two armchairs upholstered with unfashionable tapestry. Heavens, how poor they looked! Agnès wondered if she would ever get used to the luxury that surrounded the Comtesse d'Authon, the château gardens bursting with colour and fragrance where she liked to stroll and yet always felt like a visitor, and the Comte's huge library. There, she had discovered deeply moving poetry which she had whispered, entranced, or cleverly scathing texts, such as *Lai d'Aristote*, by Henri d'Andeli.[107] Aristotle, mentor to the young Alexander who has just returned from India in the company of a woman with whom he is besotted, is worried that the king is neglecting State business in favour of the heart and flesh. Annoyed with the old master's advice, one day the refined Indian lady seduces him and he lets her climb on his back as he walks on all fours like a large dog. Alexander catches the scene and laughs. However, the wise man does not allow himself to be thrown by this ridiculous situation – on the contrary. 'Sire,' he says, 'was I not right to fear love for you who are young and strong? Look at what it has reduced me to in spite of my old age.'

When she entered her chamber, the dull sadness that had been hiding there since her departure from Souarcy took hold of her. A disheartening idea began worming its way into her mind: had she become a stranger to both these places? Here and there? The simple truth was that, when all was said and done, Agnès, whether she be Dame de Souarcy or Comtesse d'Authon, had never belonged anywhere. She had clung with all her might to people she loved, but not to walls or towers. Madame Clémence de Larnay, her sweet angel who had brought her up, her daughters and Artus. She only existed, only remained standing thanks to them, because of them and, in the end, this realisation did not make her sad.

The dawn filtering through the arrow slit of his cell roused Francesco de Leone, Knight of Justice and Grace,[108] from a confused, feverish sleep which could not be explained merely by the intense heat of the night.

He left the wing that housed the cells and the dormitory, and crossed the large paved courtyard, walking towards the squat building in the middle, reserved for the care of the ill. There they would take in all the sick, be they beggars or nobles, servants, merchants or soldiers. As he drew closer to the hospital, the smell of human decay, filth and excrement got to his throat. He was not surprised by it. After all, he had been mixing with death and suffering for an eternity. The pervading heat irritated the wounds of those begging to be treated. They barely managed to clean the suffering flesh in the hope that foul vermin would not develop in it. Because of the shortage of space, means and physician knights, they no longer tried to contain the spread of infection by isolating those with respiratory or scrofulous[109] diseases, or those with diarrhoea. What they implemented now was the kind of triage no one had the heart to admit to. Those with a chance of survival were put on the first floor. The ground floor was reserved for those who were going to die, and who would shortly go down to the little cellar that had been dug beneath the hospital, and which acted as a morgue because its cool temperature reduced the pestilence the corpses gave off.

The knight Leone was overcome by a strong feeling of resentment. The King of Cyprus Henri II de Lusignan's half-hearted permission allowing the Knights Hospitaller to settle on the south coast of the island came with inflexible conditions. The number of Knights Hospitaller could not exceed seventy, in addition to their retinue of lay servants. The Knights of Christ had had to comply despite the fact that the influx of sick was five times their own number. Of course, Leone knew that Cyprus was just a stage. Guillaume de Villaret, his brother's successor[110] as the order's Grand-Master, was looking to the future, to Rhodes. However, he was overwhelmed by sadness when he thought of all the children, the old people and all those who were going to die because Lusignan dreaded expansion and especially the power of the soldierly order.

'You look lost in thought and rather sombre, my friend.'

Francesco de Leone turned towards the gentle voice.

Arnaud de Viancourt, prior and Grand-Commander, was watching him with a placid expression. He was a slight, grey man who looked ageless despite the fine lines on his forehead and cheeks. 'Why so sombre?' he insisted.

Francesco lowered his head and crossed his arms over the black monk's habit. 'So many are going to die. How many can we save?'

'Very few. Our mission isn't to succeed if that isn't God's will. It's to doggedly start from scratch every day in order to ease the suffering of His creatures.'

'And how do we know what God's will is?'

'Ah ... there's the unanswerable question I've asked myself a thousand times. Only fools think they know. As for us, we just feel our way, brother. We do our best to serve Him unfailingly, and pray that the path we take may be as pure and free of errors as possible. Come,' he said in a clearer tone, 'let us spend a few moments as friends. The early-morning air almost makes me forget that I'm now an old man. Have you noticed that about Cyprus nights? The daytime blaze carries on into the night and gradually fades. Then dawn brings a few hours of welcome but fleeting coolness, so let's take advantage of them.'

Going ahead of Leone, Arnaud de Viancourt moved away

from the walls, walking slowly and taking care not to approach the buildings. Leone understood immediately. The dawn lull had nothing to do with the prior's wish to stroll. What he wanted was to talk of important business. He feared the spies Lusignan had placed everywhere, including, no doubt, within their order, so he never engaged in important conversations except outside the walls of his office or library.

In silence, they approached a large aviary where doves and turtledoves were cooing to each other. The charming racket would drown out their exchange and Francesco wondered if the prior's insistence on the gentle birds being installed in the west corner of the courtyard was really only due to the pleasure he took in watching them, as he had maintained.

'I'm growing old, my friend,' the small man repeated, 'and I have come to lament the fact that all God's creatures don't have the useless grace of these birds.'

'If all had it, would we be able to notice and enjoy it?'

The elderly man answered with a snort of laughter.

'You have a point, Francesco. Man is made in such a way that he needs the worst before he can see the best. It's a sad fact. Will we ever change?'

His gaze swept over the courtyard slowly and with feigned indifference. He hesitated. Francesco de Leone assumed that he was searching for one of his usual preambles. Arnaud de Viancourt's mind was like a complex chessboard to him, with the pieces obeying constantly changing rules. He would move them according to a disconcerting system but then, all of a sudden, they would all fall into place and form a rigidly disciplined opening. However, the knight was wrong. Arnaud de Viancourt was weighing up the information he was about to reveal. Leone must not yet suspect that the prior had been organising their quest for decades, and that he operated from the shadows in order to counter the actions of their sworn enemy: Honorius Benedetti.

Two years earlier, Viancourt had won a decisive battle thanks to Clair Gresson, one of his most talented spies, whom he had placed near Guillaume de Plaisians, Nogaret's second in command – at least judging by what was whispered in the corridors of the Louvre. Clair Gresson had got close to Honorius by claiming that he shared his theory: that man was incapable of reaching purity and the light of Christ unless he was forced to. Gresson had managed to convince the camerlingo of his absolute faith that chaos awaited humanity if the leash that held it in check was relaxed. Only fear, established order and the Church safeguarded men from the worst: themselves. Gresson had lied with subtlety, feeding Benedetti false information about the identity of the prelate that the King of France wished to see accede to the Holy Throne. Philip the Fair needed a docile pope, even if he had to bribe other cardinals in order to ensure his election. Secret approaches had allowed the sovereign to settle on Monsieur de Got,* Archbishop of Bordeaux, since he could be sure of the Gascon vote. Moreover, Monsieur de Got had a reputation for intelligence and a sense of diplomacy, but not for stubbornness. Nogaret had therefore become certain that he would be easy to lead and that he would grant the King what the latter wanted as a mark of gratitude for his help: the posthumous trial of Boniface VIII and the unification of the soldierly orders under the banner of his son, Philippe de Poitiers. Therefore, Monsieur de Got's candidature had to be protected at all costs in order to prevent the election of Honorius Benedetti, the favourite of a few Italian prelates, and the feared enemy of most of the others. Clair Gresson had applied himself to the task. Pretending to spy on behalf of the camerlingo, he had tossed him another name, Renaud de Cherlieu, Cardinal of Troyes, and told him that the latter had declared himself agreeable to the posthumous trial of Boniface, which obsessed the King. Honorius had immediately gone on the offensive, drawing liberally from his war coffers, making promises and issuing threats. The man behind the arras, he sought the papal tiara, not that it appealed to him. All that interested him was the power it conferred upon the man wearing it – the power to save humanity from itself for the love of God.

Rumours had spread like wildfire, sown and stirred up by the camerlingo's men. Time being of the essence, Honorius had come up with an accusation that was almost impossible to counter: Monseigneur de Troyes's guilty tolerance towards heretics and religious deviants. At first, Renaud de Cherlieu, a good-humoured man, had been incredulous, and asked for Monsieur de Nogaret's advice and protection. However, the counsellor had much to do and, although unaware of where it had originated, was reasonably satisfied with the anathema[111] that threatened to strike Monseigneur de Troyes. The latter risked an Inquisition trial. This welcome diversion was convenient for the King of France and allowed Nogaret, as well as Plaisians, to push forward their pawn: Monseigneur de Got. Renaud de Cherlieu went from doubt to fear. Unable to understand the unjust ferocity of which he was the victim, he had requested an audience with Camerlingo Benedetti. If Honorius had easily concealed the surprise occasioned by the visit, he must have had to make a superhuman effort to control his rage once he had worked out that Clair Gresson, the young man so full of ardour and charming piety, had cheated him as nobody had dared do before him. Honorius Benedetti had then tried to adjust his strategy. But it was too late. All the months he had wholeheartedly devoted himself to destroying Renaud de Cherlieu had been pivotal. Monseigneur de Got would be elected, and there was nothing he could do about it.

Viancourt sighed and slipped two fingers through the wires of the aviary to stroke the breast of a turtledove that cocked its head towards him. Once again, the old man eyed his young fellow brother. Francesco de Leone must be twenty-seven. Still a young man and yet a veteran of all the battles to which he had lent his sword or his wit. Like Viancourt and so many others among them, Leone had crossed battlefields turned into slaughterhouses and mass graves by the folly of men. Like him, Leone had finished off dying companions with a blow of his sword, to spare them the avenging fury of the enemy. Like him, he had marvelled at the cool of a solitary morning, at the scent of almond trees, the song of a cicada, and felt that God was finally there. The prior noticed the first, fine wrinkles on the pale, high forehead which concealed so many things Leone believed to be secret. The knight was quite tall. His fine, well-drawn features, his darkish-blond hair and his eyes as blue as a deep sea betrayed his Northern Italian origins. His straight nose, full lips, and a smile that sometimes appeared to reach his temples, must have charmed many a woman on many a continent. However, Leone's continence of the flesh, his absolute obedience to the discipline he had committed himself to, and his ardent faith left no doubt in the prior's mind. Nor did his sharp intelligence and the purity of his goals.

'Francesco, my brave warrior, is it not sad that you should be the only man I feel I can trust?'

Leone fought a sense of rising embarrassment. For years he had been lying to the prior about the secret quest whose torch had been passed on to him by a Templar in an underground passage in Saint-Jean-d'Acre, just before the fall of the citadel. The prior sensed his unease much more clearly than the knight suspected. He sidestepped the issue out of affection.

'Each of us is so many different people at once, my dear friend, that it would be folly to claim that I know you totally ...'

Leone gave him a worried look. Just what did this remark mean? What had Viancourt guessed?

'We are, all of us, a little uncertain of others. For example, our Grand-Master, whom I consider a friend, sometimes surprises me. You see, Francesco, age doesn't necessarily make you wiser, but it does add urgency. I now consider short cuts I wouldn't have tolerated ten years ago. What is important is not to know exactly what people are, but to be certain of what they will never become, no matter what duress they may be under or what they stand to gain. I know what you could never become, and that is a great relief. No matter how harsh or unrewarding life can be, it only damages those who allow it. I do not condemn them. It's sometimes difficult to cling on to the best in oneself. Yet there lies our ultimate strength.' A subtle smile played on the slender man's lips and he sighed. 'And now look at me, pushing you towards an abyss of speculations. Your silence proves it. Forgive me, brother. What can I say? It's the privilege of old men to digress for a while and nobody dares interrupt them.'

'Digress?' Leone said, on the alert. 'On the contrary, I have the feeling all this is leading us to a specific point which I can't yet make out.'

'And you're quite right – it's your departure from Cyprus for the Kingdom of France tomorrow. Your letter of leave,[112] signed by me, is ready. It's also the reason I opened my heart to you earlier. Francesco, I don't know if we will meet again in this world.'

'What—?'

Viancourt interrupted him with a gesture.

'I do not fear death. It has been and still is our constant companion – for you, for me and for all of us in this place. Please don't worry, I don't sense it creeping towards me yet. I hope it has the courtesy to warn me of its approach. It owes me that after taking up so many days and nights of my life. In any case, it's not a matter of the amount of sand that's left in my hourglass, but of how long you'll be away.'

Francesco de Leone was torn between relief and surprise. To return to France, to his cousin Agnès d'Authon, who was unaware of their blood ties. To watch over her so that nobody would try and attack the life she was doubtless carrying. To assail Benedetti's henchmen, if that was their plan. Nevertheless, what could be the prior's reason for sending him, since the latter knew nothing of his quest, or about Agnès, or the different blood that was to be born again through her?

'I accept the mission. What is it?'

'I'm glad to hear it. Very glad. Honorius has spread his tentacles and you know all about their fearsome power.'

'What is he plotting?'

Once again, the prior hesitated. The truth would have made his heart lighter. But its time had not come yet.

'We don't know for certain,' Arnaud de Viancourt lied. 'However, it's clear that our adversary's success would mean our defeat. Does he wish to rid himself of Clément V, since he was unable to thwart his election? After all, we're convinced that it was he who gave the order to poison Benoît XI. We're trying to find our way through thick fog, my brave brother. Honorius is looking for someone we must find before he does, whether this person then turns out to be an ally or an enemy. The fact that this child should have such importance in the camerlingo's eyes makes him very precious to us.'

Leone was surprised.

'A child?'

'It's what has emerged from the information we've been able to gather.'

In truth, Clair Gresson and his spies had been criss-crossing the realm for almost two years, looking for the young Clément from Madame de Souarcy's entourage, but in vain. Arnaud de Viancourt had gradually come to believe that, since Leone knew the child well, it would be easier for him to find him and protect him. Gresson would assist him with the utmost discretion.

'A youth called Clément, a farm boy, we think, in the household of a lady, the new Comtesse d'Authon.'

Leone fought back the panic which constricted his throat. Clément! Why was Benedetti after him? Was it to recover the manuscripts the knight had entrusted to him before returning to Cyprus? The Vallombroso treatise, without which the camerlingo was unable to interpret the second subject of the prophecy, and the large notebook into which he and Eustache de Rioux, his godfather in the order, had copied the notebook given to them by the Knight Templar in the underground passage of Saint-Jean-d'Acre before dying? The two volumes must never fall into the camerlingo's hands. Not at any price.

Viancourt feigned not to notice the inner turmoil that had drained the colour from his fellow brother's lips, and continued.

'You must find this Clément. I have but few details to give you, so I'm relying on you, my friend. You must find out why he's important to Benedetti, then we'll be able to work out what plan the camerlingo has hatched.'

First and foremost, Leone had to protect the child, so that their quest might continue. Even though Viancourt did not know exactly why, the young boy had become a crucial focus.

'It will be done as you order,' Leone said, bowing, 'and, brother ... we will meet again.'

'God willing.'

Clairets Abbey, Perche, August 1306

A huge realm devoted to work and prayer, Clairets Abbey suddenly loomed up at the edge of the forest. It nestled in a valley whose hills were covered in vines that produced a reputable claret.[113]

The hundreds of acres given to the Cistercian Bernardines began on the territory of the parish of Masle.[114] The construction of the abbey – decreed by a charter in July 1204 upon the initiative of Geoffroy III, Comte de Perche, and his wife, Mathilde de Brunswick, sister of the Emperor Otto IV – had been completed in 1212.

Well equipped and exempt from bills and taxes, Clairets Abbey had the right to administer high, middle and low justice. Abbesses there had had the status of lords in that regard, including sentencing to flagellation, amputation, and even death. A gibbet had been erected on the field that extended between the abbey and Souarcy. The Abbess also judged wolves captured in the neighbouring forest for crimes against livestock. The condemned animals were immediately hanged, a few hundred feet away from the wall, in a place known as the Gallows.

Valuable advantages had been granted to this convent, one of the most important in the kingdom: the lands of Masle and Theil, as well as a large annuity which was further increased by the influx of gifts from the wealthy, lords and well-to-do peasants, not to mention those who gave alms hoping their generosity would make up for their sins.

At the time, there were about two hundred nuns there, fifty or so novices and over sixty lay servants.

The majority of the buildings – among them, in the north, the abbey church of Notre-Dame, with its choir facing Christ's tomb – had been built of *grison*, a natural black conglomerate of flint, quartz, clay and iron ore. A very long, high wall surrounded the convent, and had only three points of entry, with the main one opening to the north. Just behind it were the buildings where passing strangers were allowed: the hostelry, the parlour and the stables. On the right were the head prioress[115] and under-prioress's lodgings and the abbey palace, a squat, single-storey building that was only barely more luxurious than the nuns' dormitories. The Abbess and her secretary lived and worked there. A little further south began the cloister of Saint-Joseph. Behind it stretched the infirmary and its gardens, as well as the novitiate. Then came the *babillerie*, with its two classrooms where the teaching nuns took turns. It was where they took in children abandoned at night outside the main door or on the edge of the neighbouring woods, as well as young society ladies whose parents, hurt by their daughters' deviation from good sense, were quick to take them to the abbey so that they might give birth to their inconvenient offspring and subsequently hide there for the remainder of their lives to avoid disgracing the rest of the family.

Annelette Beaupré sighed in irritation. God in heaven! How she missed the orderly calm of her herb garden. Even so, these past months had had a profound effect on the apothecary, whom neither the years, nor the dangers, nor the reprimands had been able to bring to heel. A kind of wisdom, as well as patience, had come over her so fast that she had been astonished to suddenly notice them. Annelette had seen in them a bequest from the late Éleusie de Beaufort, her beloved Abbess, who had died in her arms from poisoning. The tall, angular woman therefore came to cherish her new character traits which, in other circumstances, would have jarred with her. After all, what use is patience when all you have to do is scold a little to obtain whatever is required? Patience is divine, her dear Éleusie always used to say, but the apothecary daughter was never entirely convinced. What does God need with patience, when He has eternity?

Annelette pushed away the register where she noted in detail, with application if not enthusiasm, the events of the day before. They had sold two barrels of young wine to an innkeeper in Nogent-le-Roux, and eight pounds of honey to an apothecary in Alençon. During the week, the woodcutters had been cutting down trees and stacking up logs for the ovens under the fussy supervision of Sylvine Taulier, the baker. She had to count them day and night in order to ascertain that one of those 'turnip bloods', as she called sisters whose health and stamina were not as robust as hers, had not stolen a log to put in the stove and warm their joints. A stag had been killed. In keeping with the abbey's tradition for charity – rare in these straitened times – one quarter had been distributed among the peasants of the area, in front of the Principal door. The rest had been cooked with fervour by a certain Elisaba Ferron, the sister in charge of organising meals and the kitchens, and who bawled at anyone wanting to hear, 'My name means "joy". Jubilation in the house of the Lord, our Father. Joy for the game that will so happily break our usual abstinence, with the permission of our Abbess – God bless her. Everything is joy. J.O.Y.' This middle-aged widow of an important tradesman from Nogent had once slapped the faces of lazy clerks as cheerfully as she had, unbeknownst to her husband, slipped a coin to young workers in love with maidens, who in turn yearned for hair ribbons admired at the market. Elisaba was large enough and fervent enough to knock out an ass. Her sturdy character, stentorian tone and market-seller manner concealed a heart as large as her bosom.

Unable to concentrate on this daily repetitive writing she considered useless, Annelette kept mulling over the events of the past months.

The deliberations of the chapter[116] had been interminable

and Annelette Beaupré's procrastinations did not help matters. Gathered together to elect their new abbess, the senior nuns had voted in favour of their apothecary. The vote was unanimous with one exception – that of the cellarer,[117] Berthe de Marchiennes, who felt that the office was hers by right and seniority. She had laid out all her arguments with her customary detail before the chapter, who had feigned to give her their full attention. After all, Berthe de Marchiennes was so foolish that only she was not aware of being so. Still, embarrassed by this mark of esteem, Annelette Beaupré had started off by declining the honour which she perceived as being too restrictive. She was queen of her herb garden and enjoyed preparing ointments and potions. She had no desire to find herself behind the austere, heavy work table where Madame de Beaufort and other abbesses before her had toiled for hours. Of course, she had to admit that she was flattered by her sisters' approval, and the recollection of her father and brother had fleetingly crossed her mind. The old quack thought he was an *aesculapius*. But the proofs of his countless medical blunders were lying six feet under the ground, so were hardly in a condition to contradict him. Grégoire, his son and worthy successor, had followed fervently in his footsteps. They had looked her up and down, humiliated her and mocked her when she had been stupid and credulous enough to believe that they would accept a demonstration of a female's scientific abilities. They had had a cheap and nasty laugh at her expense. She remembered it as though it had happened the day before. She was standing before them and her father had said, in a mocking tone, 'If you're not careful, Grégoire, this conceited young woman will be giving you lessons on how to bleed a patient!'

Annelette had picked up on their cruel joke. They clearly enjoyed putting her down. She had suddenly seen the enormity of the situation. That her intelligence, her ability to learn and use her knowledge had terrified them. However unintentionally, she had led them to see their own limitations, and they had never forgiven her for that. But strangely, the memory of their two snarling faces had suddenly vanished, and the resentment she had harboured towards them for almost thirty years had left her as though by magic. Perhaps the result of the succession of frightening months at Clairets.

Subsequently, the senior nuns had pleaded their cause before the apothecary nun, and begged her to become their Mother Superior. So Annelette had gradually been swayed by their gentle insistence. They had been so frightened while their abbey had been haunted by a demon, or rather two demon poisoners, who had turned out to be none other than Jeanne d'Amblin, their extern sister,[118] and Blanche de Blinot, who held the office of head prioress and played on her pretended senility to dupe everyone. If Annelette had not stood up to these two murderesses, the worst would have happened. Moreover, what would become of Clairets if Berthe de Marchiennes took over the reins? Everyone was saddened by the prospect. Thibaude de Gartempe, the guest mistress,[119] whose constant nervousness had always annoyed Annelette, was to sum up the situation with surprising clarity.

'Well … I hate to be uncharitable but despite her erudition and faith, Berthe is stubborn as only foolish people can be! Moreover, she has never shown the kind of compassion we would wish for in an abbess.'

Annelette had listened with astonishment to the portrait they gradually painted of her. The apothecary, whom everyone had feared because of her surly expression and sharp retorts, suddenly became their saviour and sweet, kindly angel.

Her mind was made up when she discovered in her herbarium a brief note carefully spread out on the table where she prepared and weighed the herbs, one corner secured by a small terracotta flagon. A few words were traced in tall, beautiful handwriting:

'Think about the books. Protect them.' Strangely, Annelette had never doubted the identity of the author. It was the very young woman with a dagger who had passed herself off as a novice in order to help her against Jeanne d'Amblin. Esquive d'Estouville. A pretty heart-shaped face lit by amber eyes, and dark, thick, curly hair. Annelette had vainly searched every corner of the herbarium to try and find another trace of her passage. How had Esquive managed to enter then exit again? Early that morning, the apothecary had found the door locked. The young woman was a benevolent mystery who came and went as lightly as a shadow. The idea that Mademoiselle d'Estouville could still be prowling around comforted Annelette and lightened the solitude that had stubbornly remained with her since her beloved Mother Superior had died.

The secret library at Clairets. Nobody knew of its existence except for Annelette, Francesco de Leone, the nephew or rather adoptive son of the late Madame de Beaufort, that sweet little rascal Clément, the protégé of Agnès de Souarcy, now Comtesse d'Authon, and Esquive. Perhaps also the new Pope, Clément V, but the apothecary could not have sworn to it. Even so, all it would take would be for Berthe to lift or remove the tapestry, and she would discover the low door that led to the hall. What would she do with the books then? The clumsy woman was capable of handing them over to the camerlingo Honorius Benedetti, the sworn enemy of their quest. In addition, Annelette could not stop thinking about the knowledge accumulated in that secret place, which had cost so many of her fellow sisters their lives. What prodigious secrets were hidden in those books? So much knowledge lay within those pages and parchments, which the Church was either unaware of, or forbade. Knowledge that was within arm's reach. She felt deeply sad, thinking of the fear this knowledge inspired in Éleusie de Beaufort and in so many others. Knowledge is power. Power that is, in itself, neither good nor evil, any more than science is. It is what men do with it that decides who screams and who bleeds. How did Éleusie de Beaufort fail to understand that keeping men ignorant brutes could not make them better, just more vulnerable? In any case, Annelette Beaupré had ended up accepting the senior nuns' petition, and succeeded Madame de Beaufort, but insisted on keeping her office as apothecary. After all, she had a precedent in the very erudite Hildegard of Bingen,* who had added to her wisdom as an abbess her extraordinary gift as an apothecary, as well as a marvellous talent for music and poetry. Hildegard was certainly credited with miracles Annelette doubted she could ever reproduce.

She sighed and picked up the sharpened quill that had slipped out of her hand. Until now, she had had little time to browse the shelves packed with the knowledge of past centuries. The succession of dramatic events in the abbey had left deep scars. Distrust, fear and evil deeds had broken into these austere walls devoted to prayer, work and compassion. As soon as she had been elected abbess, Annelette Beaupré had taken great care to heal wounds and revive sisterly flames, imagining that her benevolent firmness would surprise Madame de Beaufort. She had had to arrange the hasty election of nuns to the offices of those who had been killed by the two evil acolytes, and had taken advantage of this to get rid of some dead wood which Éleusie de Beaufort's kindness had kept in office even when they did not fulfil their roles. Gervaise de Puisan had been elected treasurer nun, which required common sense and application in all things; Marguerite Masurier – who also had a solid head on her shoulders – had become the bursar nun; Alice Valette had accepted the office of sacristan, while the delightful but firm Léonine de Brioure was perfect for the role of extern sister. She would be able to persuade the most reticent visitors to show generosity. Other nuns had been appointed. Berthe de Marchiennes remained the cellarer, since Annelette had not found a way to remove her and thus spare herself the sight of that large pinched face that looked like a permanent reproach. After all, was it her fault if Berthe de Marchiennes had been the only one to vote for herself? Emma de Pathus, the surly teacher[120] nun, had been judiciously moved to being a cantor[121] nun, something she considered fair recognition for a vocal range she was rather proud of. This way, her moody slaps would no longer land on innocent cheeks. All of a sudden, one started passing her in the corridors, always humming Pérotin[122] for four voices, which he had composed while he was chapel master at Notre-Dame de Paris. Emma applied herself to producing all four voices, from the deepest to the highest, annoying attentive ears with her false notes.

Annelette sighed again, irritated. She might as well finish these interminable notes as soon as possible. So, then, they had sold two geldings for harrowing to Vivien Chesnel, master tiler[123] in Colonard.

A soft knock on her heavy study door made her look up. Someone had finally come to provide her with an excuse to interrupt her unrewarding task without feeling guilty. The pleasant little face of slender Alice Valette, the sacristan sister, appeared around the half-open door.

'Reverend Mother, may I possibly have your attention? I can come back later ...'

'No, please, come in. Sit down, daughter.'

Alice crossed the large room with her odd skipping gait. The young nun did not walk but advanced with little leaps. A cheerful smile was forever quivering on her lips. Her pointy face reminded Annelette of a sweet field mouse, an impression reinforced by her dark, lively eyes. Not one of those dreadful rats who ravage food and tapestries, but one of those little creatures of the fields you sometimes come across, and which look at you with alarm, sitting on their behinds, their whiskers trembling.

'What's the purpose of your visit?' Annelette asked affably, in the tone she had adopted since she had managed to curb her former more commanding manner.

'It's a disaster,' Alice replied in a strained whisper. 'We're being attacked.'

'Excuse me? Attacked? By whom?'

'Well, not exactly us, but rather Saint Germain's tibia. The Bishop of Auxerre who fought the Picts and Saxons in England.'

'The relic given to us by the late Madame de Beaufort!' the Abbess exclaimed.

'That's right,' the young nun replied, an expression of terror on her face.

'How is this possible?'

'I don't know, Reverend Mother. You know that I take great care of it. It all started a month ago. I noticed a few grains of fine grey-white powder on the saint's tibia. At first, I thought it was dust that had got into the case despite the locks. So I cleaned it thoroughly. A week later, the same thing happened. Ever since then, I've been checking the holy relic every day ... I change the bags of juniper[124] and myrtle which protect it from insects. And, well, Reverend Mother, I don't know how to tell you ... but the powder comes from the bone, which is crumbling.'

'Sweet Lord!' the Abbess gasped and put her hand over her mouth. 'What are we going to do?'

'I don't know. I was wondering if any of your apothecary preparations could ...'

'As far as I know there isn't one that fights against this ... this disintegration of holy bones. Come, daughter, I must see this abomination for myself.'

Rue Saint-Amour, Chartres, September 1306

Hair braided with pale-blue ribbons and elegantly curled at her temples, still wearing her indoor dress of thick deep-purple silk, Mathilde de Souarcy – rechristened d'Ongeval by Madame de Neyrat to avoid indiscretion – stared with surprise at the small dish filled with little yellow-orange grains and scattered with Corinthian raisins.

'Madame, what is this?' she asked Madame de Neyrat, who was watching her with a furtive smile.

'Rice,[125] my dear, cooked at length in saffron milk and sweetened with honey.'

'Rice?'

'Try it. It's very tasty and, if you want my opinion, far better than spelt. An extravagance, but we do deserve the best, don't we?'

A contented sigh was the answer. Mathilde plunged her silver spoon into the dish, under Madame de Neyrat's hawk eye. She had already taught her that table manners betray one's origins more surely than gossip. Aude softened every light reprimand with a life lesson. Still, she had to admit that Agnès de Souarcy had done a good job in raising this restive, temperamental adolescent. The young woman had a straight posture, was well versed in the code of greetings and curtseys, knew how to lower her eyes, and expressed herself, if not with wit, then with ease.

Mathilde brought a finger up to her teeth to extract a grain of rice that had got stuck there. Aude immediately intervened. 'Now, now, Mademoiselle, what kind of boorish gesture is that?'

'I've often seen my uncle de Larnay do it.'

Aude raised her pretty blonde eyebrows and replied, ironically, 'What did I tell you?'

Mathilde sniggered behind her hand.

'Never forget the deserving work of Monsieur de Saint-Victor, who clearly advocated that we should not eat with our fingers but with the help of a spoon wherever possible, and that we should never wipe our hands on our clothes but on the tablecloth. Its primary function is to allow us to wipe grease off our fingers and we must never throw half-eaten pieces back into our plate, let alone the debris from between our teeth. My dear friend, I have already told you but it's beneficial to repeat it: there are three kinds of women. Well-born, wealthy ladies who will never know life's torments. The beggars resigned to their fate, whatever the qualities of their souls and their minds. They will, at worst, end up as whores in a brothel, at best as cloistered nuns. Then there are the foxes,[126] another kind of beggar but not resigned to their fate.'

'And are we foxes, Madame?'

'What woman in her right mind would wish to end up like a common whore or a baptistry frog? However, being a fox requires work and constant vigilance. You must develop precious skills.'

'Which ones?'

'The arts of lying, cheating and cunning. A taste for secrecy because, even if you have your back against the wall, you must never reveal your secrets, especially when you pay a high price for those of others. In addition, you need clear-headed tenacity. Some call it cynicism – this moral independence, this contempt for the rules imposed by others – and they wouldn't be far wrong. In other words, anything that, in the long run, makes you free and your own master. But beware … A clear head must remain our biggest secret and our major strength. Nobody must discover us. On the contrary, we must take great care to make everyone believe that we blindly follow accepted behaviour and do not tolerate deviations from morality, and especially not from the teachings of the Church. Do you understand?'

'Certainly, and I have totally changed because of this. So it's a question of becoming a hoaxer?'

'You've put it in a nutshell. You're so clever, my dear Mathilde.'

'I think … No, I know I'll be good at it.'

But I doubt you'll ever possess the subtlety for it, Aude thought, and cooed, 'I'm certain you will be, and I'll help you lie beautifully …' Aude seemed to hesitate. For days she had been champing at the bit, impatient to broach the subject she really cared about. 'My dear, are you pleased with my strong-arm men from Champagne?'

'Oh, Madame, I thank God every day for placing you in my path. As I've told you, this … this abduction was so easy that I would have laughed had I not been so scared it might fail. One of them lifted me, me and my bundle, as if I were a feather, up to the top of the surrounding wall. The other one was sitting astride the wall and heaved me up by the arms then tied a large leather belt around my waist. There was a ring on it, with a rope tied to it. He gently lowered me to the third man, who freed me from the harness. There was a light cart waiting for me. I was in Chartres in a few days, well guarded. I owe my release to you.'

'I'm so happy to have put an end to your torments. Of course, it was a dangerous enterprise. Still, my determination was only equalled by my compassion for you.'

Mathilde swallowed a mouthful of cool peach and honey wine. Aude curbed her impatience. The goose still did not understand where she was leading. She would have to be direct, without further delay.

'Do you remember when we first met in that sinister parlour at Argensolles Abbey, in August?'

'Every word you spoke and every one of your glances is for

ever etched in my memory, Madame,' Mathilde stated with a sad little grimace. 'How can you ever doubt it, you, who are the angel of my salvation?'

'How kind of you. I hate myself for reminding you of your promise. Still, the honour of a fox is not conventional but very demanding.'

The languid hazel eyes staring at her suddenly lit up with understanding. 'The payment,' she whispered.

'Well, let's call it the exchange. The word is ... well, less harsh.'

'You assured me that it would not be disproportionate and would not offend me.'

'Indeed. I never go back on my word, which is why I give it sparingly. The exchange, forgive me for putting it so bluntly, is as follows: it's your future in exchange for that of your mother, Madame Agnès.'

At first, there was surprise on Mathilde's face. Since she had moved into the first floor of the magnificent town house in Rue Saint-Amour, she had expected all kinds of demands but not this one. Her surprise was followed by amusement. She lowered her eyes, but not fast enough, which allowed Aude to see a nasty joy in them.

'My mother's future?' she murmured, her eyes downcast. 'What can I do about it?'

'Much, my dear. We'll come back to that. So this is the proposition I made you at Argensolles Abbey. I build, arm and equip your future, and you help me destroy that of your mother. After all, I managed to locate you easily in that ... that country jail where your odious uncle had locked you up, so how come your mother couldn't do that? Come now! She simply didn't look for you, and was only too happy to know that you were far away from her and her plans. Remember her cunning and her envy towards you, and how little she cared about her only child that she condemned her to living in a pigsty, in poverty and hardship, and forced her to consort with servants. In that sinister manor … I mean in that tumbledown farm. After all, you're a Souarcy by blood, and even if it's not the wealthiest nobility, it has nonetheless a good reputation in the county of Perche and even as far as Chartres! My dear, a family's reputation is invaluable …'

Mathilde was not listening. A tailor-made future. Two years earlier, while staying at the Château de Larnay, she had confessed to hating her mother. And her hatred had continued to grow during what she called her 'imprisonment' in Argensolles. Despite her limited intelligence, and contrary to Madame de Neyrat's insinuations, Mathilde knew she could not reproach her mother for anything except the years she had endured in Souarcy like an endless and unjust penitence. She hated her for denying her the comfort provided by her half-brother Eudes de Larnay when the latter had insisted that they go to his chateau shortly after the death of Hugues de Souarcy. Of course, just before her mother's Inquisition trial, Mathilde had understood that Eudes expected a full reward for it: Agnès as his mistress. A fine thing indeed! He would have tired of her as quickly as he had done of the others. What were a few nights in comparison to the abject poverty in which they were living? As for herself, if she had had to go through that … not that her uncle had ever charmed her. On the other hand, she had found what she thought she knew about his wealth very alluring. For a long time now, Mathilde had been devoted to herself and to satisfying her own needs and desires. The rest, all the rest, did not matter. The only recent exception to this indifference towards anything that did not concern her was the friendly gratitude she had conceived towards Madame de Neyrat, since the splendid creature represented the future Mathilde intended making her own. In truth, what had triggered a permanent rage in her was the news, received six months late, that her mother was remarried to the Comte d'Authon. What? This illegitimate woman only acknowledged at the eleventh hour had married one of the richest and most charming men in the province? On top of that he was much older than Agnès, so she could hope soon to become a wealthy widow.[127] That was dreadfully unfair! What did they all see in her? Her father, Hugues de Souarcy, that canker and rascal Clément, that idiot and simpleton Gilbert, her uncle Eudes, the nuns at Clairets who seemed honoured to have helped her, the Comte d'Authon and even that fat tub Adeline who worshipped her as if she were a manifestation of the Blessed Virgin. What was so special about her? Mathilde detested her and would finish her off with pleasure.

'Mathilde?'

'I beg your pardon, Madame. Your words bring back so many terrible memories.'

'I thought so, my poor dear.'

'I'm in your debt. We're allies, as you said. However, before proceeding any further, would you permit me to retire to my apartments for a moment?'

'I was just about to advise that. A moment to reflect on your own is important.'

Aude was no fool. She had watched every expression on Mathilde's face. The latter took pleasure at the thought of imminent revenge on her mother, her sworn enemy. What was she about to do under the pretext of retiring? No doubt admire what she had here, in this town house Aude had filled with ornaments to the point of vulgarity. What could be more inspiring to Mathilde than a display of wealth she thought would soon be hers, especially when compared to the poverty she had left behind, firmly intending never to suffer it again? As for crossing the final hurdle that separated her from indignity and a tarnished reputation, it was a fait accompli since the lying testimony with which she had tried to send her mother to the stake.

An almost dizzying contempt overcame Madame de Neyrat. She slowly stood up and decided that a long bath followed by a massage with Italian almond oil, in the ladies' steam room on Rue du Bienfait, would calm her down. She felt a pleasant certainty. Despite all the sins she had committed and lies she had told, and even the murders she had perpetrated, she was fundamentally different from this young girl. She had defended herself. All those whose demise she had arranged had been at fault, greedy or cruel, rapists or incestuous. All except, she had to admit, Agnès de Souarcy. She stifled a little laugh. It was a small consolation but it would have to do. Strangely, the memory of the blonde little girl in the shack cheered her. Angélique ... to deliver her from that hovel and restore her to purity.

Mathilde was spinning around, complimenting herself with a mischievous grimace, admiring herself in one of the countless bevelled mirrors in her apartments. She looked up and, for the umpteenth time, gazed with pleasure at the finely moulded joists and beams, a nicety reserved for the wealthier lords. The large carved bed where she liked to laze around was protected by a screen, had a canopy suspended from the ceiling and was surrounded by curtains on three sides. During the day, the one concealing the foot of the bed would be raised. Tapestries with delicate, luminous hues covered the walls, parting at the doors. A tall armoire decorated with ornamental hinges and carvings had been pushed between the two windows which – and this was the height of luxury – were made of glass and had inside blinds. On the small dressing table fitted with a swivel mirror, there were rows of brushes, combs, hair clasps and ribbons. A room fit for a princess, with an equally pretty antechamber leading into it. However, what delighted her most was the small ablutions cabinet adjoining her room. The high table with a marble top on which, every morning and evening, a basin of water scented with attar of roses was placed was so refined! She went up to the armoire and pulled open one of the richly carved doors. Heavens, what magic! Madame de Neyrat had showered her with gifts as soon as she had arrived in Chartres. There was a large collection of dresses with wide skirts and clipped sleeves in the Italian fashion, not to mention turret hats with assorted veils for tying under the chin, and fur-trimmed cloaks. She chuckled and pulled out the prettiest thing in the world: a tunic with sleeves that had slits from the elbows and was all lined with ermine. She buried her face in the silky fur which her benefactress had had the exquisite taste to have perfumed. She remembered the clothes of her aunt Apolline, which Eudes had had altered shortly after his wife's death in order to fit his niece. On top of everything else he was a miser! Her bitterness almost dampened her high spirits but then a happy thought chased it away.

She wondered if this was an ideal opportunity to haggle over the help she was glad to be able to provide Madame de Neyrat. She could ask her for the head of that rat Eudes. Of course, she would have to be even more charming and grateful than usual, but then that was one of her best talents. Despite her lack of intelligence, Mathilde understood that her protector was not the kind to be forced to do anything whatsoever.

Château d'Authon-du-Perche, Perche, September 1306

Artus d'Authon reread three times the short scroll bearing the royal seal. At first, when Ronan had brought it to him a few seconds earlier, he had felt a pleasant surprise. Ronan was waiting for his response, his face lit up with delight. A fleeting delight that vanished when his master looked up.

'It's completely baffling,' said the Comte, rising abruptly from one of the small armchairs dotted around the edge of the circular study.

Ronan, suddenly worried, waited patiently. Artus clenched his jaw and murmured, 'I'm such a fool! And I thought that perhaps the King was soon coming to visit my lands, or for some other cordial occasion!'

The old servant refrained from asking questions despite his attachment to Artus, whom he'd been watching over since childhood. The Comte began to explain, thereby demonstrating the affection that he, too, felt for Ronan. 'The King is summoning me to ... to appear before a tribunal gathered at the Inquisition headquarters in Alençon in order to clarify some ... some discrepancies regarding the outcome of the Comtesse's trial – discrepancies that seem to have come to light in testimonies.'

At the mention of the Inquisition tribunal, Ronan had turned white.

'I beg your pardon, my lord?'

'You heard me.'

'But how ... What ...' the old man muttered, stumbling over his words.

'I only know what I've just told you. It's an order from the King and not a missive from a friend to whom I taught falconry.'

Ronan got the impression that it was the fact that it was an order, more than the actual contents of the royal letter, that was hurtful to his master. As for him, he had been overwhelmed by fear. Everyone knew that when you went into the Inquisition headquarters, you never came out again.

'Is it possible that the miraculous judgement that saved Madame la Comtesse—'

'Is being put in doubt?' Artus said in an icy tone. 'I don't know, but one thing is certain: if that is the case, I will go all the way to the Pope.'

'Is there no way to obtain an explanation from the King … Surely, after the time you spent together in your youth, he must still be your friend or, at least, remember you.'

'If Philip had wished to give me any details, they would be mentioned in these lines,' Artus d'Authon replied. 'As for friendship, it's a princely vice but I believe not one that our King has.'

'So you will comply, then?'

'I have no choice but to submit to the will of the King. Especially since I have been and remain his most loyal subject.'

Artus examined the man who had watched over his days and nights for so many years. When little Gauzelin, the Comte's only son, had died, Ronan had been the only one who had dared defy his master's murderous rage. The old man possessed the strength and determination of freely offered devotion. Tight-lipped, his head lowered, he was staring at the floorboards. He hesitated, still biting back his words. Monseigneur d'Authon did not grant him the luxury of uttering them.

'I know what you're thinking. We owe loyalty and gratitude only to those who treat us with regard. However, this is the King, Ronan. So keep that opinion to yourself or I shall resent you for it.'

'I shall obey, my lord. What about the Comtesse? How shall I act with her?'

'I don't intend to inform her, at least not for the moment. I want to keep this news from her for as long as possible. No point in adding to her worries about finding young Clémence. She's exhausted by this constant search. Don't you think she's grown thinner and paler than usual?'

'It's true. I get the feeling the Comtesse has been concealing severe exhaustion under her usual calm demeanour.'

'I will ensure that she agrees to take some rest but the lady has a strong character,' said the Comte. 'Now, send for my chief bailiff, Monge de Brineux, immediately.'

'Right away, my lord,' stammered Ronan, and bowed before leaving his master's study.

Once the door was shut behind him, the old man had to pause to catch his breath. Fear was muddling his thoughts. He tried to fight off a kind of dreadful premonition. What could he do? Or even attempt to do? Of course, he was a free man, but one of so little importance. Messire de Bologne, the Comte's old physician. Now he, with all his knowledge, could perhaps devise a parry or attempt a response. Of course, Monseigneur Artus had commanded silence. However, he had only mentioned his wife. Therefore, Ronan felt justified in warning the scientist and asking for his help, especially since Messire Joseph was one of the very few people he trusted, and whose gratitude towards his master was uncompromising.

When Ronan had finished sharing the terrifying news in a faltering voice, Joseph de Bologne leant both elbows on his high lectern. He remained silent for a moment, staring at the old servant, who was fighting back tears.

'Is that all?' Joseph asked, in disbelief.

'That's all, Messire.'

'What kind of folly is this?' the scientist exclaimed.

'I can't understand it, that's why I came to seek your opinion, and hoped you might be able to explain.'

'Come, my dear Ronan. Let's go and sit for a moment, and put our heads together, and try to work out what's behind all this. One thing is certain: the papacy never does anything without excellent reason, even if those reasons are so remote and mysterious that you get lost trying to understand them.'

Ronan followed the physician. If there was any means of helping his master or simply providing an explanation, then this man would surely discover it.

Joseph de Bologne mumbled for a moment, recapitulating the events that had taken place since Agnès de Souarcy's imprisonment in *murus strictus*,[128] a dark cell where the accused were chained. Ronan waited patiently, not quite knowing where his thoughts were drifting. Just sensing that the powerful machine that was this man's intelligence was probing every corner of history made him feel calmer.

'Obviously, it's a trap!' the physician suddenly cried out. 'Only what kind of trap and to what end? The Church banned trials by ordeal over a century ago, and do you know why?'

Ronan shook his head.

'Because very few people, whether innocent or guilty, can withstand the ordeal with the red-hot iron and, in a duel, it's always the better swordsman who wins unless, of course, there's divine intervention or a miracle, and, as far as I know, many less than innocent people were acquitted during those duels. Who truly benefits from miracles? The receiver of the miracle, naturally, but also the Church which somehow has the power to trigger them, be it during a trial or a pilgrimage. So why question a miracle that involved the murder of a small-time, totally dispensable inquisitor whose reputation was so murky he would have one day ended up in the papal jails just like his dreadful precursor Robert le Bougre? Why deprive the people of Alençon and its surroundings of the happy knowledge that God intervened to destroy the monster and save the dove? This is such inept logic that it's completely unlike the Holy See.'

The scientist's face darkened and he sighed with consternation. Ronan was once again overwhelmed with anxiety. 'What do you think, Messire?' he murmured. 'I beg you, tell me the truth.'

'I think we should just take this at face value, for once. It's Monsieur d'Authon himself that they're after.'

'I cannot believe it,' Ronan argued. 'My master is a wise man who's never meddled in the politics of the kingdom, let alone Rome.'

'And how do you know that? How does he know?'

'I don't understand anything you're saying, Messire.'

'I must think alone, Ronan. I must consult various books, including *Consultationes ad inquisitores haereticae pravitatis*,[129] which should enlighten me on points of procedure. Have faith. God will not abandon us. Of that I am certain. As for my head, in His infinite generosity, He has made it very skilled.'

Messire Joseph remained sitting for a long time after the departure of the old servant, assembling and disassembling the pieces of this alarming puzzle. Perplexed, he finally went to his large study and pulled out a slender volume bound in deep-purple leather, made shiny by countless readings. With the same admiration he always felt, he began reading Emperor Marcus Aurelius Antoninus's[130] *To Myself*. It had never disappointed him and had always answered his questions. He leafed through the book he knew by heart and read:

'Get into the habit of always asking yourself, with regard to another person's every action, "What is this person's true goal?"'

Then: 'Things that follow others always have a relationship with those that preceded them.'

The true goal. The goal was Comte Artus, and not some bleak conspiracy in which he would have been a dispensable pawn. Joseph knew the Inquisition and its practices well enough to fear the worst from the impending confrontation between Monseigneur d'Authon and his judges. Honour often goes hand in hand with a lack of subtlety. The only effective strategy against an inquisitor consisted in skilful lies and cunning, even if you were as pure as a newborn lamb. Artus d'Authon would never stoop to that, certain that his good faith simply had to prevail.

As for the relationship between events, you did not have to be a genius to guess it: it was Agnès, Comtesse d'Authon. What was the papacy, or one of its tentacles, after? Was it to remove, possibly destroy, Artus d'Authon in order to weaken his wife? It was the solution that sprang to mind. But why attack this virtuous, intelligent creature whom Joseph the Wise, whose circumspection hardly ever slumbered, had never found fault with?

He lacked a crucial element to understand more of this terrifying charade. He decided to make a clean breast of it, fetched the tall walking stick with the iron tip, which stood patiently in the corner of his study, and slung his large herb bag over his shoulder.

A chiselled silver hair brush in her hand, Guillette paused mid-stroke and approached one of the windows in her mistress's apartments. She declared in a cheerful tone, 'I think your physician is going for a walk.'

'He enjoys strolling through the woods,' Agnès d'Authon answered with some hesitation. 'He brings back great quantities of medicinal herbs, most of which I'm not familiar with.'

The slow hair brushing resumed.

'You have such beautiful hair, Madame It's like fine honey. And so silky to the touch. Did you not sleep well last night, Madame? You look tired.'

'On the contrary. I slept like a log and didn't wake up till after prime.[+] It's nothing. These past few months have been exhausting.'

'Yes, of course ... Monsieur Philippe is already a strapping young lad and very lively, the little angel. Ronan says he's the spitting image of his father. And then this Clément ... I always say I can't think of many masters who'd concern themselves this much to find a little farm boy!'

Agnès was quite fond of this girl whom Barbe, who was the firm but not gratuitously harsh head of the chateau servants, had hired a few weeks earlier. Guillette was cheerful without ever becoming tiresome or too chatty. She was very bright and that had appealed to Agnès so much that she had quickly added her to her own service.

'I practically brought up Clément after his mother, my maid, died in childbirth. That's why I worry about him,' Agnès said, doing her best to keep her voice level.

'It shows you're very charitable, Madame. Then there's the mine in Souarcy ... You're certainly not short of work and worries, that's for sure!'

She braided the heavy, reddish-blonde mass of hair and coiled it on the nape of Agnès's neck before putting on the net and clips that would keep it in place.

Changing the subject, she then said, 'Monseigneur Artus requests the pleasure of your company at lunch after sext.'

A smile lit Agnès's face. 'The pleasure will be all mine,' she corrected. 'Let's hope I'll have regained my appetite by then. My husband's cook keeps surprising us with his wonders for which I've not shown due appreciation in the past few days.'

Guillette's attractive face was suddenly anxious. 'You must eat, Madame. I've noticed that your dresses seem loose. A graceful figure like yours doesn't need to lose any weight.'

'Put my turret hat on, please. Then please leave me, my dear

Guillette. I feel like reading a little before joining my husband.'

'Very well, Madame. Which book would you like me to bring you? I can't read but if you tell me where it is in the library and the colour of the binding, I'll find it.'

'There's no need,' said Agnès.

'It never leaves my bedside.' She indicated the white trunk at the foot of her bed.

As soon as the servant had left, she retrieved the book, which was beautifully delicate, and one of Artus's countless presents on the occasion of the birth of little Philippe. Madame Marie de France's *Lays*, which he had had copied in Paris and illustrated with exquisite drawings. The beautiful, long-tailed bird from *Yonec*, which turned into a lover, was displayed in it. There was the fairy from *Lanval*, dressed in a deep blue surcoat. Also, on another page, the blood-red, menacing mouth of the werewolf in *Bisclavaret*. The cover of this jewel was another marvel, with an armful of tiny flowers made of thin strips of mother-of-pearl, turquoise, emerald, ruby, amethyst and jet. On the flyleaf, her husband's nervous hand had written:

I have chosen immortal flowers so that they may testify to the constancy and depth of my love for you, my lady. For ever.

She started the lay telling the story of the hapless woman who discovers that her husband is a werewolf. The lines seemed to tremble a little and she had to read the first one twice before she could understand it. She felt so tired, she closed her eyes. What was happening? She was not with child. She would consult Messire Joseph as soon as he returned from his walk in the forest. The unreserved admiration Clémence had for him, as well as all Agnès herself had discovered about the old man, made him dear to her. Especially since he knew as much about life and its creatures as he did about the precious and mysterious books he spent his life reading. He would understand that there was no need to alarm the Comte over some silly passing tiredness and dizziness.

Despite her feeling of faintness, Agnès managed to keep a cheerful demeanour during the meal. She forced herself to eat in spite of having no appetite, enlivening the conversation with tales of her recent reading, her sometimes difficult negotiations with blacksmiths, and her walks in the park. As usual, the cook had outdone himself. After a dish of fresh fruit with sweet wine came the second course of a mushroom fricassée with onion and spices served on a thin trencher. A hare roasted on a spit with a sauce made of wine, vinegar, marjoram and cinnamon followed. Eager to entertain her love and conceal the unpleasant dizziness that sometimes came over her, Agnès did not notice the effort he made on his part to look cheerful until a servant girl placed a portion of flan with dried fruits before them.

'I talk so much that I must be making your head spin. You look rather serious.'

He shook his head slightly and smiled. 'Not at all. It's nothing – just the usual farm issues I have to settle so that everyone is happy, which is difficult to do. These are as tedious as they are constant.'

'What issues?'

'One farmer intrudes on another one's land, or so the other one claims. As you see, nothing new.'

'As for keeping them both happy, that's a job for a juggler and not a lord,' Agnès said, joking.

She barely touched the next sweet dish, a pie of fresh pears, and noticed that her husband, too, seemed to have lost his appetite. They declined the honey waffles of the fifth course and only had the *boute-hors*,[131] a mix of cardamom and aniseeds.

Artus put his arm around his beloved's waist to escort her to her apartments. Then he took his leave on the pretext of having to solve the issue of the farmers.

'Your pulse, your eyes and your breathing are perfectly satisfactory, Madame,' declared Messire Joseph, who had been studying Agnès since finishing her examination.

'I feel reassured. As I said, nothing serious, in truth. Some unexplained tiredness, a few insignificant dizzy spells.'

'And you've lost your appetite.'

'That's right.'

'Are you nauseous?'

'Sometimes, but only briefly,' she said.

'Since you're not with child and have a strong constitution, I believe this is the result of all the terrible things you endured so bravely, in addition to a temporary slowing down of the digestive system. We often see these delayed reactions. Exceptional people can endure disasters without weakening and then, as soon as the situation calms down or they are happy again, they display the symptoms of melancholy without even being aware of it. I have full confidence in your wonderful constitution. You'll get well soon. We'll give you some help with a few secret concoctions of mine.'

'Thank you very much, Messire. You have dispelled my worries and I'm already feeling better,' Agnès lied.

Joseph de Bologne was not taken in.

'With your permission, Madame, I would like to see you again two days from now, to assess the effect of the remedies I will send you shortly.'

'Is that really necessary?'

'Your husband says that physicians are like laying hens. They fuss, get anxious and spin in every direction until they have gathered all their chicks, nice and healthy, by their side.'

'In that case, I shall play my role as your chick with dedication, Messire Joseph.'

He watched her attractive, slim figure disappear. A suspicion had crossed his mind during the examination. A terrifying suspicion.

Vatican Palace, Rome, September 1306

Aude de Neyrat took a sip of malmsey wine and crunched a mouthful of French toast, one of Honorius Benedetti's favourite treats. She was surprised at how pleased she was to see him.

'How is it, my dear friend, that you are the only person in whose presence I feel at peace?' the camerlingo admitted, dabbing his forehead with a handkerchief.

'Perhaps the good news I bring you is a powerful balm.'

'It certainly seems to be. However, that doesn't fully explain it. There is in addition a feeling of trust so complete that it surprises me.'

'Why does it surprise you, since it's mutual?'

'Because we are wary creatures, and therefore solitary.' The prelate was suddenly bitter. 'This Clair Gresson is such a terrible disappointment. I'm doing my best not to give in to the resentment and hatred he inspires in me. After all, I mind less his betrayal than my own naivety in his regard.'

Aude de Neyrat seemed to reflect, gazing intently at a large hanging on the wall behind the prelate's sumptuous desk. It represented a shy, translucent Virgin bowing her head and lowering her eyes, surrounded by angels with serious smiles. Aude knew that the tapestry concealed a low passageway that had been built between the thick walls. The supreme pontiff's meeting room was situated at the other end. She began, slowly:

'Doesn't fate reserve a biting irony for creatures like us, Honorius?'

'What do you mean?'

'We scheme and cheat so much, we become incapable of feeling anything but mistrust towards all those who come near us.

If we make an exception and bestow our respect or our affections on someone, we expect it immediately to be appreciated like a rare privilege. Why should that be the case? Perhaps cunning sometimes makes us naive after all.'

'You've summed it up very well,' admitted the camerlingo, who was constantly surprised by the intelligence of the beautiful blonde cloud sitting opposite him. 'In fact, how can I possibly justify my bitterness? Gresson betrayed the friendship I felt for him, but then I, in turn, have betrayed so many friendships during my long life …'

'Isn't our conversation turning morose, my dear Honorius? Come now … I bring you excellent news, and I find you in good health. Luck is on our side, so let us rejoice.'

The prelate's lean face relaxed. 'My dear Aude, Providence showed itself to be generous when it allowed you and me to meet. Everything about you brings me delight, even during my darkest hours.'

'It was certainly very generous with me when it saved me, thanks to you, from certain death at the stake or by the executioner's rope,' she declared in an amused tone.

Despite the archbishop's admission and the feigned flippancy she displayed in order to cheer up her old friend, Madame de Neyrat sensed that he was troubled by a feeling she knew only too well. A part of her remained a mystery to the prelate, who had been gnawed by guilt for ages. Honorius wondered about her need and desire for contrition. Did she really not feel any regret for having sullied her soul? She could have enlightened him but her silence was another proof of her friendship. Of course she did. She was sometimes overwhelmed by a desire to repent, but she took care to dismiss it quickly. To brood over her vile actions would have served no purpose. She had refused the fool's bargain fate had offered her. To repent would be tantamount to admitting that she had been wrong to fight against the life that had been imposed upon her, against the injuries and the humiliations it had in store for her. It would have been to excuse the repulsive old man who had forced himself on her whenever he felt like it. As for Honorius, she would never admit to him that she sometimes had sleepless nights when she was filled with self-disgust. The camerlingo had to keep believing that some creatures were spared remorse, so that his own would perhaps seem less justified to him. Once upon a time, he had saved her life. She did her best to sweeten his dreams.

'Since it is your destiny to bring sunshine to my darkest days, tell me again about our progress.'

'I think that … that woman who was recommended to you, the one who lives not far from Ceton, has fulfilled her task, at least from what I hear from Authon-du-Perche. Madame de Souarcy is growing thin and pale. She gets so tired that she needs to lie down in the afternoon. I confess I had little faith in the powers of that witch. That's why I thought I'd join forces with Mademoiselle Mathilde, Madame Agnès's daughter. I made a mistake, that's all. Now I must find a way of getting rid of the annoying creature. A handsome dowry and a few shiny trinkets should get her off my hands, as well as the promise I made to help her take revenge on her uncle. Her mother sickening and soon dying will help dissipate the pretty pest's venom. I will not be upset if I never see her again. What else? Of course, I forgot – an inquisitor from Évreux has just been appointed to the imminent hearing of the Comte d'Authon at the Inquisition headquarters in Alençon. A godsend for us.' Aude de Neyrat wrinkled her nose charmingly. 'Although godsend probably isn't the right word, since I see your skilful hand behind the appointment.'

'Your sharpness pleases me,' said the camerlingo.

'Would it be frightfully indiscreet of me to enquire how you managed to persuade Clément V to demand that the King of France put an old friend on trial?'

'Not indiscreet at all, my dear. Clément V is a man of rare perspicacity. He's somewhat like us, although he would be outraged by the comparison. It's very hard to dupe him since he, himself, has cheated quite a few people. Having said that, his slightly tarnished past is an asset to us. His election was organised by Philip the Fair. How far Clément was involved in the dealings that were to place him on the papal throne, I do not know. However, he fears above all that the story of this bargaining might spread across the Christian West. In that case, he would more than likely be deposed. So how does Monsieur d'Authon fit into this prospect?'

'A pawn in a complex game of chess.' Aude knitted her pretty blonde eyebrows and pressed on. 'Still, I must say the strategy of the actual game escapes me. Why do you need Artus d'Authon if we're already closing in on the beautiful Agnès? What's the point of getting rid of her husband?'

Honorius Benedetti hesitated for just a moment. To anyone else, he would have lied shamelessly. But not to her.

'As you said, the game is extremely complex. In the past, I've made a serious mistake by convincing myself that Agnès de Souarcy was the principal piece on the chessboard. But now, after very long and careful thought, I have become certain that she is not the only one.'

'So is Artus d'Authon the second queen?'

'I don't know exactly what he is. However, even if he's just a protective rook, he could block our advance towards other pieces. You see, my dear friend, none of Madame d'Authon's actions is … well, innocent, contrary to what she believes.'

'Innocent?'

'All these actions are dictated to her by a plan that's totally beyond her and which she doesn't even suspect exists.'

'Do you think she chose Artus d'Authon not just for love but because he was, in some way, destined for her? This future infant whose conception – and especially birth – you're trying to avoid, is she meant to be born from him?'

He responded to her perceptiveness with a slight shake of the head.

'This is a suspicion that crosses my mind more and more. Let's be clear: Artus d'Authon does not exist without Agnès de Souarcy, at least in as far as our thousand-year-old struggle is concerned. On the other hand, I'm afraid he might be more than just a dispensable parent. I don't know … perhaps the essential procreator without whom his wife could not conceive the child who will perpetuate the lineage, as well as her protector …'

The camerlingo caught the drop of sweat that ran down his forehead to his eyebrow with a corner of his handkerchief. He let out a deep sigh.

'Aude, I can feel it. Time is speeding up and running out for us every day. They must all disappear. Madame d'Authon, since it is written that "the lineage comes through the women" and that evidence points to her being one of them. Young Clément, whose exact role I don't quite understand, and who vanished at the same time as the manuscripts. My spies inform me that Clair Gresson is desperately looking for him, as is the Comtesse d'Authon. Why? What could be the importance of a little farm boy, unless he's in possession of the Vallombroso treatise? Authon, since I don't yet know his exact role in relation to his wife. I will not surprise you, my dear, you who know me like a second self. I deeply regret that I am unable to find another solution except their deaths. I have no other means to ensure that this insane, this disastrous hope of a Second Coming[132] does not spread.'

Honorius Benedetti leant against the richly carved back of his chair, closed his eyes and murmured softly, '"And ye shall see the

Son of Man sitting on the right hand of power, and coming in the clouds of heaven."'

'It's Saint Mark's Gospel, isn't it?'

'That's correct. It echoes the Book of Daniel: "His dominion is an everlasting dominion, which shall not pass away, and his kingdom that shall not be destroyed." There are similar allusions in Matthew: "When the Son of man shall come in his glory, and all the holy angels with him, then shall he sit upon the throne of his glory". Luke describes the Second Coming in more detail: "And there shall be signs in sun and moon and stars … But when these things begin to come to pass, look up, and lift up your heads; because your redemption draweth nigh."'

'The Second Coming … Christ will be born again to deliver us once more. There will be no third, so the Holy Book says.'

'Which is why I will fight until the day I die to prevent this one from happening.'

'And oppose the will of God?'

Honorius buried his face in his hands and replied, 'By serving Him till I am damned, if that's what it takes. By protecting His creatures against themselves. By defending with my last breath the order we have established for centuries in order to restrain man's worst instincts, without which humanity would return to the chaos from which we pulled it.'

Madame de Neyrat's cheerfulness had drained away. In turn, she whispered, 'If Christ is born again—'

'What?' the camerlingo burst out, slamming his hands on his desk. 'Will man become miraculously better? It will always be as it always has been. A handful of visionaries and pure people will follow Him. The rest will try to destroy Him because He threatens their vile but profitable arrangements, and they will succeed.'

Silence fell on the room. Madame de Neyrat felt the prelate's infinite sadness. Honorius was struggling against his most absolute, his only love: God.

'So you condemn us to this imperfect world?'

'I have no alternative. I sometimes tell myself ...' He suppressed an ironic laugh. 'You will no doubt think me sentimental, my dear ... Sometimes, I feel an insane hope. That if I succeed in preventing the foretold Second Coming, if it is delayed ... Then perhaps it will occur once man has grown up, once he has repressed his ferocity, his greed, his cowardice and his stupidity and only kept his light.'

Aude smiled sadly. She sighed. 'Honorius ... My dear Honorius ... Do you believe it's possible for human beings to change so radically and so splendidly?'

His eyes filling with tears, he looked at her and said, appalled, 'No more than you do, my dear, but sometimes I need to lie to myself so that I can breathe more easily.'

Monge de Brineux bit his lip and slowly shook his head. Avoiding Comte Artus's eyes, he murmured in an upset tone, 'It's a trap, Monseigneur. The information I have gleaned confirms it.'

Artus grew irritated. 'Come now, Brineux, why would the King set me a trap? What could he possibly stand to gain by it?'

'I don't know,' the head bailiff confessed. 'On the other hand, what I do know from a reliable source is that the Bishop of Alençon has hastily appointed an inquisitor from Évreux to conduct the trial. Why Évreux, except for the fact that Louis,[133] the count of the town, takes on almost all his half-brother Philip the Fair's delicate diplomatic tasks, the Rome missions in particular?'

'So you believe I'm a bargaining counter between the King and the Vatican?'

'I'm convinced of it, and that explains the almost offensive authority of the missive you received in the first place.'

'I should feel flattered by the importance I've suddenly assumed in everybody's eyes,' Comte Artus joked darkly. He sighed and abruptly declared, 'What do you truly think, Brineux? I always know when you're trying to keep bad news from me. Your face grows as long as a day without bread and your eyes keep avoiding mine.'

'I … I could be wrong, of course … An idea has come into my head, which I hate. What if … What if they were trying to take you away from the Comtesse?'

'For what reason?' asked Artus.

Yet Monge de Brineux was certain that he was not surprised.

'She becomes easier prey without your protection. The recent attack on her by the Inquisition, the killers who would have

437

murdered her in the forest, had it not been for her strength and courage, but also the intervention of that Knight Hospitaller, too providential an intervention to be totally innocent ... Everything leads me to believe that she is vitally important to some powerful and determined people. Would their determination and their goal – even though they remain a mystery to me – suddenly have dissipated the moment you were married? I doubt it.'

'I agree with you, Brineux. You've therefore reached the same conclusion as I.'

'In other words ...' Monge de Brineux made his voice firmer in order to conceal his alarm. 'I fear that this trial is more worrying than a harmless desire for clarification on the part of Rome.'

Artus reflected before answering. 'And it's for this excellent reason that Messire Joseph has turned me into an attentive pupil this past week.'

'I beg your pardon?'

'I'm learning and analysing the *Consultations for Inquisitors* devised by the late Clément IV, a short treatise on Inquisition practices. We owe it to an anonymous inquisitor. It's edifying reading. It makes you wonder how even a single accused person has ever been able to escape their clutches!'

Monge de Brineux's face expressed relief. 'Oh, Monseigneur, I'm such a fool! There was I worrying about you, thinking you'd be throwing yourself into the lion's den without prior preparation. Such a fool!'

'Not at all,' Artus d'Authon replied in a softer voice. 'You're a good friend and I'm sorry for my own foolishness. You see, it's taken me these hours of danger to finally realise it.'

This declaration, unexpected from a man who was usually inscrutable, distant without disdain, made Brineaux's cheeks flush, and he simply murmured, 'It's my honour and my joy, Monseigneur.'

'Going back to this trial they're trying to pass off as a simple discussion, I cannot avoid it. But even if I could, I would appear before it. To dodge it would give them easy ammunition. The trial by ordeal that saved my darling wife would go from simply being questioned to being suspect and possibly even fraudulent and then void. Who says they wouldn't then try a nasty trick, which is their style, and demand a retrial, this time weighted by the murder of an inquisitor and an unpardonable sacrilege. I want to avoid that at all costs.' Artus d'Authon paused briefly before speaking again in such a flat tone that it worried the chief bailiff. 'Brineux, now that you are reassured with regard to my pugnacity, I have … This is not an order but a favour I ask you as a friend. In case events do not follow the course I am hoping for, I beg you to take the Comtesse d'Authon and little Philippe to my cousin Jacques de Cagliari, in Sardinia, as soon as possible. Despite his rather rustic manners, he has a noble heart and true courage. He is wise enough not to meddle in worldly affairs. Nobody could reach them there. I warned him as soon as I received the royal missive.'

'You'd anticipated everything, then?'

'Even the worst, God help us. My dear friend, kings have in common with popes a wonderful justification which exonerates them from feeling guilty for their shortcomings and their deceptions: it's called reason of State. Only a fool would underestimate it.'

'Does the Comtesse know that you're going to Alençon at dawn tomorrow?'

'No, and I insist you keep to the story I told her about having to travel on business. If … two or three days turn out not to be sufficient to enlighten my judges, you will come back here to comfort her and reassure her that I will be back home soon. If they arrest me, we'll know what to expect. At that point you'd have to inform the Comtesse and not leave out any detail of our conversation, then travel to Sardinia as soon as possible.'

'It will be done as you order … and in friendship, Monseigneur.'

'Thank you, Brineux … from the bottom of my heart.'

Agnès got up from her prie-dieu. Although the afternoon was warm, she was shivering. She pushed open the door of the little chapel adjoining her room and went to the white trunk at the foot of her bed. She collapsed onto it, annoyed with herself. This languor she could not seem to fight off exasperated her. The remedies prepared for her by Messire Joseph seemed powerless against the exhaustion that had been affecting her for days. In vain, she admonished herself. She had lost the desire to do anything, to go out, ride, or stroll in the park around the pond. She looked around. Where had her beautiful collection of *Lays* by Marie de France gone? A soft knock on her door made her jump. Guillette appeared, carefully holding a fine Beauvais[134] pottery goblet.

'Your eggnog, Madame. There's nothing better to perk you up, and it's pleasant on the palate.'

'You're very kind. Put it beside me.'

Obeying, the young woman asked in a worried tone, 'How are you feeling today?'

'Better,' Agnès lied.

'I'm not surprised. Messire Joseph is known to be one of the best physicians in the realm.'

'I'm sure he lives up to his reputation. Guillette, I'm looking for my collection of lays, and I cannot find it. Have you seen it?'

'No, Madame. I saw you holding it as you were going to the library. Perhaps you left it there?'

'It's precious to me. Please find it. Oh, and bring me a carafe of water. I'm thirsty, even though it's not a hot day.'

The servant girl curtseyed and left with a smile, saying, 'I shan't fail. I'm quickly going to find that little rascal of a book that's playing tricks on you.'

Agnès's gaze swept over the tables, large and small, dotted around the room. The irritation she felt towards herself increased. What a goose she was to misplace this book she cared about so much. She took small sips of the eggnog, sweetened to her taste and with a hint of cinnamon and ginger, thinking and trying to remember her comings and goings the evening before and that morning. She still had the book the night before because she had read one of the lays while in bed. Then she had fallen asleep. Had it slipped between the bed and the wall? She got up and, leaning on her hands, examined the space between the wall and the side of her bed. No luck. She knelt and lifted the counterpane to check underneath but found nothing that resembled her elegant book. She was about to get up when a strange object attracted her attention. She tried to grab it but had to lie down on the floor and slide under the bed in order to reach it. She tore off some sort of soft ball nailed to the floor and crawled out. Sitting on the floor, she examined the little black canvas bag. She untied the string that kept it closed and emptied the contents into the palm of her hand. What was it? What was this small burnt, foul-smelling cluster and these black down feathers? She suddenly fell prey to panic and her forehead grew cold with sweat. Magic. Witchcraft. Her tiredness and dizzy spells. Someone was trying to kill her by means of a spell. She hurled herself out of her antechamber and without thinking rushed to Messire Joseph's study. She ran to the old man, who was absorbed in his reading. He looked up from the lectern and remained with his mouth half open, noticing the Comtesse's devastated face. She opened her hand without a word.

'Madame …'

'This is what I've just found nailed under my bed,' she announced in a voice so detached that she did not recognise it. 'Not a word to my husband. Not yet.'

He prodded the feathers with the tip of his index finger, leant over to smell the black cluster and tipped the small mound into his own palm.

'Charred organic matter. Probably guts. Often the case. A perfect example of witchcraft, there's no doubt about it.'

'That explains my strange tiredness, my lack of appetite … I am the victim of a spell.'

'Because you believe in the power of sorcerers, do you?'

His question was answered by Agnès's deathly pallor. The old scientist went on in a reassuring tone, 'Madame, I'm an old man, I've seen many things, and have always measured them by the yardstick of science. I can promise you that the power of sorcerers lies in belief, in the terror they inspire in their clients or their victims, as the case may be.'

'So all I have to do is deny their power and I'll be rid of this growing illness?'

'Maybe not. However, don't forget, I'm at your side.'

She left him with a smile that had no joy in it.

His teeth clenched, Joseph remained for a long time with his palm open, examining the black residue. Several theories went through his mind. Only one made sense. It was so incredible, so serious that he decided to wait a little longer. An error on his part could turn out to be fatal for the Comtesse.

A rtus d'Authon and Monge de Brineux had led their mounts at lightning speed since dawn in order to reach Alençon before nones. On the way, they had dismounted for a few minutes to rest and water their horses, and taken advantage of the stop to have a goblet of wine or cider to clear the dust of the roads, which irritated their throats. Tired by the gallop and sensing his master's nervousness from the pressure of his shins, Ogier, the Comte's black stallion, had become short-tempered. When they reached the Auberge de la Taure-Attelée, where they were planning to spend the night, and Artus put his foot on the ground, the stallion snorted with exasperation.

'Gently, my beauty,' the Comte reassured him, stroking his neck. 'We've finally arrived and you're going to enjoy a well-earned rest. There, there ... calm down.'

The innkeeper, Maître Taure, who was as wide as he was tall, rushed towards them, bending forward as a sign of respect – as much as the fat around his belly allowed – bursting with pride. It was not every day that you welcomed two such prestigious guests. Maîtresse Taure had been right to persuade him to spend a few deniers to improve the interior of his establishment. Although not luxurious, the rooms were now fancy enough to welcome quality guests. Maîtresse Taure, who helped him serve in the large communal hall, showed distinction, he had to admit it. She now enjoyed rubbing shoulders with notaries or physicians who had replaced their usual old brawling clientele of pork butchers. Moreover, she now addressed her customers only in choice and even gallant language, although she sometimes mixed up the meaning of words she overheard from conversations with a haberdasher or an alderman. At first,

Maître Taure had expressed a few doubts about his wife's plan to 'raise their station', as she called it. Of course, the opinion of their neighbours was important, but not as important as the hard cash he counted in the evening, after closing time. Pork butchers are energetic people with childish pleasures. They are happy to celebrate together after a profitable transaction, and sometimes clink glasses more than they should. In other words, the drinks follow one another to the delight of the innkeeper. Maîtresse Taure had argued subtly that, in truth, pork butchers emptied bottles enthusiastically but since their shops, their kitchens and their inventories were bursting with food, they had no need to go and eat outside their homes. The new customers, however, because of their more delicate occupations would eat out and also sometimes needed a place where they could conduct their negotiations in private. And that was what Maîtresse Taure was proposing to give them. And she was eventually proved right.

'Messeigneurs, Messeigneurs ... Your rooms are ready. You'll find a basin with perfumed water there so you can freshen up after your journey. Afterwards, you can have something to eat, if you like. Your messenger said you're planning on staying two or three nights and our establishment is honoured to welcome you.'

'I might even stay longer,' the Comte d'Authon said. 'But my chief bailiff will leave the day after tomorrow at the latest. Make sure his horse is ready, innkeeper. Meanwhile, get the errand boy to take our horses to the stable and treat them gently and carefully. They're exhausted and difficult.'

'Yes, Monsieur!' the innkeeper obeyed, bowing even lower before straightening up and shouting, 'Hey! Lazy ragamuffin! Where are you hiding now?'

A little boy of about ten, skinny like a grasshopper, with dark rings around his eyes, appeared. Maître Taure launched into the outraged tirade he used in front of his clients.

'You were sleeping, as usual! Shame on you! He devours

enough food for four, eats you out of house and home and then lazes about like a lizard in the sun. Pick up your feet, you slowcoach … Do I have to box your ears before you deign to take care of these gentlemen's mounts?'

Maître Taure was a little disappointed by the unruffled face of the more prestigious of the two customers. Usually, a complicit smile would greet his outburst, repeated a thousand times, and sometimes they would reply, 'He needs the stick' or else, 'Give him stale bread and water to build his character' but, instead, Artus's attention was focused on the little boy as he approached Ogier. The Comte was ready to intervene if his moody stallion became threatening. Few people could go near the animal without fearing a hostile reaction. Agnès was one of them. She had mounted him without the slightest apprehension. But Agnès was different. The thought of his wife brought about a familiar miracle: it made him calmer.

The boy imperceptibly drew his hand close to the black stallion's mouth and touched his downy nostrils, white with froth and effort. Ogier blew without being aggressive. Instead, he stretched his neck towards the child, who stroked his forehead. The little boy grabbed the reins and walked towards the stables, followed by the horse walking in step with him without protesting.

'Boy …' Artus d'Authon stopped him and pulled out a silver denier coin from the pocket of his thick grey silk jacket. 'This is for you, from my brave four-legged companion who can be very awkward.' He turned to the innkeeper and, staring at him, repeated, 'I said it's *for you*. I would be most offended if I weren't heard correctly.'

'Such generosity!' Maître Taure exclaimed, still tempted to recover the silver coin as soon as the Comte's back was turned. 'Yet he doesn't deserve it.'

'That's not what I think,' Artus d'Authon replied in a tone that brooked no objection.

Monge de Brineux hardly uttered a word during the entire meal in the large tavern hall that had been freshly whitewashed in order to cover up the tongues of black soot left by the torches. He had also barely touched the chunks of chicken stew with broad bean purée they had been served. However, he had swallowed four goblets of wine in quick succession, which was unusual for a man who was generally sober. Speaking in veiled terms to prevent the innkeeper's wife overhearing as she fussed around them, asking with much bowing if they were satisfied, Artus d'Authon once again tried to reassure his chief bailiff about the confrontation that awaited him.

When dessert, a thick pancake with apples and raisins, was placed before them, Artus said, in an irritated tone, 'By Jove, Brineux! I've been trying to mollycoddle you like a babe for the past hour, to put your mind at rest like an old woman, when it is I who am the victim of the trap you never cease to mention.'

'I know,' the chief bailiff agreed, 'and I hate myself for adding to your worries. It's just that I so resent my own powerlessness ... Damn! I would far rather have to fight some nasty rogues!'

'These are mostly nasty rogues dressed in the robes of justice and power. However, even a good swordsman like yourself can do nothing against their breed.'

'Monseigneur, are you quite sure I can't come with you? Having had the privilege of serving you for many years, and the honour of keeping company with you, I could enlighten the judges with my testimony.'

'It's out of the question, Brineux. They'll reject anything you say precisely because you serve me. Also, I worry they might take a keen interest in you. If the worst should happen, you're the only one I respect enough to entrust the future of my wife and son to.'

Eyes lowered, Monge de Brineux nodded his head, deeply

moved. Artus d'Authon stood up and dusted off his rich brocade doublet with the back of his hand.

'I hope to see you again soon, my friend. Pray for me.'

Brineux merely nodded his head again, fearing that his voice would break and betray the emotion that made the words stick in his throat.

Artus d'Authon went through the forbidding doors which at night barricaded the surrounding wall of the Inquisition headquarters. He crossed the square courtyard of uneven cobbles with an assured step and climbed the stairs leading to a heavy door reinforced with crossbars.

A guard came towards him as he walked into the entrance hall, which was dark in spite of the flickering light that emanated from the torches on the walls. He gave his name and titles, and stated that he was expected by the Grand Inquisitor of Évreux. The guard bowed and grumbled, 'I'll go and fetch the secretary. Sit down if you feel like it,' he added, indicating the black wooden table flanked by benches, the only furniture in the large, low hall next to the entrance.

Artus approached the table but did not sit down. He waited, his mind a blank. Over the previous few days, he had forced himself to erase the very shadow of fear, knowing perfectly well that it constituted the most deadly weapon of the Inquisition.

He felt more relaxed, with a strange sense of relief, when the secretary appeared. It was Agnan, whom he had invited for dinner in the hope of obtaining information about the role played by Francesco de Leone in Florin's murder. He took a couple of steps towards the young man. His charmless ugliness – eyes close together, long, pointy nose, and weak chin – inspired mistrust as soon as you saw him. Yet Artus knew that a brave soul was concealed under the hideous mask. Strangely, as he drew near,

Agnan showed no warmth but declared with indifference:

'Monseigneur d'Authon, your judges are consulting as we speak. I don't know if they have finished the preliminaries. Please follow me. The wait will be shorter in the room adjoining the interrogation hall.'

Artus obeyed, slightly disconcerted by the young man's attitude.

They crossed a large room and turned right before going up a dark wooden staircase. Agnan walked ahead in silence. When they had reached the landing, instead of leading him into the small waiting room, he put his finger to his lips to signify silence and indicated the narrow corridor to the left, which led to a low door, that of his office. Agnan leant against the door as soon as he had bolted it. Out of breath, he murmured:

'I was afraid you might ask me downstairs about my rather disconcerting attitude. They mustn't know that we have met, except for that one time when you visited this place to try and reason with Nicolas Florin. Otherwise, they would force me to testify after swearing an oath on the four Gospels, then twist my story to serve their purposes.'

Agnan went to his little work table whose cheap wood could barely be seen beneath scrolls and registers.

'To serve Madame d'Authon, I have secretly copied the main part of the two testimonies against you. Read them to prepare yourself. The most incriminating is the one by the little street urchin. They will not summon the witnesses for the prosecution so that you will not be able to contradict them. It's usual procedure.'

Artus glanced through the copies. The stories were skilful lies, twisted to the point where you could see the agency of a clerk, and they would be easily interpreted against him.

'The interrogation – because that's what it is – that you will undergo is cloaked in unusual secrecy, which means that I know nothing about it. I was only able to glimpse the jewellery worn by that monster Florin, which has been recovered from the cesspit of the house he extorted from one of his victims. Also, there's a rumour that they're in possession of another piece of evidence against you, a decisive piece of evidence, but I don't know what it is.'

'How could they have obtained evidence, since I've never crossed the threshold of Florin's house?'

'I know. The Knight of Grace and Justice Leone has told me clearly about his own role. He rid us of the monster in order to save your wife, may God always watch over her. I cannot possibly denounce him. I beg you, do not think it's because I fear their punishment if they discover that I've concealed what the knight confessed to me one evening. I'm only afraid for Madame d'Authon. They could retry her if they could prove that the trial by ordeal was not in her favour. And I would rather die than see her suffer again. Moreover, even if I have lied by omission, my conscience is perfectly clear. Madame had to live – of that I am certain – and I have the powerful conviction that God did intervene by sending the Hospitaller to her aid.'

'You have expressed my worry in a nutshell. That is why I will not even mention Leone's name. It would be an indignity of the worst kind to denounce him and set the dogs on him. Agnès could suffer terribly as a result.'

'We must make haste. If they finished their consultations and found you here ... Monsieur ... Horrified as I am to give you this advice, I beg you – lie. Lie even under oath. To serve God. After all, don't *they* twist the Gospels and use them in order to throw innocent people into their jails and their interrogation chambers?'

'Why do you place yourself in such grave peril to help me, Agnan?'

'It's for Madame de Souarcy, the Comtesse, who has shone a

449

light on my dogged, ant-like life. Because I sense that she is the most precious of women.' He lowered his eyes and his little stone-marten face wrinkled further, then he said in such a sad voice it was almost inaudible, 'Because, you see, I used to believe them, those in the interrogation chamber and those like them, with all my naivety, my faith and my stupidity. I believed in the purity of their intentions, and the justice of their verdicts. I believed that all they wanted was to save the souls of sinners, of those who had lost their way, until I could no longer lie to myself. Some inquisitors, like Florin, are no more than vile torturers straight from hell. Others are motivated by greed. They requisition the possessions of those accused and pay themselves handsomely. An acquittal would be disastrous for them. So there is no acquittal. As for the rest, they're a crowd who weep over the suffering of our Saviour but have nothing but contempt for that of God's defenceless creatures. Is twisting bodies and torturing them to madness or death the only way to save souls? I don't believe that and I feel disgust for myself for having once believed it.' A faint smile lit up Agnan's pointy face. He concluded, 'I'd end up rotting in the cellar cages if they heard me. I beg you, Monsieur, lie, defend yourself. For the Comtesse and for your son. Once, the knight Leone assured me that you could fight fairly only against fair enemies. The contrary would be insanity. And they are not fair. Now I'm going to take you to the waiting room. They'll be coming for you soon.'

S tanding with her back to one of her chamber windows, Agnès was staring at Messire Joseph. He thought she looked even paler than the day before, and the purple rings under her eyes intensified their beautiful blue-grey colour. Despite her bold poise, he felt the fear that had been gnawing at her since she had discovered the black canvas bag nailed under her bed.

'I'm an old man and I've seen so many astonishing things, Madame, and when you analyse them in a spirit of reason, none of them can be explained by the intervention of evil powers granted to humans. It's nothing but a collection of superstitions which spread like wildfire, aided by mysteries that science isn't yet able to comprehend. As for science, it, like everything else, is God, no matter what is said by those who muzzle it because they fear, quite rightly, that it will take away their power. One day, we'll discover what thunderstorms are, and what exactly eclipses are. One day, we'll be able to fight disease. One day, so many things that we are now unable to do will become possible thanks to the progress of science.'

'And yet there are horrible stories ... There are countless testimonies from people who've suffered because of the evil practices of sorcerers, that is, when they don't die because of them. The Church condemns these devil's henchmen to the stake ... And the Church cannot be that wrong.'

Joseph de Bologne studied her for a moment, biting back the words on the tip of his tongue. Sorcerers, whom everyone feared so much, did a considerable favour to the Church, which was then believed to be the only force capable of protecting its flock. Joseph did not doubt the Comtesse's intelligence or her kindness towards him. However, he belonged to another faith, and the persecution of the Jews was almost as bad as that of sorcerers and heretics. Thanks to the Comte's hospitality, he had ceased to fear for his life and his freedom. How long for, he knew not. It would just take a royal decree and the hounds would close in on their prey. He decided to compromise.

'Some of these charlatans are so convinced by their ... their "skills", if I may use that word, that they go to the stake without a whimper. Then their reputation spreads among the cottages and everyone adds to it, exaggerating the imaginary dark deeds of these sorcerers.'

'Don't you believe in miracles, then, Messire?' Agnès asked, upset by the old man's logic.

'Of course I do, Madame. But miracles come from God, even when He chooses a human instrument for them. God is almighty and when He punishes, the punishment He sends upon us carries His divine mark. Not that of men.'

'You make me—'

A sharp abdominal pain bent her double. She stopped herself from falling by clinging to the hanging which was pulled across the window at night.

'Madame!' Messire Joseph rushed to her, panicking. 'Please, I beg you, let me sit you in this armchair.'

Clinging to his arm, Agnès went with him, taking small steps. She closed her eyes, fighting back nausea. Messire Joseph gently wiped the sweat drenching her forehead. He waited patiently for her to recover, before asking softly, 'Madame, can you describe exactly the pain you just felt?'

'It was so sharp, so sudden ...' Agnès said in a faltering voice.

'Where did it start exactly?'

'Right here, in my navel.' Agnès pointed to a specific spot.

'And does it then radiate towards your lower back and your thighs?'

'Most definitely,' she replied, staring at him.

'How have your stools[135] been recently, Madame?'

'To be honest, I've been constipated for some time.'

'How long has this been going on? Does it happen concomitantly with your tiredness, your queasiness and dizziness?'

'Now that I think about it, yes, it does. Or shortly afterwards.'

'Do you sometimes have a metallic taste in your mouth?'

'Are you a mind reader?' Agnès joked weakly.

'Sadly, only a physician,' Joseph smiled. Turning serious again, he declared, 'I'm going to have to disobey you and inform my master and his chief bailiff of your state, Madame.'

'I beg you …' the Comtesse said.

'It breaks my heart to displease you but I simply cannot obey this order. The situation is far too serious and your health is a constant concern of mine. I've no idea if some witch has cast a spell on you and, frankly, that doesn't worry me. A few hen feathers, even black ones, have never killed anyone. On the other hand, what I do know is that you're being slowly poisoned and I've even discovered the poison, although I still don't know how it's being administered to you.'

'That's impossible!' Agnès protested, her panic growing. 'Why?'

'The chief bailiff will take it upon himself to enlighten us on this point, Madame. Will you allow me to take my leave immediately?'

Unable to order her thoughts since the old physician's terrible diagnosis, Agnès nodded. Poisoning. A crime so heinous and devious that it was immediately punished by death without absolution and the poisoners were buried in unconsecrated ground.

When the physician had gone, she remained there, her fear gradually mingling with painful incomprehension. Who could hate her to the point of wishing her to die in this terrible way? What had she done to deserve such implacable hatred? The astounding stupidity of her unanswered questions finally struck her. Nothing. She had done nothing to trigger such abhorrence. It was the parchment, one of humanity's most precious, that was at the root of this poisoning. The different blood. Her blood, which she had passed on to Clémence and who, in turn, would pass it on to her daughter. However, the man who had ordered this, no doubt Camerlingo Benedetti, did not know that the young farm boy who had fled from Souarcy was none other than Agnès's youngest daughter. In his eyes, only the latter possessed that blood and no daughter of hers was to inherit it. Therefore, she had to die before conceiving again. Strangely, knowing this reassured her. Nobody knew that Clémence was a girl. Therefore, for the time being, the adolescent was safe.

Clémence, my Clémence. How I need you by my side. Your absence is torturing me. Every moment, every gesture takes me back to you. I look at little Philippe whom I love so much that my heart bursts whenever I hold him tight. He does not look like you. My son. And yet, my Clémence, it's in you that my blood throbs. I listen to its pulsations which bind me to you more strongly than a pact. I can feel you. I can sense you. You are nearby, I am certain. You are my flesh, my soul. I've been only half alive since you vanished from my life. Clémence, I've given you life and you've saved mine by allowing me to resist, to fight against the monsters who want to destroy us. Live, my Clémence. Live for me.

Aghast, Messire Joseph listened to Ronan's story. Accompanied only by the chief bailiff, Monseigneur d'Authon had left the chateau at dawn to go to the Inquisition headquarters in Alençon and Madame la Comtesse was not to know about it for the time being.

'This is a disaster! I'm merely a man of science. And an old man at that. How can I fight alone?'

Suddenly worried, Ronan asked, 'Fight against whom, Messire?'

'My good Ronan, I hesitate to confide in you. However, since our master is fond of you, I can share my extreme alarm. Our lady is being poisoned. That's certain.'

The old servant opened his mouth, unable to utter a word, his face suddenly drained of all colour.

'I beg your pardon? Poisoned? A lady who's an angel sent to make all our lives sweeter? God Almighty! What are we going to do?'

'That's what I've been trying to work out ever since I finally realised what was happening. Ronan, you're the only one I can trust. From now on, you will prepare the Comtesse's meals yourself, and every dish placed before her. All of them, do you hear? If anyone asks you anything, tell them it's the physician's orders.'

'What's happening?' the old servant lamented.

'It will become clear before long, I swear before God. We're going to fight inch by inch, Ronan.'

'Can one counter the villainy of a poisoner, Messire?'

'Certainly, if our vigilance does not falter. Even water, Ronan. You'll have to draw even her water.'

Inquisition headquarters, Alençon, Perche, September 1306

A young scribe, his writing case and inkhorn slung over his shoulder, informed Artus d'Authon in an indifferent tone that he was being summoned by the jury. The Comte stood up without haste and followed him. The young man rushed to push open the tall door they had stopped outside, and they walked into a huge room, icy despite the warm afternoon.

Five stern-looking men were sitting around a long table: a notary and his clerk, as demanded by procedure, and two Dominican brothers, as well as the Grand Inquisitor of Évreux, who had taken a seat in the tall, richly carved chair at the head of the table. There were no 'laymen of excellent reputation'. Artus wondered if the inquisitor had dispensed with them in order to ensure the support and complacency of his brothers in the order.

'Kindly state your Christian names, family name and titles, please, Monsieur.'

'Artus Charles Placide, Comte d'Authon, Lord of Masle, Béthonvilliers, Luigny, Thiron, Bonnetable and Souarcy.'

The notary rose and recited, '*In nomine Domini, Amen.* In the year 1306, on the eighteenth day of the month of September, in the presence of the undersigned Gauthier Richer, notary at Alençon, accompanied by one of his clerks and witnesses named Brother Robert and Brother Foulque, Dominicans, both from the diocese of Alençon, né respectively Ancelin and Chandars, Artus Charles Placide, Comte d'Authon, Lord of Masle, Béthonvilliers, Luigny, Thiron, Bonnetable and Souarcy appears voluntarily and in person before the venerable Brother Jacques du Pilais, Dominican, Doctor in Theology and Grand Inquisitor for the territory of Évreux, appointed to judge this matter in our good city of Alençon.'

The notary sat down again. It was the same one who had taken part in the travesty of justice intended to send his wife to the stake. Artus dismissed the bad omen. Nonsense. Alençon probably did not have that many notaries, so there was nothing to be read into this coincidence.

His eyes riveted on the dark flagstones, Jacques du Pilais approached the Comte d'Authon, holding a large black-bound book against his chest. He was a tall man and so slim that he appeared skinny under his dark, heavy habit. He raised his head and fixed his very pale blue eyes on Artus's. He spoke in a gentle, almost singsong voice.

'Monsieur d'Authon, before we get to the heart of our questions, because that's all they are, allow me to remark that your coming here voluntarily is a reflection of your untarnished reputation.' After a contented smile, the inquisitor continued. 'Artus, Comte d'Authon, here are the four Gospels. Place your right hand upon them and swear to tell the whole truth, about yourself as well as others. Do you swear on God and on your soul?'

'I swear. May God help me if I keep my oath, and condemn me if I commit perjury.'

'Very well. Notary, take note of the Comte d'Authon's oath.'

Jacques du Pilais tightened his white cape around him, as though to protect himself from the cold. Artus noticed the long, skinny, claw-like hands clutching the cloth. The inquisitor went back to the sturdy table and turned to Artus.

'In the year of Our Lord 1304, on the fifth day of November, a lady called Agnès Philippine Claire de Larnay, Dame de Souarcy, appeared in this very place before the Grand Inquisitor Nicolas Florin. The suspicions regarding her were extremely serious: complicity in heresy, or even heresy itself, aggravated by devil worship. My brothers Robert and Foulque have perused the trial records of our brother Nicolas with me. Perhaps you're aware that inquisitors are obliged to keep them with the utmost precision …'

Since Messire Joseph had guided him step by step through the labyrinth of Inquisition procedure, Artus knew that. The records were not used for checking an inquisitor's fairness. Their sole purpose was to prevent the slightest detail from escaping the judges' attention. This way, they could hope to find another reason to retry an acquitted person.

'… They contain all the stages of the trial of the lady who was soon afterwards to become your second wife, her daughter's perjury which was uncovered thanks to the vigilance of our Dominican brothers and, of course, the start of torture … The procedure was scrupulously adhered to by Nicolas Florin. A few days later, our unfortunate brother was stabbed to death by an unknown person. A hastily carried-out investigation concluded that it was an encounter with a drunkard picked up in some sordid establishment. Since Florin's death occurred the day after torture began, nobody had any doubt that in Madame de Souarcy God had judged and protected the innocent.' The inquisitor paused and stared at Artus. 'Are we in agreement so far?'

'Yes, we are. Except that, at his death, all Nicolas Florin's vices emerged. Among these were his cruelty, sins of the flesh, perversity, a taste for luxury, let alone the extortion of money and possessions that he was guilty of. I don't need to mention the damning rumours of witchcraft that circulated about him. Moreover, in his great wisdom and fairness, the bishop decided that he would be buried in unconsecrated ground.'

'We know all that,' Jacques du Pilais replied sadly. 'However, we are not gathered here today to judge a deceased man. That would be usurping the ineffable prerogative of God. Rather, we have the formidable task of working out the meaning of His judgement. Was the glory of the Almighty foully used in order to acquit Madame de Souarcy? Was blasphemy pushed to the point of murdering the Grand Inquisitor?'

'How can I help you resolve this thorny question? I only met Grand Inquisitor Florin once, in this very place, when I came to plead Madame de Souarcy's cause. He quickly dismissed me, and we never saw each other again.'

'In truth? Must I remind you that you are under oath?'

'I swear on the four Gospels that I never saw Florin again.'

A slow voice, that of Foulque de Chandars, was heard. He read out the testimony Artus had perused in Agnan's office a few minutes earlier.

> *I swear before God that I am not acting under any constraint and am not motivated by any hatred or desire for revenge. Shortly before the murder of Grand Inquisitor Florin, Seigneur d'Authon offered me a pretty clutch of silver deniers if I followed the aforementioned Florin, whom he would point out to me when he came out of the Inquisition headquarters. In order to get the second half of the sum, I was supposed to go to Monsieur d'Authon at the Auberge de la Jument-Rouge and let him know the personal address of the Grand Inquisitor. And that's what I did.*

'That's a lie,' Artus d'Authon declared flatly. 'I never saw the rascal again. I did wait for him at the inn, but in vain.'

'That's not what Maître Rouge, the owner of the establishment, declares,' the inquisitor replied. 'Notary, please read out the declaration under oath of the witness.'

> *I swear before God that I am not acting under any constraint and am not motivated by any hatred or desire*

for revenge. On the twelfth day of the month of November 1304, Seigneur d'Authon met a little street urchin in my inn. They were acquainted and had evidently already had dealings with each other. The rascal spoke to him in confidence, so that I was only able to hear the name of a street, Rue de l'Ange. Then Monsieur d'Authon gave the boy a coin, and the latter ran off.

'I never found out the Grand Inquisitor's address. As I've already said, the urchin let me down. As for Maître Rouge, his memory is astonishing. He remembers the exact day a customer came – although he sees dozens every day – and two years after the event. I'm envious,' the Comte said ironically.

'It's often the case with these innkeepers,' the inquisitor argued. 'That's how they inform provosts and bailiffs and it's in their interest to remember bad payers and troublemakers.' He turned to the two Dominicans and asked, 'Do these two testimonies seem questionable to you, brothers?'

Two heads were shaken in reply.

'Notary, please record that these testimonies have been judged to be true and acceptable both by me and by my Dominican advisers. What was the reason you wished to know the address of the Grand Inquisitor conducting your future wife's trial, Monseigneur d'Authon?'

Artus remembered the advice given to him by his bailiff, Agnan and Messire Joseph. There was no shame in lying to judges who fabricated evidence. 'I've heard about Florin's peculiar understanding of his mission and duty.'

'No slander regarding the deceased will be allowed in this court, Messire d'Authon,' the Grand Inquisitor interrupted.

'It's not slander or even a rumour. You know as well as I that Florin would get paid for some trials by impatient heirs or enemies bent on vengeance. I have no doubt that a thorough episcopal investigation into his … his arrangements must have taken place after his death.'

The pale-blue eyes bored into him as Jacques du Pilais replied, 'We're not gathered here to judge the actions of our late brother but to check the validity of the trial by ordeal that was invoked in order to exonerate your wife from all suspicion. So why did you wish to know the Grand Inquisitor's address?'

'In order to bribe him, which, I insist, was his common practice.'

'For shame, Messire! Bribe an inquisitor?'

'The shame is his, Monsieur,' Artus d'Authon counterattacked in a commanding voice. 'You can only bribe those who wish to be corrupted by money. Unfortunately, as I have explained, the little rascal who was supposed to supply me with information double-crossed me. And I deplore this fact. After all, if he had accepted my money, Florin would perhaps still be alive.'

'Take care, Monsieur!' Pilais exclaimed, sickened.

'I am taking care, but nobody will make me pretend that Florin's death was a sad event.'

Jacques du Pilais wondered how to proceed. He was used to panicking defendants, whether they were innocent or guilty. Of course, he had expected Seigneur d'Authon to put up more of a fight and to show impertinence. However, he was facing a wall of calm stubbornness which he did not know how to attack.

'Scribe, produce the items found in the cesspit of the house in Rue de l'Ange.'

The young man sprang up, picked up the small bundle in front of him, and rushed to the inquisitor, who commanded, 'Show them to the judges, the notary, and finally to Monseigneur d'Authon.'

The Dominicans pretended to be absorbed in the silent contemplation of the jewels which they had no doubt examined earlier. With his bony index finger, the notary turned over the heavy rings wrapped in cloth. Artus d'Authon gave them a quick glance. There was a huge, rectangular topaz in a gold claw setting, probably an index finger ring, next to a wide ring set with large pearls and sapphires. Then a narrower one, a serpent with ruby eyes, which Florin must have worn on his little finger.

'Do you recognise these rings, Messire d'Authon?' the inquisitor asked in his soft voice.

'No.'

'You can assure me that you have never seen them before?'

'I assure you on my honour.'

'Monseigneur d'Authon ... What do you make of this charade? A rascal, a drunkard allegedly encountered in a tavern, follows the Grand Inquisitor to his dwelling. They drink some more, as the two broken glasses found at the scene demonstrate. Perhaps there's a quarrel. In any case, the drunkard in question kills Nicolas Florin and snatches his rings ... which the investigators of the supreme pontiff, blessed he be, find in the cesspit two years later. Isn't that astounding?'

'Nothing men do surprises me. If you will allow me, I had no idea my opinion was required to explain the motives of a vile murderer.'

Jacques du Pilais was disconcerted by the Comte's offhand tone in which there was no arrogance.

'You're a gentleman of the finest reputation. Don't you think that abandoning the loot like that, an incomprehensible act for a scoundrel, is, however, easily explained if the murder wasn't motivated by drunkenness and theft but was committed in cold blood by a man of noble birth wishing to protect the woman who had so captured his heart that he married her? Stealing the rings would throw the investigators off the scent. Which is what happened. However, this man of noble birth would not have stooped so low as to keep them.'

'Your reasoning is skilful, I admit, my Lord Inquisitor. It only has one important flaw in it. Would this man of noble birth have been so foolish as to throw the incriminating rings into the cesspit of Florin's house – the only place where they could be found?'

Pilais was expecting this answer. 'It might have been the emotion of the moment, remorse at having killed one of God's creatures.'

'Didn't you just say that this man of noble birth had murdered Florin in cold blood? Let us put an end to all this cavilling, my Lord Inquisitor. I doubt I was the only gentleman not to be upset by Florin's death. I wager that others must have thanked heaven when they heard news of his demise. If this feeling of satisfaction is uncharitable, it does not for all that constitute a crime.'

Jacques du Pilais had conducted many interrogations, and tracked down many guilty people. He had uncovered the shrewdest deceptions, confused liars so charming that they would otherwise have been pardoned without hesitation. He had cornered some cunning felons disguised as gentle lambs, and sometimes delivered from the putrid jails of the Inquisition headquarters some clumsy innocents whose lack of wit would have led them straight to the stake. In other words, the human soul and its traps held few secrets for him. Absolute faith and an unwavering ardour kept him going through these trials. He was saving lost souls for the love of God.[136] In fact, his passion for God set him alight, devoured him so exquisitely that Jacques du Pilais would never have tarnished it with a flagrant injustice, a shameful or a lenient verdict. Of course, he had left Évreux convinced that Monseigneur d'Authon was guilty, influenced by the damning portrait painted by the bishop. However, he had been growing increasingly uncertain in the past few minutes.

He remembered for the umpteenth time since early that morning the short missive he had received from Rome a week earlier, which bore the papal seal and was signed by the hand of the camerlingo Honorius Benedetti.

It is of the most crucial importance that we be enlightened about the ineffable purity of the judgement by God that apparently manifested itself in the matter of Madame Agnès de Souarcy, now Comtesse d'Authon. It appears to us that the aforementioned judgement has been misrepresented, an unpardonable sacrilege. We demand from you the utmost severity and most complete vigilance towards the godless man who could have committed this defilement for personal gain.

In other words, he was to incriminate Artus d'Authon even if he was not convinced of his guilt any more, or at least, draw out his trial. Jacques du Pilais compressed his lips with displeasure. He could envisage only one solution. For the sake of the Sublime and Divine Lamb, he would not push an innocent onto the torture table. However, to content the bishop and the camerlingo, the procedure could drag on for months, possibly years. Sometimes a lifetime.

'Notary, please produce the item we have placed in your care so that it might be safe from any interference that could prejudice our investigation.'

Maître Gauthier Richer bounced up as though propelled by a spring and walked briskly and nervously over to the inquisitor. He pulled a purse out of his legal robes and emptied its contents into his hand, studied them for a long time and declared, 'We, Gauthier Richer, notary in Alençon, certify that this item is the one given to us by the Grand Inquisitor Jacques du Pilais so that we might protect it from any attempt to tamper with it.'

He tipped the contents from his hand into the inquisitor's hand, turned on his heel and went back to his seat with his peculiar, jerky walk.

Jacques du Pilais went right up to Artus d'Authon, opened his hand and asked, 'Messire, do you recognise this object?'

For a fleeting moment, Artus's mind was a blank. What was this thin ring of iridescent white stone, broken into three pieces? He felt a mixture of anger and sadness when he finally recognised it. It was the opal ring from his marriage to Mademoiselle Madeleine d'Omoy, a marriage of convenience, a business arrangement, which had sealed the bargain between him and his father. The gentle and transparent Madeleine's appetite for life had deserted her as soon as she had been forced to leave her parents and the family manor. He had but a faint memory of that frail, tragic little bird. She had given herself up to death with sad indifference, the same way she had welcomed the first cry of their son Gauzelin, who was also to die a few years later.

'It's my wedding ring from my first marriage to Mademoiselle d'Omoy.'

'You confirm that this jewel belongs to you.'

'Yes.'

Jacques du Pilais paused a while. Artus took it for a trick aimed at impressing the other two Dominicans. However, he was wrong. Pilais hated himself for taking part in this lamentable farce. Still, he could not go back. His only consolation was that Monsieur d'Authon could have had an inquisitor determined to please the camerlingo at any price, even the life of an innocent man.

'How do you explain this mystery, Monsieur d'Authon, since you say that you never knew Nicolas Florin's address, and never crossed his threshold?'

'It's the truth.'

'Really? Did this ring then find its way to him by magic?'

The sadness vanished, leaving just anger.

'What?' Artus almost shouted. 'Are you claiming you found my wedding ring at the Grand Inquisitor's house?'

'Calm down! I'm claiming nothing. I'm only using the evidence that has been supplied by investigators above suspicion.'

Artus lashed out. 'From one gentleman to another, I am telling you, Monsieur, this charade should make you blush!'

The snub was worse than a slap across the face. Jacques du Pilais blinked and swallowed. An aura of strange, unshakeable faith surrounded Authon. Pilais was now certain that the Comte's tall, slightly heavy build was deceptive. The politeness and impeccable manners concealed an ardent, passionate man. A man who would never compromise his honour or go back on his word. He recovered, thinking of how Artus d'Authon would never know the efforts he had made to save him from the worst.

'The ring was recently found shattered, the pieces stuck between the floorboards in front of the fireplace, in the precise spot where the Grand Inquisitor died.'

'Almost two years later, when the first investigators didn't see anything? Has the house been unoccupied since then?'

'Scribe, what do we know about the house being occupied?'

The young secretary consulted the notes piled up on his writing case.

'Er ... Three months after the death of our lamented Grand Inquisitor Florin it was sold to a salt merchant, Jean Chauvet, who's been living there with his family ever since.'

The Comte d'Authon lost his temper.

'So are we to believe that the mistress of the house and her servants didn't discover the opal fragments? She should punish them right away. Her home must be appallingly kept if nobody scrubs the dirt between the floorboards!'

'Do not play the fool with me, Messire d'Authon,' the inquisitor ventured, having run out of arguments.

'Play the fool? You mock me, Monsieur! What kind of carnival is this interrogation? My wife died shortly before my son. The bereavement, I mean that of my heir, nearly made me lose my mind. I will not pretend that I despaired when my wife died. With infinite respect to her, she and I were but strangers sharing the same house. This may shock your so-called investigators. I took the wedding ring off my third finger as soon as my wife died, and that was many years ago. There were too many hurtful memories, and I never wore it again.' Overcome with rage, Artus spat through clenched teeth, 'In other words, whoever stole the ring from me in order to please whoever it was, did not know me well. The henchman made a basic mistake, because all my entourage will testify to the fact that I've not worn it for ages.'

Jacques du Pilais defended himself half-heartedly.

'We appreciate your change of heart. However, you must admit that we need to check. The Inquisition is charitable and just. Our mission consists in making every possible effort to clear people and to understand them. If what you say turns out to be true, we will be overjoyed to consider you a soul belonging to Our Lord. However, since I must complete the investigation with the sole aim of exonerating you, you will have to accept our hospitality. Naturally, it bears no comparison to the comfort you're accustomed to. However, the *murus strictus* will not be applied in your case, and neither will the daily ration of water, three bowls of milk and root vegetables[137] and a quarter of starvation bread,[138] a penance generally inflicted on true suspects so that they might examine their souls.'

'How generous!' Artus d'Authon said with irony. 'However, to please you, I will content myself with milk soup and starvation bread. My wife endured it, and although I am not sure I possess her willpower, my stubbornness is certainly equal to hers.'

The inquisitor did not react to the remark. Instead, without showing the slightest irritation, he asked, 'Monsieur d'Authon, do I have your word that you will be allow yourself to be led away, or do I have to resort to fetters?'

'You have my word, Monsieur.'

'Notary, take note that the interrogation is over for today, and that it will resume as soon as possible.'

Without a glance and without acknowledging the other members of the jury, Artus d'Authon followed the Grand Inquisitor, flanked by his scribe, and was immediately joined by a stone-faced Agnan.

When they reached the hallway, Jacques du Pilais summoned one of the armed guards on duty. 'You, walk ahead of us.'

Taking one of the torches, which cast a feeble light, the man walked diagonally across the large hall. He opened one side of a low door which concealed a winding stone staircase that plunged into a dark cellar. The guard walked ahead to light their way. An acrid stench of mould hit them as they went deeper and deeper beneath the Inquisition headquarters. Soon, it mingled with the smells of excrement and sanies, as well as physical decay. Human decay.

The staircase led to an earthen floor, muddy from the nearby river Sarthe. Their heads down, they walked under arches that were too low for a man to stand upright, past the dungeons and the hapless, tortured creatures crammed within. A strange silence reigned over the place. A silence of terror, disturbed only by the scraping of chains against the walls, and an occasional groan.

Artus knew this silence. It was the silence of the most sinister dungeons, where everyone was wondering who they were coming to fetch for an interminable session of torture or an execution. He clenched his fists. Agnès, his friend, his lover, his wife, had been thrown into this cesspit, this vast dungeon, like an animal. Her flesh as well as her soul had been torn. Yet she bore no marks of it, as though a higher power had decided to spare her the scars left on its victims by human barbarism.

He suddenly felt calm again at the prospect of following the example of the splendid creature who had lit up his life ever since he had first seen her, wearing breeches and gathering honey from her beehives. He had to resist. For Agnès's sake and that of his son. Resist in order to keep his faith in justice.

Artus's boots made a sucking noise as he pulled them free of the swampy ground. They were probably approaching the river bed. The huge cellar stretched on and on in the flickering light of the torch carried by the guard. A stray question flashed through the Comte's mind: how many poor wretches were awaiting torment or death here? How many were hoping for the latter?

The inquisitor stopped and addressed Artus for the first time since they had begun their nauseating underground journey. 'We've arrived, Monseigneur d'Authon. You'll remain in this cell until we can provide the clarifications the Holy Father expects. Although it's austere and damp, it's reserved for witnesses. As such, you will receive a basin of fresh water every day for your ablutions, as well as a cess bucket.'

Artus d'Authon thanked him with a nod. He suddenly felt that this man was not an enemy intent on destroying him. Unless he was so crafty that he donned a mask of integrity in order to throw his adversary off guard.

Aude de Neyrat had been awake for an hour and was lounging in bed. Propped up by a large number of pillows and cushions covered in silk and lace, she was trying in vain to fight off the mood that had been affecting her for several days. It was about that pest, the tiresome young girl she had welcomed into her home.

Mathilde spent all her time changing her hairstyle or her outfit, taking hours to choose between a taffeta dress and a silk tunic trimmed with ermine, and almost fainted when she put over her close-fitting sleeves the thick wool *coudières*[139] embroidered with gold thread, the latest gift from her 'dear friend' Madame de Neyrat. She would then whirl around for the sole benefit of her benefactress, simpering, 'I beg you, Madame, tell me how I look.'

'Stunning,' Aude would invariably reply. 'You would take even the most discerning person's breath away.'

The Dame de Souarcy's condition was deteriorating every day, just as the witch had promised her. Aude did not need to use her daughter against her. There was just one consideration that prevented her from getting rid of her without delay. Almost a superstition. It was wiser to wait until the beautiful Comtesse d'Authon had departed this life. Amen.

Unwillingly, she got up and summoned a servant by pulling on the braided cord that hung near the head of the bed.

She would have to go and join her protégée, and once again endure the pretty young fool's comments.

They were sitting at a large, oval pedestal table pushed against a window, having their breakfast. Today, finery was not in the forefront of Mathilde's mind. According to her, these few weeks spent in the company of her protector and mentor had changed her substantially. She had gone from child to woman. And women take revenge.

'When do you wish me to start my mission against my mother, as you wanted, Madame?'

'I'm still waiting for information that will be of great help to you in your task of destruction, my dear,' the splendid creature lied. 'Don't forget that our skill, as foxes, is first and foremost to reconnoitre the area before we venture into it.'

Looking serious, Mathilde shook her head:

'And what about that vile scoundrel Eudes de Larnay? Have you thought of a way I can take glorious revenge on him, Madame?'

The little importance Mathilde now had in Aude de Neyrat's eyes had made her forget that commitment. Heavens! How would she extricate herself from this annoyance? She slowly sipped her lavender and sage tea with honey, taking time to think.

She replaced the elegant Beauvais pottery goblet adorned with silver circles, and began, with feigned uncertainty:

'I want nothing other than to help you. Your anger is justified and I share it, as well as your impatience. Having said that, my people have not been idle, they've been working for you. That nasty rascal Larnay still enjoys the support of people we have yet to tackle,' she said, making it up as she went along.

Mathilde was hanging on her every word to such an extent that she did not wonder who was supporting the indebted baron whose iron mines were exhausted, whose reputation had been sullied for a while, and whose enemies had found a second wind.

Madame de Neyrat could have perfectly well offered her help as an expert poisoner. However, she did not trust the young girl, who had given ample proof that she was capable of denouncing someone simply because she had a taste for comfort, or on a whim. A boorish idea suddenly crossed her mind. A coarse, indecent but cheerful idea. Looking thoughtful, she said, 'I have spent hours thinking about your justifiable desire for revenge, my dear. What we need, as you have so cleverly said, is a glorious and total revenge. However, you must not be tainted by it in any way. If that were to happen, your reputation would be tarnished, and that would break my heart.'

'You're so kind, my dear Madame, to take such good care of me,' said the goose gratefully, with tears in her eyes since she was the centre of her benefactress's attention.

'I have thought of several stratagems, some too risky for me to consider. Allow me to explain my thinking. I've asked myself what injurious damage, what unforgivable harm can a villain cause an adorable girl from a good family who's about to make her mark in society? In other words, what dreadful villainy could Eudes de Larnay have committed against you that would earn him an implacable punishment? Certainly not placing you behind the forbidding doors of a nunnery. If anything, it's an extra stain on your reputation. Especially since he could then trot out the ridiculous tale of your sensual excesses to his judges, and thus justify your retreat from the world ...'

Her mouth half open with admiration, surrounded by wafts of Madame de Neyrat's iris and rose fragrance, Mathilde marvelled at this beautiful woman's intelligence.

'Incest, my dear. Brutal incest which you bravely tried to resist. But what could you possibly do, you poor, frail virgin? After all, didn't you tell me about your uncle's passionate declarations in your apartments at Château de Larnay? The beast had little regard for the fact that the room had belonged to his recently deceased wife. In addition, there is against him his terrible reputation as a womaniser, which has no doubt reached the ears of Monge de Brineux. Neither our chief bailiff nor, for that matter, the Comte d'Authon, can be unaware of Larnay's unhealthy desire for your mother, whom he'd been pursuing since childhood.' Aude let out a tinkling little laugh. 'If, as I think, he's condemned, he'll be emasculated then quartered. That's for sure.'

Emasculation would have been more than enough to satisfy Mathilde. Still, she was not going to be fussy, especially as she could refuse to watch the punishment. However, a doubt crossed her mind. 'My uncle will demand an examination by a midwife, and I'm a virgin.'

This was becoming truly delicious for Aude, who pretended to take offence.

'I never doubted that! A young lady like yourself, deflowered? What a dreadful thought! My dear, we have two options to settle ... to settle this troublesome detail. Although I'd prefer the first option, it's not without risk. I can find us a midwife and pay her handsomely so that she discreetly rids us of your hymen. The danger, as you can guess, is that you can't trust these lowly people. She could always talk if paid cash or after a few drinks.'

'What's the second option,' Mathilde asked impatiently, not thrilled by the prospect of an intervention by a midwife.

'A man, what else? A man who could never recognise you. We can arrange that, if the solution appeals to you. Take your time and think about it calmly.'

A pleasant thrill ran up the young girl's body. Finally, she would find out what people whispered about in hushed tones.

'May I ask you an improper question, Madame?'

'Of course, my dear. I have no secrets from you.'

'When were you ... deflowered?' the young girl asked almost in a whisper.

The expression in the emerald eyes turned blank. If Mathilde had been interested in anyone but herself, she would have noticed the pretty heart-shaped mouth tighten. Still, Aude de Neyrat answered in a light tone:

'I was younger than you. The deflowerer, or rather the brutal rapist, was none other than my uncle. A dreadful memory. I would have preferred it a thousand times to have been a stranger who would have shown some gentleness. Still, what's past is past. In any case, you see how much we have in common.'

Despite her lack of intelligence, Mathilde was clever enough where her future was concerned. She grew worried.

'This hymen is so precious to girls that I fear its disappearance might then harm my marriage. What well-born heir would want a deflowered young girl, unless she were very wealthy, which I am not?'

'I admire your candour. It makes me feel younger. Hymens are like cats. They have more than one life. I myself have given up more than three. It's a simple female skill. I'll teach you. Men are so easy to dupe, especially when passion grabs them by the loins.'

Mathilde clapped her hands with relief and satisfaction.

'How can you be so many things at once? Kind, intelligent, learned and so beautiful.'

The adjective 'kind' amused Madame de Neyrat. Was Mathilde forgetting that they were plotting to have a man emasculated and quartered who, despite all his vices, was innocent of committing incest with his niece, a niece who would not have been remotely sad to have been bedded by her half-uncle. She would find her a rough lad the little virgin would remember for a long time. There were plenty who were used to performing that kind of task. Some society ladies, who were unhappily married and not bedded often enough, enjoyed a rustic thrust of the loins and did not baulk at paying a stranger for an intimate service outside the marriage bed, as long as they were guaranteed total discretion.

The man's face was drawn from tiredness and his clothes grey with road dust. He was leading an exhausted hired nag by the reins. When he entered the huge courtyard of the chateau, which gave onto the gently sloping gardens, Ronan knew that he was not just some poor traveller in need of hospitality and the offer of a glass of water and a crust of bread. Something about the approaching man's gait and bearing spoke of his rank.

The man greeted him with a nod. The dust had traced black lines around his sea-blue eyes.

'You're Ronan, aren't you?' the man enquired in a pleasant voice.

The old servant was only partly surprised that the visitor knew his name.

'I wish to see your master and seek his permission to speak to Madame d'Authon. Please announce Francesco Leone, knight of the order of Hospitallers.'

Ronan gave a deep bow. So this was the Hospitaller who had saved Madame. It was he who had braved that monster Florin. He who had annoyed the Comte and made him jealous by his intervention in favour of the woman he loved. Moved, the old man murmured, 'Knight, I thank you for myself and on behalf of all the others who have the privilege of serving Madame.'

Leone immediately understood that he was referring to the trial by ordeal.

'Thanks be to God, my good Ronan. Could you warn your master that I have arrived?'

'Alas … He's gone to the Inquisition headquarters in order to present himself voluntarily … but upon orders from the King.

Messire Monge de Brineux, his chief bailiff, has gone with him. As for Madame ... Oh, God ...'

Despite being exhausted after his long journey from Cyprus, Leone noticed Ronan becoming increasingly agitated and his eyes filling with tears.

'Knight, it's Providence that sends you here again. I don't know what to think any more ... In truth, I've started to believe that evil forces have been attacking us since our poor Raimonde, an old servant, was murdered by a thief ... I feel so guilty for refusing to go with her on market days ... May she rest in peace. Quick, come with me. Messire Joseph de Bologne, the Comte's physician, will tell you about our dreadful situation better than I can. I feel there's an evil hand at work here, so powerful that it has influenced the King and has made him suddenly end his childhood friendship with my master. But I must stop making your head spin with my incoherent babble ... I'm only confusing you. I just don't know what to do,' the old servant panicked. 'I feel helpless. Just a powerless old fool!'

An hour later, having listened to Messire Joseph's account without a single interruption, Francesco de Leone finished the meal Ronan had prepared for him. He carefully crumbled the trencher soaked in meat juices and swallowed it to the last mouthful. A poor man's habit he cherished. Rich people would throw their trenchers to their dogs, or give them to the beggars waiting at their gates. Today, however, this humble act brought him no pleasure. He was angry as well as worried. Head lowered towards the hem of his garment, which brushed the floor with every step, arms crossed behind his back, Messire Joseph finished his story on a gloomy note.

'Now you know everything, knight. I have spared no detail, at least none that I have been given, in order to enlighten you. I must confess ... I possess but few means to slow down the effects of the poison Madame is being administered. Vomiting triggered by drinking milk but that's effective only if the poison is still in the stomach, a lot of cheese[140] in addition to all the dishes which Ronan personally prepares so that no one else can get near them. If the poisoner is not discovered as soon as possible, she will die.'

His throat dry from anxiety, Leone asked, 'Which poison is it?'

'Unless I am very much mistaken – and I don't think I am – it's lead.* The most skilled poisoners have been using it since the dawn of time. However, few people are aware of its terrible power, as evidenced by the fact that we use it to sweeten our most prized wines.'[141]

'Do you have a suspicion, no matter how small, as to the poisoner's identity?'

'I confess we began to suspect young Guillette, her maid, even though she seems so fond of our lady. But it can't be her because, like everyone else, she is forbidden from taking her food or drink – even water. Yet this poison is ingested … You see, knight, Madame is an exceptional being, which is why it took me so long to see the unacceptable truth. Who would resent and attack a beam of light to destroy it, when there are so few of them in this world?'

'Those who benefit from the darkness. Since this is a poisoning, why this hoax involving the black bag containing charred debris and feathers?'

'I've been asking myself that for a long time. It's a clever ruse for which I can see many reasons.'

'Please sit down, Messire,' Leone suggested again. 'Let's share a glass of mead.'

Joseph obeyed, somewhat half-heartedly. He thought better on his feet, pacing up and down the room, his eyes fixed on an invisible spot in space, fully immersed in his own mind. However, the comfort brought to him by the presence of this knight, young as he was, and the ruthless determination he sensed in him, as well as the reputation for courage and integrity of the Hospitallers, were surely worth a small deviation from his thinking habits. However, before accepting the goblet proffered by Leone, he said, 'We do not belong to the same faith, and you are a soldier of your God.'

Leone smiled. 'I know that, and my God has been yours for much longer. In addition, I've learnt much from my contact with your people and the Saracens against whom we fight so hard. Messire Joseph, it's only the weight of their souls that distinguishes men. Apparently, our two souls are light. Let's drink to men of goodwill and strong faith.' After taking a sip, Leone put down his glass of mead and continued, 'You say it's a clever ruse?'

'Of course. I don't know your opinion of these witches and sorcerers but mine is unequivocal: they're charlatans who live off people's gullibility, or else poor fools intoxicated by their faith in supernatural powers.'

'I've reached the same conclusion. And yet I've seen so many surprising things.'

'Madame ... is not immune from fear of them. I was surprised by how terrified she was of that bag, even though I've frequently found her to be very intelligent.'

'So far, she has lived surrounded by superstitious farm boys who swallow whole any kind of tale as long as it's served garnished with spells.'

'That's right. The fact still remains that these cheap creatures' only true power lies in the terror they inspire. The main reason I can see is that the poisoner wished to increase the damage caused by the poison by creating panic in Madame. If you think of it, the bag was not at all well hidden. In fact, I'm surprised a servant didn't come across it sooner when sweeping under our mistress's bed.'

'Evil and clever,' Leone commented.

'The other reason is even more perverse, yet I find it plausible. They say that spells are allegedly cast at a distance. Perhaps whoever placed the spell bag was hoping that it would be linked to the Comtesse's failing health. That means that any investigation to discover the culprit would be destined to fail from the outset since, according to legend, the sorcerer can be leagues[+] away from his victim, unlike a poisoner who hands out his lethal substance on a daily basis. This way, the monster could hope to continue to operate calmly, even after the Comtesse's physical decline had started to alert her close circle.'

'Can't lead be used to kill someone quickly?'

'Absolutely, but it's dangerous because then you know that the victim was poisoned. The aim of the poisoner was to make us believe that it was a languishing illness very much like the one from which the first Dame d'Authon, as well as her son Gauzelin, died. Then there's no culprit. All they'd have to do at that point is spread the rumour of a family curse, or perhaps even direct suspicions towards the Comte d'Authon.'

'You'd make a fearsome investigator, Messire.'

Joseph de Bologne studied him for a moment.

'It's only that, like you, I've penetrated so many mysteries of the human soul. Some wonderful, others repugnant. We are capable of everything – evil as well as good. Did you know that?'

'I've discovered it.'

'So the battlefields have given you the opportunity to overtake me by several decades,' Joseph murmured.

'They allow men to reveal their fear, their bravery, their cowardice or their betrayal. Only God knows which way we're going to lean.'

'Only God knows,' the old physician agreed. 'One more theory has crossed my mind about the little bag. Some sorcerers are well established, their reputation extends beyond the province, and they nurse it like a baby. As their success spreads, they keep up the myth. The fear they inspire protects them and guarantees them a constant flow of customers. And what if we're dealing with one of those sorcerers for whom Madame's death would act as a kind of ... recommendation, unless we believe that it's caused by infernal forces under his or her command? In that case, nobody would suspect a poisoning, a simple murder which, after all, anyone could easily commit. On the contrary, everything would have to suggest that it's the power of the spell he or she cast.'

'Your three theories are troubling. All three are plausible.'

'Please understand, knight, that they're not mutually exclusive, and that we may be facing a being of dark but real intelligence.'

'And we're going to defeat him,' Leone promised, standing up. 'Permit me to take my leave, Messire. I want to greet and reassure Madame.'

Joseph also stood up. Uncertain and emotional, he stammered, 'Oh, Monsieur, you're sent by God. There's no doubt about it. With the Comte and the chief bailiff away, Ronan and I were like two old women – powerless and desperate. You're the miracle we summoned with our wishes to save our beloved mistress.'

'We'll see if that's true once the monstrous assassin is swinging at the end of a rope. Have you noticed any improvement in Madame's health since you started treating her and Ronan began preparing her meals? Or is it too soon to tell?'

'The pains in her stomach should have become less frequent, but that's not the case,' the physician said, sounding distressed.

'Then the poisoner is still operating and we need to find out how without delay. I'll get to work straight away. Would you be so kind as to have them put a straw mattress outside the door of the Comtesse's bedchamber? I'll not move from there until I have solved this fiendish riddle.'

The physician closed his eyes with relief and resisted the impulse to take the knight in his arms, as he would have done with a son. However, a new worry took the place of the previous one.

'What about Monseigneur d'Authon? How can we rescue him from this Inquisition interrogation that looks more like a trial?'

Leone said gently, 'Have no fear, Messire Joseph. I have every confidence in your master's skill and audacity. Authon is no coward and his splendid reputation stands him in good stead. Moreover, I know Jacques du Pilais. He is a stickler for the rules, wily and fearsome – but an absolute stickler for the rules. I have an infallible way of getting Monseigneur d'Authon out of the Inquisition headquarters. If you do not mind, for the time being I shall keep silent as to its nature. However, be assured that I will not hesitate to use it.'

The old man's eyes filled with tears and he thanked God for allowing him to witness this miracle. Men who were straight, good and brave without any hope of payment, even if death was their only reward, did exist after all.

'No need to tell me its nature, as I think I understand by a process of deduction. You were the one chosen by God to carry out His judgement, weren't you? You would give yourself up for the murder of Nicolas Florin.'

'If it came down to it, I'd do it without hesitation.'

'Of course you know what they would do to you.'

'Down to every gruesome detail,' Leone said with a sigh. 'When I chose to join God with all my love and obedience, I accepted the possibility of a terrible death. I've never regretted it. Come now, my wise and perceptive physician,' Leone joked, 'I am nothing, and yet I am everything as long as He gives me the means. Let us not think about these ugly stories for the time being. Our one imperative, our sole imperative, is Madame d'Authon.'

*

Agnès stood up with difficulty when he entered. He had seen her so weak, so haggard and yet so sublime once before. It had been in that putrid cellar in the Inquisition headquarters. He was overcome with the same emotion. She was the one for whom he would be happy to give his life. She rushed to him, her arms outstretched.

'Knight, sweet Jesus, my prayers have been answered. To see you again. My husband should be back soon and he'll welcome you like a brother, since he's now so sorry that he has no other beside the King.'

Leone did not disabuse her. Artus d'Authon would not be back soon. He had thought it wise to keep his wife in the dark in order to protect her, but he had made a grave mistake. They had removed him with the sole aim of killing his beloved. However, God, whose darling daughter she was, had decided otherwise, and Leone had rushed to her aid. Of that he had no doubt.

'Madame, Messire Joseph has just told me in every detail about the recent events. Someone is trying to kill you. I intend to take my place outside your door, like a dog, until your husband returns.'

'If anyone else had given me this diagnosis, I would have dismissed it as nonsense.'

'And of course you know why this is happening.'

'Of course, knight. That very reason you discovered in the secret library at Clairets. Women with green blood, different blood. They want to kill me to stop me from passing on this blood to one of my daughters, and prevent the Second Coming.'

Leone nodded. 'Madame, never forget that they are fearsome and ready to do anything. Benedetti is behind all this but you knew that already. He has even managed to muzzle Clément V, probably by threatening that the royal help that led to his election might be disclosed. Naturally, it would be impossible to prove that. Do not trust anyone, never lower your guard. Until your husband and his chief bailiff return, you have three allies here you can trust: your physician, old Ronan and myself.'

'So you'll be my guard dog,' she said, trying to joke.

'I promise I won't bark during the night.'

Monge de Brineux paused and waited for Maîtresse Taure to finish filling their goblets with hydromel,[142] which Agnan had preferred to wine.

Once again, he marvelled at the young man's charmless ugliness, even though the Comte had described him so that he could be recognised. Artus d'Authon had specified that the clerk was a good soul and probably the only kindness he could count on at the Inquisition headquarters. Therefore, Monge de Brineux had waited for him at the exit of the sinister building, to ask him for news. He had followed him for a few yards before going up to him and inviting him to the inn, which was quite distant from the Inquisition headquarters, so that they could speak without being disturbed. Agnan's face had lit up at the mention of his name and position, and he had whispered, 'I was very much hoping that someone close to the Comte would approach me, Lord bailiff. Things are happening … Things I don't understand but that I spend hours worrying about.'

Once the innkeeper's wife had left, Monge said, in a low voice, 'What are the things you were alluding to earlier, Monsieur?'

'I can't understand. Their famous irrefutable piece of evidence was a wedding ring and that's another sign that God is on our side. The thief stole the wedding band from Monseigneur d'Authon's first marriage. Yet the Comte claims that he took it off his finger as soon as his wife died and has never worn it again. I believe him.'

'And you're right to,' the chief bailiff said. 'I'd testify to it in court, as would everyone in the Comte's immediate circle.'

Agnan took a slow sip of his drink and hesitated.

'You see, Monsieur, I got the definite impression that there was something troubling the Grand Inquisitor Jacques du Pilais when he came to my office to give me the legal documents. I'd swear he didn't know that the ring had been stolen in order to incriminate the Comte. He, too, believed in his sincerity.'

'In that case, the situation is looking promising for us,' Monge de Brineux said cheerfully. 'Artus d'Authon will be cleared of all suspicion and the trial by ordeal will be ratified.'

'You're jumping to conclusions, I'm afraid …'

Agnan began speaking fast and Monge de Brineux signalled to him to lower his voice, for fear of eavesdroppers.

'The Grand Inquisitor has requested a further inquiry regarding the ring allegedly found two years after Florin's death. Given Monseigneur d'Authon's character and his honourable reputation, he could very well have allowed him to return to his lands upon his word that he would not leave them. In that case, why has Jacques du Pilais ordered that the Comte be kept at the Inquisition headquarters? Of course, he will be treated as a witness and not a defendant, but the only explanation I can think of is terrifying: that they want to get to the Comtesse. The Comte is in their way, so he needs to be removed. Therefore, I beg you to act quickly. Madame is in serious danger.'

An icy wave swept over the chief bailiff. He stood up abruptly and shouted, 'Maîtresse Taure – your husband, quick! Prepare my bill and saddle my horse immediately. Monseigneur Artus's horse will stay in your stables and you will be paid for looking after it properly.'

Arriving at lightning speed, Maître Taure said, 'But, Monsieur, it'll be night soon. You can't—'

'If any brigand stands in my way, I'll slice off his ears!' the chief bailiff replied, his hand flat on the sword banging against his calf.

Settled, like a soldier in the field, on the straw mattress Ronan had had pushed against the wall adjoining the door to Madame's apartments, Francesco de Leone was reading a psalter. He had spent so many nights in makeshift tents or out in the open, he barely remembered how many.

A young servant girl approached him stealthily and he looked up at her serious face. She curtseyed.

'I'm Guillette, in Madame's service. Er ... Please, Messire, do not reproach me for my curiosity. It's due to my concern for my good mistress. Is she in danger that you are outside her door?'

The knight answered gently, 'No danger, since I am here.'

'May I stay with her in order to comfort her? I could sleep at the foot of her bed. She's so generous and kind to us.'

'Carry out your usual duties for her, then let her rest and have no fear. She's in no danger.'

Leone glanced discreetly at the girl to make sure that she was not holding a sweet or a drink.

She came back out after less than an hour, looking worried, and said, 'Madame is in her nightclothes and will be going to bed soon. Please do not disturb her. She really needs rest. Good God, she doesn't look well at all. What's happening here? You outside her door, our lady so weak, Ronan completely inscrutable. He says nothing except to forbid me from bringing her sweetmeats ... I feel she's being threatened and my heart is constricted with fear.'

'All is well now, Guillette, you can go without concern.'

'Aren't you going to have any supper, sitting outside this door, Monseigneur?'

'Yes, I am. Ronan will soon bring me my meal.'

'In that case, I wish you goodnight.'

The girl turned on her heel. She briefly looked back at him before disappearing at the end of the corridor.

Leone picked up the psalter he had abandoned on the mattress. Suddenly, without any thought on his mind except for his reading, without even being aware of any suspicion, he leapt up and violently struck Agnès's door with his fist.

'Who goes there?'

'Leone, Madame. Allow me to come in this very minute, I beg you.'

'It's just that I am … I am in my nightclothes …'

'Please, Madame, I'm a monk first and a man second. Quickly!'

Panic caused his stomach to knot and he nearly pushed the door open without waiting for permission.

'All right … Come in.'

He forced himself to be calm, in order not to show his terror to the Comtesse.

'Your supper will be here soon.'

'I have no appetite, knight. This constant nausea puts me off my food. I'm an awful hostess. I'm so happy to see you and yet I spoil your meals. What must you think of me? It's just that this tiredness … This tiredness is making me reel.'

'Madame, my impression of you is so glowing, it couldn't tarnish. Guillette was with you a long time, wasn't she?'

'She's charming and looks after me most attentively. She suspects something is wrong with me, but I've followed your advice and not told her anything.'

'Did she read to you?'

'The poor girl can't read, which is a great shame because she's very bright.'

'Please don't think I am intruding on your privacy, but what did you do exactly? I know nothing about how a lady gets undressed, but an hour seems like rather a long time.'

Agnès's surprised blue eyes studied him. 'What are you getting at, knight?'

'I'd just like to know what you did together during this hour. Every detail.'

'How strange that you should insist on it. Well, Guillette helped me undress and told me stories about the chateau as she usually does. She never gossips but she's very observant, so she often makes me laughs. Not much, really.'

'Is that all, Madame?'

'I don't think ... Oh, there's just something very small. I doubt you'll be interested. She warmed up the rest of the eggnog that I drink every afternoon, and which Ronan has been preparing for me and bringing with the rest of my meals, for the past few days ... He doesn't make it as well as Guillette but please don't tell him. It's just that it had too much honey in it.'

'Did she warm it up in this fireplace?' Leone persisted, trying to control his voice, and indicating the hearth diagonally across from them, which heated the Comtesse's chamber.

'No, over the burner that lights my chapel,' Agnès said, motioning to the door that led to it – a place Agnès couldn't watch and where Guillette was free to do as she chose.

'Did you finish your eggnog, Madame?'

Leone pushed away the paralysing thought he had had for the past few seconds: she is going to die. My God, no, never!

'Not all of it. It was too sickly sweet.'

In a panic, he said abruptly, 'I'm calling your physician immediately. Don't go out, don't say anything to anyone, and don't open your door.'

'What ... But, Monsieur!' she called after him, but Leone had rushed out of the room.

Barely a few seconds later, Joseph de Bologne, the colour drained even from his lips, came in without knocking, followed by the knight, whose face betrayed his fear. Leone was holding a small jug against him, and Joseph put down on the chest the basin and cloths he was carrying. Joseph took the jug, poured out a full goblet of milk and handed it to Agnès.

'Drink this, Madame.'

She drank three goblets.

'Do you wish to be on your own in order to disgorge?'

'Again?' the Comtesse moaned.

'I beg you, Madame, quickly, before the poison is digested. We're going to repeat this unpleasant purging three times.'

Agnès picked up the basin and went to the chapel adjoining her room, murmuring with despair, 'It's impossible. Not Guillette. Not her.'

Soon, they heard her vomiting.

Joseph shouted towards the chapel, 'Force everything out, Madame, it's our only hope.'

When she came out, Agnès was as white as a sheet, her eyes red from all the effort. The purging started again.

She began vomiting anew.

'What about the monster?' Joseph asked in a low voice.

'I'll take care of her,' the knight replied in a tone so flat you could sense the rage he was trying to conceal.

'Are you going to kill her?'

'Of course not, even though it would give me much pleasure to do so. She has to talk and she will talk. Then she'll be sorry I didn't run her through immediately. The chief bailiff's men will do their duty.'

Guillette was coming out of the servants' hall. She looked astonished.

'The chateau is so large. Are you lost, Messire?'

'It's you who are lost,' Francesco de Leone replied. A hand roughly grabbed Guillette's arm, pushing up her sleeve and revealing a large strawberry mark in the crook of her elbow.

'What are you doing?' the girl protested. 'You're hurting me!'

Leone was struggling to contain the rage that had filled him ever since he had guessed the identity of the poisoner. A murderous rage. He searched the folds of her tunic with his hand until he felt a small purse concealed under her belt.

Guillette understood. She kicked out, tried to scratch him and knee him in the crotch. Leone flung her in front of him with a sharp movement and twisted her arm behind her back so that she cried out in genuine pain.

'Listen to me. I'd be deeply ashamed to strike a woman but you're no woman, you're the worst kind of viper, so I'll have no qualms about it. Start walking without putting up any resistance or I'll give you a thrashing and drag you if need be. Don't tempt me. At this very moment I'm fighting against the hatred and disgust you inspire in me.'

She obeyed, her teeth chattering with fear. Leone pushed her towards the spiral staircase which led to the dungeons and the cellars. Ronan was expecting them, holding a torch.

'I beg you,' Guillette sobbed. 'It's all a terrible mistake. I don't even know what you're accusing me of. I've done nothing wrong. I've not stolen anything.'

'Ronan, remove the purse she's hidden under her belt. Fear not, I'm holding her. The evil snake is capable of attacking.'

The old servant removed the small canvas bag, and poured a fine blue-grey powder into his hand.

'Blast, what could this be?' Leone asked with menacing sarcasm. 'Would you care to swallow it now in front of us? It tastes nice and sweet.'

The murderer's eyes widened and she shook her head in refusal.

Leone pushed her into a dungeon and Ronan promptly bolted the door. She stumbled and fell, but stood back up immediately. Her fear had vanished. Disfigured by her own wickedness, she screamed and tried to kick them through the bars she was clinging to.

'Drop dead! Drop dead, all of you! You don't scare me. She'll kill you and save me. She knows. She knows all the secrets.'

Leone had no doubt that she was referring to whoever had prepared the little bag found under the Comtesse's bed and ordered that she be poisoned. He had to lay his hands on her. Only she would enable them to trace everything back to Honorius or one of his henchmen in France. Choking with anger, he said, 'Do you really think so? If I were you, I'd be very worried. If her knowledge of evil is so powerful, then why did she need the help of a common poisoner?'

Guillette's eyes narrowed and she spat in his face, hurling insults at him.

Shortly before lauds,[+] an exhausted Monge de Brineux dismounted in the chateau courtyard, crying out to the servants to look after his horse, which was exceedingly tired after such a hard gallop. Ronan rushed to meet him and tried to give him an account of the situation but got so tangled up in his explanations that Brineux understood only two things: that Madame had almost died from poisoning and that the knight Francesco de Leone had only just saved her.

Brought up to date by the Knight of Grace and Justice and by Messire Joseph de Bologne, Brineux enquired with an impassive face, 'How is our lady?'

'She's resting. This evening she narrowly escaped death. I'll bet when the poisoner found out that Madame's food was being watched, she decided to do away with her as soon as possible. If it hadn't been for the knight and the immediate purging ... I can't bear to think about it.'

'Since these are extraordinary circumstances, I can assume the Comte's role in his absence and dispense justice. The girl will be interrogated forthwith, and I'll send for the executioner. She has an hour to give answers of her own accord. Then … Then she'll answer anyway. Do you wish to be present at the questioning, knight?'

'No, I care little about what happens to her. What I do want, however, is to find out who the powerful witch she mentions is.'

'You will, and soon.'

Leone stood up and was about to say goodbye to Brineux when the latter held him back and offered his hand.

'I am for ever indebted to you, Monsieur. I beg you never to let me forget it.'

'The honour is mine, Monsieur.'

'As for you, Messire Joseph, you were brought to this house by God himself.'

The old man's face wrinkled deeply in a smile. He murmured, 'I'm starting to believe that, my lord.'

Shaking the bars of her cell with wild frenzy, Guillette spent an hour hurling abuse, obscenities and threats at them. She uttered such monstrous curses that the secretary appointed by Brineux to take note of her confession crossed himself several times. The two guards standing with their backs against a nearby cell kept nudging each other, enjoying the scene as true connoisseurs.

The deep revulsion the chief bailiff felt for her made things easier. Brineux's weakness for the fair sex – further encouraged by a perfect marriage – the pleasure he took in their company, their cheerful disposition and their charming faces would have made his task unbearable. He considered it an abomination to torture a woman. But not this one. He hated her for having tried to kill the Comtesse, fussing over her and taking good care of her yet all the while cunningly plotting her demise. He said, in an even tone, 'Time is running out, you monster. There isn't much sand left,' he added, indicating the hourglass standing on the earth floor.

'I'll shit on you, you swine! You'll die like the pig that you are! The same goes for your brats and your wife!'

The sound of heavy footsteps made them turn round. A huge figure in a bloodied leather apron came towards them, holding a metal lantern.

'Prepare the room, executioner,' Brineux ordered. 'And no need for the consideration[143] normally reserved for women – she deserves none.'

'As you command,' the man muttered, bowing his bald head with its leather cap.

'Poor fool,' Guillette bawled, frothing at the mouth. 'I'll feel nothing. It won't hurt me. I'm protected.'

'We'll soon find out,' Brineux said, unruffled.

Lying strapped to the torture table, naked, she opened her eyes wide with surprise for a split second when the iron, white-hot from the embers, came in contact with the delicate skin of her belly and produced a sizzling sound. Immediately there was a revolting smell of burnt flesh. She screamed.

'Stop, executioner,' the chief bailiff commanded.

The brute with the impassive face paused and stuck the two metal blades back into the red embers.

'Speak,' Brineux ordered, his face sweaty from the stifling heat in the room. 'Not being an inquisitor, it's not a confession I'm after but simply the name of the witch you're wrongly protecting. I want to know where I can find her. I care nothing about your repentance. God will be your judge and His sentence will be terrible.'

'I curse you with all the demons of hell!' Guillette roared, her sobs getting the better of her.

'Executioner, resume your duty.'

She screamed for a long time. Whenever the metal blades were lowered, her cries would echo through the low vaults of the cellar. Brineux looked at the stripes of red, swollen wounds across her stomach, and could not allow himself to remember that this was a woman's body. It was just the flesh of a wicked poisoner who had tried and almost succeeded in killing the perfect and gentle Madame d'Authon. The screaming stopped abruptly. Guillette had fallen unconscious. But not for long. The tub of water her torturer threw in her face made her come to. As soon as she opened her eyes, Monge de Brineux knew that her hatred and hope of being saved had drained from her. She was now nothing but suffering and terror.

'Speak. Can't you see she lied to you, tricked you in order to make you do her dirty work without taking any risks herself? She has no power. Can't you see that now?'

Choking with sobs and begging, Guillette confessed.

'She doesn't have a name ... The Witch, that's all. It's she who ordered me to stab old Raimonde so that they'd hire me at the chateau. I swear! It's a tumbledown cottage ... in the Forest of Trahant, not far from Ceton ... I beg you ... for the love of God ... please ...'

'Executioner, let the fire go out, dress her wounds and then let the guards take her back to her cell. She must be treated charitably, fed and watered.' Bending over the tortured body, he added in a voice that was almost friendly, 'You've done well. Once I've checked your information, you'll be hanged. The rope will be short and you'll be pushed from a height so that your neck will break and your death throes will be brief. I give you my word. If, however, you've lied to me ...'

'I'm not lying, I swear,' she mumbled, terrified.

'I hope the Comte will be back by then. If only to confirm my sentence.'

Château de Larnay, Perche, September 1306

Lying across his bed, Eudes had not sobered up for a week. He felt pressure in his temples and his tongue was furry. The smell of his clothes – filthy with grime, sweat and vomited wine – sickened him. Yet the mere prospect of changing them made him feel tired. He had called out for a servant just before collapsing in a drunken stupor. At least that was what he remembered. Nobody had come. The few chateau residents kept a low profile and tried to make themselves scarce, since their master's fury tended to explode for no reason except that by lashing out he vainly hoped to calm down.

He rolled onto his side and got up with great difficulty, still drunk from the night before. What time was it? He had no idea. Daylight was already peeping through a grey mist. He stumbled to the bevelled mirror and examined the marks of his debauchery. The face of a tavern drunkard. A fine network of tiny thread veins criss-crossed his yellow corneas. His purplish cheeks looked even more crumpled than the day before. He stretched his hand out before him. It was shaking so much that he clenched his fist.

A wave of self-pity was added to the rage that had been eating away at him for months and years. Alone. He was alone. Ruined and discredited. It never occurred to him that he had caused his own downfall. Even the servants made fun of him behind his back. He was sure of it. Dishonourable, ungrateful beggars. He had forgotten the hardship and cruelty he had inflicted on them since childhood. He had forgotten that he bedded the girls whenever he pleased, never hesitating to use a few slaps to persuade them if they were ever unwilling.

Even a woman's belly no longer attracted him. He had lost his taste for everything except the wine which burnt his throat and slowly drowned his memory. Wine was his only weapon against the memory of Agnès which gnawed at him relentlessly.

She had been on his mind for as long as he could remember. Even as a child, he had watched her coming and going, making sure he came upon her when she least expected it and thought she was out of his reach. The anxiety he then saw in her blue-grey eyes intoxicated him. He wanted so much to bend her to his will and force her to love him that he developed an unhealthy desire for her that was so stifling not a night went by without his dreaming he was putting his hand on her proffered belly. But, instead, he had bedded so many beggars and whores that he had lost count. He had fulfilled his marital duties with Apolline solely to have a son. Her flabby flesh repulsed him and only seemed capable of producing daughters. The image of his dead wife's pretty, despairing face flashed through his mind but he chased it away. He had no use for remorse. Why should he? He had never loved her, barely tolerating her presence, treating her harshly, and had been unfaithful to her even in her bedchamber. What of it? She joined the legion of women whose offspring mattered only if it was male.

The powerful tensing of Agnès's long thighs in breeches, while he was teaching her to ride bareback – he had pictured them squeezing his ribs a thousand times.

At first, he had convinced himself that she did not understand, that she could not feel it. He had persuaded himself that their blood ties alone explained the way in which she was forever reminding him of their consanguinuity. So he had shown her consideration and showered her with expensive gifts that ruined him further. Then, a few years after Hugues de Souarcy's death, he had been forced to admit that it was she who had been taking him for a ride when he was the one who should have been in charge of the horse. She feigned not to see in order to keep him at a distance. A feeling of hatred had combined with the lust that never left him. A desire to destroy, to pillage this perfection which was denied him, since all he had left was his power over her. Or so he thought. Even revenge had been denied him. The skilfully hatched plan to terrorise her and leave her with but one option – him – had nearly cost Agnès her life. Powers Eudes de Larnay had never been able to discover had tried to push her towards torture and death. And if she died, there would be no reason left for Eudes to outlive her. As for living, he had lost any desire for that a long time ago.

A surge of anger swept away the self-indulgence he was wallowing in. With a violent kick, he sent the pedestal table from his bedchamber flying across the room. The top of the table could not withstand the shock and split with a sudden crack. Had God been against him from the start? Agnès had become his suzerain by marriage, so he could no longer reach her. She had given Artus d'Authon a son. And the mine he sometimes had his people watch kept producing iron.

Why? He sometimes had the insidious fear that God had protected Agnès just in order to punish him for having been born, and to warn him that the rest of his life would be his worst nightmare.

In the high bevelled mirror, a drunkard held his gaze. In that expression, he sensed fear.

His fist smashed into the mirror. A thick line ran through the glass, splitting it across, but Eudes did not see it. Instead, a smile on his lips, he was looking at the blood dripping lazily from his knuckles.

Agnan jumped up as Jacques du Pilais, the Grand Inquisitor, walked in. He looked down at his records since the pale-blue eyes made him feel so ill at ease. They seemed to bore through your skull and read your innermost thoughts.

'Agnan, have you finished writing up the notes?'

'Yes, my lord. Er ... with regard to the further investigation into Lord d'Authon's wedding ring, the messenger brought back seven testimonies. They all concur and certify that, in fact, the Comte has never worn the wedding ring since his first wife died. One of them comes from the Bishop of Authon. Should Maître Richer and our brothers Robert Ancelin and Foulque de Chandars be called in for a second confrontation?'

Jacques du Pilais studied him for a moment, a strange smile hovering on his lips, then replied in a smooth tone, 'That would be premature.'

'Are we expecting further testimonies?' Agnan continued, at the same time wondering if he was being dangerously reckless.

'Not really. Let's just say that I am searching my soul in order to dispense justice as irreproachably as possible.'

'Oh ...'

Jacques du Pilais walked to the door and paused before going out. Without turning to the clerk, he said, in the same calm, soft tone, 'You're a good example of the charity and openness of spirit of our Inquisition. You show so much concern for Lord d'Authon's fate!'

Agnan felt cold sweat on his back. He had been imprudent. If the Grand Inquisitor had the slightest suspicion of any collusion between him and Artus d'Authon ... he couldn't bear to think of what awaited him.

Yet that was not what was bothering Jacques du Pilais as he closed the door of the secretary's little office. How much longer would this farce have to go on for Rome to be satisfied?

For the time being, he would have to go down to the cellars of the Inquisition headquarters, as he had already done several times. This contemptible game consisted in trying to persuade Lord d'Authon that his judges were still awaiting the outcome of further enquiries.

Jacques du Pilais was overwhelmed by a feeling of shame. Despite his relentless tracking down of heretics, ungodly people and sorcerers, in spite of the unfailing severity he had always demonstrated, he had only resorted to the ultimate punishment on rare occasions. His mission was to bring souls back to God, convince the defendants of their errors and make them aware that they had strayed. He had dispensed countless penances, imposed barefoot pilgrimages and even public floggings, but death seemed to him to have too divine a nature to become a human recourse.

Vatican Palace, Rome, September 1306

Honorius Benedetti wiped the beads of sweat from his forehead with two fingers, then looked at the moisture on them with disgust.

Bartolomeo was patiently waiting for the prelate's verdict. Would Benedetti consider the lack of information he had just admitted to as a failure? Strangely, even though the young Dominican was certain of the archbishop's formidable power, he felt no fear in his presence. One thing he had grown certain of over the past few months was that no wickedness guided the camerlingo's actions, no matter how ruthless these were.

Finally, Honorius Benedetti said in an irked tone, 'Honestly – hundreds of spies are looking without success for a farm boy, young Clément, who keeps slipping through our fingers. Not only that, but we can't even find any trace of him. And now Sulpice de Brabeuf, a penniless little monk, has also vanished into thin air. Blast this bad luck that seems to pursue us! We absolutely have to get hold of this Vallombroso treatise, or at least its rough draft.'

'It's just that Brother Sulpice doesn't seem to have sought shelter in any other monastery after he disappeared from Vallombroso, Your Eminence, not even under an assumed name. And, apparently, he hasn't asked his relatives for help – at least not those contacted by our investigators. They've not heard from him again, much to his mother's chagrin.'

'He must have gone back into the world,' the camerlingo concluded. 'Might as well look for a needle in a haystack.'

'If I might be so bold as to contradict you, not necessarily. I agree with you that Brabeuf has probably gone back into the world. Being without means, he couldn't survive without help, except by practising some kind of trade. Now I've suddenly remembered a detail from my conversation with the Abbot of Vallombroso. Father Eligius told me that, in addition to having a talent for mathematics, Sulpice de Brabeuf is also a good musician, and plays the lute and hurdy-gurdy very well.'

'Do you think he's become a minstrel? Such people are always on the road, going between chateaux and manors, and you never know where to look for them.'

'Maybe, but I doubt it, Your Eminence. From the description I've been given of Brabeuf, nothing leads me to believe that he is fearless or experienced in trade, which are qualities necessary in a troubadour. He's a very young, very shy and retiring man. Rather, I can picture him as a stringed-instrument maker in a large city. Where else can you hide your identity better than in a large city?'

Honorius Benedetti sat up, leant his elbows on his imposing desk and examined the young Dominican's face intensely.

'You see, Bartolomeo, wasn't I right when I said I was a better judge of your efficiency? I have a gut feeling that you're right. We've got no time to lose. Our investigators must contact all the stringed-instrument makers or repairers in the large cities as soon as possible. Start with the cities where there's an Inquisition headquarters. They'll help us and your task will be easier. I am going to write a mission note to that effect. Thanks to the description we have of Brabeuf, who can't have changed that much over just a few years, our bloodhounds will unearth him – that's if your insight is correct.'

Forest of Trahant, Perche, September 1306

Despite being wrapped in a sable-[144] lined cloak and having her hood up, Madame de Neyrat was shuddering. A kind of monotonous chant rose in the distance, coming from the glow she could see through the rows of chestnut trees, and sometimes interrupted by the shrill cry of a woman.

She stifled the anxiety that was threatening to occupy her mind. She would soon accomplish her task, she thought, and get what she wanted. Then she would go south, to her fiefdom. It would be such a pleasure to see, once again, the large pink stones of the manor she had obtained at the death of Monsieur de Neyrat, vigorously defending it against the avidity of her late husband's blood heirs. All had died, more or less quickly, depending on her interest in them. Also on her affection for them, because even though you can kill to protect yourself, you can still feel some tenderness towards your victims. At least that was Madame de Neyrat's absolute conviction. Only the most sensible ones had survived, perceiving vaguely that insisting on their inheritance would trigger the discontent of the pretty Aude, who would try to dispatch them to join their ancestors. The plentiful water irises which, in the morning, gave a purple and yellow glow to the pond she had had dug. The endless song of cicadas that kept her company for hours. On rare occasions, you would discover them stuck to a tree trunk and marvel at their having been so near all the while. The peacocks striding towards her, cocking their heads to see what treat she was holding. It was a game she never tired of. Peacocks are temperamental animals and can peck you very hard. Holding a piece of bread or brioche in her fingers, Aude would reach out and touch them, without taking her eyes off them. Up to now, she had never been pecked. She roused herself from the blissful reverie she was slipping into. Later.

She closed her eyes for a moment and breathed in the cool, dry night air, open-mouthed.

Already twenty-five years old. Only twenty-five. It had been an endless succession of moments that led nowhere, a sea of faces she could not remember. Forgotten, barely uttered words, sighs she had immediately wished she had not uttered. In a way, her life had been nothing but an interminable process of preparation. She had built up the means to defend herself, money and connections who were keen on keeping her happy since she knew many ugly little secrets about them. She had traded in human filth, certain that it was the most infallible way to pull herself out of it for ever. The much-awaited moment had finally arrived. It would require courage but she had no lack of that. Or of cruelty, either. Who cared, if it was in order to find something pleasant? Another moment, another face, no memories.

The man she had met in Ceton had been adamant as soon as she had got him thoroughly drunk. In a slurred voice, he had said, 'It's someone who meddles in un-Christian things, I tell you! Mating when it's full moon. Better stay away, it's not healthy stuff. Apparently, they get up to all sorts of filthy things, like rubbing their rude bits together and even doing it with black goats.'

She had managed to get the precise location of the devilish sabbath out of the man before he slid to the ground, dead drunk. A full moon was due two days later.

Escorted by one of her armed guards, aware that night covers tracks and confuses points of reference, Aude had done a reconnaissance of the location the day before, as soon as she had heard about Guillette being tortured.

She did not mind the solitude she had chosen for this final night. On the contrary, she feared that an armed guard would probably let something slip, so had decided to bring her plan to fruition by herself. The overwhelming fear she had felt as she mounted her horse had vanished. She had inspired enough fear in others in order to bend them to her will that she considered it as her sister. She was no longer fearful. Why should she be afraid of the night, her long-time accomplice? As for the forest surrounding her, it was so black and thick that it gave her a feeling of expectancy. An almost serene expectancy.

Its bridle attached to a low branch, her dun filly was patiently waiting, its eyes fixed on its feet, which had been wrapped in hessian in order not to make a sound.

The moon was full. It was an ideal night. The first night of one life and the last of another. The chanting had ceased in the distance. There was an almost surreal silence. A large silver veil brushed Madame de Neyrat's face without a sound, then vanished. She jumped, then reprimanded herself for the foolishness that had crossed her mind. No, it was not a witch on a reconnaissance mission. An aggressive whistling sound soon put her right. It was a barn owl, and they brought luck. Only gullible folk believed that a soul can be traded in exchange for alleged powers and improbable recipes! Souls cannot be traded since their price is only what God puts on them. She remembered the exorbitantly expensive book she had bought when she still believed in the power of magic. She had studied it in every detail until she had read a passage that made her burst out laughing: 'To cause deafness and then restore hearing: eat powdered broad bean root, then, when you want hearing to return, press some onions and put the juice into your ears.'

She had then closed the book and only read it again in order to laugh at its ridiculous advice.

Stepping on a tree stump and placing her foot in the single stirrup, Madame de Neyrat got nimbly back on her horse, sorry, as usual, that ladies' saddles were so foolishly restrictive and unsuitable for trotting and galloping, except perhaps for highly skilled horsewomen. The harness of women's horses was only slightly better than the old *sambue* of the past century – a comfortable armchair placed on the horse's hindquarters, which did not permit the rider to control the horse. A servant would lead it at walking pace.

She pushed the bottom of her cloak out of the way and shuddered again. With a movement of her heel, she started her horse. Its cloth-wrapped shoes made no sound. She went towards the place she had noted the day before. Once she reached the clearing, she stopped her horse by pulling on the reins.

There was a sound of footsteps and crushed leaves. A drunken laugh. Someone exclaimed:

'I can't walk straight. I'm going to end up going head over heels! Help me, you clumsy fool. At least show some gratitude for the food I give you, if nothing else. You can't see a thing here. It's like the arsehole of hell! Help me, I tell you, or as soon as I've slept off this bad wine I'll give you a thrashing you won't forget.'

Aude pursed her lips with displeasure. She had considered this possibility even though she had wished she would not have to face it. Too bad. As God wishes!

The sounds were drawing close to her. Aude pulled out the quiver hanging from her stirrup leather and fitted a short, quilled, two-foot arrow with a metal point to the bow. The weapon could send a projectile over a hundred yards and they said that the best archers could shoot twelve per minute. More than satisfactory.

The witch came out from behind a hawthorn bush, leaning on Angélique, who was staggering under her weight. In her drunken state, she did not immediately notice the horsewoman a few feet from her. Angélique, on the other hand, recognised her straight away and a radiant smile lit up her face, which was tense with effort.

Madame de Neyrat's voice rose, calm and serious.

'Stand aside, my darling, and close your eyes – quickly.'

With a leap, the little girl was out of range of the weapon.

Aude drew the bow.

Despite being drunk, the woman finally saw that she was the target and bawled, 'You will die in atrocious suffering and be for ever damned … Whoever makes an attempt on my life will know worse torments than hell! They promised, those below, and they always keep their word!'

Aude chuckled, then replied, in an amused tone, 'What childish nonsense.'

She aimed at the woman. The witch fell to her knees and curled up in a ball on the leafy carpet, shielding her head with her folded arms, shouting, 'Is it the girl you want? Take her, then. Take her. I'm giving her to you, for what she's worth!'

'Now that's a lot more reasonable. It's a deal. I'm taking Angélique. Come, my sweet.'

Despite Madame de Neyrat's order, the child's eyes shifted from one woman to the other.

The witch got up and took three steps towards the horsewoman. The arrow flew through the air with an angry whistling sound and stuck in her throat. She staggered and clutched the shaft with both hands, trying to stop the flow of blood pouring from her wound, then collapsed.

Aude sighed and moved her horse forward. She looked at the groaning woman and confessed with a smile of regret, 'I lied. But then when it comes to lies, I give as good as I get, if not better. The time for bargaining is over. You cheated me and I hate being cheated. Your spells, your potions and your stinking slaughtered hens have no effect except to make one want to vomit, since you had to employ the help of a poisoner. And a mediocre poisoner at that. If you're dead, you can't reveal our little dealings.' In a tone of disappointment, she added, 'I really have no luck, but I'll manage somehow.'

The witch's legs relaxed after a final spasm. Aude turned to Angélique, who was watching the scene, and smiling contentedly, with her lips parted.

'Come, my darling, you'll sit behind me. We're going home. Unfortunately, I'm going to have to inflict someone's company on you, someone I hope you'll find as dull as I do, because that will mean that we have much more in common than our outward appearance. The annoying thing is that the goose is now useful again because her mother has just escaped death. Hang all incompetence! It's a good thing I've kept her on my side. Truly, there's no one you can count on except yourself, my darling. Meanwhile, let's put a stop to this coarse, informal way of speaking, only good for beggars and servants.'

Aude stretched out her fine hand in its purple leather glove to the little girl and helped her climb up behind her.

'Come, my pretty damsel, my daughter. Do you have a bundle to pick up? I beg you, give up all your ugly rags. They're unworthy of you.'

'Just a little box where I keep some small trinkets,' Angélique replied gently. 'Not much, really. Just a few silly good-luck charms I've collected here and there. I used to touch them in secret – otherwise the witch would have taken them away from me – hoping and praying that one day a splendid princess would come and rescue me. And she's finally here. You came, my lady mother. There is no other in my heart.'

Madame de Neyrat was overcome by an emotion she did not know she was capable of. She savoured this unexpected, precious title, 'my lady mother'.

Her life was finally changing. The world was becoming a kinder place. Angélique was going to sweep away the clouds that had been looming for so long.

She started the horse, silently, afraid that her voice would betray her emotion.

When they reached the cottage, Aude helped the child slide off the horse.

'Hurry, my sweetheart. Let's leave the past behind us quickly and for ever.'

There was just one cloud on the horizon. A dark cloud. How would she tell the camerlingo that the Souarcy woman had escaped death for the third time? Once again, Mathilde became indispensable. Only she could get close enough to her mother, feigning repentance, in order to complete what these clumsy fools had left unfinished. Madame de Neyrat did not entirely like her new strategy. She had considered using Mathilde to undermine her mother's future with espionage, more or less made-up evidence that could be used against Agnès if need be. But there was no time for that. Agnès was still young and in good health. She could produce more children. Therefore, she had to die as soon as possible. In other words, Madame de Neyrat had to teach that goose Mathilde a little of the poisoner's knowledge and provide the poison. However, Aude had no confidence in that pest of a girl. If she were caught and accused, she would not hesitate to reveal all, including the name of her benefactress, the person behind the crime. How awkward that would be! Unless, of course, Mathilde were soon afterwards to join her mother and her Maker. Soon enough for the judges not to have time to question her. What an excellent idea.

Angélique came out of the cottage with a small box wedged under her arm. Her laughter cheered Madame de Neyrat.

A weak early-autumn sun shone over the surroundings when, the following day, Monge de Brineux, escorted by three armed guards, approached the cottage. They soon discovered the body, with the arrow through its throat.

'A skilful archer,' the chief bailiff commented.

He was not altogether surprised. Those the witch had been

working for must have been highly disappointed by her failure. Moreover, she had become an inconvenient witness.

Following his order, one of the men threw the corpse over the back of his brown rouncy without concealing his feeling of repulsion. Monge reassured him.

'As soon as a few folks from Ceton have identified her, we'll get rid of her. Fear not – she had no power while she was alive, so it's no different now she's dead.'

Rue Saint-Amour, Chartres, September 1306

Mathilde de Souarcy, newly d'Ongeval, was making a worthy effort to create a good impression on the blonde child. The latter's arrival, a week earlier, at the town house where she now felt like a second mistress had vexed her extremely. Everything about Angélique exasperated her: her youth, her beauty and her quick mind. That and the obvious tenderness with which Madame de Neyrat treated her. A plague on this girl, her beautiful hair, her eyes as blue as cold water, her charming facial expressions. It was not exactly jealousy, since Mathilde did not feel any true affection for her mentor. However, she needed the latter, her advice and her money in order to further an education she felt would be very useful to her future. And now Angélique was a rival. Madame de Neyrat had dressed her like a little princess, and Mathilde had scrutinised her finery in order to satisfy herself that it was not more sumptuous than her own. One detail had placated her. No jewel had been purchased to adorn her protector's latest whim. Angélique was still a child.

The little girl seemed unaware of Mathilde's latent animosity and in order to please her complimented her on her poise, the perfect pitch of her voice, the alluring warmth of her hazel eyes, and the delicate pallor of her skin. She followed her everywhere like a little dog, went with her for walks, and sat quietly next to her while Mathilde pretended to read in an attempt to get rid of her.

Mathilde looked up from the lines of the poem she was not reading, let alone understanding.

Angélique's beaming smile, after she had spent half an hour waiting patiently, sitting up straight as Madame de Neyrat demanded, met her eyes. Her voice filled with hope, the little girl said, 'I can help you by changing the perfumed water in your water closet, Mademoiselle.'

'Don't even think about it, Mademoiselle,' Mathilde rebuffed her. 'That's the servant's task. Don't go demeaning yourself in everyone's eyes with such low occupations.'

'Oh …' Angélique murmured, looking put out. 'Then what can I do to please you? I'm upset that I'm so young and unrefined that my conversation doesn't interest a damsel as accomplished as yourself.'

Mathilde nearly replied, 'You could disappear immediately and for ever.' Instead, she played for time in order not to incur the disapproval of her benefactress. Trying, without much success, to tone down the sharp annoyance in her voice, she explained, 'Angélique, you're an angel and shouldn't have such a poor impression of yourself. However, it's true that you're still a child, of an age for games, when I am already a woman. Therefore, I will tell you honestly while begging you to forgive me, my exchanges with Madame de Neyrat are more … how can I put it? More …'

'Fascinating? Entertaining?' the little girl suggested, looking serious and sad.

'Not at all. Let's say more appropriate.'

'Of course, I understand,' Angélique said with a deep sigh. 'With your permission, Mademoiselle, I'll take my leave, then you can go back to your reading in peace. Some day soon, I'll be able to read as well as you do. It must be such a delight.'

'It is,' Mathilde agreed, although she was indifferent to the appeal of reading.

Still, as Madame de Neyrat always said, 'Never mind, whether it's a book or needlework, it gives a lady a certain countenance and proves that she isn't just an idle fool.'

Agnès could not shake off a frightening premonition. Thanks to Messire de Boulogne's constant care and, especially, the arrest of the poisoner, her health was improving. Naturally, her physician had warned her that lead poisoning, as well as being insidious, was also quite long-lasting. Still, she was slowly coming back to life, although the dark mood that haunted her, and which she had attributed to her physical weakness of the previous days, continued and would seize her at the first moment of idleness.

Her beloved husband had been away for five days on business, much longer than usual. No messenger had brought her news of him. He never neglected to send her a loving missive if he knew he would have to stay away from his estate for longer than two days. She would have thought Monge de Brineux's efforts to avoid her bordered on discourtesy if she had not sensed that his reticence concealed some unpleasant secrets. He had barely told her anything about Guillette's confession, and Agnès had not sought to know more. Deep in her heart, she knew. After all, a new offensive on the part of her enemies was hardly surprising, even if she had prayed to God every night to shield them all from the hostility of their adversaries. As for Francesco de Leone, sometimes he disappeared and only returned at night, exhausted, and went, without even eating anything, to the tiny room he had chosen in the outbuildings in order to avoid any gossip while the Comte was absent. When she occasionally came across him, she asked him about his long walks, but without being too intrusive. He would then evade the question with one of those strange smiles of his that stretched his deep-blue eyes towards his temples, and give her some non-committal response.

She realised that she had been pacing up and down her room for several minutes, like a lion in its cage, so she stopped by the tall Italian pedestal table. Her heart suddenly began to race and her head throbbed. Her skull felt as though it was being squeezed. Strangely, she knew this was not a symptom of the poisoning. Her mind went blank and she was forced to lean the palms of her hands on the pedestal table to avoid staggering. At the same time, there was no fear. Just the impression of someone whispering to her. Madame Clémence de Larnay, who had brought her up, and whose name she had given her beloved daughter. Madame Clémence, who had helped her resist the Grand Inquisitor from beyond the grave.

'My angel – is that you?' she heard herself murmur, her eyes closed.

Agnès's shoes sank into the thick mud. They were certainly close to the river. A damp, unhealthy chill caused her to shiver, and the idea that she would soon be alone, shut in with this foul odour, undermined her resolve not to allow her fear to show. Strangely, even Florin's evil presence felt preferable to this void full of horrors that awaited her. All of a sudden something slippery gripped her ankle and she screamed.

A guard rushed over and, pulling her roughly to one side, stamped his heavy wooden clog onto a hand … A bloodstained hand drooping through the bars of one of the cages. There was a wail, then whimpering ending in a sob.

'Madame … there is no hope of salvation here. Die, Madame, die quickly.'

She opened her eyes, panting. The Inquisition headquarters. She remembered the scene, the hand, and the man's voice. Florin had just pushed her into her cell. It was two years earlier. Her throat was dry with panic. What were they concealing from her? Her palms left a damp patch on the rosewood. She rushed out of her chamber.

Monge de Brineux had left the chateau to go back to his estate. Agnès sharply commanded Messire Joseph to confess the truth.

'Immediately, Monsieur. Your silence is reprehensible and I will reproach you if it persists. Where's my husband? I know that everyone here is hiding bad news from me, I can feel it.'

Joseph de Bologne lowered his head and replied, 'True, Madame. Nevertheless, I cannot tell you. Lord d'Authon has ordered me to say nothing, as he did Ronan.'

'This explains Monsieur de Brineux calling on me so rarely!'

'He has been much engaged with your would-be murderer,' the physician said, with so little conviction that the Comtesse lost her temper.

'I beg you, Monsieur, stop this ridiculous nonsense! Do you think I am so foolish? I want the truth and I will get it!'

Having said that, she left him standing there, and went to the outbuildings.

She must not be afraid yet. Fear dissipates courage. First, she must know. Then she would act.

Francesco de Leone had installed himself in a tiny room above the stables, where the blacksmith usually stayed when waiting for a mare to give birth. Agnès pounded at the door and waited barely a second before entering. They were stubbornly lying to her, concealing something sinister, so ladylike manners were out of place here. Francesco de Leone must have gone out on one of his long errands. The knight's few worldly clothes lay on a stool, neatly folded. So few things: a threadbare linen undershirt, peasant breeches, and a boiled-wool overall of an indefinable colour. On a small poplar work table, there was a psalter, scrolls of paper covered in the Hospitaller's tall, nervous handwriting, and an inkhorn. There was no basin or water pitcher. No doubt he washed in the tub in the courtyard. The chamber pot stood in a corner. Despite her panic, Agnès was suddenly overcome with tenderness for the passion that had prompted Leone to forsake the fortune that made his family one of the richest in Italy, and a future of ease and leisure, in order to live his faith in full.

She approached the table and, lifting the scrolls, discovered a blank strip of paper she had torn off after writing a short message. This meant she could now avoid wasting a whole new sheet. Once again, she told herself that she would never forget the habit of penury. A good thing, too, since she never wished to forget it. Knowing how to treat the most mundane objects without ever forgetting their value, remembering how they are missed when they are not available. She sat on the small chair and drew the inkhorn closer to her. Her long *coudière* brushed against a few of the scrolls, and one of them fell to the floor.

She leant over to pick it up and her eyes unwittingly fell on the first lines of a letter dated that morning.

My dearest cousin,

I have had so much to do since arriving in Angers that I have not had the time to inform you with regard to my search. I hope with all my heart that you will not hold this against me. Despite my efforts to find the diptych your father sold, I can still find no trace of it. Please rest assured that I am seeking it relentlessly and am fully aware of the urgency of the mission with which you have entrusted me.

Your humble and devoted Guillaume.

What did this mean? The handwriting was undeniably that of the knight. Why did he speak of Angers and a diptych? Why sign with a name that was not his? A doubt crossed her mind. It was a prearranged message. The recipient would know its exact meaning but it would mean nothing if it were to fall into the wrong hands. She suddenly felt certain that Leone was looking for Clémence, whom he still thought was a boy, on behalf of his so-called cousin. Did the latter know about the prophecy? Was he aware that the second birth chart referred to Agnès's daughter? Did he know that a manuscript depicting women with green blood had been discovered in the secret library at Clairets? She had no idea, but she would stop Leone from finding Clémence. She would fight to the death against his forcing upon her daughter the glorious, murderous future revealed in the stars.

Trying to steady her hand, she wrote on a strip of paper.

Monsieur,
It seems to me that our paths have crossed even less since you returned from Cyprus. Please do me the honour of dining with me this evening, so that we can talk a little as friends.
Your devoted Agnès d'Authon.

She placed the brief note in full view on the low bed, and left the room.

She had ordered the servants to notify her as soon as the knight Leone returned, and to set a table for two. Then she had waited, sitting on a chair in her room, an open book on her lap. It would soon be compline.[+] Where had her thoughts drifted during all that time? She could not tell. Even her impatience seemed to have evaporated. She was just waiting, that was all. Waiting for heavy, fast footsteps to tell her that Artus was about to walk into her chamber. That was all she was waiting for. Waiting for a throaty laugh to tell her that Clémence was about to run into her arms. Waiting for relief while fighting bravely against the fear assailing her. Fear, her sworn enemy. 'Fear does not spare its bite,' the Baronne de Larnay had once said. She had to prick up her ears and raise her tail. Keep fear on a leash. Muzzle it.

There was a soft knock on the door and a little servant girl she could not remember having seen before popped her head through the opening.

'Madame …' she murmured shyly, 'Ronan has sent me. Messire the knight is back. He's just washing the day's dirt off his face and says he'll accept your invitation.'

The girl disappeared before Agnès had had time to dismiss her. She was probably a scullery maid. A crowd of people, always working, with whom she barely had dealings.

She struggled against the inertia that made her want to remain sitting there and headed to the small dining room that was reserved for intimate gatherings.

Collapsing on her chair, her mind focused on just one purpose: to conquer fear, no matter what she was about to find out. She waited a little longer.

Whether an hour or just a few minutes had elapsed before the knight joined her, she could not tell. His forced cheerfulness concealed exhaustion and worry. She matched his feigned lightheartedness.

'Thank you for doing me the honour of dining with me, knight.'

He bowed. 'The honour is mine, Madame, as well as the pleasure of your company.' He smiled his beautiful slow smile. 'Not to mention the fact that you have a hungry dog here at your side.'

She remembered. Even during the worst moments of doubt

or anguish, Leone's presence had always made her feel calm. Strangely, she felt no attraction towards him as a man, yet he seemed to cast a benevolent, soothing shade over her. She could have fallen asleep in that shade, like a child that had finally been comforted. Was it because they both shared heavy, painful secrets Artus was not aware of? The fact that her children had been conceived outside the marriage bed? The prophecy? Perhaps.

Benoîte, a middle-aged servant, placed the first course before them: pea soup with rosemary and sage, and a carafe of Épernon wine. Softly, Leone thanked God for His munificence.

Agnès was prey to a disconcerting sensation, as though she had left her body. They ate their soup in silence, occasionally smiling at each other in order to fill the gaps in their conversation.

Agnès struggled to act normally. Benoîte reappeared with the second course, chunks of mutton with a hint of hyssop, and a vinaigrette that was delicate because it contained no soured wine, as Agnès explained to the knight, who, delighted to have a pleasant topic of conversation, said, 'It's truly wonderful. How does your cook make it?'

'He guards his secrets rather jealously, and we only know them in part. It's all we can do to obtain a few details from him. You must mix cinnamon, pepper and some ginger with good red wine diluted with beef stock, then add to this blend finely chopped onion, pork liver, as well as some stale bread.' Then without even meaning to, she said, 'Knight, I am waiting.'

Leone raised his inscrutable eyes. He could have pretended not to understand, but not with her. This extraordinary woman deserved better.

'My mission is to try to find Clément, Madame. And up to now, all my efforts have been fruitless.'

'Mine, too. But why this mission? Who entrusted it to you?' She barely recognised her own voice, which was soft and almost detached. The voice of a stranger.

'The prior of Limassol. Others, too, are looking for Clément. They are our enemies, Madame, even if Arnaud de Viancourt doesn't think they are enemies of the Hospitallers. Clément was trying to hide the manuscripts I entrusted him with, wasn't he?'

'Apparently so,' she lied.

'If our enemies were to lay their hands on your son before I do … May God save him. I confess, at first I wanted to keep this from you, but now I can see it's pointless to do so.' His blue-grey eyes searched her face.

Thank you, Lord. I have missed you so much, my darling, but He is watching over us. He has prevented me finding you so that you may be kept safe from the camerlingo's henchmen. Hide, my angel. Hide well. After all, didn't they almost succeed in killing me? How can I possibly protect you when I'm not even able to sense when an adder is close to me?

'Where's my husband? I demand to know the truth, since I've been denied it for days.'

Leone clenched his jaw and lowered his gaze. His high forehead creased.

'Monsieur?' she insisted.

'I cannot, Madame,' he murmured, looking down at his trencher.

The Comtesse's tone grew peremptory. 'The truth, this minute, and look me in the eye, Monsieur. I have a right to know.'

Finally, Leone looked up and she saw such deep sorrow in his eyes that she shuddered. She froze, expecting the worst. He got straight to the point.

'He has gone to the Inquisition headquarters by the King's command, and ordered everyone to keep silent so as not to alarm you.'

She let out a long sigh through her parted lips. Her earlier daydream. Her shoes sinking into the mud of the dungeons. Something slippery squeezing her ankle. Artus.

Leone panicked. 'Madame, are you faint? You're white as a sheet.' He stood up, about to rush and get a servant to help, but she stopped him with a gesture of her hand.

'Stay. I am not among those women who are permitted the brief respite of swooning or losing consciousness. And for that I am the sorrier. Knight, tell me a nice story about your past. Tell me that honour and courage can prevail. I beg of you.'

'Right now?'

'Right now.'

'It's just that I have so few nice stories compared to so many unbearable memories. A nice story then, for your sake, Madame. It was in Cyprus, many years ago. I was tending to the sick that week. My task consisted in going around farmhouses and hovels on the coast, administering basic help to those confined to their beds by common illnesses, and loading others onto the cart and bringing them back to our hospital. You see, many don't come of their own accord because they're very poor and afraid we'll ask their already starving families for money, despite all our reassurances to the contrary. When I arrived in the small courtyard of this derelict cottage, I immediately saw that something terrible had happened just a little earlier. Everything had been pillaged, and an enormous fire was burning not far from the buildings. I saw two charred human corpses on top of it. I stepped off—'

'But you were alone,' she interrupted, 'and the robbers could have been hiding. They were vile looters, were they not? Do you not know any fear?'

He threw his head back and laughed mirthlessly.

'Fear, Madame? It's all I do know. It's my most faithful companion and, it seems to me, it has been dogging my footsteps for an eternity. I know all its tricks aimed at reducing a man of honour and faith to the most infamous cowardice. However, you see, fear has a weak spot and, once you've discovered it, it vanishes.'

'What weak spot?'

'The gift. The gift of oneself. To accept the idea of dying is to stifle fear. It then retreats sheepishly. Of course, it returns at the slightest chink in your defences. Then all you need to do is defy it, and let it know you're ready for the sacrifice. As soon as it senses you're sincere, it beats a retreat.'

'What a happy formula. Please continue your story, Monsieur.'

'Drawing my sword, I inspected every building, room and outbuilding. Everything was wretched, and yet the villains had turned everything upside down, hoping to find a few coins or jewellery. No doubt they had tortured the residents and, tired of that, killed them and burnt them like animal carcasses. These foul creatures who torture their victims with fire can be found in every country. There was nothing for me to do there. I was about to climb back on my cart when a yelping dog on my right attracted my attention. I went towards it until I came across a kind of large kennel. A mouth full of rage, blood and anger barred the entrance. Baring its bluish fangs, it snarled to warn me off. Dogs possess a dignity we should envy and, instead, we use it to torment them. They never attack without prior warning. I heard a small child's weeping through the menacing growls. I sat next to the kennel, emptied my mind of any haste and anxiety, and spoke to the beast. To no avail. It was protecting the child. I had to make a choice: to kill the dog or risk its wrath. It would have been easy to strike it down with a blow of my sword. It was not aware of the damage a blade can cause the bravest of defenders. Dogs never distrust humans enough. I plunged my arm into the opening of the kennel in order to catch the animal by the throat.

I meant to strangle it just a little to control it. It did not give in. I still have the bite marks on my left arm. A good memory of a brave enemy. They're the only totally disinterested wounds that were ever inflicted on me ...'

Leone pulled up the sleeve of his undershirt and she saw them. Long white bumps, scars streaking his forearm.

'... I managed to pull the animal out by taking it by the scruff of the neck and choking it. It was a large bitch, a farm mongrel, one of those guard dogs that don't back down even before two or three wolves. I stunned it with a blow of my fist against its temple, then climbed inside the kennel. There was a little girl, perhaps four or five years old, crying silently, her hand on her mouth so as not to be noticed. Her mother had probably pushed her into the kennel and entrusted her to the dog as soon as she knew she was going to die.'

After holding back her tears despite all the disastrous revelations concerning Artus and Clémence, Agnès could contain them no longer.

'What became of them?'

'The child is a young girl who can read and count. And the dog guarded our herds for years until she died.'

'So it's a story of a dog's valour and honour you're telling me.'

'Indeed. Dogs, like other animals, are God's creatures and share some of our traits, although they're spared many of our vices.'

'Do you mean you don't remember any nice story of "valour and honour" about humans?'

'Certainly I do, but I need longer to think of one.'

He cut up his trencher and ate it to the last mouthful. This beautiful gesture of a humble man who knows the bite of true hunger made Agnès even sadder.

'Guillette is to be strung up at dawn. The chief bailiff will honour his promise and her death throes will be brief. She … she begs you to forgive her.'

The Comtesse pursed her lips in an expression of uncertainty. She thought for a moment.

'In all conscience, why would I? Only God can absolve her. You see, if a stranger had tried to hurt me, I'd forgive them without hesitation, for the love of the Saviour. But Guillette showed me such kindness with the sole aim of killing me slowly, slyly,[145] in the worst possible way.'

'If I were addressing any other woman, I wouldn't dare say what I am about to.' Leone hesitated. 'But they will not stop here, Madame. Other killers will soon draw near. I shudder with terror as I say this.'

'I'm fully aware of that,' she replied in a detached tone.

'As well as finding Clément, I must discover who is organising Benedetti's base acts against you. The camerlingo cannot be acting all the way from Rome, so he must have enlisted the services of an associate, or even a cunning accomplice who is highly intelligent and formidable. If this person could be eliminated, Benedetti would have trouble overcoming this defeat, which would give us the chance to act and counter him directly this time.'

'It's some vile creature that's been prowling around us for years and we haven't even seen its shadow. How do you intend to go about it?'

'I have no shortage of allies,' said Leone, sidestepping the issue, thinking of Clair Gresson and his spies.

He paused when Benoîte came in to serve the next course, crayfish in jelly.

'I have eaten my fill, Madame. Many thanks for your generosity. For the love of Christ, give the rest of my meal to the poor.'

'I've also lost my appetite. Tomorrow I leave for Alençon,' she said in a tone that brooked no contradiction.

'Certainly not,' Leone replied abruptly. 'You'd make it easier for them.'

'I'm going to my husband, to get him out of jail.'

'Madame, don't you know their tricks and lies yet? Florin … Florin had to be murdered in order to get you out of their clutches. Artus made his decision in full consciousness. Refusing this confrontation would be tantamount to giving you up to them. He knew that, and has acted like a man of honour and love.'

'If they want me that much, they'll free my husband.'

'Madame, they want to kill you.'

'Didn't you say that to accept the idea of dying is to stifle fear? That it would then sheepishly retreat? I leave tomorrow at dawn.'

'No.'

'I beg your pardon?'

'No.' Leone closed his eyes and swept his dark-blond hair back. 'Madame, my life's task and only purpose is to watch over you. I would die for you, Madame. I will not allow you to dispose of your life on a whim, no matter how brave and loving it might be …' Then, in a suddenly icy tone, he added, 'Stand up, Madame. I'm taking you back to your room.'

'What—'

'I hate myself for what I intend to do. It would be pointless to beg your forgiveness, so I will spare you that. Stand up, Madame. You'll remain confined to your apartments and I will guard the door. You will not go to Alençon and throw yourself into the lion's den. I swear it before God. Monseigneur d'Authon has sacrificed himself knowing perfectly well what he was doing.'

'Come now, Monsieur!' Agnès protested. 'Do you mean to treat me like a prisoner in my own home?'

'Indeed, Madame, and I beg you at least to hear me even if you can't forgive me. You are far too precious for me to tolerate your plan. Follow me to your room, Madame. I beg you not to resist, or I shall be obliged to force you, much to my shame. I will warn your chief bailiff immediately and have no doubt that he will second me. Your servants will be forbidden to saddle your horse or hitch up your travelling cart.'

She stood up before him, very straight.

'Don't you even think of forbidding me to help my husband, Monsieur!'

'Not at all, but I won't allow you to throw yourself into the lion's den, when that's exactly what your enemies want. None of us belongs completely to ourselves, Madame. You belong to your husband, to your two sons, a little also to me, and to all those who love you and are ready to perish so that you might live. Above all, you belong to a future that was decreed by the most almighty powers. Now follow me, I beg of you.'

'Why is it that I don't hate you?' Agnès asked, with surprise in her voice.

'Maybe because a part of you knows that I'm right. Come, Madame.'

Agnès followed him with a meekness that puzzled her. Leone had seen correctly. One part of her would have rushed to the aid of her love, while another was calculating, evaluating. She had to remain here in order to protect Clémence and little Philippe. If she presented herself at the Inquisition headquarters, they would never let her out again, but would not, for all that, free Artus. Then Clémence would have no one to turn to if she were in danger. And danger was near. Leone's admission over supper had confirmed Agnès's gut feeling. Although the little girl would be coming of age in a few weeks' time, she was not yet twelve. Leone pushed the door open and stood aside to let her through. 'Madame, I'd hate to have to bolt the door. Do I have your word before God that you will not try to leave the chateau?'

'You have my word, knight. And may I be damned if I go back on it.'

'Very well. I wish you a good night.'

But it was not so. Sinister thoughts preoccupied her until dawn. They had tried to kill her three times to ensure that she would never conceive again. No doubt they would try again. They were after Clémence only because they hoped to recover the manuscripts. If they discovered that she was a girl, they would hunt her down like an animal. One question had been haunting her for months. How could a little girl, with no support and no money, survive alone, when the camerlingo's henchmen were trying relentlessly to track her down?

It was bitterly cold in Agnan's office early that morning. The young clerk had stuffed his hands into the sleeves of his ugly homespun habit in the vain hope of warming them up. He was listening attentively to Brother Vieuvie, who was sitting before him. His chubby, cheerful face inspired trust. His large, myopic eyes seemed to rest on everything with benevolence. The Dominican Henri Vieuvie had come to ask the Inquisition headquarters for help, as authorised by the mission note given to him by the camerlingo Honorius Benedetti. The monk had spent the last quarter of an hour getting tangled up in such vague explanations that Agnan struggled to follow him. Evidently, Brother Vieuvie had no wish to reveal the exact nature of his mission, while attempting to acquire information.

'My brother in Christ,' Agnan tried to sum up, 'if I understand you correctly, you're looking for a stringed-instrument maker and yet not really looking for him.'

The other man sighed with what might have been relief or annoyance – Agnan could not tell.

'In a way,' he replied, hesitating. 'Of course, I'm being helped in my task by three laymen … since my habit and my tonsure are too obvious … Still, how can I put this … We must exercise the utmost discretion.'

'But why, since we're talking about a heretic here?' Agnan asked, intrigued by the other man's palpable embarrassment but treading carefully.

Brother Vieuvie tried clumsily to evade the question.

'Your knowledge of the city – I'm told you were born here – and of its inhabitants makes you very valuable to me. We're looking for a stringed-instrument maker. He'd be about your age, perhaps a little older, and they say he is puny and ...' He hesitated, looking away from the secretary, then continued, '... and very ugly. These characteristics should give you an idea.'

Agnan thought as fast as he could. Why did Henri Vieuvie and his laymen not simply go and see all the stringed-instrument makers in town? The power of the Church, represented by the Dominican opposite him, authorised them to do so. In order to prevent word from spreading, and the man they were after being warned and escaping. In other words, the story provided by the brother did not add up. Nobody would help a heretic, unless he was willing to become his accomplice and risk an almost equally severe punishment. Brows knitted, pretending to think things over, Agnan sidestepped the issue.

'Well, there are three stringed-instrument makers in our city. The first one is so old that he's not the man you're looking for. The second one is middle-aged, and such a mountain of a man that one wonders how his coarse fingers can produce the delicate marvels he is renowned for. The third one could match your description, although he is rather handsome. I think Alençon is probably not the city where this henchman of Satan is hiding, brother, unless he's changed profession.'

Agnan was certain that God would forgive him his lie. Since Madame de Souarcy's trial, he had been sickened by the schemes, lies and traps of the Inquisition. It was good and right not to take part in them, and even to oppose them for the glory of the Holy Lamb.

A look of disappointment mixed with mute anger spread across his interlocutor's face, suddenly making him less agreeable.

Agnan enjoyed his little victory. He, a hard-working little ant, was contributing to the eternal battle for the Light. And the Light was intoxicating, as Agnan had discovered when he had met Madame de Souarcy, who shone with it, though she was not even aware of it. Having come close to the Light and been sustained by it, albeit briefly, had produced in him an irreversible transformation and a deep-rooted revulsion for the shadows. And if anyone ever reproached him for having described the stringed-instrument maker Denis Laforge as 'handsome', he would reply that everything was relative. For once, his own ugliness would serve him well. In truth, compared to Agnan, Lafarge could claim to have a plain appearance but was not particularly ugly.

Vieuvie left shortly afterwards, without even thanking him. Agnan was exultant. Agnès would be proud of him. He decided to follow his rebellion through.

He waited until sext, unable to concentrate on his work, which consisted in endlessly copying recent trial papers. Then Agnan left the Inquisition headquarters, walking calmly like a lowly secretary. He headed towards Rue de la Poêle-Percée and walked into the Auberge du Chat-Borgne, where he usually had his midday meal. The grub that passed for a meal there lacked refinement but was edible and affordable. In addition, Maître Borgne would serve him generous portions, so he could eat his fill and save on supper. No doubt the man was seeking forgiveness for a long and venial life, his past excesses betrayed by his drunkard's face and large belly. The Chat-Borgne also prided itself on two other assets that were unknown to the shadow that had been following Agnan since he had left the Inquisition headquarters but which, in his state of alert, he had immediately noticed.

Maître Borgne rushed towards him.

'It's quite a treat today! Fish stew with bittersweet sauce. I'm sure you'll like it. The fish was fresh, with bright eyes.'

'Seigneur Borgne, please come closer. I want to confide a church secret.'

Flattered and thinking that he was taking a step closer to

heaven, the tavern keeper sat down at the table and leant towards Agnan.

'I repeat, this is a secret.'

'I'm as silent as the grave.'

'A Grand Inquisitor has given me a task of the utmost importance. I'm being followed ... by enemies of our faith,' he added for good measure.

His mouth half open, the other man encouraged him with small nods.

'I must use your privy ... and come back only when your wonderful food is served piping on the table.'

'I understand.'

'If, in the meantime, some vile scoundrels who are trying to stop me from fulfilling my mission were to question you, tell them I have answered the call of nature and that it usually causes me lengthy embarrassment.'

'Er ...?'

'In other words, that I usually have persistent constipation.'

Having finally understood, the innkeeper laughed, and his large face, purple from decades of looking into the bottom of a tankard, lit up.

'It can happen to any of us to have to push and push! Don't worry. I lie so well that sometimes even I can't remember what the truth is. I'll prepare your fish with bittersweet sauce while you go and answer the call of nature, brother,' he said, laughing heartily.

Agnan left through the back door and headed quickly towards the wooden hut with the privy – a hole dug in the ground. He climbed over the wall and emerged in a street parallel to Rue Poêle-Percée. He lifted his habit above his ankles with both hands, and ran.

The second advantage of the Chat-Borgne was its geographical location, fifty yards from the workshop of the stringed-instrument maker Denis Laforge. Without even catching his breath, he pushed the door open. Laforge was bent over a lyre with a broken pegbox. He automatically looked up and smiled. Agnan got straight to the point. Time was of the essence.

'They're looking for you. An Inquisition Dominican and some laymen. I recognised you immediately from their description.'

The instrument maker turned pale, obviously not surprised by the news.

'God Almighty, will this never end?' Sulpice de Brabeuf murmured gently.

'They're trying to make out that you're a dangerous heretic. If they arrest you, they'll keep you in a secret place and nobody will be able to help you. As for evidence, they'll invent it. They're experienced at that. I don't know why they're looking for you so assiduously but we've no time to discuss it. My advice is to run away as quickly as you can. I think I've delayed them with my lies.'

The former monk from the monastery of Vallombroso studied Agnan's face.

'Why are you helping me? You're a Dominican, and if they find out you betrayed them—'

'For the love of God, brother. So that the Light might shine.'

Having said that, he ran back to the Chat-Borgne. The wooden soles of his clogs slid on the uneven flagstones but he did not care. He felt as though he had wings and was being transported by an immense force. Although he was so skinny and puny, he was only slightly out of breath when he sat down before his piping-hot fish with bittersweet sauce. Maître Borgne reassured him. Nobody had enquired after him during his brief absence.

Contrary to the tavern keeper's optimistic assurances – which bordered on swindling – the food smelt like old, leftover market fish. Despite the large amount of ginger and cardamom, and a generous helping of vinegar which Maître Borgne had hoped would cover the smell, it gave off a strange odour. No matter. Victory had increased Agnan's appetite.

When the young clerk came back out an hour later, the shadow followed him at a distance back to the Inquisition headquarters.

A mischievous smile on his lips, he sat back down at his work table. He had another one of his tricks in store for them this evening.

Rue Saint-Amour, Chartres, October 1306

Early that morning, Madame de Neyrat summoned Mathilde to her chamber. Propped up on her cosy pillows, in her fine nightclothes and with her puff of blonde hair, she looked like a good fairy. Before coming to the point, she said, 'My room seemed like a discreet place, my dear. Angélique must on no account know the nature of our alliance.'

'You have my word, Madame,' Mathilde murmured, flattered by this pact that bound just the two of them.

'Come and sit by me.'

Mathilde sat on the bed and marvelled at the smooth, milky skin of Aude's arms.

'Yesterday, I received the information that was still missing. My dear friend, the time for your revenge is finally approaching, and you deserve it. I need to go away for two days to see to my affairs. As soon as I return, I'll explain in detail what I expect of you as a friend. Think about it, Mathilde ... Soon, the world will be your oyster.'

Of course, you'll have to poison your mother first, Madame de Neyrat added to herself, so don't leave me in the lurch, you little goose!

It was a radically different plan from the one she had previously proposed to Mathilde, who would have been content to ruin her mother's future for ever. There is a world of difference between causing someone's ruin and murder. She would have to play it very carefully in order to manoeuvre Mathilde to the conclusion that it was really just a trifle. Still, she trusted the girl's favourable disposition and the fact that her one true passion was herself. Only the first cold-blooded murder matters to the person who breaks the laws of God and those, less stern but also less clear-cut, of men. There is only one option, in that case. Relentless remorse that eats away at you day and night. The kind that Honorius Benedetti had been suffering for ages. Either that, or a sort of rebellious excitement at having transgressed as others had not. The murders that follow become just simple copies – trifles.

'Soon, you'll go to your mother as a loving and repentant daughter. I wager she's so desperate to find you that she'll swallow all your lies whole. You should find it easy. I'll miss you so much, my dear friend,' Madame de Neyrat said, placing her fine, beautiful hand on her heart. 'Still, let's be thankful that it'll be only a brief separation and that we'll be together again very soon.'

Half an hour later, when Mathilde left her benefactress's room, she was so happy and excited that she did not see a faint shadow quickly bend down behind the tall chest. Crouching, tight-lipped, Angélique waited for the sound of her footsteps to die away at the bottom of the stairs before standing up again.

'Look what I've made for you, Mademoiselle. Black nougat with pieces of hazelnut and almond, and cinnamon, to go with your evening malmsey.'

The child was so silly. How many times did one have to tell her that a young lady did not stoop to fiddling with pots and pans in the kitchen! But of course she was nothing more than a beggar who had had the immense privilege of being picked out by Madame de Neyrat, despite her grime. Even so!

Mathilde's irritation had done nothing but increase and blossom since her protector's departure that morning. This Angélique and her sickly-sweet attentions really got on her nerves. The little girl overdid it with her consideration. However, since their recent discussion, she had been doing her best not to annoy Mathilde and followed her around less, but that was no use since it was her very existence that drove Mathilde to distraction.

Still, she would be rid of her in a few days' time, so she forced herself to be affable.

'How very kind of you. Nougat. One of my little foibles.'

Angélique blushed with happiness and curtseyed. She placed the wooden board with a handle on the pedestal table, next to the glass of malmsey.

'I will let you enjoy your treat in peace and quiet, Mademoiselle.'

Mathilde sighed with relief at the prospect of resuming the daydream that never left her: about herself, what she would become, and do.

That night, Mathilde woke up with an unbearable pain. She tried getting up to call for help but collapsed on her bed, moaning. She slid to the floor, trying to hold on to the sheets, which were soaked in perspiration and pinkish fluid. She wanted to scream but the pain made it impossible. She dragged herself to the door, dripping with sweat, sobbing with terror, shaken by violent nausea. A jet of blood poured from her mouth. Fighting for breath, she managed to emit a weak cry. Light footsteps approached her door.

'Help me, please … a fit.'

The door partly opened and Angélique's face appeared in the chink.

The little girl rushed to her. She panicked when she saw the pool of blood darkening the pale floorboards.

'Oh, my God … My God! I'll run for help … the physician …'

She ran out of the room, abandoning Mathilde, who was slumped on her side, writhing in pain.

Two manservants managed to put her on the bed. A maidservant insisted on dabbing her forehead with a wet cloth until the physician, roused from sleep, finally arrived. Mathilde was as pale as wax. Semi-conscious, she was hardly complaining any more. She occasionally groaned, trying to take in a deep breath. The physician felt her belly and her throat and recommended bleeding her in order to lighten her humours.

Mathilde de Souarcy passed away early in the morning without regaining consciousness, shortly after Madame de Neyrat's chaplain had hastily given her the last rites.

Pale and tired, Angélique went back to her room. After bolting the door, she leant against it and put her hand over her pretty mouth to stifle the giggle that had been threatening to erupt for the past hour. The physician had assisted her by recommending bleeding when that pretentious bitch was already bleeding profusely thanks to the crushed glass she had added to the nougat, hoping that the pieces of hazelnut would explain the hard bits between Mathilde's teeth, in case she wondered about them.

Two protégées was one too many. Angélique had no intention of sharing her adopted mother's generosity with a bossy goose. She had been a good pupil and had benefited from the vile knowledge imparted by the witch. She took out of her armoire the little box she had brought with her when she had left the witch's hovel. All those years, she had rotted there, waiting for an opportunity to escape for ever. Why did they all want to make her their child, anyway? Still, she was not complaining. She looked at the thin booklet blackened with the witch's sinister recipes – recipes that were very much of this world and aimed at killing someone more or less slowly – as well as the little bottles. Which poison would she use on the Neyrat woman when she no longer needed her? Perhaps in a few years' time … She did not know yet. She had much to learn before then; as well as getting herself loved by the woman so that she would inherit her name and riches, she would also charm her to the point of making her lose her common sense and caution.

When, the following day, Aude de Neyrat returned, her rage was mixed with incomprehension. Delighted by her 'mother's' display of nerves, Angélique, huddled in an armchair in the small reading room, pretended to snivel and twisted her hands in distress.

'It's enough to drive you out of your wits!' Madame de Neyrat roared at her physician, forsaking her usual elegant composure. 'Only fourteen years old, and died from a fit, you say?'

'Yes, Madame,' he replied in a knowledgeable tone. 'Do you know if she was prone to them as a child?'

'I don't know and I don't care!'

'The violent spasms that shook Mademoiselle d'Ongeval triggered intestinal bleeding.'

'Then why on earth did you bleed her for so long, as my daughter and servants have reported?'

'Madame,' he replied, taking offence, 'it's how one proceeds in such circumstances.' Wishing to act as a teacher, the physician explained, 'There are different types of blood. There is black harmful blood that must be drained through bleeding, and pure dynamic blood that must be preserved. Bleeding allows us to get rid of one, to the benefit of the other.'

'Leave me, Monsieur. I need to think.'

'What about the burial? We were waiting to receive your orders.'

'As soon and as simply as possible – I have enough on my plate as it is,' Aude de Neyrat snapped.

'We should inform the next of kin of your late protégée, and—'

'I appreciate your concern but it's unnecessary. Mathilde d'Ongeval was ... was an orphan, which is why I took her under my protection. Take care of the arrangements. I must think now, I tell you.'

Once the physician had left, she gave free rein to her foul

mood. 'She simply had to go and annoy me to the very end, didn't she?' she exploded.

In truth, Madame de Neyrat was beginning to panic. With Mathilde dead, how was she going to keep her word of honour to the camerlingo? An unpleasant but persistent doubt was worming its way into her mind. There were so many and such implacable coincidences that she was struck by a kind of superstitious fear. Did this Agnès de Souarcy enjoy divine protection, for all the attempts against her to fail like this? Strangely, she could not bring herself to hate her, let alone curse her. It is true that hatred is a most powerful feeling, as is love, and Madame de Neyrat did not trust either, so had excluded them from her life. Only recently had she found tenderness again, thanks to Angélique. Love, true love, would come soon, she felt. What could she think up in order to get rid of this Authon woman once and for all? Not Angélique. She could have trained her to become a fearsome poisoner thanks to her age and her pure appearance. Never. Angélique would be protected from all this wickedness. Aude would see to that. An idea entered her confused mind. What about her? Neither Agnès d'Authon nor her entourage knew her. She would just have to avoid meeting any of the nuns from Clairets. After all, if you want a task done well, you have to do it yourself, especially when it comes to crime.

'Damn that foolish maiden!' she burst out, stamping her foot. 'If she were still alive, I'd happily slap her to soothe my anger.'

A plaintive sniff could be heard.

'Oh, my sweet ... I'm burdening you with foolish tales.' Forcing a cheerfulness she was far from feeling, Madame de Neyrat said, 'Come, my dearest, let me read you a fairy tale. A tale about a beautiful princess, like you. And beautiful princesses should never concern themselves with ugly things.'

Rue de la Poêle-Percée, Chartres, October 1306

H is leather apron still tied around his waist, the metal beater was waiting, drinking his glass of wine in small sips. He had carefully folded his cloak, made of thick wool and lined with rabbit fur, and placed it on the chair opposite him. A clear message to the Chat-Borgne regulars that he did not wish for company, especially not that of some lonely chatterbox whose desire for conversation would lead him to sit at his table, then ask if his presence bothered him.

At last, the man he was waiting for pushed open the tavern door and he welcomed him with a discreet smile.

Agnan took off his cloak, soaked by the downpour, and gave a sigh of relief before murmuring, 'Kni—'

'Hush – I'm François here. Sit down, my dear Agnan. I thank God for the joy of seeing you again.'

'As for me, the letters we exchanged after you left for Cyprus, in which I gave you any news I was able to gather about the Comtesse, were a great comfort. François … do you know that I had to end up in the Inquisition headquarters, swarming with people, to discover the desert of solitude? It is strange, isn't it, that I suddenly realised I had no friend, nobody to confide in, except you, whom I'd only known a few hours, and who was so far away?'

'Strange? I think not. We have the friends we deserve. After all, you were living an orderly existence, determined by the laws and commands of others. Your friends were like you. With no regard for your own safety, you joined me in an endless fight against the dark forces. Few people wish to be part of it. They vaguely feel that we are not like them and stay away from us because we bring turmoil to their minds. I don't blame them.

However, you and I are not alone, Agnan. We're a multitude. Let's raise a glass to the greatness of men.'

One evening, two years earlier, Leone had invited the young clerk to dine at the Auberge de la Jument-Rouge. The worse for drink, Agnan had made a clean breast of his disappointment and the remorse that was beginning to eat away at him for having taken part, even from a distance, in what he described as infamy. Stammering from anxiety and hippocras, tears in his eyes, he had confessed his wilful blindness. After all, he had known, without admitting it, that many of the Inquisition procedures were nothing but sinister, bloody farces. The purpose of the Inquisition was to terrorise and nip any idea of disobedience in the bud, and in that it succeeded brilliantly. When he had set upon the noble Agnès de Souarcy, the diabolical Nicolas Florin had, in the process, opened Agnan's eyes. Nothing more. Leone had studied his small stone-marten face. A consuming passion shone in his eyes. Strangely, he had not in the least doubted the clerk's ardent faith and considerable strength. Strangely, even though their paths had only just crossed, the knight's customary caution had abandoned him. Dropping his voice to a barely audible whisper, he had told Agnan about the quest, and about the extraordinary importance of Agnès de Souarcy, of her future daughter, of the different blood they would pass on until the Second Coming. Overwhelmed, the young secretary had stared at him, speechless, for a long time. Finally, he whispered, 'So I was right. Madame de Souarcy is an angel who has transformed my pathetic, ant-like life. My slender means, but also my obstinacy ... my life, knight, is yours. Yours and theirs – hers and that of her daughter who is to be born.'

Thus, Agnan had joined the troops of the shadows of light, who had been hiding for centuries in order to protect the Second Coming. Over that dinner, Leone had decided that the young man would remain at the Inquisition headquarters so that he could keep an eye on their closest enemies. As for Agnès de Souarcy, Agnan would be on the alert for the slightest detail concerning her, and would inform Leone, who had to return to the Cypriot citadel of Limassol as soon as possible.

Agnan quickly told him about the Dominican Henri Vieuvie's visit, and about having warned the stringed-instrument maker Denis Laforge.

'Why does he need the help of the Inquisition headquarters to the extent of actually demanding it if – and you seem certain of this – he is not a heretic?' Leone asked.

'Absolutely not. However, since the mission note was signed by the camerlingo, we must assume that Laforge has links with what has been concerning us for years. I couldn't wait for you to come to Alençon. They were about to arrest him. I also advised him to escape immediately, without asking him any questions.'

'You did the right thing,' Leone reassured him. 'What about Monseigneur d'Authon?'

'He's rotting in his cell. Still, he's being treated with respect. I think Jacques du Pilais, the Grand Inquisitor in charge of his interrogation, is a man of honour and seems very embarrassed. He definitely wanted to know the truth about the wedding ring that was so conveniently discovered at the scene of the crime two years after the event. And yet, using procedure as authorisation, he's continuing with this farce. If he wanted him to, Monseigneur d'Authon could spend the rest of his life in that dungeon.'

'He's obeying orders,' Leone said. 'But I'm surprised they didn't pick another Florin to see their heinous schemes through. The kind of inquisitor who has no scruples about manipulating evidence and testimonies.'

'Pilais isn't that sort, I'd swear it. He's a stern, austere man but not an unjust one.'

'Then they've made a mistake in choosing him, which is

another proof that God is watching over us.'

'I have no doubt about that,' Agnan replied. 'I think Pilais was chosen because he's the cousin of Monseigneur d'Évreux, the King's half-brother. The order Monseigneur d'Authon received to present himself at the Inquisition hearing came from the hand of a sovereign eager to secure the favour of Clément V. The Bishop of Évreux must have hoped that Jacques du Pilais, placed under his direct authority, would do his cousin d'Évreux a favour by proving to be extremely rigorous with the Comte d'Authon, even if that involved falsifying the charges.'

'I think you're right,' the knight said. 'Still, I'm afraid for Madame d'Authon's life, Agnan. Benedetti could have entrusted her poisoning only to a dependable and intimate accomplice. I must find my way to him and destroy him. Of course, that will not mean that the war is over, since I'm sure Benedetti will replace him sooner or later, but it will give us some breathing space.'

'Do you think this accomplice is in Alençon?'

'I don't know, but there aren't many large cities nearby where you can blend into the crowd, recruit killers and hatch plots.'

'Alençon and Chartres. Authon-du-Perche would be highly imprudent. As for Mortagne, it's a small town, so a stranger would immediately stand out. I'll take care of Alençon, François.'

'And I'll take Chartres. I hope to see you again very soon, my friend.'

'Please God.'

Château d'Authon-du-Perche, Perche, October 1306

An almost suffocating silence. The cold, grey light of a late winter's afternoon. The acrid smell of altar candles. Footsteps echoing on the brown flagstones.

Francesco de Leone glided through the interminable ambulatory of the church. His black coat, ornamented with a cross, its eight branches fused together in pairs, flapped around his leather boots.

He was following a silently moving figure, her presence betrayed only by the soft rustle of fabric, a yellow robe of heavy silk. A woman, a woman hiding. A woman almost the same height as he. The candle flames cast an intermittent glow on her undulating hair. A silky wave descending below her knees and merging with her dress. Hair with a copper sheen, like honey. A sudden breathlessness made Leone gasp with pain, even as the icy chill froze his lips.

With his left hand he tried to wipe away the sweat running down his brow, stinging his eyes, and scratched his face with his gauntlet. Why was he wearing it? Was he about to go into combat?

Gradually he had become accustomed to the semi-darkness. By the dim light filtering in through the dome and the flickering candlelight, he strained to see into the enveloping gloom obscuring the columns and engulfing the walls. What church was he in? Did it matter? It was a smallish church, and yet he had been circling inside it for what seemed like hours.

He was chasing the woman, without urgency. Why? She did not try to run away, but maintained an equal distance between them. She kept a few steps ahead of him, as though anticipating his movements, staying on the outside of the ambulatory while he moved along on the inside.

He paused. A step, one step, and then she stopped. The sound of steady breathing. The woman's breathing. As he moved off again so did his shadow.

Francesco de Leone's hand reached slowly for the pommel of his sword even as a feeling of tenderness made him gasp. He looked down incredulously at his right hand clutching the metal sphere. He had aged terribly. Great veins bulged beneath the wrinkled skin.

Suddenly he was aware of a third presence hiding in the darkness. A bloody, murderous presence. A ruthless presence. The woman had stopped. Had she sensed the ferocious shadow? A voice murmured: 'Help me, knight, for the love of God.' A pale feminine hand brushed the sleeve of his long tunic, causing him to tremble with almost intolerable delight. The other hand disappeared into the folds of her dress and emerged clutching the handle of a glinting short sword. He hadn't noticed that she was armed. He whispered, 'I will give my life for you, Madame,' then turned slowly towards her. The saffron yellow of her silk dress was stretched tightly over her belly. She was with child. Ready for battle in order to protect the fruit of her womb. The child all the evil spectres wished to destroy. Leone looked up at the fine heart-shaped face, and the blue-green eyes searching the menacing darkness. He knew that face. He knew it well. Yet he could not remember exactly where he had seen it.

She raised the short sword and pointed east, at one of the apses studding the circumference of the church. There was no aggressiveness in the whisper which said, 'It's the woman who must be killed. She's the one who gives them their orders, even though she has almost forgotten that she was on the side of evil.'

Leone frowned, uncertain, and walked slowly towards the little chapel. A profusion of candles cast some light onto the darkness. Before the statue of a serene Virgin presenting the Divine Child to the world, a woman was kneeling. A woman so beautiful and calm that she seemed to be another vessel for endless love. Without haste, she stood up and stretched her hand out towards him, smiling. She *opened her mouth, as though about to welcome him into that place. A stream of red blood trickled down her chin, dripping languidly onto the front of her white dress.*

Leone suddenly opened his eyes, and with some difficulty recognised the little room above the stables where he was staying. He struggled to sit up in bed. Strange. Usually, this recurring dream upset him so much he would wake up drenched in sweat, his heart racing, the blood throbbing in the veins of his neck. But not today. Instead, he felt a kind of inexorable calm. The kind of calm that precedes a battle, when the die has been cast, and nothing can change the present any more.

A blonde woman with eyes like emeralds. A woman who looked like an angel. A fallen angel. Her face was indelibly etched in Leone's memory.

The dream had turned from obsessive premonition to a message of war.

The upper part of his body naked, he splashed his face and bathed his arms in the cold water of the alveus. The shudders that ran through him chased the remnants of sleep from his mind. He called out to a farm boy, and ordered that his horse be saddled and two days' worth of food be prepared for him.

Agnès was reading in the library. True to her word, the only walks she had allowed herself had been from one end of the large garden to the other.

'Madame, urgent business requires my attention. I'm going to Chartres and will probably remain there for several days.'

She nodded in agreement.

'With your permission, Monge de Brineux will stay at the chateau during my absence.'

She replied, amused, 'I'm no longer a child whose hand needs holding, knight.'

'They're not children either, Madame.'

'I know. I must go to Souarcy to see my people, Monsieur. Since I've given you my word not to leave the chateau grounds, I need you to grant me an exemption.'

'You have it, Madame. However, I need your promise that your trip will be limited to your manor and back, and that you'll be escorted by at least two of the Comte's armed guards.'

'I promise, Monsieur, upon my honour.'

In the kitchens, he ate a piece of cheese and a slice of bread spread with suet, then jumped into the saddle.

The fallen angel was in Chartres. He had sensed it even before he discovered that it was a woman. Now he was certain of it. He must not think of her as a woman, since he had to kill her.

As he rode, Leone was gripped by deep anguish. Had he been wrong to allow Agnès to go to Souarcy? The roads were not safe, even if she had an escort. Of course, the lady would defend herself bravely, but what could she do if faced with five or six brigands or hired killers? Still, she would be protected by her two armed guards and, besides, nobody knew she was planning to go to her manor.

Leone was seized by a desire to see Clairets again and to relive, however briefly, that moment of total bliss when he had discovered the incomprehensible manuscript. He was galloping past the enormous abbey. Unable to resist, he turned off the road.

Leone dismounted outside the main entrance of Clairets after nones. He felt a pang in his heart at the memory of the beautiful smile of his aunt and adoptive mother Éleusie de Beaufort, the former Abbess who had been poisoned within these walls.

The elegant Éleusie, who would burst out laughing like a girl when her dress got tangled up around her ankles and made her trip as she was teaching him to play *soule*. Sometimes, on a summer's evening, she would point a slender finger at the brightest star and, her eyes closed in sorrow and affection, say, 'Say goodnight to your mother, my sweetheart.'

'Is that star my mother?'

'Of course. It's my sister, my Claire, the brightest of all.'

Éleusie had met with a terrible death within these walls when all she had wanted to find here was peace.

Leone fought back the hatred he felt surging within him. Éleusie de Beaufort would not have tolerated it.

With his forehead pressed against the spy-hole in the door, he had to provide lengthy explanations to convince an obtuse lay porteress of the purity of his intentions, and that he was a Knight Hospitaller.

'Then where's your surcoat with the eight-pointed cross?' she asked, mistrustful.

'I'm travelling incognito, on the instructions of my order. May I please see your new Abbess for a few minutes?' the knight repeated for the twentieth time.

The porteress looked down and examined him through the

grid. 'Except for the way you speak and your travelling boots, you look more like a beggar to me!'

Curbing his exasperation, Francesco de Leone insisted politely, 'Could you please send for the apothecary sister, Annelette Beaupré? She knows me very well and will vouch for me.'

'Our Mother Superior?'

'Annelette?'

'Well, yes – she's our Mother Superior now, thank God. She's not someone you'd want to upset! Other than that, she's a sweet, compassionate angel towards us. A real angel, I tell you.'

Hearing this seraphic description – and had he not been struggling to contain his irritation – Leone would have doubted they were talking about the same Annelette Beaupré.

'Will you please go and tell her, then?'

The lay porteress's eyes narrowed and she pursed her lips like a hen's bottom. 'Er … I'll go.'

The spy-hole was shut abruptly, notifying the visitor that the conversation was over.

Not three minutes later, a hurricane blew out through the forbidding door. A tall woman rushed towards him, arms open.

'Sweet Jesus, Mother of God … What joy! Oh, I am so happy … knight … knight …'

Such happy ardour made the knight smile.

'Reverend Mother, I'm so lucky, so relieved to see you again. To tell the truth, I've so often thought of you and missed you. I couldn't have hoped for anything better for Clairets than your being elected abbess.'

The former apothecary was bursting with pride.

'Oh, I don't deserve such praise! But please come in … What are we doing standing around the front door like a pair of broomsticks! Our lovely Elisaba will bring you a meal and an invigorating infusion in the study.'

He followed her along endless corridors. The vaults, so high they vanished in the shadows, echoed with their footsteps, and the steam of their breath blended together. Francesco de Leone stopped without meaning to before entering the large study where he had often visited his aunt. Annelette gave him a sad smile.

'I know how you feel. I also … I feel so comfortable in this study, it calms me and gives me support. Here, I spend my days and a large part of my nights in friendly company. And yet I feel as though I'm trespassing.'

'Nobody else would have been better suited to take her place than you, my dear Reverend Mother. The wonderful Éleusie loved you as one of her daughters, of course, but also as a friend.'

Annelette walked around the heavy work table and stared far into space before she admitted, 'I've always been foolishly vain enough to think I was stronger than the others. However, I must confess that I miss your aunt terribly.'

Searching for any pretext at all to dispel the emotional moment that made her vulnerable, she picked up a wad of papers, burst out laughing and exclaimed, 'And all these papers, lists, cartularies, registers … It never ends! It's enough to drive the most meticulous woman insane! In addition, my sight is deteriorating … I have to write holding my quill at arm's length and sitting back. Of course, our bishop has promised to bring me back a pair of besicles[146] when he next goes to Italy. I'm going to look like a wretched invalid!'

'Everybody else keeps it a secret, but you talk of it so openly,' said Leone, trying to comfort her. 'I think you'll do very well with this tool which few of us will manage to escape.'

'It's true that everybody's eyesight gets weaker as they get older. I don't see why people need to pretend they can see as well as a small child. That they're still young and vigorous.'

A surprising smile, which Leone had never seen, made the stern face he had in the past found to be surly look younger. She said again, in a whisper, 'I'm happy you're here. It's like a gift from heaven. However, I fear that your duty calls you and that, sadly, you won't be staying here long.'

'When our quest is successful, Reverend Mother, I shall come back for longer.'

'Will it ever be successful?' Annelette asked, without a trace of bitterness.

'Perhaps not in our lifetime. God only knows, and I put my trust in Him.'

'Amen.'

A young kitchen *semainier*[147] nun knocked at the door.

'Enter!' Annelette replied in a stentorian voice.

Somewhat anxiously, the young nun placed a tray on the floor, next to the armchair where the knight was sitting, and said, 'Reverend Mother, our kind Elisaba Ferron begs to know if she has been too stingy in feeding your guest. If so, a second helping will be brought to him.'

Leone looked down. This Elisaba must have been used to feeding hungry men in her lay past. There were five thick slices of bread and suet, covered so generously in smoked trout fillets that you could barely see them. A huge chunk of sheep's cheese formed the second course, and, to finish, a dish of dried fruit soaked in wine.

'By Jove!' Leone exclaimed. 'There's enough here to fill the bellies of two hungry men.'

The *semainier* nun disappeared. As a soldier familiar with hunger, Leone asked, 'Might I take the rest of this feast to help me on my journey?'

'Gladly. It's a gift from God and it's wonderful to share it with you. Now tell me the reason for your visit.'

'The pleasure of seeing you again—'

She interrupted him, certain that this was not just a simple courtesy.

'Is it the other manuscripts of the secret library? The ones you didn't take with you? Rest assured that I'm guarding them and nobody had better try and play any tricks on me!'

He burst out laughing. He found the energy of this intelligent woman, capable of moving mountains in spite of her age, invigorating. 'They'd be foolish to try,' he said. Then, growing serious again, he searched for the right words. 'Reverend Mother,' he said, 'I've been having a dream, the same recurring dream for many years. The details are not important, but I want to say that it's becoming more and more specific, and also increasingly cruel ...'

Resting her elbows on the desk, she leant towards him, not missing a word.

'Last night, another character appeared, emerging from the shadows of a church apse. The dream had never revealed her to me before ... You'll think that I'm losing my mind but ... I got it into my head that you are the only person able to help me solve this riddle. With your intelligence, your knowledge ...'

At any other time, Annelette would have purred with delight. For her, intelligence was God's supreme gift. However, Leone's gravity made her forget the happiness this kind of compliment generally brought her.

'Knight ... I beg your pardon, my son – I can't get used to this ... dreams are not necessarily premonitions. Some are nothing more than muddled ideas and memories that our mind reconstructs in such an incoherent way that we don't understand anything at all. Then we are very much tempted to see them as prophetic.'

He liked her cut-and-dried scientific way of sweeping away the superstitious jumble most people clung to.

'But some are, aren't they?'

'If I were to trust serious testimonies, from people who have their heads screwed on tight and their feet firmly on the ground, it would seem that some rare dreams are indeed premonitions. I don't know whether they are warnings from God, who chooses to guide us, or an intuition that at night breaks free from the constraints imposed upon it by the mind. Probably both, since our intuition comes from the Lord.'

'This dream does, of that I am certain.'

'Coming from you, I believe it unreservedly.'

'So then, last night, this woman, an abomination, appeared in my dream.'

'Do you know her? I mean, have you ever met her?'

'No. I'd remember if I had. She is breathtakingly beautiful. Tall, slim, with beautiful wavy hair cascading over her shoulders. Eyes like mountain lakes, almond-shaped, emerald-green. She suddenly came out of the apse and as she was about to speak to me, a stream of dark-red blood—'

'Madame de Neyrat!' Annelette burst out. She leapt to her feet, slammed her fist on the heavy oak table and cried, 'That monster ... A demon straight out of hell with the face of an angel. Your dream is a premonition, I can assure you!' She suddenly panicked, slumped into her armchair and buried her face in her hands, stammering, 'Sweet Jesus ... My God ... Holy Mother, watch over us.'

Leone rushed to the desk. Panic-stricken, he begged, 'Reverend Mother, Reverend Mother ... I beseech you, explain yourself.'

She motioned him to be silent. A few moments elapsed which seemed filled with an invisible, malevolent presence.

Then she dropped her hands, half opened her eyes and fixed her pale-blue gaze on Leone. In an oddly detached tone, Annelette Beaupré explained, 'Shortly after your aunt died, an abbess was appointed. Such charm, such friendliness. She displayed such tenderness towards us. But I wasn't fooled. So she made no effort towards me. She's the associate, I tell you – the camerlingo's accomplice. It was she who recruited Jeanne d'Amblin, our old extern sister, to do her dirty work. It was she who poisoned her when she was no longer useful. Did you know she threatened me in order to lay her hands on the manuscripts? They had already left Clairets thanks to the brave Esquive d'Estouville. I confess that Madame Aude de Neyrat was a good loser. She left the abbey as soon as she could to avoid the bailiff's men, and didn't even think to take revenge on me. I can't find the words to describe her. When, earlier, I called her "a demon straight out of hell", don't think I was using an easy set phrase. It's much worse than that. She's neither possessed nor devilish. Strangely, and unlike Jeanne d'Amblin and Blanche de Blinot, I saw no corroding hatred in her, but rather … the combination of these three words to describe a murderess will surprise you but it's the only thing that comes to mind: she has a cheerful and steely determination.'

When Leone left the abbey, he was choked by a deep sense of anguish. Evil was drawing closer. Agnès d'Authon had decided to go to Souarcy. The two armed guards, heavy and clumsy, whom she had promised to requisition, would not be able to fight the scourge with emerald eyes. This woman acted in the shadows, from behind the scenes, and had been doing so for years. She had caused the death of several nuns and of his beloved aunt Éleusie. She had managed to get herself appointed abbess, a mask that would have allowed her to recover the manuscripts on behalf of the camerlingo. She had not hesitated to recruit a so-called witch in order to poison Madame d'Authon without even needing to get close to her. In other words, this was one of the most cunning, most efficient enemies Leone had ever had to face. Yet it was by a simple coincidence, his friendship with Annelette, that Leone had been able to identify her. That, and his dream. God was on their side.

To protect Agnès. For a fleeting moment, he almost postponed his trip to Chartres. But he could not. He had to destroy the very root of evil, to eradicate it as soon as possible so that it would take a long time to be reborn. Because evil is always reborn. To gain time. To gain time in order to save Agnès. To destroy the viper.

Manoir de Souarcy-en-Perche, October 1306

Francesco de Leone reached the large, square towers at nightfall. It was cool and humid. The only sign of life was the light from the torches in the large communal hall, which flickered behind the oilskins concealing the narrow windows.

Leone dismounted and tied the reins of his horse to one of the rings embedded in the wall of an outbuilding.

'We're going to spend the night here, my sweet,' he whispered into the horse's ear. 'It would be imprudent to continue. You'll be well fed and groomed.'

He had to bang his fist on the door several times before a wary voice shouted from behind the thick wooden panel, 'Who's there at this ungodly hour?'

'It's the Knight Hospitaller Francesco de Leone, Adeline. I've been a guest of your mistress and I need hospitality for one night. For myself and my horse.'

He heard the scraping noise of the heavy iron bar that secured the door.

Adeline appeared, and made a curtsey, holding on to the side of the door firmly while at the same time trying to straighten her bonnet, so that she nearly fell sideways.

'Oh, look … It's really you, knight. Sweet Jesus, but our good lady didn't warn us you were coming … What am I going to find for you to eat?'

'Some thick soup and a piece of bread will be a feast for me, my good Adeline. I ate not long ago. Can Gilbert take care of my horse? Afterwards, I'd like to speak to him.'

'We've got what's left of some pea soup with lard and the leftovers of just about everything else in it. It's filling. The simpleton must be snoring by now. He sleeps like a log, that one. I'll put the pot on the fire and go and wake him up.'

Adeline finally got around to opening the large door and letting him in. She disappeared to the kitchens, leaving him alone in the sinister great hall, its walls blackened with long tongues of soot from the torches. Memories suddenly flooded over the Hospitaller. This was where she had lost her temper, demanding that he answer her questions. Where she had practically threatened him lest anything happen to Clément, her natural son. Where she had confessed, with a blank stare, that her children were by other men than her barren husband. She had insulted herself, called herself a common whore, when she was the most dazzling, the most magical woman he had ever met.

Pushing the kitchen door open with her hip, Adeline returned with an armful of logs and kindling.

'I'll take care of the fire, Adeline. Wake Gilbert, please. My horse is exhausted, its muscles warmed up by its exertions, and I'm afraid it'll catch a chill.'

The heavy-set girl obeyed.

Leone busied himself with the fire, then slumped against the dresser next to the huge fireplace.

After so many years, so many steps, so many nights spent worrying, so many disappointments, he had finally arrived. Of that he was certain. There was just one heavy door left to push open. And Light would shine forth behind it.

'It's our knight, our good fairy's friend!' boomed Gilbert the Simpleton, holding his felt hat in his hand.

Cheerful despite looking sleepy and his hair being all tousled, he stood at the entrance to the great hall, shifting from one foot to the other. Leone rose and took a few steps towards him. 'Come in, my good Gilbert, and shut the door. It's chilly tonight.'

Gilbert did not have to be asked twice and pushed the door shut as though it were no heavier than a curtain.

'Your horse's got a bucket of good water and a bucket of oats. It'll get a good night's sleep.'

'Thank you, Gilbert,' said Leone in the same slow, gentle voice that Agnès used with the simpleton. 'I'm leaving tomorrow at dawn, so please have it saddled. Now come closer. I need to explain something very important to you.'

'Oh, yes, yes …' Gilbert obeyed, wrinkling his short forehead.

'It's about your good fairy, our lady.'

Concentration immediately gave way to alarm in the gentle giant's face.

'What's the matter?' he asked in an abrupt and menacing tone.

Leone realised that the titan sensed other people's emotions before they were even expressed. Trying not to add to his worry, and certain that he could become dangerous and even kill if he thought his fairy was in danger, the knight continued, 'Unfortunately, there are bad people who don't like good fairies …'

'Nasty villains. I'll stick their heads up their arses, them swines,' he spat, opening his hands, hands capable of breaking a horse's neck.

'Calm yourself, Gilbert, for our lady's sake.'

The words worked like magic. The angry redness disappeared from the giant's cheeks. His mouth opened in a blissful smile.

'Yes, yes!' he stammered. 'She saved me, my fairy. When I was just a titch. They wanted to throw me into that stinking hole with the rotting corpses. But they didn't manage. She gave them a beating, she did. It was so cold. She filled my belly, my fairy, she did. She defended me.'

Leone understood from this that some villagers had obviously tried to dispatch an extra mouth to feed – that of a half-wit – to a better world, but that the Dame de Souarcy had firmly opposed it. She must have been very young at the time. He gave a deep sigh in order to expel the choking tenderness that swelled in his chest.

'She is truly magnificent.'

'Oh, yes, that she is,' Gilbert agreed with a vigorous nod.

'Listen carefully, my good Gilbert. I need to go away for a while, so I won't be by her side to protect her from nasty villains, as you call them. Do you understand?'

'Yes, yes.'

'Your fairy is coming to Souarcy soon, and will spend a few days here.'

'Oh, sweet Jesus.' The simpleton clapped his huge hands with delight.

'She'll be escorted by two armed guards, but I'm still worried. The demons sent against our fairy are very powerful.'

'I'm not scared of demons!' the giant roared. 'Sweet Jesus watches over the fairy and Gilbert.'

'Yes, but they're very crafty. I want you to protect our fairy, to watch her constantly. Do you understand? If you suspect that something bad is about to happen, send a servant immediately to warn the chief bailiff in Authon-du-Perche.'

'Yes, of course. I saddle a horse and ride as fast as I can with my arse up, and then the chief bailiff's going to cut the villains' heads off.'

'That's right. There may be a woman among them. A very beautiful blonde woman with green eyes. She passes herself off as a good fairy but really she's a demon. The worst.'

Gilbert clenched his jaw and wrung his hands.

'I'll squash her like an adder, I will. She's not going to hurt my fairy.'

'You can't do that, Gilbert. She's a noblewoman. You can't touch her or they'll have the right to torture you to death, and that will make our good fairy very sad. Terribly sad. And you don't want to make her cry, now, do you?'

Gilbert immediately forgot about the torture he'd suffer if he as much as hit the 'vile demon'. He remembered only what was most important in his eyes, and that was his lady. His large face crumpled in sorrow at the prospect of upsetting her.

'Oh, no, no, no,' he moaned. 'I don't want my fairy to be sad.'

Leone did not even want to think about the fate justice would have in store for this giant with the mind of a child if he were to manhandle Honorius Benedetti's accomplice.

'Swear before God that you won't try and do anything except protect your fairy, and that you'll never touch the pretty monster directly. You know what would happen to you if you broke a promise to God.'

'Oh, yes, yes. My fairy explained it to me.' He suddenly became excited and began flapping his arms like a spiteful goose, stammering and salivating from the corners of his mouth. 'Flames ... Roasting for eternity. Bad, very bad! And I'd never see my fairy again because she'll be in heaven.'

Leone clung to the only thing that was important to the simpleton: his fairy. He had to convince Gilbert, and terrify him with the help of what he cherished more than life itself or even the prospect of hell.

'That's right. You would never see her again for all eternity. So if you notice that woman, only stop her from approaching our fairy. Stop her from coming any nearer than six feet. She's a poisoner and she knows some terrible secrets. Let the chief bailiff know immediately. Did you understand that?'

He was answered with a nod. His weak mind overwhelmed by despair, the simpleton left without a word. He could not find the right words to describe the void he felt inside, the terror and hatred he suddenly felt. Violent, boundless hatred. For the first time since Clément's disappearance, he missed the boy. Clément would understand this better than him, and would find a solution. That night, Gilbert would sleep among his horses, comforted by their smell. That night, an angel would come to him in his sleep, and tell him how to defend his fairy. Gilbert had no doubt. Hadn't his good fairy once told him, smiling with her eyes and tousling his hair, that, 'Angels love the simple-hearted. They allow them to rest for a while.'

Gilbert alternated between a state of semi-wakefulness and confused, worrying nightmares that were too complicated for him to understand, except that they all told him the same thing: that he had to find a way to protect his good fairy from the viper, without, however, committing a sin that would stop him from going to heaven. Gilbert was ready for anything, except to be separated from his lady, whether in this world or the next. The prospect was so unacceptable, so frightening, that he burst into tears, hating that dull-witted, incomplete brain of his. Raging against himself, he angrily pummelled his thighs and his arms with his fists. He was such an idiot, such an animal. He deserved the punishment he was inflicting on himself, deserved even more than that. He sobbed for a long time, snot trickling down his chin – it never even occurred to him to wipe it off. Dazed from exhaustion and panic, he finally fell asleep towards morning, surrounded by the powerful breath of Perche horses.

And the angel did come to him.

Hamlet of Loges, near Authon-du-Perche, Perche, October 1306

Joseph de Bologne dropped his satchel of medicinal herbs on the beaten-earth floor of the cottage.

'Pauline?' he called out gently.

There was a sudden stampede upstairs, then light footsteps coming down the wooden stepladder that led to the bedroom. A very young woman, with hair blonde as wheat, rushed into his arms, laughing.

'I'm so happy to see you! But I should be somewhat jealous. You didn't visit me quite so often before she arrived.'

He shook his head, smiling, then indicated his bag.

'I've brought some food that looks rather tasty.'

'You shouldn't have,' she scolded him, as she always did. 'After all, you're stealing from the Comte and Comtesse who are good masters, aren't you?'

'I certainly am not,' Messire Joseph protested. 'It's the leftovers that Ronan gives every morning to the poor. And, after all, you're not rich. It's not kosher ... Still, we have no choice. If we have to observe *kashrut*[148] in order to remember just what fallible creatures we are, who mix things that should not be mixed, and are led to the stake because of strict observance, God would not be pleased.'

Pauline lowered her gaze, hesitating. 'I often wonder,' she said, 'why He tests us so, and has been doing it for so long. Don't bother answering, or I'll say something terribly blasphemous. Intelligence is a gift from Y——,[149] and not to use it would be a sin.'

'I don't know, my dear Sarah – Pauline,' he corrected himself. The young woman stared at him with her unsteady, troubling eyes. The bullying and recriminations had not ceased since the sixth century, except perhaps during the time Louis le Pieux had placed the Jews under his protection. The lull had lasted for a while, with ups and downs, only to come to an end when Philip Augustus, taking advantage of the people's animosity, had expelled them, confiscating their possessions and annulling the debts of their borrowers, among whom was the realm. It was a good deal. Philip the Fair had been following in his illustrious ancestor's footsteps when, a few months earlier,[150] he had ordered the expulsion of all the Jews in the realm, despite the opposition of some of his lords, who were reluctant to lose the commercial manna which fell thanks to these once again undesirable subjects. Some, like Monseigneur d'Authon, took offence at this witch hunt that occurred periodically, especially when the kingdom got into heavy debt with Jewish bankers.

'Are they going to hunt us down like animals?' Pauline asked.

'Probably, if they find out that we're Jews.'

'She knows we are.'

'She'll say nothing, even if they torture her. Don't worry. My master promised to help me leave for Provence or the Kingdom of Naples, where Philip the Fair's cousin, Charles II of Anjou, is aware of the profit he can make from our work. If these raids were to come too close to us, I would never abandon you, Sarah. You'd come with me. Artus d'Authon is one of those men who are truly honourable and would never go back on their word, even if they might suffer because of it. For the time being, our best defence is to remain under his protection and conceal our faith. Where's your younger sister Adèle?'

'She's working in the henhouse.'

'I'll go and see her.'

Her eyes followed the back that the years had not managed to bow. She remembered. She hated remembering. Nevertheless, despite her efforts, the horror of that early evening and the agony of those months would remain imprinted in her mind and her flesh for ever.

She was returning home to the Rue aux Juifs, where they had been cooped up in order to be watched more easily. Sarah was not offended by this measure. It allowed them to be together and draw comfort from one another. But not that evening. She walked fast, worried by the approaching darkness. At that moment, they had come out of a tavern and mocked her veil. They had started following her, laughing. She had quickened her pace. Drunkenness had quickly transformed their joviality into obscene aggressiveness. One of them had torn off her veil, and another had pushed her so violently that she had nearly fallen full length into the gutter. She knew she must not run, or they would immediately start chasing after her. She had to get back to the Rue aux Juifs. The odd passer-by had noticed the scene but not intervened.

'Well then, you beautiful beggar!' a drunken voice behind her shouted. 'Apparently your kind doesn't care for Christian caresses. You're wrong not to. We know how to treat a lady!'

'Except that this isn't a lady. It's a Jewess.'

'Apparently they're voluptuous and sensual,' said the third one in a bawdy voice.

There was hatred beneath the drunken lustful comments. Sarah felt it as clearly as a solid wall.

Then, the nightmare. They dragged her through a carriage entrance and towards a small building in a back yard. She screamed and screamed. They slapped and punched her. They took it in turns to rape her while laughing hysterically. She saw an oilskin fall down over one of the windows of the small building. A resident who had tired of the show. She stopped screaming. After they left, the minutes seemed an eternity, as Sarah sat on the flagstones, and finally wept. An elderly woman came out of the building.

'No use crying, my girl, believe me,' she sighed. 'At least they didn't cut your throat. Come with me. I'll get you a basin so you can wash. Make sure you wash deep inside. Then maybe you'll avoid a child.'

She hadn't avoided it. She had returned to Rue aux Juifs, her head bare, her cheeks swollen from the blows. Sarah had admitted that she had been attacked and beaten up. Nothing else. When she discovered that she was pregnant, she felt as though she were being raped a second time. To carry the child of one of the boors who had dishonoured her revolted her so much, she had considered suicide as a better option. The resentment she felt for this child terrified her. The solid reputation enjoyed within their community by Joseph de Bologne, an unequalled physician, humanist and philosopher, had become her only hope of salvation. He would be able to save her, even though only women looked after women's bellies. Hearing that he often consulted books at the prestigious library of the Sorbonne, she had rushed there, hiding her veil in her bag as soon as she was far enough from Rue aux Juifs. She had waited outside for Messire Joseph for over an hour, in the teeming rain. Relying on the description she had been given by those who knew him, she had hurried towards him as soon as he had appeared at the top of the steps.

He had listened to her in silence, not interrupting once, just raising an eyebrow when the rage that was choking her emerged from her mouth in insults and violent words. Finally, he had said, in a gentle but categorical tone, 'I cannot do what you ask, young lady. Even if it's rape, I will not put an end to a pregnancy unless I know the mother is at risk of dying. And that's not the case here. You're young and in rude health.'

'I abhor this child, I don't want it! They've dishonoured me for ever, Messire. If anyone found out – and in a few weeks' time

I'll no longer be able to hide it …'

'But it's not your fault. You were alone against three of them, all drunk. You struggled. Moreover, if you have this child, it means you're able to conceive others. There's nothing worse than barrenness in a couple.'

She shed no tears. The old woman who had allowed her to wash and tidy her clothes was right. There was no use crying. She had stared at him and, clenching her teeth, had said, 'I hate you, too. You're condemning me to give birth to a disgraced child and to suffer it at my side when I already hate it.'

'You will learn to love it.'

'Never. I'll leave Paris … I'll find someone … There are women who—'

'They're butchers. They'll damage your insides so badly, you'll never be able to conceive again – that's if you don't die of a fever a few days later.'

'Too bad. Either way, I'll have you to thank. I'd rather that than the dishonour and the stain on my reputation. I won't survive the shame of this hateful belly.'

He had looked closely at her stunning face, her large, childlike blue eyes, her small, tight, determined mouth. Fearing she might commit a folly, the consequences of which she could not anticipate, he made up his mind.

'In that case, come with me. I shall watch over your pregnancy, and then if you still want to get rid of the child, I'll see to it.'

Sarah, now Pauline, had gone to Perche, to the hamlet of Loges, where she had been living for three years now. The child, a girl, had lived for barely an hour after birth. Joseph looked after Pauline, who, sensing the fate that awaited them, had preferred not to return to Rue aux Juifs. When Messire Joseph had asked her to welcome Adèle and pass her off as her younger sister, since they looked alike, she had neither hesitated nor asked any questions.

*

Adèle was collecting eggs when he approached her. He gave a little cough. She stood up and turned to him, a happy smile lighting up her face.

'Master, what joy to see you. What are we studying today? Astronomy, the art of mathematics or Greek philosophy?'

He looked at the girl. Her honey-coloured hair, shoulder-length now, her blue-green eyes, her slim figure. She was already tall for such a young girl. God, how much like her she looked. Like Agnès de Souarcy. Clémence.

For the umpteenth time, Messire Joseph tried to reason with her. 'She misses you terribly. She's tormented with worry. Why won't you let me tell her that her darling daughter is hiding just around the corner from her, and is safe?'

The beautiful face suddenly became closed. 'She knows I'm safe. She feels it just as I feel her. There's such a tight bond between us.' Clémence looked down and said softly, 'Messire Joseph, it's still too soon to endanger our safety. As for the Comte d'Authon, he mustn't find out that I'm his beloved's daughter.'

'He'll never hear it from me; I've given you my word.'

'Some men passed through the village a month ago, asking after a boy. I don't know if they were friends or enemies. If anything were to happen to my dear mother, it would be the end of me. Please believe me, Messire Joseph. I dream of nothing else but throwing myself into her arms and talking to her for hours … However, since it's obvious our enemies must be watching my mother, they might come as far as Loges without her even noticing. The manuscripts are in a safe place, where nobody will think to look. Nevertheless, I am afraid of the camerlingo's henchmen. Their methods are so vile, so powerful and cruel. Who's to say they couldn't make me confess where they are hidden?' The smile returned to the youthful face. 'How is she?'

Joseph looked away, certain that she would be able to read in his face everything he had kept concealed in order to spare her endless hours of terror. The attempted poisoning of Madame, the Comte's arrest.

'Apart from her missing you cruelly, which eats away at her for hours, she's in excellent health and lights up that huge chateau so much, it seems to sigh with relief. When can I tell her the splendid news? I can just picture her joy—'

'I doubt that, Messire Joseph,' a voice broken by emotion said behind them.

They turned with a start. Agnès, Dame de Souarcy, Comtesse d'Authon, was standing before them, even her lips drained of all colour. She covered her mouth with her hand, as though to stifle a cry or perhaps a moan. Her happiness was mixed with sorrow sharper than a blade. She raised her eyebrows, catching her breath, searching for words.

'I followed you, Messire. Your frequent walks in the forest, from which you return with an empty satchel, aroused my curiosity.' She stared with eyes almost identical to her daughter's. Unable to move or take a step forward, she whispered, 'Talk to me for hours, my darling. Talk to me till evening. And afterwards, you're right, I shan't come back until our enemies are vanquished. They're too cunning and too fearsome. Even more than I had imagined. But this way, I'll be able to carry within me the memory of each of your words, and repeat them until I fall asleep.'

Clémence rushed to her mother and flung her arms around her almost roughly. For a long time she wept, clinging to this woman she adored, whom she had missed to the point of distraction and pain.

Overwhelmed and relieved, Joseph de Bologne went back to Pauline's cottage.

G ilbert was ecstatically happy. A strong earthy smell came from his canvas bag. His fairy would be pleased and proud of him when she saw the splendid mushrooms he had gathered, some with caps as large as his hand. Adeline would dry a batch above the kitchen fireplace, and they would be used to stuff the pig that would be slaughtered next December.

Pleased with his pickings, he swung the heavy canvas bag over his shoulder and started on his way back. His instinct told him to hide and he slipped behind an oak tree just in time. Two horsemen were riding along the edge of the forest, or rather a horsewoman and her escort. They passed a few feet away from the simpleton without noticing him. Panicking, Gilbert remained frozen for a long minute, incoherent thoughts passing through his mind, although he was unable to grasp a single one.

His good fairy. His good fairy would shortly be coming back from La Haute-Gravière, where she had gone to inspect the progress of the ore extraction. He dashed off in the direction of the manor, running without stopping to catch his breath, as though the devil were after him.

Gilbert the Simpleton was shaking with terror. His throat was dry. She was there, he had seen her, the vile witch with hair like clouds and eyes of green stone. She was prowling around Souarcy, escorted by a sinister-looking brute. One of those mercenaries who, in peacetime, supplemented their meagre salary by hiring themselves out to do dirty work and thus spare their employers' guilt.

The simpleton felt a mixture of frustration and fear. He could have killed the viper, crushed her thin neck with his hands in a matter of seconds. After all, she was not a true creature of God but a nasty witch. However, the knight had been adamant that he would then lose his place in heaven next to his good fairy. And that man with eyes like lakes knew what he was talking about because, two years earlier, Agnès de Souarcy had told him he was a knight of Christ. At the time, Gilbert had found this combination of words so beautiful that his heart was touched and he had never forgotten it – unlike so many other things. The angel – the one who had come to him while he was sleeping like an animal beside Églantine – had been very clear. His hands must not be stained with blood. He must not kill this monster. Had it really been a seraph? Gilbert was not sure. What do angels look like? He could not remember its face. Even so, waking up the following morning, he had the solution. Had his wretched, backward mind found it by itself? Probably not. Only an angel, he thought, could have whispered it to him. In any case, in its infinite goodness, the heavenly creature had given him the means to protect both his fairy and his place, later, at her side in heaven.

His fear vanished. Gilbert burst out laughing, his huge hand over his mouth. He headed towards the woodshed and spread a large cloth on the ground so that he could stack up firewood and small logs on it. He added an armful of damp straw and hoisted the bundle onto his shoulder, all the while whistling cheerfully. That was something he was good at, since he was used to doing it.

'Hey, you there!' Madame de Neyrat shouted as she entered the great court of the manor, shielding her eyes from the setting sun with her hand.

Gilbert's stomach was knotted with anxiety as he pretended to be busy examining Églantine's hooves. An anxiety mixed with fierce, murderous joy. He stifled a laugh, thinking of the surprise he had in store for them. Madame de Neyrat's bodyguard studied him with an unfriendly air when he approached his mistress's brown filly.

'Keep at a respectful distance, unless you want a taste of my sword!' he barked.

'Oh, really? … What are you on about? How am I supposed to hear the beautiful lady unless I get nearer! You're a bit of an idiot, aren't you?'

'He's a half-wit, Madame,' the man said.

For the first and only time, Gilbert was grateful for his idiot's face and his speech difficulty. Still, he was not as stupid as people thought. His good fairy had made sure that his child's intelligence had awakened a little, even though it had never quite grown up.

Clever Aude decided to be charming. 'I'm looking for Madame d'Authon, Agnès de Souarcy. She's a friend, but I lost touch with her a long time ago. Can you tell me where I can find her? That would be kind of you.'

'Yes, yes.'

'Where is she?' Aude de Neyrat insisted with a softness she was proud of.

'Over there,' Gilbert replied, waving his arms towards the fields at the back of the manor.

'Could you lead us there, so that I may take my friend in my arms?'

The hat pin coated in antiaris,[151] which she had prepared and kept safe in the purse hanging from her belt, would do the rest. The natives of Africa and Asia had been dipping the tips of their arrows in it since the dawn of time to kill large game. It took just one arrow to kill a buffalo. A deep scratch, and the beautiful Agnès would quickly collapse. Her death throes would last fifteen minutes, then her heart would stop beating. A formidable poison, and a pleasing one, since there are not many that can kill with just a wound.

'Yes, of course … It's just that our lady's busy with the honey flies right now. She's smoking them out so she can gather the honey. It's the last of the year.'

Heavens above, how awful, Madame de Neyrat thought. Would she never lose her peasant habits? The lady was the Comtesse d'Authon! How could she sink to such a menial task?

'Well, then, we'll help her,' Aude de Neyrat suggested, repressing a grimace of disgust. 'Take me there, please. As for you,' she said to her guard, 'wait here.'

The man looked surprised but did not argue. He was paid handsomely to obey. As for Aude, the last thing she wanted was a witness who could some day do her harm. There would be just the three of them: Agnès, the dimwit servant, and her. Two would come out alive, and who would believe the rantings of a born idiot, if it ever came to it? Especially since he wouldn't understand what had caused his mistress's death.

A delicious tension made her sit up in her saddle as she prodded her horse into motion behind the Simpleton, who was muttering something she could not make out. Actually, she had no interest whatsoever in what he had to say. She had to act with lightning speed. Slide off her saddle, put on an air of delight, rush to Agnès, take her in her arms and stick the hat pin into her shoulder. Agnès must not have sufficient time to realise she did not know her and stand back. Just a few seconds' hesitation would seal her fate.

A curtain of thick smoke blurred the edges of the groves thirty yards away. Aude made out a figure. Agnès.

The simpleton kept advancing. With a gesture of annoyance and fear, Aude waved away a few bothersome bees flying around her. Gilbert paused.

'It's not prudent to go any further. They get angry because their honey's being taken. I'll go and warn our lady. You better dismount. I'll take the horse back a bit so it doesn't panic.'

As he said this, he grabbed Madame de Neyrat by the waist before she had time to protest, lowered her to the ground and carefully brushed the road dust from her thick purple silk dress.

'Will you leave me alone! Go and fetch my friend, your mistress.'

'Yes, yes.'

Gilbert walked fearlessly through the thick curtain, which seemed to swallow him. He gave a conspiratorial wave to the scarecrow he had dragged there earlier. Suddenly, he took off like an arrow towards the beehive and gave it a powerful kick with his clog, knocking it over. He ran as fast as he could to the woods, to the pond, ready to leap into it if need be. A panic-stricken swarm shot out of the toppled beehive with a thunderous buzz. Hesitating at first, the bees finally sensed the distinctive smell of their king,[152] some distance away. A huge cloud darkened the sky and rushed towards the king to surround and protect him. Aude watched it sweep down upon her. She tried to run, pushing away tens of thousands of insects[153] by waving her arms around, screaming as though she were possessed. Disorientated and puzzled by their king's reaction, the bees attacked. Collapsing to the ground, Madame de Neyrat died of asphyxia less than a quarter of an hour later, her angelic face disfigured by swelling and stings. During that time, which felt like an infinity, and before she lost consciousness, many horrible memories came back to her, punctuated by the witch's threat: *You will die in atrocious suffering and be for ever damned ... Whoever makes an attempt on my life will know worse torments than hell! They promised, those below, and they always keep their word!* Strangely, in her death throes, the only comfort she found amid her terror at not having been able to balance the scales of her soul was not Angélique, but Honorius. Deprived of air, her brain shutting down in death, her one prayer was for him.

Gilbert washed his hands at length, rubbing them with soil. He felt guilty for the nasty trick he had played on his friendly allies. Still, they would understand his reasons and forgive him. The day before, he had smoked out the beehives in order to get a king, which he had then squashed between two pebbles. He had carefully collected the juice from the little corpse and rubbed it on the nasty witch's dress while pretending to dust her off. He giggled with relief. He had not broken his word to the knight; he had not soiled his hands with blood. He had not killed her. The bees had seen to that. After all, if the bad fairy hadn't started gesticulating and yelling like a pig being slaughtered, then the nice honey flies would not have stung her. Nevertheless, he was worried: had he deprived them of heaven? Quick, he had to return to the manor. His good lady would be there soon. In his joy at the prospect of seeing her, any alarm he might have felt about the bees' souls vanished.

Château d'Authon-du-Perche, Perche, October 1306

In his room above the stables, Leone hesitated. He had been considering the pros and cons for hours. For once in his life, he could not bear his solitude, and Agnès, for all her wisdom and alert mind, could not advise him in a matter too close to her heart. In other circumstances, to give himself up to the Inquisition for the murder of Nicolas Florin so that Monseigneur d'Authon might be cleared of all suspicion would have seemed to him like the only option. However, he had to watch over Agnès and find Clément before the camerlingo's men did. You can only have a clean fight with worthy enemies. The opposite would be foolish madness.

Grim-faced, Monge de Brineux sat in the Comte's small circular study, sorting out current business. The confidences he had gathered here and there all coincided. A sort of alarming inertia seemed to have fallen over the Inquisition headquarters at Alençon. Jacques du Pilais claimed to still be waiting for the results of further enquiries. Monseigneur d'Authon had not appeared again before the judges, and was rotting in the cell reserved for witnesses; in other words those they had not yet been able to charge. This uncertainty made the chief bailiff angry. Everything was ready for him to honour his promise to the Comte and dispatch Madame and her son to Sardinia in order to ensure their safety. Perhaps, though, the person who was not ready was the one from whom he was concealing her husband's decision. Telling her would be tantamount to informing her of a death sentence. Yet Monge de Brineux was still hopeful.

*

He stood up to welcome the knight Leone, who declined with a shake of his head his invitation to sit down.

'Monsieur, you're a man of honour and the Comte trusts you.'

'And I cherish that trust.'

'Since I don't know the area very well, I need your help. Time is of the essence; therefore, at the risk of seeming abrupt, I shall not beat about the bush.'

Monge de Brineux remained silent, waiting.

'Arranging a false testimony. Would you consider that an infamy?'

'So as to save Monseigneur d'Authon? Certainly not. The infamy was in doubting his word and trying to accuse him of a crime he has not committed. I'm at your service, Monsieur. With all my heart. Just tell me how I can be of help to you.'

Clairets Abbey, Perche, October 1306

The heightened anxiety of Thibaude de Gartempe, the guest mistress, since she had entered her study, breathless, a few seconds earlier was making Annelette Beaupré so tense that she could barely hold back the curses that were on the tip of her tongue. Thibaude was walking round and round, waving her arms about like a panic-stricken goose, opening and closing her mouth spasmodically like a carp that had leapt out of a pond. Still, Annelette heard herself give measured advice.

'Calm yourself, dear daughter, and tell me why you're so upset.'

'Oooh ...' was the only response at first. Familiar with Thibaude's nervous excesses, Annelette refused to be unduly alarmed and managed to keep her angelic smile while the other woman gathered her wits.

'Reverend Mother ... It's your brother ...'

'My brother? Which one?'

'Your own brother.'

'Grégoire?'

'Yes, yes ... He's waiting in the parlour ... and has requested the honour of speaking to you.'

Annelette Beaupré jumped up. A wave of bitter memories swept over her and she had difficulty breathing. What was Grégoire doing in Clairets, thirty years after his only sister's departure from the family home? Neither he nor their father had ever deigned to send her news of the household, let alone enquire after her health. Annelette had heard of her mother's death years after the event. Her father and brother had shared the little grey woman's inheritance between themselves while she waited, sighing, for the gardens of angels she imagined all day long.

Naturally, having renounced her worldly possessions, Annelette would have given her share to the abbey, which over the years had become her only family, her only world. Still, she would have liked to keep the psalter with the binding her mother had embroidered with a multitude of winged and smiling creatures.

As she walked into the parlour, Grégoire rose and stood rooted to the spot, evidently feeling uneasy. The quack had grown fat. A white, flabby kind of fat. As for his son, who was about fifteen and was with him, he looked alarmingly like his father.

Annelette waited, having no wish to make his task easier, and not inviting him to sit down, if only to let him know that the interview would be brief.

'My dear sister – Er ... Reverend Mother ...'

'My son, my brother,' she echoed in a flat voice.

'I can't tell you how happy, how delighted we were when we heard you had been elected by the chapter.'

'Really? Then you're better informed than I am, since I don't know if our father is still alive.'

His heavy jowls drooped a little more. 'Alas,' he announced, his voice faltering with grief, 'he passed away about ten years ago. A nasty lung fever which, despite my knowledge and my best efforts, I couldn't cure.'

Another medical blunder, Annelette thought. At least her father was the victim this time.

'Sister ... Reverend Mother ... Allow me to present your nephew, Thibaud, my youngest from my second marriage. Alas, fate has it in for our family. My wife died in childbirth, like the first one.'

Because you insisted on delivering her yourself instead of using the services of an experienced midwife whom you would have had to pay. What do you want from me, Grégoire, to make you bow and scrape so? Hurry up. I have little patience and certainly not for you.

'I have much to do, my son. I suspect your journey to Clairets must have been exhausting, so I will give you hospitality for one night, and supper in our hostelry. '

'Oh, I don't wish to take up your time; I know how busy you are. The reason for my visit, besides my happiness at seeing you in such good health … Well, it's a little delicate. As you know, everything is so dreadfully expensive …'

And you're as tight-fisted as your father.

'I have four sons to place. Fortunately, no daughters … er … with all the respect I have for the fairer sex. Whether it's the army, the Church or medicine, setting them up will cost me a fortune.'

'And since I own nothing, how can I possibly help?'

He perked up at the opening, relieved.

'Well … Given the great importance of your position, your splendid reputation and the illustrious name of the abbey you manage with such remarkable skill … I wondered if …'

The pale-blue eyes studying him made him go to pieces, causing him to forget the words – aimed at touching the heart – which he had been rehearsing all the way here.

'Wondered if——?'

'Er … If perhaps you would consider interceding in our favour … in Rome.'

'Rome?'

'An usher's position for my youngest. He's bright and hard-working, and I'm certain he would give full satisfaction and soon be rewarded with a more prestigious rank. Maybe a chamberman.'

She looked at him, unmoved.

He lowered his head until his chin dug into the fat that padded his neck.

'Sister … Reverend Mother, I have felt guilty, terribly guilty about our father's harshness towards you. I should have stood up to him. I was too obedient and for that I beg you to forgive me.'

A strange feeling took the place of Annelette's bitterness. So he had come to beg a favour from the very woman he would happily have confined to the back of the scullery to wash his patients' soiled laundry. She had every right to take revenge, or at least seek legitimate satisfaction. But she did not. Her brother's presence at Clairets irritated her. As for her nephew, who kept flashing smiles at her, he left her indifferent. Yet she did not resent them. Not Grégoire, and not their father. They had vanished from her world. Finally.

'For heaven's sake, Grégoire! You used to take me for a fool and still do. My son, we do not love each other, so let's stop this emotional play-acting. The only satisfaction I shall take from your visit is yet more proof that we are fundamentally different. Yes, I will intercede. Farewell, brother. Please accept my hospitality for tonight, and leave early in the morning.'

'Aunt ...' the nephew gratefully stammered.

'Reverend Mother!' she interrupted in an icy tone. She turned on her heel and said, over her shoulder, 'Oh, and Grégoire, no need to come back and thank me once you have obtained what you came for. You will not be in my debt. You see, without even knowing it, you've just done me a big favour.'

Annelette thought she felt Éleusie de Beaufort place a kiss on her forehead. She had made peace with her memories after so, so many years.

Inquisition headquarters, Alençon, Perche, October 1306

Bernadette Carlin waited, her hands folded over her belly. With her slim figure, she must have been pleasant to look at once, but life had taken its toll on her perfect oval face and extinguished the light in her pretty grey eyes.

A heavy silence reigned in the interrogation room, disturbed only by the rustling of the short sheet of paper which the Grand Inquisitor was turning over and over.

'Kindly state your name, surname and position, Madame.'

'Bernadette Jeanne Marie Carlin, née Bardeau. Widow, much-praised orphrey embroiderer.'

The notary stood up and, with a pinched air, recited, '*In nomine Domini, Amen.* In the year 1306, on the twenty-fourth of the month of October, in the presence of the undersigned Gauthier Richer, notary at Alençon, accompanied by one of his clerks and by the witnesses called Brother Robert and Brother Foulque, Dominicans, both from the diocese of Alençon, né respectively Ancelin and Chandars, Bernadette Jeanne Marie Carlin, née Bardeau, appears voluntarily and in person before the venerable Brother Jacques du Pilais, Dominican, Doctor of Theology, Grand Inquisitor for the territory of Évreux, appointed to judge this matter in our good city of Alençon.'

Jacques du Pilais approached the woman, boring into her with his pale eyes.

'Bernadette Carlin, here are the four Gospels. Place your right hand upon them and swear to tell the truth, about yourself as well as others. Do you swear it on God and on your soul?'

'I swear,' she stated in a voice that lacked conviction.

'Of course, you know that perjury, as well as irredeemably

sullying your soul, would incur the wrath of this court.'

'I know, my lord. But my soul is pure, and God can examine it.'

'Now, then. A few days ago, you sent us a very strange confession. Rather belated but well written.'

'I cannot read, let alone write, my lord, so I dictated the contents to a public scribe.'

'Hmm ... That explains the pretty turns of phrase. What do you tell us in it?' Jacques du Pilais began reading with a gentle voice:

> *To the Grand Inquisitor in charge of shedding light on the murder of the Dominican Nicolas Florin.*
>
> *My lord,*
>
> *The secret I have kept for almost two years has become too heavy a burden to bear since there is a rumour in town that a man, the Comte d'Authon, may be accused of the Grand Inquisitor Nicolas Florin's murder. He is innocent and I could keep quiet no longer. I have said nothing in order to protect the name of my children and spare them further shame. Their father's dreadful reputation weighs too heavily on their young shoulders as it is. As for me, that drunken thief, womaniser and liar has ruined my life. God called him back to Him six months ago, and I shall not pretend that we're beside ourselves with grief. He died as he had lived. A good-for-nothing stabbed coming out of a tavern by a drinking companion to whom he was refusing to pay his gambling debt. I tell you before God and with great shame that it was my husband who murdered the Grand Inquisitor Florin. He said he was a burgher he'd met in a tavern, with whom he got so drunk that the other began making faces like a girl at him. My*

rogue of a husband discovered his victim's true identity only a few days later. Panic-stricken, he decided to get rid of the jewels he'd stolen and, at night, went back to Seigneur Florin's house and threw them into the cesspit.

I have no doubt that your investigators will confirm his despicable reputation and enlighten you as to mine.

This is the exact truth. I swear it before God.

Your humble Bernadette Carlin.

'Do you deny this statement, Madame?'

'Not at all. I swear it's the truth. An innocent man shouldn't suffer because of the crimes of that scoundrel, my husband. We have suffered from them sufficiently as it is.'

Brother Ancelin's thin, unpleasant voice asked, 'Who has paid you, and how much, to contrive this testimony?'

Bernadette Carlin blinked as though she had just been slapped. She studied him then answered firmly, 'Monsieur, it may be true that I am a pauper who slaves away day and night in order to feed my children. However, I have never stolen. As for perjuring myself after placing my hand on the Gospels – I'd rather die right now.'

She crossed herself and turned to Jacques du Pilais, who had not looked away from her for a second. Something about her bearing puzzled him. Despite her threadbare but obsessively clean clothes, her thick linen bonnet, and her fingers, deformed by holding the gold thread taut, this woman carried herself with a natural elegance that made one want to believe her. In addition, there were the many testimonies in her favour, gathered during the preliminary investigation, testimonies which, conversely, had not spared her brutal drunkard of a husband. Bernadette Carlin almost led the life of a recluse, leaving her work to go home and take care of her children, who were said to be well kept and well behaved. Her rare outings were to the market and to Mass. Nobody recalled ever having seen her sitting at a tavern table or gossiping with other matrons. Moreover, if they trusted her with reels of gold and silver thread, it meant they knew she was honest. And yet, as a formidable reader of souls, Jacques du Pilais was certain she was lying. Did she know that he could get the truth out of her under torture? Perhaps. After all she was clever. But then, why take that risk, so terrifying that many men would have promptly turned from it? For the money, for her children, of course. In the dense silence of the room, he listened to her breathing, which she was trying to keep regular. Strange breed, women, he thought. They are scared of a mouse but defy an Inquisition tribunal in order to improve the lives of their offspring. Pilais procrastinated for a few more minutes. After all, wasn't this woman providing a wonderful remedy for the increasing unease he felt at the wrongful imprisonment of Monseigneur d'Authon, whom he knew to be innocent? Playing the political game as he was, he had not been able to free him, not even after receiving the further information he had demanded. This testimony, on the other hand, delivered before ecclesiastical witnesses, was as providential as it was contrived. And Jacques du Pilais, who, during his long life, had relentlessly hunted down lies, heard himself saying in a falsely vexed tone, 'Brothers, in all conscience I believe we can have faith in what this woman is saying. However, she will have to say three novenas in order for God to forgive her for having concealed the truth for so long. Notary, kindly record this judgement. Monseigneur d'Authon is therefore free. Agnan, go and tell him immediately.'

The young clerk darted to the door without looking at Bernadette Carlin, whom he had approached a few days earlier in order to propose a lucrative deal. At dawn tomorrow, he would give her the promised purse. A year from now, in order to eliminate any suspicion, Bernadette would move to Chartres, where she would finally be able to live a life which was not one of constant fear for the next day.

A comforting thought crossed the young man's mind. The murder of the monster Florin had brought some handsome compensations.

'Who is this missive from?'

'I know not, Your Excellency,' the usher replied, bowing even lower. 'One of the guards by the wall said that an exhausted horseman, a French messenger, had given it to him. So I thought it couldn't be one of the countless beggars who bother you every day, even though the sender didn't deem it appropriate to place his seal on the wax, or write his name on the scroll.'

Honorius Benedetti dismissed the man with a small movement of his head and turned the missive over in his hands before unrolling it. His eyes searched in vain for a signature. His lips tightened in displeasure. What was it? An anonymous letter. What arrogance! Nevertheless, he read it. His heart began to race as he deciphered the tall, nervous handwriting. He felt as though his brain were being violently torn apart and had to reread the senseless, unacceptable words before fully understanding them.

Your Eminence,

We feel it is a matter of courtesy to inform you of the death of Madame Aude de Neyrat, who, we are told, was a friend of yours. A terrible accident is the cause. It seems that Madame de Neyrat unwittingly disturbed a beehive, and the swarm attacked her.

Madame de Neyrat has been buried in Chartres, where she lived, following a religious service at the cathedral.

Nothing else. Nothing. An infinity of nothing. There was a void in his mind, an abyss in his chest. A sharp pain, like a sword, made him double over at his desk. He panted, his mouth open, struggling not to suffocate. The horde of his worst memories was let loose, as though only those almond-shaped emerald eyes had been able to keep them at bay. He was deafened by a steady moan and it took him a while to realise that it was coming from his own throat. Tears streamed down his face, soaking the hand which, like a heartbroken child, he had pressed to his cheek. Did all this, did everything for which he had been fighting for such a long time really have no meaning? Had he been misguided from the first? Was God sending him a final warning?

Benoît, whom he loved more than a brother, more than his own elder brother, whose poisoning he had ordered and who had died in his arms. Aude, splendid Aude, whom he had saved from the executioner at Auxerre, and whose death he had later caused. He dismissed the image of the sublime face swollen by bee stings. The only two beings he had truly loved. The only two capable of lightening his days.

Alone. His life was a sinister cemetery where he drifted alone. No gentle phantom would escort him on his wanderings amidst the nameless, unforgiving tombs. It was the price of his damnation. He had wanted to save men from themselves for the love of the Divine Lamb. Instead, he had destroyed the only thing that remained pure within him: his infinite tenderness towards Benoît, his immeasurable need for Aude. Strange. He, who had never been interested in profit, who had never been dazzled by money, glory or even power, was now alone in the centre of a realm of shadows that he had built stone by stone, bolting every door. This labyrinth of traps, of tricks, of hideous and grotesque masks, now sickened him so much it choked him. Huge grief. Endless. The grief of a titan who suddenly realises that his power has abandoned him. The grief of an old man who turns around and sees the extent of the desert he has left behind. Desert and nothing else.

He straightened up and wiped his face with the back of his

sleeve, trying to stifle the obstinate sobs in his throat.

What had Benoît XI whispered with his dying breath? 'Light. I can see the light. I am bathed in it ... Farewell, my dear brother.' Then the Pope's fingers had gripped Honorius's. But then the pressure had suddenly lessened, leaving the camerlingo alone in the world, and chilled.

What had she said the last time he had relaxed while admiring her smile? 'So you condemn us to this imperfect world?' For a brief moment, a puzzled sadness had extinguished the light in those splendid emerald eyes.

Ineffable Lamb, I can no longer lie to myself. I admit that my blindness was only matched by my obstinacy. It's because I love You so much. I humbly beg Your forgiveness for having deceived You, for not having understood the signs You deigned to send me in Your infinite indulgence. You see, strangely, I'm still certain that I was right. Only the order we have imposed can save men from chaos. However, I am no more than an insect. I know only the past and the present. You know the future. You are the future. Will the future be illuminated by Your glory or will it end in a bloodbath? I know not. Strangely, it's no longer important since You have just shown me that I am not the one who will make the future happen. As for the rest – my bloody crimes, the appalling acts I have been guilty of – I await my speedy sentence and punishment. At last, I will pay. I will shake off remorse. At last, I will sleep.

He had explained it one day – it seemed like an eternity ago – to Bartolomeo. There are some extraordinary moments in our lives, details we are wrong to ignore. The grotesque human haste to bring matters to a conclusion and our presumptuous desire to think that we can control time are the cause. These moments are the turning points of our existence. Once they are shut behind us, the doors are closed for ever. With no hope or will to go back.

Honorius Benedetti slumped against the tall back of his armchair and closed his eyes, carefully studying the present moment. No delight and no apprehension. Just the certainty that time had stood still.

He reached out for the long paper knife and admiringly examined its ivory handle, carved with the precision of lace. He lifted his robe and examined the pale, wrinkled skin of his thighs. He gently touched his groin until he felt beneath his fingers the now-slowed throbbing of his blood. With steady pressure, he pushed in the blade. There was a sharp pain that was not his any more. A warm, crimson stream soaked his thigh and trickled lazily towards his calf. Another. And another. He considered counting these little flurries that drained his blood from him, but chose instead to go back, one last time, to Aude's smile, to Benoît's slow and sometimes uncertain voice, to the shrimp-fishing excursions his brother used to take him on, to his mother's throaty laughter.

An impertinent thought made him laugh. How would the ushers and chambermen go about erasing all trace of the red flood that was slowly soaking the rug? They had quite a task ahead of them to clean all this up. Then Clément V would be able to announce that his beloved brother had died from a weakness of the heart, his soul at peace.

Château d'Authon-du-Perche, November 1306

Days had drifted by since Artus's return, days of long silences interspersed with polite conversation. After the huge relief of knowing that he was free and cleared of all suspicion, after the feverish joy that had made her quiver when she had finally glimpsed his figure, grown thin, walking up the courtyard, after the joy of nights together again during which she had sobbed with womanly happiness and gratitude to God, the time had come for unuttered questions. Questions that poison the hours because one so much fears their answers. Agnès sensed them turning over and over in her husband's mind. That elegant, generous man could not bring himself to ask them and corner her. She hated herself for the cowardice she was discovering in herself, and against which she had fought so hard. Love makes one a coward towards the beloved, for fear of losing him. For all her repeating to herself that nothing sapped the will like uncertainty, her courage failed her. Sometimes, she would rush to her husband's study, determined to tell him everything about her past: her daughters, Clémence, the prophecy, Leone's true role, the quest. But a few paces away from his door, she would stop abruptly and walk back to her apartments feeling defeated. Countless times, she had hoped that a word or a sigh would lead her, even unwittingly, to confide in him. But it was all in vain.

Agnès had found dinner inordinately long. Although she usually could not get enough of her husband's company, his smiles and his loving glances, she was now counting the minutes between courses. She was stupefied by her own inconsistency. The confessions were pressing on her, demanding to be let out. Nevertheless, the terror of their consequences stilled them in her throat. She never grew weary of Artus, or of his slightest gesture. Yet tonight his presence was oppressive to her. A servant girl placed the third course before them – a *chaudumé* – grilled fish with bread sauce and verjuice with white wine, seasoned with a pinch of saffron and ginger. The tangy sauce blended perfectly with the tender flesh.

'You look lost in thought, my darling ... and not very talkative. Are you recovering from the monstrous acts that nearly cost you your life? When I think of it, Madame, my legs turn to lead. I can't stop thinking with horror of what would have become of my life, which you make so complete.' Then, humour soothing retrospective fear, he added, smiling, 'You may well say it's yet more proof of male selfishness.'

'Absolutely not, my dear. It's wonderful proof of love for a lady to have the certainty that she has deeply affected her beloved's life. As for your question, yes, I am getting stronger every day, thanks to your being back and to Messire Joseph's constant care. The frightful tiredness that took away any desire to do anything has diminished considerably.'

Once again, a veil of silence fell over them. Agnès was racking her brains to think of some appropriate story to relaunch the conversation, but her need to speak, to finally explain, was choking her.

'Madame, perhaps you miss the knight Leone's company, since he has not been to see you much.'

'No,' she replied, forcing a smile. 'He's very busy. Something about a diptych sold by a cousin of his who is now trying to buy it back, if I understand correctly.'

'That's also the reason he gave me when he said he was sorry for his frequent absences.' He frowned as though trying to recall something. 'Though I don't really believe it.'

Agnès shuddered, but managed to conceal the alarm this comment triggered in her.

'You mean that he was sorry?'

'No, I mean that story about a diptych. Come now, would Leone come back from Cyprus and undertake a long, exhausting journey merely in order to recover a work of art? Such a paltry excuse might put me off the track if I didn't sense, behind it, a totally different truth – a much darker one – being concealed. At least that's what I think.'

'The order of the Hospitallers, like others, is known to possess secrets the uninitiated may not know,' Agnès said, stalling.

He gave her a sharp look, the kind of look he usually gave those whose integrity he doubted. It was a look she hated.

'That's true,' he agreed in a tone that was too casual to reassure her.

A fresh silence replaced what was beginning to feel like a courtly joust where each competitor evaluates the strengths and weaknesses of his opponent. Agnès felt rocked by a slight dizziness that had nothing to do with having been the victim of poisoning. God Almighty! She cursed herself for this shift in feelings, for the mistrust and sorrow she felt in him. It was her fault. What had she expected? One had to be foolish indeed, or mad, to think that this intelligent, refined man would be fooled for ever by a few clumsy lies. Of course, his love for her had blinded him for a time, but then her terror that he might be angry with her for taking advantage of his weakness as a man in love had dissuaded Agnès from revealing the entire history of her existence.

The servant girl delicately brought in the sweet course – bowls of doughnuts – and for a while her presence filled their silence, that increasingly uncomfortable wait for the other person to speak. In truth, Agnès was honest enough to admit that all she wanted was for him to order and demand that she explain herself. That way, she would not be able to shy away from it any longer. That way, he would take away the doubts that hounded her. What was she afraid of exactly? That he would suddenly disappoint her by being narrow-minded. That he might misjudge her. That he would not understand that her youthful actions, reprehensible though they might be, had been engendered by nothing else but the terror of falling back into Eudes's clutches and having to submit to his lust. To escape him, she had needed a child. Hughes de Souarcy being sterile, a stranger encountered by chance, about whom she remembered nothing, had saved her from a fate worse than death.

She had lost her appetite. Still, she tackled the doughnuts, to compose herself if nothing else. Artus drained his glass in one draught and sighed wearily.

'Are you bored, Monsieur?'

'With you next to me? Never, Madame.' Suddenly tense, he continued, 'Agnès, they say that love frays after a while, especially after a child is born. Do you believe that?'

'No,' she replied vehemently. 'My love for you, at least, keeps growing so much, it makes me dizzy.' Suddenly worried, she asked, 'Is that a polite way of warning me that yours is cooling?'

Artus could not help chuckling. 'I cannot believe that a lady as intelligent as yourself could possibly believe such a thing. Every moment of my life is filled with you. When I was exhausted by my imprisonment, my one dream was to lie by your side and deprive you of sleep for nights on end. Is that the sign of a man falling out of love?'

'You wouldn't doubt my love, would you? It would be mad—'

'My darling, I don't doubt it,' he replied so sadly that she went to him and seized his hands in order to kiss them. 'It's your reluctance to fully trust me that pains me. Have I ever given you reason to believe that you would be disappointed?'

'My dearest husband,' she protested. 'You're the most honourable, most trustworthy man, and I know you would die rather than break your word ... How can you say that?'

'And yet, Madame …'

'And yet …?' she managed to say, her heart throbbing with pain. So she had sensed correctly. Artus had noticed her evasions and half-truths. She prepared herself for the worst.

'I beg you, go back to your seat, Madame. I need to see your eyes.'

She obeyed and walked around the table in the wavering light of the torches and the fire that crackled in the hearth. For a few seconds, her figure dissolved and vanished in the flicker of the flames, then returned again. Artus refused to see it as an ill omen. The idea that Agnès could one day disappear. The certainty that the countless ties that bound them together would leave nothing of him that was worthwhile if she were to turn away from him. Once again, he hesitated. Should he force her to make revelations? Would she resent him for making her admit a secret she had been protecting so jealously? He was so scared of displeasing her. But this masquerade had gone on long enough. He was not motivated by a husband's worry. His speculations were far more frightening. In truth, the story Agnès had told him two years earlier, to explain her anxiety when Clément, the young farm boy, had disappeared, had only partly convinced Artus. Nonetheless, Agnès's attitude in the months that followed had first intrigued, then alarmed him. However much of a kind and generous angel she might have been, losing sleep and her appetite over being unable to find a little illegitimate girl born to a dead servant seemed wildly disproportionate. He had heard her pacing up and down her room at night. He had not been fooled by her feigned appetite every time Monge de Brineux brought her the same news: that their search had been unsuccessful. He had noticed her suddenly look away at the garden so that he would not see her tears whenever he mentioned Clémence.

His beloved's voice drew him from his reverie.

'Well, Monsieur, I am sitting down.'

He studied her Italian-style dress. The heavy bronze velvet emphasised the honey colour of her hair. He remembered her in the poor grey dress she wore to Mass. The Dame de Souarcy's best outfit. He remembered how moved he was when she had mounted Ogier, dressed in peasant breeches, elegant as a queen. He dismissed the emotion that had brought a lump to his throat. The time for procrastination, for fear of displeasing, was over. He had to know.

'And yet, Madame,' he said, gently, 'what terrible secret are you keeping from me?'

She closed her eyes and sighed, her lips parted, her face drained of colour. Pale even to her lips, she warned him, 'All will be revealed to you, Monsieur. If, afterwards, you consider me unworthy of your love, then please do not hesitate to say so in order to spare my feelings. Tell me without any evasions.'

Strangely, this warning did not worry Artus. Nothing that was a part of her could be bad. Nothing in her could deceive him. He would have bet his life on that certainty. She wet her lips with a sip of wine, and began. She spoke in a calm, strangely flat voice he barely recognised.

'Clémence is my daughter. So is Mathilde. Neither of them is a Souarcy.'

She told him all the twists and turns of the events that had pained her so much, omitting nothing, not even dwelling on her excuses. Everything was listed with an economy of words and emotions. Eudes's incestuous desire, her angel Madame de Larnay, her marriage to Hugues, the atrocious death throes of that loyal, honourable man whose demise had once again made her vulnerable to her half-brother's vile concupiscence, the arrival of Leone, the discovery of the holy papyrus in Clairets, the camerlingo Honorius Benedetti and his henchmen, the poisoned nuns, the quest, the different blood. Life seemed to have drained from her, only returning when she remembered their meeting, near the beehives, his embarrassment as a man in love, her own panic.

For a whole hour, he listened without interrupting, barely daring to blink or raise the glass to his lips, for fear that she might break off. With a discreet gesture, he dismissed the servant bringing them the last course. Immersed in the recounting of her nightmare, Agnès did not even notice. Several times, he fought against a powerful desire to rush to her and hold her tight in his arms, so tight as to take her breath away.

She paused to take a sip of wine. He stretched his hands out to her. She declined them with a shake of her head. She took a deep breath and continued:

'As I told the knight Leone, who must never know that Clémence is a girl, you must think of me now as a common whore.'

'You, Madame ...' he whispered, fighting back tears. 'You are a beam of divine light. Your relentless courage, your determination without hatred, your ... your strange strength. I didn't think I could love you any more than I already did, but I was wrong. You have led me deep into your soul, and my dearest wish is to remain there for ever. It is now the only place where I have ever felt totally content. Will you grant me that?'

His intense blue-green eyes fixed on hers. She did not need words. And besides, were there any? He knew now that nothing could ever damage their love. He gently stood up and walked steadily towards her. She rested her forehead on the stomach of the man she loved, and wept. They remained like that for a long time. He cradled her while her tears flowed, not knowing if they were tears of sorrow or peace. Finally, she looked up and he kissed her lips. Suddenly, she repeated in an urgent voice, 'Leone must never know that Clémence is a girl.'

'Won't he be able to protect her?'

'Oh, he'd give every drop of his blood to do so. But I am certain he is known to our enemies. Wherever he goes, they will follow. And Leone is a man of God. Worse – he is a man who sees only God. If he finds out that the different blood has been passed on to Clémence, he will not rest until the prophecy has been fulfilled.' In a biting tone, she added, 'I don't want that for my daughter. I don't want her to become a prize for powers that are beyond us and would crush us in order to reach their aims, be they of the dark or of the light.'

'Do you know where Clémence is?' Artus asked gently.

'Not far from here, in the hamlet of Loges. I only recently discovered this. Messire de Bologne's constant walks in the forest, from which he returned with an empty satchel, intrigued me, so I followed him. He has been hiding and protecting Clémence from the moment she disappeared. I am torn between infinite gratitude towards him and resentment, I confess. Having said that, Clémence had demanded that he keep it a secret, for the excellent reason that I would immediately rush to her hiding place and risk our enemies following me. A charming young woman, Pauline, Joseph's protégée, has taken her in and has been passing her off as her younger sister. They raise hens.'

'Oh, Madame, my darling … It was folly to conceal the truth from me for so long. You must have had such a low opinion of me!'

'Are you mad?' Agnès almost shouted. 'A low opinion when I knew you were the person most worthy of knowing the truth? I was afraid. Afraid you might not love me any more, that you might misjudge me. Afraid, also, that my revelations would place you in danger.'

'But it's your silence that endangers me since it exposes you more to risk! But enough of my loving reproaches … We must act. Clémence cannot remain there. Has she changed? Physically, I mean.'

Agnès's face lit up with delight. 'She is so beautiful, so … so wonderful. She is much taller, and her figure has become more womanly. Her hair has grown. You'd be surprised by her erudition … Messire Joseph is teaching her mysteries.'

'We must find a safe place to protect her.'

'But where? I deceived myself that I could defend her and, look … they almost managed to kill me, and I didn't even suspect they were so close to me.'

'Nobody here knows Clément or Clémence except you, my physician, this Pauline and Leone. In other words, people of integrity. Clémence could … I don't know… enter your service. All we need is for Leone never to meet her and for her never again to go to Souarcy or to Clairets.'

'She looks so much like me that anyone would know at a glance that we are related by blood,' Agnès argued.

'Blast!' Artus snapped, pacing up and down the room, his arms clasped behind his back. He suddenly froze. 'Sardinia. My kind cousin Jacques de Cagliari, to whom I planned to send you and Philippe if I wasn't able to escape the trap that had been set for me. He's a bear, but a bear who would rather be wounded than give in. He has always hated orders and intimidation. No one will look for Clémence in his wild, arid hills. We'll have her travel with an escort, dressed as a young burgher going to meet her intended. They're all looking for a boy. A farm boy.'

Her eyes wide with sadness, Agnès murmured, 'Sardinia? Sweet Jesus, it's the other side of the world. Still, I know you're right … It's just that the idea of her being so far away …'

'Out of reach, Madame. It's only for a few months or, at worst, one or two years. Let's give Leone and his shadow companions time to complete their task and destroy for ever those who wish to harm your daughter and you.'

'Will they be able to, some day?'

'Please God.'

Agnès stood up, went to her husband and put her head on his shoulder. He stroked the precious mass of hair, letting it glide between his fingers like silk.

'My love, before she leaves, I would so much like to spend a whole day with her, dine with her, get breathless telling her so many little things, show her around the park … stock up on memories.'

'Pauline will come and bring us a basket of eggs, accompanied by her sister. She will then leave alone. An armed guard will escort Clémence back early in the morning.' He smiled, and she felt like kissing him. 'Will you invite me to share your supper or will I be in the way? It's high time I met my daughter by marriage, the very one who threatened to strike me with a sword if I were to bother you at your manor. Do you remember? Heavens – and she wasn't joking, either! Still, the apple doesn't fall far from the tree!'

The following morning, shortly before prime, Artus d'Authon had Ogier saddled. The Comte hesitated as he put his foot into the stirrup. He stroked the neck of his splendid steed, who was troubled by this uncertainty on his master's part, and whispered into his ear, 'Ogier, my brave Ogier … You know nothing of men's lives. How lucky you are!'

He called out to a stable boy, handed him the reins and said, 'I'm delaying my departure by a few minutes. Tie him up.' He walked slowly towards the stables. So what? He and Leone now shared the same secret, so it was natural that they should discuss it, man to man. He increased his stride.

Artus found Leone sitting at the table in his little room. He told him in a few words about his wife's revelation.

'I am relieved that Madame d'Authon has decided to tell you

the truth. It allows you to appreciate the huge danger hanging over her head. I was putting off my departure, afraid to leave her vulnerable. That is no longer the case. You are a brave, intelligent man and you will not shy away from any enemy in order to protect your wife. I can therefore leave, my heart lighter, to pursue my search.'

'To find Clément and the manuscripts,' Artus d'Authon said.

'That's right.'

'Monsieur, I am for ever in your debt. You have saved the most precious creature in my life. You have watched over her when they were trying to keep me away in order to get to her. Moreover, you have rescued me from the clutches of the Inquisition. It's good that one should feel indebted. It reminds us to be humble. One becomes once again aware of one's weaknesses. I am not sure I will ever be able to repay such a debt.'

Leone gave him one of those strange smiles that seemed to come from afar, from unfathomable depths.

'There is no debt, Monsieur, I tell you in truth. Serving God cannot be considered like a usury note.'

The Comte said in a more abrupt tone, 'The fact remains, Monsieur, with all due respect, that I would have preferred to help you, assist you – social positions are not relevant here – rather than be kept in ignorance, an ignorance that made me a dead weight when I could have added my vigilance and my sword to yours.'

'I beg your pardon, Monsieur, from the bottom of my heart. However, as you can understand, the decision wasn't mine to make but Madame's alone. Moreover, the people we have been fighting against for centuries rarely use the sword. Their weapons are a lot more cunning.'

'No doubt,' the Comte murmured in agreement. 'When will we have the sadness of seeing you leave, knight?'

'Tomorrow. With your permission, I shall go and say goodbye

to the Comtesse and wish her well. It's such a relief to know that you are near her, fully aware of the threat hanging over her. Remember, Monsieur: her enemies are formidable and ready for anything. Let the slightest clue alert you, the smallest detail alarm you. For the time being, they are disorganised, but they will soon regroup.'

Artus felt convinced that these were not empty words. As well as fear for his wife, he was conscious of a nagging question: why had she chosen him? Was it a whim of the heart or was she unwittingly following an incomprehensible plan? It was a flattering question, since it implied that they had been destined for each other since the dawn of time.

'When will you return, knight?'

'When I have finally found Clément. He is hiding so well that the camerlingo's spies still haven't been able to track him down … But for how long? He's still so young and they will not spare him.'

'I hope we see you soon, knight.'

'God willing.'

APPENDIX I: HISTORICAL REFERENCES

Archimedes, 287–212 BC. Greek mathematical genius and inventor to whom we owe very many mathematical advances, including the famous hydrostatic principle, which is named after him. He also gave the first precise definition of the number pi, and set himself up to be the advocate of experimentation and demonstration. Archimedes is credited with being the author of several inventions including the catapult, the Archimedes screw, the pulley and the cog.

A palimpsest was recently auctioned at Christie's for US$2 million. It recounted the progress made by Archimedes in getting to grips with infinity. The document, which had been overwritten with the copy of a religious text, also contained the first crucial steps towards differential calculus, a branch of mathematics that had to be re-invented after the Renaissance. It is rumoured that Bill Gates was the successful bidder for the document, which has been donated to the Walters Art Museum in Baltimore, where it has been subjected to sophisticated analysis.

Benoît XI, Pope, Nicolas Boccasini, 1240–1304. Relatively little is known about him. Coming from a very poor background, Boccasini, a Dominican, remained humble throughout his life. One of the few anecdotes about him demonstrates this: when his mother paid him a visit after his election, she made herself look pretty for her son. He gently explained that her outfit was too ostentatious and that he preferred women to be simply dressed. Known for his conciliatory temperament, Boccasini, who had been Bishop of Ostia, tried to mediate in the disagreements between the Church and Philip the Fair, but he showed his disapproval of Guillaume de Nogaret and the Colonna brothers. He died after eight months of the pontificate, on 7 July 1304, poisoned by figs or dates.

Bingen (Hildegard of), 1098–1179. She took her vows at the age of fifteen and became abbess in 1136. A poet and a musician, she corresponded with the prominent personalities of the world during the latter half of the twelfth century. She is said to have performed miracles and had her visions come true. Of a frail constitution, she soon took an interest in medicinal plants. She compiled, among other things, a medical book which is now considered the first 'modern' work of herbal medicine. Despite her poor health, she lived to the age of eighty-four, a record at the time. Perhaps we should consider it proof of the effectiveness of her therapeutic recipes! Although she is often called a saint, she has never been canonised.

Blood that is different. Blood-profiling was unknown in the fourteenth century. The blood from the Turin Shroud, which was supposedly wrapped around the body of Christ, the blood from the holy Tunic of Argenteuil, which Christ is said to have worn on His way to Calvary and crucifixion, and the blood from the Shroud of Oviedo, the cloth wrapped around Christ's head after He died, are all from a man with the blood group AB. As only one and a half million of the human population have this blood group, it is hard to believe that the three samples are all from the same group by simple coincidence. In addition, blood group AB developed about two thousand years ago in the Middle East. It apparently emerged in France at the beginning of the second millennium. Group AB is recessive and it is therefore strange that it is still in existence. An AB group couple (which is in itself statistically very unlikely) has only a one in two chance of having children who are also AB, whereas parents who have O group blood will always have O group children. From a strictly statistical point of view, group AB should have disappeared, particularly as it is more vulnerable to certain types of illness. Yet it persists, albeit in small numbers.

According to carbon-14 dating methods, the Turin Shroud dates from 1250 to 1340, the Tunic of Argenteuil from the year 800 and the Shroud of Oviedo from 500. However, the samples authorised by the

Church, at least in the case of the Turin Shroud, were taken from the edges of the cloth, which would have been more prone to general decay and less reliable for the purposes of establishing a date. Rumour has it that the Church did not really want the Shroud to be attributed to Christ, as it would have engendered a sort of hysteria among the faithful. Whether this is true or not, it cannot be ruled out. And there is one more point to note: scientists have not been able to solve the enigma of the Tunic of Argenteuil. White blood cells were apparently found intact on the Tunic, whereas normally these cells perish shortly after death (and the Tunic is at least 1,200 years old). The following hypothesis has been formulated to explain the mystery: white blood cells were preserved thanks to the vegetable-conserving agents used at the time of Christ. As for the face of the man who appears quite distinctly on the Turin Shroud, several different explanations have been put forward, from a holy miracle, to the cloth having been exposed to sun behind a window.

Boniface VIII, Pope, Benedetto Caetani, *c*.1235–1303. Cardinal and legate in France, then Pope. He was a passionate defender of pontifical theocracy, which was opposed to the new authority of the State. He was openly hostile to Philip the Fair from 1296 onwards and the affair continued even after his death – France attempted to try him posthumously.

Clairets Abbey, Orne. Situated on the edge of Clairets Forest, in the parish of Masle, the abbey was built by a charter issued in July 1204 by Geoffroy III, Comte du Perche, and his wife Mathilde of Brunswick, sister of Emperor Otto IV. The abbey's construction took seven years and finished in 1212. Its consecration was co-signed by the commander of the Knights Templar, Guillaume d'Arville, about whom little is known. The abbey is only open to Bernardine nuns of the Cistercian order, who have the right to all forms of seigneurial justice.

Got, Bertrand de, c.1270–1314. He is best known as a canon and counsellor to the King of England. He was, however, a skilled diplomat, which enabled him to maintain cordial relations with Philip the Fair even though England was at war with France. He became Archbishop of Bordeaux in 1299 then succeeded Benoît XI as Pope in 1305, taking the name Clément V. He chose to install himself in Avignon, because he was wary of the politics of Rome, which he knew little about. He was good at handling Philip the Fair in their two major differences of opinion: the posthumous trial of Boniface VIII and the suppression of the Knights Templar. He managed to rein in the spite of the sovereign in the first case, and to contain it in the second case.

The Hospitallers of Saint John of Jerusalem were recognised by Pope Paschal II in 1113. Unlike the other soldier orders, the original function of the Hospitallers was charitable. It was only later that they assumed a military function. After the Siege of Acre in 1291, the Hospitallers withdrew to Cyprus, then Rhodes and finally Malta. The order was governed by a Grand-Master, elected by the general chapter made up of dignitaries. The chapter was subdivided into provinces, governed in their turn by priors. Unlike the Templars and in spite of their great wealth, the Hospitallers always enjoyed a very favourable reputation, no doubt because of their charitable works, which they never abandoned, and because of the humility of their members.

Jews. Bullying, discrimination and executions had not stopped since the sixth century, except for when Louis le Pieux (814–840) placed Jews under his protection and created the office of 'Master of the Jews', responsible for ensuring that his support of them was respected. This led to a period of relative peace, especially thanks to the openness of Saint Bernard, who was alarmed by the animosity of some Crusaders who tried to revive antisemitic hatred by drawing attention to the Jews' responsibility for the Passion of Christ. This peace did not last. Rumours of ritual killings subsequently revived the hatred. Some Jewish communities were accused of sacrificing Christian children, with no evidence or even the discovery of any bodies. It was these unfounded rumours that led to the extermination of the Jewish community in Blois, who were burnt at the stake (1171). Taking advantage of the people's hatred, Philip Augustus subsequently expelled the Jews in 1182, seizing their possessions and declaring void the debts of their borrowers, among whom was the Kingdom of France. Louis IX (Saint Louis) did not remain idle when the Inquisition started to liken Judaism to heresy. He had twenty-four carts full of Talmudic manuscripts burnt in Paris, under the pretext that they diverted the faithful from the one and only Book – the Bible. At that point, there were many forced conversions to Christianity, not counting those inspired by fear. The Fourth Lateran Council represented a turning point, since it gave a ruling on the Jews, whether in matters of usury, distinctive clothing so that they might be immediately recognised, blasphemy or conversions that lacked sincerity. The persecution of the Jews became one of the Inquisition's principal missions, so all the faithful were obliged to wear badges and women the veil. In 1294, the grouping of Jews in certain streets became compulsory throughout the entire kingdom. In 1290, the case of the Paris Jew Jonathas, who was accused – in spite of contradictory testimonies – of profaning a consecrated host, stirred up antisemitism. This also gave Philip the Fair an excuse to expel all the Jews from the kingdom in 1306, despite the open reservations of some lords, some of whom were reluctant to lose out on the commercial advantage which accrued to them thanks to the Jews, while others were convinced that this discrimination had been conceived as a radical method of erasing the debts of the State.

Knights Templar. The order was created in 1118 in Jerusalem by the knight Hugues de Payens and other knights from Champagne and Burgundy. It was officially endorsed by the Church at the Council of Troyes in 1128, having been championed by Bernard of Clairvaux.

The order was led by a Grand-Master, whose authority was backed up by dignitaries. The order owned considerable assets (3,450 chateaux, fortresses and houses in 1257). With its system of transferring money to the Holy Land, the order acted in the thirteenth century as one of Christianity's principal bankers. After the Siege of Acre in 1291 – which was ultimately fatal to the order – the Templars almost all withdrew to the West. Public opinion turned against them and they were regarded as indolent profiteers. Various expressions of the period bear witness to this. For example, 'Going to the Temple' was a euphemism for going to a brothel. When the Grand-Master Jacques de Molay refused to merge the Templars with the Hospitallers, the Templars were arrested on 13 October 1307. An investigation followed, confessions were obtained (in the case of Jacques de Molay, some historians believe, with the use of torture), followed by retractions. Clément V, who feared Philip the Fair for various unrelated reasons, passed a decree suppressing the order on 22 March 1312. Jacques de Molay again stood by the retraction of his confession and on 18 March 1314 was burnt at the stake along with other Templars. It is generally agreed that the seizure of the Templars' assets and their redistribution to the Hospitallers cost Philip the Fair more money than it gained him.

Lays of Marie de France. Twelve lays generally attributed to a certain Marie, originally from France but living at the English court. Some historians believe she was the daughter of Louis VII or of the Comte de Meulan. The *Lays* were written before 1167 and the *Fables* around 1180. Marie de France was also the author of a novel, *The Legend of the Purgatory of St Patrick*.

Lead. Humans have been using lead for three and a half thousand years. It is essential for growth but only in tiny doses. For a long time, it was a favourite among poisoners. It has had multiple uses: in alloys, waterproofing, pipes, roofing, kitchen utensils and for sealing tinned foods. It was also one of history's first sweeteners, since the Romans used it to sweeten their fine wines. Lead poisoning, or saturnism, was the first job-related illness to be recognised in France. The range of symptoms varies depending on the dose ingested and duration of the period of poisoning. Chronic poisoning (small doses over a long time) manifests itself as cognitive difficulties that are hard and sometimes impossible to reverse, and neurotoxicity to which foetuses and children are particularly sensitive. Medium poisoning (higher doses) leads to a metallic taste in the mouth, anorexia, violent abdominal pains, nausea, vomiting and diarrhoea. Acute poisoning (very high doses) is characterised by either agitation or, on the contrary, sleepiness, hypotension, convulsions and coma.

Medieval Inquisition. It is important to distinguish the Medieval Inquisition from the Spanish Inquisition. The repression and intolerance of the latter were incomparably more violent than anything known in France. Under the leadership of Tomás de Torquemada alone, there were more than two thousand deaths recorded in Spain.

The Medieval Inquisition was at first enforced by the bishops. Pope Innocent III (1160–1216) set out the regulations for the inquisitorial procedure in the papal bull *Vergentis in senium* of 1199. The aim was not to eliminate individuals – as was proved by the Fourth Council of the Lateran, called by Innocent III a year before his death, which emphasised that it was forbidden to inflict the Ordeal on dissidents. (The Ordeal or 'judgement of God' was a trial by fire, water or the sword to test whether an accused person was a heretic or not.) What the Pope was aiming for was the eradication of heresies that threatened the foundation of the Church by promoting, amongst other things, the poverty of Christ as a model way to live – a model that was obviously rarely followed if the vast wealth earned by most of the monasteries from land tax is anything to go by. Later the Inquisition was enforced by the Pope, starting with Gregory IX, who conferred inquisitorial powers on the Dominicans in 1232 and, in a lesser way, on the Franciscans. Gregory's motives in reinforcing the powers of the Inquisition and placing them under his sole control were entirely political. He was ensuring that on no account would Emperor Frederick II be able to control the Inquisition for reasons that had nothing to do with spirituality. It was Innocent IV who took the ultimate step in authorising recourse to torture in his papal bull *Ad extirpanda* of 15 May 1252. Witches as well as heretics were then hunted down by the Inquisition.

The real impact of the Inquisition has been exaggerated. There were relatively few inquisitors to cover the whole territory of the kingdom of France and they would have had little effect had they not received the help of powerful lay people and benefited from numerous denunciations. But thanks to their ability to excuse each other for their faults, certain inquisitors were guilty of terrifying atrocities that sometimes provoked riots and scandalised many prelates.

In March 2000, roughly eight centuries after the beginnings of the Inquisition, Pope John Paul II asked God's pardon for the crimes and horrors committed in its name.

Nogaret, Guillaume de, *c*.1270–1313. Nogaret was a professor of civil law and taught at Montpellier before joining Philip the Fair's Council in 1295. His responsibilities grew rapidly more widespread. He was involved, at first more or less clandestinely, in the great religious debates that were shaking France, for example the trial of Bernard Saisset. Nogaret progressively emerged from the shadows and played a pivotal role in the campaign against the Knights Templar and the King's struggle with Pope Boniface VIII. Nogaret was of unshakeable faith and great intelligence. He would go on to become the King's chancellor and, although he was displaced for a while by Enguerran de Marigny, he took up the seal again in 1311.

Philip the Fair, 1268–1314. The son of Philip III (known as Philip the Bold) and Isabelle of Aragon. With his consort Joan of Navarre, he had three sons who would all become kings of France – Louis X (Louis the Stubborn), Philip V (Philip the Tall) and Charles IV (Charles the Fair). He also had a daughter, Isabelle, whom he married to Edward II of England. Philip was brave and an excellent war leader, but he also had a reputation for being inflexible and harsh. It is now generally agreed, however, that perhaps that reputation has been overstated, since contemporary accounts relate that Philip the Fair was manipulated by his advisers, who flattered him whilst mocking him behind his back.

Philip the Fair is best known for the major role he played in the suppression of the Knights Templar, but he was above all a reforming king whose objective was to free the politics of the French kingdom from papal interference.

Robert le Bougre, also known as Robert the Small, was possibly Bulgarian in origin. He originally embraced Catharism and acceded to the highest rank and became an expert in that faith. But he later converted to Catholicism and became a Dominican monk. Gregory IX (1227–1241) valued him for his extraordinary ability to expose heretics. He seemed capable of trapping even the most skilled at concealment. In 1233 he was appointed Inquisitor General of Charité-sur-Loire, after his predecessor Conrad de Marbourg was assassinated, and was then responsible for cruel mistreatment and horrifying torture. The Archbishops of Sens and Rheims, amongst others, scandalised by the accounts that were reaching their ears, protested about Robert's behaviour. After the first written report on the methods used by Robert, he was stripped of his powers in 1234. Yet he returned to favour in August of the following year, and immediately took up his 'amusements' again. It was not until 1241 that he was permanently removed from power and imprisoned for life.

Vallombroso (or *Vall'Ombrosa*, or *Vallombreuse*, or *Vallombrosa*, from the Latin *Vallis Ombrosa*). Tuscan abbey at an altitude of about 1,000 metres. Founded in 1036 by Saint John Gualbert, it became the centre of a Benedictine congregation. It was closed in 1808 then restored by Ferdinand III in 1866. In the twelfth century, the congregation was formed of twenty-three monasteries. Galileo studied there.

Valois, Charles de, 1270–1325. Philip the Fair's only full brother. The King showed Charles a somewhat blind affection all his life and conferred on him missions that were probably beyond his capabilities. Charles de Valois, who was father, son, brother, brother-in-law, uncle and son-in-law to kings and queens, dreamt all his life of his own crown, which he never obtained.

Waldensians or Poor Men of Lyons. One of the most important 'heresies' of the time, not only because of its extent but also its impact on people. The movement, which advocated destitution, evangelical purity and equality for all, was founded in 1170 by Peter Waldo, a rich merchant from Lyons who gave away all his possessions. As in the case of Catharism, the success of the Waldensians owed much to the religious malaise of the time. It primarily expressed the longing of wealthy strata of society for increasing purity. Women could be ordained. Rejecting anything that diverged from a strict reading of the Gospels, the faithful were soon persecuted by the Inquisition. Some would join the Poor Catholics, while others would spread throughout Europe, which explains the existence of communities even in the present day.

APPENDIX II: GLOSSARY

Liturgical Hours

Aside from Mass – which was not strictly part of them – ritualised prayers, as set out in the sixth century by the Regulation of Saint Benoît, were to be said several times a day. They regulated the rhythm of the day. Monks and nuns were not permitted to dine before nightfall, that is, until after vespers. This strict routine of prayers was largely adhered to until the eleventh century, when it was reduced to enable monks and nuns to devote more time to reading and manual labour.

Matins: at 2.30 a.m. or 3 a.m.

Lauds: just before dawn, between 5 a.m. and 6 a.m.

Prime: around 7.30 a.m., the first prayers of the day, as soon as possible after sunrise and just before Mass.

Terce: around 9 a.m.

Sext: around midday.

Nones: between 2 p.m. and 3 p.m. in the afternoon.

Vespers: at the end of the afternoon, at roughly 4.30 p.m. or 5 p.m., at sunset.

Compline: after vespers, the last prayers of the day, sometime between 6 p.m. and 8 p.m.

Measurements

It is quite difficult to translate some measurements into their modern-day equivalents, as the definitions varied from region to region.

Bushel: a measure of volume equal to about 8 gallons (36 litres).

Denier: currency in the Middle Ages.

League: about 2½ miles (4 kilometres).

Ell: about 45 inches (114 centimetres) in Paris, 37 inches (94 centimetres) in Arras.

Foot: as today, 12 inches (30 centimetres).

APPENDIX III: NOTES

1. Similar to Lent, Advent included the four preceding Sundays ending in the festival of Nativity, which was then a religious festival. The custom of giving presents only appeared later on.

2. Unfounded rumours were rife at the time, accusing Boniface of dabbling in witchcraft and occult practices in order to strengthen his power.

3. Known as a *daguette* in French, these were often fluted and ornamented. Ladies would sometimes carry them as protection when they travelled.

4. Uranus, Neptune and Pluto.

5. Known as *oblatus*: 'offering'. Anyone (often children) who offered themselves or were offered to God and to a monastery or nunnery.

6. A good physician.

7. In what is now the Aisne.

8. Nun whose task it was to look after the chevet or round point in the church, the treasure house and the candles. She was also in charge of surveying and paying the blacksmiths, singers, veterinarians and so on.

9. Administrator and bursar.

10. Castor oil.

11. An arbitrary tax levied upon feudal dependants by their superiors.

12. Girls came of age then at twelve and boys at fourteen.

13. Secular society.

14. It is thought that towards the end of the seventh century, the counts of Perche imported Arab horses in order to cross them with the local percherons to improve the breed. This explanation dates back to the

nineteenth century, though the idea is not uncontested. It is generally accepted that Perche mares were crossed early on with stallions from Boulogne or Belgium in order to produce a heavier and more hardy breed.

15. The origin of the Anglo-Saxon name for magnet, meaning 'attraction'.

16. The stone was supposed to ward off evil spirits and cure illnesses.

17. It is thought that he drafted the letter in 1269 while mounting the guard during the siege of Lucera.

18. It was not until William Gilbert's experiments in 1600 that the properties of magnetism began to be understood.

19. The iron blade fixed in front of a plough.

20. Landless peasants who hired their labour.

21. This law was almost the norm in France at the time.

22. Collections of copies of charters in the general sense of the term. These appeared in France from the ninth century onwards. These could be files containing rights and titles pertaining to lords or to an abbey, bills of sale, exchange and contract, or of administration of an estate, and inventories. There were also registers of chronicles made up of a mixture of charters and historical accounts, etc.

23. Marrow, pumpkin and squash originating from the Americas were still unknown in Europe.

24. Used as a plate in relatively well-to-do society, this slice of stale bread was afterwards given to the needy or to the dogs.

25. These were seats with a raised pommel and just one stirrup, which meant the rider could use only her left leg to command her mount. The horn, which later made it easier for the horsewoman to keep her balance, was not invented until the sixteenth century and is attributed to Catherine de Medici, herself an outstanding horsewoman.

26. A smaller horse with a smooth ambling gait that was considered a suitable mount for women.

27. Ring-shaped loaf made of choux pastry with cheese.

28. ?–1226.

29. An alexandrine comprising twenty-nine quatrains.

30. A woman speaks an average of twenty thousand words a day, compared to a man who averages seven thousand.

31. The universe of angels was divided into three orders.

32. ?–c.1313.

33. In the Middle Ages the concept of time was not universal, but varied according to the divine, angelic or human 'substances' to which it related.

34. Used as a remedy for respiratory infections.

35. Used to cure horse flu.

36. Nominated by the regional or national chapters, the abbots and abbesses were appointed by the Pope.

37. An early forerunner of football, rugby and hockey.

38. A type of lantern made of wood or metal designed so that they could be carried without the flame blowing out.

39. The seeds of the nux vomica tree are rich in strychnine and brucine. They also contain vomicine and novacine, etc. Nux vomica was commonly used from the fifteenth to the sixteenth century onwards as a rodenticide and in very small doses as a stimulant. The symptoms of poisoning in humans are similar to those of tetanus and include a hypersensitivity to noise and light, which can cause convulsions. Death results from paralysis of the diaphragm. The victim is conscious throughout. The lethal dose in human beings varies between 30 and 120 milligrams, though some people have resisted up to one gram.

40. One grain = 0.053 grams

41. It was the custom in those days to name a landlord after his tavern.

42. 'Whomsoever bathes in the divine blood cleanses his sins and acquires the beauty of the angels.'

43. The first gargoyles appeared in the eleventh to twelfth century. Gutters date back to ancient times.

44. Dawn Mass had been held since the second century.

45. 'Not for our sakes, oh Lord, not for our sakes but for the glory of Your name.'

46. Lemon tree.

47. 300–390, an Egyptian monk of the desert who is thought to have some points in common with Francis of Assisi.

48. Depression.

49. Uranus, Neptune and Pluto were discovered later.

50. A *serfouette* was a combined hoe and fork.

51. 950–1012 (?).

52. According to Pliny, this tree, native to Syria, was brought to Italy by Sextus Papirus.

53. Also known as *sauve-chrétien*, this is a brandy-based liqueur made with sweet white wine, raisins, honey, vanilla, cinnamon, nutmeg and ginger, thickened with egg yolk.

54. A window divided into two parts.

55. Church with semicircular apse opening onto the transept.

56. This fashion, possibly originating in Italy, allowed the sleeves of a dress to be changed to vary in style and colour.

57. Turret hats became fashionable in France towards the middle of the thirteenth century.

58. Latex is a powerful cardiotoxic not dissimilar to digitalis, taken from the ako or iroko (African teak) tree (or in Asia the upas or ipho

tree – *Antiaris toxicaria*). The wood is commonly used as a veneer.

59. ?–1272.

60. 'We adore You, Christ.'

61. The only wood that could be collected without the permission of the local landowning lord.

62. On barges the backs of which opened to allow the animals to be loaded into stalls, where they were secured to avoid falls.

63. *Preceptor* was the name given in Latin for the commander.

64. A tenth of the harvest, given in taxes to the landlords, was kept in such barns.

65. Eight yards in diameter, it was later converted into a dovecote by the Hospitallers.

66. 'Robert d'Avelin, Templar commander at Arville, 1208.'

67. It was not until the thirteenth century that recumbent effigies became true likenesses of the deceased people they represented. Up until then they were made to look young, beautiful and strong.

68. The names of the commanders and the dates when they held office are taken from the journal *Templarium*, special edition no.1, which, among other things, is devoted to the Templar commandery at Arville.

69. A noble and delicate instrument which up until the middle of the fourteenth century, when it became definitively five-stringed, could possess between three and five strings.

70. The skin of a stillborn calf.

71. Latinisation of the Greek word *bibliothêkê*, literally meaning 'box of books'.

72. 546 BC.

73. The equivalent of today's brioche.

74. 14:62. The Gospel according to Saint Mark contains many such evocations that combined to convince Christians in past centuries of

the return 'in person' of Christ on earth in some unspecified future. Ancient calculations fixed the date in 1666, encouraging Oliver Cromwell (1599–1658) to authorise the return of the Jews to England.

75. Inspired by the indecipherable manuscript known as 'Voynich', which is kept at the Benicke Rare Book and Manuscript Library at Yale University in the United States. It is thought that the manuscript dates from the fourteenth century and it is written in an unknown language.

76. Known as the *ferrons de Normandie*, they organised the production and sale of iron and dictated the conditions of work and even the recourse to middlemen.

77. Snails were allowed on fast days as well as ordinary days. They were served everywhere.

78. A kind of long shirt worn against the skin under the clothes.

79. Head of the Apostolic Camera and treasurer, as well as close adviser, to the Pope.

80. At the time, bishops' houses were on the site of the present Saint Peter's Basilica, the building of which began in 1452 and continued for over a century.

81. Pope from 1277 to 1280.

82. Second century BC. Author of a totally rigid and incorrect theory that the universe was flat and finite, with the Earth motionless at its centre. Favoured by the Church, this theory persisted for seventeen centuries.

83. A fortune at the time.

84. Nun who collected the gifts of charitable people or those forced by a court to be generous.

85. The term 'Lombard' referred to all bankers, whether Italians or Jews.

86. Man's headdress ending in a long strip that would be wound around

the neck, like a scarf.

87. 1165–1223, only son of Louis VII and Adèle de Champagne. Saint Louis's grandfather.

88. See *Got (Bertrand de)*.

89. See Volume I. *The Season of the Beast.*

90. An unforgivable crime at that time.

91. Most inquisitors would take over the possessions of the people they had condemned.

92. A physical trial (red-hot iron, immersion in icy water, duel, etc.) aiming to prove innocence or guilt. It was a Judgement of God which went out of fashion in the eleventh century and was condemned by the Fourth Lateran Council in 1215.

93. In his encyclical *Dura nimis*.

94. In 1224.

95. Nowadays known as Moslins. There were many mills in the area at the time which probably explains the medieval name.

96. The village would be integrated with Molin two years later.

97. The doors were generally watched by lay servants.

98. As opposed to important State barons.

99. From *oblatus*; see Note 5.

100. Provision usually bestowed upon a widow from her husband's possessions. In the Paris region, this constituted half the husband's possessions. In Normandy one-third.

101. Castrated horse trained to amble in order to allow female riders, disadvantaged by the saddles of the time, to keep their balance.

102. At the time, mines were mostly in the open air, since people lacked the technology to dig underground tunnels and especially to prop them up.

103. Their intervention was compulsory in order to regulate

transactions. They were forbidden from trading in the goods whose weight and volume they assessed.

104. Like the Judgement of God, it was a way of deciding between two camps. Even though, at the time, the Church no longer considered it irrefutable proof of the winner's innocence, the notion still held sway for a long time.

105. Wednesdays, Fridays and Saturdays, and on the eve of a holy day, as well as during Lent and Advent.

106. They were only used in the larger rooms because of their strong smell and because they darkened the walls.

107. Probably written between 1230 and 1250.

108. A Knight of Justice could pride himself on having at least eight quarters of nobility in France and Italy, and sixteen in Germany. The title of Knight of Grace, however, was acquired strictly on merit.

109. At the time, this term referred to any skin-disease symptoms, whether the disease was contagious, like leprosy, or not.

110. In 1296.

111. Originally, a person publicly subject to a curse on the part of Church authority. Formal curse of excommunication issued against enemies of the Catholic faith and heretics.

112. The brothers could not travel without it. Any commander coming across a Hospitaller unable to produce one was obliged to arrest him immediately and have him tried by the order.

113. Claret, locally produced wine, probably gave its name to Clairets Abbey.

114. Nowadays called Mâle.

115. The abbess's second in command.

116. Assembly of monks or nuns responsible for organising the life of the monastery or convent. At first, abbots and abbesses were elected

by regional or general chapters but were subsequently appointed by the Pope.

117. Nun in charge of managing the abbey, including provisions and food. She supervised the barns, mills, breweries, storehouses and food stores. She also oversaw the provision of furniture, various objects and outside visits.

118. Nun responsible for her abbey's relations with the outside world.

119. Nun in charge of guests and their care. She oversaw cleanliness, the fire, the kitchen, the candles, and guests' behaviour in the abbey.

120. Nun in charge of teaching children and novices and the only one allowed to hit them and punish them.

121. Nun who led and conducted the singing.

122. Famous early-thirteenth-century composer. Author of religious works for four voices, which were very innovative for the time, since hymns were generally composed for two voices.

123. Earthenware tiles appeared in France at the end of the thirteenth century and quickly became fashionable since they were considered less cold than stone slabs.

124. Besides being an effective pesticide, it was used for some skin ailments and to treat mange in domestic animals.

125. Contrary to popular belief, rice had been grown in France – in Roussillon in particular – since the thirteenth century. However, it remained for a long time a gastronomical curiosity.

126. While wolves, despite the fear they inspired, were considered foolish gluttons, foxes were admired for their intelligence, cunning and courage.

127. Being a widow, especially if she had a child, was a convenient status for wealthy ladies of the time. So much so that many burghers and noblewomen, having finally become their own mistresses and

not having to account to anyone, as long as their behaviour was not scandalous, were reluctant to remarry.

128. 'Narrow wall'.

129. *Consultations à l'usage de l'inquisiteur* by Gui Foulques (Guy Faucoi), counsellor of Saint Louis, and subsequently Pope Clément IV.

130. Marcus Aurelius, 121–180.

131. The final part of the meal, often consisting of wine and spices.

132. Some calculations estimated the Second Coming would take place in 1666. This encouraged Oliver Cromwell to allow the Jews to return to England, since it was said that Jesus Christ would be reborn of a Jewish woman.

133. 1276–1319, son of Philip III and Marie de Brabant.

134. Enamelled pottery from Beauvais had been very valuable since the twelfth century.

135. They were then a major diagnostic tool.

136. Unacceptable as this might sound nowadays, this was the primary justification of the Inquisition.

137. Root vegetables were reserved for peasants. Noblemen preferred vegetables that grew above the ground.

138. A mixture of straw, clay, tree bark, acorn flour and ground grass.

139. Long strips of fabric that trailed down to the floor, and which were worn over the sleeves, at the elbow.

140. Fermented milk, somewhat like yoghurt, and cheese were supposed to reduce the absorption of lead, as was eating wholemeal bread.

141. A custom that persisted until the nineteenth century. Some recipes show that there were wines containing up to 800 mg of lead per litre, while the maximum dose tolerated by an adult is 3 mg per week. Some historians have used this to explain the fall of the Roman Empire, since

the aristocracy drank wine containing large amounts of this heavy metal.

142. Fermented honey and water, to which white wine or brandy was added in order to preserve it. It had been drunk since Antiquity.

143. Flagellation was normally used on women. Men would be subjected to strappado.

144. All furs were prized in the Middle Ages. The most expensive ones (sable, marten and ermine), which came mainly from Russia and Scandinavia, were worn by the wealthy classes. Poorer people made do with rabbit, goat and white sheep, while the middle classes wore lamb, otter, beaver and fox. In the thirteenth century, the burghers' right to wear the more expensive furs was restricted, as they were a symbol of the aristocracy.

145. Poisoning was considered the most unpardonable crime because of its slyness and because it was almost impossible to protect oneself against it.

146. Spectacles, worn in France since the thirteenth century, but seen as a sign of grave infirmity and thus often kept hidden.

147. A nun without a permanent job title, who performed a different task every week.

148. A list of Judaic laws pertaining to food.

149. God (Yahweh) is neither named nor represented in Judaism.

150. July 1306.

151. *Antiaris toxicaria*, contains a powerful cardiac toxin.

152. Until late-seventeenth-century Dutch physician Jan Swammerdam observed otherwise, it was a commonly held belief that bee colonies had a king at their centre.

153. A beehive can have up to 80,000 bees. Side by side, they would cover a football pitch.